WITHDRAWN

D1071343

THE BEST OF KAGE BAKER

THE BEST OF KAGE BAKER

KAGE BAKER

Illustrated by J. K. Potter

Subterranean Press 2012

First Edition

ISBN
978-1-59606-442-3

Subterranean Press
PO Box 190106
Burton, MI 48519

www.subterraneanpress.com

TABLE OF CONTENTS

Story-telling is like building half a bridge into the fog—
the other half is anchored by the readers.
This book is dedicated to Kage's Dear Readers:
You know who you are.

Noble Mold

For a while I lived in this little town by the sea. Boy, it was a soft job. Santa Barbara had become civilized by then: no more Indian rebellions, no more pirates storming up the beach, nearly all the grizzly bears gone. Once in a while some bureaucrat from Mexico City would raise hell with us, but by and large the days of the old Missions were declining into forlorn shades, waiting for the Yankees to come.

The Company operated a receiving, storage, and shipping terminal out of what looked like an oaken chest in my cell. I had a mortal identity as an alert little padre with an administrative career ahead of him, so the Church kept me pretty busy pushing a quill. My Company duties, though, were minor: I logged in consignments from agents in the field and forwarded communiqués.

It was sort of a forty-year vacation. There were fiestas and fandangos down in the pueblo. There were horse races along the shore of the lagoon. My social standing with the De La Guerra family was high, so I got invited out to supper a lot. And at night, when the bishop had gone to bed and our few pathetic Indians were tucked in for the night, I would sneak a little glass of Communion wine and then relax out on the front steps of the church. There I'd sit, listening to the night sounds, looking down the long slope to the night sea. Sometimes I'd sit there until the sky pinked up in the east and the bells rang for Matins. We Old Ones don't need much sleep.

One August night I was sitting like that, watching the moon drop down toward the Pacific, when I picked up the signal of another immortal somewhere out there in the night. I tracked it coming along the shoreline, past the point at Goleta; then it crossed the Camino Real and came straight uphill at me. Company business. I sighed and broadcast, *Quo Vadis?*

Hola, came the reply. I scanned, but I knew who it was anyway. *Hi, Mendoza,* I signaled back, and leaned up on my elbows to await her arrival. Pretty soon I picked her up on visual, too, climbing up out of the mists that flowed along the little stream; first the wide-brimmed hat, then the shoulders bent forward under the weight of the pack, the long walking skirt, the determined lope of the field operative without transportation.

Mendoza is a botanist, and has been out in the field too long. At this point she'd been tramping around Alta California for the better part of twelve decades. God only knew what the Company had found for her to do out in the back of beyond; I'd have known, if I'd been nosy enough to read the Company directives I relayed to her from time to time. I wasn't her case officer anymore, though, so I didn't.

She raised burning eyes to me and my heart sank. She was on a Mission, and I don't mean the kind with stuccoed arches and tile roofs. Mendoza takes her work way too seriously. "How's it going, kid?" I greeted her in a loud whisper when she was close enough.

"Okay." She slung down her pack on the step beside me, picked up my wine and drank it, handed me back the empty glass and sat down.

"I thought you were back up in Monterey these days," I ventured.

"No. The Ventana," she replied. There was a silence while the sky got a little brighter. Far off, a rooster started to crow and then thought better of it.

"Well, well. To what do I owe the pleasure, et cetera?" I prompted.

She gave me a sharp look. "Company Directive 080444-C," she said, as though it were really obvious.

I'd developed this terrible habit of storing incoming Green Directives in my tertiary consciousness without scanning them first. The soft life, I guess. I accessed hastily. "They're sending you after grapes?" I cried a second later.

"Not just grapes." She leaned forward and stared into my eyes. "*Mission* grapes. All the cultivars around here that will be replaced by the varieties the Yankees introduce. I'm to collect genetic material from every remaining vine within a twenty-five-mile radius of this building." She looked around disdainfully. "Not that I expect to find all that many. This place is a wreck. The Church has really let its agricultural program go to hell, hasn't it?"

"Hard to get slave labor nowadays." I shrugged. "Can't keep 'em down on the farm without leg irons. We get a little help from the ones who really bought into the religion, but that's about it."

"And the Holy Office can't touch them." Mendoza shook her head. "Never thought I'd see the day."

"Hey, things change." I stretched out and crossed my sandaled feet one over the other. "Anyway. The Mexicans hate my poor little bishop and are doing their level best to drive him crazy. In all the confusion with the Missions being closed down, a lot of stuff has been looted. Plants get dug up and moved to people's gardens in the dark of night. There are still a few Indian families back in some of the canyons, too, and a lot of them have tiny little farms. Probably a lot of specimens out there, but you'll really have to hunt around for them."

She nodded, all brisk. "I'll need a processing credenza. Bed and board, too, and a cover identity. That's your job. Can you arrange them by 0600 hours?"

"Gosh, this is just like old times," I said without enthusiasm. She gave me that look again.

"I have work to do," she explained with exaggerated patience. "It is very important work. I'm a good little machine and I love my work. Nothing is more important than *My Work*. You taught me that, remember?"

Which I had, so I just smiled my most sincere smile as I clapped her on the shoulder. "And a damned good machine you are, too. I know you'll do a great job, Mendoza. And I feel that your efficiency will be increased if you don't rush this job. Take the time to do it right, you know? Mix a little rest and rec into your schedule. After all, you really deserve a holiday, a hard-working operative like you. This is a great place for fun. You could come to one of our local cascaron balls. Dance the night away. You used to like to dance."

Boy, was that the wrong thing to say. She stood up slowly, like a cobra rearing back.

"I haven't owned a ballgown since 1703. I haven't attended a mortal party since 1555. If you've chosen to forget that miserable Christmas, I can assure you I haven't. *You* play with the damned monkeys, if you're so fond of them." She drew a deep breath. "I, myself, have better things to do." She stalked away up the steps, but I called after her:

"You're still sore about the Englishman, huh?"

She didn't deign to respond but shoved her way between the church doors, presumably to get some sleep behind the altar screen where she wouldn't be disturbed.

She was still sore about the Englishman.

▲▼▲

I may have a more relaxed attitude toward my job than some people I could mention, but I'm still the best at it. By the time Mendoza wandered squinting into morning light I had her station set up, complete with hardware, in one of the Mission's guest cells. For the benefit of my fellow friars she was my cousin from Guadalajara, visiting me while she awaited the arrival of her husband from Mexico City. As befitted the daughter of an old Christian family the señora was of a sober and studious nature, and derived much innocent pleasure from painting flowers and other subjects of natural history.

She didn't waste any time. Mendoza went straight out to what remained of the Mission vineyard and set to work, clipping specimens, taking soil samples, doing all those things you'd have to be an obsessed specialist to enjoy. By the first evening she was hard at work at her credenza, processing it all.

When it came time to loot the private gardens of the *Gentes de Razon* her social introductions went okay, too, once I got her into some decent visiting clothes. I did most of the talking to the Ortegas and Carrillos and the rest, and the fact that she was a little stiff and silent while taking grape brandy with them could easily be explained away by her white skin and blue veins. If you had any Spanish blood you were sort of expected to sneer about it in that place, in those days.

Anyway it was a relief for everybody when she'd finished in the pueblo and went roving up and down the canyons, pouncing on unclaimed vines. There were a few Indians settled back in the hills, ex-neophytes scratching out a living between two worlds, on land nobody else had wanted. What they made of this woman, white as their worst nightmares, who spoke to them in imperious and perfectly accented Barbareño Chumash, I can only imagine. However she persuaded them, though, she got samples of their vines too. I figured she'd soon be on her way back to the hinterlands, and had an extra glass of Communion wine to celebrate. Was *that* ever premature!

I was hearing confessions when her scream of excitement cut through the subvocal ether, followed by delighted profanity in sixteenth-century Galician. My parishioner went on:

"…which you should also know, Father, was that I have coveted Juana's new pans. These are not common iron pans but enamelware, white with a blue stripe, very pretty, and they came from the Yankee trading ship. It disturbs me that such things should imperil my soul."

Joseph! Joseph! Joseph!

"It is good to be concerned on that account, my child." I shut out Mendoza's transmission so I could concentrate on the elderly mortal woman on the other side of the screen. "To covet worldly things is very sinful indeed, especially for the poor. The Devil himself sent the Yankees with those pans, you may be certain." But Mendoza had left her credenza and was coming

down the arcade in search of me, ten meters, twenty meters, twenty-five…
"For this, and for your sinful dreams, you must say thirty Paternosters and
sixty Ave Marias…" Mendoza was coming up the church steps two at a
time…"Now, recite with me the Act of Contrition—"

"Hey!" Mendoza pulled back the door of the confessional. Her eyes were
glowing with happiness. I gave her a stern look and continued the Act of
Contrition with my somewhat disconcerted penitent, so Mendoza went out
to stride up and down in front of the church in her impatience.

"Don't you know better than to interrupt me when I'm administering
a sacrament?" I snapped when I was finally able to come out to her. "Some
Spaniard you are!"

"So report me to the Holy Office. Joseph, this is important. One of my
specimens read out with an F-M Class One rating."

"And?" I put my hands in my sleeves and frowned at her, refusing to
come out of the role of offended friar.

"Favorable Mutation, Joseph, don't you know what that means? It's a
Mission grape with a difference. It's got Saccharomyces with style and
Botrytis in rare bloom. Do you know what happens when a field operative
discovers an F-M Class One, Joseph?"

"You get a prize," I guessed.

"Si Señor!" She did a little dance down the steps and stared up at me in blazing jubilation. I hadn't seen her this happy since 1554. "I get a Discovery Bonus!
Six months of access to a lab for my own personal research projects, with the
very finest equipment available! Oh joy, oh rapture. So I need you to help me."

"What do you need?"

"The Company wants the parent plant I took the specimen from, the
whole thing, root and branch. It's a big vine, must have been planted years
ago, so I need you to get me some Indians to dig it up and bring it back here
in a carreta. Six months at a Sciences Base, can you imagine?"

"Where did you get the specimen?" I inquired.

She barely thought about it. "Two kilometers south-southeast. Just some
Indian family back in the hills, Joseph, with a hut in a clearing and a garden.
Kasmali, that was what they called themselves. You know the family? I suppose we'll have to pay them something for it. You'll have to arrange that for
me, okay?"

I sighed. Once again the kindly padre was going to explain to the Indian
why it was necessary to give up yet another of his belongings. Not my favorite
role, all things considered.

▲▼▲

But there we were that afternoon, the jolly friar and his haughty cousin, paying a call on the Kasmali family.

They were good parishioners of mine, the old abuela at Mass every day of the week, rain or shine, the rest of the family lined up there every Sunday. That was a lot to expect of our Indians in this day and age. They were prosperous, too, as Indians went: they had three walls of a real adobe house and had patched in the rest with woven brush. They had terraced their tiny hillside garden and were growing all kinds of vegetables on land not fit for grazing. There were a few chickens, there were a few little brown children chasing them, there were a few cotton garments drying on the bushes. And, on the crest of the hill, a little way from the house, there was the vineyard: four old vines, big as trees, with branches spreading out to shade most of an acre of land.

The children saw us coming and vanished into the house without a sound. By the time we reached the top of the winding stony path, they had all come out and were staring at us: the toothless old woman from daily Mass, a toothless old man I did not know, the old son, the two grown grandsons, their wives, and children of assorted ages. The elder of the grandsons came forward to greet us.

"Good evening, little Father." He looked uneasily at Mendoza. "Good evening, lady."

"Good evening, Emidio." I paused and pretended to be catching my breath after the climb, scanning him. He was small, solidly built, with broad and very dark features; he had a stiff black moustache. His wide eyes flickered once more to Mendoza, then back to me. "You have already been introduced to my cousin, I see."

"Yes, little Father." He made a slight bow in her direction. "The lady came yesterday and cut some branches off our grapevines. We did not mind, of course."

"It is very kind of you to permit her to collect these things." I eyed Mendoza, hoping she'd been tactful with them.

"Not at all. The lady speaks our language very well."

"That is only courtesy, my son. Now, I must tell you that one of your vines has taken her fancy, for its extraordinary fruit and certain virtues in the leaves. We have come back here today, therefore, to ask you what you will accept for that near vine at the bottom of the terrace."

The rest of the family stood like statues, even the children. Emidio moved his hands in a helpless gesture and said, "The lady must of course accept our gift."

"No, no," said Mendoza. "We'll pay you. How much do you want for it?" I winced.

"She must accept the gift, please, Father." Emidio's smile was wretched.

"Of course she shall," I agreed. "And, Emidio, I have a gift I have been meaning to give you since the feast of San Juan. Two little pigs, a boar and a sow, so they may increase. When you bring down the vine for us you may collect them."

The wives lifted up their heads at that. This was a good deal. Emidio spread out his hands again. "Of course, little Father. Tomorrow."

▲▼▲

"Well, that was easy," Mendoza remarked as we picked our way down the hill through the chaparral. "You're so good with mortals, Joseph. You just have to treat Indians like children, I guess, huh?"

"No, you don't," I sighed. "But it's what they expect you to do, so they play along." There was more to it than that, of course, but something else was bothering me. I had picked up something more than the usual stifled resentment when I had voiced my request: someone in the family had been badly frightened for a second. Why? "You didn't do anything to, like, scare those people when you were there before, did you, Mendoza? Didn't threaten them or anything, did you?"

"Heavens, no." She stopped to examine a weed. "I was quite polite. They weren't comfortable around me, actually, but then mortals never are. Look at this! I've never seen this blooming so late in the year, have you?"

"Nice." I glanced at it. I don't know from plants. I know a lot about mortals, though.

▲▼▲

So I was surprised as hell next day when Emidio and his brother appeared at the Mission, trundling a cart full of swaying leaves into the open space by the fountain. I went out to greet them and Mendoza was behind me like a shadow. She must have been prowling her room, listening for the squeak of wheels.

"This is very good, my sons, I am proud of you—" I was saying heartily, when Mendoza transmitted a blast of subvocal fury.

Damn it, Joseph, this is wrong! These are just clippings, they haven't brought the whole vine!

"—but I perceive there has been a misunderstanding," I continued. "My cousin requested the vine itself, with its roots, that she may replant it. You have brought only cut branches, apparently." The Indians exchanged glances.

"Please forgive us, little Father. We did not understand." They set down the traces and Emidio reached into the back. "We did bring all the grapes that were ripe. Maybe it was these the lady wanted?" And he proffered a big woven dish of grapes. I looked close and noticed they did have a funny look to them, a bloom on the skin so heavy it was almost…furry?

"No," said Mendoza, in clearest Chumash. "Not just the grapes. I want the vine. The whole plant. You need to dig it up, roots and all, and bring it here. Do you understand now?"

"Oh," said Emidio. "We're very sorry. We didn't understand."

"But you understand now?" she demanded.

"I am certain they do," I said smoothly. "What remarkable grapes these are, my sons, and what a beautiful basket! Come in and rest in the shade, my sons, and have a cool drink. Then we will go catch one of the little pigs I promised you."

By the time we got back, Mendoza had vanished; the grapes and the vine cuttings were gone too. The brothers trudged away up the hill with their cart and one squealing shoat, his legs bound with twine. Pig Number Two remained in the Mission pen, to be paid on delivery of the vine. I figured if the wives got that message they'd see to it the job got done.

Mendoza came out when they were gone. She looked paler than usual. She handed me a sheet of paper from her credenza. "This is a Priority Order," she told me. "I sent them the codes on the grapes and clippings anyway, but it's not enough."

I read the memo. She wasn't kidding; it was a first-class transdepartmental Priority Gold telling me I was to do everything in my power to facilitate, expedite and et cetera. "What have we got here, anyway, cancer cures from grapes?" I speculated.

"You don't need to know and neither do I," said Mendoza flatly. "But the Company means business now, Joseph. We must get that vine."

"We'll get it tomorrow," I told her. "Trust me."

▲▼▲

Next day, same hour, the brothers came with hopeful smiles and a big muddy mess of a vine trailing out of their cart. Such relief! Such heartfelt praise and thanks the kindly friar showered on his obedient sons in Christ! Mendoza heard their arrival and came tearing out into the courtyard, only to pull up short with an expression of baffled rage.

THAT'S NOT THE VINE! she transmitted, with such intensity I thought for a second we were having an earthquake.

"…And yet, my sons, I am afraid we have not understood each other once again," I went on wearily. "It appears that, although you have brought us *a* whole vine, you have not brought *the* particular vine that was specifically asked for by my cousin."

"We are so sorry," replied Emidio, averting his eyes from Mendoza. "How stupid we were! But, Father, this is a very good vine. It's in much better condition than the other one and bears much prettier grapes. Also, it was very difficult to dig it all up and we have brought it a long way. Maybe the lady will be satisfied with this vine instead?"

Mendoza was shaking her head, not trusting herself to speak, although the air around her was wavering like a mirage. Hastily I said:

"My dearest sons, I am sure it is an excellent vine, and we would not take it from your family. You must understand that it is the *other* vine we want, the very one you brought cuttings from yesterday. That vine and no other, and all of that vine. Now, you have clearly worked very hard and in good faith, so I will certainly send you home with your other pig, but you must come back tomorrow with the right vine."

The brothers looked at each other and I picked up a flash of despair from them, and some weird kind of fear too. "Yes, little Father," they replied.

▲▼▲

But on the next day they didn't come at all.

Mendoza paced the arcade until nine in the evening, alarming the other friars. Finally I went out to her and braced myself for the blast.

"You know, you lost yourself two perfectly good pigs," she informed me through gritted teeth. "Damned lying Indians."

I shook my head. "Something's wrong here, Mendoza."

"You bet something's wrong! You've got a three-day delay on a Priority Gold."

"But there's some reason we're not getting. Something is missing from this picture…"

"We never should have tried to bargain with them, you know that? They offered it as a gift in the first place. We should have just taken it. Now they know it's really worth something! I'll go up there with a spade and dig the damned vine up myself, if I have to."

"No! You can't do that, not now. They'll know who took it, don't you see?"

"One more crime against the helpless Indians laid at the door of Spain. As if it mattered any more!" Mendoza turned on her heel to stare at me. Down at the other end of the arcade one of my brother friars put his head out in discreet inquiry.

It does matter! I dropped to a subvocal hiss. *It matters to them and it matters to me! I call them my beloved sons, but they know I've got the power to go up there and confiscate anything they have on any excuse at all because that's how it's always been done! Only I don't. They know Father Rubio won't do that to them. I've built up a cover identity as a kindly, honorable guy because I've got to live with these people for the next thirty years! You'll get your damn specimen and go away again into the sagebrush, but I've got a character to maintain!*

My God, she sneered, *He wants his little Indians to love him.*

Company policy, baby. It's easier to deal with mortals when they trust you. Something you used to understand. So just you try screwing with my cover identity! Just you try it and see what happens.

She widened her eyes at that, too furious for words, and I saw her knuckles go white; little chips of whitewash began falling from the walls. We both looked up at them and cooled down in a hurry.

Sorry. But I mean what I say, Mendoza. We handle this my way.

She threw her hands up in the air. *What are you going to do, then, smart guy? You have to do* something.

▲▼▲

Day four of the Priority Gold, and Company Directive 081244-A anxiously inquired why no progress on previous transdepartmental request for facilitation?

Situation Report follows, I responded. *Please stand by.* Then I put on my walking sandals and set off up the canyon alone.

Before I had toiled more than halfway, though, I met Emidio coming in my direction. He didn't try to avoid me, but as he approached he looked down the canyon past me in the direction of the Mission. "Good morning, little Father," he called.

"Good morning, my son."

"Is your cousin lady with you?" He dropped his voice as he drew close.

"No, my son. We are alone."

"I need to speak with you, little Father, about the grapevine." He cleared his throat. "I know the lady must be very angry, and I am sorry. I don't mean to make you angry too, little Father, because I know she is your cousin—"

"I understand, my son, believe me. And I am not angry."

"Well then." He drew a deep breath. "This is the matter. The grapevines do not belong to me, nor to my father. They belong to our grandfather Diego. And he will not let us dig up the vine the lady wants."

"Why will he not?"

"He won't tell us. He just refuses. Don't be stupid, we told him. Father Rubio has been good to us, he has treated us fairly. Look at the fine pigs he has given us, we said. He just sits in the sun and rocks himself, and refuses us. And our grandmother came and touched his feet and cried, though she didn't say anything, but he wouldn't even look at her."

"I see."

"We have said everything we could say to him, but he will not let us dig up that vine. We tried to fool the lady twice by pretending to make mistakes (and that was a sin, little Father, and I'm sorry), but it didn't work. Somehow she knew. Then our grandfather—" he paused in obvious embarrassment. "I don't know how to say this, little Father—you know the old people are superstitious and still believe foolish things—I think he somehow has the idea that your cousin lady is a *nunasis*. Please don't take this the wrong way—"

"No, no, go on—"

"We have an old story about a spirit who walks on the mountains and wears a hat like hers, you see, throwing a shadow cold as death. I know it's stupid. Even so, Grandfather won't let us dig up that vine. Now, you might say, our grandfather is only an old man and a little bit crazy now, and we're strong, so he can be put aside as though he were a little baby; but if we did that, we would be breaking the commandment about honoring the old people. It seems to us that would be a worse sin than the white lady not getting what she wanted. What do you think, little Father?"

Boy, oh, boy. "This is very hard, my son," I said, and I meant it. "But you are right."

Emidio studied me in silence for a long moment, his eyes narrowed. "Thank you," he said at last. After another pause he added, "Is there anything we can do that will make the lady happy? She'll be angry with you, now."

I found myself laughing. "She will make my life a Purgatory, I can tell you," I said. "But I will offer it up for my sins. Go home, Emidio, and don't worry. Perhaps God will send a miracle."

▲▼▲

I wasn't laughing when I got back to the Mission, though, and when Mendoza came looking for me she saw my failure right away.

"No dice, huh?" She squinted evilly. "Well. This is no longer a matter of me and my poor little bonus now, Joseph. *The Company wants that vine.* I suggest you think of something fast or there are liable to be some dead Indians around here soon, pardon my indelicate phrasing."

"I'm working on it," I told her.

And I was. I went to the big leatherbound books that held the Mission records. I sat down in a corner of the scriptorium and went over them in minute detail.

1789—here was the baptism of Diego Kasmali, age given as thirty years. 1790, marriage to Maria Concepción, age not given. 1791 through 1810, a whole string of baptisms of little Kasmalis: Agustin, Xavier, Pablo, Juan Bautista, Maria, Dolores, Guadalupe, Dieguito, Marta, Tomas, Luisa, Bartolomeo. First Communion for Xavier Kasmali, 1796. One after the other, a string of little funerals: Agustin age two days, Pablo age three months six days, Juan Bautista age six days, Maria age two years…too sad to go on down the list, but not unusual. Confirmation for Xavier Kasmali, 1802. Xavier Kasmali married to Juana Catalina of the Dos Pueblos rancheria, age 18 years, 1812. Baptism of Emidio Kasmali, 1813. Baptism of Salvador Kasmali, 1814. Funeral of Juana Catalina, 1814. First Communions, Confirmations, Marriages, Baptisms, Extreme unctions…not a sacrament missed. Really good Catholics.

Why there was the old, old woman was at Mass every single day of the year, rain or shine, though she was propped like a bundle of sticks in the shadows at the back of the church. Maria Concepción, wife of Diego Kasmali. But Diego never, ever at Mass. Why not? On a desperate hunch I went to my transmitter and typed in a request for something unusual.

The reply came back: *Query: first please resolution Priority Gold status?*

Request relates Priority, I replied. *Resolving now. Requisition Sim ParaN Phenom re: Priority resolution?*

That gave them pause. They verified and counterverified my authority, they re-scanned the original orders and mulled over their implications. At least, I guessed they were doing that, as the blue screen flickered. Feeling I had them on the run, I pushed for a little extra, just for my own satisfaction: *Helpful Priority specify mutation. What? Why?*

Pause while they verified me again, then the bright letters crawled on-screen in a slow response:

Patent Black Elysium.

I fell back laughing, though it wasn't exactly funny. The rest of the message followed in a rapid burst: *S-P Requisition approved. Specify Tech support?*

I told them what I needed.

Estimate resolution time Priority Gold?

I told them how long it would take.

Expecting full specimen consign & report then, was the reply, and they signed off.

▲▼▲

"Why don't they ever put convenient handles on these things?" grumbled Mendoza. She had one end of the transport trunk and a shovel; I had the other end of the trunk and the other shovel. It was long after midnight and we were struggling up the rocky defile that led to the Kasmali residence.

"Too much T-field drag," I explained.

"Well, you would think that an all-powerful cabal of scientists and businessmen, with advance knowledge of every event in recorded history *and* infinite time in which to take every possible advantage of said events, *and* every possible technological resource at their command, *and* unlimited wealth—" Mendoza shifted the trunk again and we went on—"you'd think they could devise something as simple as a recessed handle."

"They tried it. The recess cuts down on the available transport space inside," I told her.

"You're kidding me."

"No. I was part of a test shipment. Damn thing got me right in the third cervical vertebra."

"I might have known there'd be a reason."

"The Company has a reason for everything, Mendoza."

We came within earshot of the house, so conversation ended. There were three big dogs in the yard before the door. One slept undisturbed, but two raised their heads and began to growl. We set down the trunk. I opened it and from the close-packed contents managed to prize out the hush unit. The bigger of the dogs got to his feet, preparing to bark.

I switched on the unit. Good dog, what a sleepy doggie; he fell over with a woof and did not move again. The other dog dropped his head on his paws. Dog Number Three would not wake at all now, nor would any of the occupants of the house, not while the hush field was being generated.

I carried the unit up to the house and left it by the dogs, Mendoza dragging the trunk after me. We removed the box of golden altar vessels and set off up the hill with it.

The amazing mutated vine was pretty sorry-looking now, with most of its branches clipped off in the attempt to appease Mendoza. I hoped to God their well-meaning efforts hadn't killed it. Mendoza must have been thinking the same thing, but she just shrugged grimly. We began to dig.

We made a neat hole, small but very deep, just behind the trunk and angled slightly under it. There was no way to hide our disturbance of the earth, but fortunately the ground had already been so spaded up and trampled over that our work shouldn't be that obvious.

"How deep does this have to be?" I panted when we had gone about six feet and I was in the bottom passing spadefuls up to Mendoza.

"Not much deeper; I'd like it buried well below the root ball." She leaned in and peered.

"Well, how deep is that?" Before she could reply my spade hit something with a metallic clank. We halted.

Mendoza giggled nervously. "Jesus, don't tell me there's *already* buried treasure down there!"

I scraped a little with the spade. "There's something like a hook," I said. "And something else." I got the spade under it and launched it up out of the hole with one good heave. The whole mass fell on the other side of the dirt heap, out of my view. "It looked kind of round," I remarked.

"It looks kind of like a hat—" Mendoza told me cautiously, bending down and turning it over. Abruptly she yelled and danced back from it. I scrambled up out of the hole to see what was going on.

It was a hat, all right, or what was left of it; one of the hard-cured leather kind Spain had issued to her soldiers in the latter half of the last century. I remembered seeing them on the presidio personnel. Beside the hat, where my spade-toss had dislodged it, was the head that had been wearing it. Only a brown skull now, the eyes blind with black earth. Close to it was the hilt of a sword, the metallic thing I'd hit.

"Oh, *gross*!" Mendoza wrung her hands.

"Alas, poor Yorick," was all I could think of to say.

"Oh, God, how disgusting. Is the rest of him down there?"

I peered down into the hole. I could see a jawbone and pieces of what might have been cavalry boots. "Looks like it, I'm afraid."

"What do you suppose he's doing down there?" Mendoza fretted, from behind the handkerchief she had clapped over her mouth and nose.

"Not a damn thing nowadays," I guessed, doing a quick scan of the bones. "Take it easy: no pathogens left. This guy's been dead a long time."

"Sixty years, by any chance?" Mendoza's voice sharpened.

"They must have planted him with the grapevine," I agreed. In the thoughtful silence that followed I began to snicker. I couldn't help myself. I leaned back and had myself a nice sprawling guffaw.

"I fail to see what's so amusing," said Mendoza.

"Sorry. Sorry. I was just wondering: do you suppose you could cause a favorable mutation in something by planting a dead Spaniard under it?"

"Of course not, you idiot, not unless his sword was radioactive or something."

"No, of course not. What about those little wild yeast spores in the bloom on the grapes, though? You think they might be influenced somehow by the close proximity of a gentleman of Old Castile?"

"What are you talking about?" Mendoza took a step closer.

"This isn't a cancer cure, you know." I waved my hand at the vinestock, black against the stars. "I found out why the Company is so eager to get hold of your Favorable Mutation, kid. This is the grape that makes Black Elysium."

"The dessert wine?" Mendoza cried.

"The very expensive dessert wine. The hallucinogenic-controlled-substance dessert wine. The absinthe of the twenty-fourth century. The one the Company holds the patent on. That stuff. Yeah."

Stunned silence from my fellow immortal creature. I went on:

"I was just thinking, you know, about all those decadent technocrats sitting around in the future getting bombed on an elixir produced from…"

"So it gets discovered here, in 1844," said Mendoza at last. "It isn't a genetically engineered cultivar at all. And the wild spores somehow came from…?"

"But nobody else will ever know the truth, because we're removing every trace of this vine from the knowledge of mortal men, see?" I explained. "Root and branch and all."

"I'd sure better get that bonus," Mendoza reflected.

"Don't push your luck. You aren't supposed to know." I took my shovel and clambered back into the hole. "Come on, let's get the rest of him out of here. The show must go on."

Two hours later there was a tidy heap of brown bones and rusted steel moldering away in a new hiding place, and a tidy sum in gold plate occupying the former burial site. We filled in the hole, set up the rest of the equipment we'd brought, tested it, camouflaged it, turned it on and hurried away back down the canyon to the Mission, taking the hush unit with us. I made it in time for Matins.

▲▼▲

News travels fast in a small town. By nine there were Indians, and some of the *Gentes de Razon* too, running in from all directions to tell us that the Blessed Virgin had appeared in the Kasmalis' garden. Even if I hadn't known already, I would have been tipped off by the fact that old Maria Concepción did not show up for morning Mass.

By the time we got up there, the bishop and I and all my fellow friars and Mendoza, a cloud of dust hung above the dirt track from all the traffic. The Kasmalis' tomatoes and corn had been trampled by the milling crowd. People ran everywhere, waving pieces of grapevine; the other plants had been stripped as bare as the special one. The rancheros watched from horseback, or urged their mounts closer across the careful beds of peppers and beans.

Around the one vine, the family had formed a tight circle. Some of them watched Emidio and Salvador, who were digging frantically, already about five feet down in the hole; others stared unblinking at the floating image of the Virgin of Guadalupe who smiled upon them from midair above the vine. She was complete in every detail, nicely three-dimensional and accompanied by heavenly music. Actually it was a long tape loop of Ralph Vaughan Williams's *Fantasia on a Theme by Thomas Tallis*, which nobody would recognize because it hadn't been composed yet.

"Little Father!" One of the wives caught me by my robe. "It's the Mother of God! She told us to dig up the vine, she said there was treasure buried underneath!"

"Has she told you anything else?" I inquired, making the sign of the cross. My brother friars were falling to their knees in raptures, beginning to sing the *Ave Maria*; the bishop was sobbing.

"No, not since this morning," the wife told me. "Only the beautiful music has gone on and on."

Emidio looked up and noticed me for the first time. He stopped shoveling for a moment, staring at me, and a look of dark speculation crossed his face. Then his shovel was moving again, clearing away the earth, and more earth, and more earth.

At my side, Mendoza turned away her face in disgust. But I was watching the old couple, who stood a little way back from the rest of the family. They clung to each other in mute terror and had no eyes for the smiling Virgin. It was the bottom of the ever-deepening hole they watched, as birds watch a snake.

And I watched them. Old Diego was bent and toothless now, but sixty years ago he'd had teeth, all right; sixty years ago his race hadn't yet learned never to fight back against its conquerors. Maria Concepción, what had she been sixty years ago when those vines were planted? Not a dried-up shuffling old thing back then. She might have been a beauty, and maybe a careless beauty.

The old bones and the rusting steel could have told you, sixty years ago. Had he been a handsome young captain with smooth ways, or just a soldier who took what he wanted? Whatever he'd been, or done, he'd wound up buried under that vine, and only Diego and Maria knew he was there. All those years, through the children and grandchildren and great-grandchildren, he'd been there. Diego never coming to Mass because of a sin he couldn't confess. Maria never missing Mass, praying for someone.

Maybe that was the way it had happened. Nobody would ever tell the story, I was fairly sure. But it was clear that Diego and Maria, alone of all those watching, did not expect to see treasure come out of that hole in the ground.

So when the first glint of gold appeared, and then the chalice and altar plate were brought up, their old faces were a study in confusion.

"The treasure!" cried Salvador. "Look!"

And the rancheros spurred their horses through the crowd to get a better look, lashing the Indians out of the way; but I touched the remote hidden in my sleeve and the Blessed Virgin spoke, in a voice as sweet and immortal as a synthesizer:

"This, my beloved children, is the altar plate that was lost from the church at San Carlos Borromeo, long ago in the time of the pirates. My beloved Son has caused it to be found here as a sign to you all that ALL SINS ARE FORGIVEN!"

I touched the remote again and the Holy Apparition winked out like a soap bubble, and the beautiful music fell silent.

Old Diego pushed his way forward to the hole and looked in. There was nothing else there in the hole now, nothing at all. Maria came timidly to his side and she looked in too. They remained there staring a long time, unnoticed by the mass of the crowd, who were watching the dispute that had already erupted over the gold.

The bishop had pounced on it like a duck on a June bug, as they say, asserting the right of Holy Mother Church to her lost property. Emidio and Salvador had let it be snatched from them with hard patient smiles. One of the *Gentes de Razon* actually got off his horse to tell the bishop that the true provenance of the items had to be decided by the authorities in Mexico City, and until they could be contacted the treasure had better be kept under lock and key at the alcalde's house. Blessed Virgin? Yes, there had seemed to be an apparition of some kind; but then again, perhaps it had been a trick of the light.

The argument moved away down the hill—the bishop had a good grip on the gold and kept walking with it, so almost everyone had to follow him. I went to stand beside Diego and Maria, in the ruins of their garden.

"She forgave us," whispered Diego.

"A great weight of sin has been lifted from you today, my children," I told them. "Rejoice, for Christ loves you both. Come to the church with me now and I will celebrate a special Mass in your honor."

I led them away with me, one on either arm. Unseen behind us, Mendoza advanced on the uprooted and forgotten vine with a face like a lioness kept from her prey.

▲▼▲

Well, the old couple made out all right, anyway. I saw to it that they got new grapevines and food from the Mission supplies to tide the family over until their garden recovered. Within a couple of years they passed away, one after the other, and were buried reasonably near one another in the consecrated ground of the Mission cemetery, in which respect they were luckier than the unknown captain from Castile, or wherever he'd come from.

They never got the golden treasure, but being Indians there had never been any question that they would. Their descendants lived on and multiplied in the area, doing particularly well after the coming of the Yankees, who (to the mortification of the *Gentes de Razon*) couldn't tell an Indian from a Spanish Mexican and lumped them all together under the common designation of Greaser, treating one no worse than the other.

Actually I never kept track of what happened to the gold. The title dispute dragged on for years, I think, with the friars swearing there had been a miracle and the rancheros swearing there hadn't been. The gold may have been returned to Carmel, or it may have gone to Mexico City, or it may have gone into a trunk underneath the alcalde's bed. I didn't care; it was all faked Company-issue reproductions anyway. The bishop died and the Yankees came and were the new conquerors, and maybe nothing ever did get resolved either way.

But Mendoza got her damned vine and her bonus, so she was as happy as she ever is. The Company got its patent on Black Elysium secured. I lived on at the Mission for years and years before (apparently) dying of venerable old age and (apparently) being buried in the same cemetery as Diego and Maria. God forgave us all, I guess, and I moved on to less pleasant work.

Sometimes, when I'm in that part of the world, I stop in as a tourist and check out my grave. It's the nicest of the many I've had, except maybe for that crypt in Hollywood. Well, well; life goes on.

Mine does anyway.

Old Flat Top

The boy has the firm chin and high-domed brow of the Cro-Magnon hominids—might be a member of any racial group—and is dressed in somewhat inadequate Neolithic clothing of woven grass and furs. He didn't bring any useful Neolithic tools with him on this journey, however. He had come to see if God was really on the mountain as he'd always been told, and he hadn't thought tools would be any use in finding God. In this he was reasonably correct. No instrument his people could produce, at their present level of technology, would help him now.

Far enough up a mountain to peer above the clouds, the boy is in serious trouble. Above him is ice and thin air; all around him a sliding waste of black blasted rock, immense, pitiless. The green valley of his ancestors lies a long way below him, and he could return there in slightly under a minute if he didn't mind arriving in a red smashed mass.

That would scarcely win him the admiration of his peers, however, and he clings now desperately to a narrow handhold, and gazes up at the mouth of the cave he has come so far to find. He can neither jump nor climb any higher. He can't climb back down, either; his hands and feet have gone numb. He realizes he is going to die.

To his left, a few meters away, there is sudden movement.

He turns his head to stare. What he had taken to be an outcropping of particularly weathered rock is looking at him. It is in fact a man, easily twice his size, naked but for a belted bearskin and a great deal of dun-colored hair and beard.

The giant's body is powerfully built, nearly human as the boy understands human, but with a slightly odd articulation of the arms and shoulders. The head is not human at all. The skull is long and low, helmet-shaped, and with its heavy orbital ridges and forward-projecting face it reminds the boy of those stocky little villagers in the next valley, the ones who scatter flowers over their dead and make such unimaginative flint tools. Like them, too, the giant has an immense protruding nose. Its cheekbones are high and broad, its jaw heavy, its teeth terrifyingly long. The boy knows this because the giant is grinning at him.

"Boo," says the giant, in a light and rather pleasant voice.

This syllable means nothing to the boy, but he is so thoroughly unnerved that he loses his grip on the mountain and totters backward, screaming.

The next moment is a blur. All his breath is knocked out of him, and before he can grasp what has happened, he finds himself crouching inside the cave that was so unattainable a moment before. The giant is squatting beside him, considering him with pale inhuman eyes.

Seen close to, the giant is even more unnerving. He cocks his head and the angle at which he does this is not human either, nor is the strong strange musk of his body. The boy drags himself swiftly backward, stares around the interior of the cave for a weapon. The giant chuckles at him.

There are plenty of weapons, but it's doubtful the boy would be able to lift any of these tremendous stone axes, let alone defend himself with one. He looks further, and then his frantic gaze stops dead at the battered cabinet against one wall.

The fact that its central screen glows with tiny cryptic symbols is almost beside the point. It's a *box*, and the boy's world has no such geometry. He has never seen a rectangle, a square. This fully convinces him that he has found the object of his quest. Slowly, he turns back to face the giant.

He makes obeisance, and the giant snorts. Sitting timidly upright, the boy explains that he has come in search of God on the mountain for the purpose of learning the Truth.

The boy's language is a combination of hand gestures and sounds. The giant's eyes narrow; he leans close, keenly observing, listening. When the boy has finished, the giant clears his throat and replies in the same manner.

He communicates for some time. His hands are clever, capable of facile and expressive gestures, and his vocal apparatus produces a wider range of syllables, enunciated with greater precision; so it will be understood that he is a far more eloquent speaker than the boy, who listens as though spellbound.

▲▼▲

Yes, I'll tell you the Truth. Why not? In all these generations, you're the first mortal to climb up here, so you've earned an answer; but I don't think you'll like it much.

I'm not your God. I'm the highest authority you'll ever encounter, though, mortal man. Really. I was created to judge you and punish you, you and all your fathers. Would you like to know how that happened? Watch.

I'll draw something in the dust for you, here. This is called a circle, all right? It's the wheel of Time. Never mind what a wheel is. This part here, almost at the beginning, is where your people began to exist.

Life was a lot harder back then, mortal. Your people almost didn't make it. You know why? Because, almost from the time your fathers stood up on their little hind legs, they made war on one another. Winters weren't bitter enough! Leopards and crocodiles weren't hungry enough! Famine wasn't terrible enough either. They had to keep whittling away at their numbers themselves, stupid monkeys.

The worst were a bunch who called themselves the Great Goat Cult. They found a weed that filled them with holy visions when they chewed it. They heard voices that told them to go out and kill. Became screaming tattooed maniacs who made a lot of converts, believe me, but they killed more than they converted.

Now, look here at this part of the circle. This is up at the other end of Time. The people up there are, let's say they're powerful shamans. And they're very nervous. Being so close to the end of Time, they want to save as much of the past as they can.

They looked back into Time through a, uh, a *magic eye* they had. They looked at their oldest fathers and saw that if this Great Goat Cult wasn't stopped, they themselves might never come to exist. Who had time to learn how to make fire, or sew furs into clothing or make pots out of clay, if crazy people were always chasing and killing everybody?

I'm simplifying this for you, mortal, but here's what they did.

The shamans found a way to step across from their part of the circle into the beginning part. They took some of your fathers' children and made them slaves, but magic slaves: immortal and strong and really smart. They sent those slaves to try to reason with the Great Goat Cult.

It didn't work.

The slaves were great talkers, could present many clever arguments, but the Great Goat Cult wouldn't listen. In fact, they sent the slaves back to their shaman masters with spears stuck in inconvenient places, and one or two had to carry their own lopped-off body parts. So the shamans had to come up with another idea.

Can you guess yet what it was? No? Well, you're only a mortal. I'll tell you.

They took some more slaves, not just from your fathers but from some of the other tribes running around back then—those little guys in the next valley, for example, and some big people from a valley you've never seen, and a few others who're all extinct now.

You know how you can put a long-legged ram with long fleece in the pen with a short-legged ewe with short fleece, and you'll get a short-legged lamb with long fleece? Eventually? Breeding experiments, right, you've got it. Well, that's what the shamans did with all these people. Bred the big ones and the little ones to get what they wanted.

What did they want? What were they breeding for? You can't guess? I'm disappointed. They wanted their very own screaming killing maniacs to counter the cultists.

Except we're not really maniacs. We just have a great sense of humor.

We're the optimum morphological design for a humanoid fighting machine, oo-rah! We're not afraid of being hurt, like you. And of course we too were made immortal and smart. Three thousand of us were bred. That was a lot of people, back then. They raised us in cadet academies, trained us in camps, me and all my brother warriors.

This was all done back here at the beginning of time, by the way. The shamans were scared to death to have us up there at their end. There are no warriors in their time, or so we were always told.

And we were all programmed—no, you don't know what that is. Indoctrinated? Convinced with extreme prejudice?

We were given the absolute Truth.

But it's our Truth, not yours, mortal. Our Truth is that we have the joyous right and duty to kill, instantly and without question, any dirty little mortals we find making war on each other. *You* don't have the right to kill yourselves. You're supposed to live in peace, herd beasts, plant crops, tell stories, have babies. Do that and we'll let you alone. But if you decide to make war, not love—whack, there we are with flint axes and bloody retribution, you see? Simplicity itself.

It was the law. Perfect and beautiful justice. You do right, we punish wrong. No questions. No whining.

The shamans from the other end of Time created us as the consummate weapon against the Great Goat Cult. We were bigger and faster, and we killed without pity or hesitation. Our faith was stronger than theirs. So we made mincemeat out of the little bastards.

Oh, those were great times. So much work to do! Because, while the shamans had dithered around about whether or not we should be created, the Cult had spread across the world. It took centuries to stamp them all out. We rode in endless pursuit and it was one long happy party, mortal. Summer campaigns, year after year. Winter raids, damn I loved them: bloodspray's beautiful on new-fallen snow, and corpses stay fresh so much longer…

Don't be scared. I'm just reminiscing.

When we slaughtered the last of the Goats, your fathers were set free, don't you understand? Instead of running and hiding in holes like animals, they could settle down to become people. They had time at last, to learn to count on their fingers and toes, to look at the stars and wonder what they were. Time to drill holes in deer bone and make music. Time to paint bison on cave walls. And the other immortals (we called them Preservers), had time at last to go among your fathers and collect cultural artifacts the shamans wanted saved, now that there *was* culture.

But what were we Enforcers supposed to do, with our great purpose in life gone? We loved to kill. It was all we knew, all we were made for. So our officers met together, to talk over the question of where the masters expected us to fit, in this new peacetime we'd made possible for mortals.

There was a lot of debate. Most of us in the rank and file were pretty optimistic; we just figured they'd reprogram us to do some other job. But one colonel, an asshole named Marco, thought we could never be sure the mortals wouldn't relapse into being cultists, and that maybe we ought to make some preemptive strikes: you know, kill all the mortals who looked as though they *might* make war, so they'd never get a chance to.

Everyone roared him down, except the men under his command. See, that would have been absolutely wrong! That would have been killing innocents, and we don't do that. Noncombatants are to be protected at all times. But our masters, who as I mentioned are nervous people, shit themselves in terror when they found out what Marco'd said.

Marco's faith was imperfect. We should have done something about him right then…but that's another story.

Anyway, Budu told him he was a fool, and that shut him up.

Budu was our general, our supreme commanding officer. He was one of the oldest of us and he was the best, the strongest, the biggest. And he was righteous, I tell you, our Truth was strong in his heart! I'd have died for him, if I wasn't immortal, and as it was I had my head lopped off twice fighting under him. I didn't care; the masters stuck it on again and I was proud to go right from the regeneration tank back to the front lines, as long as Budu was out there too.

(Regeneration tank. It's…think of it as a big pot, no, a *big* pot, do you know what a cauldron is? All right, imagine a big one full of, uh, *magic juice*, and whenever one of us immortals would be damaged too badly to repair ourselves, we'd be carted off the field and put in one of these magic cauldrons to heal. We'd come out good as new.)

Anyway. Budu was also the smartest of us. Budu studied future history, between this age and the time in which our masters live. He figured out what scared them the most. He said the mortal masters might think they didn't need us anymore, but they'd find they were mistaken soon enough. He ordered us to wait. Something would happen.

And, Father of Justice, the old man was right!

Now you're going to find the story more interesting, mortal, because this part of it deals with your own people.

Let's see, how do I explain the concept of mitochondrial DNA to you?

I've already told you how the shamans at the other end of Time want to be sure nothing happens to endanger their own existence, right? Causality really worries them. So they're obsessive about tracing their ancestors, finding out for certain where they came from. And they've been careful to chart something called *genetic drift*. It's like a map, you know what a map is, that shows where their fathers have been.

Well, they found that a lot of their fathers—actually, mothers—started out right below this mountain, mortal, right down in that nice green valley of yours. It's sort of a crossroads—uh, game trail—for humanity. It's where a lot of important human traits came together to make something special.

But back then this hadn't happened yet. There was a tribe living down there, all right, nicely settled into a farming community, but they only had some of the genetic markers, the special blood, that our masters expected to find.

So the masters sent in a Preserver to watch them. He was what we call an *anthropologist,* which meant he didn't mind working with the monkeys. His name was Rook. He became a member of their tribe, lived in their huts with them. I couldn't do it, but I guess there's no accounting for tastes.

Rook was expecting another tribe to appear from somewhere and intermarry with the farmers, and that other tribe would provide the missing pieces, so to speak, and their descendants would become our masters' fathers. He was all set to record it, when it happened; but it didn't quite happen the way he'd expected.

The other tribe came along, all right, hunter-gatherers on a long leisurely migration to greener pastures, and that valley below was nice and green. The newcomers had the right genes, too, just as Rook had predicted.

What he hadn't predicted, though, was that the peaceful farming folk would treat the newcomers just like they treated any other migratory species. Like elk, or caribou. You see, agrarian societies sometimes have a problem getting enough protein...

That means meat. I mean they were catching the hunter-gatherers and eating them.

You're embarrassed to learn that your fathers were cannibals? Think how the shamans at the other end of Time felt!

So the old Enforcers weren't demobilized quite yet, ha ha. But this was a slightly more complicated situation than we were used to, understand? We couldn't just wade in there and wipe out the peaceful farming folk. Negotiation was called for. And we never negotiate.

So our masters assigned us a liaison with the mortals, a new kind of Preserver they'd invented, called a Facilitator.

Facilitators are different. We Enforcers were designed to love killing, and the regular Preservers were designed to love the things they preserved. The Facilitators, though, were designed to be more objective, to operate in the big civilizations that were about to be born. They would be politicians, intriguers, councilors to mortal kings. What do those words mean?...I guess the best translation would be *liars*.

I remember the staff meeting as though it were yesterday, mortal man.

It was raining. We'd made camp on that high meadow you passed on your way up here, and most of us had fanned out into the landscape. Budu had only brought the Fifth Infantry Division, which I was in. I was one of his aides, so all I had to do was set up the tent where the meeting was to be held. The old man stood there quietly in the open, staring down the trail; he didn't care if he got wet.

We'd had a report from a patrol that they were on their way. Pretty soon I caught a whiff of Preserver in the wind though Budu had picked it up before I did; he had already turned to watch them come down from the pass. Rook was on foot, a little miserable-looking guy in a wet cloak, but the Facilitator was riding a horse, and Rook was having to tilt his head back to look up at him as he talked earnestly, waving his arms.

The Facilitator was tall, for one of them anyway, and wore nice tailored clothes. His name was Sarpa. He wasn't paying attention to Rook much, just sort of nodding his head as he rode and scanning the landscape, and when he spotted us I saw his eyes widen. I don't know what he'd been told about Enforcers at his briefing, but he hadn't expected what he found.

They were escorted in, and I took Sarpa's horse away and tethered it. The old man wanted to start the meeting right then. The Preservers asked for something hot to drink first, which seemed stupid to me—had they come there to talk, or to have a party?—but Budu just told me to get them something. All we had was water, but I brought it in a couple of polished Great Goat skulls, the nicest ones in camp. The Preservers stared with big round eyes when I set their drinks before them, and didn't touch a drop. There's no pleasing some people.

At least they got down to business. Rook made his report first, about how the farming tribe had been fairly peaceable until the newcomers had arrived, when they had suddenly shown a previously-unknown talent for hunting hunters. They watched the hunters' trails, lay in wait with sharp sticks, and almost never failed to carry off one of the younger or weaker of the new tribe, whom they butchered and parceled out among themselves. Rook had seen all this firsthand.

The Facilitator Sarpa asked him why he hadn't tried to stop them.

"I did try," he said wretchedly. "I told them they shouldn't eat other people. They told me (with their mouths full) that the strangers weren't people. There were quite calm about it, and nothing I said could convince them otherwise. Anyway, I can't say much without blowing my cover; they thought it was funny enough I wouldn't touch the ribs they offered me."

Sarpa wanted to know what his cover was, and Rook told him he was an adopted member of the tribe, and had himself avoided any "unpleasantness" by volunteering to work in the fields even in bad weather. Sarpa stared harder at that than he'd stared at the skull cups.

"You're maintaining your cover by *good attitude*?" he said, as though he couldn't believe it.

"That's what a participant observer does," Rook explained.

"But when you're one of *us*? It never occurred to you to exploit your superior abilities, or your knowledge? Why didn't you pose as a spirit? A magician, at least, and impress them with a few tricks?"

"That would have been lying," said Budu, and Rook said:

"Well, but that would have created an artificial dynamic in our relationship. I'm supposed to observe and document the way they live in their natural state. If I'd said I was a magical being, they wouldn't have behaved in a natural way toward me, would they?"

Sarpa exhaled hard through his little thin nose, and drummed his fingers on his knees. "All right," he said, "it's clearly time a specialist was brought in. I'll make contact with them immediately."

Budu wanted to know what he was going to do, and Sarpa waved his hand. "Textbook procedure for managing primitives. I'll put them in awe of me with an exhibition of juggling, or something. Once I've got their attention, I'll explain the health risks involved in eating the flesh of their own species."

"And if they won't listen?" asked Budu. Sarpa smiled at him in a patronizing kind of way, I guess because he was frightened of the old man. I could smell his fear from clear over where I was standing, playing dumb like a good orderly.

"Why, then we send in the troops, don't we?" Sarpa said lightly. "But it won't come to that. I know my job."

"Good," said Budu. "What do you need now?"

"I need to download all possible data on them from Rook, here," Sarpa replied. (What's that mean? Just that Rook was going to tell him a lot of things very very fast, mortal.) "We can retire to my field quarters for that; I'd like to get into dry clothes first. Where's our camp?"

"You're in it," said Budu.

Sarpa looked around in dismay. "You haven't put up the other tents yet?" he asked.

Budu told him we don't need tents, but offered him the one in which they were squatting. "And I'll assign you Flat Top for an aide," he said.

(He meant me. I was designated Joshua when I was born, but everybody in my unit went by a nickname. Skullcracker, Crunchmaster, Terminator, that kind of thing. I earned my nickname when we had a contest to see how many beers we could balance on top of our heads. I got five up there.)

Sarpa didn't look too happy about it, but I made myself useful after the old man left: hung some more skins around the tent and brought in some springy bushes for bedding. I unloaded his saddlebags and set up the field unit—uh, the *magic box* that let us talk to the shamans. Like that one over there, see? Only smaller—while he downloaded from Rook. Rook went back to the farmstead after that, poor little drone, couldn't leave his mortals for long.

Sarpa got up and spread his hands over the back of his field unit to get them warm. He asked me, "What time are rations served out?" and I told him we were foraging on this campaign, but that I'd get him part of somebody's kill if he wanted, or maybe some wild onions. He shuddered and said he'd manage on the Company-issued provisions he'd brought with him. So I set that out for him instead, little tiny portions of funny-smelling stuff.

I don't think Sarpa understood yet that he was supposed to dismiss me or I couldn't go. I just stood at ease while he ate, and after a few minutes he offered me a packet of crackers. I could have inhaled the damn things, they were so small. To be polite I nibbled at the edges and made them last a while, which was hard with teeth like mine, believe me.

When he was finished I tidied up for him, and he settled down at his field unit. He didn't work, though. He just stared out over the edge of the meadow at the smoke rising from the mortals' farmstead. I figured I'd better give him a clue, so I said, "Sir, will there be anything else, sir?"

"No…" he said, in a way that meant there would be. I waited, and after a minute he said, not meeting my eyes: "Tell me something, Enforcer. What does a man have to do to—ah—fraternize with the female mortals?"

By which he meant he wanted to couple with one of your mothers.

I said, "Sir, I don't know, sir."

His attention came away from the smoke and he looked up at me sharply. "So it's true, then, about Enforcers?" he asked me. "That you're really not, ah, interested?"

"Sir, that's affirmative, sir," I told him.

"No sex at all?"

"Sir, no sir."

"But…" He looked out at the smoke again. "How on earth do you manage?"

I felt like asking him the same question: Why would our masters have created his kind with the need to go through the motions of reproduction, when they can't actually reproduce?

(No, mortal, we can't. We're immortal, so we don't need to.)

I mean, I can see why you mortals are obsessed with it; I'd be too, if that was my only shot at immortality. But we've always wondered why the Preserver class were given such a stupid appetite. Budu used to say it was because they needed to be able to understand the mortals' point of view if they were to function correctly, and I guess that makes sense. Still, if it was me, I'd find it a distraction.

So I just told Sarpa, "Sir, nothing to manage. Everybody knows that killing's a lot easier than making life, and for us it's a lot more fun, sir."

He shivered at that, and said, "I suppose it's really just sports taken to the extreme, isn't it? Very well; Rook will probably know how to set me up with a girl."

I didn't say anything, and he looked at me sidelong, trying to read my expression.

"You probably disapprove," he said. "With the morality the Company programmed into you."

"Sir, strictly speaking, you're exploiting the mortals, sir," I said.

"And you think that's wrong."

"Sir, it would be for me. Not my place to say what's wrong for you, sir. You're a Preserver, and one of the new models at that, sir."

"So I am," he said, smiling. "You won't judge *me*, eh? I like the way your conscience works, Flat Top. And after all, if I can get the creatures' females on my side, it'll be easier to persuade them to behave themselves."

I don't know why he should have cared what I thought of him, but the Preservers were all like that; the damndest things bothered them. I just told him, "Yes Sir." and he dismissed me after that. The guys in my mess had saved me a leg of mountain goat. Not much meat, but there was a lot of marrow in the bones. Crack, yum.

Well, so the next day the Facilitator went out and did his stuff.

He dressed in his best clothes, dyed all kinds of bright colors to dazzle the mortals, and he put on makeup. He rode on his horse, which your fathers hadn't got around to domesticating yet. It was a pretty animal, nothing like the big beasts our cavalry ride: slender legs, little hooves, kind of on the stupid side but elegant as you please.

We went with Sarpa, though of course we were undercover. There were maybe a hundred of us flanking him as he rode down to their patchwork fields, slipping through the trees and the bushes, keeping ourselves out of sight. So close we came I could have popped open any one of their little round heads with a rock, as Sarpa rode back and forth in plain sight and got their attention.

They froze with their deer-antler hoes in their hands, they watched him with their mouths open, and slowly drew into a crowd as he approached them. He staged it nicely, I have to say, let his long cloak blow out behind him so its rainbow lining showed, and there were grunts and cries of wonder from the mortals.

Sarpa told them he was a messenger from their ancestors, and to prove it he did a stunt with some special-effects charges that sent red smoke and fireballs shooting from his fingertips. The mortals almost turned and ran at that, but he kept them with his voice, saying he had an important message to deliver. Then he said the ancestors demanded to know why their children had been eating their own kind?

His audience just looked blank at that, and I spotted Rook running up from behind and pushing his way through the crowd. He yelled out that he'd warned them this would happen. Falling flat before Sarpa, he begged the ancestors for mercy and promised that the farmers would never do such a terrible thing again.

At this point, though, the farmstead's lady raised her voice and said there must be some mistake, because her people weren't eating their own kind.

Sarpa asked, were they not lying in wait for the strangers who had recently come into the valley, the harmless people who hunted and gathered? Were they not stabbing them with spears, cutting them open, roasting them over coals?

The lady smiled and shrugged and said yes, the invaders were being treated so; but they were not her own kind, and certainly not children of the ancestors!

Sarpa didn't win them over nearly as easy as he'd thought he could. They argued back and forth for about an hour, as I remember. He told them why it was wrong to eat other human beings, told them all about the diseases they could catch, even told them a lot of malarkey about what would happen to them in the next world if they didn't cut it out right now.

The mortals were clearly impressed by him, but refused to consider the newcomers as people and in fact argued quite confidently against such a silly idea. Not only did they point out a whole lot of physical differences that were obvious to them (though it was lost on me; I've never been able to tell one of your races from another), they explained how vitally necessary it was to protect their sacred home turf from the alien interlopers, and protect their limited resources.

Sarpa was kind of taken aback that these little mortal things had the gall to argue with him. I saw he was beginning to lose his temper, and in the shadows beside me Budu noticed it, too; the old man snorted, but he just narrowed his eyes and watched. At last the Facilitator fell back on threatening the mortals, letting fly with a couple of thunderbolts that set fire to a bush and working a few other alarming-looking tricks.

That got instant capitulation. The mortals abased themselves, and the lady apologized profusely for them all being so stupid as not to understand the mighty Son of Heaven sooner. She asked him what they could possibly do to please the Son of Heaven. Maybe he'd like a beautiful virgin?

And a mortal girl was pushed forth, looking scared, and Budu grunted, because Sarpa's eyes fixed on her with an expression like a hungry dog's. Then he was all smiles and gracious acceptance, and congratulated the mortals for being so wise as to see things his way. The girl squealed a bit, but he assured her she'd live through his embrace and even have pretty things afterward. I don't think she believed him, but her mother fixed her with an iron glare, and she gulped back her terror and went with Sarpa.

He took her back up to camp—she squealed a lot more when she saw us at last, but Sarpa sweet-talked her some more—and to celebrate his success he took her to his tent, stripped her bare as a skinned rabbit, and had his fun.

There was a lot of muttering from us about that, and not just because we thought what he was doing was wrong. We were disgusted because he hadn't realized the mortals were lying to him.

See, mortal, *we* can tell when you're lying. You smell different then. You smell afraid. But Sarpa had been distracted by his lusts and his vanity, sniffing after something else. We knew damned well the mortals were only giving him the girl to make him go away.

And oh, mortal, it was hard not to go down there and punish them. It was our duty, it was our programmed and ancient desire. By every law we understood, those mortals were ours now. Budu wouldn't give the order yet, all the same. He just bided his time, though he must have known what was going to happen.

Well—three days later, as Sarpa was in his tent with his little friend while I was busting my ass to find a way to boil water in a rock basin because the great Facilitator wanted a *hot* bath, thank you very much—Rook came slinking up from the farmstead to tell us that the mortals had done it again. They'd caught a party of strangers, and even now they were whacking them up into bits to be skewered over the cookfire.

I can't say I was surprised, and I know the old man wasn't. He just stalked to Sarpa's tent, threw back one of the skins and said:

"Son of Heaven, it seems that your in-laws have backslid."

Sarpa was furious. He yelled at the mortal girl, demanded to know what was wrong with her people, even took a swing at her. Budu growled and fetched him out by his arm, and told him to stop being an ass. He added that if this was the way the hotshot Facilitators operated, the Company—the shamans, I mean—should have saved themselves the trouble of designing a new model, or at least not sent one into the field until they'd got the programming right.

Sarpa just drew himself up and yelled for me to bring his horse. He jumped into the saddle and rode off hell-for-leather, with Rook racing after him. Budu watched them go, and I think he actually considered for a minute whether or not it was worth it to send an armed escort after the fool. In the end he did, which turned out to be a wise precaution.

I wasn't there to see what happened. I was babysitting Sarpa's little girl-friend, watching as she cowered in the bedding and cried. I felt sorry for her. We do feel sorry for you sometimes, you know. It's just that you can be so stupid, you mortals.

Anyway I missed quite a scene. Apparently it didn't go at all well: Sarpa went galloping down and caught the farm-tribe with their mouths full of hunter-tribe. He shouted terrible threats at them, and put on another show of smoke and noises. Maybe he should have waited until there was an eclipse or a comet scheduled, though, because the farmers weren't as impressed with his stunts this time. The upshot was, they killed his horse from under him and he had to run for it, and Rook too. If the armed escort hadn't stepped out and scared the mortals off, there'd have been a couple of badly damaged Preservers doing time in regeneration vats, and maybe some confused farmers puking up bits of biomechanical implants.

But Sarpa and Rook got back up to camp safely enough, though they were fuming at each other, Rook especially because now he'd lost his cover and wouldn't be able to collect any more anthropological data. He said a lot of cutting things about Facilitators in general. Sarpa was just gibbering with rage. I got between him and the girl until he calmed down a little and I respectfully suggested, sir, that he might want to keep her safe as a hostage, sir, and whatever he might have retorted, he shut up when Budu came into the tent and looked at him.

"Well, Facilitator," said Budu, "what are you going to do now?"

But Sarpa had an answer for that. He was through dealing with the lying, grubbing little farmers. He'd go straight to the hunter-gatherers and present himself as their good angel, and show them how to defend themselves against the other tribe.

Budu told him he couldn't do that, because it directly contravened orders. The monkeys were supposed to interbreed, not fight.

Sarpa said something sarcastic about Budu's grasp of subtleties and explained that he'd manage that; if the hunter-gatherers captured the farmers' females, they could keep them as slaves and impregnate them. It wouldn't exactly be the peace and harmony our masters had wanted imposed, but it would at least guarantee the requisite interbreeding took place.

Budu shrugged, and told him to go ahead and try.

Next day, he did. Rook stayed in camp this time, but I went along because Sarpa, having lost his mount, insisted on me carrying him around on my shoulders. I guess he felt safe up there. He had a good view, anyway, because he was the first in our party to spot the hunter-gatherers' camp on the far side of the valley.

Our reconnaissance team had reported the hunter-gatherers were digging in and fortifying a position for themselves, finally. Nice palisade of sharpened sticks, and inside they were chipping flint points just as fast as they could. Budu studied them from all angles before he just sent me walking up to the stockade so that Sarpa could look over the fence at them.

He—that is, I—had to dodge quite a few spears and thrown flints before he got them to listen to his speech. They did listen, I have to hand them that much.

But they weren't buying it. They had every intention of descending on the farmer-tribe and getting revenge for the murder of their brethren. Sarpa tried to persuade them that the best way to do this was to make more children, but that wouldn't wash either.

It turned out they weren't just a migratory tribe. They apparently had a long-standing cultural imperative to expand, to take new land for themselves whenever they needed it, and if other tribes got in the way they'd push them out or kill them off—though they *never* ate them, they hastened to add, because they were a morally superior people, which was why they deserved to have the land in the first place.

Sarpa argued against this until they began to throw things at him again, and we beat an inglorious retreat. What was worse, when we got back we discovered that Rook had let the mortal girl go. He'd known her since her childhood, evidently, and didn't want to see her hurt. He and Sarpa almost came to blows and it's not pretty to see Preservers do that, mortal, they're not designed for it. Budu had to step in again and threaten to knock their heads together if they didn't back off.

Anyway, the damage was done, because the girl ran right back to her tribe and told them what was going on. How she'd figured out that Sarpa was going to woo the enemy, I don't know, unless Rook was dumb enough to tell her. Then, too, you people aren't always as stupid as you look. She might have figured out on her own that matters were coming to a head.

Which they did, in the gray cold hour before the next dawn.

Our patrols spotted them long before they got within a kilometer of each other: two little armies carrying as much weaponry as they could hold, men and boys and strong women, with their faces painted for war. Guilty, guilty, guilty, mortal! We watched from our high place and danced where we stood, we were so hungry to go after them. Sarpa didn't desire his naked girl as much as we desired the sound of our axes on their guilty skulls, pop-chop! They were sinning, the worst of sins, and their blood was ours.

But the old man held us back. Orders were, the mortals were to be given every chance. That's why he was our commander, mortal! He loved the law. His faith was stronger than anyone's, but *he* had the strength to hold back from the purest pleasure in the world, which is being the law's instrument, you see?

So he sent me down with Sarpa riding on my shoulder, and I walked out before the mortal armies, who had just seen each other in the growing light and were working themselves up to charge, the way the monkeys do. They fell silent when Sarpa and I appeared, and clear in the morning they heard the voices of our men, because we couldn't help singing now, the ancient song, and it welled up so beautiful behind Sarpa's voice as he shouted for them to lay down their arms and go home!

Oh, mortal man, you'd have thought they'd listen to him, in that cold morning when the sun was just rising and making the high snow red as blood, lighting the meadows up green, reaching bright fingers down through deeps of blue air to touch their thatched roofs and palisade points with gold. So brief their lives are in this glorious world, you'd think they'd have grabbed at any excuse not to make them briefer.

But the one side jeered and the other side screamed, and the next thing I knew I had a spear sticking out of my leg.

I swear, it felt good. The suspense was over.

They charged, and were at each other's throats in less time than it takes to say it. So Budu gave the order.

I just shoved Sarpa up into a tree, drew my axes, and waded in.

You can't imagine the pleasure, mortal. It would be wrong, anyway; that joy is reserved to us, forbidden to the likes of you. War is *the* Evil, and we make war on war, we strike that wickedness into bloody pulp! The little bone bubbles burst under our axes and the gray matter of their arrogance and presumption flies, food for crows.

Oh, it was over too soon. There'll always be those who get the lesson at the last minute, but once we've shown them what true evil is they do get it, and throw down their weapons and scream their repentance on their knees. Those we spared; those we accorded mercy. Budu himself herded the terrified survivors into a huddle, and stood guard while we mopped up.

I was stringing together a necklace of ears I'd taken when I spotted Rook at the edge of the battlefield, weeping. I was feeling so friendly I almost went over and patted him on the back, with the idea of saying something to cheer him up; but they don't see things the way we do, the Preservers. And seeing him put me in mind of Sarpa, and when I looked around for the Facilitator, damned if he wasn't still up in the tree where I'd left him.

So I went over and offered him a helpful hand down, but he drew back at the sight of all the blood on it. I can't blame him. I was red to the elbows, actually. Sarpa was so pale he looked green, staring at the field as though he'd never be able to close his eyes again.

I told him it was all right, that the slaughter was over. He just looked down at me and asked me how I could do such things.

Well, I had to laugh at that. It's my duty! Who couldn't love doing his duty? It's the best work in the world, mortal, in the best cause: seeing that Evil is punished and Good protected. I told him so, and he said it was obscene; I replied that when the mortals took it into their heads to usurp our jobs, that would be obscene. Sarpa didn't say anything to that, just scrambled awkwardly down and staggered out on the field.

Maybe he shouldn't have done that. The boys were still having a little fun, taking heads that weren't too smashed and cutting off other things that took their fancies, and Sarpa took one look and doubled over, vomiting. The poor guy was a Preserver at heart, after all. The problem was, this was the big dramatic moment when he was supposed to address the surviving mortals of each tribe and point out how disobeying him had brought them to this sorry state.

I told him to pull himself together. Budu, kind of impatient, sent over a runner to ask if the Facilitator was ready to give his speech, and I tried to drag Sarpa along but he'd take a few steps and start retching again, especially when he saw the women lying dead. I hoisted him up on my shoulders to give him a ride, but he got sick again, right in my hair, which the other guys in my unit thought was hilarious; they stopped stacking corpses to point and laugh.

I growled at them and set Sarpa down. He put his hands over his face, crying like a baby. It was hopeless. I looked over at Budu and shrugged, holding out my hands in a helpless kind of way. The old man shook his head, sighing.

In the end, Budu was the one who made the speech, rounding up what was left of the two tribes and penning them together to listen to him.

It wasn't a long speech, no flowers of rhetoric such as Sarpa might have come up with. Budu just laid it out for them, simple and straight. From now on, they were all to live together in peace. They would intermarry and have children. There would be no more cannibalism. There would be no more fighting. The penalty for disobedience would be death.

Then Budu told them that we were going, and they were to bury what we'd left them of their dead. He warned them, though, that we were only going up the mountain, above the tree line into the mist, and we'd be watching them always from the high places.

And we did. We were up here thirty years. It turned out to be a good thing for us, too, because while we were overseeing the integration of the two tribes, Budu worked out a proposal for our masters.

I told you he'd studied their future history. He knew what kind of an opening they needed, and he gave them one. He pointed out the nearly universal existence of places we could fit in the mortals' mythology. Not just of your village, mortal; every village there is, anywhere.

Legends of gods, or giants or trolls or demons, who live up somewhere high and bring judgment on mankind. Sometimes terrible, sometimes benign, but not to be screwed with, ever! Sometimes they're supposed to live on one specific mountain, like this one; sometimes the story gets garbled and they're thought to live in the clouds, or the sky. Someplace *up*. Hell, there's even a story about a big man with a beard who lives at the North Pole, who rewards and punishes children. I think he's called Satan…or was it Nobodaddy? It doesn't matter.

Anyway, Budu showed our masters that his proposal fit right in with recorded history, was in fact vital to the development of mortal religion. And, while I understand they don't approve of religion much up there in the future, they do like to be absolutely sure that history rolls along smoothly. Messing with causality scares them.

What was his proposal, mortal? Come on, can't you think? What if I give you three guesses? No?

Well, Budu said that since civilization was still a little shaky on its legs, our masters needed to keep us around a while as a peacekeeping force. We'd go to each little community and lay down the law, or give them law if they didn't have it: no eating each other, no murder, don't inbreed, don't steal. Basic stuff. Then we'd run patrols and administer justice when and as needed, and contain any new mortal aggression that might threaten to wipe out humanity before it could become established. The final clever touch was that he signed Sarpa's name to it.

The masters accepted that proposal, mortal. It's bought us generations of time, even with Marco's idiot rebellion. The masters may not have trusted us anymore, but they still needed us.

And it worked for their good, too; it certainly got *your* village established. You wouldn't be here now if not for what we did that day, on that bloody field. And neither would our masters, and they know it.

We watched your fathers, from up here in the rocks and the snow, until we could be certain they wouldn't backslide again. Then Budu pulled the Fifth Infantry out, all but a garrison of three of us, me and Bouncer and Longtooth, and we watched over your little valley down the long centuries while he went off to give law to other mortals.

But time marched on, and eventually Bouncer got reassigned somewhere else, and later on Longtooth was transferred out too. Now there's only me.

And the word's just come down from the top, mortal: they're sending me back to my old unit, after all this time. I'll see battle again, I'll serve under the old man! My hands will steam with the blood of sinners. It'll be wonderful! I've gotten so tired of sitting up here, freezing my ass off. If you'd climbed this mountain a day later than you did, you'd have missed out on your chance to get the Truth. Life's funny, isn't it? Death is even funnier.

▲▼▲

The words and gestures cease, as the old monster settles back on his haunches, momentarily lost in a happy dream. The boy watches him. Terrified as he is, he cannot help wondering whether his host isn't something of a fool. It has of course occurred to him, as he listened unwilling to this story, that people as clever as the Time Shamans must have long since found some way of outwitting their servants. How can the creature trust his masters? How can he not know that times change?

For even in his village below, where there are still those who can remember glimpsing God, skepticism is blooming. Nowadays children are frightened into good behavior by the old stories, but not men. Once nobody would have dared climb this mountain, seek out this cave; it would have been sacrilegious. Yet the boy's friends had laughed at him when he'd set out for the mountain, and the village elders had just shrugged, smiling, and watched him go.

The boy is musing to himself, thinking of the methods fabled heroes had always used to defeat ogres, and wondering what sort of magical devices the Time Shamans might have employed, when he becomes aware that the old monster has turned his pale eyes on him again. Flat Top's expression has lost its warmth. He looks remote, stern, sad.

The boy feels a chill go down his spine, wondering if his thoughts have been read somehow. The giant extends one of his eloquent hands and picks up a stone axe. He runs his thumb along its scalloped edge. Holding the boy's gaze with his own, he lays the axe across his knees and resumes their conversation:

...But enough about me.

I want to hear your story now, mortal man. I want to know if you're one of the righteous. You'll tell me everything you've ever done, your whole life story, and then I'll judge you. Take as long as you like. My patience is limitless.

The boy gulps, wondering how convincingly he can lie.

Hanuman

So there I was playing billiards with an *Australopithecus afarensis*, and he was winning.

I don't usually play with lower hominids, but I was stuck in a rehab facility during the winter of 1860, and there was nothing else to do but watch holoes or listen to the radio programs broadcast by my owner/employer, Dr. Zeus Incorporated. And the programs were uniformly boring; you'd think an all-powerful cabal of scientists and investors, having after all both the secrets of immortality and time travel, could at least come up with some original station formats. But anyway...

Repair and Rehabilitation Center Five was neatly hidden away in a steep cliff overlooking a stretch of Baja coastline. Out front, lots of fortunate convalescing operatives sprawled on golden sand beside a bright blue sea. Not me, though. When you're growing back skin, the medical techs don't like you sunbathing much.

Even when I looked human again, I couldn't get an exit pass. They kept delaying my release pending further testing and evaluation. It drove me crazy, but cyborgs are badly damaged so seldom that when the medical techs do get their hands on a genuine basket case, they like to keep it as long as possible for study.

Vain for me to argue that it was an event shadow and not a mysterious glitch in my programming that was to blame. I might as well have been talking to the wall. Between tests I sat interminably in the Garden Room among the bromeliads and ferns, thumbing through old copies of *Immortal Lifestyles Monthly* and trying to adjust my bathrobe so my legs didn't show.

"Oh, my! Nice gams," said somebody one morning. I lowered my magazine, preparing to fix him with the most scathing glare of contempt I could muster. What I saw astonished me.

He was about four and a half feet tall and looked something like a pint-sized Alley Oop, or maybe like a really racist caricature of an Irishman, the way they were being drawn back then. Tiny head, face prognathous in the extreme, shrewd little eyes set in wrinkles under heavy orbital ridges. The sclerae of his eyes were white, like a *Homo sapiens*. White whiskers all around his face. Barrel chest, arms down to his knees like a chimpanzee. However, he stood straight; his feet were small, narrow and neatly shod. He was impeccably dressed in the fashion of the day, too, what any elderly gentleman might be wearing at this very moment in London or San Francisco.

I knew the Company had a few cyborgs made from Neanderthals in its ranks—I'd even worked with a couple—but they looked human compared to this guy. Besides, as I scanned him I realized that he wasn't a cyborg. He was mortal, which explained the white whiskers.

"What the hell are you?" I inquired, fairly politely under the circumstances.

"I'm the answer to your prayers," he replied. "You want to come upstairs and see my etchings?"

"No," I said.

"It's because I'm a monkey, isn't it?" he snapped, thrusting his face forward in a challenging kind of way.

"Yeah," I said.

"Well, at least you're honest about being a bigot," he said, subsiding.

"Excuse me!" I slammed my magazine down in my lap. "Anyway, you aren't a monkey. Are you? You're a member of the extinct hominid species *Australopithecus afarensis.*"

"I love it when you people talk like computers," he mused. "Sexy, in a perverse kind of way. Yes, *Afarensis,* all right, one of Lucy's kindred. Possibly explaining my powerful attraction to ditzy redheads."

"That's an awful lot of big words to keep in such a teeny little skull," I said, rolling up my magazine menacingly. "So you think cyborgs are sexy, huh? Did you ever see *Alien?*"

"And you're a hot-blooded cyborg," he said, smiling. "Barely suppressed rage is sexy, too, at least I find it so. Yes, I know a lot of big words. I've been augmented. I'd have thought a superintelligent machine-human hybrid like yourself would have figured that out by now."

I was almost startled out of my anger. "A mortal being augmented? I've never heard of that being done!"

"I was an experiment," he explained. "A prototype for an operative that could be used in deep Prehistory. No budget for the project, unfortunately, so I'm unique. Michael Robert Hanuman, by the way." He extended his hand. It had long curved fingers and a short thumb, like an ape's hand. I took it gingerly.

"Botanist Grade Six Mendoza," I said, shaking his hand.

"A cyborg name," he observed. "What was your human name, when you had one?"

"I don't remember," I told him. "Look, I haven't been calling you a monkey during this conversation. How about you stop throwing around the word *cyborg*, okay?"

"No c-word, got it," he agreed. "You're sensitive about what you are, then?"

"Aren't you?"

"No, oddly enough," said Hanuman. He sat down in the chair next to mine. "I've long since come to terms with my situation."

"Well, three cheers for you," I said. "What are you doing in rehab, anyway?"

"I live here, at Cabo Rehabo," he said. "I'm retired now and the Company gave me my choice of residences. It's warm and I like the sea air. Also—" He fished an asthma inhaler from an inner pocket and waved it at me. "No fluorocarbons in the air during this time period. One of the great advantages to living in the past. What are you doing here, if you don't mind my asking?"

"There was an accident," I said.

"Really! You malfunctioned?"

"No, there was an error in the Temporal Concordance," I explained. "Some idiot input a date wrong and I was somewhere I shouldn't have been when a hotel blew up. Just one of those things that happen in the field."

"So you're—say! Would you be the one they brought in from Big Sur? I heard about you." He regarded my legs with renewed interest.

"That was me," I said, wishing he'd go away.

"Well, well." His gaze traveled over the rest of me. "I'd always heard you people never had accidents. You're programmed to dodge bullets and anything else that comes flying your way."

"You try dodging a building," I muttered.

"Is that why you're so angry?" he inquired, just as a repair tech stuck his head around the doorway.

"Botanist Mendoza? Please report to Room D for a lower left quadrant diagnostic."

"It's been fun," I told Michael Robert Hanuman, and made my exit gratefully. He watched me go, his small head tilted on one side.

▲▼▲

But I saw him the next day, waiting outside the lounge. He wrinkled his nose at my flannel pajama ensemble, then looked up and said, "We meet again! Can I buy you a drink?"

"Thanks, but I don't feel like going down to the bar dressed like this," I told him.

"There's a snack bar in the Rec Room," he said. "They serve cocktails."

I had just been informed I faced a minimum of two more months of tests, and the idea of dating a superannuated hominid seemed slightly less degrading than the rest of what I had to look forward to. "Why not?" I sighed.

The Rec Room had two pool tables and a hologame, as well as an entire wall of bound back issues of *Immortal Lifestyles Monthly*. There were tasteful Mexican-themed murals on the walls. There was a big picture window through which you could look out at the happy, well-rested operatives sunning themselves on the beach instead of having intrusive repair diagnostics done. Cocktails were available, at least, and Hanuman brought a pair of mai tais to our card table and set them down with a flourish.

"Yours has no alcohol in it," I said suspiciously, scanning.

"Can't handle the stuff," he informed me, and rapped his skull with his knuckles. "This tiny little monkey brain, you know. You don't want me hooting and swinging from the light fixtures, do you? Or something even less polite?"

"No, thank you," I said, shuddering.

"Not that I swing from anything much, at my age," he added, and had a sip of his drink. He set it down, pushed back in his chair and considered me. "So," he said, "What's it like being immortal?"

"I don't care for it," I replied.

"No?"

"No."

"Why not? Is it the Makropolous syndrome? You know, an overpowering sense of meaninglessness with the passage of enough time? Or does it have to do with being a cyb—sorry, with feeling a certain distance from humanity due to your unique abilities?"

"Mostly it's having to be around monkeys," I said, glaring at him. "Mortal *Homo sapiens*, I mean."

"Touché," he said, raising his drink to me. "I can't say I'm crazy about them, either."

"I'm happy when I'm alone," I continued, and tasted my drink. "I like my work. I don't like being distracted from my work."

"Human relationships are irrelevant, eh?" Hanuman said. "How lucky you've met me, then."

"You're human," I said, studying him.

"Barely," he said. "Oh, I know my place. If the Leakeys had had their way I wouldn't even get to play in the family tree! I'm just a little animal with a lot of wit and some surgical modification."

"Suit yourself," I said, and shrugged.

"So it isn't being immortal that bothers you, it's the company you have to keep?" he inquired. "Immortality itself is good?"

"I guess so," I said. "I certainly wouldn't want to have a body that decayed while I was wearing it. And I've got way too much work for one human lifespan."

"What do you do? Wait, you're a botanist. You were doing something botanical in Big Sur?"

"I was doing a genetic survey on *Abies bracteata*," I told him. "The Santa Lucia fir. It's endangered. The Company wants it."

"Ah. It has some terribly valuable commercial use?" He scratched his chin-whiskers.

"Why does the Company ever want anything?" I replied. "But if it was all that valuable, you'd think they'd let me out of here to get back to the job."

"They probably sent another botanist up there in your place," Hanuman pointed out. "And, after all, you haven't recovered yet. Have you? How are your new hands working? And the feet?"

"They're not new hands," I said irritably, wondering how he knew so much. "Just the skin. And some other stuff underneath. What do you care, anyway?"

"I'm wondering how well you'd be able to hold a billiards cue," he said. "Feel like a game?"

"Are you kidding?" I felt like laughing for the first time since I'd been there. "I'm a cyborg, remember? You're only a mortal, even if you have been augmented. I'd cream you."

"That's true," he said imperturbably, draining his glass. "In that case, what would you say to playing with a handicap? So a poor little monkey like me has a chance?"

Like an idiot, I agreed, and that was how I found out that augmented lower hominids have all the reflexes that go with the full immortality process.

"Boy, I'm glad we're not playing for money," I said, watching gloomily as he completed a ten-point bank shot and neatly sank three balls, *clunk clunk clunk.*

"How could we?" Hanuman inquired, hopping down from the footstool. "I've always heard the Company doesn't pay you people anything. That's one of the reasons they made you, so they'd have an inexpensive work force."

"For your information, we cost a lot," I snapped. "And I suppose you get paid a salary?"

"I did, before I retired," he told me smugly, chalking his cue. "Now I've got a nice pension."

"What'd you get paid for?" I asked. "You told me you were a prototype that never got used."

"I said the program budget got cut," he corrected me, climbing up for his next shot. "You ought to know the Company finds a use for everything they create. I gave them thirty years of service."

"Doing what?"

He took his time answering, frowning at the table, clambering down, kicking the stool around to a better spot and climbing up to survey the angles again. "Mostly impersonating a monkey, if you must know," he said at last.

I grinned. "Dancing while an organ grinder played? Collecting change in a tin cup to augment somebody's departmental budget?"

He grimaced, but it didn't throw his shot off, *click, clunk,* and another ball dropped into a corner pocket.

"No, as a matter of fact," he said. "I worked on some delicate missions. Collected sensitive information. Secrets. You wouldn't believe the things people will say in front of you when they think you're not human."

"Oh, wouldn't I?" I paced around the table, trying to distract him while he took aim again. It didn't work; another flawless bank shot, and it was clear I was never going to get a turn. He straightened up on the stool, now at eye level with me.

"My memoirs would make interesting reading, I can tell you. What about yours?"

I shivered. "Boring. "Unless you'd be spellbound by my attempts to produce a maize cultivar with high lysine content."

"I'd be interested in hearing how you happened to be in a hotel when it blew up," he said, surveying the table for his next shot. "Especially in the wilds of Big Sur."

"I was looking for a glass of iced tea," I said.

"Really." *Smack, clunk*, another ball down.

"With lemon," I said, taken by the stupidity of it in retrospect. "I was miles from the nearest humans, working my way along a ridge four thousand feet above a sheer drop into the Pacific…and suddenly I had this vision of a glass of iced tea, with lemon." For a moment I saw it again, with all the intensity of hallucination. "The glass all beaded in frost, and the ice cubes floating, and the lemon slice, with its white cold rind and stinging aromatic zest, and the tart pulp in the glass lending a certain juicy piquancy to the astringent tea…God, I was thirsty.

"I went back to my base camp, but I guess I'd been away a while. Lichen was growing on my processing credenza. My bivvy tent was collapsed and full of leaves. Raccoons had been into my field rations and strewn little packets of stuff everywhere."

"No tea, eh?" Hanuman jumped down, circled the table and leaned up on tiptoe for a shot.

"Nope," I said, watching him sink another ball. "And then I got to thinking about other things I hadn't done in a while. Like…sitting at a table and eating with a fork and knife. Sleeping in a room. Having clean fingernails. All the things you take for granted when you don't live out of a base camp."

"And this was enough to make you go into a hazard zone, and endure the company of the mortal monkeys you so despise—" Hanuman set up for another shot, "—the refinements of civilization?" *Whack! Clunk.*

"It sounds so dumb," I said wonderingly, "but that's how it was. So I broke camp, cached my stuff, picked the moss out of my hair and took a transverse ridge down to Garrapatta Landing."

"The town that exploded?" Hanuman cleared the table and jumped down. "I win, by the way."

"The town didn't explode; it burned to the ground after the hotel exploded," I explained. "Garrapatta Landing was only about three shacks anyway. Nasty little boom town."

"And how," chuckled Hanuman. "Care for another game?"

"No, thank you." I glared at the expanse of green felt, empty but for the cue ball.

"We could play for articles of clothing."

"Not a chance in hell." I set my cue back in its rack.

"Okay." Hanuman set his cue beside mine and waved for another round of cocktails. "I'm still curious. How did the hotel explode? I thought you Preserver drones were programmed to avoid hazardous structures."

"It wasn't hazardous when I got there," I said. "And I don't like the word *drone* either, all right? I knew the place was doomed, but because the Concordance had the date wrong on when it was set to blow, I thought I'd be safe going there when I did. What happened was, some miners going into the south range came into town late with a wagonload of blasting powder. Damned mortal morons parked it right under my window. I don't know how the explosion happened. I was asleep at the time. But it happened, and the whole hotel sort of leaned over sideways and became a mass of flaming wreckage."

"With you in it? Ouch," commented Hanuman.

"Yes. Ouch," I said, sitting down again. "Look, I'm tired of explaining this. Why don't we talk about you, instead? What did the Company do with an operative disguised as a monkey?"

"Lots of things," he said, sitting down too. "But I've never been debriefed, so I can't tell you about them."

"Okay; but can you tell me why the Company decided it needed to resurrect an *Afarensis*, rather than just taking a chimpanzee for augmentation?" I persisted. "If they needed a talking monkey? And how'd they do it, anyway?"

Hanuman looked thoughtful. It was amazing how quickly I'd adjusted to seeing human expressions in his wizened face, human intelligence in his eyes. They fixed on me now, as he nodded.

"I can tell you that," he said. The waiter brought our drinks, and Hanuman leaned back in his chair and said:

"You know the Company has a lot of wealthy clients in the twenty-fourth century. Dr. Zeus takes certain special orders from them, fetching certain special items out of the dead past. Makes a nice profit off the trade, too. You Preservers think all the stuff you collect goes for science, or to museums; not by a long shot, honey. Most of it goes into private collections."

"I'd heard that," I said. Not often, but it was one of the rumors continually circulating among operatives. "So what?"

"So somebody placed an order once for Primeval Man," Hanuman went on. "And the Company needed to know what, exactly, was meant by primeval. Was he talking cavemen? Little skinny monkey-faced fellows scavenging hyena kills? Bigfoot? What? But the plutocrat placing the order had trouble being specific. He wanted something that walked upright, but he wanted… an animal. An animal perhaps a little smarter than a performing dog."

"This is so illegal," I said.

"Isn't it? But the client could afford to make it profitable for Dr. Zeus. The only trouble was nailing down the definition of the merchandise. Finally the Company sent him an image of a reconstructed *Afarensis*. Was that primeval enough? Yes! That was what he'd had in mind. Fifteen breeding pairs, if you please."

"This is SO illegal," I said. He smiled at me, not the gum-baring grin of a chimpanzee but tight-lipped, pained.

"Big money," was all he said.

"I guess so! What was he going to do with them once he had them?"

"Play God, one assumes." Hanuman shrugged. "Or perhaps Tarzan. In any case, I suppose you've heard that the Company has a genetic bank on ice somewhere, with reproductive tissue and DNA from every race the planet's ever produced? Neanderthal, Cro-Magnon, Crewkerne, the whole works?"

"That's what I've heard. They have *Afarensis* in there too?"

Hanuman nodded. He did it differently from a *Homo sapiens sapiens*, I guess because of the way his skull was positioned on his vertebrae. It's difficult to describe, an odd abrupt bobbing motion of his head.

"The Company took what they had and filled the order. Produced fifteen female embryos, sixteen males. I was number sixteen."

"Why'd they make one extra?" I inquired.

"Because they could," said Hanuman, a little wearily. "The client was throwing ridiculous amounts of money at them, after all; why not skim a bit for R&D on a new project? The idea persons involved thought it would be great to find out whether sentience could be enhanced in a lower hominid.

"So the client got his thirty assorted *Afarensis* babies and I went off to a private lab for augmentation and years of training."

"But not the immortality process," I said.

"Prototypes aren't made immortal," said Hanuman. "I can see the reasoning: why risk setting a mistake in stone? If the project proposal had been approved they'd have cranked out any number of immortal monkeys, I don't doubt, but as it was…the Company decided it didn't need a specialized operative for Prehistory. Apparently they were already having problems integrating their Neanderthal operatives and such into human society, and the last thing they wanted was another set of funny-looking immortals. So…"

"So there was just you," I said.

"Just me," he agreed. "Can you wonder I'm sex-starved?"

"I'd rather not wonder, okay?" I said. "But that's pretty awful, I have to admit. Were you raised in a cage?"

"Good lord, no!" Hanuman looked indignant. "Were you?"

"No, I was raised at a Company base school," I said.

"Then I had a more human upbringing than you had," he told me. "I had adoptive parents. Dr. Fabry, the head of the project, took me home to his wife. She was a primate liaison and delighted to get me. They were a very loving couple. I had quite a pleasant childhood."

"You're kidding. How'd they get away with it? Isn't it illegal to keep pets up at that end of time?"

"I wasn't a pet," he said stiffly. "I was raised as their child. They told everyone I was microcephalic."

"And the mortals believed that?"

"Oh, yes. By the twenty-fourth century, there hadn't been a microcephalic born in generations, and people were a little hazy about what the word meant. Everyone I met was kind and sympathetic as a consequence."

"The *mortals* were?" I couldn't believe this.

"The twenty-fourth century has its faults," Hanuman told me, "but people from that time can't bear to be perceived as intolerant."

"But they are," I protested. "I've met some, and they are."

"Ah, but you're a—excuse me—a cyborg, you see?" Hanuman reached over and patted my hand. "Better than mortals, so of course they're not going to waste their sympathy on you! But I had every advantage. Why, I myself thought I was a challenged human being until I hit puberty, when I was five."

"You didn't know you were an *Afarensis*?"

"I thought all the cranial operations were to compensate for my condition," he said. "And my parents were too kind-hearted to tell the truth until I became interested in sex, at which time they sat me down and explained that it wasn't really an option for me."

"That's kind-hearted, all right," I said.

"Mm. I was crushed, of course. Went through denial. Mumums and Daddums were so dreadfully sorry because they really did love me, you see, and so they hastened to provide me with all sorts of self-image-improving material. I was told I could be anything I set out to be! Except, of course, a human being, but that didn't mean I couldn't enjoy a full life. Et cetera."

"What did you do?" I asked.

"Raged. Rebelled. Gave poor kind Dr. and Mrs. Fabry no end of grief. Decided at last to embrace my hominid heritage and turn my back on *Homo sapiens*." Hanuman picked the fruit spear out of his mai tai and considered it critically. "Demanded to meet my biological parents." He bit off a chunk of pineapple.

"But you came out of a DNA bank," I said.

"Yes, they pointed that out too. The best that could be managed was an interview with the host mother who had given birth to me." Hanuman leaned forward, still munching pineapple, and waggled his eyebrows. "And, talk about illegal! It turned out that the lady in question lived at Goodall Free Township."

I did a fast access and was shocked. "You mean the chimpanzee commune? That place set aside for the Signers after the split happens in the Beast Liberation Party? But I thought that'll be off-limits to humans."

Hanuman lifted his cocktail and drained it, gracefully extending one long pinky as he drank. "Of course it is," he said, setting the glass down. "Tell me, how long have you worked for the Company now? And you still think laws matter to Dr. Zeus?"

I was speechless.

"The Company had sent in a fast-talking—or should I say fast-signing?—person to negotiate with the females at Goodall," Hanuman said. "One of you people, I believe. A Facilitator, isn't that what the political ones are called? He offered a contract for surrogate maternity to thirty-one chimpanzees. They were implanted with the embryos, they carried them to term and delivered as per contract. Handsomely paid off, too, though presumably not in bananas alone."

Something beeped and Hanuman started slightly. "Oops! Excuse me a moment." He fished a pillbox out of his vest pocket and shook a few capsules into his palm. When he looked around for something to take them with, I pushed my glass forward.

"No, thank you," he said delicately, getting up and filling a disposable cup at the water cooler. I narrowed my eyes. Certain mortals from the twenty-fourth century are reluctant to touch utensils or other personal items a cyborg has used. Probably he just didn't want to take a sip of something with rum in it, but I was hair-trigger sensitive to anti-cyborg bigotry.

"You know what? I've just remembered I have an appointment," I said, getting to my feet and stalking out of the room. "Great story, but we'll have to do this some other time, okay? Bye now."

"Aw," he said sadly, looking after me as I stormed away.

▲▼▲

I didn't get the rest of the story until a week later.

The people responsible for my new lungs cautiously admitted that sea air might be good for them, so I was permitted to go outside if I wore a long coat, wide-brimmed hat and a face mask that made me look like Trona the Robot Woman. I reclined in a deck chair on the beach and gazed out at the sea for hours on end, telling myself I didn't give a damn that other immortals were staring at me. The dark lenses of the mask made the sea a deep violet blue, gave everything an eerie cast like an old day-for-night shot, and I could watch the waves rolling in and pretend I was anywhere but here, anyone but me.

One morning I heard a clatter as another deck chair was set up beside mine.

"There you are," said someone cheerfully, and turning my head I saw Hanuman settling into the chair. He was nicely dressed as usual, in a white linen suit today, with a Panama hat that must have been specially made for his little coconut head. He drew a pair of sunglasses from an inner pocket and slipped them on. "Bright, isn't it?"

I just turned my robot face back to regard the sea, hoping its expressionlessness would intimidate him into silence.

"Strange mask," he observed. "Not the most attractive design they could have chosen. Much more angular than, say, the police in *THX 1138*. Nowhere near as human as Robot Maria in *Metropolis*. Even the Tin Man in—"

"I think they were going for Art Deco," I said. "Buck Rogers Revival."

"Yes!" He leaned forward to study the mask again. "Or *Flesh Gordon*."

"Flash Gordon."

He chuckled wickedly. "I meant what I said. Did you ever see it? Surprisingly good for a porn film. Great special effects."

I was silent again, wishing I really was a robot, one perhaps with the ability to extend an arm and fire missiles at unwelcome companions.

"I was telling you the story of my life," he said.

"So you were."

"Still interested?"

"Go right ahead."

He folded his hands on his stomach and began again.

▲▼▲

"Goodall Free Township is a grand name, but the reality's sort of squalid. After the Signer scandal, the Beast Liberation Party gave the signing chimpanzees a thousand acres of tropical woodland for their very own, hoping they'd just disappear into the forest and return to whatever the Beast equivalent of Eden is. I had decided to go there to live, and celebrate my true *Afarensis* nature.

"All the way there in the car, Mrs. Fabry told me about the wonderful paradise I was going to be privileged to see, where beasts lived in dignity and self-sufficiency, and how this was only one of the modern examples of mankind atoning for its crimes against the natural world.

"So I was expecting rainbows and unicorns and waterfalls, you see, quite illogically, but I was, and when we pulled up to the big electrified fence with barbed wire at the top it was jarring, to say the least. Beyond the fence was a thicket of cane solid as a wall, nothing visible behind it, growing to left and right along the fence as far as the eye could see.

"Even Mrs. Fabry looked stunned. A ranger emerged from a little shack by the locked gate and saluted snappily, but she demanded to know why the barbed wire was there. He told her it was to keep poachers out, which she accepted at once. Personally I think—well, you decide, once you've heard.

"The ranger stared at me, but didn't question. He just stepped inside and got a jotpad, which he handed to Mrs. Fabry with the explanation that she needed to state for the record that she was going in of her own free will, and released the Goodall Free Township Committee from any responsibility in the event of unpleasantness. As she was listening to the plaquette and recording her statement, I began to remove my clothes.

"At this, the ranger looked concerned and signed to me, *What are you doing?*

"'What's it look like I'm doing?' I said indignantly. 'Besides talking, which I can do, thank you very much.' And I explained that I was going to meet my brothers and sisters in nature and wanted no effete *Homo sapiens* garments to set me apart. He just shook his head and told me I might want to reconsider.

"Mrs. Fabry, who knew more about chimpanzees than I did, kept her clothing on. Even so, the ranger advised her she'd do well to take a gift for the inhabitants. She asked him if he had any fruit and he went inside his shack, to emerge a moment later with a bottle of Biodyne.

"'Take this,' he said. 'They got all the fruit they need.'

"Mrs. Fabry took it reluctantly. Giving renaturalized primates any kind of medical assistance was strictly forbidden, as I was later to find out, but then so were visitors to this particular paradise. Anyway, the ranger dropped the perimeter security and let us in, pointing out a tiny gap between the cane stalks where we might squeeze through; then he locked up after us and I heard the faint *hummzap* of the fences going back on.

"As we picked our way through the jungle (where I very much regretted I hadn't worn my shoes), Mrs. Fabry said, 'Now, Michael dear, when we meet the chimpanzees, it might be a good idea if you got down in a crouch. They'll be more comfortable.'

"'Won't they understand what I am?' I demanded. 'The whole point of this is that I'm returning to my true state.'

"'Well—' she said, and then we were through the jungle and out in a clearing, and there they were.

"I have to admit it was sort of breathtaking, mostly because of the scenery. Forested mountains rose straight into clouds, below which four chimpanzees were doing something in a meadow. Other than the noise my fellow primates were making, there was a dull sleepy silence over everything. The chimpanzees turned to look at us, and Mrs. Fabry dropped at once into a crouch. I didn't, which was why I got a glimpse of what they'd been doing before they noticed we were there. They'd been beating a scrap of sheet metal into a curve around the tip of a stick, taking turns hammering it with river cobbles. It looked rather like a spear.

"The minute they spotted us, however, they closed rank and one of them tossed the stick behind the big rock they'd been using for an anvil. They advanced on us cautiously and I saw they were all males. They'd been focusing on Mrs. Fabry, I suppose because she was bigger than I was, only glancing at me, but one by one they did double takes and stopped, staring.

"The biggest male, who had a lot of silver on his muzzle, signed, *What that thing?* to Mrs. Fabry, indicating me with a flick of his hand.

"She winced for me, and signed back, *My baby sort of chimpanzee.*

"The big male gave me an incredulous look. The younger males began to—I think it's called displaying, where they get erections and start behaving badly? Acting in a vaguely threatening manner. Rushing at me and pulling up short, then retreating. I did a bit of retreating myself, not quite cowering behind Mrs. Fabry, and seeing their bared fangs I wished very much I'd kept my pants on at least.

"The old male ignored them, staring earnestly into Mrs. Fabry's face. *Not chimpanzee,* he signed. *Lie lie. Wrong feet. What that thing?*

"She signed, *Friend,* and offered the bottle of Biodyne hopefully. He regarded it a moment, sighed, and put out his long hand and took it from her. He loped off to the big rock, dropped it, picked up something else and loped back.

"Holding the object up before her eyes a moment—it was a six-centimeter Phillips-head screw—he signed, *You come again bring this. Many this. Need this. Yes?*

"Mrs. Fabry hesitated, and I yelped, 'Tell him yes, Mom!' because one of the other youths had made another rush and snapped his fangs perilously close to my ass. The old male started up and snarled at the others, baring his own fangs. *Sit stupid dirt,* he signed. *I talk!* Whereupon the juveniles snorted but turned away, and went to groom each other beside the big rock, but they watched me balefully.

"*That not chimpanzee,* the old male continued, indicating me. *Sound like you. Lie. Pink pink pink. Why here?*

"Mrs. Fabry signed, *Come visit chimpanzee Gamma 18.* Which, I discovered, was my host-mother's name."

"I thought they all had names like Lucy and Washoe," I said.

"Not after Beast Liberation. It was decided human names would be insulting and patronizing," Hanuman explained. "So they went with letter-number combinations instead. As soon as the old male saw my mother's name, an expression of sudden comprehension crossed his face. Very human looking. In some excitement he signed, *Doctor babies! Old time. Babies take away. Baby big now? This thing?*

"I was getting a little tired of this, so I signed, *I not thing. I good ape.*

"He just laughed at me—oh, yes, they laugh—and signed, *You good thing.* He looked back at Mrs. Fabry and signed, *Come visit Gamma 18.*

"By this time I was ready to turn around and go home, but Mrs. Fabry wasn't going to waste this chance to socialize with her favorite study subjects. She grabbed my hand and we set off after our host. He led us away, detouring just long enough to grab the Biodyne from the juveniles, who had opened it and were applying it to their cuts and sores. They sulked after us, making rude noises, until the old male (Tau 47, as he introduced himself) turned back and barked at them.

"We followed a trail over a shoulder of mountain and, what a surprise! They'd built themselves a township all right: eleven huts made of corrugated tin and aluminum panels from aircraft wreckage. The huts were arranged in a rough circle, with a fire pit in the center. Yes indeed, they even had fire. Mrs. Fabry caught her breath and Tau 47 glanced up at her warily. In a defensive kind of way he signed, *Fire good. Chimpanzee careful careful.*

"'I thought this was supposed to be pristine primeval wilderness,' I said under my breath.

"'They must have found a crash site the Goodall Free Township Committee was unaware of,' replied Mrs. Fabry.

"There were several chimpanzees sitting in the center clearing, mostly females with young. They all looked up and stared as we came down the hillside. Some of the smaller juveniles screamed and ran, or threw things, but most of them watched us intently.

"One or two females signed *Look look*. Tau 47 led us right up to a female with an infant at her breast and signed, *Remember doctor babies gone. Big baby now. Visit.* He turned and indicated us. Mrs. Fabry crouched at once and I hastily followed suit. I couldn't take my eyes off the female. *This Gamma 18,* he signed to us.

"Remarkable how different their faces are, one from another, when you see them all in a group. My host-mother had a more pronounced muzzle, and the hair on her head seemed longer than elsewhere, like a woman's. Taken all in all the effect was a little like that famous parody of the Mona Lisa. But, you understand, by this time she no longer seemed like an animal to me. She looked like the Madonna of the Forest.

"I signed, *Mother,* and reached out to her, but she drew back, glancing at me sidelong. Her baby ignored us, snuffling at her long flat breast. After a moment she reached out a tentative hand and knuckled my foot.

"*Funny foot,* she signed. *Remember. Doctor pull out, take gone. See funny foot. You my baby old now?*

"I signed back, *I your baby, good ape now.* Mrs. Fabry had tears in her eyes.

"Gamma 18 signed *Good good* in an uncertain way. Then she turned to Mrs. Fabry and signed, *Comb?*

"We thought she was asking Mrs. Fabry to groom her, and Mrs. Fabry was breathless at the honor and acceptance that implied, but when she hitched herself closer Gamma 18 backed off and repeated *Comb?* And she carefully and unmistakably mimed running a comb through her hair, as opposed to a flea-picking gesture.

"Mrs. Fabry said out loud, 'Oh, you mean you want one!'

"She happened to be wearing one of those hikers' pouches at her waist, and she unzipped it and dug around for her comb. She handed it over to Gamma 18, and was instantly surrounded by other females who all wanted things too, and I must say asked for them very politely.

"Mrs. Fabry, looking radiantly happy, passed out tissues and breath mints and offered little squirts of cologne from a vial she had in there. Gamma 18 moved in closer, and soon they were all sitting around, Mrs. Fabry included, signing to one another and blowing their noses, or taking turns passing the comb through their hair.

"I sat to one side, dumfounded. Tau 47, who had been watching me, caught my eye and signed, *You thing come.* He paced away a little distance, looking over his shoulder at me. I got up and followed, feeling sullen and miserable. I had to stand to follow him, because I've never been able to walk on my knuckles very well, and of course my rising to my full height set off another round of screams and abuse from the juveniles in the group. One very little male galloped close, pulled up and signed, *Ugly ugly pink pink.*

"Angrily I signed back, *Dirty stupid.* Tau 47 stood up and snarled at the little male, who drew back at once. But he sat there watching us, and to my annoyance began to sign slyly: *Pretty pretty pink pink.* The other juveniles took it up too, laughing to themselves. I was nearly in tears.

"Tau 47 huffed and signed, *Stupid babies. You smart thing?*

"*Not thing,* I insisted. *Good ape.* Tau 47 rolled his eyes as if to say 'Whatever' and then signed, *You see how lock work?*

"I signed confusion at this. He grunted, sat down and with great care signed slowly: *You go in gate. Here. You see how gate lock work? How open?*

"I signed back, *Not know. Sorry. You want leave here?*

"*I leave leave,* he signed. *I go back people houses.*

"I was astonished. *Why?* I signed. *This good here. I come here live.* It was his turn to look astonished.

"*Come here live,* he repeated, as though he couldn't believe what he'd seen. *Why why why? Cold here. Wet here. Bad food. Bugs. Fight bad chimpanzees.*

"I didn't know what he meant by this, because the Goodall Free Township Committee had selected wilderness that was not only virgin, it was empty of any other chimpanzees. So I signed, *Who bad chimpanzees?*

"Tau 47 looked threateningly up at the mountain and signed, *Bad bad Iota 34. Bad chimpanzee, friends. Fight. Eat babies. Steal.* By which he meant, I suppose, that some family group had split off from the original settlement and taken up residence in a distant corner of the preserve, and now there were territorial conflicts. It didn't surprise me; chimpanzees in the wild had used to do that, and it might be lamentable but it was, after all, natural. So I signed, *Iota 34 steal food?*

"He considered me a moment and then signed, *Come hide quiet.* So signing, he knuckle-loped away a few paces and looked back over his shoulder at me. I followed uneasily, and he led me through bushes and along a jungle trail, taking us deeper into the hills.

"Within a couple of minutes we were out of sight of the village and I began to hear warning calls from the brush around us, and glimpse here and there a chimpanzee peering down from high branches. Finally a big male dropped into the path before us, followed by two other males and a big female without young. They bared their teeth at me. Tau 47 signed, *Good chimpanzee-thing no bite.* He put an arm around me and made a cursory grooming motion.

"They blinked and looked away, then vanished back into the leaf cover as suddenly as they had appeared. *Chimpanzees watch,* explained Tau 47. I wondered what they were watching, but he led me forward and as we came out on the edge of a ravine it became clear why they guarded that patch of forest.

"There, filling the ravine and spilling down it in a river of squalor, was a trash landfill. It was overgrown with creepers, overhung with trees, which was perhaps why the Goodall Free Township Committee hadn't known it was there. Two chimpanzees worked the heap immediately below us, poking through it with sticks and now and then pulling out a useful scrap of salvage, old wiring or broken furniture."

"I guess it wasn't quite virgin wilderness," I said.

"I guess so. Something the survey parties for the Goodall Free Township Committee missed, evidently, or were bribed to overlook. I just stood there gaping at it. The two chimpanzees below looked up at me and froze; after watching Tau 47 and me a moment they seemed to accept my presence and got back to their work. Tau 47 signed to me, *This secret. Good things here. Make house. Make knife. Live good.* He looked up once again at the mountain and bared his teeth. *Iota 34 want secret. Dirty bad bad.*

"*Iota 34 make house too?* I signed.

"*No no,* signed Tau 47. *Iota 34 make,* and he paused and made a motion of gripping a shaft of something with both hands, stabbing with it. Then he signed, *Stick knife hunt hurt.*

"I saw the whole problem in a flash: it was much more than a Tree of Knowledge in Eden. It was like the twentieth-century dilemma over atomic power. Here these poor creatures had this unexpected gift, from which they could derive all sorts of comforts for their wretched existence; but it had to be prevented from falling into the enemy's hands at all costs, or it could be used against them."

"Though they were obviously using it to make weapons themselves," I said.

"Naturally." Hanuman tilted his hat forward to shade his face. "They were chimpanzees. It was in their nature. They're decent enough people but they're not peace-loving, you know, any more than *Homo sapiens* is. What a Cold War scenario, eh? Being signers, they had the ability to communicate ideas; they had seen enough of what *Homo sapiens* has in the way of enriched environments to want to make one for themselves, and now they had the potential to do so.

"But as long as most of their tribe's resources had to be expended on guarding this trash pile, how much time could they afford to do anything else?"

"It's always something," I muttered.

"So there I was, standing on this height, and suddenly it flashed before my eyes: what if I became one of these people? What if I led them, used my augmented intelligence to give them the edge in their arms race? I might become a lower-hominid Napoleon! We'd take on the dastardly Iota 34 and force his tribe to become peaceful citizens of a new primate civilization! Made of recycled trash, admittedly, but unlike anything that had ever existed.

"Or perhaps—dare I even think it—force the *Homo sapiens* world to face the monstrous injustice of what had been done to these poor creatures by letting them get an earful of the Black Monolith, so to speak, and then removing any way for them to fulfill their hitherto unguessed-at potential by insisting they live like primitives?

"Good heavens, I thought to myself, it might even be a plot to keep us from moving into Man's neighborhood! Having transmitted the divine spark of reason to us, what if Man had now regretted and sought to keep us mere animals? How dare he deny our humanity? Why, I might lead a crusade to bring apes everywhere to a higher level of being. Shades of Roddy McDowall in a monkey mask!"

"But you saw the futility of such an exercise in ego?" I inquired.

"Actually, it was the cold realization that I'd probably be remembered as Pretty Pink General," said Hanuman. "Plus the fact that just then I felt something bite me, and looked down at myself and realized I was covered in fleas.

"*Good secret*, I signed to Tau 47. *I quiet quiet.*

"He looked out over it all, sighed and signed, *You go. No stay here. Go houses.*

"I signed, *You miss houses?*

"*Miss houses,* he signed back. *Want good food. Good blanket good. Miss pictures. Miss music. Miss game. Good good all. I sad. Cry like baby.*

"*Sorry,* I signed. He just huffed and looked out over the landfill.

"We went back to the village.

"The ladies were all sitting around grooming one another, Mrs. Fabry included. She looked up as we approached and said, 'Michael, dear, I've been trying to explain that you want to stay with them, but—'

"I told her it was all right, that I'd changed my mind. Before she could explain this, though, Gamma 18 broke away from the group and approached me. Looking at me seriously, she signed, *You no stay here.*

"*No stay,* I agreed bitterly.

"She came closer on all fours—her baby was still hanging under her—and put her hand on my shoulder, quite gently. Then she signed, *You no chimpanzee. You no man. You other thing. Sad thing here. You go houses, be happy thing.*

"By which motherly advice I guess she meant that the bananas grow at the top of the tree, not at the roots, and since I didn't belong at either end (evolutionarily speaking) I might as well climb up and eat rather than slide back down and starve. You get what life deals you, and you'd better make the best of it.

"I went back home with Mrs. Fabry. The dear woman didn't mind all the flea bites she'd incurred on my behalf in the least; I do believe she got more out of the whole ape-bonding experience than I had. I settled down to try to be a good adoptive son to her and Dr. Fabry. Tried not to think of my chimp-mother's plight, though I lived by her wise words."

"And that was it? You came all that way, and that was all she had to tell you?" I demanded.

"Well, she was a chimpanzee, after all, not a vocational guidance counselor." Hanuman looked at me over his sunglasses. "And if you think about it, it's good advice. Certainly I've let it guide me through a long and occasionally trying life. You might consider doing the same."

"I fail to see how our problems are in any way similar," I snapped.

"Aren't they?" Hanuman regarded me. "When I discovered I was neither an ape nor a man, I tried to be an ape. It was a waste of my time. All the advantage is on the human side.

"You—during a similar adolescent crisis, I'd bet bananas to coconuts—discovered you are neither a machine nor a woman. So you've tried to be a machine."

"Go to hell, you little hominid bastard!"

"No, no, hear me out: your work habits, your preference for physical and emotional isolation, are part of your attempts to ignore your human heritage. But your heart is human so you can't do it, any more than I could, and the stress of the conflict drove you to seek out human companionship.

"Or possibly, by sleeping in a place you knew to be hazardous, you were indulging in a covert suicide attempt. Was it really tea you were thirsty for, Mendoza?"

"I can't believe this!" I leaped out of my chair and tore off my mask, glaring at him. "You're one of the Company's psychiatrists! Aren't you?"

"Let's just say I'm not completely retired. You must have suspected all along," he added calmly, "clever cyborg that you are."

"How many times do I have to tell you people, it was an accident?" I shouted, and all up and down the beach, heads turned and other operatives stared at us.

"But you're programmed not to have accidents," he said. "And the Company would like to know how it happened, and whether it's likely to happen again. Is it just your neurosis that leads you to take unnecessary risks, or is it a design flaw they need to know about? They have a lot of money invested in you cyborgs, you know. Who were you hoping to find in the fire, Mendoza?"

"Oh, now we get to the truth," I said, sitting down again. "Now we drop the crap about how I'm really human. I'm an expensive *machine* and the Company's doing a diagnostic to see whether I'm still malfunctioning?"

Hanuman shrugged, holding my gaze with his own. "You look at me and all you see is a monkey, no matter how cleverly I speak. They look at you and all they see is a machine they can't seem to repair. It's insulting. Unfair. Yet the hard truth is, neither one of us belong in the natural world. I know it hurts; who'd know better than I? But it won't change. I've accepted that. Can you?"

I put my mask back on and, without another word to him, strode away up the beach.

▲▼▲

I managed to avoid speaking to him the rest of the time I was there, and he didn't try to speak to me, though he watched me somberly from a distance and tipped his hat once or twice when our paths crossed. Maybe he'd found out all the Company wanted him to find out, or maybe he knew there was no way on earth I was ever going to let him any further into my head than he'd gotten already.

The Company discharged me for active service at last; they had to. They'd repaired me good as new, right? So I took off for the coastal mountains and made a new base camp up in the big trees, and got right back to work happily collecting genetic variants of *Abies bracteata*. I had all I wanted in the wilderness.

Stupid chimpanzees, wanting to go back to the cities of humanity! Maybe they needed an enriched environment, but not me. I'd stripped away such irrelevant nonsense from my life, hadn't I?

I had the looming mountains to myself, and the vast empty sea and the immensity of cold white stars at night and, thank God, the silence of my own heart. It never makes a sound of complaint. It's a perfectly functioning machine.

SON, OBSERVE THE TIME
AND FLY FROM EVIL. ECC. IV. 23.

Son Observe the Time

On the eve of destruction we had oysters and Champagne.

Don't suppose for a moment that we had any desire to lord it over the poor mortals of San Francisco, in that month of April in that year of 1906; but things weren't going to be so gracious there again for a long while, and we felt an urge to fortify ourselves against the work we were to do.

London before the Great Fire, Delhi before the Mutiny, even Chicago—I was there and I can tell you, it requires a great deal of mental and emotional self-discipline to live side by side with mortals in a Salvage Zone. You must look, daily, into the smiling faces of those who are to lose all, and walk beside them in the knowledge that nothing you can do will affect their fates. Even the most prosaic of places has a sort of haunted glory at such times; judge then how it looked to us, that gilded fantastical butterfly of a city, quite unprepared for its approaching holocaust.

The place was made even queerer by the fact that there were so many Company operatives there at the time. The very ether hummed with our transmissions. In any street you might have seen us dismounting from carriages or the occasional automobile, we immortal gentlemen tipping our derbies to the ladies, our immortal ladies responding with a graceful inclination of their picture hats, smiling as we met each others' terrified eyes. We dined at the Palace and as guests at Nob Hill mansions; promenaded in Golden Gate Park, drove out to Ocean Beach, attended the theater and everywhere saw the pale, set faces of our own kind, busy with their own particular preparations against what was to come.

Some of us had less pleasant places to go. I was grateful that I was not required to brave the Chinese labyrinth by Waverly Place, but my associate Pan had certain business there amongst the Celestials. I myself was obliged to venture, too many times, into the boarding houses south of Market Street. Beneath the Fly Trap was a Company safe house and HQ; we'd meet there sometimes, Pan and I, at the end of a long day in our respective ghettoes, and we'd sit shaking together over a brace of stiff whiskeys. Thus heartened, it was time for a costume change: dock laborer into gentleman for me, coolie into cook for him, and so home by cable car.

I lodged in two rooms on Bush Street. I will not say I slept there; one does not rest well on the edge of the maelstrom. But it was a place to keep one's trunk, and to operate the Company credenza necessary for facilitating the missions of those operatives whose case officer I was. Salvaging is a terribly complicated affair, requiring as it does that one hide in history's shadow until the last possible moment before snatching one's quarry from its preordained doom. One must be organized and thoroughly coordinated; and timing is everything.

On the morning of the tenth of April I was working there, sending a progress report, when there came a brisk knock at my door. Such was my concentration that I was momentarily unmindful of the fact that I had no mortal servants to answer it. When I heard the impatient tapping of a small foot on the step, I hastened to the door.

I admitted Nan D'Arraignee, one of our Art Preservation specialists. She is an operative of West African origin with exquisite features, slender and slight as a doll carved of ebony. I had worked with her briefly near the end of the previous century. She is quite the most beautiful woman I have ever known, and happily married to another immortal, a century before I ever laid eyes on her. Timing, alas, is everything.

"Victor." She nodded. "Charming to see you again."

"Do come in." I bowed her into my parlor, acutely conscious of its disarray. Her bright gaze took in the wrinkled laundry cast aside on the divan, the clutter of unwashed teacups, the half-eaten oyster loaf on the credenza console, six empty sauterne bottles, and one smudgily thumb-printed wineglass. She was far too courteous to say anything, naturally, and occupied herself with the task of removing her gloves.

"I must apologize for the condition of the place," I stammered. "My duties have kept me out a good deal." I swept a copy of the *Examiner* from a chair. "Won't you sit down?"

"Thank you." She took the seat and perched there, hands folded neatly over her gloves and handbag. I pulled over another chair, intensely irritated at my clumsiness.

"I trust your work goes well?" I inquired, for there is of course no point in asking one of us if *we* are well. "And, er, Kalugin's? Or has he been assigned elsewhere?"

"He's been assigned to Marine Transport, as a matter of fact," she told me, smiling involuntarily. "We are to meet on the *Thunderer* afterward. I am so pleased! He's been in the Bering Sea for two years, and I've missed him dreadfully."

"Ah," I said. "How pleasant, then, to have something to look forward to in the midst of all this…"

She nodded quickly, understanding. I cleared my throat and continued: "What may I do for you, Nan?"

She averted her gaze from dismayed contemplation of the stale oyster loaf and smiled. "I was told you might be able to assist me in requisitioning additional transport for my mission."

"I shall certainly attempt it." I stroked my beard. "Your present arrangements are unsuitable?"

"Inadequate, rather. You may recall that I'm in charge of presalvage at the Hopkins Gallery. It seems our original estimates of what we can rescue there were too modest. At present, I have five vans arranged for to evacuate the gallery contents, but really, we need more. Would it be possible to requisition a sixth? My own case officer was unable to assist me, but felt you might have greater success."

This was a challenge. Company resources were strained to the utmost on this operation, which was one of the largest on record. Every operative in the United States had been pressed into service, and many of the European and Asian personnel. A handsome allotment had been made for transport units, but needs were swiftly exceeding expectations.

"Of course I should like to help you," I replied cautiously, "if at all possible. You are aware, however, that horsedrawn transport utilization is impossible, due to the subsonic disturbances preceding the earthquake—and motor transports are, unfortunately, in great demand—"

A brewer's wagon rumbled down the street outside, rattling my windows. We both leaped to our feet, casting involuntary glances at the ceiling; then sat down in silent embarrassment. Madame D'Arraignee gave a little cough. "I'm so sorry—my nerves are simply—"

"Not at all, not at all, I assure you—one can't help flinching—"

"Quite. In any case, Victor, I understand the logistical difficulties involved; but even a handcart would greatly ease our difficulties. So many lovely and unexpected things have been discovered in this collection, that it really would be too awful to lose them to the fire."

"Oh, certainly." I got up and strode to the windows, giving in to the urge to look out and assure myself that the buildings hadn't begun to sway yet. Solid and seemingly as eternal as the pyramids they stood there, for the moment. I turned back to Madame D'Arraignee as a thought occurred to me. "Tell me, do you know how to operate an automobile?"

"But of course!" Her face lit up.

"It may be possible to obtain something in that line. Depend upon it, madame, you will have your sixth transport. I shall see to it personally."

"I knew I could rely on you." She rose, all smiles. We took our leave of one another with a courtesy that belied our disquiet. I saw her out and returned to my credenza keyboard.

QUERY, I input, *RE: REQUISITION ADDTNL TRANSPORT MOTOR VAN OR AUTO? PRIORITY RE: HOPKINS INST.*

HOPKINS PROJECT NOT YOUR CASE, came the green and flashing reply.

NECESSARY, I input. *NEW DISCV OVRRIDE SECTION AUTH. PLEASE FORWARD REQUEST PRIORITY.*

WILL FORWARD.

That was all. So much for my chivalrous impulse, I thought, and watched as the transmission screen winked out and returned me to my status report on the Nob Hill presalvage work. I resumed my entry of the Gilded Age loot tagged for preservation.

When I had transmitted it, I stood and paced the room uneasily. How long had I been hiding in here? What I wanted was a meal and a good stretch of the legs, I told myself sternly. Fresh air, in so far as that was available in any city at the beginning of this twentieth century. I scanned the oyster loaf and found it already pulsing with bacteria. Pity. After disposing of it in the dustbin I put on my coat and hat, took my stick and went out to tread the length of Bush Street with as bold a step as I could muster.

It was nonsense, really, to be frightened. I'd be out of the city well before the first shock. I'd be safe on air transport bound for London before the first flames rose. London, the other City. I could settle into a chair at my club and read a copy of *Punch* that wasn't a month old, secure in the knowledge that the oak beams above my head were fixed and immovable as they had been since the days when I'd worn a powdered wig, as they would be until German shells came raining down decades from now…

Shivering, I dismissed thoughts of the Blitz. Plenty of *life* to think about, surely! Here were bills posted to catch my eye: I might go out to the Pavilion to watch the boxing exhibition—Jack Joyce and Bob Ward featured. There was delectable vaudeville at the Orpheum, I was assured, and gaiety girls out at the Chutes, to say nothing of a spectacular sideshow recreation of the Johnstown flood…perhaps not in the best of taste, under the present circumstances.

I might imbibe Gold Seal Champagne to lighten my spirits, though I didn't think I would; Veuve Cliquot was good enough for me. Ah, but what about a bottle of Chianti, I thought, arrested by the bill of fare posted in the window of a corner restaurant. Splendid culinary fragrances wafted from within. Would I have grilled veal chops here? Would I go along Bush to the Poodle Dog for Chicken *chaud-froid blanc*? Would I venture to Grant in search of yellow silk banners for duck roasted in some tiny Celestial kitchen? Then again, I knew of a Swiss place where the cook was a Hungarian, and prepared a light and crisply fried Wienerschnitzel to compare with any I'd had… or I might just step into a saloon and order another oyster loaf to take home…

No, I decided, veal chops would suit me nicely. I cast a worried eye up at the building—pity this structure wasn't steel-framed—and proceeded inside.

It was one of those dark, robust places within, floor thickly strewn with fresh sawdust not yet kicked into little heaps. I took my table as any good operative does, back to the wall and a clear path to the nearest exit. Service was poor, as apparently their principal waiter was late today, but the wine was excellent. I found it bright on the palate, just what I'd wanted, and the chops when they came were redolent of herbs and fresh olive oil. What a consolation appetite can be.

Yes, life, that was the thing to distract one from unwise thoughts. Savor the wine, I told myself, observe the parade of colorful humanity, breathe in the fragrance of the joss sticks and the seafood and the gardens of the wealthy, listen to the smart modern city with its whirring steel parts at the service of its diverse inhabitants. The moment is all, surely.

I dined in some isolation, for the luncheon crowd had not yet emerged from the nearby offices and my host remained in the kitchen, arguing with the cook over the missing waiter's character and probable ancestry. Even as I amused myself by listening, however, I felt a disturbance approaching the door. No temblor yet, thank heaven, but a tempest of emotions. I caught the horrifying mental images before ever I heard the stifled weeping. In another moment he had burst through the door, a young male mortal with a prodigious black mustache, quite nattily dressed but with his thick hair in wild disarray. As soon as he was past the threshold his sobs burst out unrestrained, at a volume that would have done credit to Caruso.

This brought his employer out of the back at once, blurting out the first phrases of furious denunciation. The missing waiter (for so he was) staggered forward and thrust out that day's *Chronicle*. The headlines, fully an inch tall, checked the torrent of abuse: MANY LOSE THEIR LIVES IN GREAT ERUPTION OF VESUVIUS.

The proprietor of the restaurant, struck dumb, went an ugly sallow color. He put the fingertips of one hand in his mouth and bit down hard. In a broken voice, the waiter described the horrors: roof collapsed in church in his own village. His own family might even now lie dead, buried in ash. The proprietor snatched the paper and cast a frantic eye over the columns of print. He sank to his knees in the sawdust, sobbing. Evidently he had family in Naples, too.

I stared at my plate. I saw gray and rubbery meat, congealing grease, seared bone with the marrow turned black. In the midst of life we are in death, but it doesn't do to reflect upon it while dining.

"You must, please, excuse us, sir," the proprietor said to me, struggling to his feet. "There has been a terrible tragedy." He set the *Chronicle* beside my plate so I could see the blurred rotogravure picture of King Victor Emmanuel. REPORT THAT TOTAL NUMBER OF DEAD MAY REACH SEVEN HUNDRED, I read. TOWNS BURIED UNDER ASHES AND MANY CAUGHT IN RUINED BUILDINGS. MANY BUILDINGS CRUSHED BY ASHES. Of course, I had known about the coming tragedy; but it was on the other side of the world, the business of other Company operatives, and I envied them that their work was completed now.

"I am so very sorry, sir," I managed to say, looking up at my host. He thought my pallor was occasioned by sympathy: he could not know I was seeing his mortal face like an apparition of the days to come, and it was livid and charring, for he lay dead in the burning ruins of a boardinghouse in the Mission district. Horror, yes, impossible not to feel horror, but one cannot empathize with them. One must not.

They went into the kitchen to tell the cook and I heard weeping break out afresh. Carefully I took up the newspaper and perused it. Perhaps there was something here that might divert me from the unpleasantness of the moment? Embezzlement. A crazed admirer stalking an actress. Charlatan evangelists. Grisly murder committed by two boys. Deadly explosion. Crazed derelict stalking a bank president. Los Angeles school principals demanding academic standards lowered.

I dropped the paper, and, leaving five dollars on the table, I fled that place.

I walked briskly, not looking into the faces of the mortals I passed. I rode the cable car, edging away from the mortal passengers. I nearly ran through the green expanse of Golden Gate Park, dodging around the mortal idlers, the lovers, the nurses wheeling infants in perambulators, until at last

I stood on the shore of the sea. Tempting to turn to look at the fairy castles perched on its cliffs; tempting to turn to look at the carnival of fun along its gray sand margin, but the human comedy was the last thing I wanted just then. I needed, rather, the chill and level grace of the steel-colored horizon, sun-glistering, wide-expanding. The cold salt wind buffeted me, filled my grateful lungs. Ah, the immortal ocean.

Consider the instructive metaphor: every conceivable terror dwells in her depths; she receives all wreckage, refuse, corruption of every kind, she pulls down into her depths human calamity indescribable: but none of this is any consideration to the sea. Let the screaming mortal passengers fight for room in the lifeboats, as the wreck belches flame and settles below the extinguishing wave; next morning she'll still be beautiful and serene, her combers no less white, her distances as blue, her seabirds no less graceful as they wheel in the pure air. What perfection, to be so heartless. An inspiration to any lesser immortal.

As I stood so communing with the elements, a mortal man came wading out of the surf. I judged him two hundred pounds of athletic stockbroker, muscles bulging under sagging wet wool, braving the icy water as an act of self-disciplinary sport. He stood for a moment on one leg, examining the sole of his other foot. There was something gladiatorial in his pose. He looked up and saw me.

"A bracing day, sir," he shouted.

"Quite bracing." I nodded and smiled. I could feel the frost patterns of my returning composure.

And so I boarded another streetcar and rode back into the mortal warren, and found my way by certain streets to the Barbary Coast. Not a place a gentleman cares to admit to visiting, especially when he's known the gilded beauties of old Byzantium or Regency-era wenches; the raddled pleasures available on Pacific Street suffered by comparison. But appetite is appetite, after all, and there is nothing like it to take one's mind off unpleasant thoughts.

▲▼▲

"Your costume." The attendant pushed a pasteboard carton across the counter to me. "Personal effects and field equipment. Linen, trousers, suspenders, boots, shirt, vest, coat, and hat." He frowned. "Phew! These should have been laundered. Would you care to be fitted with an alternate set?"

"That's all right." I took the offending rags. "The sweat goes with the role, I'm afraid. Irish laborer."

"Ah." He took a step backward. "Well, break a leg."

Fifteen minutes later I emerged from a dressing room the very picture of an immigrant yahoo, uncomfortably conscious of my clammy and odiferous clothing. I sidled into the canteen, hoping there wouldn't be a crowd in the line for coffee. There wasn't, at that: most of the diners were clustered around one operative over in a corner, so I stood alone watching the food service technician fill my thick china mug from a dented steel coffee urn. The fragrant steam was a welcome distraction from my own fragrancy. I found a solitary table and warmed my hands on my dark brew there in peace, until an operative broke loose from the group and approached me.

"Say, Victor!"

I knew him slightly, an American operative so young one could scan him and still discern the scar tissue from his augmentations. He was one of my Presalvagers.

"Good morning, Averill."

"Say, you really ought to listen to that fellow over there. He's got some swell stories." He paused only long enough to have his cup refilled, then came and pulled out a chair across from me. "Know who he is? He's the guy who follows Caruso around!"

"Is he?"

"Sure is. Music Specialist Grade One! That boy's wired for sound. He's caught every performance Caruso's ever given, even the church stuff when he was a kid. Going to get him in *Carmen* the night before you-know-what, going to record the whole performance. He's just come back from planting receivers in the footlights! Say, have you gotten tickets yet?"

"No, I haven't. I'm not interested, actually."

"Not interested?" he exclaimed. "Why aren't you—how *can't* you be interested? It's *Caruso*, for God's sake!"

"I'm perfectly aware of that, Averill, but I've got a prior engagement. And, personally, I've always thought de Reszke was much the better tenor."

"De Reszke?" He scanned his records to place the name and, while doing so, absently took a great gulp of coffee. A second later he clutched his ear and gasped. "Christ almighty!"

"Steady, man." I suppressed a smile. "You don't want to gulp beverages over sixty degrees Celsius, you know. There's some very complex circuitry placed near the Eustachian tube that gets unpleasantly hot if you do."

"Ow, ow, ow!" He sucked in air, staring at me with the astonishment of the very new operative. It always takes them a while to discover that immortality and intense pain are not strangers, indeed can reside in the same eternal house for quite lengthy periods of time. "Should I drink some ice water?"

"By no means, unless you want some real discomfort. You'll be all right in a minute or so. As I was about to say, I have some recordings of Jean de Reszke I'll transmit to you, if you're interested in comparing artists."

"Thanks, I'd like that." Averill ran a hasty self-diagnostic.

"And how is your team faring over at the New Brunswick, by the way? No cases of nerves, no blue devils?"

"Hell no." Averill started to lift his coffee again and then set it down respectfully.

"Doesn't bother you that the whole place will be ashes in a few days' time, and most of your neighbors dead?"

"No. We're all O.K. over there. We figure it's just a metaphor for the whole business, isn't it? I mean, sooner or later this whole world"—he made a sweeping gesture, palm outward—"as we know it, is going the same way, right? So what's it matter if it's the earthquake that finishes it now, or a wrecking ball someplace further on in time, right? Same thing with the people. There's no reason to get personally upset about it, is there? No, sir. Specially since *we'll* all still be alive."

"A commendable attitude." I had a sip of my coffee. "And your work goes well?"

"Yes, *sir.*" He grinned. "You will be so proud of us burglary squad fellows when you get our next list. You wouldn't believe the stuff we're finding! All kinds of objets d'art, looks like. One-of-a-kind items, by God. Wait'll you see."

"I look forward to it." I glanced at my chronometer and drank down the rest of my coffee, having waited for it to descend to a comfortable fifty-nine degrees Celsius. "But, you know, Averill, it really won't do to think of yourselves as burglars."

"Well—that is—it's only a figure of speech, anyhow!" Averill protested, flushing. "A joke!"

"I'm aware of that, but I cannot emphasize enough that we are not stealing anything." I set my coffee cup down, aware that I sounded priggish, and looked sternly at him. "We're preserving priceless examples of late Victorian craftsmanship for the edification of future generations."

"I know." Averill looked at me sheepishly, "But—aw, hell, do you mean to say not one of those crystal chandeliers will wind up in some Facilitator General's private HQ somewhere?"

"That's an absurd idea," I told him, though I knew only too well it wasn't. Still, it doesn't do to disillusion one's subordinates too young. "And now, will you excuse me? I mustn't be late for work."

"All right. Be seeing you!"

As I left he rejoined the admiring throng about the fellow who was telling Caruso stories. My way lay along the bright tiled hall, steamy and echoing with the clatter of food preparation and busy operatives; then through the dark security vestibule, with its luminous screens displaying the world without; then through the concealed door that shut behind me and left no trace of itself to any eyes but my own. I drew a deep breath. Chill and silent morning air; no glimmer of light, yet, at least not down here in the alley. Half past-five. This time three days hence—

I shivered and found my way out in the direction of the waterfront.

Not long afterward I arrived at the loading area where I had been desultorily employed for the last month. I made my entrance staggering slightly, doing my best to murder "You Can't Guess Who Flirted With Me" in a gravelly baritone.

The mortal laborers assembled there turned to stare at me. My best friend, an acquaintance I'd cultivated painstakingly these last three weeks, came forward and took me by the arm.

"Jesus, Kelly, you'd better stow that. Where've you been?"

I stopped singing and gave him a belligerent stare. "Marching in the Easter parade, O'Neil."

"O, like enough." He ran his eyes over me in dismay. Francis O'Neil was thirty years old. He looked enough like me to have been taken for my somewhat bulkier, clean-shaven brother. "What're you doing this for, man? You know Herlihy doesn't like you as it is. You look like you've not been home to sleep nor bathe since Friday night!"

"So I have not." I dropped my gaze in hungover remorse.

"Come on, you poor stupid bastard, I've got some coffee in my dinner pail. Sober up. Was it a letter you got from your girl again?"

"It was." I let him steer me to a secluded area behind a mountain of crates and accepted the tin cup he filled for me with lukewarm coffee. "She doesn't love me, O'Neil. She never did. I can tell."

"You're taking it all the wrong way, I'm sure. I can't believe she's stopped caring, not after all the things you've told me about her. Just drink that down, now. Mary made it fresh not an hour ago."

"You're a lucky man, Francis." I leaned on him and began to weep, slopping the coffee. He forbore with the patience of a saint and replied: "Sure I am, Jimmy, And shall I tell you why? Because I know when to take my drink, don't I? I don't swill it down every payday and forget to go home, do I? No indeed. I'd lose Mary and the kids and all the rest of it, wouldn't I? It's self-control you need, Jimmy, and the sorrows in your heart be damned. Come on now. With any luck Herlihy won't notice the state you're in."

But he did, and a litany of scorn was pronounced on my penitent head. I took it with eyes downcast, turning my battered hat in my hands, and a dirtier nor more maudlin drunk could scarce have been seen in that city. I would be summarily fired, I was assured, but they needed men today so bad they'd employ even the likes of me, though by God next time—

When the boss had done excoriating me I was dismissed to help unload a cargo of copra from the *Nevadan*, in from the islands yesterday. I sniveled and tottered and managed not to drop anything much. O'Neil stayed close to me the whole day, watchful lest I pass out or wander off. He was a good friend to the abject caricature I presented; God knows why he cared. Well, I should repay his kindness, at least, though in a manner he would never have the opportunity to appreciate.

We sweated until four in the afternoon, when there was nothing left to take off the *Nevadan*; let go then with directions to the next day's job, and threats against slackers.

"Now, Kelly." O'Neil took my arm and steered me with him back toward Market Street. "I'll tell you what I think you ought to do. Go home and have a bit of a wash in the basin, right? Have you clean clothes? So, put on a clean shirt and trousers and see can you scrape some of that off your boots. Then come over to supper at our place. Mary's bought some sausages, we thought we'd treat ourselves to a dish of coddle now that Lent's over. We've plenty."

"I will, then." I grasped his hand. "O'Neil, you're a lord for courtesy."

"I am not. Only go home and wash, man!"

We parted in front of the Terminal Hotel and I hurried back to the HQ to follow his instructions. This was just the sort of chance I'd been angling for since I'd sought out the man on the basis of the Genetic Survey Team report.

An hour later, as cleanly as the character I played was likely to be able to make himself, I ventured along Market Street, heading down in the direction of the tenement where O'Neil and his family lived, the boardinghouses in the shadow of the Palace Hotel. I knew their exact location, though O'Neil was of course unaware of that; accordingly he had sent a pair of his children down to the corner to watch for me.

They failed to observe my approach, however, and I really couldn't blame them; for proceeding down Market Street before me, moving slowly between the gloom of twilight and the electric illumination of the shop signs, was an apparition in a scarlet tunic and black shako.

It walked with the stiff and measured tread of the automaton it was pretending to be. The little ragged girl and her littler brother stared open-mouthed, watching its progress along the sidewalk. It performed a brief business of marching mindlessly into a lamppost and walking inexorably in place there a moment before righting itself and going on, but now on an oblique course toward the children.

I too continued on my course, smiling a little. This was delightful: a mortal pretending to be a mechanical toy being followed by a cyborg pretending to be a mortal.

There was a wild reverberation of mirth in the ether around me. One other of our kind was observing the scene, apparently; but there was a gigantic quality to the amusement that made me falter in my step. Who was that? That was someone I knew, surely. *Quo Vadis?* I transmitted. The laughter shut off like an electric light being switched out, but not before I got a sense of direction from it. I looked across the street and just caught a glimpse of a massive figure disappearing down an alley. My visual impression was of an old miner, one of the mythic founders of this city. Old gods walking? What a ridiculous idea, and yet…what a moment of panic it evoked, of mortal dread, quite irrational.

But the figure in the scarlet tunic had reached the children. Little Ella clutched her brother's hand, stock-still on the pavement: little Donal shrank behind his sister, but watched with one eye as the thing loomed over them.

It bent forward, slowly, in increments, as though a gear ratcheted in its spine to lower it down to them. Its face was painted white, with red circles on the cheeks and a red cupid's bow mouth under the stiff black mustaches. Blank glassy eyes did not fix on them, did not seem to see anything, but one white-gloved hand came up jerkily to offer the little girl a printed handbill.

After a frozen motionless moment she took it from him. "Thank you, Mister Soldier," she said in a high clear voice. The figure gave no sign that it had heard, but unbent slowly, until it stood ramrod-straight again; pivoted sharply on its heel and resumed its slow march down Market Street.

"Soldier go." Donal pointed. Ella peered thoughtfully at the handbill.

"'CH—IL—DREN'," she read aloud. What an impossibly sweet voice she had. "And that's an exclamation point, there. 'Babe—Babies, in, To—Toy—'"

"'Toyland'," I finished for her. She looked up with a glad cry.

"There you are, Mr. Kelly. Donal, this is Mr. Kelly. He is Daddy's good friend. Supper will be on the table presently. Won't you please come with us, Mr. Kelly?"

"I should be delighted to." I touched the brim of my hat. They pattered away down an alley, making for the dark warren of their tenement, and I followed closely.

They were different physical types, the brother and sister. Pretty children, certainly, particularly Ella with her glossy black braids, with her eyes the color of the twilight framed by black lashes. But it is not beauty we look for in a child.

It was the boy I watched closely as we walked, a sturdy three-year-old trudging along holding tight to the girl's hand. I couldn't have told you the quality nor shade of his skin, nor his hair nor his eyes; I cared only that his head appeared to be a certain shape, that his little body appeared to fit a certain profile, that his limbs appeared to be a certain length in relation to one another. I couldn't be certain yet, of course: that was why I had maneuvered his father into the generous impulse of inviting me into his home.

They lived down a long dark corridor toward the back of the building, its walls damp with sweat, its air heavy with the odors of cooking, of washing, of mortal life. The door opened a crack as we neared it and then, slowly, opened wide to reveal O'Neil standing there in a blaze of light. The blaze was purely by contrast to our darkness, however; once we'd crossed the threshold, I saw that two kerosene lamps were all the illumination they had.

"There now, didn't I tell you she'd spot him?" O'Neil cried triumphantly. "Welcome to this house, Jimmy Kelly."

"God save all here." I removed my hat. "Good evening, Mrs. O'Neil."

"Good evening to you, Mr. Kelly." Mary O'Neil turned from the stove, bouncing a fretful infant against one shoulder. "Would you care for a cup of tea, now?" She was like Ella, if years could be granted Ella to grow tall and slender and wear her hair up like a soft thundercloud. But there was no welcoming smile for me in the gray eyes, for on the previous occasion we'd met I'd been disgracefully intoxicated—at least, doing my best to appear so. I looked down as if abashed.

"I'd bless you for a cup of tea, my dear, I would," I replied. "And won't you allow me to apologize for the condition I was in last Tuesday week? I'd no excuse at all."

"Least said, soonest mended." She softened somewhat at my obvious sobriety. Setting the baby down to whimper in its apple-box cradle, she poured and served my tea. "Pray seat yourself."

"Here." Ella pulled out a chair for me. I thanked her and sat down to scan the room they lived in. Only one room, with one window that probably looked out on an alley wall but was presently frosted opaque from the steam of the saucepan wherein their supper cooked. Indeed, there was a fine layer of condensation on everything: it trickled down the walls, it lay in a damp film on the oilcloth cover of the table and the blankets on the bed against the far wall. The unhappy infant's hair was moist and curling with it.

Had there been any ventilation it had been a pleasant enough room. The table was set with good china, someone's treasured inheritance, no doubt. The tiny potbellied stove must have been awkward to cook upon, but O'Neil had built a cabinet of slatwood and sheet tin next to it to serve as the rest of a kitchen. The children's trundle was stored tidily under the parent's bed. Next to the painted washbasin on the trunk, a decorous screen gave privacy to one corner. Slatwood shelves displayed the family's few valuables: a sewing basket, a music box with a painted scene on its lid, a cheap mirror whose frame was decorated with glued-on seashells, a china dog. On the wall was a painted crucifix with a palm frond stuck behind it.

O'Neil came and sat down across from me.

"You look grand, Jimmy." He thumped his fist on the table approvingly. "Combed your hair, too, didn't you? That's the boy. You'll make a gentleman yet."

"Daddy?" Ella climbed into his lap. "There was a soldier came and gave us this in the street. Will you ever read me what it says? There's more words than I know, see." She thrust the handbill at him. He took it and held it out before him, blinking at it through the steamy air.

Here I present the printed text he read aloud, without his many pauses as he attempted to decipher it (for he was an intelligent man, but of little education):

CHILDREN!

Come see the Grand Fairy Extravaganza BABES IN TOYLAND
Music by Victor Herbert—Book by Glen MacDonough—
Staged by Julian Mitchell Ignacio Martinetti and 100 Others!
Coming by Special Train of Eight Cars!
Biggest Musical Production San Francisco Has Seen In Years!

An Invitation from Mother Goose Herself:

MY dear little Boys and Girls,

I DO hope you will behave nicely so that your Mammas and Papas will treat you to a performance of Mr. Herbert's lovely play Babes in Toyland at the Columbia Theater, opening Monday, the 16th of April. Why, my dears, it's one of the biggest successes of the season and has already played for ever so many nights in such far-away cities as New York, Chicago and Boston. Yes, you really must be good little children, and then your dear parents will see that you deserve an outing to visit me. For, make no mistake, I myself, the only true and original MOTHER GOOSE, shall be there upon the stage of the Columbia Theater. And so shall so many of your other friends from my delightful rhymes such as Tom, Tom the Piper's Son, Bo Peep, Contrary Mary, and Red Riding Hood. The curtain will rise upon Mr. Mitchell's splendid production, with its many novel effects, at eight o'clock sharp.

OF course, if you are very little folks you are apt to be sleepyheads if kept up so late, but that need not concern your careful parents, for there will be a matinee on Saturday at two o'clock in the afternoon.

WON'T you please come to see me?

Your affectionate friend, Mother Goose.

"O, dear," sighed Mary.

"Daddy, can we go?" Ella's eyes were alight with anticipation. Donal chimed in: "See Mother Goose, Daddy!"

"We can't afford it, children," Mary said firmly. She took the saucepan off the stove and began to ladle a savory dish of sausage, onions, potatoes, and bacon onto the plates. "We've got a roof over our heads and food for the table. Let's be thankful for that."

Ella closed her little mouth tight like her mother's, but Donal burst into tears. "I wanna go see Mother Goose!" he howled.

O'Neil groaned. "Your mother is right, Donal. Daddy and Mummy don't have the money for the tickets, can you understand that?"

"You oughtn't to have read out that bill," said Mary in a quiet voice.

"I want go see the soldier!"

"Donal, hush now!"

"Donal's the boy for me," I said, leaning forward and reaching out to him. "Look, Donal Og, what's this you've got in your ear?"

I pretended to pull forth a bar of Ghirardelli's. Ella clapped her hands to her mouth. Donal stopped crying and stared at me with perfectly round eyes.

"Look at that! Would you ever have thought such a little fellow'd have such big things in his ears? Come sit with your Uncle Jimmy, Donal." I drew him onto my lap. "And if you hush your noise, perhaps Mummy and Daddy'll let you have sweeties, eh?" I set the candy in the midst of the oil-cloth, well out of his reach.

"Bless you, Jimmy," said O'Neil.

"Well, and isn't it the least I can do? Didn't know I could work magic, did you, Ella?"

"Settle down, now." Mary set out the dishes. "Frank, it's time to say grace."

O'Neil made the sign of the Cross and intoned, with the little ones mumbling along, "Bless-us-O-Lord-and-these-Thy-gifts-which-we-are-about-to-receive-from-Thy-bounty-through-Christ-Our-Lord-Amen."

Mary sat down with us, unfolding her threadbare napkin. "Donal, come sit with Mummy."

"Be easy, Mrs. O'Neil, I don't mind him." I smiled at her. "I've a little brother at home he's the very image of. Where's his spoon? Here, Donal Og, you eat with me."

"I don't doubt they look alike." O'Neil held out his tumbler as Mary poured from a pitcher of milk. "Look at you and me. Do you know, Mary, that was the first acquaintance we had—? Got our hats mixed up when the wind blew 'em both off. We wear just the same size."

"Fancy that."

So we dined, and an affable mortal man helped little Donal make a mess of his potatoes whilst chatting with Mr. and Mrs. O'Neil about such subjects as the dreadful expense of living in San Francisco and their plans to remove to a cheaper, less crowded place as soon as they'd saved enough money. The immortal machine that sat at their table was making a thorough examination of Donal, most subtly: an idle caress of his close-cropped little head measured his skull size, concealed devices gauged bone length and density and measured his weight to the pound; data was analyzed and preliminary judgment made: optimal morphology. Augmentation process possible. Classification pending blood analysis and spektral diagnosis.

"That's the best meal I've had in this country, Mrs. O'Neil," I told her as we rose from the table.

"How kind of you to say so, Mr. Kelly," she replied, collecting the dishes.

"Chocolate, Daddy?" Donal stretched out his arm for it. O'Neil tore open the waxed paper and broke off a square. He divided it into two and gave one to Donal and one to Ella.

"Now, you must thank your uncle Jimmy, for this is good chocolate and cost him dear."

"Thank you, Uncle Jimmy," they chorused, and Ella added, "But he got it by magic. It came out of Donal's ear. I saw it."

O'Neil rubbed his face wearily. "No, Ella, it was only a conjuring trick. Remember the talk we had about such things? It was just a trick. Wasn't it, Jimmy?"

"That's all it was, sure," I agreed. She looked from her father to me and back.

"Frank, dear, will you help me with these?" Mary had stacked the dishes in a washpan and sprinkled soap flakes in.

"Right. Jimmy, will you mind the kids? We're just taking these down to the tap."

"I will indeed," I said, and thought: *Thank you very much, mortal man, for this opportunity.* The moment the door closed behind them I had the device out of my pocket. It looked rather like a big old-fashioned watch. I held it out to the boy.

"Here you go, Donal, here's a grand timepiece for you to play with."

He took it gladly. "There's a train on it!" he cried. I turned to Ella.

"And what can I do for you, darling?"

She looked at me with considering eyes. "You can read me the funny papers." She pointed to a neatly stacked bundle by the stove.

"With pleasure." I seized them up and we settled back in my chair, pulling a lamp close. The baby slept fitfully, I read to Ella about Sambo and Tommy Pip and Herr Spiegleburger, and all the while Donal pressed buttons and thumbed levers on the diagnostic toy. It flashed pretty lights for him, it played little tunes his sister was incapable of hearing; and then, as I had known it would, it bit him.

"Ow!" He dropped it and began to cry, holding out his tiny bleeding finger.

"O, dear, now, what's that? Did it stick you?" I put his sister down and got up to take the device back. "Tsk! Look at that, the stem's broken." It vanished into my pocket. "What a shame. O, I'm sorry, Donal Og, here's the old hankie. Let's bandage it up, shall we? There, there. Doesn't hurt now, does it?"

"No," he sniffled. "I want another chocolate."

"And so you'll have one, for being a brave boy." I snapped off another square and gave it to him. "Ella, let's give you another as well, shall we? What have you found there?"

"It's a picture about Mother Goose." She had spread out the Children's Page on the oilcloth. "Isn't it? That says Mother Goose right there."

I looked over her shoulder. "'Pictures from Mother Goose,'" I read out, "'Hot Cross Buns. Paint the Seller of Hot Cross Buns.' Looks like it's a contest, darling. They're asking the kiddies to paint in the picture and send it off to the paper to judge who's done the best one."

"Is there prize money?" She had an idea.

"Two dollars for the best one," I read, pulling at my lower lip uneasily. "And paintboxes for everyone else who enters."

She thought that over. Dismay came into her face. "But I haven't got a paintbox to color it with at all! O, that's stupid! Giving paintboxes out to kids that's got them already. O, that's not fair!" She shook with stifled anger.

"What's not fair?" Her mother backed through the door, holding it open for O'Neil with the washpan.

"Only this Mother Goose thing here," I said.

"You're never on about going to that show again, are you?" said Mary sharply, coming and taking her daughter by the shoulders. "Are you? Have you been wheedling at Mr. Kelly?"

"I have not!" the little girl said in a trembling voice.

"She hasn't, Mrs. O'Neil, only it's this contest in the kids' paper," I hastened to explain. "You have to have a set of paints to enter it, see."

Mary looked down at the paper. Ella began to cry quietly. Her mother gathered her up and sat with her on the edge of the bed, rocking her back and forth.

"O, I'm so sorry, Ella dear, Mummy's so sorry. But you see, now, don't you, the harm in wanting such things? You see how unhappy it's made you? Look how hard Mummy and Daddy work to feed you and clothe you. Do you know how unhappy it makes us when you want shows and paintboxes and who knows what, and we can't give them to you? It makes us despair. That's a Mortal Sin, despair is."

"I want to see the fairies," wept the little girl.

"Dearest dear, there aren't any fairies! But surely it was the devil himself you met out in the street, that gave you that wicked piece of paper and made you long after vain things. Do you understand me? Do you see why it's wicked, wanting things? It kills the soul, Ella."

After a long, gasping moment the child responded, "I see, Mummy." She kept her face hidden in her mother's shoulder. Donal watched them uncertainly, twisting the big knot of handkerchief on his finger. O'Neil sat at the table and put his head in his hands. After a moment he swept up the newspaper and put it in the stove. He reached into the slatwood cabinet and pulled a bottle of Wilson's Whiskey up on the table, and got a couple of clean tumblers out of the washpan.

"Will you have a dram, Kelly?" he offered.

"Just the one." I sat down beside him.

"Just the one," he agreed.

You must not empathize with them.

▲▼▲

When I let myself into my rooms on Bush Street, I checked my messages. A long green column of them pulsed on the credenza screen. Most of it was the promised list from Averill and his fellows; I'd have to pass that on to our masters as soon as I'd reviewed it. I didn't feel much like reviewing it just now, however.

There was also a response to my request for another transport for Madame D'Arraignee: *DENIED. NO ADDITIONAL VEHICLES AVAILABLE. FIND ALTERNATIVE.*

I sighed and sank into my chair. My honor was at stake. From a drawer at the side of the credenza I took another Ghirardelli bar and, scarcely taking the time to tear off the paper, consumed it in a few greedy bites. Waiting for its soothing properties to act, I paged through a copy of the *Examiner*. There were automobile agencies along Golden Gate Avenue. Perhaps I could afford to purchase one out of my personal operation's expense account?

But they were shockingly expensive in this city. I couldn't find one for sale, new or used, for less than a thousand dollars. Why couldn't *her* case officer delve into his own pocket to deliver the goods? I verified the balance of my account. No, there certainly wasn't enough for an automobile in there. However, there was enough to purchase four tickets to *Babes in Toyland*.

I accessed the proper party and typed in my transaction request.

TIX UNAVAILABLE FOR 041606 EVENT, came the reply. *041706 AVAILABLE OK?*

OK, I typed. *PLS DEBIT & DELIVER.*

DEBITED. TIX IN YR BOX AT S MKT ST HQ 600 HRS 041606.

TIBI GRATIAS! I replied, with all sincerity.

DIE DULCE FRUERE. OUT.

Having solved one problem, an easy solution to the other suggested itself to me. It involved a slight inconvenience, it was true: but any gentleman would readily endure worse for a lady's sake.

▲▼▲

My two rooms on Bush Street did not include the luxury of a bath, but the late Mr. Adolph Sutro had provided an alternative pleasure for his fellow citizens.

Just north of Cliff House Mr. Sutro had purchased a rocky little purgatory of a cove, cleaned the shipwrecks out of it and proceeded to shore it up against the more treacherous waves with several thousand barrels of cement. Having constructed not one but six saltwater pools of a magnificence to rival old Rome, he had proceeded to enclose it in a crystal palace affair of no less than four acres of glass.

Ah, but this wasn't enough for San Francisco! The entrance, on the hill above, was as near a Greek temple as modern artisans could produce; through the shrine one wandered along the museum gallery lined with exhibits both educational and macabre and descended a vast staircase lined with palm trees to the main level, where one might bathe, exercise in the gymnasium, or attend a theater performance. Having done all this, one might then dine in the restaurant.

However, my schedule today called for nothing more strenuous than bathing. Ten minutes after descending the grand staircase I was emerging from my changing room (one of five hundred), having soaped, showered, and togged myself out in my rented bathing suit, making my way toward the nearest warm-water pool under the bemused eyes of several hundred mortal idlers sitting in the bleachers above.

I was not surprised to see another of my own kind backstroking manfully across the green water; nothing draws the attention of an immortal like sanitary conveniences. I must confess my heart sank when I recognized Lewis. I hadn't seen him since that period at New World One, when I'd been obliged to monitor him again. His career was in ruins, of course. Rather a shame, really. A drone, but a gentleman for all that.

He felt my regard and glanced up, seeing me at once. He smiled and waved.

Victor! he broadcast. *How nice to see you again.*

It's Lewis, isn't it? I responded, though I knew his name perfectly well, and far more of his history than he knew himself. I had been assigned to monitor his activities once, to my everlasting shame. Still, it had been centuries, and he had never shown any sign of recovering certain memories. I hoped, for his sake, that such was the case. Memory effacement is not a pleasant experience.

He pulled himself up on the coping of the pool and swept his wet hair out of his eyes. I stepped to the edge, took the correct diver's stance and leapt in, transmitting through bubbles: *So you're here as well? Presalvaging books, I suppose?*

The Mercantile Library, he affirmed, and there was nothing in his pleasant tone to indicate he'd remembered what I'd done to him at Eurobase One.

God! That must be a Herculean effort, I responded, surfacing.

He transmitted rueful amusement. *You've heard of it, I suppose?*

Rather, I replied, practicing my breast stroke. *All those Comstock Lode silver barons went looting the old family libraries of Europe, didn't they? Snatched up medieval manuscripts at a tenth their value from impoverished Venetian princes, I believe? Fabulously rare first editions from London antiquarians?*

Something like that, he replied. *And brought them back home to the States for safekeeping.*

Ha!

Well, how were they to know? Lewis made an expressive gesture taking in the vast edifice around us. *Mr. Sutro himself had a Shakespeare first folio. What a panic it's been tracking* that *down! And you?*

I'm negotiating for a promising-looking young recruit. Moreover, I drew Nob Hill detail, I replied casually. *I've coordinated a team of quite talented youngsters set to liberate the premises of Messrs. Towne, Crocker, Huntington et al. as soon as the lights are out. All manner of costly bric-a-brac has been tagged for rescue—Chippendales, Louis Quatorzes—to say nothing of jewels and cash.*

My, that sounds satisfying. You'll never guess what I found, only last night! Lewis transmitted, looking immensely pleased with himself.

Something unexpected? I responded.

He edged forward on the coping. *Yes, you might say so. Just some old papers that had been mislaid by an idiot named Pompeo Leoni and bound into the wrong book. Just something jotted down by an elderly left-handed Italian gentleman!*

Not Da Vinci? I turned in the water to stare at him, genuinely impressed.

Who else? Lewis nearly hugged himself in triumph. *Not just any doodlings or speculation from the pen of Leonardo, either. Something of decided interest to the Company! It seems he devoted some serious thought to the construction of articulated human limbs—a clockwork arm, for example, that could be made to perform various tasks!*

I've heard something of the sort, I replied, swimming back toward him.

Yes, well, he seems to have taken the idea further than robotics. Lewis leaned down in a conspiratorial manner. *From a human arm he leapt to the idea of an entire articulated human skeleton of bronze, and wondered whether the human frame might not be merely imitated but improved in function.*

By Jove! Was the man anticipating androids? I reached the coping and leaned on it, slicking back my hair.

No! No, he was chasing another idea entirely, Lewis insisted. *Shall I quote? I rather think I ought to let him express his thoughts.* He leaned back and, with a dreamy expression, transmitted in flawless fifteenth-century Tuscan: *It has been observed that the presence of metal is not in all cases inimical to the body of man, as we may see in earrings, or in crossbow bolts, spearpoints, pistol balls, and other detritus of war that have been known to enter the flesh and remain for some years without doing the bearer any appreciable harm, or indeed in that practice of physicians wherein a small pellet of gold is inserted into an incision made near an aching joint, and the sufferer gains relief and ease of movement thereby.*

'Take this idea further and think that a shattered bone might be replaced with a model of the same bone cast in bronze, identical with or even superior to its original.

'Go further and say that where one bone might be replaced, so might the skeleton entire, and if the articulation is improved upon the man might attain a greater degree of physical perfection than he was born with.

'The flaw in this would be the man's pain and the high likelihood he would die before surgery of such magnitude could be carried out.

'Unless we are to regard the theory of alchemists who hold that the Philosopher's Stone, once attained, would transmute the imperfect flesh to perfection, a kind of supple gold that lives and breathes, and by this means the end might be obtained without cutting, the end being immortality.' Lewis opened his eyes and looked at me expectantly. I smacked my hand on the coping in amusement.

By Jove, I repeated. *How typical of the Maestro. So he was all set to invent us, was he?*

To say nothing of hip replacements.

But what a find for the Company, Lewis!

Of course, to give you a real idea of the text I ought to have presented it like this: Lewis began to rattle it out backwards. I shook my head, laughing and holding up my hands in sign that he should stop. After a moment or two he trailed off, adding: *I don't think it loses much in translation, though.*

I shook my head. *You know, old man, I believe we're treading rather too closely to a temporal paradox here. Just as well the Company will take possession of that volume, and not some inquisitive mortal! What if it had inspired someone to experiment with biomechanicals a century or so too early?*

Ah! No, we're safe enough, Lewis pointed out. *As far as history records those da Vinci pages at all, it records them as being lost in the Mercantile Library fire. The circle is closed. All the same, I imagine it was a temptation for any operatives stationed near Amboise in da Vinci's time. Wouldn't you have wanted to seek the old man out as he lay dying, and tell him that something would be done with this particular idea, at least? Immortality and human perfection!*

Of course I'd have been tempted; but I shook my head. *Not unless I cared to face a court-martial for a security breach.*

Lewis shivered in his wet wool and slid back into the water. I turned on my back and floated, considering him.

The temperature doesn't suit you? I inquired.

Oh…They've got the frigidarium all right, but the calidaria here aren't really hot enough, Lewis explained. *And of course there's no sudatorium at all.*

Nor any slaves for a good massage, either, I added, glancing up at the mortal onlookers. *Sic transit luxuria, alas.* Lewis smiled faintly; he had never been comfortable with mortal servants, I remembered. Odd, for someone who began mortal life as a Roman, or at least a Romano-Briton.

Weren't you recruited at Bath…? I inquired, leaning on the coping.

Aquae Sulis, it was then, Lewis informed me. *The public baths there.*

Of course. I remember now! You were rescued from the temple. Intercepted child sacrifice, I imagine?

Oh, good heavens, no! The Romans never did that sort of thing. No, I was just left in a blanket by the statue of Apollo. Lewis shrugged, and then began to grin. *I hadn't thought about it before, but this puts a distinctly Freudian slant on my visits here! Returning to the womb in time of stress? I was only a few hours old when the Company took me, or so I've always been told.*

I laughed and set off on a lap across the pool. *At least you were spared any memories of mortal life.*

That's true, he responded, and then his smile faded. *And yet, you know, I think I'm the poorer for that. The rest of you may have some harrowing memories, but at least you know what it was to be mortal.*

I assure you it's nothing to be envied, I informed him. He set out across the pool himself, resuming his backstroke.

I think I would have preferred the experience, all the same, he insisted. *I'd have liked a father—or mother—figure in my life. At the very least, those of you rescued at an age to remember it have a sort of filial relationship with the immortal who saved you. Haven't you?*

I regret to disillusion you, sir, but that is absolutely not true, I replied firmly.

Really? He dove and came up for air, gasping. *What a shame. Bang goes another romantic fantasy. I suppose we're all just orphans of one storm or another.*

At that moment a pair of mortals chose to roughhouse, snorting and chuckling as they pummeled each other in their seats in the wooden bleachers; one of them broke free and ran, scrambling apelike over the seats, until he lost his footing and fell with a horrendous crash that rolled and thundered in the air, echoing under the glassed dome, off the water and wet coping.

I saw Lewis go pale; I imagine my own countenance showed reflexive panic. After a frozen moment Lewis drew a deep breath.

"One storm or another," he murmured aloud. "Nothing to be afraid of here, after all. Is there? This structure will survive the quake. History says it will. Nothing but minor damage, really."

I nodded. Then, struck in one moment by the same thought, we lifted our horrified eyes to the ceiling, with its one hundred thousand panes of glass.

"I believe I've got a rail car to catch," I apologized, vaulting to the coping with what I hoped was not undignified haste.

"I've a luncheon engagement myself," Lewis said, gasping as he sprinted ahead of me to the grand staircase.

▲▼▲

On the 16th of April I entertained friends, or at least my landlady received that impression; and what quiet and well-behaved fellows the gentlemen were, and how plain and respectable the ladies! No cigars, no raucous laughter, no drunkenness at all. Indeed, Mrs. McCarty assured me she would welcome them as lodgers at any time in the future, should they require desirable Bush Street rooms. I assured her they would be gratified at the news. Perhaps they might have been, if her boardinghouse were still standing in a week's time. History would decree otherwise, regrettably.

My parlor resembled a war room, with its central table on which was spread a copy of the Sanborn map of the Nob Hill area, up-to-date from the previous year. My subordinates stood or leaned over the table, listening intently as I bent with red chalk to delineate the placement of salvage apparatus generators.

"The Hush Field generators will arrive in a baker's van at the corner of Clay and Taylor Streets at midnight precisely," I informed them. "Delacort, your team will approach from your station at the end of Pleasant Street and take possession of them. There will be five generators. I want them placed at the following intersections: Bush and Jones, Clay and Jones, Clay and Powell, Bush and Powell and on California midway between Taylor and Mason." I put a firm letter X at each site. "The generators should be in place and switched on by no later than five minutes after midnight. Your people will remain in place to remove the generators at half past three exactly, returning them to the baker's van, which will depart promptly. At that moment a private car will pull up to the same location to transport your team to the central collection point on Ocean Beach. Is that clear?"

"Perfectly, sir," Delacort saluted. Averill looked at her slightly askance and turned a worried face to me.

"What're they going to do if some cop comes along and wants to know what they're doing there at that time of night?"

"Any cop coming in range of the Hush Field will pass out, dummy," Philemon informed him. I frowned and cleared my throat. Cinema Standard (the language of the schoolroom) is not my preferred mode of expression.

"If you please, Philemon!"

"Yeah, sorry—"

"Your team will depart from their station at Joice Street at five minutes after midnight and proceed to the intersection of Mason and Sacramento, where a motorized drayer's wagon will be arriving. You will be responsible for the contents of the Flood mansion." I outlined it in red. "Your driver will provide you with a sterile containment receptacle for item number thirty-nine on your acquisitions list. Kindly see to it that this particular item is salvaged first and delivered to the driver separately."

"What's item thirty-nine?" Averill inquired. There followed an awkward silence. Philemon raised his eyebrows at me. Company policy discourages field operatives from being told more than they strictly need to know regarding any given posting. Upon consideration, however, it seemed wisest to answer Averill's question; there was enough stress associated with this detail as it was without adding mysteries. I cleared my throat.

"The Flood mansion contains a 'Moorish' smoking room," I informed him. "Among its features is a lump of black stone carefully displayed in a glass case. Mr. Flood purchased it under the impression that it is an actual piece of the Qaaba from Mecca, chipped loose by an enterprising Yankee adventurer. He was, of course, defrauded; the stone is in fact a meteorite, and preliminary spectrographic analysis indicates it originated on Mars."

"Oh," said Averill, nodding sagely. I did not choose to add that plainly visible on the rock's surface is a fossilized crustacean of an unknown kind, or that the rock's rediscovery (in a museum owned by Dr. Zeus, incidentally) in the year 2210 will galvanize the Mars colonization effort into making real progress at last.

I bent over the map again and continued: "All the items on your list are to be loaded into the wagon by twenty minutes after three. At that time, the wagon will depart for Ocean Beach and your team will follow in the private car provided. Understood?"

"Understood."

"Rodrigo, your team will depart from their Taylor Street station at five minutes after midnight as well. Your wagon will arrive at the corner of California and Taylor; you will proceed to salvage the Huntington mansion." I marked it on the map. "Due to the nature of your quarry you will be allotted ten additional minutes, but all listed items must be loaded and ready for removal by half past three, at which time your private transport will arrive. Upon arrival at Ocean Beach you will be assisted by Philemon's team, who will already (I should hope) have loaded most of their salvage into the waiting boats."

"Yes, sir." Rodrigo made a slight bow.

"Freytag, your team will be stationed on Jones Street. You depart at five after midnight, like the rest, and your objective is the Crocker mansion, here." Freytag bent close to see as I shaded in her area. "Your wagon will pull up to Jones and California; you ought to be able to fill it in the allotted time of two hours and fifteen minutes precisely, and be ready to depart for Ocean Beach without incident. Loong? Averill?"

"Sir!" Both immortals stood to attention.

"Your teams will disperse from their stations along Clay and Pine Streets and salvage the lesser targets shown here, here, here, and here—" I chalked circles around them. "I leave to your best judgment individual personnel assignments. Two wagons will arrive on Clay Street at one o'clock precisely and two more will arrive on Pine five minutes later. You ought to find them more than adequate for your purposes. You will need to do a certain amount of running to and fro to coordinate the efforts of your ladies and gentlemen, but it can't be helped."

"I don't anticipate difficulties, sir." Loong assured me.

"No indeed; but remember the immensity of this event shadow." I set down the chalk and wiped my hands on a handkerchief. "Your private transports will be waiting at the corner of Bush and Jones by half past three. Please arrive promptly."

"Yes, *sir*." Averill looked earnest.

"In the entirely likely event that any particular team completes its task ahead of schedule, and has free space in its wagon after all the listed salvage has been accounted for, I will expect that team to lend its assistance to Madame D'Arraignee and her teams at the Mark Hopkins Institute." I swept them with a meaningful stare. "Gentlemen doing so can expect my personal thanks and commendation in their personnel files."

That impressed them, I could see. The favorable notice of one's superiors is invariably one's ticket to the better sort of assignment. Clearing my throat, I continued: "I anticipate arriving at no later than half past two to oversee the final stages of removal. Kindly remain at your transports until I transmit your signal to depart for the central collection point. Have you any further questions, ladies and gentlemen?"

"None, sir," Averill said, and the others nodded agreement.

"Then it's settled," I told them, and carefully folded shut the map book. "A word of warning to you all: you may become aware of precursors to the shock in the course of the evening. History will record a particularly nasty seismic disturbance at two A.M. in particular, and another at five. Control your natural panic, please. Upsetting as you may find these incidents, they will present no danger whatsoever, will in fact go unnoticed by such mortals as happen to be awake at that hour."

Averill put up his hand. "I read the horses will be able to feel it," he said, a little nervously. "I read they'll go mad."

I shrugged. "Undoubtedly why we have been obliged to confine ourselves to motor transport. Of course, *we* are no brute beasts. I have every confidence that we will all resist any irrational impulses toward flight before the job is finished.

"Now then! You may attend to the removal of your personal effects and prepare for the evening's festivities. I shouldn't lunch tomorrow; you'll want to save your appetites for the banquet at Cliff House. I understand it's going to be rather a Roman experience!"

The tension broken, they laughed; and if Averill laughed a bit too loudly, it must be remembered that he was still young. As immortals go, that is.

▲▼▲

Astute mortals might have detected something slightly out of the ordinary on that Tuesday, the seventeenth of April; certainly the hired-van drivers must have noticed an increase in business, as they were dispatched to house after house in every district of the city to pick up nearly identical loads, these being two or three ordinary-looking trunks and one crate precisely fifty centimeters long, twenty centimeters wide, and twenty centimeters high, in which a credenza might fit snugly. And it would be extraordinary if none of them remarked upon the fact that all these same consignments were directed to the same location on the waterfront, the berth of the steamer *Mayfair*.

Certainly in some cases mortal landladies noticed trunks being taken down flights of stairs, and put anxious questions to certain of their tenants regarding hasty removal; but their fears were laid to rest by smiling lies and ready cash.

And did anyone notice, as twilight fell, when persons in immaculate evening dress were suddenly to be seen in nearly every street? Doubtful; for it was, after all, the second night of the opera season, and with the Metropolitan company in town all of Society had turned out to do them honor. If a certain number of them converged on a certain warehouse in an obscure district, and departed therefrom shortly afterward in gleaming automobiles, that was unlikely to excite much interest in observers, either.

I myself guided a brisk little four-cylinder Franklin through the streets, bracing myself as it bumped over the cable car tracks, and steered down Gough with the intention of turning at Fulton and following it out to the beach. At the corner of Geary I glimpsed for a moment a tall figure in a red coat, and wondered what it was doing so far from the theater district; but a glance over my shoulder made it plain that I was mistaken. The red-clad figure shambling along was no more than a bum, albeit one of considerable stature. I dismissed him easily from my thoughts as I contemplated the O'Neil family's outing to the theater.

Had I a warm, sentimental sensation thinking of them, remembering Ella's face aglow when she saw me present her father with the tickets? Certainly not. One magical evening out was scarcely going to make up for their ghastly deaths, in whatever cosmic scale might be supposed to balance such things. Best not to dwell on that aspect of it at all. No, it was the convenience of their absence from home that occupied my musings, and the best way to take advantage of it with regard to my mission.

At the end of Fulton I turned right, in the purple glow of evening over the vast Pacific. Far out to sea—well beyond the sight of mortal eyes—the Company transport ships lay at anchor, waiting only for the cover of full darkness to approach the shore. In a few hours I'd be on board one of them, steaming off in the direction of the Farallones to catch my air transport, with no thought for the smoking ruin of the place I'd lived in so many harrowing weeks.

Cliff House loomed above me, its turreted mass a blaze of light. I saw with some irritation that the long uphill approach was crowded with carriages and automobiles, drawn in on a diagonal; I was obliged to go up as far as the rail depot before I could find a place to leave my motor, and walk back downhill past the baths.

I dare say the waiters at Cliff House could not recall an evening when so large a party, of such unusual persons, had dined with such hysterical gaiety as on this seventeenth of April, 1906.

If I recall correctly, the reservation had been made in the name of an international convention of seismologists. San Francisco was ever the most cosmopolitan of cities, so the restaurant staff expressed no surprise when elegantly attired persons of every known color began arriving in carriages and automobiles. If anyone remarked upon a certain indefinable similarity in appearance among the conventioneers that transcended race, why, that might be explained by their common avocation—whatever seismology might be; no one on the staff had any clear idea. Only the queer nervousness of the guests was impossible to account for, the tendency toward uneasy giggling, the sudden frozen silences and dilated pupils.

I think I can speak for my fellow operatives when I say that we were determined to enjoy ourselves, terror notwithstanding. We deserved the treat, every one of us; we faced a long night of hard work, the culmination of months of labor, under circumstances of mental strain that would test the resolution of the most hardened mercenaries. The least we were owed was an evening of silk hats and tiaras.

▲▼▲

There was a positive chatter of communication on the ether as I approached. We were all here, or in the act of arriving; not since leaving school had I been in such a crowd of my own kind. I thought how we were to feast here, a company of immortals in an airy castle perched on the edge of the Uttermost West, and flit away well before sunrise. It is occasionally pleasant to embody a myth.

I saw Madame. D'Arraignee stepping down from a carriage, evidently arriving with other members of the Hopkins operation team. No bulky Russian sea captain in sight, of course, yet; I hastened to her side and tipped my hat.

"Madame, will you do me the honor of allowing me to escort you within?"

"M'sieur Victor." She gave me a dazzling smile. She wore a gown of pale blue green silk, a shade much in fashion that season, which brought out beautifully certain copper hues in her intensely black skin. Diamonds winked from the breathing shadow of her bosom. She took my arm and we proceeded inside, where we had the remarkable experience of having to shout our transmissions to one another, so crowded was the ether: *I am very pleased to inform you I have arranged for an automobile for your use this evening,* I told her as we paused at the cloakroom for checks.

Oh, I am so glad! I do hope you weren't put to unnecessary trouble.

Through the door to the dining room we caught glimpses of napery like snow, folded in a wilderness of sharp little peaks, with here and there a gilt epergne rising above them.

Not what I'd call unnecessary trouble, no, though it proved impossible to requisition anything at this late date. However, I did have a vehicle allocated for my own personal use and that fine runabout is entirely at your disposal.

Merci, merci mille fois! But will this not impede your own mission?

Not at all, dear lady. I shall be obliged to you for transportation as far as the Palace, I think, after we've dined; but since my mission involves nothing more strenuous than carrying off a child, I anticipate strolling back across the city with ease.

You are too kind, my friend.

A gentleman could do no less. I pulled out a chair for her.

We chatted pleasantly of trifling matters as the rest of the guests arrived. We studied the porcelain menu in some astonishment—the Company had spent a fortune here tonight, certainly enough to have allotted me one extra automobile. I was rather nettled, but my irritation was mollified somewhat by the anticipation of our *carte du jour:*

Green Turtle Soup   Consommé Divinesse
Salmon in Sauce Veloute   Trout Almondine Crab Cocktail
Braised Sweetbreads   Roast Quail Andaluz
Le Faux Mousse Faison Lucullus

Early Green Peas   White Asparagus   Risotto Milanese
Roast Saddle of Venison with Port Wine Jelly
Curried Tomatoes   Watercress Salad
Chicken Marengo Plovers' Eggs   Virginia Ham Croquettes
Lobster Salad   Oysters in Variety
Gateau d'Or et Argent   Assorted Fruits in Season
Rose Snow   Tulip Jellies   Water Ices
Surprise Yerba Buena

All accompanied. of course, by the appropriate vintages, and service *à la russe*. We *were* being rewarded.

A shift in the black rock, miles down, needle-thin fissures screaming through stone, perdurable clay bulging like the head of a monstrous child engaging for birth, straining, straining, STRAINING!

The smiling chatter stopped dead. The waiters looked around, confused, at that elegant assembly frozen like mannequins. Not a scrape of chair moving, not a chime of crystal against china. Only the sound that we alone listened to: the cello-string far below us, tuning for the dance of the wrath of God. I found myself staring across the room directly into Lewis' eyes, where he had halted at the doorway in midstep. The immortal lady on his arm was still as a painted image, a perfect profile by da Vinci.

The orchestra conductor mistook our silence for a cue of some kind. He turned hurriedly to his musicians and they struck up a little waltz tune, light, gracious accompaniment to our festivities. With a boom and a rush of vacuum the service doors parted, as the first of the waiters burst through with tureens and silver buckets of ice. Champagne corks popped like artillery. As the noises roared into our silence, an immortal in white lace and spangles shrieked; she turned it into a high trilling laugh, placing her slender hand upon her throat.

So conversation resumed, and a server appeared at my elbow with a napkined bottle. I held up my glass for Champagne. Madame D'Arraignee and I clinked an unspoken toast and drank fervently.

Twice more while we dined on those good things, the awful warning came. As the venison roast was served forth, its dish of port jelly began to shimmer and vibrate—too subtly for the mortal waiters to notice more than a pretty play of light, but we saw. On the second occasion the oysters had just come to table, and what subaudible pandemonium of clattering there was: half-shell against half-shell with the sound of basalt cliffs grinding

together, and the staccato rattle of all the little sauceboats with their scarlet
and yellow and pink and green contents; though of course the mortal waiters couldn't hear it. Not even the patient horses waiting in their carriage-
traces heard it yet. But the sparkling bubbles ascended more swiftly through
the glasses of Champagne.

The waiters began to move along the tables bearing trays: little cut-crystal
goblets of pink ices, or red and amber jellies, or fresh strawberries drenched
in liqueur, or cakes. We heard the ringing note of a dessert spoon against a
wineglass, signaling us all to attention.

The Chief Project Facilitator rose to address us. Labienus stood poised
and smiling in faultless white tie and tuxedo. As he waited for the babble of
voices to fade he took out his gold chronometer on its chain, studied its tiny
screen, then snapped its case shut and returned it to the pocket of his white
silk waistcoat.

"My fellow seismologists." His voice was quiet, yet without raising it
he reached all corners of the room. Commanding legions confers a certain
ease in public speaking. "Ladies." He bowed. "I trust you've enjoyed the bill
of fare. I know that, as I dined, I was reminded of the fact that perhaps in
no other city in the world could such a feast be so gathered, so prepared,
so served to such a remarkable gathering. Where but here by the Golden
Gate can one banquet in a splendor that beggars the Old World, on deli-
cacies presented by masters of culinary sophistication hired from all civilized nations—all the while in sight of forested hills where savages roamed
within living memory, across a bay that *within living memory* was innocent
of any sail?

"So swiftly has she risen, this great city, as though magically conjured by
djinni out of thin air. Justifiably her citizens might expect to wake tomorrow
in a wilderness, and find that this gorgeous citadel had been as insubstantial
as their dreams."

Archly exchanged glances between some of our operatives as his irony
was appreciated.

"But if that were to come to pass—if they were to wake alone, unhoused
and shivering upon a stony promontory, facing into a cold northern ocean
and a hostile gale—why, you know as well as I do that within a few short
years the citizens of San Francisco would create their city anew, with spires
soaring ever closer to heaven, and mansions yet more gracious."

Of course we knew it, but the poor mortal waiters didn't. I am afraid
some of our younger operatives were base enough to smirk.

"Let us marvel, ladies and gentlemen, at this phoenix of a city, at once ephemeral and abiding. Let us drink to the imperishable spirit of her citizens. I give you the city of San Francisco."

"The city of San Francisco," we chorused, raising our glasses high.

"And I *give* you"—smiling, he extended his hand—"the city of San Francisco!"

Beaming the waiters wheeled it in, on a vast silver cart: an ornate confection of pastry, of spun-sugar and marzipan and candies, a perfect model of the City. It was possible to discern a tiny Ferry Building rising above chocolate wharves, and a tiny Palace, and Nob Hill reproduced in sugared peel and nonpareils. Across the familiar grid of streets Golden Gate Park was done in green fondant, and beyond it was the hill where Sutro Park rose in nougat and candied violets, and beyond that Cliff House itself, in astonishing detail.

We applauded.

Then she was destroyed, that beautiful city, with a silver cake knife and serving wedge, and parceled out to us in neat slices. One had to commend Labienus's sense of humor, to say nothing of his sense of ritual.

▲▼▲

It was expected that we would wish to dance after dining; the ballroom had been reserved for our use, and at some point during dessert the orchestra had discreetly risen and carried their instruments up to the dais.

I thought the idea of dancing in rather poor taste, under the circumstances, and apparently many of my fellow operatives agreed with me; but Averill and some of the other young ones got out on the floor eagerly enough, and soon the stately polonaise gave way to ragtime tunes and two-stepping.

Under the pretense of going for a smoke I went out to the terrace, to breathe the clean night air and metabolize my portion of magnificent excess in peace. By ones and twos several of the older immortals followed me. Soon there was quite an assemblage of us out there between two worlds, between the dark water surging around Seal Rock and the brilliant magic lantern of the Cliff House.

"Victor?" Madame D'Arraignee was making her way to me through the crowd. Her slippers, together with her diamonds, had gone into the leather case she was carrying, and she had donned sensible walking shoes; she had also buttoned a long motorist's duster over her evening gown. The radiant Queen of the Night stood now before me as the Efficient Modern Woman.

"You didn't care to dance either, I see," she remarked.

"Not I, no," I replied. Within the giddy whirl, Averill pranced by in the arms of an immortal sylph in pink satin; their faces were flushed and merry. Don't think them heartless, reader. They did not understand yet. Horror, for Averill, was still a lonely prairie and a burning wagon; for the girl, still a soldier with a bayonet in a deserted orchard. *Those* nightmares weren't here in this bright room with its bouncing music, and so all must be right with the world.

But we were old ones, Madame D'Arraignee and I, and we stood outside in the dark and watched them dance.

Down, miles down, the slick water on the clay face and the widening fissure in darkness, dead shale trembling like an exhausted limb, granite crumbling, rock cracking with the strain and crying out in a voice that rose up, and up at last through the red brick, through the tile and parquet, into the warm air and the music!

The mortal musicians played on, but the dancers faltered. Some of them stopped, looking around in confusion; some of them only missed a step or two and then plunged back into the dance with greater abandon, determined to celebrate something.

Madame D'Arraignee shivered. I threw my unlit cigar over the parapet into the sea.

"Shall we go, Nan?" I offered her my arm. She took it readily and we left Cliff House.

Outside on the carriage drive, and all the way up the steep hill to where my motor was parked, the waiting horses were tossing their heads and whickering uneasily.

Madame D'Arraignee took the wheel, easily guiding us back down into the City through the spangled night.

Even now, at the Grand Opera House, Enrico Caruso was striking a pose before a vast Spanish mountain range rendered on canvas and raising his carbine to threaten poor Bessie Abott. Even now, at the Mechanic's Pavilion, the Grand Prize Masked Carnival was in full swing, with throngs of costumed roller skaters whirling around the rink that would be a triage hospital in twelve hours and a pile of smoking ashes in twenty-four. Even now, the clock on the face of Old St. Mary's Church—bearing its warning legend SON OBSERVE THE TIME AND FLY FROM EVIL—was counting out the minutes left for heedless passersby. Even now, the O'Neil children were sitting forward in their seats, scarcely able to breathe as the cruel Toymaker recited the incantation that would bring his creations to life.

And we rounded the corner at Devisadero and sped down Market, with Prospero's *après*-pageant speech ringing in our ears. At the corner of Third I pointed and Madame D'Arraignee worked the clutch, steered over to the curb and trod on the brake pedal.

"You're quite sure you won't need a ride back?" she inquired over the chatter of the cylinders. I put my legs out and leapt down to the pavement.

"Perfectly sure, Nan." I shot my cuffs and adjusted the drape of my coat. Reaching into the seat, I took my stick and silk hat. "Give my seat to the Muse of Painting. I'm off to lurk in shadows like a gentleman."

"*Bonne chance,* then, Victor." She eased up on the brake, clutched, and cranked the wheel over so the Franklin swung around in a wide arc to retrace its course up Market Street. I tipped my hat and bowed; with a cheery wave and a double honk on the Franklin's horn, she steered away into the night.

So far, so good. The night was yet young and there were plenty of debonair socialites in evening dress on the street, arriving and departing from the restaurants, the hotels, the theaters. For a block I was one of their number; then accomplished my disappearance down a black alleyway into another world, to thread my way through the boardinghouse warren.

Rats were out and scuttling everywhere, sensing the coming disaster infallibly. In some buildings they were cascading down the stairs like trickling water, and cats ignored them and drunkards stood watching in stupefied amazement, but there was nobody else there to remark upon it; these streets did not invite promenaders.

I found the O'Neils' building and made my way up through the unlit stairwell, here and there kicking vermin out of my way. I left the landing and proceeded down their corridor, past doors tight shut showing only feeble lines of light at floor level to mark where the occupants were at home. I heard snores; I heard weeping; I heard a drunken quarrel; I heard a voice raised in wistful melody.

No light at the O'Neils' door, naturally; none at the door immediately opposite theirs. I scanned the room beyond but could discern no occupant. Drawing out a skeleton key from my waistcoat pocket, I gained entrance and shut the door after me.

No tenant at all; good. It was death-cold in there and black as pitch, for a roller shade had been drawn down on the one window. A slight tug sent it wobbling upward but failed to let much more light into the room. Not that I needed light to see my chronometer as I checked it; half past eleven, and even now my teams were assembling at their stations on Nob Hill. I leaned against a wall, folded my arms and composed myself to wait.

Time passed slowly for me, but in Toyland it sped by. Songs and dances, glittering processions came to their inevitable close; fairies took wing. Innocence was rewarded and wickedness resoundingly punished. The last of the ingenious special effects guttered out, the curtain descended, the orchestra fell silent, the house lights came up. A little while the magic lingered, as the O'Neil family made their way out through the lobby, a little while it hung around them like a perfume in the atmosphere of red velvet and gilt and fashionably attired strangers, until they were borne out through the doors by the receding tide of the crowd. Then the magic left them, evaporating upward into the night and the fog, and they got their bearings and made their way home along the dark streets.

I heard them, coming heavily up the stairs, O'Neil and Mary each carrying a child. Down the corridor their footsteps came, and stopped outside.

"Slide down now, Ella, Daddy's got to open the door."

I heard the sound of a key fumbling in darkness for its lock, and a drowsy little voice singing about Toyland, the paradise of childhood to which you can never return.

"Hush, Ella, you'll wake the neighbors."

"Donal's asleep. He missed the ending." Ella's voice was sad. "And it was such a beautiful, beautiful ending. Don't you think it was a beautiful ending, Daddy?"

"Sure it was, darling." Their voices receded a bit as they crossed the threshold. I heard a clink and the sputtering hiss of a match; there was the faintest glimmer of illumination down by the floor.

"Sssh, sh, sh. Home again. Help Mummy get his boots off, Ella, there's a dear."

"I'll just step across to Mrs. Varian's and collect the baby."

"Mind you remember his blanket."

"I will that."

Footsteps in the corridor again, discreet rapping on a panel, a whispered conversation in darkness and a sleepy wail; then returning footsteps and a pair of doors closing. Then, more muffled but still distinct to me, the sound of the O'Neils going to bed.

Their lamps were blown out. Their whispers ceased. Still I waited, listening as the minutes ticked away for their mortal souls to rest.

Half past one on the morning of Wednesday, the eighteenth of April in the year 1906, in the city of San Francisco. Francis O'Neil and his wife and their children asleep finally and forever, and the world had finished with them. In the gray morning, at precisely twelve minutes after the hour of five, this boarding house would lurch forward into the street, bricks tumbling as mortar blew out like talcum powder, rotten timbers snapping. That would be the end of Frank's strength and Mary's care and Ella's dreams, the end of the brief unhappy baby, and no one would remember them but me.

And, perhaps, Donal. I stepped across the hall and let myself into their room, perfectly silent.

The children lay in their trundle on the floor, next to their parent's bed. Donal slept on the outer edge, curled on his side, both hands tucked under his chin. I stood for a moment observing, analyzing their alpha patterns. When I was satisfied that no casual noise would awaken them, I bent and lifted Donal from his bed. He sighed but slept on. After a moment's hesitation I drew the blanket up around Ella's shoulders.

I stood back. The boy wore a nightshirt and long black stockings, but the night was cold. Frank's coat hung over the back of a chair: I appropriated it to wrap his son. Shifting Donal to one arm, I backed out of the room and shut the door.

Finished.

No sleeper in that building woke to hear our rapid descent of the stairs. On the first landing a drunk sat upright, leaning his head on the railings, sound asleep with his lower jaw dropped open like a corpse's. We fled lightly past him, Donal and I, and he never moved.

Away through the maze, then, away forever from the dirt and stench and poverty of that place. In twelve hours it would have ceased to exist, and the wind would scatter white ashes so the dead could never be named nor numbered.

Even Market Street was dark now, its theaters shut down. Over at the Grand Opera House on Mission, Enrico Caruso's costumes hung neatly in his dark dressing room, ready for a performance of *La Bohème* that would never take place. Up at the Mechanic's Pavilion, the weary janitor surveyed the confetti and other festive debris littering the skating rink and decided to sweep it up in the morning. Toyland, at the Columbia, was shut away in its properties room: fairy tinsel, butterfly wings, bear heads peering down from dusty shelves into the darkness.

Even now my resolute gentlemen and ladies were despoiling Nob Hill, flitting through its darkened drawing rooms at hyperspeed like so many whirring ghosts, bearing with them winking gilt and crystal, calfskin and morocco, canvas and brass, all the very best that money could buy but couldn't hope to preserve against the hour to come. Without the Franklin I'd have a tedious walk uphill to join them, but at a brisk pace I might arrive with time to spare.

Donal stretched and muttered in his sleep. I shifted him to my other shoulder, changed hands on my walking stick, and was about to hurry on when I caught a whiff of some familiar scent on the air. I halted.

It was not a pleasant scent. It was harsh, musky, like blood or sweat but neither; like an animal smell, but other; it summoned in me a sudden terror and confusion. When I tried to identify it, however, I had only a mental image of a bear costume hanging on a hook, the head looking down from a shelf. When had I seen that? *I* hadn't seen that! *Whose memories were these?*

I controlled myself with an effort. Some psychic disturbance was responsible for this, my own nerves were contributing to this, there was no real danger. Why, of course: it must be nearly two o'clock, when the first of the major subsonic disruptions would occur.

Yes, here it came now. I could hear nearby horses begin to scream and stamp frantically, I could feel the paving bricks grind against one another under the soles of my boots, and the air groaned as though buried giants were praying to God for release.

Yes, I thought, this must be it. I balanced my stick against my knee and drew out my chronometer, trying to verify the event. As I peered at it, the door of a stable directly across the street burst open, and a white mare came charging out, hooves thundering. Donal jerked and cried.

Timing is everything. My assailant chose that perfect moment of distraction to strike. I was enveloped in a choking wave of *that smell* as a hand closed on my face and pulled my head back. Instantly I clawed at it, twisted my head to bite; but a vast arm was wrapping around me from the other side and cold steel entered my throat, opened the artery, wrenched as it was pulled out again.

So swiftly had this occurred that my stick was still falling through mid-air, had not yet struck the pavement. Donal was pulled upward and backward, torn from me, and I heard his terrified cry mingle with the clatter of the stick as it landed, the rumbling earth, the running horse, a howling laughter I knew but could not place. I was sinking to my knees, clutching at my cut throat as my blood fountained out over the starched front of my dress shirt and stained the diamond stud so it winked like Mars. Ares, God of War. *Thor.* I was conscious of a terrible anger as I descended to the shadows and curled into fugue.

▲▼▲   ·

"Will you get on to this, now? Throat cut and he's not been robbed! Here's his watch, for Christ's sake!"

"Stroke of luck for us, anyhow."

I sat up and glared at them. The two mortal thieves backed away from me, horrified; then one mustered enough nerve to dart in again, aiming a kick at me while he made a grab for my chronometer. I caught his wrist and broke it. He jumped back, stifling an agonized yell; his companion took to his heels and after only a second's hesitation he followed.

I remained where I was, huddled on the pavement, running a self-diagnostic. The edges of my windpipe and jugular artery had closed and were healing nicely at hyperspeed; if the thieves hadn't roused me from fugue I'd be whole now. Blood production had sped up to replace that now dyeing the front of my previously immaculate shirt. The exterior skin of my throat was even now self-suturing, but I was still too weak to rise.

My hat and stick remained where they had fallen, but of Donal or my assailant there was no sign. I licked my dry lips. There was a vile taste in my mouth. My chronometer told me it was a quarter past two. I dragged myself to the base of a wall and leaned there, half swooning, drowning in unwelcome remembrance.

That smell. Sweat, blood, the animal and smoke. Yes, they'd called it the Summer of Smoke, that year the world ended. What world had that been? The world where I was a little prince, or nearly so; better if my mother hadn't been a Danish slave, but my father had no sons by his lady wife, and so I had fine clothes and a gold pin for my cloak.

When I went to climb on the beached longship and play with the gear, a warrior threatened me with his fist; then another man told him he'd better not, for I was Baldulf's brat. That made him back down in a hurry. And once, my father set me on the table and put his gold cup in my hand, but I nearly dropped it, it was so heavy. He held it for me and I tasted the mead and his companions laughed, beating on the table. The ash-white lady, though, looked down at the floor and wrung her hands.

She told me sometimes that if I wasn't good the Bear would come for me. She was the only one who would ever dare to talk to me that way. And then he *had* come, the Bear and his slaughtering knights. All in one day I saw our tent burned and my father's head staring from a pike. Screaming, smoke and fire, and a banner bearing a red dragon that snaked like a living flame, I remember.

My mother had caught me up and was running for the forest, but she was a plump girl and could not get up the speed. Two knights chased after us on horseback, whooping like madmen. Just under the shadow of the oaks, they caught us. My mother fell and rolled, loosing her hold on me, and screamed for me to run; then one of the knights was off his horse and on her. The other knight got down too and stood watching them, laughing merrily. One of her slippers had come off and her bare toes kicked at the air until she died.

I had been sobbing threats, I had been hurling stones and handfuls of oak-mast at the knights, and now I ran at the one on my mother and attacked him with my teeth and nails. He reared up on his elbows to shake me off; but the other knight reached down and plucked me up as easily as if I'd been a kitten. He held me at his eye level while I shrieked and spat at him. His shrill laughter dropped to a chuckle, but never stopped.

A big shaven face, dun-drab hair cropped. Head of a strange helm shape, tremendous projecting nose and brows, and his wide gleeful eyes so pale a blue as to be colorless, like the eyes of my father's hounds. He had enormous broad cheekbones and strange teeth. That smell, that almost-animal smell, was coming from him. That had been where I'd first encountered it, hanging there in the grip of that knight.

The other knight had got up and came forward with his knife drawn and ready for me, but my captor held out his huge gauntleted hand.

"*Sine eum!*" he told him pleasantly. "*Noli irritare leones.*"

"*Faciam quicquid placet, o ingens simi tu!*" the other knight growled, and brandished his knife. My captor's eyes sparkled; he batted playfully at my assailant, who flew backward into a tree and lay there twitching, blood running from his ears. Left in peace, my knight held me up and sniffed at me. He sat down and ran his hands all over me, taking his gauntlets off to squeeze my skull until I feared it would break like an egg. I had stopped fighting, but I whimpered and tried to wriggle away.

"Do you want to live, little boy?" he asked me in perfectly accented Saxon. He had a high-pitched voice, nasally resonant.

"Yes," I replied, shocked motionless.

"Then be good, and do not try to run away from me. I will preserve you from death. Do you understand?"

"Yes."

"Good." He forced my mouth open and examined my teeth. Apparently satisfied, he got up, thrusting me under one arm. Taking the two horses' bridles, he walked back to the war camp of the Bear with long rolling strides.

It was growing dark, and new fires had been lit. We passed pickets who challenged my captor, and he answered them with smiles and bantering remarks. At last he stopped before a tent and gave a barking order, whereupon a groom hurried out to take the horses and led them away for him. Two other knights sat nearby, leaning back wearily as their squires took off their armor for them. One pointed at me and asked a question.

My captor grinned and said something in fluting reply, hugging me to his chest. One knight smiled a little, but the other scowled and spat into the fire. As my captor bore me into his tent I heard someone mutter "*Amator puer!*" in a disgusted tone.

It was dark in the tent, and there was no one there to see as he stripped off my clothes and continued his examinations. I attempted to fight again but he held me still and asked, very quietly, "Are you a stupid child? Have you forgot what I said?"

"No." I was so frightened and furious I was trembling, and I hated the smell of him, so close in there.

"Then listen to me again, Saxon child. I will not hurt you, neither will I outrage you. But if you want to die, keep struggling."

I held still then and stood silent, hating him. He seemed quite unconcerned about that; he gave me a cup of wine and a hard cake, and ignored me while I ate and drank. All his attention was on the two knights outside. When he heard them depart into their respective tents, he wrapped me in a cloak and bore me out into the night again.

At the other end of the camp there was a very fine tent, pitched a little distance from the others. Two men stood before it, deep in conversation. After a moment one went away. The other remained outside the tent a moment, breathing the night air, looking up at the stars. When he lifted the flap and made to go inside, my captor stepped forward.

"*Salve, Emres.*"

"*Invenistine novum tironem, Budu?*" replied the other. He was a tall man and elderly—I thought: his hair and eyebrows were white. His face, however, was smooth and unlined, and there was an easy suppleness to his movements.

He was very well dressed, as Britons went. They had a brief conversation and then the one called Emres raised the flap of the tent again, gesturing us inside.

It was so brilliantly lit in there it dazzled my eyes. I was again unrobed, in that white glare, but I dared do no more than clench my fists as the old one examined me. His hands were remarkably soft and clean, and *he* did not smell bad. He stuck me with a pin and dabbed the blood onto the tongue of a little god he had, sitting on a chest; it clicked for a moment and then chattered to him in a tinny voice. He in his turn had a brief conversation with my captor. At its conclusion, Emres pointed at me and asked a question. My captor shrugged. He turned his big head to look at me.

"What is your name, little boy?" he asked in Saxon.

"Bricta, son of Baldulf," I told him. He looked back at Emres.

"*Nomen ei Victor est*," he said.

▲▼▲

The taste in my mouth was unbearable. I hadn't wanted this recollection, this squalid history! I much preferred time to begin with that first memory of the silver ship that rose skyward from the circle of stones, taking me away to the gleaming hospital and the sweet-faced nurses.

I got unsteadily to my feet, groping after my hat and stick. As I did so I heard the unmistakable sound of an automobile approaching. In another second a light runabout rattled around the corner and pulled up before me. Labienus sat behind the wheel, no longer the jovial master of ceremonies. He was all hard-eyed centurion now.

"We received your distress signal. Report, please, Victor."

"I was attacked," I said dully.

"Tsk! Rather obviously."

"I...I know it sounds improbable, sir, but I believe my assailant was another operative," I explained. To my surprise he merely nodded.

"We know his identity. You'll notice he's sending quite a distinct signal."

"Yes." I looked down the street in wonderment. The signal lay on the air like a trail of green smoke. Why would he signal? "He's...somewhere in Chinatown."

"Exactly," agreed Labienus. "Well, Victor, what do you intend to do about this?"

"Sir?" I looked back at him, confused. Something was wrong here, some business I hadn't been briefed about, perhaps? But why—?

"Come, come, man, you've a mission to complete! He took the mortal boy! Surely you've formed a plan to rescue him?" he prompted.

The hideous taste welled in my mouth. I suppressed an urge to expectorate.

"My team on Nob Hill is more than competent to complete the salvage there without my supervision," I said, attempting to sound coolly rational. "That being the case, I believe, sir, that I shall seek out the scoundrel who did this to me and jolly well kill him. Figuratively speaking, of course."

"Very good. And?"

"And, of course, recapture my mortal recruit and deliver him to the collection point as planned and according to schedule," I said. "Sir."

"See that you do." Labienus worked both clutch and brake expertly and edged his motor forward, cylinders idling. "Report to my cabin on the *Thunderer* at seven hundred hours for a private debriefing. Is that clear?"

"Perfectly clear, sir." So there was some mystery to be explained. Very well.

"You are dismissed."

"Sir." I doffed my hat and watched as he drove smoothly away up Market Street.

I replaced my hat and turned in the direction of the signal, probing. My dizziness was fading, burned away by my growing sense of outrage. The filthy old devil, how dare he do this to me? What was he playing at? I began to walk briskly again, my speed increasing with my strength.

Of course, the vow to kill him hadn't been meant literally. We do not die. But I'd find some way of paying him out in full measure, I hadn't the slightest doubt about that. He had the edge on me in strength, but I was swifter and in full possession of my faculties, whereas he was probably drooling mad, the old troll.

Yes, mad, that was the only explanation. There had always been rumors that some of the oldest operatives were flawed somehow, those created earliest, before the augmentation process had been perfected. Budu had been one of the oldest I'd ever met. He had been created more than forty thousand years ago, before the human races had produced their present assortment of representatives.

Now that I thought of it, I hadn't seen an operative of his racial type *in the field* in years. They held desk jobs at Company bases, or were air transport pilots. I'd assumed this was simply because the modern mortal race was now too homogenous for Budu's type to pass unnoticed. What if the true reason was that the Company had decided not to take chances with the earlier models? What if there was some risk that all of that particular class were inherently unstable?

Good God! No wonder I was expected to handle this matter without assistance. Undoubtedly our masters wanted the whole affair resolved as quietly as possible. They could count on my discretion; I only hoped my ability met their expectations.

Following the signal, I turned left at the corner of Market and Grant. The green trail led straight up Grant as far as Sacramento. What was his game? He was drawing me straight into the depths of the Celestial quarter, a place where I'd be conspicuous were it daylight, but at no particular disadvantage otherwise.

He must intend some kind of dialogue with me. The fact that he had taken a hostage indicated that he wanted our meeting on his terms, under his control. That he felt he needed a hostage could be taken as a sign of weakness on his part. Had his strength begun to fail somehow? Not if his attack on me had been any indication. Though it had been largely a matter of speed and leverage…

I came to the corner of Grant and Sacramento. The signal turned to the left again. It traveled up a block, where it could be observed emanating from a darkened doorway. I stood considering it for a moment, tapping my stick impatiently against my boot. I spat into the gutter, but it did not take the taste from my mouth.

I walked slowly uphill, past the shops that sold black and scarlet lacquerware and green jade. Here was the Baptist mission, smelling of starch and good intentions. From this lodging-house doorway a heavy perfume of joss sticks; from this doorway a reek of preserved fish. And from this doorway…

It stood ajar. A narrow corridor went straight back into darkness, with a narrower stair ascending to the left. The bottommost stair tread had been thrown open like the lid of a piano bench, revealing a black void below.

I scanned. He was down there, and making no attempt to hide himself. Donal was there with him, still alive. There were no other signs of mortal life, however.

I paced forward into the darkness and stood looking down. Chill air was coming up from below. It stank like a crypt. Rungs leading down into a passageway were just visible, by a wavering pool of green light. So was a staring dead face, contorted into a grimace of rage.

After a moment's consideration, I removed my hat and set it on the second step. My stick I resolved to take with me, although its sword would be useless against my opponent. No point in any further delay; it was time to descend into yet another hell.

At the bottom of the ladder the light was a little stronger. It revealed more bodies, lying in a subterranean passage of brick plastered over and painted a dull green. The dead had been Celestials, and seemed to have died fighting, within the last few hours. They were smashed like so many insects. The light that made this plain was emanating from a wide doorway that opened off the passage, some ten feet farther on. The smell of death was strongest in there.

"Come in, Victor," said a voice.

I went as far as the doorway and looked.

In that low-ceilinged chamber of bare plaster, in the fitful glow of one oil lamp, more dead men were scattered. These were all elderly Chinese, skeletally emaciated, and they had been dead some hours and they had not died quietly. One leaned in a chair beside the little table with the flickering lamp; one was hung up on a hook that protruded from a wall; one lay half in, half out of a cupboard passage, his arm flung out as though beckoning. Three were sprawled on the floor beside slatwood bunks, in postures suggesting they had been slain whilst in the lethargy of their drug and tossed from the couches like rags. The apparatus of the opium den lay here and there; a gold-wrapped brick of the poisonous substance, broken pipes, burnt dishes, long matches, bits of wire.

And there, beyond them, sat the monster of my long nightmares.

"You don't like my horrible parlor," chuckled Budu. "Your little white nose has squeezed nearly shut, your nostrils look like a fish's gills."

"It's just the sort of nest you'd make for yourself, you murdering old fool," I told him. He frowned at me.

"I have never murdered," he told me seriously. "But these were murderers, and thieves. Who else would keep such a fine secret cellar, eh? A good place for a private meeting." He leaned back against the wall, lounging at his ease across the top tier of a bunk, waving enormous mud-caked boots. His dress consisted of stained blue-jean trousers, a vast shapeless red coat made from a blanket, and a battered black felt hat. He had let his hair and beard grow long; they trailed down like pale moss over his bare hairy chest. He looked rather like St. Nicholas turned monster.

Donal sat stiffly beside him. Budu had placed his great hand about the boy's neck, as easily as I might take hold of an axe handle.

"Uncle Jimmy," moaned Donal.

"Explain yourself, sir," I addressed Budu, keeping my voice level and cold. He responded with gales of delighted laughter.

"I was the Briton, and you were the little barbarian," he said. "Look at us now!"

I stepped into the room, having scanned for traps. "I followed your signal," I told him. "You certainly made it plain enough. May I ask why you thought it was necessary to cut my throat?"

He shrugged, regarding me with hooded eyes. "How else to get your attention but to take your quarry from you? And how to do that but by disabling you? What harm did it do? Spoiled your nice white shirt, yes, and made you angry."

I tapped my stick in impatience. "What was your purpose in calling me here, old man?"

"To tell you a few truths, and see what you do when you've heard them. You were wondering about us, we oldest Old Ones, wondering what became of us all. You were thinking we're like badly made clockwork toys, and our Great Toymakers decided to pull us off the shelves of the toyshop." He stretched luxuriously. Donal tried to turn his head to stare at him, but was held fast as the old creature continued: "No, no. We're not badly made. I was better made than you, little man. It's a question of purpose." He thrust his prognathous face forward at me through the gloom. "I was made a war axe. They made you a shovel. Is the metaphor plain enough for you?"

"I take your meaning." I moved a step closer.

"You've been told all your life that our masters wish only to save things, books and pretty pictures and children, and for this purpose we were made, to creep into houses like mice and steal away loot before time can eat it."

"That's an oversimplification, but essentially true."

"Is it?" He stroked his beard in amusement. I could see the red lines across the back of his hand where I'd clawed him. He hadn't bothered to heal them yet. "You pompous creature, in your nice clothes. You were made to save things, Victor. I wasn't. Now, hear the truth: I, and all my kind, were made because our perfect and benign masters wanted *killers* once. Can you guess why?"

"Well, let me see." I swallowed back bile. "You say you're not flawed. Yet it's fairly common knowledge that flawed immortals were produced, during the first experiments with the process. What did the Company do about them? Perhaps you were created as a means of eliminating them."

"Good guess." He nodded his head. "But wrong. They were never killed, those poor failed things. I've seen them, screaming in little steel boxes. No. Guess again."

"Then…perhaps at one time it was necessary to have agents whose specialty was defense." I tried. "Prior to the dawn of civilization."

"An easy guess. You fool, of course it was. You think our masters waited, so gentle and pure, for sweet reason to persuade men to evolve? Oh, no. Too many wolves were preying on the sheep. They needed operatives who could kill, who could happily kill fierce primitives so the peaceful ones could weave baskets and paint bison on walls." He grinned at me with those enormous teeth, and went on: "We made civilization dawn, I and my kind. We pushed that bright ball over the horizon at last, and we did it by killing! If a man raised his hand against his neighbor, we cut it off. If a tribe painted themselves for war, we washed their faces with their own blood. Shall I tell you of the races of men you'll never see? They wouldn't learn peace, and so we were sent in to slay them, man, woman and child."

"You mean," I exhaled, "the Company decided to accelerate mankind's progress by selectively weeding out its sociopathic members. And if it did? We've all heard rumors of something like that. It may be necessary, from time to time, even now. Not a pretty thought, but one can see the reasons. If you hadn't done it, mankind might have remained in a state of savagery forever." I took another step forward.

"We did good work," he said plaintively. "And we weren't hypocrites. It was fun." His pale gaze wandered past me to the doorway. There was a momentary flicker of something like uneasiness in his eyes, some ripple across the surface of his vast calm.

"What is the point of telling me this, may I ask?" I pressed.

"To show you that you serve lying and ungrateful masters, child," he replied, his attention returning to me. "Stupid masters. They've no understanding of this world they rule. Once we cleared the field so they could plant, how did they reward us? We had been heroes. We became looters.

"And you should see how they punished the ones who argued! No more pruning the vine, they told us, let it grow how it will. You're only to gather the fruit now, they told us. Was that fair? Was it, when we'd been created to gather heads?"

"No, I dare say it wasn't. But you adapted, didn't you?" To my dismay I was shaking with emotion. "You found ways to satisfy your urges in the Company's service. You'd taken your share of heads the day you caught me!"

"Rescued you," he corrected me. "You were only a little animal, and if I hadn't taken you away, you'd have grown into a big animal like your father.

There were lice crawling in his hair, when I stuck his head on the pike. There was food in his beard."

I spat in his face. I couldn't stop myself. The next second I was sick with mortification, to be provoked into such operatic behavior, and dabbed hurriedly at my chin with a handkerchief. Budu merely wiped his face with the back of his hand and smiled, content to have reduced my stature.

"Your anger changes nothing. Your father was a dirty beast. He was an oathbreaker and an invader, too, as were all his people. You've been taught your history, you know all this! So don't judge me for enjoying what I did to exterminate his race. And see what happened when I was ordered to stop killing Saxons! When Arthur died, Roman order died with him. All that we'd won at Badon Hill was lost and the Saxon hordes returned, never to leave. What sense did it make, to have given our aid for a while to one civilized tribe, and then leave it to be destroyed?"

His gaze traveled past me to the doorway again. Who was he expecting? They weren't coming to join him, that much was clear.

"We do not involve ourselves in the petty territorial squabbles of mortals," I recited. "We do not embrace their causes. We move amongst them, saving what we can, but we are never such fools as to be drawn into their disputes."

"Yes, you're quoting Company policy to me. But don't you see that your fine impartiality has no purpose? It accomplishes nothing! It's wasteful! You know the house will burn, so you creep in like thieves and steal the furniture beforehand, and then watch the flames. Wouldn't it be more efficient use of your time to prevent the fire in the first place?" He paused a moment and looked at the back of his hand with a slight frown. I saw the red lines there fade to pink as he set them to healing over.

"It would be more efficient, yes," I said, "but for one slight difficulty. You couldn't prevent the fire happening. It isn't possible to change history."

"*Recorded* history." He bared his big teeth in amusement once more. "It isn't possible to change recorded history. And do you think even that sacred rule's as unbreakable as you've been told? I have made the history that was written and read. It disappoints me. I will make something new now."

"Shall you really?" I folded my arms. Doubtless he was going to start bragging about being a god. It went with the profile of this sort of lunatic.

"Yes, and you'll help me, if you're wise. Listen to me. In the time before history was written down, in those days, our masters were bold. All mortals have inherited the legend that there was once a golden age when men lived simply in meadows, and the Earth was uncrowded and clean, and there was no war, but only arts of peace.

"But when recorded history began—when we were forbidden to exterminate the undesirables—that paradise was lost. And our masters let it be lost, and that is the condemnation I fling in their teeth." He drew a deep breath.

"Your point, sir?"

"I'll make an end of recorded history. I can so decimate the races of men that their golden age will come again, and never again will there be enough of them to ravage one another or the garden they inhabit. And we immortals will be their keepers. Victor, little Victor, how long have you lived? Aren't you tired of watching them fight and starve? You creep among them like a scavenger, but you could walk among them like—"

"Like a god?" I sneered.

"I had been about to say, an angel," Budu sneered back. "I remember the service I was created for. Do you, little man? Or have you ever even known? Such luxuries you've had, among the poor mortals! Have you never felt the urge to *really* help them? But the time's soon approaching when you can."

"Ridiculous." I stated. "You know as well as I do that history won't stop. There'll be just as much warfare and mortal misery in this new century as in the centuries before, and nothing anyone can do will alter one event." I gauged the pressure of his fingers on Donal's neck. How quickly could I move to get them loose?

"Not one event? You think so? Maybe." He looked sly. "But our masters will turn what can't be changed to their own advantage, and why can't I? Think of the great slaughters to come, Victor. How do you know I won't be working there? How do you know I haven't been at work already? How do you know I haven't got disciples among our people, weary as I am of our masters' blundering, ready as I am to mutiny?"

"Because history states otherwise," I told him flatly. "There will be no mutiny, no war in heaven if you like. Civilization will prevail. It is recorded that it will."

"Is it?" He grinned. "And can you tell me who recorded it? Maybe I did. Maybe I will, after I win. Victor, such a simple trick, but it's never occurred to you. History is only writing, and *one can write lies!*"

I stared at him. No, in fact, it never had occurred to me. He rocked to and fro in his merriment, dragging Donal with him. Silent tears streamed down the child's face.

Budu lurched forward, fixing me with his gaze. "Listen now. I have my followers, but we need more. You'll join me because you're clever, and you're weary of this horror, too, and you owe me the duty of a son, for I saved you from death. You're a Facilitator and know the Company codes. You'll work in secret, you'll obtain certain things for me, and we'll take mortal children and work the augmentation process on them, and raise them as our own operatives, for our own purposes, loyal to us. Then we'll pull the weeds from the Garden. Then we'll geld the bull and make him pull the plough. Then we'll slaughter the wolf that preys on the herd. Just as we used to do! There will be order.

"For this reason I came as a beggar to this city and followed you, watching. Now I've made you listen to me." He looked at the doorway again. "Tell me I'm not a fool, little Victor, tell me I haven't walked into this trap with you to no purpose."

"What will you do if I refuse?" I demanded. "Break the child's neck?"

This was too much for the boy, who whimpered like a rabbit and started forward convulsively. Budu looked down, scowling as though he had forgotten about him. "Are you a stupid child?" he asked Donal. "Do you want to die?"

I cannot excuse my next act, though he drove me to it; he, and the horror of the place, and the time that was slipping away and bringing this doomed city down about our ears if we tarried. I charged him, howling like the animal he was.

He reared back. Instead of closing about Donal's throat, his fingers twitched harmlessly. As his weight shifted, his right arm dropped to his side, heavy as lead. My charge threw him backward so that his head struck the wall with a resounding thud.

All the laughter died in his eyes, and they focused inward as he ran his self-diagnostic. I caught up Donal in my arms and backed away with him, panting.

Budu looked out at me.

"A virus," he informed me. "It was in your saliva. It's producing inert matter even now, at remarkable speed. Blocking my neuroreceptors. I don't think it will kill me, but I doubt if even your masters could tell. I'm sure they hope so. You're surprised. You had no knowledge of this weapon inside yourself?"

"None," I said.

Budu was nodding thoughtfully, or perhaps he was beginning to be unable to hold his head up. "They didn't tell you about this talent of yours, because if you'd known about it I would have seen it in your thoughts, and then I'd never have let you spit on me. At the very least I wouldn't have wiped it away with my wounded hand."

"A civilized man would have used a handkerchief," I could not resist observing.

He giggled, but his voice was weaker when he spoke.

"Well. I guess we'll see now if our masters have at long last found a way to unmake their creations. Or I will see; you can't stay in this dangerous place to watch the outcome, I know. But you'll wish you had, in the years to come, you'll wish you knew whether or not I was still watching you, following you. For I know your defense against me now, think of that! And I know who betrayed me, with his clever virus." Budu's pale eyes widened. "I was wrong. The rest of them may be shovels, but you, little Victor—you are a poisoned knife. *Victor veneficus!*" he added, and laughed thickly at his joke. "Oh, tell him—never sleep. If I live—"

"We're going now, Donal Og, Uncle Jimmy'll get you safe out of here," I said to the child, turning from Budu to thread my way between the stinking corpses on the floor.

I heard Budu cough once as his vocal centers went, and then the ether was filled with a cascade of images: a naked child squatting on a clay floor, staring through darkness at a looming figure in a bearskin. Flames devouring brush huts, goatskin tents, cottages, halls, palaces, shops, restaurants, hotels. Soldiers in every conceivable kind of uniform, with every known weapon, in every posture of attack or defense the human form could assume.

If these were his memories, if this was the end of his life, there was no emotion of sorrow accompanying the images; no fear, no weariness, no relief either. Instead, a loud yammering laughter grew ever louder, and deafened the inner ear at the last image: a hulking brute in a bearskin, squatting beside a fire, turning and turning in his thick fingers a gleaming golden axe; and on the blade of the axe was written the word VIRUS.

Halfway up the ladder, the trap opening was occluded by a face that looked down at me and then drew back. I came up with all speed; I faced a small mob of Chinese, grim men with bronze hatchets. They had not expected to see a man in evening dress carrying a child.

I addressed them in Cantonese, for I could see they were natives of that province.

"The devil who killed your grandfathers is still down there. He is asleep and will not wake up. You can safely cut him to pieces now."

I took up my hat and left the mortals standing there, looking uncertainly from my departing form to the dark hole in the stair.

The air was beginning to freshen with the scent of dawn. I had little more than an hour to get across the city. In something close to panic I began to run up Sacramento, broadcasting a general assistance signal. Had my salvage teams waited for me? Donal clung to me and did not make a sound.

Before I had gone three blocks, I heard the noise of an automobile echoing loud between the buildings. It was climbing up Sacramento toward me. I turned to meet it. Over the glare of its brass headlamps I saw Pan Wen-Shi. His tuxedo and shirtfront, unlike mine, were still as spotless as when he'd left the Company banquet. On the seat beside him was a tiny almond-eyed girl. He braked and shifted, putting out a hand to prevent her from tumbling off and rolling away downhill.

"Climb in," he shouted. I vaulted the running board and toppled into the backseat with Donal. Pan stepped on the gas and we cranked forward again.

"Much obliged to you for the ride," I said, settling myself securely and attempting to pry Donal's arms loose from my neck. "Had a bit of difficulty."

"So had I. We must tell one another our stories some day," Pan acknowledged, rounding the corner at Powell and taking us down toward Geary. The baby had turned in her seat and was staring at us. Donal was quivering and hiding his eyes.

"Now then, Donal Og, now then," I crooned to him. "You've been a brave boy and you're all safe again. And isn't this grand fun? We're going for a ride in a real motorcar!"

"Bad Toymaker gone?" asked the little muffled voice.

"Sure he is, Donal, and we've escaped entirely."

He consented to lower his hands, but shrank back at the sight of the others. "Who's that?"

"Why, that's a China doll that's escaped the old Toymaker, same as you, and that's the kind Chinaman who helped her. They're taking us to the sea, where we'll escape on a big ship."

He stared at them doubtfully. "I want Mummy," he said, tears forming in his eyes.

The little girl, who till this moment had been solemn in fascination, suddenly dimpled into a lovely smile and laughed like a silver bell. She pointed a finger at him and made a long babbling pronouncement, neither in

Cantonese nor Mandarin. For emphasis, she reached down beside her and flung something at him over the back of the seat, with a triumphant cry of "*Dah!*" It was a wrapped bar of Ghirardelli's, only slightly gummy at one corner where she'd been teething on it. I caught it in midair.

"See now, Donal, the nice little girl is giving us chocolates." I tore off the wrapper hastily and gave him a piece. She reached out a demanding hand and I gave her some as well. "Chocolates and an automobile ride and a big ship! Aren't you the lucky boy, then?"

He sat quiet, watching the gregarious baby and nibbling at his treat. His memories were fading. As we rattled up Geary, he looked at me with wondering eyes.

"Where Ella?" he asked me.

When I had caught my breath, I replied: "She couldn't come to Toyland, Donal Og. But you're a lucky, lucky boy, for you shall. You'll have splendid adventures and never grow old. Won't that be fun, now?"

He looked into my face, not knowing what he saw there. "Yes," he answered in a tiny voice.

Lucky boy, yes, borne away in a mechanical chariot, away from the perishable mortal world, and all the pretty nurses will smile over you and perhaps sing you to sleep before they take you off to surgery. And when you wake, you'll have been improved; you'll be ever so much cleverer, Donal, than poor mortal monkeys like your father. A biomechanical marvel, fit to stride through this new century in company with the internal combustion engine and the flying machine.

And you'll be so happy, boy, and at peace, knowing about the wonderful work you'll have to do for the Company. Much happier than poor Ella would ever have been, with her wild heart, her restlessness and anger. Surely no kindness to give her eternal life, when life's stupidities and injustice could never be escaped?

…But you'll enjoy your immortality, Donal Og. You will, if you don't become a thing like me.

The words came into my mind unbidden, and I shuddered in my seat. Mustn't think of this just now: too much to do. Perhaps the whole incident had been some sort of hallucination? There was no foul taste in my mouth, no viral poison sizzling under my glib tongue. The experience might have been some fantastic nightmare brought on by stress, but for the blood staining my elegant evening attire.

I was a gentleman, after all. No gentleman did such things.

Pan bore left at Mason, rode the brakes all the way down to Fulton, turned right and accelerated. We sped on, desperate to leave the past.

▲▼▲

There were still whaleboats drawn up on the sand, still wagons waiting there, and shirtsleeved immortals hurriedly loading boxes from wagon to boat. We'd nearly left it too late: those were my people, that was my Nob Hill salvage arrayed in splendor amid the driftwood and broken shells. There were still a pair of steamers riding at anchor beyond Seal Rock, though most of the fleet had already put out to sea and could be glimpsed as tiny lights on the gray horizon, making for the Farallones. As we came within range of the Hush Field both of the children slumped into abrupt and welcome unconsciousness.

We jittered to a stop just short of the tavern, where an impatient operative from the Company's motor agency took charge of the automobile. Pan and I jumped out, caught up our respective children, and ran down the beach.

Past the wagons loaded with rich jetsam of the Gilded Age, we ran: lined up in the morning gloom and salt wind were the grand pianos, the crystal chandeliers, the paintings in gilt frames, the antique furniture. Statuary classical and modern; gold plate and tapestries. Cases of rare wines, crates of phonograph cylinders, of books and papers, waited like refugees to escape the coming morning.

I glimpsed Averill, struggling through the sand with his arms full of priceless things. He was sobbing loudly as he worked; tears coursed down his cheeks, his eyes were wide with terror, but his body served him like the clockwork toy, like the *fine machine* it was, and bore him ceaselessly back and forth between the wagon and the boat until his appointed task should be done.

"Sir! Where did you get to?" he said, gasping. "We waited and waited—and now it's going to cut loose any second, and we're still not done!"

"Couldn't be helped, old man," I told him as we scuttled past. "Carry on! I have every faith in you."

I shut my ears to his cry of dismay and ran on. A boat reserved for passengers still waited in the surf. Pan and I made for the boarding officer and gave our identification.

"You've cut it damned close, gentlemen," he grumbled.

"Unavoidable," I told him. His gaze fell on my gore-drenched shirt and he blinked, but waved us to our places. Seconds later we were seated securely, and the oarsmen pulled and sent us bounding out on the receding tide to the *Thunderer* where she lay at anchor.

We'd done it, we were away from that fated city, where even now bronze hatchets were completing the final betrayal—

No. A gentleman does not betray others. Nor does he leave his subordinates to deal with the consequences of his misfortune.

Donal shivered in the stiff breeze, waking slowly. Frank's coat had been lost somewhere in Chinatown; I shrugged out of my dinner jacket and put it around Donal's shoulders. He drew closer to me, but his attention was caught by the operatives working on the shore. As he watched, something disturbed the earth, and the sand began to flurry and shift. Another warning was sounding up from below. It hit the bottom of our boat as though we'd struck a rock, and I feared we'd capsize.

The rumbling carried to us over the roar of the sea, as did the shouts of the operatives trying to finish the loading. One wagon settled forward a few inches, causing the unfortunate precipitation of a massive antique clock into the arms of the immortals who had been gingerly easing it down. They arrested its flight, but the shock or perhaps merely the striking hour set in motion its parade of tiny golden automata. Out came its revolving platforms, its trumpeting angels, its pirouetting lovers, its minute Death with raised scythe and hourglass. Crazily it chimed five.

Pan and I exchanged glances. He checked his chronometer. Our boatmen increased the vigor of their strokes.

Moment by moment the east was growing brighter, disclosing operatives massed on the deck of the *Thunderer*. Their faces were turned to regard the sleeping city. Pan and I were helped on deck and our mortal charges handed up after us. A pair of white-coifed nurses stepped forward.

"Agent Pan? Agent Victor?" inquired one, as the other checked a list.

"Here, now, Donal, we're on our ship at last, and here's a lovely fairy to look after you." I thrust him into her waiting arms. The other received the baby from Pan, and the little girl went without complaint; but as his nurse turned to carry him below decks, Donal twisted in her arms and reached out a desperate hand for me.

"Uncle Jimmy," he screamed. I turned away quickly as she bore him off. Really, it was for the best.

I made my way along the rail and emerged on the aft deck, where I nearly ran into Nan D'Arraignee. She did not see me, however; she was fervently kissing a great bearded fellow in a brass-buttoned blue coat, which he had opened to wrap about them both, making a warm protected place for her in his arms. He looked up and saw me. His eyes, timid and kindly, widened, and he nodded in recognition.

"Kalugin," I acknowledged with brittle courtesy, tipping my hat. I edged on past them quickly, but not so quickly as to suggest I was fleeing. What had I to flee from? Not guilt, certainly. No gentleman dishonorably covets another gentleman's lady.

As I reached the aft saloon we felt it beginning, in the rising surge that lifted the *Thunderer* with a crash and threatened to swamp the fleeing whale-boats. We heard the roar coming up from the earth, and in the City some mortals sat up in their beds and frowned at what they could sense but not quite hear yet.

I clung to the rail of the *Thunderer*. My fellow operatives were hurrying to the stern of the ship to be witness to history, and nearly every face bore an expression compounded of mingled horror and eagerness. There were one or two who turned away, averting their eyes. There were those like me, sick and exhausted, who merely stared.

And really, from where we lay offshore, there was not much to see; no DeMille spectacle. No more at first than a puff of dust rising into the air. But very clear across the water we heard the rumbling, and then the roar of bricks coming down, and steel snapping, and timbers groaning, and the high sweet shattering of glass, and the tolling in all discordance of bronze-throated bells. Loud as the Last Trumpet, but not loud enough to drown out the screams of the dying. No, the roar of the earthquake even paused for a space, as if to let us hear mortal agony more clearly; then the second shock came, and I saw a distant tower topple and fall slowly, and then the little we had been able to see of the City was concealed in a roiling fog the color of a bloodstain.

I turned away, and chanced to look up at the open doorway of a state-room on the deck above. There stood Labienus, watching the death of three thousand mortals with an avid stare. That was when I knew, and knew beyond question whose weapon I was.

I hadn't escaped. My splendid mansion, with all its gilded conceits, had collapsed in a rain of bricks and broken plaster.

A hand settled on my shoulder and I dropped my gaze to behold Lewis, of all people, looking into my face with compassion.

"I know," he murmured, "I know, old fellow. At least it's finished now, for those poor mortals and for us. Brace up! Can I get you a drink?"

What did he recognize in my sick white face? Not the features of a man who had emptied a phial into an innocent-looking cup of wine. Why, I'd always been a poisoner, hadn't I? But it had happened long ago, and he had no memory of it anyway. I'd seen to that. And Lewis would never suspect me of such behavior in any case. We were both gentlemen, after all.

"No, thank you," I replied, "I believe I'll just take the air for a little while out here. It's a fine restorative to the nerves, you know. Sea air."

"So it is," he agreed, stepping back. "That's the spirit! It's not as though you could have done anything more. You know what they say: history cannot be changed." He gave me a final helpful thump on the arm and moved away, clinging to the rail as the deck pitched.

Alone, I fixed my eyes on the wide horizon of the cold and perfect sea. I drew in a deep breath of chill air.

One can write lies. And live them.

Two operatives in uniform were making their way toward me through the press of the crowd. "Executive Facilitator Victor?"

I nodded. They shouldered into place, one on either side of me.

"Sir, your presence is urgently requested. Mr. Labienus sends his apologies for unavoidably revising your schedule," one of them recited.

"Certainly." I exhaled. "By all means, gentlemen, let us go."

We made our way across deck to the forward compartments, avoiding the hatches where the crew were busily loading down the art, the music, the literature, the fine flowering of the humanity that we had, after all, been created to save.

Welcome to Olympus, Mr. Hearst

Opening Credits: 1926

"*Take Ten!*" called the director, and lowering his megaphone he settled back in his chair. It sank deeper into the sand under his weight, and irritably settling again he peered out at the stallion galloping across the expanse of dune below him, its burnoosed rider clinging against the scouring blast of air from the wind machines.

"Pretty good so far…" chanted the assistant director. Beside him, Rudolph Valentino (in a burnoose that matched the horseman's) nodded grimly. They watched as the steed bore its rider up one wave of sand, down the next, nearer and nearer to that point where they might cut away—

"Uh-oh," said the grip. From the sea behind them a real wind traveled forward across the sand, tearing a palm frond from the seedy-looking prop trees around the Sheik's Camp set and sending it whirling in front of the stallion. The stallion pulled up short and began to dance wildly. After a valiant second or so the rider flew up in the air and came down on his head in the sand, arms and legs windmilling.

"Oh, Christ," the director snarled. "*Cut! Kill the wind!*"

"*You O.K., Lewis?*" yelled the script boy.

The horseman sat up unsteadily and pulled swathing folds of burnoose up off his face. He held up his right hand, making an OK sign.

"*Set up for take eleven!*" yelled the assistant director. The horseman clambered to his feet and managed to calm his mount; taking its bridle, he slogged away with it, back across the sand to their mark. Behind them the steady salt wind erased the evidence of their passage.

"This wind is not going to stop, you know," Valentino pointed out gloomily. He stroked the false beard that gave him all the appearance of middle age he would ever wear.

"Ain't there any local horses that ain't spooked by goddam palm leaves?" the grip wanted to know.

"Yeah. Plowhorses," the director told them. "Look, we paid good money for an Arabian stallion. Do you hear the man complaining? I don't hear him complaining."

"I can't even *see* him," remarked the assistant director, scanning the horizon. "Jeez, you don't guess he fell down dead or anything out there?"

But there, up out of the sand came the horse and his rider, resuming position on the crest of the far dune.

"Nah. See?" the director said. "The little guy's a pro." He lifted the megaphone, watching as Lewis climbed back into the saddle. The script boy chalked in the update and held up the clapboard for the camera. *Crack!*

"Wind machines go—and—take eleven!"

Here they came again, racing the wind and the waning light, over the lion-colored waves as the camera whirred, now over the top of the last dune and down, disappearing—

Disappearing—

The grip and the assistant director groaned. Valentino winced.

"I don't see them, Mr. Fitzmaurice," the script boy said.

"So where are they?" yelled the director. "*Cut! Cut, and kill the goddam wind.*"

"Sorry!" cried a faint voice, and a second later Lewis came trudging around the dune, leading the jittering stallion. "I'm afraid we had a slight spill back there."

"*Wranglers!* Jadaan took a fall," called the assistant director in horrified tones, and from the camp on the beach a half dozen wranglers came running. They crowded around the stallion solicitously. Lewis left him to their care and struggled on toward the director.

The headpiece of his burnoose had come down around his neck, and his limp fair hair fluttered in the wind, making his dark makeup—what was left after repeated face-first impact with dunes—look all the more incongruous. He spat out sand and smiled brightly, tugging off his spirit-gummed beard.

"Of course, I'm ready to do another take if you are, Mr. Fitzmaurice," Lewis said.

"No," said Valentino. "We will kill him or we will kill the horse, or both."

"Oh, screw it," the director decided. "We've got enough good stuff in the can. Anyway, the light's going. Let's see what we can do with that take, as far as it went."

Lewis nodded and waded on through the sand, intent on getting out of his robes; Valentino stepped forward to put a hand on his shoulder. Lewis squinted up at him, blinking sand from his lashes.

"You work very hard, my friend," Valentino said. "But you should not try to ride horses. It is painful to watch."

"Oh—er—thank you. It's fun being Rudolph Valentino for a few hours, all the same," said Lewis, and from out of nowhere he produced a fountain pen. "I don't suppose I might have your autograph, Mr. Valentino?"

"Certainly," said Valentino, looking vainly around for something to autograph. From another nowhere Lewis produced a copy of the shooting script, and Valentino took it. "Your name is spelled?"

"L-e-w-i-s, Mr. Valentino. Right there?" he suggested. "Right under where it says *The Son Of The Sheik?*" He watched with a peculiarly stifled glee as Valentino signed: *For my "other self" Lewis. Rudolph Valentino.*

"There," said Valentino, handing him the script. "No more falls on the head, yes?"

"Thank you so much. It's very kind of you to be worried, but it's all right, you know," Lewis replied. "I can take a few tumbles. I'm a professional stunt man, after all."

He tucked the script away in his costume and staggered down to the water's edge, where the extras and crew were piling into an old stakebed truck. The driver was already cranking up the motor, anxious to begin his drive back to Pismo Beach before the tide turned and they got bogged down again.

Valentino watched Lewis go, shaking his head.

"Don't worry about that guy, Rudy," the director told him, knocking sand out of his megaphone. "I know he looks like a pushover, but he never gets hurt, and I mean never."

"But luck runs out, like sand." Valentino smiled wryly and waved at the dunes stretching away behind them, where the late slanting sunlight cast his shadow to the edge of the earth. "Doesn't it? And that one, I think he has the look of a man who will die young."

Which was a pretty ironic thing for Valentino to say, considering that he'd be dead himself within the year and that Lewis happened to be, on that particular day in 1926, just short of his eighteen hundred and twenty-third birthday.

If we immortals had birthdays, anyway.

▲▼▲

Flash Forward: 1933

"Oh, look, we're at Pismo Beach," exclaimed Lewis, leaning around me to peer at it. The town was one hotel and a lot of clam stands lining the highway. "Shall we stop for clams, Joseph?"

"Are you telling me you didn't get enough clams when you worked on *Son of the Sheik*?" I grumbled, groping in my pocket for another mint Lifesaver. The last thing I wanted right now was food. Usually I can eat anything (and have, believe me) but this job was giving me butterflies like crazy.

"Possibly," Lewis said, standing up in his seat to get a better view as we rattled past, bracing himself with a hand on the Ford's windshield. The wind hit him smack in the face and his hair stood out all around his head. "But it would be nice to toast poor old Rudy's shade, don't you think?"

"You want to toast him? Here." I pulled out my flask and handed it to Lewis. "It would be nice to be on time for Mr. Hearst, too, you know?"

Lewis slid back down into his seat and had a sip of warm gin. He made a face.

"*Ave atque vale,* old man," he told Valentino's ghost. "You're not actually nervous about this, are you, Joseph?"

"Me, nervous?" I bared my teeth. "Hell no. Why would I be nervous meeting one of the most powerful men in the world?"

"Well, precisely," Lewis had another sip of gin, made another face. "Thank God you won't be needing this bootlegger any more. *Vale* Volstead Act, too! You must have known far more powerful men in your time, mustn't you? You worked for a Byzantine emperor once, if I'm not mistaken."

"Three or four of 'em," I corrected him. "And believe me, not one had anything like the pull of William Randolph Hearst. Not when you look at the big picture. Anyway, Lewis, the rules of the whole game are different now. You think a little putz like Napoleon could rule the world today? You think Hitler'd be getting anywhere without the media? Mass communication is where the real power is, kiddo."

"He's only a mortal, after all," Lewis said. "Put it into perspective! We're simply motoring up to someone's country estate to spend a pleasant weekend with entertaining people. There will be fresh air and lovely views. There will be swimming, riding, and tennis. There will be fine food and decent drink, at least one hopes so—"

"Don't count on booze," I said. "Mr. Hearst doesn't like drunks."

"—and all we have to do is accomplish a simple document drop for the Company," Lewis went on imperturbably, patting the briefcase in which he'd brought the autographed Valentino script. "A belated birthday present for the master of the house, so to speak."

"That's all you have to do," I replied. "I have to actually negotiate with the guy."

Lewis shrugged, conceding my point. "Though what was that story you were telling me the other night, about you and that pharaoh, what was his name—? It's not as though there will be jealous courtiers ordering our executions, after all."

I made a noise of grudging agreement. I couldn't explain to Lewis why this job had me so on edge. Probably I wasn't sure. I lie to myself a lot, see. I started doing it about thirteen thousand years ago and it's become a habit, like chain-sucking mints to ward off imaginary nervous indigestion.

Immortals have a lot of little habits like that.

▲▼▲

We cruised on up the coast in my Model A, through the cow town of San Luis Obispo. This was where Mr. Hearst's honored guests arrived in his private rail car, to be met at the station by his private limousines. From there they'd be whisked away to that little architectural folly known to later generations as Hearst Castle, but known for now just as The Ranch or, if you were feeling romantic, *La Cuesta Encantada*.

You've never been there? Gee, poor you. Suppose for a moment you owned one of the more beautiful hills in the world, with a breathtaking view of mountains and sea. Now suppose you decided to build a house on top of it, and had all the money in the world to spend on making that house the place of your wildest dreams, no holds barred and no expense spared, with three warehouses full of antiques to furnish the place.

Hell yes, you'd do it; anybody would. What would you do then? If you were William Randolph Hearst, you'd invite guests up to share your enjoyment of the place you'd made. But not just any guests. You could afford to lure the best minds of a generation up there to chat with you, thinkers and artists, Einsteins and Thalbergs, Huxleys and G.B. Shaws. And if you had a blonde mistress who worked in the movies, you got her to invite her friends, too: Gable and Lombard, Bette Davis, Marie Dressler, Buster Keaton, Harpo Marx, Charlie Chaplin.

And the occasional studio small fry like Lewis and me, after I'd done a favor for Marion Davies and asked for an invitation in return. The likes of us didn't get the private railroad car treatment. We had to drive all the way up from Hollywood on our own steam. I guess if Mr. Hearst had any idea who was paying him a visit, he'd have sent a limo for us too; but the Company likes to play its cards close to the vest.

And we didn't look like a couple of immortal cyborg representatives of an all-powerful twenty-fourth-century Company, anyway. I appear to be an ordinary guy, kind of dark and compact (O.K., *short*) and Lewis… well, he's good-looking, but he's on the short side, too. It's always been Company policy for its operatives to blend in with the mortal population, which is why nobody in San Luis Obispo or Morro Bay or Cayucos wasted a second glance on two average cyborg joes in a new Ford zipping along the road.

Anyway we passed through little nowhere towns-by-the-sea and rolling windswept seacoast, lots of California scenery that was breathtaking, if you like scenery. Lewis did, and kept exclaiming over the wildflowers and cypress trees. I just crunched Pep-O-Mints and kept driving. Seventeen miles before we got anywhere near Mr. Hearst's castle, we were already on his property.

What you noticed first was a distant white something on a green hilltop: two pale towers and not much more. I remembered medieval hill towns in Spain and France and Italy, and so did Lewis, because he nudged me and chuckled: "Rather like advancing on Le Monastier, eh? Right about now I'd be practicing compliments for the lord or the archbishop or whoever, and hoping I'd brought enough lute strings. What about you?"

"I'd be praying I'd brought along enough cash to bribe whichever duke it was I had to bribe," I told him, popping another Lifesaver.

"It's not the easiest of jobs, is it, being a Facilitator?" Lewis said sympathetically. I just shook my head.

The sense of displacement in reality wasn't helped any by the fact that we were now seeing the occasional herd of zebra or yak or giraffe, frolicking in the green meadows beside the road. If a roc had swept over the car and carried off a water buffalo in its talons, it wouldn't have seemed strange. Even Lewis fell silent, and took another shot of gin to fortify himself.

He had the flask stashed well out of sight, though, by the time we turned right into an unobtrusive driveway and a small sign that said HEARST RANCH. Here we paused at a barred gate, where a mortal leaned out of a shack to peer at us inquiringly.

"Guests of Mr. Hearst's," I shouted, doing my best to look as though I did this all the time.

"Names, please?"

"Joseph C. Denham and Lewis Kensington," we chorused.

He checked a list to be sure we were on it and then, "Five miles an hour, please, and the animals have right-of-way at all times," he told us, as the gates swung wide.

"We're in!" Lewis gave me a gleeful dig in the ribs. I snarled absently and drove across the magic threshold, with the same jitters I'd felt walking under a portcullis into some baron's fortress.

The suspense kept building, too, because the road wound like five miles of corkscrew, climbing all that time, and there were frequent stops at barred gates as we ascended into different species habitats. Lewis had to get out and open them, nimbly stepping around buffalo pies and other things that didn't reward close examination, and avoiding the hostile attentions of an ostrich at about the third gate up. Eventually we turned up an avenue of orange trees and flowering oleander.

"Oh, this is very like the south of France," said Lewis. "Don't you think?"

"I guess so," I muttered. A pair of high wrought-iron gates loomed in front of us, opening unobtrusively as we rattled through, and we pulled up to the Grand Staircase.

We were met by a posse of ordinary-looking guys in chinos and jackets, who collected our suitcases and made off with them before we'd even gotten out of the car. I managed to avoid yelling anything like "Hey! Come back here with those!" and of course Lewis was already greeting a dignified-looking lady who had materialized from behind a statue. A houseboy took charge of the Model A and drove it off.

"...Mr. Hearst's housekeeper," the lady was saying. "He's asked me to show you to your rooms. If you'll follow me—? You're in the Casa del Sol."

"Charming," Lewis replied, and I let him take the lead, chatting and being personable with the lady as I followed them up a long sweeping stair-case and across a terrace. We paused at the top, and there opening out on my left was the biggest damn Roman swimming pool I've ever seen, and I worked in Rome for a couple of centuries. The statues of nymphs, sea gods, et cetera, were mostly modern or museum copies. Hearst had not yet imported what was left of an honest-to-gods temple and set it up as a backdrop for poolside fun. He would, though.

Looming above us was the first of the "little guest bungalows". We craned back our heads to look up. It would have made a pretty imposing mansion for anybody else.

"Delightful," Lewis said. "Mediterranean Revival, isn't it?"

"Yes, sir," the housekeeper replied, leading us up more stairs. "I believe this is your first visit here, Mr. Kensington? And Mr. Denham?"

"Yeah," I said.

"Mr. Hearst would like you to enjoy your stay, and has asked that I provide you with all information necessary to make that possible," the housekeeper recited carefully, leading us around the corner of the house to its courtyard. The door at last! And waiting beside it was a Filipino guy in a suit, who bowed slightly at the waist when he saw us.

"This is Jerome," the housekeeper informed us. "He's been assigned to your rooms. If you require anything, you can pick up the service telephone and he'll respond immediately." She unlocked the door and stepped aside to usher us in. Jerome followed silently and vanished through a side door.

As we stood staring at all the antiques and Lewis made admiring noises, the housekeeper continued: "You'll notice Mr. Hearst has furnished much of this suite with his private art collection, but he'd like you to know that the bathroom—just through there, gentlemen—is perfectly up-to-date and modern, with all the latest conveniences, including shower baths."

"How thoughtful," Lewis answered, and transmitted to me: *Are you going to take part in this conversation at all?*

"That's really swell of Mr. Hearst," I said. *I'm even more nervous than I was before, O.K.?*

The housekeeper smiled. "Thank you. You'll find your bags are already in your assigned bedrooms. Jerome is unpacking for you."

Whoops. "Great," I said. "Where's my room? Can I see it now?"

"Certainly, Mr. Denham," said the housekeeper, narrowing her eyes slightly. She led us through a doorway that had probably belonged to some sixteenth-century Spanish bishop, and there was Jerome, laying out the contents of my cheap brown suitcase. My black suitcase sat beside it, untouched.

"If you'll unlock this one, sir, I'll unpack it too," Jerome told me.

"That's O.K.," I replied, taking the black suitcase and pushing it under the bed. "I'll get that one myself, later."

In the very brief pause that followed, Jerome and the housekeeper exchanged glances, Lewis sighed, and I felt a real need for another Lifesaver. The housekeeper cleared her throat and said, "I hope this room is satisfactory, Mr. Denham?"

"Oh! Just peachy, thanks," I said.

"I'm sure mine is just as nice," Lewis offered. Jerome exited to unpack for him.

"Very good." The housekeeper cleared her throat again. "Now, Mr. Hearst wished you to know that cocktails will be served at Seven this evening in the assembly hall, which is in the big house just across the courtyard. He expects to join his guests at Eight; dinner will be served at Nine. After dinner Mr. Hearst will retire with his guests to the theater, where a motion picture will be shown. Following the picture, Mr. Hearst generally withdraws to his study, but his guests are invited to return to their rooms or explore the library." She fixed me with a steely eye. "Alcohol will be served only in the main house, although sandwiches or other light meals can be requested by telephone from the kitchen staff at any hour."

She thinks you've got booze in the suitcase, you know, Lewis transmitted.

Shut up. I squared my shoulders and tried to look open and honest. Everybody knew that there were two unbreakable rules for the guests up here: no liquor in the rooms and no sex between unmarried couples. Notice I said "for the guests". Mr. Hearst and Marion weren't bound by any rules except the laws of physics.

The housekeeper gave us a few more helpful tidbits like how to find the zoo, tennis court, and stables, and departed. Lewis and I slunk out into the garden, where we paced along between the statues.

"Overall, I don't think that went very well," Lewis observed.

"No kidding," I said, thrusting my hands in my pockets.

"It'll only be a temporary bad impression, you know," Lewis told me helpfully. "As soon as you've made your presentation—"

"Hey! Yoo hoo! Joe! You boys made it up here O.K.?" cried a bright voice from somewhere up in the air, and we turned for our first full-on eyeful of La Casa Grande in all its massive glory. It looked sort of like a big Spanish cathedral, but surely one for pagans, because there was Marion Davies hanging out a third-story window waving at us.

"Yes, thanks," I called, while Lewis stared. Marion was wearing a dressing gown. She might have been wearing more, but you couldn't tell from this distance.

"Is that your friend? He's *cute*," she yelled. "Looks like Freddie March!"

Lewis turned bright pink. "I'm his stunt double, actually," he called to her, with a slightly shaky giggle.

"What?"

"I'm his stunt double."

"Oh," she yelled back. "O.K.! Listen, do you want some ginger ale or anything? You know there's no—" she looked naughty and mimed drinking from a bottle, "until tonight."

"Yes, ginger ale would be fine," bawled Lewis.

"I'll have some sent down," Marion said, and vanished into the recesses of La Casa Grande.

We turned left at the next statue and walked up a few steps into the court-yard in front of the house. It was the size of several town squares, big enough to stage the riot scene from *Romeo and Juliet* complete with the Verona Police Department charging in on horseback. All it held at the moment, though, was another fountain and some lawn chairs. In one of them, Greta Garbo sat moodily peeling an orange.

"Hello, Greta," I said, wondering if she'd remember me. She just gave me a look and went on peeling the orange. She remembered me, all right.

Lewis and I sat down a comfortable distance from her, and a houseboy appeared out of nowhere with two tall glasses of White Rock over ice.

"Marion Davies said I was cute," Lewis reminded me, looking pleased. Then his eyebrows swooped together in the middle. "That's not good, though, is it? For the mission? What if Mr. Hearst heard her? Ye gods, she was shout-ing it at the top of her lungs."

"I don't think it's going to be any big deal," I told him wearily, sipping my ginger ale. Marion thought a lot of people were cute, and didn't care who heard her say so.

We sat there in the sunshine, and the ice in our drinks melted away. Garbo ate her orange. Doves crooned sleepily in the carillon towers of the house and I thought about what I was going to say to William Randolph Hearst.

Pretty soon the other guests started wandering up, and Garbo wouldn't talk to them, either. Clark Gable sat on the edge of the fountain and got involved in a long conversation with a sandy-haired guy from Paramount about their mutual bookie. One of Hearst's five sons arrived with his girl-friend. He tried to introduce her to Garbo, who answered in monosyllables, until at last he gave it up and they went off to swim in the Roman pool. A couple of friends of Marion's from the days before talkies, slightly threadbare guys named Charlie and Laurence who looked as though they hadn't worked lately, got deeply involved in a discussion of Greek mythology.

I sat there and looked up at the big house and wondered where Hearst was, and what he was doing. Closing some million-dollar media deal? Giving some senator or congressman voting instructions? Placing an order with some antiques dealer for the contents of an entire library from some medieval duke's palace?

He did stuff like that, Mr. Hearst, which was one of the reasons the Company was interested in him.

I was distracted from my uneasy reverie when Constance Talmadge arrived, gaining on forty now but still as bright and bouncy as when she'd played the Mountain Girl in *Intolerance*, and with her Brooklyn accent just as strong. She bounced right over to Lewis, who knew her, and they had a lively chat about old times. Shortly afterward the big doors of the house opened and out came, not the procession of priests and altar boys you'd expect, but Marion in light evening dress.

"Hello, everybody," she hollered across the fountain. "Sorry to keep you waiting, but you know how it is—Hearst come, Hearst served!"

There were nervous giggles and you almost expected to see the big house behind her wince, but she didn't care. She came out and greeted everybody warmly—well, almost everybody; Garbo seemed to daunt even Marion—and then welcomed us in through the vast doorway, into the inner sanctum.

"Who's a first-timer up here?" she demanded, as we crossed the threshold. "I know you are, Joe, and your friend—? Get a load of this floor." She pointed to the mosaic tile in the vestibule. "Know where that's from? Pompeii! Can you beat it? People actually died on this floor."

If she was right, I had known some of them. It didn't improve my mood.

The big room beyond was cool and dark after the brilliance of the courtyard. Almost comfortable, too: had contemporary sofas and overstuffed chairs, little ashtrays on brass stands. If you didn't mind the fact that it was also about a mile long and full of Renaissance masterpieces, with a fireplace big enough to roast an ox and a coffered ceiling a mile up in the air, it was sort of cozy. Here, as in all the other rooms, were paintings and statues representing the Madonna and Child. It seemed to be one of Mr. Hearst's favorite images.

We milled around aimlessly until servants came out bearing trays of drinks, at which time the milling became purposeful as hell. We converged on those trays like piranhas. The Madonna beamed down at us all, smiling her blessing.

The atmosphere livened up a lot after that. Charlie sat down at a piano and began to play popular tunes. Gable and Laurence and the guy from Paramount found a deck of cards and started a poker game. Marion worked the rest of the crowd like the good hostess she was, making sure that everybody had a drink and nobody was bored.

The Hearst kid and his girlfriend came in with wet hair. A couple of Hearst's executives (slimy-looking bastards) came in too, saw Garbo and hurried over to try to get her autograph. A gaunt and imposing grande dame with two shrieking little mutts made an entrance, and Marion greeted her enthusiastically; she was some kind of offbeat novelist who'd had one of her books optioned, and had come out to Hollywood to work on the screenplay.

I roamed around the edges of the vast room, scanning for the secret panel that concealed Hearst's private elevator. Lewis was gallantly dancing the Charleston with Connie Talmadge. Marion made for them, towing the writer along.

"—And this is Dutch Talmadge, you remember her? And this is, uh, what was your name, sweetie?" Marion waved at Lewis.

"Lewis Kensington," he said, as the music tinkled to a stop. The pianist paused to light a cigarette.

"Lewis! That's it. And you're even cuter up close," said Marion, reaching out and pinching his cheek. "Isn't he? Anyway you're Industry too, aren't you, Lewis?"

"Only in a minor sort of way," Lewis demurred. "I'm a stunt man."

"That just means you're worth the money they pay you, honey," Marion told him. "Unlike some of these blonde bimbos with no talent, huh?" She whooped with laughter at her own expense. "Lewis, Dutch, this is Cartimandua Bryce! You know? She writes those wonderful spooky romances."

The imposing-looking lady stepped forward. The two chihuahuas did their best to lunge from her arms and tear out Lewis's throat, but she kept a firm grip on them.

"A-and these are her little dogs," added Marion unnecessarily, stepping back from the yappy armful.

"My familiars," Cartimandua Bryce corrected her with a saturnine smile. "Actually, they are old souls who have re-entered the flesh on a temporary basis for purposes of the spiritual advancement of others."

"Oh," said Connie.

"O.K.," said Marion.

"This is Conqueror Worm," Mrs. Bryce offered the smaller of the two bug-eyed monsters, "and this is Tcho-Tcho."

"How nice," said Lewis gamely, and reached out in an attempt to shake Tcho-Tcho's tiny paw. She bared her teeth at him and screamed frenziedly. Some animals can tell we're not mortals. It can be inconvenient.

Lewis withdrew his hand in some haste. "I'm sorry. Perhaps the nice doggie's not used to strangers?"

"It isn't that—" Mrs. Bryce stared fixedly at Lewis. "Tcho-Tcho is attempting to communicate with me telepathically. She senses something unusual about you, Mr. Kensington."

If she can tell the lady you're a cyborg, she's one hell of a dog, I transmitted.

Oh, shut up, Lewis transmitted back. "Really?" he said to Mrs. Bryce. "Gosh, isn't that interesting?"

But Mrs. Bryce had closed her eyes, I guess the better to hear what Tcho-Tcho had to say, and was frowning deeply. After a moment's uncomfortable silence, Marion turned to Lewis and said, "So, you're Freddie March's stunt double? Gee. What's that like, anyway?"

"I just take falls. Stand in on lighting tests. Swing from chandeliers," Lewis replied. "The usual." Charlie resumed playing: *I'm the Sheik of Araby.*

"He useta do stunts for Valentino, too," Constance added. "I remember."

"You doubled for Rudy?" Marion's smile softened. "Poor old Rudy."

"I always heard Valentino was a faggot," chortled the man from Paramount. Marion rounded on him angrily.

"For your information, Jack, Rudy Valentino was a real man," she told him. "He just had too much class to chase skirts all the time!"

"Soitain people could loin a whole lot from him," agreed Connie, with the scowl of disdain she'd used to face down Old Babylon's marriage market in *Intolerance.*

"I'm just telling you what I heard," protested the man from Paramount.

"Maybe," Gable told him, looking up from his cards. "But did you ever hear that expression, 'Say nothing but good of the dead'? Now might be a good time to dummy up, pal. That or play your hand."

Mrs. Bryce, meanwhile, had opened her eyes and was gazing on Lewis with a disconcerting expression.

"Mr. Kensington," she announced with a throaty quaver, "Tcho-Tcho informs me you are a haunted man."

Lewis looked around nervously. "Am I?"

"Tcho-Tcho can perceive the spirit of a soul struggling in vain to speak to you. You are not sufficiently tuned to the cosmic vibrations to hear him," Mrs. Bryce stated.

Tell him to try another frequency, I quipped.

"Well, that's just like me, I'm afraid." Lewis shrugged, palms turned out. "I'm terribly dense that way, you see. Wouldn't know a cosmic vibration if I tripped over one."

Cosmic vibrations, my ass. I knew what she was doing; carney psychics do it all the time, and it's called a cold reading. You give somebody a close once-over and make a few deductions based on the details you observe. Then you start weaving a story out of your deductions, watching your subject's reactions to see where you're accurate and tailoring your story to fit as you go on. All she had to work with, right now, was the mention that Lewis had known Valentino. Lewis has *Easy Mark* written all over him, but I guessed she was up here after bigger fish.

"Tcho-Tcho sees a man—a slender, dark man—" Mrs. Bryce went on, rolling her eyes back in her head in a sort of alarming way. "He wears Eastern raiment—"

Marion downed her cocktail in one gulp. "Hey, look, Mrs. Bryce, there's Greta Garbo," she said. "I'll just bet she's a big fan of your books."

Mrs. Bryce's eyes snapped back into place and she looked around.

"Garbo?" she cried. She made straight for the Frozen Flame, dropping Lewis like a rock, though Tcho-Tcho snapped and strained over her shoulder at him. Garbo saw them coming and sank further into the depths of her chair. I was right. Mrs. Bryce was after bigger fish.

I didn't notice what happened after that, though, because I heard a clash of brass gates and gears engaging somewhere upstairs. The biggest fish of all was descending in his elevator, making his delayed entrance.

I edged over toward the secret panel. My mouth was dry, my palms were sweaty. I wonder if Mephistopheles ever gets sweaty palms when he's facing a prospective client?

Bump. Here he was. The panel made no sound as it opened. Not a mortal soul noticed as W.R. Hearst stepped into the room, and for that matter Lewis didn't notice either, having resumed the Charleston with Connie Talmadge. So there was only me to stare at the very, very big old man who sat down quietly in the corner.

I swear I felt the hair stand on the back of my neck, and I didn't know why.

William Randolph Hearst had had his seventieth birthday a couple of weeks before. His hair was white, he sagged where an old man sags, but his bones hadn't given in to gravity. His posture was upright and powerfully alert.

He just sat there in the shadows, watching the bright people in his big room. I watched him. This was the guy who'd fathered modern journalism, who with terrifying energy and audacity had built a financial empire that included newspapers, magazines, movies, radio, mining, ranching. He picked and chose presidents as though they were his personal appointees. He'd ruthlessly forced the world to take him on his own terms; morality was what *he* said it was; and yet there wasn't any fire that you could spot in the seated man, no restless genius apparent to the eye.

You know what he reminded me of? The Goon in the *Popeye* comic strips. Big as a mountain and scary too, but at the same time sad, with those weird deep eyes above the long straight nose.

He reminded me of something else, too, but not anything I wanted to remember right now.

"Oh, you did your trick again," said Marion, pretending to notice him at last. "Here he is, everybody. He likes to pop in like he was Houdini or something. Come on, W.R., say hello to the nice people." She pulled him to his feet and he smiled for her. His smile was even scarier than the rest of him. It was wide, and sharp, and hungry, and young.

"Hello, everybody," he said, in that unearthly voice Ambrose Bierce had described as the fragrance of violets made audible. Flutelike and without resonance. Not a human voice; jeez, *I* sound more human than that. But then, I'm supposed to.

And you should have seen them, all those people, turn and stare and smile and bow—just slightly, and I don't think any of them realized they were bowing to him, but I've been a courtier and I know a grovel when I see one. Marion was the only mortal in that room who wasn't afraid of him. Even Garbo had gotten up out of her chair.

Marion brought them up to him, one by one, the big names and the nobodies, and introduced the ones he didn't know. He shook hands like a shy kid. Hell, he *was* shy! That was it, I realized: he was uneasy around people, and Marion—in addition to her other duties—was his social interface. O.K., this might be something I could use.

I stood apart from the crowd, waiting unobtrusively until Marion had brought up everybody else. Only when she looked around for me did I step out of the shadows into her line of sight.

"And—oh, Joe, almost forgot you! Pops, this is Joe Denham. He works for Mr. Mayer? He's the nice guy who—"

Pandemonium erupted behind us. One of the damn chihuahuas had gotten loose and was after somebody with intent to kill, Lewis from the sound of it. Marion turned and ran off to deal with the commotion. I leaned forward and shook Hearst's hand as he peered over my shoulder after Marion, frowning.

"Pleased to meet you, Mr. Hearst," I told him quietly. "Mr. Shaw asked me to visit you. I look forward to our conversation later."

Boy, did that get his attention. Those remote eyes snapped into close focus on me, and it was like being hit by a granite block. I swallowed hard but concentrated on the part I was playing, smiling mysteriously as I disengaged my hand from his and stepped back into the shadows.

He wasn't able to say anything right then, because Tcho-Tcho was herding Lewis in our direction and Lewis was dancing away from her with apologetic little yelps, jumping over the furniture, and Marion was laughing hysterically as she tried to catch the rotten dog. Mrs. Bryce just looked on with a rapt and knowing expression.

Hearst pursed his lips at the scene, but he couldn't be distracted long. He turned slowly to stare at me and nodded, just once, to show he understood.

A butler appeared in the doorway to announce that dinner was served. Hearst led us from the room, and we followed obediently.

The dining hall was less homey than the first room we'd been in. Freezing cold in spite of the roaring fire in the French Gothic hearth, its gloom was brightened a little by the silk Renaissance racing banners hanging up high and a lot of massive silver candlesticks. The walls were paneled with fifteenth-century choir stalls from Spain. I might have dozed off in any one of them, back in my days as a friar. Maybe I had; they looked familiar.

We were seated at the long refectory table. Hearst and Marion sat across from each other in the center, and guests were placed by status. The nearer you were to the master and his mistress, the higher in favor or more important you were. Guests Mr. Hearst found boring or rude were moved discreetly further out down the table.

Well, we've nowhere to go but up, Lewis transmitted, finding our place cards clear down at the end. I could see Hearst staring at me as we took our plates (plain old Blue Willow that his mother had used for camping trips) and headed for the buffet.

I bet we move up soon, too, I replied.

Ah! Have you made contact? Lewis peered around Gable's back at a nice-looking dish of venison steaks.

Just baited the hook. I tried not to glance at Hearst, who had loaded his plate with pressed duck and was pacing slowly back to the table.

Does this have to be terribly complicated? Lewis inquired, sidling in past Garbo to help himself to asparagus soufflé. *All we want is permission to conceal the script in that particular Spanish cabinet.*

Actually we want a little more than that, Lewis. I considered all the rich stuff and decided to keep things bland. Potatoes, right.

I see. This is one of those need-to-know things, isn't it?

You got it, kiddo. I put enough food on my plate to be polite and turned to go back to my seat. Hearst caught my eye. He tracked me like a lighthouse beam all the way down the table. I nodded back, like the friendly guy I really am, and sat down across from Lewis.

I take it there's more going on here than the Company has seen fit to tell me? Lewis transmitted, unfolding his paper napkin and holding out his wine glass expectantly. The waiter filled it and moved on.

Don't be sore, I transmitted back. *You know the Company. There's probably more going on here than even I know about, O.K.?*

I only said it to make him feel better. If I'd had any idea how right I was…

So we ate dinner, at that baronial banqueting table, with the mortals. Gable carried on manful conversation with Mr. Hearst about ranching, Marion and Connie joked and giggled across the table with the male guests, young Hearst and his girl whispered to each other, and a servant had to take Tcho-Tcho and Conqueror Worm outside because they wouldn't stop snarling at a meek little dachshund that appeared under Mr. Hearst's chair. Mrs. Bryce didn't mind; she was busy trying to tell Garbo about a past life, but I couldn't figure out if it was supposed to be hers or Garbo's. Hearst's executives just ate, in silence, down at their end of the table. Lewis and I ate in silence down at our end.

Not that we were ignored. Every so often Marion would yell a pleasantry our way, and Hearst kept swinging that cold blue searchlight on me, with an expression I was damned if I could fathom.

When dinner was over, Mr. Hearst rose and picked up the dachshund. He led us all deeper into his house, to his private movie theater.

Do I have to tell you it was on a scale with everything else? Walls lined in red damask, gorgeous beamed ceiling held up by rows of gilded caryatids slightly larger than lifesize. We filed into our seats, I guess unconsciously preserving the order of the dinner table because Lewis and I wound up off on an edge again. Hearst settled into his big leather chair with its telephone, called the projectionist and gave an order. The lights went out, and after a fairly long moment in darkness, the screen lit up. It was *Going Hollywood,* Marion's latest film with Bing Crosby. She greeted her name on the screen with a long loud raspberry, and everyone tittered.

Except me. I wasn't tittering, no sir; Mr. Hearst wasn't in his big leather chair anymore. He was padding toward me slowly in the darkness, carrying his little dog, and if I hadn't been able to see by infrared I'd probably have screamed and jumped right through that expensive ceiling when his big hand dropped on my shoulder in the darkness.

He leaned down close to my ear.

"Mr. Denham? I'd like to speak with you in private, if I may," he told me.

"Yes, sir, Mr. Hearst," I gasped, and got to my feet. Beside me, Lewis glanced over. His eyes widened.

Break a leg, he transmitted, and turned his attention to the screen again.

I edged out of the row and followed Hearst, who was walking away without the slightest doubt I was obeying him. Once we were outside the theater, all he said was, "Let's go this way. It'll be faster."

"O.K.," I said, as though I had any idea where we were going. We walked back through the house. There wasn't a sound except our footsteps echoing off those high walls. We emerged into the assembly hall, eerily lit up, and Hearst led me to the panel that concealed his elevator. It opened for him. We got in, he and I and the little dog, and ascended through his house.

▲▼▲

My mouth was dry, my palms were sweating, my dinner wasn't sitting too well…well, that last one's a lie. I'm a cyborg and I can't get indigestion. But I felt like a mortal with a nervous stomach, know what I mean? And I'd have given half the Renaissance masterpieces in that house for a roll of Pep-O-Mints right then. The dachshund watched me sympathetically.

We got out at the third floor and stepped into Hearst's private study. This was the room from which he ran his empire when he was at La Cuesta Encantada, this was where phones connected him directly to newsrooms all over the country; this was where he glanced at teletype before giving orders to the movers and shakers. Up in a corner, a tiny concealed motion picture camera began to whir the moment we stepped on the carpet, and I could hear the click as a modified Dictaphone hidden in a cabinet began to record. State-of-the-art surveillance, for 1933.

It was a nicer room than the others I'd been in so far. Huge, of course, with an antique Spanish ceiling and golden hanging lamps, but wood-paneled walls and books and Bakhtiari carpets gave it a certain warmth. My gaze followed the glow of lamplight down the long polished mahogany conference table and skidded smack into Hearst's life-size portrait on the far wall. It was a good portrait, done when he was in his thirties, the young emperor staring out with those somber eyes. He looked innocent. He looked dangerous.

"Nice likeness," I said.

"The painter had a great talent," Hearst replied. "He was a dear friend of mine. Died too soon. Why do you suppose that happens?"

"People dying too soon?" I stammered slightly as I said it, and mentally yelled at myself to calm down: it was just business with a mortal, now, and the guy was even handing me an opening. I gave him my best enigmatic smile and shook my head sadly. "It's the fate of mortals to die, Mr. Hearst. Even those with extraordinary ability and talent. Rather a pity, wouldn't you agree?"

"Oh, yes," Hearst replied, never taking his eyes off me a moment. "And I guess that's what we're going to discuss now, isn't it, Mr. Denham? Let's sit down."

He gestured me to a seat, not at the big table but in one of the comfy armchairs. He settled into another to face me, as though we were old friends having a chat. The little dog curled up in his lap and sighed. God, that was a quiet room.

"So George Bernard Shaw sent you," Hearst stated.

"Not exactly," I said, folding my hands. "He mentioned you might be interested in what my people have to offer."

Hearst just looked at me. I coughed slightly and went on: "He spoke well of you, as much as Mr. Shaw ever speaks well of anybody. And, from what I've seen, you have a lot in common with the founders of our Company. You appreciate the magnificent art humanity is capable of creating. You hate to see it destroyed or wasted by blind chance. You've spent a lot of your life preserving rare and beautiful things from destruction.

"And—just as necessary—you're a man with vision. Modern science, and its potential, doesn't frighten you. You're not superstitious. You're a moral man, but you won't let narrow-minded moralists dictate to you! So you're no coward, either."

He didn't seem pleased or flattered, he was just listening to me. What was he thinking? I pushed on, doing my best to play the scene like Claude Rains.

"You see, we've been watching you carefully for quite a while now, Mr. Hearst," I told him. "We don't make this offer lightly, or to ordinary mortals. But there are certain questions we feel obliged to ask first."

Hearst just nodded. When was he going to say something?

"It's not for everybody," I continued, "what we're offering. You may think you want it very much, but you need to look honestly into your heart and ask yourself: are you ever tired of life? Are there ever times when you'd welcome a chance to sleep forever?"

"No," Hearst replied. "If I were tired of life, I'd give up and die. I'm not after peace and tranquillity, Mr. Denham. I want more time to live. I have things to do! The minute I slow down and decide to watch the clouds roll by, I'll be bored to death."

"Maybe." I nodded. "But here's another thing to consider: how much the world has changed since you were a young man. Look at that portrait. When it was painted, you were in the prime of your life—*and so was your generation.* It was your world. You knew the rules of the game, and everything made sense.

"But you were born before Lincoln delivered the Gettysburg address, Mr. Hearst. You're not living in that world anymore. All the rules have changed. The music is so brassy and strident, the dances so crude. The kings are all dying out, and petty dictators with dirty hands are seizing power. Aren't you, even a little, bewildered by the sheer speed with which everything moves nowadays? You're only seventy, but don't you feel just a bit like a dinosaur sometimes, a survivor of a forgotten age?"

"No," said Hearst firmly. "I like the present. I like the speed and the newness of things. I have a feeling I'd enjoy the future even more. Besides, if you study history, you have to conclude that humanity has steadily improved over the centuries, whatever the cynics say. The future generations are bound to be better than we are, no matter how outlandish their fashions may seem now. And what's fashion, anyway? What do I care what music the young people listen to? They'll be healthier, and smarter, and they'll have the benefit of learning from our mistakes. I'd love to hear what they'll have to say for themselves!"

I nodded again, let a beat pass in silence for effect before I answered. "There are also," I warned him, "matters of the heart to be considered. When a man has loved ones, certain things are going to cause him grief—if he lives long enough to see them happen. Think about that, Mr. Hearst."

He nodded slowly, and at last he dropped his eyes from mine.

"It would be worse for a man who felt family connections deeply," he said. "And every man ought to. But things aren't always the way they ought to be, Mr. Denham. I don't know why that is. I wish I did."

Did he mean he wished he knew why he'd never felt much paternal connection to his sons? I just looked understanding.

"And as for love," he went on, and paused. "Well, there are certain things to which you have to be resigned. It's inevitable. Nobody loves without pain."

Was he wondering again why Marion wouldn't stop drinking for him?

"And love doesn't always last, and that hurts," I condoled. Hearst lifted his eyes to me again.

"When it does last, that hurts too," he informed me. "I assure you I can bear pain."

Well, those were all the right answers. I found myself reaching up in an attempt to stroke the beard I used to wear.

"A sound, positive attitude, Mr. Hearst," I told him. "Good for you. I think we've come to the bargaining table now."

"How much can you let me have?" he said instantly.

Well, this wasn't going to take long. "Twenty years," I replied. "Give or take a year or two."

Yikes! What an expression of rapacity in his eyes. Had I forgotten I was dealing with William Randolph Hearst?

"Twenty years?" he scoffed. "When I'm only seventy? I had a grandfather who lived to be ninety-seven. I might get that far on my own."

"Not with that heart, and you know it," I countered.

His mouth tightened in acknowledgment. "All right. If your people can't do any better—twenty years might be acceptable. And in return, Mr. Denham?"

"Two things, Mr. Hearst," I held up my hand with two fingers extended. "The Company would like the freedom to store certain things here at La Cuesta Encantada from time to time. Nothing dangerous or contraband, of course! Nothing but certain books, certain paintings, some other little rarities that wouldn't survive the coming centuries if they were kept in a less fortified place. In a way, we'd just be adding items to your collection."

"You must have an idea that this house will 'survive the coming centuries', then," said Hearst, looking grimly pleased.

"Oh, yes, sir." I told him. "It will. This is one thing you've loved that won't fade away."

He rose from his chair at that, setting the dog down carefully, and paced away from me down the long room. Then he turned and walked back, tucking a grin out of sight. "O.K., Mr. Denham," he said. "Your second request must be pretty hard to swallow. What's the other thing your people want?"

"Certain conditions set up in your will, Mr. Hearst," I said. "A secret trust giving my Company control of certain of your assets. Only a couple, but very specific ones."

He bared his smile at me. It roused all kinds of atavistic terrors; I felt sweat break out on my forehead, get clammy in my armpits.

"My, my. What kind of dumb cluck do your people think I am?" he inquired jovially.

"Well, you'd certainly be one if you jumped at their offer without wanting to know more," I smiled back, resisting the urge to run like hell. "They don't want your money, Mr. Hearst. Leave all you want to your wife and your boys. Leave Marion more than enough to protect her. What my Company wants won't create any hardship for your heirs, in any way. But—you're smart enough to understand this—there are plans being made now that won't bear fruit for another couple of centuries. Something you might not value much, tonight in 1933, might be a winning card in a game being played in the future. You see what I'm saying here?"

"I might," said Hearst, hitching up the knees of his trousers and sitting down again. The little dog jumped back into his lap. Relieved that he was no longer looming over me, I pushed on.

"Obviously we'd submit a draft of the conditions for your approval, though your lawyers couldn't be allowed to examine it—"

"And I can see why." Hearst held up his big hand. "And that's all right. I think I'm still competent to look over a contract. But, Mr. Denham! You've just told me I've got something you're going to need very badly one day. Now, wouldn't you expect me to raise the price? And I'd have to have more information about your people. I'd have to see proof that any of your story, or Mr. Shaw's for that matter, is true."

What had I said to myself, that this wasn't going to take long?

"Sure," I said brightly. "I brought all the proof I'll need."

"That's good," Hearst told me, and picked up the receiver of the phone on the table at his elbow. "Anne? Send us up some coffee, please. Yes, thank you." He leaned away from the receiver a moment to ask: "Do you take cream or sugar, Mr. Denham?"

"Both," I said.

"Cream and sugar, please," he said into the phone. "And please put Jerome on the line." He waited briefly. "Jerome? I want the black suitcase that's under Mr. Denham's bed. Yes. Thank you." He hung up and met my stare of astonishment. "That is where you've got it, isn't it? Whatever proof you've brought me?"

"Yes, as a matter of fact," I replied.

"Good," he said, and leaned back in his chair. The little dog insinuated her head under his hand, begging for attention. He looked down at her in mild amusement and began to scratch between her ears. I leaned back, too, noting that my shirt was plastered to my back with sweat and only grateful it wasn't running down my face.

"Are you a mortal creature, Mr. Denham?" Hearst inquired softly.

Now the sweat was running down my face.

"Uh, no, sir," I said. "Though I started out as one."

"You did, eh?" he remarked. "How old are you?"

"About twenty thousand years," I answered. Wham, he hit me with that deadweight stare again.

"Really?" he said. "A little fellow like you?"

I ask you, is five foot five really so short? "We were smaller back then," I explained. "People were, I mean. Diet, probably."

He just nodded. After a moment he asked: "You've lived through the ages as an eyewitness to history?"

"Yeah. Yes, sir."

"You saw the Pyramids built?"

"Yes, as a matter of fact." I prayed he wouldn't ask me how they did it, because he'd never believe the truth, but he pushed on:

"You saw the Trojan War?"

"Well, yes, I did, but it wasn't exactly like Homer said."

"The stories in the Bible, are they true? Did they really happen? Did you meet Jesus Christ?" His eyes were blazing at me.

"Well—" I waved my hands in a helpless kind of way. "I didn't meet Jesus, no, because I was working in Rome back then. I never worked in Judea until the Crusades, and that was way later. And as for the stuff in the Bible being true...Some of it is, and some of it isn't, and anyway it depends on what you mean by true." I gave in and pulled out a handkerchief, mopping my face.

"But the theological questions!" Hearst leaned forward. "Have we got souls that survive us after physical death? What about Heaven and Hell?"

"Sorry." I shook my head. "How should I know? I've never been to either place. I've never died, remember?"

"Don't your masters know?"

"If they do, they haven't told me," I apologized. "But then there's a lot they haven't told me."

Hearst's mouth tightened again, and yet I got the impression he was satisfied in some way. I sagged backward, feeling like a wrung-out sponge. So much for my suave, subtle Mephistopheles act.

On the other hand, Hearst liked being in control of the game. He might be more receptive this way.

Our coffee arrived. Hearst took half a cup and filled it the rest of the way up with cream. I put cream and four lumps of sugar in mine.

"You like sugar," Hearst observed, sipping his coffee. "But then, I don't suppose you had much opportunity to get sweets for the first few thousand years of your life?"

"Nope," I admitted. I tasted my cup and set it aside to cool. "No Neolithic candy stores."

There was a discreet double knock. Jerome entered after a word from Mr. Hearst. He brought in my suitcase and set it down between us. "Thanks," I said.

"You're welcome, sir," he replied, without a trace of sarcasm, and exited as quietly as he'd entered. It was just me, Hearst and the dog again. They looked at me expectantly.

"All right," I said, drawing a deep breath. I leaned down, punched in the code on the lock, and opened the suitcase. I felt like a traveling salesman. I guess I sort of was one.

"Here we are," I told Hearst, drawing out a silver bottle. "This is your free sample. Drink it, and you'll taste what it feels like to be forty again. The effects will only last a day or so, but that ought to be enough to show you that we can give you those twenty years with no difficulties."

"So your secret's a potion?" Hearst drank more of his coffee.

"Not entirely," I said truthfully. I was going to have to do some cryptosurgery to make temporary repairs on his heart, but we never tell them about that part of it. "Now. Here's something I think you'll find a lot more impressive."

I took out the viewscreen and set it up on the table between us. "If this were, oh, a thousand years ago and you were some emperor I was trying to impress, I'd tell you this was a magic mirror. As it is…you know that Television idea they're working on in England right now?"

"Yes," Hearst replied.

"This is where that invention's going to have led in about two hundred years," I said. "Now, I can't pick up any broadcasts because there aren't any yet, but this one also plays recorded programs." I slipped a small gold disc from a black envelope and pushed it into a slot in the front of the device, and hit the PLAY button.

Instantly the screen lit up pale blue. A moment later a montage of images appeared there, with music booming from the tiny speakers: a staccato fanfare announcing the evening news for April 18, 2106.

Hearst peered into the viewscreen in astonishment. He leaned close as the little stories sped by, the attractive people chattering brightly: new mining colonies on Luna, Ulster Revenge League terrorists bombing London again, new international agreement signed to tighten prohibitions on Recombinant DNA research, protesters in Mexico picketing Japanese-owned auto plants—

"Wait," Hearst said, lifting his big hand. "How do you stop this thing? Can you slow it down?"

I made it pause. The image of Mexican union workers torching a sushi bar froze. Hearst remained staring at the screen.

"Is that," he said, "what journalism is like, in the future?"

"Well, yes, sir. No newspapers anymore, you see; it'll all be online by then. Sort of a print-and-movie broadcast," I explained, though I was aware the revelation would probably give the poor old guy future shock. This had been his field of expertise, after all.

"But, I mean—" Hearst tore his gaze away and looked at me probingly. "This is only snippets of stuff. There's no real coverage; maybe three sentences to a story and one picture. It hasn't got half the substance of a newsreel!"

Not a word of surprise about colonies on the Moon.

"No, it'll be pretty lightweight," I admitted. "But, you see, Mr. Hearst, that'll be what the average person wants out of news by the twenty-second century. Something brief and easy to grasp. Most people will be too busy—and too uninterested—to follow stories in depth."

"Play it over again, please," Hearst ordered, and I restarted it for him. He watched intently. I felt a twinge of pity. What could he possibly make of the sound bites, the chaotic juxtaposition of images, the rapid, bouncing, and relentless pace? He watched, with the same frown, to about the same spot; then gestured for me to stop it again. I obeyed.

"Exactly," he said. "Exactly. News for the fellow in the street! Even an illiterate stevedore could get this stuff. It's like a kindergarten primer." He looked at me sidelong. "And it occurs to me, Mr. Denham, that it must be fairly easy to sway public opinion with this kind of pap. A picture's worth a thousand words, isn't it? I always thought so. This is mostly pictures. If you fed the public the right little fragments of story, you could manipulate their impressions of what's going on. Couldn't you?"

I gaped at him.

"Uh—you could, but of course that wouldn't be a very ethical thing to do," I found myself saying.

"No, if you were doing it for unethical reasons," Hearst agreed. "If you were on the side of the angels, though, I can't see how it would be wrong to pull out every trick of rhetoric available to fight for your cause! Let's see the rest of this. You're looking at these control buttons, aren't you? What are these things, these hieroglyphics?"

"Universal icons," I explained. "They're activated by eye movement. To start it again, you look at this one—" Even as I was pointing, he'd started it again himself.

There wasn't much left on the disc. A tiny clutch of factoids about a new fusion power plant, a weather report, a sports piece, and then two bitty scoops of local news. The first was a snap and ten seconds of sound, from a reporter at the scene of a party in San Francisco commemorating the two-hundredth anniversary of the 1906 earthquake. The second one—the story that had influenced the Company's choice of this particular news broadcast for Mr. Hearst's persuasion—was a piece on protesters blocking the subdivision of Hearst Ranch, which was in danger of being turned into a planned community with tract housing, golf courses, and shopping malls.

Hearst caught his breath at that, and if I thought his face had been scary before I saw now I had had no idea what scary could be. His glare hit the activation buttons with almost physical force: replay, replay, replay. After he'd watched that segment half a dozen times, he shut it off and looked at me.

"They can't do it," he said. "Did you see those plans? They'd ruin this coastline. They'd cut down all the trees! Traffic and noise and soot and—and where would all the animals go? Animals have rights, too."

"I'm afraid most of the wildlife would be extinct in this range by then, Mr. Hearst," I apologized, placing the viewer back into its case. "But maybe now you've got an idea about why my Company needs to control certain of your assets."

He was silent, breathing hard. The little dog was looking up at him with anxious eyes.

"All right, Mr. Denham," he said quietly. "To paraphrase Dickens: Is this the image of what will be, or only of what may be?"

I shrugged. "I only know what's going to happen in the future in a general kind of way, Mr. Hearst. Big stuff, like wars and inventions. I'm not told a lot else. I sincerely hope things don't turn out so badly for your ranch—and if it's any consolation, you notice the program was about protesting the *proposed* development only. The problem is, history can't be changed, not once it's happened."

"History, or recorded history, Mr. Denham?" Hearst countered. "They're not at all necessarily the same thing, I can tell you from personal experience."

"I'll bet you can," I answered, wiping away sweat again. "O.K., you've figured something out: there are all kinds of little zones of error in recorded history. My Company makes use of those errors. If history can't be changed, it can be worked around. See?"

"Perfectly," Hearst replied. He leaned back in his chair and his voice was hard, those violets of sound transmuted to porphyry marble. "I'm convinced your people are on the level, Mr. Denham. Now. You go and tell them that twenty years is pretty much chickenfeed as far as I'm concerned. It won't do, not by a long way. I want nothing less than the same immortality you've got, you see? Permanent life. I always thought I could put it to good use and, now that you've shown me the future, I can see my work's cut out for me. I also want shares in your Company's stock. I want to be a player in this game."

"But—" I sat bolt upright in my chair. "Mr. Hearst! I can manage the shares of stock. But the immortality's impossible! You don't understand how it works. The immortality process can't be done on old men. We have to start with young mortals. I was only a little kid when I was recruited for the Company. Don't you see? Your body's too old and damaged to be kept running indefinitely."

"Who said I wanted immortality in this body?" said Hearst. "Why would I want to drive around forever in a rusted old Model T when I could have one of those shiny new modern cars? Your masters seem to be capable of darned near anything. I'm betting that there's a way to bring me back in a new body, and if there isn't a way now, I'll bet they can come up with one if they try. They're going to have to try, if they want my cooperation. Tell them that."

I opened my mouth to protest, and then I thought—why argue? Promise him anything. "O.K.," I agreed.

"Good," Hearst said, finishing his coffee. "Do you need a telephone to contact them? My switchboard can connect you anywhere in the world in a couple of minutes."

"Thanks, but we use something different," I told him. "It's back in my room and I don't think Jerome could find it. I'll try to have an answer for you by tomorrow morning, though."

He nodded. Reaching out his hand, he took up the silver bottle and considered it. "Is this the drug that made you what you are?" He looked at me. His dog looked up at him.

"Pretty much. Except my body's been altered to manufacture the stuff, so it pumps through me all the time," I explained. "I don't have to take it orally."

"But you'd have no objection to sampling a little, before I drank it?"

"Absolutely none," I said, and held out my empty coffee cup. Hearst lifted his eyebrows at that. He puzzled a moment over the bottlecap before figuring it out, and then poured about three ounces of Pineal Tribrantine Three cocktail into my cup. I drank it down, trying not to make a face.

It wasn't all PT3. There was some kind of fruit base, cranberry juice as far as I could tell, and a bunch of hormones and euphoriacs to make him feel great as well as healthy, and something to stimulate the production of telomerase. Beneficial definitely, but not an immortality potion by a long shot. He'd have to have custom-designed biomechanicals and prosthetic implants, to say nothing of years of training for eternity starting when he was about three. But why tell the guy?

And Hearst was looking young already, just watching me: wonderstruck, scared, and eager. When I didn't curl up and die, he poured the rest of the bottle's contents into his cup and drank it down, glancing furtively at his hidden camera.

"My," he said. "That tasted funny."

I nodded.

And of course he didn't die either, as the time passed in that grand room. He quizzed me about my personal life, wanted to hear about what it was like to live in the ancient world, and how many famous people I'd met. I told him all about Phoenician traders and Egyptian priests and Roman senators I'd known. After a while Hearst noticed he felt swell—I could tell by his expression—and he got up and put down the little dog and began to pace the room as we talked, not with the heavy cautious tread of the old man he was but with a light step, almost dancing.

"So I said to Apuleius, 'But that only leaves three fish, and anyway what do you want to do about the flute player—'" I was saying, when a door in the far corner opened and Marion stormed in.

"W-w-where *were* you?" she shouted. Marion stammered when she was tired or upset, and she was both now. "Thanks a lot for s-sneaking out like that and leaving me to t-t-talk to everybody. They're your guests too, y-you know!"

Hearst turned to stare at her, openmouthed. I really think he'd forgotten about Marion. I jumped up, looking apologetic.

"Whoops! Hey, Marion, it was my fault. I needed to ask his advice about something," I explained. She turned, surprised to see me.

"Joe?" she said.

"I'm sorry to take so long, dear," said Hearst, coming and putting his arms around her. "Your friend's a very interesting fellow." He was looking at her like a wolf looks at a lamb chop. "Did they like the picture?"

"N-n-no!" she said. "Half of 'em left before it was over. You'd think they'd s-stay to watch Bing C-Crosby."

If there's one thing I've learned over the millennia, it's when to exit a room.

"Thanks for the talk, Mr. Hearst," I said, grabbing my black case and heading for the elevator. "I'll see if I can't find that prospectus. Maybe you can look at it for me tomorrow."

"Maybe," Hearst murmured into Marion's neck. I was ready to crawl down the elevator cable like a monkey to get out of there, but fortunately the car was still on that floor, so I jumped in and rattled down through the house like Mephistopheles dropping through a trapdoor instead.

▲▼▲

It was dark when I emerged into the assembly hall, but as soon as the panel had closed after me light blazed up from the overhead fixtures. I blinked, looking around. Scanning revealed a camera mount, way up high, that I hadn't noticed before. I saluted it Roman style and hurried out into the night, over the Pompeiian floor. As soon as I had crossed the threshold, the lights blinked out behind me. More surveillance. How many faithful Jeromes did Hearst have, sitting patiently behind peepholes in tiny rooms?

The night air was chilly, fresh with the smell of orange and lemon blossoms. The stars looked close enough to fall on me. I wandered around between the statues for a while, wondering how the hell I was going to fool the master of this house into thinking the Company had agreed to his terms. Gee: for that matter, how was I going to break it to the Company that they'd underestimated William Randolph Hearst?

Well, it wasn't going to be the first time I'd had to be the bearer of bad news to Dr. Zeus. At last I gave it up and found my way back to my wing of the guest house.

There was a light on in the gorgeously gilded sitting room. Lewis was perched uncomfortably on the edge of a sixteenth-century chair. He looked guilty about something. Jumping to his feet as I came in, he said: "Joseph, we have a problem."

"We do, huh?" I looked him over wearily. All in the world I wanted right then was a hot shower and a few hours of shuteye. "What is it?"

"The, ah, Valentino script has been stolen," he said.

My priorities changed. I strode muttering to the phone and picked it up. After a moment a blurred voice answered.

"Jerome? How you doing, pal? Listen, I'd like some room service. Can I get a hot fudge sundae over here at La Casa del Sol? Heavy on the hot fudge?"

"Make that two," Lewis suggested. I looked daggers at him and went on:

"Make that two. No, no nuts. And if you've got any chocolate pudding or chocolate cake or some Hershey bars or anything, send those along, too. O.K? I'll make it worth your while, chum."

▲▼▲

"...so I just thought I'd have a last look at it before I went to bed, but when I opened the case it wasn't there," Lewis explained, licking his spoon.

"You scanned for thermoluminescence? Fingerprints?" I said, putting the sundae dish down with one hand and reaching for cake with the other.

"Of course I did. No fingerprints, and judging from the faintness of the thermoluminescence, whoever went through my things must have been wearing gloves," Lewis told me. "About all I could tell was that a mortal had been in my room, probably an hour to an hour and a half before I got there. Do you think it was one of the servants?"

"No, I don't. I know Mr. Hearst sent Jerome in here to get something out of my room, but I don't think the guy ducked into yours as an afterthought to go through your drawers. Anybody who swiped stuff from Mr. Hearst's guests wouldn't work here very long," I said. "If any guest had ever had something stolen, everybody in the Industry would know about it. Gossip travels fast in this town." I meant Hollywood, of course, not San Simeon.

"There's a first time for everything," Lewis said miserably.

"True. But I think our buddy Jerome has *faithful retainer* written all over him," I said, finishing the cake in about three bites.

"Then who else could have done it?" Lewis wondered, starting on a dish of pudding.

"Well, you're the Literary Specialist. Haven't you ever accessed any Agatha Christie novels?" I tossed the cake plate aside and pounced on a Hershey bar. "You know what we do next. Process of elimination. Who was where and when? I'll tell you this much, it wasn't me and it wasn't Big Daddy Hearst. I was with him from the moment we left the rest of you in the theater until Marion came up and I had to scram." I closed my eyes and sighed in bliss, as the Theobromos high finally kicked in.

"Well—" Lewis looked around distractedly, trying to think. "Then—it has to have been one of us who were in the theater watching *Going Hollywood*."

"Yeah. And Marion said about half the audience walked out before it was over," I said. "Did you walk out, Lewis?"

"No! I stayed until the end. I can't imagine why anybody left. I thought it was delightful," Lewis told me earnestly. "It had Bing Crosby in it, you know."

"You've got pudding on your chin. O.K; so you stayed through the movie." I said, realizing my wits weren't at their sharpest right now but determined to thrash this through. "And so did Marion. Who else was there when the house lights came up, Lewis?"

Lewis sucked in his lower lip, thinking hard through the Theobromine fog. "I'm replaying my visual transcript," he informed me. "Clark Gable is there. The younger Mr. Hearst and his friend are there. The unpleasant-looking fellows in the business suits are there. Connie's there."

"Garbo?"

"Mm—nope."

"The two silents guys? Charlie and Laurence?"

"No."

"What's his name, Jack from Paramount, is he there?"

"No, he isn't."

"What about the crazy lady with the dogs?"

"She's not there either." Lewis raised horrified eyes to me. "My gosh, it could have been any one of them." He remembered the pudding and dabbed at it with his handkerchief.

"Or the thief might have sneaked out, robbed your room and sneaked back in before the end of the picture," I told him.

"Oh, why complicate things?" he moaned. "What are we going to do?"

"Damned if I know tonight," I replied, struggling to my feet. "Tomorrow you're going to find out who took the Valentino script and get it back. I have other problems, O.K.?"

"What do you mean?"

"Mr. Hearst is upping the ante on the game. He's given me an ultimatum for Dr. Zeus," I explained.

"Wowie." Lewis looked appalled. "He thinks he can dictate terms to the Company?"

"He's doing it, isn't he?" I said, trudging off to my bedroom. "And guess who gets to deliver the messages both ways? Now you see why I was nervous? I knew this was going to happen."

"Well, cheer up," Lewis called after me. "Things can't go more wrong than this."

I switched on the light in my room, and found out just how much more wrong they could go.

Something exploded up from the bed at my face, a confusion of needle teeth and blaring sound. I was stoned, I was tired, I was confused, and so I just slapped it away as hard as I could, which with me being a cyborg and all was pretty hard. The thing flew across the room and hit the wall with a crunch. Then it dropped to the floor and didn't move, except for its legs kicking, but not much or for long.

Lewis was beside me immediately, staring. He put his handkerchief to his mouth and turned away, ashen-faced.

"Ye gods!" he said. "You've killed Tcho-Tcho!"

"Maybe I just stunned her?" I staggered over to see. Lewis staggered with me. We stood looking down at Tcho-Tcho.

"Nope," Lewis told me sadly, shaking his head.

"The Devil, and the Devil's dam, and the Devil's…insurance agent," I swore, groping backward until I found a chair to collapse in. "Now what do we do?" I averted my eyes from the nasty little corpse and my gaze fell on the several shreddy parts that were all that remained of my left tennis shoe. "Hey! Look what the damn thing did to my sneaker!"

"How did she get in here, anyway?" Lewis wrung his hands.

"So much for my playing tennis with anybody tomorrow," I snarled.

"But—but if she was in here long enough to chew up your shoe..." Lewis paused, eyes glazing over in difficult thought. "Oh, I wish I hadn't done that Theobromos. Isn't that the way it always is? Just when you think it's safe to relax and unwind a little—"

"Hey! This means Cartimandua Bryce took your Valentino script," I said, leaping to my feet and grabbing hold of the chair to steady myself. "See? The damn dog must have followed her in unbeknownst!"

"You're right." Lewis's eyes widened. "Except—well, no, not necessarily. She didn't have the dogs with her, don't you remember? They wouldn't behave at table. They had to be taken back to her room."

"So they did." I subsided into the chair once more. "Hell. If somebody was sneaking through the rooms, the dog might have got out and wandered around until it got in here, chewed up my shoe, and went to sleep on my bed."

"And that means—that means—" Lewis shook his head. "I'm too tired to think what that means. What are we going to do about the poor dog? I suppose we'll have to go tell Mrs. Bryce."

"Nothing doing," I snapped. "When I'm in the middle of a deal with Hearst? Hearst, who's fanatic about kindness to animals? Sorry about that, W.R., but I just brutally murdered a dear little chihuahua in La Casa del Sol. Thank God there aren't any surveillance cameras in here!"

"But we have to do something," Lewis protested. "We can't leave it here on the rug! Should we take it out and bury it?"

"No. There's bound to be a search when Mrs. Bryce notices it's gone," I said. "If they find the grave and dig it up, they'll know the mutt didn't die naturally, or why would somebody take the trouble to hide the body?"

"Unless we hid it somewhere it'd never be found?" Lewis suggested. "We could pitch it over the perimeter fence. Then, maybe the wild animals would remove the evidence!"

"I don't think zebras are carrion eaters, Lewis." I rubbed my temples wearily. "And I don't know about you, but in the condition I'm in, I don't think I'd get it over the fence on the first throw. All I'd need then would be for one of Hearst's surveillance cameras to pick me up in a spotlight, trying to stuff a dead chihuahua through a fence. Hey!" I brightened. "Hearst has a zoo up here. What if we shotput Tcho-Tcho into the lion's den?"

Lewis shuddered. "What if we missed?"

"To hell with this." I got up. "Dogs die all the time of natural causes."

So we wound up flitting through the starry night in hyperfunction, leaving no more than a blur on any cameras that might be recording our passage, and a pitiful little corpse materialized in what we hoped was a natural attitude of canine demise on the front steps of La Casa Grande. With any luck it would be stiff as a board by morning, which would make foul play harder to detect.

▲▼▲

Showered and somewhat sobered up, I opened the field credenza in my suitcase and crouched before it to tap out my report on its tiny keys.

WRH WILLING, HAD PT3 SAMPLE, BUT HOLDING OUT FOR MORE. TERMS: STOCK SHARES PLUS IMMORTALITY PROCESS. HAVE EXPLAINED IMPOSSIBILITY. REFUSES TO ACCEPT.

SUGGEST: LIE. DELIVER 18 YEARS PER HISTORICAL RECORD WITH PROMISE OF MORE, THEN RENEGOTIATE TERMS WITH HEIRS.

PLEASE ADVISE.

It didn't seem useful to tell anybody that the Valentino script was missing. Why worry the Company? After all, we must be going to find it and complete at least that part of the mission successfully, because history records that an antiques restorer will, on Christmas 20, 2326, at the height of the Old Hollywood Revival, find the script in a hidden compartment in a Spanish cabinet, once owned by W.R. Hearst but recently purchased by Dr. Zeus Incorporated. Provenance indisputably proven, it will then be auctioned off for an unbelievably huge sum, even allowing for twenty-fourth-century inflation. And history cannot be changed, can it?

Of course it can't.

I yawned pleasurably, preparing to shut the credenza down for the night, but it beeped to let me know a message was coming in. I scowled at it and leaned close to see what it said.

TERMS ACCEPTABLE. INFORM HEARST AND AT FIRST OPPORTUNITY PERFORM REPAIRS AND UPGRADE. QUINTILIUS WILL CONTACT WITH STOCK OPTIONS.

I read it through twice. Oh, O.K; the Company must mean they intended to follow my suggestion. I'd promise him the moon but give him the eighteen years decreed by history, and he wouldn't even be getting those if

I didn't do that repair work on his heart. What did they mean by *upgrade,* though? Eh! Details.

And I had no reason to feel lousy about lying to the old man. How many mortals even get to make it to eighty-eight, anyway? And when my stopgap measures finally failed, he'd close his eyes and die—like a lot of mortals—in happy expectation of eternal life after death. Of course, he'd get it in Heaven (if there is such a place) and not down here like he'd been promised, but he'd be in no position to sue me for breach of contract anyway.

I acknowledged the transmission and shut down at last. Yawning again, I crawled into my fabulous priceless antique Renaissance-era hand-carved gilded bed. The chihuahua hadn't peed on it. That was something, at least.

▲▼▲

I slept in next morning, though I knew Hearst preferred his guests to rise with the sun and do something healthy like ride five miles before breakfast. I figured he'd make an exception in my case. Besides, if the PT3 cocktail had delivered its usual kick he'd probably be staying in bed late himself, and so would Marion. I squinted up at the left-hand tower of La Casa Grande, making my way through the brilliant sunlight.

No dead dog in sight anywhere, as I hauled open the big front doors; Tcho-Tcho's passing must have been discovered without much commotion. Good. I walked through the cool and the gloom of the big house to the morning room at the other end, where sunlight poured in through French doors. There a buffet was set out with breakfast.

Lewis was there ahead of me, loading up on flapjacks. I heaped hash browns on my plate and, for the benefit of the mortals in various corners of the room, said brightly: "So, Lewis! Some swell room, huh? How'd you sleep?"

"Fine, thanks," he replied. *Other than a slight Theobromos hangover.* "But, you know, the saddest thing happened! One of Mrs. Bryce's little dogs got out in the night and died of exposure. The servants found it this morning."

"Gee, that's too bad." *Anybody suspect anything?*

No. "Yes, Mrs. Bryce is dreadfully upset." *I feel just awful.*

Hey, did you lure the damn mutt into my room? We've got worse things to worry about this morning. I helped myself to coffee and carried my plate out into the dining hall, sitting down at the long table. Lewis followed me.

Right, the Valentino script. Have you had any new ideas about who might have taken it?

No. I dug into my hash browns. *Has anybody else complained about anything missing from their rooms?*

No, nobody's said a word.

The thing is—nobody knew you had it with you, right? You didn't happen to mention that you were carrying around an autographed script for The Son Of the Sheik?

No, of course not! Lewis sipped his coffee, looking slightly affronted. *I've only been in this business for nearly two millennia.*

Maybe one of the guests was after Garbo or Gable, and got into your room by mistake? I turned nonchalantly to glance into the morning room at Gable. He was deeply immersed in the sports section of one of Mr. Hearst's papers.

Well, if it was an obsessive Garbo fan he'd have seen pretty quickly that he wasn't in a woman's room. Lewis put both elbows on the table in a manly sort of way. *So if it was one of the ladies after Gable—? Though it still doesn't explain why she'd steal the script.*

I glanced over at Connie, who was sitting in an easy chair balancing a plate of scrambled eggs on her knees as she ate. *Connie wouldn't have done it, and neither would Marion. I doubt it was the Hearst kid's popsy. That leaves Garbo and Mrs. Bryce, who left the movie early.*

But why would Garbo steal the script? Lewis drew his eyebrows together.

Why does Garbo do anything? I shrugged. Lewis looked around uneasily.

I can't see her rifling through my belongings, however. And that leaves Mrs. Bryce.

Yeah. Mrs. Bryce. Whose little dog appeared mysteriously in my bedroom.

I got up and crossed back into the morning room on the pretext of going for a coffee refill. Mrs. Bryce, clad in black pajamas, was sitting alone in a prominent chair, with Conqueror Worm greedily wolfing down Eggs Benedict from a plate on the floor. Mrs. Bryce was not eating. Her eyes were closed and her face turned up to the ceiling. I guess she was meditating, since she was doing the whole lotus position bit.

As I passed, Conqueror Worm left off eating long enough to raise his tiny head and snarl at me.

"I hope you will excuse him, Mr. Denham," said Mrs. Bryce without opening her eyes. "He's very protective of me just now."

"That's O.K., Mrs. Bryce," I said affably, but I kept well away from the dog. "Sorry to hear about your sad loss."

"Oh, Tcho-Tcho remains with us still," she said serenely. "She has merely ascended to the next astral plane. I just received a communication from her, in fact. She discarded her earthly body in order to accomplish her more important work."

"Gee, that's just great," I replied, and Gable looked up from his paper at me and rolled his eyes. I shrugged and poured myself more coffee. I still thought Mrs. Bryce was a phony on the make, but if she wanted to pretend Tcho-Tcho had passed on voluntarily instead of being swatted like a tennis ball, that was all right with me.

You think she might have done it, after all? Lewis wondered as I came back to the table. *She had sort of fixated on me, before Marion turned her on Garbo.*

Could be. I think she's too far off on another planet to be organized enough for cat burglary, though. And why would she steal the script and nothing else?

I can't imagine. What are we going to do? Lewis twisted the end of his paper napkin. *Should we report the theft to Mr. Hearst?*

Hell no. That'd queer my pitch. Some representatives of an all-powerful Company we'd look, wouldn't we, letting mortals steal stuff out of our rooms? No. Here's what you do: see if you can talk to the people who left the theater early, one by one. Just sort of engage them in casual conversation. Find out where each one of the suspects went, and see if you can cross-check their stories with others.

Lewis looked panicked. *But—I'm only a Literature Preservation Specialist. Isn't this interrogation sort of thing more in your line of work, as a Facilitator?*

Maybe, but right now I've got my hands full, I responded, just as the lord of the manor came striding into the room.

Mr. Hearst was wearing jodhpurs and boots, and was flushed with exertion. He hadn't gotten up late after all, but had been out on horseback surveying his domain, like one of the old Californio dons. He hit me with a triumphant look as he marched past, but didn't stop. Instead he went straight up to Mrs. Bryce's chair and took off his hat to address her. Conqueror Worm looked up and him and cowered, then ran to hide behind the chair.

"Ma'am, I was so sorry to hear about your little dog! I hope you'll do me the honor of picking out another from my kennels? I don't think we have any chihuahuas at present, but in my experience a puppy consoles you a good deal when you lose an old canine friend," he told her, with a lot more power and breath in his voice than he'd had last night. The PT3 was working, that much was certain.

Mrs. Bryce looked up from her meditation, startled. Smiling radiantly she rose to her feet.

"Why, Mr. Hearst, you are too kind," she replied. No malarkey about ascendance to astral planes with him, I noticed. He offered her his arm and they swept out through the French doors, with Conqueror Worm running after them desperately.

What happens when we've narrowed down the list of suspects? Lewis tugged at my attention.

Then we steal the script back, I told him.

But how? Lewis tore his paper napkin clean in half. *Even if we move fast enough to confuse the surveillance cameras in the halls—*

We'll figure something out, I replied, and then shushed him, because Marion came floating in.

Floating isn't much of an exaggeration, and there was no booze doing the levitation for her this morning. Marion Davies was one happy mortal. She spotted Connie and made straight for her. Connie looked up and offered a glass.

"I saved ya some arranch use, Marion," she said meaningfully. The orange juice was probably laced with gin. She and Marion were drinking buddies.

"Never mind that! C'mere," Marion told her, and they went over to whisper and giggle in a corner. Connie was looking incredulous.

And are you sure we can rule the servants out? Lewis persisted.

Maybe, I replied, and shushed him again, because Marion had noticed me and broken off her chat with Connie, her smile fading. She got up and approached me hesitantly.

"J-Joe? I need to ask you about something."

"Please, take my seat, Miss Davies." Lewis rose and pulled the chair out for her. "I was just going for a stroll."

"Gee, he's a gentleman, too," Marion said, giggling, but there was a little edge under her laughter. She sank down across from me, and waited until Lewis had taken his empty plate and departed before she said: "Did you— um—come up here to ask Pops for m-money?"

"Aw, hell, no," I said in my best regular guy voice. "I wouldn't do something like that, Marion."

"Well, I didn't really think so," she admitted, looking at the table and pushing a few grains of spilled salt around with her fingertip. "He doesn't pay blackmailers, you know. But—y-you've got a reputation as a man who knows a lot of secrets, and I just thought—if you'd used me to get up here to talk to him—" She looked at me with narrowed eyes. "That wouldn't be very nice."

"No, it wouldn't," I agreed. "And I swear I didn't come up here to do anything like that. Honest."

Marion just nodded. "The other thing I thought it might be," she went on, "was that you might be selling some kind of patent medicine. A lot of people know he's interested in longevity, and it looked like he'd been drinking something red out of his coffee cup, you see." Her mouth was hard. "He may be a millionaire and he's terribly smart, but people take advantage of him all the time."

"Not me," I said, and looked around as though I wanted to see who might be listening. I leaned across the table to speak close to her ear. "Listen, honey, the truth is—I really did need his advice about something. And he was kind enough to listen. But it's a private matter and believe me, *he's* not the one being blackmailed. See?"

"Oh!" She thought she saw. "Is it Mr. Mayer?"

"Why, no, not at all," I answered hurriedly, in a tone that implied exactly the opposite. Her face cleared.

"Gee, poor Mr. Mayer," she said. She knitted her brows. "So you didn't give W.R. any kind of…spring tonic or something?"

"Where would I get something like that?" I looked confused, as I would be if I were some low-level studio dick who handled crises for executives and had never heard of PT3.

"Yeah." Marion reached over and patted my hand. "I'm sorry. I just wanted to be sure."

"I don't blame you," I said, getting to my feet. "But please don't worry, O.K.?"

She had nothing to worry about, after all. Unlike me. I still had to talk to Mr. Hearst.

I strolled out through the grounds to look for him. He found me first, though, looming abruptly into my path.

"Mr. Denham." Hearst grinned at me. "I must commend you on that stuff. It works. Have you communicated with your people?"

"Yes, sir, I have," I assured him, keeping my voice firm and hearty.

"Good. Walk with me, will you? I'd like to hear what they had to say." He started off, and I had to run to fall into step beside him.

"Well—they've agreed to your terms. I must say I'm a little surprised." I laughed in an embarrassed kind of way. "I never thought it was possible to grant a mortal what you're asking for, but you know how it is—the rank and file aren't told everything, I guess."

"I suspected that was how it was," Hearst told me placidly. His little dachshund came racing to greet him. He scooped her up and she licked his face in excitement. "So. How is this to be arranged?"

"As far as the shares of stock go, there'll be another gentleman getting in touch with you pretty soon," I said. "I'm not sure what name he'll be using, but you'll know him. He'll mention my name, just as I mentioned Mr. Shaw's."

"Very good. And the other matter?"

Boy, the other matter. "I can give you a recipe for a tonic you'll drink on a daily basis," I said, improvising. "Your own staff can make it up."

"As simple as that?" He looked down at me sidelong, and so did the dog. "Is it the recipe for what I drank last night?"

"Oh, no, sir," I told him truthfully. "No, this will be something to prolong your life until the date history decrees that you *appear* to die. See? But it'll all be faked. One of our doctors will be there to pronounce you dead, and instead of being taken away to a mortuary, you'll go to one of our hospitals and be made immortal in a new body."

That part was a whopping big bald-faced lie, of course. I felt sweat beading on my forehead again, as we walked along through the garden and Hearst took his time about replying.

"It all sounds plausible," he said at last. "Though of course I've no way of knowing whether your people will keep their word. Have I?"

"You'd just have to trust us," I agreed. "But look at the way you feel right now! Isn't that proof enough?"

"It's persuasive," he replied, but left the sentence unfinished. We walked on. O.K, I needed to impress him again.

"See that pink rose?" I pointed to a bush about a hundred yards away, where one big bloom was just opening.

"I see it, Mr. Denham."

"Count to three, O.K.?"

"One," Hearst said, and I was holding the rose in front of his eyes. He went pale. Then he smiled again, wide and genuine. The little dog *whuffed* at me uncertainly.

"Pretty good," he said. "And can you 'put a girdle round about the earth in forty minutes'?"

"I might, if I could fly," I said. "No wings, though. You don't want wings too, do you, Mr. Hearst?"

He just laughed. "Not yet. I believe I'll go wash up now, and then head off to the tennis court. Do you play, Mr. Denham?"

"Gee, I just love tennis," I replied, "but, you know, I got all the way up here and discovered I'd only packed one tennis shoe."

"Oh, I'll have a pair brought out for you." Hearst looked down at my feet. "You're, what, about a size six?"

"Yes, sir," I said with a sinking feeling.

"They'll be waiting for you at the court," Hearst informed me. "Try to play down to my speed, will you?" He winked hugely and ambled away.

I was on my way back to the breakfast room with the vague hope of drinking a bottle of pancake syrup or something when I came upon Lewis. He was creeping along a garden path, keenly watching a flaxen-haired figure slumped on a marble bench amid the roses.

"What are you doing, Lewis?" I said.

"What does it look like I'm doing?" he replied *sotto voce*. "I'm stalking Garbo."

"All right…" I must have looked dubious, because he drew himself up indignantly.

"Can you think of any other way to start a casual conversation with her?" he demanded. "And I've worked out a way—" he looked around and transmitted the rest, *I've worked out quite a clever way of detecting the guilty party.*

Oh yeah?

You see, I just engage Garbo in conversation and then sort of artlessly mention that I didn't catch the end of Going Hollywood *because I had a dreadful migraine headache, so I went back to my room early, and would she tell me how it came out? And if she's not the thief, she'll just explain that she left early too and has no idea how it turned out. But! If she's the one who took the script, she'll know I'm lying, because she'll have been in my room and seen I wasn't there. And she'll be so disconcerted that her blood pressure will rise, her pulse will race, her pupils will dilate, and she'll display all the other physical manifestations that would show up on a polygraph if I happened to be using one! And then I'll know.*

Ingenious, I admitted. *Worked all the time for me, when I was an Inquisitor.*

Thank you. Lewis beamed.

Of course, first you have to get Garbo to talk to you.

Lewis nodded, looking determined. He resumed his ever-so-cautious advance on the Burning Icicle. I shrugged and went back to La Casa del Sol to change into tennis togs.

Playing tennis with W.R. Hearst called for every ounce of the guile and finesse that had made me a champion in the Black Legend All-Stars, believe me. I had to demonstrate all kinds of hyperfunction stunts a mortal wouldn't be able to do, like appearing on both sides of the net at once, just to impress him with my immortalness; and yet I had to avoid killing the old man with the ball, and—oh yeah—let him win somehow, too. I'd like to see Bill Tilden try it some time.

It was hell. Hearst seemed to think it was funny, at least; he was in a great mood watching me run around frantically while he kept his position in center court, solid as a tower. He returned my sissy serves with all the force of cannon fire. His dog watched from beyond the fence, standing up on her hind legs to bark suspiciously. She was *sure* there was something funny about me now. Thank God Gable put in an appearance after about an hour of this, and I was able to retire to the sidelines and wheeze, and swear a tougher hour was never wasted there. Hearst paused before his game long enough to make a brief call from a courtside phone. Two minutes later, there was a smiling servant offering me a glass of ice-cold ginger ale.

Gable didn't beat Hearst, either, and I think he actually tried. Clark wasn't much of a toady.

I begged off to go shower—dark hairy guys who play tennis in hyper-function tend to stink—and slipped out afterward to do some reconnoitering.

Tonight I planned to slip in some minor heart surgery on Hearst as he slept, to guarantee those eighteen years the Company was giving him. The trick was going to be getting in undetected. There had to be another way to reach Hearst's rooms besides his private elevator, but there were no stairs visible in any of the rooms I'd been in. How did the servants get up there?

Prowling slowly around the house and bouncing sonar waves off the outside, I found a couple of ways to ascend. The best, for my purposes, was a tiny spiral staircase that was entered from the east terrace. I could sneak through the garden, go straight up, find my way to Hearst's bedroom, and depart the same way once I'd fixed his heart. I could even wear the tennis shoes he'd so thoughtfully loaned me.

I was wandering in the direction of the Neptune pool when there was a hell of a racket from the shrubbery ahead of me. Conqueror Worm came darting out, yapping savagely. I was composed enough not to kick him as he raced up to my ankles. He growled and backed away when I bared my teeth at him in my friendliest fashion.

"Hi, doggie," I said. "Poor little guy, where's your mistress?"

A dark-veiled figure that had been standing perfectly still on the other side of the hedge decided to move, and Cartimandua Bryce walked forward calling out: "Conqueror! Oh! Conqueror, you mustn't challenge Mr. Denham." She came around the corner and saw me.

There was a pause. I think she was waiting for me to demand in astonishment how she'd known it was me, but instead I inquired: "Where's your new dog?"

"Still in Mr. Hearst's kennels," she replied, with a proud lift of her head. "Dear Mr. Hearst is having a traveling basket made for her. Such a kind man!"

"He's a swell guy, all right," I agreed.

"And just as generous in this life as in his others," she went on. "But, you know, being a Caesar taught him that. Ruling the Empire either ennobled a man or brought out his worst vices. Clearly, our host was one of those on whom the laurel crown conferred refinement. Of course, he is a very old soul."

"No kidding?"

"Oh, yes. He has come back many, many times. Many are the names he has borne: Pharaoh, and Caesar, and High King," Mrs. Bryce told me, in as matter-of-fact a voice as though she was listing football trophies. "He has much work to do on this plane of existence, you see. Of course, you may well wonder how I know these things."

"Gee, Mrs. Bryce, how do you know these things?" I asked, just to be nice.

"It is my gift," she said, with a little sad smile, and she sighed. "My gift and my curse, you see. The spirits whisper to me constantly. I described this terrible and wonderful affliction in my novel *Black Covenant,* which of course was based on one of my own past lives."

"I don't think I've read that one," I admitted.

"A sad tale, as so many of them are," she said, sighing again. "In the romantic Scottish Highlands of the thirteenth century, a beautiful young girl discovers she has an uncanny ability to sense both past and future lives of everyone she meets. Her gift brings inevitable doom upon her, of course. She finds her long-lost love, who was a soldier under Mark Antony when she was one of Cleopatra's handmaidens, and is now a gallant highwayman—I mean her lover, of course—and, sensing his inevitable death on the gallows, she dares to die with him."

"That's sad, all right." I agreed. "How'd it sell?"

"It was received by the discerning public with their customary sympathy," Mrs. Bryce replied.

"Is that the one they're doing a screenplay on?" I inquired.

"No," she said, looking me up and down. "That's *Passionate Girl,* the story of Mary, Queen of Scots, told from the unique perspective of her faithful terrier. I may yet persuade Miss Garbo to accept the lead role But,

Mr. Denham—I am sensing something about you. Wait. You work in the film industry—"

"Yeah, for Louis B. Mayer," I said.

"And yet—and yet—" She took a step back and shaded her eyes as she looked at me. "I sense more. You cast a long shadow, Mr. Denham. Why—you, too, are an old soul!"

"Oh yeah?" I said, scanning her critically for Crome's radiation. Was she one of those mortals with a fluky electromagnetic field? They tend to receive data other mortals don't get, the way some people pick up radio broadcasts with tooth fillings, because their personal field bleeds into the temporal wave. I couldn't sense anything out of the ordinary in Mrs. Bryce, though. Was she buttering me up because she thought I could talk Garbo into starring in *Passionate Girl* at MGM? Well, she didn't know much about my relationship with Greta.

"Yes—yes—I see you in the Mediterranean area—I see you dueling with a band of street youths—is it in Venice, in the time of the Doges? Yes. And before that...I see you in Egypt, Mr. Denham, during the captivity of the Israelites. You loved a girl...yet there was another man, an overseer..." Conqueror Worm might be able to tell there was something different about me, but his mistress was scoring a big metaphysical zero.

"Really?"

"Yes," she said, lowering her eyes from the oak tree above us, where she had apparently been reading all this stuff. "Do you experience disturbing visions, Mr. Denham? Dreams, perhaps of other places, other times?"

"Yeah, actually," I couldn't resist saying.

"Ah. If you desire to seek further—I may be able to help you." She came close and put her hand on my arm. Conqueror Worm prowled around her ankles, whining like a gnat. "I have some experience in, shall we say, arcane matters? It wouldn't be the first time I have assisted a questing soul in unraveling the mystery of his past lives. Indeed, you might almost call me a detective...for I sense you enjoy the works of Mr. Dashiell Hammett," she finished, with a smile as enigmatic as the Mona Lisa.

I smiled right back at her. Conqueror Worm put his tail between his legs and howled.

"Gosh, Mrs. Bryce, that's really amazing," I said, reaching for her hand and shaking it. "I do like detective fiction." And there was no way she could have known it unless she'd been in my room going through my drawers, where she'd have seen my well-worn copy of *The Maltese Falcon*. "Did your spirits tell you that?"

"Yes," she said modestly, and she was lying through her teeth, if her skin conductivity and pulse were any indication. Lewis was right, you see: we can tell as much as a polygraph about whether or not a mortal is truthful.

"You don't say?" I let go her hand. "Well, well. This has been really interesting, Mrs. Bryce. I've got to go see how my friend is doing now, but, you know, I'd really like to get together to talk with you about this again. Soon."

"Ah! Your friend with the fair hair," she said, and looked wise. Then she stepped in close and lowered her voice. "The haunted one. Tell me, Mr. Denham…is he…inclined to the worship of Apollo?"

For a moment I was struck speechless, because Lewis does go on sometimes about his Roman cultural identity, but then I realized that wasn't what Mrs. Bryce was implying.

"You mean, is he a homo?"

"Given to sins of the purple and crimson nature," she rephrased, nodding.

Now I knew she had the Valentino script, had seen Rudy's cute note and leaped to her own conclusion. "Uh…gee. I don't know. I guess he might be. Why?"

"There is a male spirit who will not rest until he communicates with your friend," Mrs. Bryce told me, breathing heavily. "A fiery soul with a great attachment to Mr. Kensington. One who has but recently passed over. A beautiful shade, upright as a smokeless flame."

The only question now was, why? One thing was certain: whether or not Lewis had ever danced the tango with Rudolph Valentino, Mrs. Bryce sure wished she had. Was she planning some stunt to impress the hell out of all these movie people, using her magic powers to reveal the script's whereabouts if Lewis reported it missing?

"I wonder who it is?" I said. "I'll tell him about it. Of course, you know, he might be kind of embarrassed—"

"But of course." She waved gracefully, as though dismissing all philistine considerations of closets. "If he will speak to me privately, I can do him a great service."

"O.K., Mrs. Bryce," I said, winking, and we went our separate ways through the garden.

I caught up with Lewis in the long pergola, tottering along between the kumquat trees. His tie was askew, his hair was standing on end, and his eyes shone like a couple of blue klieg lights.

"The most incredible thing just happened to me," he said.

"How'd you make out with Garbo?" I inquired, and then my jaw dropped, because he drew himself up and said, with an effort at dignity:

"I'll thank you not to speculate on a lady's private affairs."

"Oh, for crying out loud!" I hoped he'd had the sense to stay out of the range of the surveillance cameras.

"But I can tell you this much," he said, as his silly grin burst through again, "she absolutely did not steal my Valentino script."

"Yeah, I know," I replied. "Cartimandua Bryce took it after all."

"She—Really?" Lewis focused with difficulty. "However did you find out?"

"We were talking just now and she gave the game away." I explained. "Oldest trick in the book, for fake psychics: snoop through people's belongings in secret so you know little details about them you couldn't have known otherwise, then pull 'em out in conversation and wow everybody with your mystical abilities.

"What do you want to bet that's what she was doing when she sneaked out of the theater? She must have used the time to case people's rooms. That's how the damn dog got in our suite. It must have followed her somehow and gotten left behind."

"How sordid," Lewis said. "How are we going to get it back, then?"

"We'll think of a way." I said. "I have a feeling she'll approach you herself, anyhow. She's dying to corner you and give you a big wet kiss from the ghost of Rudolph Valentino, whom she thinks is your passionate dead boyfriend. You just play along."

Lewis winced. "That's revolting."

I shrugged. "So long as you get the script back, who cares what she thinks?"

"I care," Lewis protested. "I have a reputation to think about!"

"Like the opinions of a bunch of mortals are going to matter in a hundred years!" I said. "Anyway, I'll bet you've had to do more embarrassing things in the Company's service. I know I have."

"Such as?" Lewis demanded sullenly.

"Such as I don't care to discuss just at the present time," I told him, flouncing away with a grin. He grabbed a pomegranate and hurled it at me, but I winked out and reappeared a few yards off, laughing. The lunch bell rang.

▲▼▲

I don't know what Lewis did with the rest of his afternoon, but I suspect he spent it hiding. Myself, I took things easy; napped in the sunlight, went swimming in the Roman pool, and relaxed in the guest library with a good book. By the time we gathered in the assembly hall for cocktail hour again, I was refreshed and ready for a long night's work.

The gathering was a lot more fun now that I wasn't so nervous about Mr. Hearst. Connie got out a Parcheesi game and we sat down to play with Charlie and Laurence. The Hearst kid and his girlfriend took over one of the pianos and played amateurish duets. Mrs. Bryce made a sweeping entrance and backed Gable into a corner, trying out her finder-of-past-lives routine on him. Marion circulated for a while, before getting into a serious discussion of real estate investments with Jack from Paramount. Mr. Hearst came down in the elevator and was promptly surrounded by his executives, who wanted to discuss business. Garbo appeared late, smiling to herself as she wandered over to the other piano and picked out tunes with one finger.

Lewis skulked in at the last moment, just as we were all getting up to go to dinner, and tried to look as though he'd been there all along. The ladies went in first. As she passed him, Garbo reached out and tousled his hair, though she didn't say a word.

The rest of us—Mr. Hearst included—gaped at Lewis. He just straightened up, threw his shoulders back, and swaggered into the dining hall after the ladies.

My place card was immediately at Mr. Hearst's right, and Lewis was seated on the other side of me. It didn't get better than this. I looked nearly as smug as Lewis as I sat down with my loaded plate. Cartimandua Bryce had been given the other place of honor, though, at Marion's right, I guess as a further consolation prize for the loss of Tcho-Tcho. Conqueror Worm was allowed to stay in her lap through the meal this time. He took one look at me and cringed down meek as a lamb, only lifting his muzzle for the tidbits Mrs. Bryce fed him.

She held forth on the subject of reincarnation as we dined, with Marion drawing her out and throwing the rest of us an occasional broad wink, though not when Hearst was looking. He had very strict ideas about courtesy toward guests, even if he clearly thought she was a crackpot.

"So what you're saying is, we just go on and on through history, the same people coming back time after time?" Marion inquired.

"Not all of us," Mrs. Bryce admitted. "Some, I think, are weaker souls and fade after the first thundering torrent of life has finished with them. They are like those who retire from the ball after but one dance, too weary to respond any longer to the fierce call of life's music."

"They just soita go ova to da punchbowl and stay there, huh?" said Connie.

"In a sense," Mrs. Bryce told her, graciously ignoring her teasing tone. "The punchbowl of Lethe, if you will; and there they imbibe forgetfulness and remain. Ah, but the stronger souls plunge back headlong into the maelstrom of mortal passions!"

"Well, but what about going to Heaven and all that stuff?" Marion wanted to know. "Don't we ever get to do that?"

"Oh, undoubtedly," Mrs. Bryce replied, "for there are higher astral planes beyond this mere terrestrial one we inhabit. The truly great souls ascend there in time, as that is their true home; but even they yield to the impulse to assume flesh and descend to the mundane realms again, especially if they have important work to do here." She inclined across the table to Hearst. "As I feel *you* have often done, dear Mr. Hearst."

"Well, I plan on coming back after this life, anyhow," he replied with a smile, and nudged me under the table. I nearly dropped my fork.

"I don't know that I'd want to," said Marion a little crossly. "My g-goodness, I think I'd rather have a nice rest afterwards, and not come back and have to go fighting through the whole darned business all over again."

Hearst lifted his head and regarded her for a long moment.

"Wouldn't you, dear?" he said.

"N-no," Marion insisted, and laughed. "It'd be great to have some peace and quiet for a change."

Mrs. Bryce just nodded, as though to show that proved her point. Hearst looked down at his plate and didn't say anything else for the moment.

"But anyway, Mrs. Bryce," Marion went on in a brighter voice, "who else do you think's an old soul? What about the world leaders right now?"

"Chancellor Hitler, certainly," Mrs. Bryce informed us. "One has only to look at the immense dynamism of the man! This, surely, was a Teutonic Knight, or perhaps one of the barbarian chieftains who defied Caesar."

"Unsuccessfully," said Hearst in a dry little voice.

"Yes, but to comprehend reincarnation is to see history in its true light," Mrs. Bryce explained. "Over the centuries his star has risen inexorably, and will continue to rise. He is a man with true purpose."

"You don't feel that way about Franklin Delano Roosevelt, do you?" Hearst inquired.

"Roosevelt strives," said Mrs. Bryce noncommittally. "But I think his is yet a young soul, blundering perhaps as it finds its way."

"I think he's an insincere bozo, personally," Hearst said.

"Unlike Mussolini! Now there is another man who understands historical destiny, to such an extent one knows he has retained the experience of his past lives."

"I'm afraid I don't think much of dictators," said Hearst, in that castle where his word was law. Mrs. Bryce's eyes widened with the consciousness of her misstep.

"No, for your centuries—perhaps even eons—have given you the wisdom to see that dictatorship is a crude substitute for enlightened rule," she said.

"By which you mean good old American democracy?" he inquired. Wow, Mrs. Bryce was sweating. I have to admit it felt good to sit back and watch it happen to somebody else for a change.

"Well, of course she does," Marion said. "Now, I've had enough of all this history talk, Pops."

"I wanna know more about who *we* all were in our past lives, anyway," said Connie. Mrs. Bryce joined in the general laughter then, shrill with relief.

"Well, as I was saying earlier to Mr. Gable—I feel certain he was Mark Antony."

All eyes were on Clark at this pronouncement. He turned beet red but smiled wryly.

"I never argue with a lady," he said. "Maybe I was, at that."

"Oh, beyond question you were, Mr. Gable," said Mrs. Bryce. "For I myself was one of Cleopatra's maidens-in-waiting, and I recognized you the moment I saw you."

Must be a script for *Black Covenant* in development, too.

There were chuckles up and down the table. "Whaddaya do to find out about odda people?" Connie persisted. "Do ya use one of dose Ouija boards or something?"

"A crude parlor game," Mrs. Bryce said. "In my opinion. No, the best way to delve into the secrets of the past is to speak directly to those who are themselves beyond the flow of time."

"Ya mean, have a seance?" Connie looked intrigued. Marion's eyes lit up.

"That'd be fun, wouldn't it? Jeepers, we've got the perfect setting, too, with all this old stuff around!"

"Now—I don't know—" said Hearst, but Marion had the bit in her teeth.

"Oh, come on, it can't hurt anybody. Are you all done eating? What do you say, kids?"

"Aren't you supposed to have a round table?" asked Jack doubtfully.

"Not necessarily," Mrs. Bryce told him. "This very table will do, if we clear away dinner and turn out the lights."

There was a scramble to do as she suggested. Hearst turned to look at me sheepishly, and then I guess the humor of it got to him: an immortal being sitting in on a seance. He pressed his lips together to keep from grinning. I shrugged, looking wise and ironic.

Marion came running back from the kitchen and took her place at table. "O.K.," she yelled to the butler, and he flicked an unseen switch. The dining hall was plunged into darkness.

"Whadda we do now?" Connie asked breathlessly.

"Consider the utter darkness and the awful chill for a moment," replied Mrs. Bryce in somber tones. "Think of the grave, if you are tempted to mock our proceedings. And now, if you are all willing to show a proper respect for the spirits—link hands, please."

There was a creaking and rustling as we obeyed her. I felt Hearst's big right hand enclose my left one. Lewis took my other hand. *Good Lord, it's dark in here,* he transmitted.

So watch by infrared, I told him. I switched it on myself; the place looked really lurid then, but I had a suspicion about what was going to happen and I wanted to be prepared.

"Spirits of the unseen world," intoned Mrs. Bryce. "Ascended ones! Pause in your eternal meditations and heed our petition. We seek enlightenment! Ah, yes, I begin to feel the vibrations—there is one who approaches us. Can it be? But yes, it is our dear friend Tcho-Tcho! Freed from her disguise of earthly flesh, she once again parts the veil between the worlds. Tcho-Tcho, I sense your urgency. What have you to tell us, dear friend? Speak!"

I think most of the people in the room anticipated some prankster barking at that point, but oddly enough nobody did, and in the strained moment of silence that followed Mrs. Bryce let her head sag forward. Then, slowly, she raised it again, and tilted it way back. She gasped a couple of times and then began to moan in a tiny falsetto voice, incoherent sounds as though she were trying to form words.

"*Woooooo,*" she wailed softly. "*Woooo woo woo woo! Woo woooo!*"

There were vibrations then, all right, from fourteen people trying to hold in their giggles. Mrs. Bryce tossed her head from side to side.

"*Wooooo,*" she went on, and Conqueror Worm sat up in her lap and pointed his snout at the ceiling and began to talk along with her in that way that dogs will, sort of *wou-wou, wou-wou wou,* and beside me Hearst was shaking with silent laughter. Mrs. Bryce must have sensed she was losing her audience, because the woo-woos abruptly began to form into distinct words:

"*I have come back,*" she said. "*I have returned from the vale of felicity because I have unfinished business here. Creatures of the lower plane, there are spirits waiting with me who would communicate with you. Cast aside all ignorant fear. Listen for them!*"

After another moment of silence Marion said, in a strangling kind of voice:

"Um—we were just wondering—can you tell us who any of us were in our past lives?"

"*Yes...*" Mrs. Bryce appeared to be listening hard. "*There is one...she was born on the nineteenth day of April.*"

Connie sat up straight and peered through the darkness in Mrs. Bryce's direction. "Why, dat's my boithday!" she said in a stage whisper.

"*Yes...I see her in Babylon, Babylon that is fallen...yea, truly she lived in Babylon, queen of cities all, and carried roses to lay before Ishtar's altar.*"

"Jeez, can ya beat it?" Connie exclaimed. "I musta been a priestess or something."

"*Pass on now...I see a man, hard and brutal...he labors with his hands. He stands before towers that point at heaven...black gold pours forth. He has been too harsh. He repents...he begs forgiveness...*"

I could see Gable gritting his teeth so hard the muscles in his jaws stood out. His eyes were furious. I wondered if she'd seen a photograph of his father in his luggage. Or had Mrs. Bryce scooped this particular bit of biographical detail out of a movie magazine?

Anyway he stubbornly refused to take the bait, and after a prolonged silence the quavery voice continued:

"*Pass on, pass on...There is one here who has sailed the mighty oceans. I see him in a white cap...*"

There was an indrawn breath from one of Hearst's executives. Somebody who enjoyed yachting?

"*Yet he has sailed the seven seas in another life...I see him kneeling before a great queen, presenting her with all the splendor of the Spanish fleet...this entity bore the name of Francis Drake.*"

Rapacious little pirate turned cutthroat executive? Hey, it could happen.

"*Pass on now...*" I could see Mrs. Bryce turn her head slightly and peer in Lewis's direction through half-closed eyes. "*Oh, there is an urgent mes-*

sage…there is one here who pleads to speak…this spirit with his dark and smoldering gaze…he begs to be acknowledged without shame, for no true passion is shameful…he seeks his other self."

Yikes! transmitted Lewis, horrified.

O.K. She wanted to convince us Rudolph Valentino was trying to say something? He was going to say something, all right. I didn't care whether Lewis *or* Rudy were straight or gay or swung both ways, but this was just too mean-spirited.

I pulled my right hand free from Lewis's and wriggled the left one loose from Hearst's. He turned his head in my direction and I felt a certain speculative amusement from him, but he said nothing to stop me.

So here's what Hearst's surveillance cameras and Dictaphones recorded next: a blur moving through the darkness and a loud crash, as of cymbals. Tcho-Tcho's voice broke off with a little scream.

Next there was a man's voice speaking out of the darkness, but from way high up in the air where no mortal could possibly be—like on the tiny ledge above the wall of choir stalls. If you'd ever heard Valentino speak (like I had, for instance) you'd swear it was him yelling in a rage: "*I am weary of lies! There is a thief here, and if what has been stolen is not returned tonight, the djinni of the desert will avenge. The punishing spirits of the afterlife will pursue! Do you DARE to cross me?*"

Then there was a hiss and a faint smell of sulfur, and gasps and little shrieks from the assembled company as an apparition appeared briefly in the air: Valentino's features, and who could mistake them? His mouth was grim, his eyes hooded with stern determination, just the same expression as Sheik Ahmed had worn advancing on Vilma Banky. Worse still, they were eerily pallid against a scarlet shadow. Somebody screamed, really screamed in terror.

The image vanished, there was another crash, and then a confused moment in which the servants ran in shouting and the lights were turned on.

Everybody was sitting where they had been when the lights had gone out, including me. Down at the end of the table, though, where nobody was sitting, one of Mr. Hearst's collection of eighteenth-century silver platters was spinning around like a phonograph record.

Everyone stared at it, terrified, and the only noise in that cavernous place was the slight rattling as the thing spun slowly to a stop.

"Wow," said the Hearst kid in awe. His father turned slowly to look at me. I met his eyes and pulled out a handkerchief. I was sweating again, but you would be, too, you know? And I used the gesture to drop the burnt-out match I had palmed.

"What the hell's going on?" said Gable, getting to his feet. He stalked down the table to the platter and halted, staring at it.

"What is it?" said Jack.

Gable reached out cautiously and lifted the platter in his hands. He tilted it up so everybody could see. There was a likeness of Valentino smeared on the silver, in some red substance.

"Jeez!" screamed Connie.

"What *is* that stuff?" said Laurence. "Is it blood?"

"Is it ectoplasm?" demanded one of the executives.

Gable peered at it closely.

"It's ketchup," he announced. "Aw, for Christ's sake."

Everyone's gaze was promptly riveted on the ketchup bottle just to Mr. Hearst's right. Hard as they stared at it, I don't think anybody noticed that it was five inches further to his right than it had been when the lights went out.

Or maybe Mr. Hearst noticed. He pressed his napkin to his mouth and began to shiver like a volcano about to explode, squeezing his eyes shut as tears ran down.

"P-P-Pops!" Marion practically climbed over the table to him, thinking he was having a heart attack.

"I'm O.K.—" He put out a hand to her, gulping for breath, and she realized he was laughing. That broke the tension. There were nervous guffaws and titters from everyone in the room except Cartimandua Bryce, who was pale and silent at her place. Conqueror Worm was still crouched down in her lap, trembling, trying to be The Little Dog Who Wasn't There.

"Gee, that was some neat trick somebody pulled off!" said young Hearst.

Mrs. Bryce drew a deep breath and rose to her feet, clutching Conqueror Worm.

"Or—was it?" she said composedly. She swept the room with a glance. "If anyone here has angered the spirit of Rudolph Valentino, I leave it to his or her discretion to make amends as swiftly as possible. Mr. Hearst? This experience has taken much of the life force from me. I must rest. I trust you'll excuse me?"

"Sure," wheezed Hearst, waving her away.

She made a proudly dignified exit. I glanced over at Lewis, who stared back at me with wide eyes.

Nice work, he transmitted. I grinned at him.

I wouldn't go off to your room too early, I advised. *Give her time to put the script back.*

O.K.

"Well, I don't know about the rest of you," Hearst said at last, sighing, "but I'm ready for some ice cream, after that."

So we had ice cream and then went in to watch the movie, which was *Dinner at Eight.* Everybody stayed through to the end. I thought it was a swell story.

▲▼▲

Lewis and I walked back to La Casa del Sol afterwards, scanning carefully, but nobody was lurking along the paths. No horrible little dog leaped out at me when I turned on the light in my room, either.

"It's here," I heard Lewis crowing.

"The script? Safe and sound?"

"Every page!" Lewis appeared in my doorway, clutching it to his chest. "Thank God. I think I'll sleep with it under my pillow tonight."

"And dream of Rudy?" I said, leering.

"Oh, shut up." He pursed his lips and went off to his room.

I relaxed on my bed while I listened to him changing into his pajamas, brushing his teeth, gargling and all the stuff even immortals have to do before bedtime. He climbed into bed and turned out the light, and maybe he dreamed about Rudy, or even Garbo. I monitored his brainwaves until I was sure he slept deeply enough. Time for the stuff he didn't need to know about.

I changed into dark clothes and laced up the tennis shoes Hearst had loaned me. Opening my black case, I slid out its false bottom and withdrew the sealed prepackaged medical kit I'd been issued from the Company HQ in Hollywood before coming up here. With it was a matchbox-sized Hush Field Unit.

I stuck the Hush Unit in my pocket and slid the medical kit into my shirt. Then I slipped outside, and raced through the gardens of La Cuesta Encantada faster than Robin Goodfellow, or even Evar Swanson, could have done it.

The only time I had to pause was at the doorway on the east terrace, when it took me a few seconds to disable the alarm and pick the lock; then I was racing round and round up the staircase, and so into Hearst's private rooms.

I had the Hush Field Unit activated before I came anywhere near him, and it was a good thing. There was still a light on in his bedroom. I tiptoed in warily all the same, hoping Marion wasn't there.

She wasn't. She slept soundly in her own room on the other end of the suite. I still froze when I entered Hearst's room, though, because Marion gazed serenely down at me from her life-sized nude portrait on the wall. I looked around. She kept pretty strange company: portraits of Hearst's mother and father hung there too, as well as several priceless paintings of the Madonna and Child. I wondered briefly what the pictures might have to say to one another, if they could talk.

Hearst was slumped unconscious in the big armchair next to his telephone. Thank God he hadn't been using it when the Hush Field had gone on, or there'd be a phone off the hook and a hysterical night operator sending out an alarm now. He'd only been working late, composing an editorial by the look of it, in a strong confident scrawl on a lined pad. His dachshund was curled up at his feet, snoring. I set it aside gently and, like an ant picking up a dead beetle, lifted Hearst onto his canopied bed. Then I turned on both lamps, stripped off Hearst's shirt and took out the medical kit.

The seal hissed as I broke it, and I peeled back the film to reveal...

The wrong medical kit.

I stared into it, horrified. What was all this stuff? This wasn't what I needed to do routine heart repair on a mortal! This was one of our own kits, the kind the Base HQ repair facilities stocked. I staggered backward and collapsed into Hearst's comfy chair. Boy, oh boy, did I want some Pep-O-Mints right then.

I sat there a minute, hearing my own heart pounding in that big quiet house.

All right, I told myself, talented improvisation is your forte, isn't it? You've done emergency surgery with less, haven't you? Sure you have. Hell, you've used flint knives and bronze mirrors and leeches and...there's bound to be something in that kit you can use.

I got on my feet and poked through it. O.K., here were some sterile Scrubbie Towelettes. I cleansed the area where I'd be making my incision. And here were some sterile gloves, great; I pulled those on. A scalpel. So far, so good. And a hemostim, and a skin plasterer, yeah, I could do this! And here was a bone laser. This was going to work out after all.

I gave Hearst a shot of metabolic depressant, opened him up, and set to work, telling myself that somebody was going to be in big trouble when I made my report to Dr. Zeus...

Hearst's ribs looked funny.

There was a thickening of bone where I was having to use the laser, in just the places I needed to make my cuts. Old trauma? Damned old. Funny-looking.

His heart looked funny too. Of course, I expected that. Hearst had a heart defect, after all. Still, I didn't expect the microscopic wired chip attached to one chamber's wall.

I could actually taste those Pep-O-Mints now. My body was simulating the sensation to comfort me, a defense against the really amazing stress I was experiencing.

I glanced over casually at the medical kit and observed that there was an almost exact duplicate of the chip, but bigger, waiting for me in a shaped compartment. So were a bunch of other little implants.

Repairs and upgrade. This was the right kit after all.

I set down my scalpel, peeled off my gloves, took out my chronophase, and opened its back. I removed a small component. Turning to Hearst's phone, I clamped the component to its wire and picked up the receiver. I heard weird noises and then a smooth voice informing me I had reached Hollywood HQ.

"This is Facilitator Joseph and *what the hell is going on here?*" I demanded.

"Downloading file," the voice replied sweetly.

I went rigid as the encoded signal came tootling through the line to me. Behind my eyes flashed the bright images: I was getting a mission report, filed in 1862, by a Facilitator Jabesh…assigned to monitor a young lady who was a passenger on a steamer bound from New York to the Isthmus of Panama, and from there to San Francisco. She was a recent bride, traveling with her much older husband. She was two months pregnant. I saw the pretty girl in pink, I saw the rolling seas, I saw the ladies in their bustles and the top-hatted guys with muttonchop whiskers.

The girl was very ill. Ordinary morning sickness made worse by *mal de mer*? Jabesh—there, man in black, tipping his stovepipe hat to her—posing as a kindly doctor, attended her daily. One morning she fainted in her cabin and her husband pulled Jabesh in off the deck to examine her. Jabesh sent him for a walk around the ship and prepared to perform a standard obstetric examination on the unconscious girl.

Jabesh's horrified face: almost into his hands she miscarried a severely damaged embryo. It was not viable. His frantic communication, next, on the credenza concealed in his doctor's bag. The response: PRIORITY GOLD, with an authorization backed up by Executive Facilitator General Aegeus. The child was to live, at all costs. He was to make it viable. Why? Was the

Company making certain that history happened *as written* again? But how could he save this child? With what? Where did he even start?

He downloaded family records. Here was an account of the husband having had a brother "rendered helpless" by an unspecified disease and dying young. Some lethal recessive? Nobody could make this poor little lump of flesh live! But the Company had issued a Priority Gold.

I saw the primitive stateroom, the basin of bloody water, Jabesh's shirtsleeves rolled up, his desperation. The Priority Gold blinking away at him from his credenza screen.

We're not bound by the laws of mortals, but we do have our own laws. Rules that are never broken under any circumstances, regulations that carry terrible penalties if they're not adhered to. We can be punished with memory effacement, or worse.

Unless we're obeying a Priority Gold. Or so rumor has it.

Jabesh repaired the thing, got its heart-bud beating again. It wasn't enough. Panicked, he pulled out a few special items from his bag (I had just seen one of them) and did something flagrantly illegal: he did a limited augmentation on the embryo. Still not enough.

So that was when he rolled the dice, took the chance. He did something even more flagrantly illegal.

He mended what was broken on that twisted helix of genetic material. He did it with an old standard issue chromosome patcher, the kind found in any operative's field repair kit. They were never intended to be used on mortals, let alone two-month-old embryos, but Jabesh didn't know what else to do. He set it on automatic and by the time he realized what it was doing, he was too late to stop the process.

It redesigned the baby's genotype. It surveyed the damage, analyzed what was lacking, and filled in the gaps with material from its own preloaded DNA arsenal. It plugged healthy chromosome sequences into the mess like deluxe Tinkertoy units until it had an organism with optimal chances for survival. That was what it was programmed to do, after all. But it had never had to replace so much in a subject, never had to dig so deeply into its arsenal for material, and some of the DNA in there was very old and very strange indeed. Those kits were first designed a hundred thousand years ago, after all, when *Homo sapiens* hadn't quite homogenized.

By the time the patcher had finished its work, the embryo had been transformed into a healthy hybrid of a kind that hadn't been born in fifty millennia, with utterly unknown potential.

I could see Jabesh managing to reimplant the thing and get the girl all tidy by the time her gruff husband came back. He was telling the husband she needed to stay off her feet and rest, he was telling him that nothing in life is certain, and tipping his tall hat, good day, sir, and staggering off to sit shaking in his cabin, drinking bourbon whiskey straight out of a case bottle without the least effect.

He knew what he'd done. But Jabesh had obeyed the Priority Gold.

I saw him waiting, afraid of what might happen. Nothing did, except that the weeks passed, and the girl lost her pallor and became well. I could see her crossing at Panama—there was the green jungle, there was the now visibly pregnant mother sidesaddle on a mule—and here she was disembarking at San Francisco.

It was months before Jabesh could summon the courage to pay a call on her. Here he was being shown into the parlor, hat in hand. Nothing to see but a young mother dandling her adored boy. Madonna and child, to the life. One laughing baby looks just like another, right? So who'd ever know what Jabesh had done? And here was Jabesh taking his leave, smiling, and turning to slink away into some dark corner of history.

The funny thing was, what Jabesh had done wasn't even against the mortals' law. Yet. It wouldn't become illegal until the year 2093, because mortals wouldn't understand the consequences of genetic engineering until then.

But I understood. And now I knew why I'd wanted to turn tail and run the moment I'd laid eyes on William Randolph Hearst, just as certain dogs cowered at the sight of me.

The last images flitted before my eyes, the baby growing into the tall youth with something now subtly different about him, that unearthly voice, that indefinable quality of endlessly prolonged childhood that would worry his parents. Then! Downloaded directly into my skull before I could even flinch, the flashing letters: PRIORITY GOLD. *REPAIR AND UPGRADE.* Authorized by Facilitator General Aegeus, that same big shot who'd set up Jabesh.

I was trapped. I had been given the order.

So what could I do? I hung up the phone, took back my adapter component, pulled on a fresh pair of gloves, and took up my scalpel again.

How bad could it be, after all? I was coming in at the end of the story, anyway. Eighteen more years weren't so much, even if Hearst never should have existed in the first place. Any weird genetic stuff he might have passed on to his sons seemed to have switched off in them. And, looking at the big picture, had he really done any harm? He was even a decent guy, in his way.

Too much money, enthusiasm, appetite for life, an iron will, and unshakable self-assurance…and a mind able to think in more dimensions than a human mind should. O.K., so it was a formula for disaster.

I knew, because I remembered certain men with just that kind of zeal and ability. They had been useful to the Company, back in the old days before history began, until they had begun to argue with Company policy. Then the Company had had a problem on its hands, because the big guys were immortals. Then the Company had had to fight dirty, and take steps to see there would never be dissension in its ranks again.

But that had been a long time ago, and right now I had a Priority Gold to deal with, so I told myself Hearst was human enough. He was born of woman, wasn't he? There was her picture on the wall, right across from Marion's. And he had but a little time to live.

I replaced the old tired implants with the fresh new ones and did a repair job on his heart that ought to last the required time. Then I closed him up and did the cosmetic work, and got his shirt back on his old body.

I set him back in his chair, returned the editorial he had been writing to his lap, set the dog at his feet again, gathered up my stuff, turned off the opposite lamp, and looked around to see if I'd forgotten anything. Nope. In an hour or so his heart would begin beating again and he'd be just fine, at least for a few more years.

"Live forever, oh king," I told him sardonically, and then I fled, switching off the hush field as I went.

But my words echoed a little too loudly as I ran through his palace gardens, under the horrified stars.

▲▼▲

Hearst watched, intrigued, as Lewis slid the Valentino script behind the panel in the antique cabinet. With expert fingers Lewis worked the panel back into its grooves, rocking and sliding it gently, until there was a click and it settled into the place it would occupy for the next four centuries.

"And to think, the next man to see that thing won't even be born for years and years," Hearst said in awe. He closed the front of the cabinet and locked it. As he dropped the key in his waistcoat pocket, he looked at Lewis speculatively.

"I suppose you're an immortal too, Mr. Kensington?" he inquired.

"Well—yes, sir, I am," Lewis admitted.

"Holy Moses. And how old are you?"

"Not quite eighteen hundred and thirty, sir."

"Not quite! Why, you're no more than a baby, compared to Mr. Denham here, are you?" Hearst chuckled in an avuncular sort of way. "And have *you* known many famous people?"

"Er—I knew Saint Patrick," Lewis offered. "And a lot of obscure English novelists."

"Well, isn't that nice?" Mr. Hearst smiled down at him and patted him on the shoulder. "And now you can tell people you've known Greta Garbo, too."

"Yes, sir," said Lewis, and then his mouth fell open, but Hearst had already turned to me, rustling the slip of paper I had given him.

"And you say my kitchen staff can mix this stuff up, Mr. Denham?"

"Yeah. If you have any trouble finding all the ingredients, I've included the name of a guy in Chinatown who can send you seeds and plants mail-order," I told him.

"Very good," he said, nodding. "Well, I'm sorry you boys can't stay longer, but I know what those studio schedules are like. I imagine we'll run into one another again, though, don't you?"

He smiled, and Lewis and I sort of backed out of his presence salaaming.

Neither one of us said much on the way down the mountain, through all those hairpin turns and herds of wild animals. I think Lewis was scared Hearst might still somehow be able to hear us, and actually I wouldn't have put it past him to have managed to bug the Model A.

Myself, I was silent because I had begun to wonder about something, and I had no way to get an answer on it.

I hadn't taken a DNA sample from Hearst. It wouldn't have been of any use to anybody. You can't make an immortal from an old man, because his DNA, no matter how unusual it is, has long since begun the inevitable process of deterioration, the errors in replication that make it unusable for a template.

This is one of the reasons immortals can only be made from children, see? The younger you are, the more bright and new-minted your DNA pattern is. I was maybe four or five when the Company rescued me, not absolute optimum for DNA but within specs. Lewis was a newborn, which is supposed to work much better. Might fetal DNA work better still?

That being the case…had Jabesh kept a sample of the furtive work he'd done, in that cramped steamer cabin? Because if he had, if Dr. Zeus had it on file somewhere…it would take a lot of work, but the Company *might* meet the terms of William Randolph Hearst.

But they wouldn't actually ever really do such a thing, would they?

We parked in front of the general store in San Simeon and I bought five rolls of Pep-O-Mints. By the time we got to Pismo Beach I had to stop for more.

▲▼▲

End Credits: 2333

The young man leaned forward at his console, fingers flying as he edited images, superimposed them, and rearranged them into startling visuals. When he had a result that satisfied him, he put on a headset and edited in the sound, brief flares of music and dialogue. He played it all back and nodded in satisfaction. His efforts had produced thirty seconds of story that would hold the viewers spellbound, and leave them with the impression that Japanese Imperial troops had brutally crushed a pro-Republic riot in Mazatlan, and Californians from all five provinces were rallying to lend aid to their oppressed brothers and sisters to the south.

Nothing of the kind had occurred, of course, but if enough people thought it had, it just might become the truth. Such things were known to happen.

And it was for everyone's good, after all, because it would set certain necessary forces in motion. He believed that democracy was the best possible system, but had long since quietly acknowledged to himself that government by the people seldom worked because people were such fools. That was all right, though. If a beautiful old automobile wouldn't run, you could always hook it up to something more efficient and tow it, and pretend it was moving of its own accord. As long as it got where you wanted it to go in the end, who cared?

He sent the story for global distribution and began another one, facts inert of themselves but presented in such a way as to paint a damning picture of the Canadian Commonwealth's treatment of its Native American neighbors on the ice mining issue. When he had completed about ten seconds of the visual impasto, however, an immortal in a gray suit entered the room, carrying a disc case.

"Chief? These are the messages from Ceylon Central. Do you want to review them before or after your ride?"

"Gosh, it's that time already, isn't it?" the young man said, glancing at the temporal chart in the lower left hand corner of the monitor. "Leave them here, Quint. I'll go through them this evening."

"Yes, sir." The immortal bowed, set down the case, and left. The young man rose, stretched, and crossed the room to his living suite. A little dog rose from where it had been curled under his chair and followed him sleepily.

Beyond his windows the view was much the same as it had been for the last four centuries: the unspoiled wilderness of the Santa Lucia mountains as far as the eye could see in every direction, save only the west where the sea lay blue and calm. The developers had been stopped. He had seen to it.

He changed into riding clothes and paused before a mirror, combing his hair. Such animal exploitation as horseback riding was illegal, as he well knew, having pushed through the legislation that made it so himself. It was good that vicious people weren't allowed to gallop around on poor sweating beasts anymore, striking and shouting at them. He never treated his horses that way, however. He loved them and was a gentle and careful rider, which was why the public laws didn't apply to him.

He turned from the mirror and found himself facing the portrait of Marion, the laughing girl of his dreams, forever young and happy and sober. He made a little courtly bow and blew her a kiss. All his loved ones were safe and past change now.

Except for his dog; it was getting old. They always did, of course. There were some things even the Company couldn't prevent, useful though it was.

Voices came floating up to him from the courtyard.

"…because when the government collapsed, of course Park Services didn't have any money anymore," a tour docent was explaining. "For a while it looked as though the people of California were going to lose La Cuesta Encantada to foreign investors. The art treasures were actually being auctioned off, one by one. How many of you remember that antique movie script that was found in that old furniture? A few years back, during the Old Hollywood Revival?"

The young man was distracted from his reverie. Grinning, he went to the mullioned window and peered down at the tour group assembled below. His dog followed him and he picked it up, scratching between its ears as he listened. The docent continued: "Well, that old cabinet came from here! We know that Rudolph Valentino was a friend of Marion Davies, and we think he must have left it up here on a visit, and somehow it got locked in the cabinet and forgotten until it was auctioned off, and the new owners opened the secret drawer."

One of the tourists put up a hand.

"But if everything was sold off—"

"No, you see, at the very last minute a miracle happened." The docent smiled. "William Randolph Hearst had five sons, as you know, but most of their descendants moved away from California. It turned out one of them was living in Europe. He's really wealthy, and when he heard about the Castle being sold, he flew to California to offer the Republic a deal. He bought the Castle himself, but said he'd let the people of California go on visiting Hearst Castle and enjoying its beauty."

"How wealthy is he?" one of the visitors wanted to know.

"Nobody knows just how much money he has," said the docent after a moment, sounding embarrassed. "But we're all very grateful to the present Mr. Hearst. He's actually added to the art collection you're going to see and—though some people don't like it—he's making plans to continue building here."

"Will we get to meet him?" somebody else asked.

"Oh, no. He's a very private man," said the docent. "And very busy, too. But you will get to enjoy his hospitality, as we go into the Refectory now for a buffet lunch. Do you all have your complimentary vouchers? Then please follow me inside. Remember to stay within the velvet ropes…"

The visitors filed in, pleased and excited. The young man looked down on them from his high window.

He set his dog in its little bed, told it to stay, and then left by a private stair that took him down to the garden. He liked having guests. He liked watching from a distance as their faces lit up, as they stared in awe, as they shared in the beauty of his grand house and all its delights. He liked making mortals happy.

He liked directing their lives, too. He had no doubt at all of his ability to guide them, or the wisdom of his long-term goals for humanity. Besides, it was fun.

In fact, he reflected, it was one of the pleasures that made eternal life worth living. He paused for a moment in the shade of one of the ancient oak trees and looked around, smiling his terrible smile at the world he was making.

The Catch

The barn stands high in the middle of backcountry nowhere, shimmering in summer heat. It's an old barn, empty a long time, and its broad planks are silvered. Nothing much around it but yellow hills and red rock.

Long ago, somebody painted it with a mural. Still visible along its broad wall are the blobs representing massed crowds, the green diamond of a baseball park, and the figure in a slide, seeming to swim along the green field, glove extended. His cartoon eyes are wide and happy. The ball, radiating black lines of force, is sailing into his glove. Above him is painted the legend:

WHAT A CATCH! And, in smaller letters below it:

1951, The Golden Year!

The old highway snakes just below the barn, where once the mural must have edified a long cavalcade of DeSotos, Packards, and Oldsmobiles. But the old road is white and empty now, with thistles pushing through its cracks. The new highway runs straight across the plain below.

Down on the new highway, eighteen-wheeler rigs hurtle through, roaring like locomotives, and they are the only things to disturb the vast silence. The circling hawk makes no sound. The cottonwood trees by the edge of the dry stream are silent too, not a rustle or a creak along the whole row; but they do cast a thin gray shade, and the men waiting in the Volkswagen Bug are grateful for that.

They might be two cops on stakeout. They aren't. Not exactly.

▲▼▲

"Are you going to tell me why we're sitting here, now?" asks the younger man, finishing his candy bar.

His name is Clete. The older man's name is Porfirio.

The older man shifts in his seat and looks askance at his partner. He doesn't approve of getting stoned on the job. But he shrugs, checks his weapon, settles into the most comfortable position he can find.

He points through the dusty windshield at the barn. "See up there? June 30, 1958, family of five killed. '46 Plymouth Club Coupe. Driver lost control of the car and went off the edge of the road. Car rolled seventy meters down that hill and hit the rocks, right there. Gas tank blew. Mr. and Mrs. William T. Ross of Visalia, California, identified from dental records. Kids didn't have any dental records. No relatives to identify bodies.

"Articles in the local and Visalia papers, grave with the whole family's names and dates on one marker in a cemetery in Visalia. Some blackening on the rocks up there. That's all there is to show it ever happened."

"Okay," says the younger man, nodding thoughtfully. "No witnesses, right?"

"That's right."

"The accident happened on a lonely road, and state troopers or whoever found the wreck after the fact?"

"Yeah."

"And the bodies were so badly burned they all went in one grave?" Clete looks pleased with himself. "So...forensic medicine being what it was in 1958, maybe there weren't five bodies in the car after all? Maybe one of the kids was thrown clear on the way down the hill? And if there was *somebody* in the future going through historical records, looking for incidents where children vanished without a trace, this might draw their attention, right?"

"It might," agrees Porfirio.

"So the Company sent an operative to see if any survivors could be salvaged," says Clete. "Okay, that's standard Company procedure. The Company took one of the kids alive, and he became an operative. So why are we here?"

Porfirio sighs, watching the barn.

"Because the kid didn't become an operative," he says. "He became a problem."

▲▼▲

1958. Bobby Ross, all-American boy, was ten years old, and he loved baseball and cowboy movies and riding his bicycle. All-American boys get bored on long trips. Bobby got bored. He was leaning out the window of his parents' car when he saw the baseball mural on the side of the barn.

"Hey, look!" he yelled, and leaned *way* out the window to see better. He slipped.

"Jesus Christ!" screamed his mom, and lunging into the back she tried to grab the seat of his pants. She collided with his dad's arm. His dad cursed;

the car swerved. Bobby felt himself gripped, briefly, and then all his mom had was one of his sneakers, and then the sneaker came off his foot. Bobby flew from the car just as it went over the edge of the road.

He remembered afterward standing there, clutching his broken arm, staring down the hill at the fire, and the pavement was hot as fire, too, on his sneakerless foot. His mind seemed to be stuck in a little circular track. He was really hurt bad, so what he had to do now was run to his mom and dad, who would yell at him and drive him to Dr. Werts, and he'd have to sit in the cool green waiting room that smelled scarily of rubbing alcohol and look at dumb *Humpty Dumpty Magazine* until the doctor made everything all right again.

But that wasn't going to happen now, because…

But he was really hurt bad, so he needed to run to his mom and dad—

But he couldn't do that ever again, because—

But he was really hurt bad—

His mind just went round and round like that, until the spacemen came for him.

▲▼▲

They wore silver suits, and they said "Greetings, Earth boy; we have come to rescue you and take you to Mars," but they looked just like ordinary people and in fact gave Bobby the impression they were embarrassed. Their spaceship was real enough, though. They carried Bobby into it on a stretcher and took off, and a space doctor fixed his broken arm, and he was given space soda pop to drink, and he never even noticed that the silver ship had risen clear of the hillside, one step ahead of the state troopers, until he looked out and saw the curve of the Earth. He'd been lifted from history, as neatly as a fly ball smacking into an outfielder's mitt.

The spacemen didn't take Bobby Ross to Mars, though. It turned out to be some place in Australia. But it might just as well have been Mars.

Because, instead of starting fifth grade, and then going on to high school, and getting interested in girls, and winning a baseball scholarship, and being drafted, and blown to pieces in Viet Nam—Bobby Ross became an immortal.

▲▼▲

"Well, that happened to all of us," says Clete, shifting restively. "One way or another. Except I've never heard of the Company recruiting a kid as old as ten."

"That's right." Keeping his eyes on the barn, Porfirio reaches into the backseat and gropes in a cooler half full of rapidly melting ice. He finds and draws out a bottle of soda. "So what does that tell you?"

Clete considers the problem. "Well, everybody knows you can't work the immortality process on somebody that old. You hear rumors, you know, like when the Company was starting out, that there were problems with some of the first test cases—" He stops himself and turns to stare at Porfirio. Porfirio meets his gaze but says nothing, twisting the top off his soda bottle.

"*This* guy was one of the test cases!" Clete exclaims. "And the Company didn't have the immortality process completely figured out yet, so they made a mistake?"

▲▼▲

Several mistakes had been made with Bobby Ross.

The first, of course, was that he was indeed too old to be made immortal. If two-year-old Patty or even five-year-old Jimmy had survived the crash, the process might have been worked successfully on them. Seat belts not having been invented in 1946, however, the Company had only Bobby with whom to work.

The second mistake had been in sending "spacemen" to collect Bobby. Bobby, as it happened, didn't like science fiction. He liked cowboys and baseball, but rocket ships left him cold. Movie posters and magazine covers featuring bug-eyed monsters scared him. If the operatives who had rescued him had come galloping over the hill on horseback, and had called him "Pardner" instead of "Earth boy," he'd undoubtedly have been as enchanted as they meant him to be and he would have bought into the rest of the experience with a receptive mind. As it was, by the time he was offloaded into a laboratory in a hot red rocky landscape, he was far enough out of shock to have begun to be angry, and his anger focused on the bogusness of the spacemen.

The third mistake had been in the Company's choice of a mentor for Bobby.

Because the Company hadn't been in business very long—at least, as far as its stockholders knew—a lot of important things about the education of young immortals had yet to be discovered, such as: no mortal can train an immortal.

Only another immortal understands the discipline needed, the pitfalls to be avoided when getting a child accustomed to the idea of eternal life.

But when Bobby was being made immortal, there weren't any other immortals yet—not successful ones, anyway—so the Company might be excused that error, at least. And if Professor Bill Riverdale was the last person who should have been in charge of Bobby, worse errors are made all the time. Especially by persons responsible for the welfare of young children.

After all, Professor Riverdale was a good, kind man. It was true that he was romantically obsessed with the idyll of all-American freckle-faced boyhood to an unhealthy degree, but he was so far in denial about it that he would never have done anything in the least improper.

All he wanted to do, when he sat down at Bobby's bedside, was help Bobby get over the tragedy. So he started with pleasant conversation. He told Bobby all about the wonderful scientists in the far future who had discovered the secret of time travel, and how they were now working to find a way to make people live forever.

And Bobby, lucky boy, had been selected to help them. Instead of going to an orphanage, Bobby would be transformed into, well, nearly into a superhero! It was almost as though Bobby would never have to grow up. It was every boy's dream! He'd have super-strength and super-intelligence and never have to wash behind his ears, if he didn't feel like it! And, because he'd live forever, one day he really would get to go to the planet Mars.

If the immortality experiment worked. But Professor Riverdale—or Professor Bill, as he encouraged Bobby to call him—was sure the experiment would work this time, because such a lot had been learned from the last time it had been attempted.

Professor Bill moved quickly on to speak with enthusiasm of how wonderful the future was, and how happy Bobby would be when he got there. Why, it was a wonderful place, according to what he'd heard! People lived on the moon and on Mars, too, and the problems of poverty and disease and war had been licked, by gosh, and there were *no Communists*! And boys could ride their bicycles down the tree-lined streets of that perfect world, and float down summer rivers on rafts, and camp out in the woods, and dream of going to the stars…

Observing, however, that Bobby lay there silent and withdrawn, Professor Bill cut his rhapsody short. He concluded that Bobby needed psychiatric therapy to get over the guilt he felt at having caused the deaths of his parents and siblings.

And this was a profound mistake, because Bobby Ross—being a normal ten-year-old all-American boy—had no more conscience than Pinocchio before the Cricket showed up, and it had never occurred to him that he had been responsible for the accident. Once Professor Bill pointed it out, however, he burst into furious tears.

So poor old Professor Bill had a lot to do to help Bobby through his pain, both the grief of his loss and the physical pain of his transformation into an immortal, of which there turned out to be a lot more than anybody had thought there would be, regardless of how much had been learned from the last attempt.

He studied Bobby's case, paying particular attention to the details of his recruitment. He looked carefully at the footage taken by the operatives who had collected Bobby, and the mural on the barn caught his attention. Tears came to his eyes when he realized that the sight of the ballplayer must have been Bobby's last happy memory, the final golden moment of his innocence.

▲▼▲

"What'd he do?" asks Clete, taking his turn at rummaging in the ice chest. "Wait, I'll bet I know. He used the image of the mural in the kid's therapy, right? Something to focus on when the pain got too bad? Pretending he was going to a happy place in his head, as an escape valve."

"Yeah. That was what he did."

"There's only root beer left. You want one?"

"No, thanks."

"Well, so why was this such a bad idea? I remember having to do mental exercises like that, myself, at the Base school. You probably did, too."

"It was a bad idea because the professor didn't know what the hell he was doing," says Porfirio. The distant barn is wavering in the heat, but he never takes his eyes off it.

▲▼▲

Bobby's other doctors didn't know what the hell they were doing, either. They'd figured out how to augment Bobby's intelligence pretty well, and they already knew how to give him unbreakable bones. They did a great job of convincing his body it would never die, and taught it how to ward off viruses and bacteria.

But they didn't know yet that even a healthy ten-year-old's DNA has already begun to deteriorate, that it's already too subject to replication errors for the immortality process to be successful. And Bobby Ross, being an all-American kid, had got all those freckles from playing unshielded in ultraviolet light. He'd gulped down soda pop full of chemicals and inhaled smoke from his dad's Lucky Strikes and hunted for tadpoles in the creek that flowed past the paper mill.

And then the doctors introduced millions of nanobots into Bobby's system, and the nanobots' job was to keep him perfect. But the doctors didn't know yet that the nanobots had to be programmed with an example to copy. So the nanobots latched onto the first DNA helix they encountered, and made it their pattern for everything Bobby ought to be. Unfortunately, it was a damaged DNA helix, but the nanobots didn't know that.

Bobby Ross grew up at the secret laboratory, and as he grew it became painfully obvious that there were still a few bugs to be worked out of the immortality process. There were lumps, there were bumps, there were skin cancers and deformities. His production of Pineal Tribrantine Three was sporadic. Sometimes, after months of misery, his body's chemistry would right itself. The joint pain would ease, the glands would work properly again.

Or not.

Professor Bill was so, so sorry, because he adored Bobby. He'd sit with Bobby when the pain was bad, and talk soothingly to send Bobby back to that dear good year, 1951—and what a golden age 1951 seemed by this time, because it was now 1964, and Bobby had become Robert, and the world seemed to be lurching into madness. Professor Bill himself wished he could escape back into 1951. But he sent Robert there often, into that beautiful summer afternoon when Hank Bauer flung his length across the green diamond—and the ball had smacked into his leather glove—and the crowds went wild!

Though only in Robert's head, of course, because all this was being done with hypnosis.

Nobody ever formally announced that Robert Ross had failed the immortality process, because it was by no means certain he wasn't immortal. But it had become plain he would never be the flawless superagent the Company had been solving for, so less and less of the laboratory budget was allotted to Robert's upkeep.

What did the Company do with unsuccessful experiments? Who knows what might have happened to Robert, if Professor Bill hadn't taken the lad under his wing?

He brought Robert to live with him in his own quarters on the Base, and continued his education himself. This proved that Professor Bill really was a good man and had no ulterior interest in Robert whatsoever; for Bobby, the slender kid with skin like a sun-speckled apricot, was long gone. Robert by this time was a wizened, stooping, scarred thing with hair in unlikely places.

Professor Bill tried to make it up to Robert by giving him a rich interior life. He went rafting with Robert on the great river of numbers, under the cold and sparkling stars of theory. He tossed him physics problems compact and weighty as a baseball, and beamed with pride when Robert smacked them out of the park of human understanding. It made him feel young again, himself.

He taught the boy all he knew, and when he found that Robert shone at Temporal Physics with unsuspected brilliance, he told his superiors. This pleased the Company managers. It meant that Robert could be made to earn back the money he had cost the Company after all. So he became an employee, and was even paid a modest stipend to exercise his genius by fiddling around with temporal equations on the Company's behalf.

▲▼▲

"And the only problem was, he was a psycho?" guesses Clete. "He went berserk, blew away poor old Professor Riverdale and ran off into the sunset?"

"He was emotionally unstable," Porfirio admits. "Nobody was surprised by that, after what he'd been through. But he didn't kill Professor Riverdale. He did run away, though. Walked, actually. He walked through a solid wall, in front of the professor and about fifteen other people in the audience. He'd been giving them a lecture in advanced temporal paradox theory. Just smiled at them suddenly, put down his chalk, and stepped right through the blackboard. He wasn't on the other side when they ran into the next room to see."

"Damn," says Clete, impressed. "*We* can't do that."

"We sure can't," says Porfirio. He stiffens, suddenly, seeing something move on the wall of the barn. It's only the shadow of the circling hawk, though, and he relaxes.

Clete's eyes have widened, and he looks worried.

"You just threw me a grenade," he says. *Catching a grenade* is security slang for being made privy to secrets so classified one's own safety is compromised.

"You needed to know," says Porfirio.

▲▼▲

The search for Robert Ross had gone on for years, in the laborious switchback system of time within which the Company operated. The mortals running the 1964 operation had hunted him with predictable lack of success. After the ripples from that particular causal wave had subsided, the mortal masters up in the twenty-fourth century set their immortal agents on the problem.

The ones who were security technicals, that is. The rank-and-file Preservers and Facilitators weren't supposed to know that there had ever been mistakes like Robert Ross. This made searching for him that much harder, but secrecy has its price.

It was assumed that Robert, being a genius in Temporal Physics, had somehow managed to escape into time. Limitless as time was, Robert might still be found within it. The operatives in charge of the case reasoned that a needle dropped into a haystack must gravitate toward any magnets concealed in the straw. Were there any magnets that might attract Robert Ross?

"Baseball!" croaked Professor Riverdale, when Security Executive Tvashtar had gone to the nursing home to interview him. "Bobby just loved baseball. You mark my words, he'll be at some baseball game somewhere. If he's in remission, he'll even be on some little town team."

With trembling hands he drew a baseball from the pocket of his dressing gown and held it up, cupping it in both hands as though he presented Tvashtar with a crystal wherein the future was revealed.

"He and I used to play catch with this. You might say it's the egg out of which all our hopes and dreams hatch. Peanuts and Crackerjack! The crack of the bat! The boys of summer. Bobby was the boy of summer. Sweet Bobby…He'd have given anything to have played the game…It's a symbol, young man, of everything that's fine and good and American."

Tvashtar nodded courteously, wondering why mortals in this era assumed the Company was run by Americans, and why they took it for granted that a stick-and-ball game had deep mystical significance. But he thanked Professor Riverdale, and left the 1970s gratefully. Then he organized a sweep through Time, centering on baseball.

▲▼▲

"And it didn't pan out," says Clete. "Obviously."

"It didn't pan out," Porfirio agrees. "The biggest search operation the Company ever staged, up to that point. You know how much work was involved?"

▲▼▲

It had been a lot of work. The operatives had to check out every obscure minor-league player who ever lived, to say nothing of investigating every batboy and ballpark janitor and even bums who slept under the bleachers, from 1845 to 1965. Nor was it safe to assume Robert might not be lurking beyond the fruited plains and amber waves of grain; there were Mexican, Cuban and Japanese leagues to be investigated. Porfirio, based at that time in California, had spent the Great Depression sweeping up peanut shells from Stockton to San Diego, but neither he nor anyone else ever caught a glimpse of Robert Ross.

It was reluctantly concluded that Professor Riverdale hadn't had a clue about what was going on in Robert's head. But, since Robert had never shown up again anywhere, the investigation was quietly dropped.

Robert Ross might never have existed, or indeed died with his mortal family. The only traces left of him were in the refinements made to the immortality process after his disappearance, and in the new rules made concerning recruitment of young operatives.

The Company never acknowledged that it had made any defectives.

▲▼▲

"Just like that, they dropped the investigation?" Clete demands. "When this guy knew how to go places without getting into a time transcendence chamber? Apparently?"

"What do you think?" says Porfirio.

Clete mutters something mildly profane and reaches down into the paper bag between his feet. He pulls out a can of potato chips and pops the lid. He eats fifteen chips in rapid succession, gulps root beer, and then says: "Well, obviously they *didn't* drop the investigation, because here we are. Or something happened to make them open it again. They got a new lead?"

Porfirio nods.

▲▼▲

1951. Porfirio was on standby in Los Angeles. Saturday morning in a quiet neighborhood, each little house on its square of lawn, rows of them along tree-lined streets. In most houses, kids were sprawled on the floor reading comic books or listening to Uncle Whoa-Bill on the radio, as long low morning sunlight slanted in through screen doors. In one or two houses, though, kids sat staring at a cabinet in which was displayed a small glowing image brought by orthicon tube; for the future, or a piece of it anyway, had arrived.

Porfirio was in the breakfast room, with a cup of coffee and the sports sections from the *Times,* the *Herald Express,* the *Examiner,* and the *Citizen News,* and he was scanning for a certain profile, a certain configuration of features. He was doing this purely out of habit, because he'd been off the case for years; but, being immortal, he had a lot of time on his hands. Besides, he had all the instincts of a good cop.

But he had other instincts, too, even more deeply ingrained than hunting, and so he noticed the clamor from the living room, though it wasn't very loud. He looked up, scowling, as three-year-old Isabel rushed into the room in her nightgown.

"What is it, *mi hija?*"

She pointed into the living room. "Maria's bad! The scary man is on the TV," she said tearfully. He opened his arms and she ran to him.

"Maria, are you scaring your sister?" he called.

"She's just being a dope," an impatient little voice responded.

He carried Isabel into the living room, and she gave a scream and turned her face over his shoulder so she wouldn't see the television screen. Six-year-old Maria, on the other hand, stared at it as though hypnotized. Before her on the coffee table, two little bowls of Cheerios sat untasted, rapidly going soggy in their milk.

Porfirio frowned down at his great-great-great-great-(and several more greats) grand-niece. "Don't call your sister a dope. What's going on? It sounded like a rat fight in here."

"She's scared of the Amazing No Man, so she wanted me to turn him off, but he's *not* scary," said Maria. "And I want to see him."

"You were supposed to be watching *Cartoon Circus,*" said Porfirio, glancing at the screen.

"Uh-huh, but Mr. Ringmaster has people on sometimes, too," Maria replied. "See?"

Porfirio looked again. Then he sat down beside Maria on the couch and stared very hard at the screen. On his arm, Isabel kicked and made tiny complaining noises over his shoulder until he absently fished a stick of gum from his shirt pocket and offered it to her.

"Who is this guy?" he asked Maria.

"The Amazing No Man," she explained. "Isn't he *strange?*"

"Yeah," he said, watching. "Eat your cereal, honey."

And he sat there beside her as she ate, though when she dripped milk from her spoon all over her nightgown because she wasn't paying attention as she ate, he didn't notice, because he wasn't paying attention either. It was hard to look away from the TV.

A wizened little person wandered to and fro before the camera, singing nonsense in an eerily high-pitched voice. Every so often he would stop, as though he had just remembered something, and grope inside his baggy clothing. He would then produce something improbable from an inner pocket: a string of sausages. A bunch of bananas. A bottle of milk. An immense cello and bow. A kite, complete with string and tail.

He greeted each item with widely pantomimed surprise, and a cry of "*Woooowwwwww!*" He pretended he was offering the sausages to an invisible dog, and made them disappear from his hand as though it were really eating them. He played a few notes on the cello. He made the kite hover in midair beside him, and did a little soft-shoe dance, and the kite bobbed along with him as though it were alive. His wordless music never stopped, never developed into a melody; just modulated to the occasional *Wowww* as he pretended to make another discovery.

More and more stuff came out of the depths of his coat, to join a growing heap on the floor: sixteen bunches of bananas. A dressmaker's dummy. A live sheep on a leash. An old-fashioned Victrola, complete with horn. A stuffed penguin. A bouquet of flowers. A suit of armor. At last, the pile was taller than the man himself. He turned, looked full into the camera with a weird smile, and winked.

Behind Porfirio's eyes, a red light flashed. A readout overlaid his vision momentarily, giving measurements, points of similarity and statistical percentages of matchup. Then it receded, but Porfirio had already figured out the truth.

The man proceeded to stuff each item back into his coat, one after another.

"See? Where does he make them all go?" asked Maria, in a shaky voice. "They can't all fit in there!"

"It's just stage magicians' tricks, *mi hija*," said Porfirio. He observed that her knuckles were white, her eyes wide. "I think this is maybe too scary for you. Let's turn it off, okay?"

"I'm not scared! He's just...funny," she said.

"Well, your little sister is scared," Porfirio told her, and rose and changed the channel, just as Hector wandered from the bedroom in his pajamas, blinking like an owl.

"Papi, Uncle Frio won't let me watch Amazing No Man!" Maria complained.

"What, the scary clown?" Hector rolled his eyes. "Honey, you know that guy gives you nightmares."

"I have to go out," said Porfirio, handing Isabel over to her father.

"You were living with mortals? Who were these people?" asks Clete.

"I had a brother, when I was mortal," says Porfirio. "I check up on his descendants now and then. Which has nothing to do with this case, okay? But that's where I was when I spotted Robert Ross. All the time we'd been looking for a baseball player, he'd been working as the Amazing Gnomon."

"And a gnomon is the piece on a sundial that throws the shadow," says Clete promptly. He grins. "Sundials. Time. Temporal physics. They just can't resist leaving clues, can they?"

Porfirio shakes his head. Clete finishes the potato chips, tilting the can to get the last bits.

"So when the guy was programmed with a Happy Place, it wasn't baseball he fixated on," he speculates. "It was 1951. 'The Golden Year'. He had a compulsion to be there in 1951, maybe?"

Porfirio says nothing.

"So, how did it go down?" says Clete, looking expectant.

▲▼▲

It hadn't gone down, at least not then.

Porfirio had called for backup, because it would have been fatally stupid to have done otherwise, and by the time he presented his LAPD badge at the studio door, the Amazing Gnomon had long since finished his part of the broadcast and gone home.

The station manager at KTLA couldn't tell him much. The Amazing Gnomon had his checks sent to a post office box. He didn't have an agent. Nobody knew where he lived. He just showed up on time every third Saturday and hit his mark, and he worked on a closed set, but that wasn't unusual with stage magicians.

"Besides," said the mortal with a shudder, "he never launders that costume. He gets under those lights and believe me, brother, we're glad to clear the set. The cameraman has to put VapoRub up his nose before he can stand to be near the guy. Hell of an act, though, isn't it?"

The scent trail had been encouraging, even if it had only led to a locker in a downtown bus station. The locker, when opened, proved to contain the Amazing Gnomon's stage costume: a threadbare old overcoat, a pair of checked trousers, and clown shoes. They were painfully foul, but contained no hidden pockets or double linings where anything might be concealed, nor any clue to their owner's whereabouts.

By this time, however, the Company had marshaled all available security techs on the West Coast, so it wasn't long before they tracked down Robert Ross.

Then all they had to do was figure out what the hell to do next.

▲▼▲

Clete's worried look has returned.

"Holy shit, I never thought about that. How do you arrest one of *us?*" he asks.

Porfirio snarls in disgust. His anger is not with Clete, but with the executive who saddled him with Clete.

"Are you ready to catch another grenade, kid?" he inquires, and without waiting for Clete's answer he extends his arm forward, stiffly, with the palm up. He has to lean back in his seat to avoid hitting the Volkswagen's windshield. He drops his hand sharply backward, like Spiderman shooting web fluid, and Clete just glimpses the bright point of a weapon emerging from Porfirio's sleeve. Pop, like a cobra's fang, it hits the windshield and retracts again, out of sight. It leaves a bead of something pale pink on the glass.

"Too cool," says Clete, though he is uneasily aware that he has no weapon like that. He clears his throat, wondering how he can ask what the pink stuff is without sounding frightened. He has always been told operatives are immune to any poison.

"It's not poison," says Porfirio, reading his mind. "It's derived from Theobromos. If I stick you in the leg with this, you'll sleep like a baby for twelve hours. That's all."

"Oh. Okay," says Clete, and it very much isn't okay, because a part of the foundation of his world has just crumbled.

"You can put it in another operative's drink, or you can inject it with an arm-mounted rig like this one," Porfirio explains patiently. "You can't shoot it in a dart, because any one of us could grab the dart out of the air, right? You have to close with whoever it is you're supposed to take down, go hand to hand.

"But first, you have to get the other guy in a trap."

▲▼▲

Robert Ross had been in a trap. He seemed to have chosen it.

He turned out to be living in Hollywood, in an old residency hotel below Franklin. The building was squarely massive, stone, and sat like a megalith under the hill. Robert had a basement apartment with one tiny window on street level, at the back. He might have seen daylight for an hour at high summer down in there, but he'd have to stand on a stool to do it. And wash the window first.

The sub-executive in charge of the operation had looked at the reconnaissance reports and shaken his head. If an operative wanted a safe place to hide, he'd choose a flimsy frame building, preferably surrounding himself with mortals. There were a hundred cheap boardinghouses in Los Angeles that would have protected Robert Ross. The last place any sane immortal would try to conceal himself would be a basement dug into granite with exactly one door, where he might be penned in by other immortals and unable to break out through a wall.

The sub-executive decided that Robert *wanted* to be brought in.

It seemed to make a certain sense. Living in a place like that, advertising his presence on television; Robert must be secretly longing for some kindly mentor to find him and tell him it was time to come home. Alternatively, he might be daring the Company problem solvers to catch him. Either way, he wasn't playing with a full deck.

So the sub-executive made the decision to send in a psychologist. A *mortal* psychologist. Not a security tech with experience in apprehending immortal fugitives, though several ringed the building and one—Porfirio, in fact—was stationed outside the single tiny window that opened below the sidewalk on Franklin Avenue.

Porfirio had leaned against the wall, pretending to smoke and watch the traffic zooming by. He could hear Robert Ross breathing in the room below. He could hear his heartbeat. He heard the polite double knock on the door, and the slight intake of breath; he heard the gentle voice saying "Bobby, may I come in?"

"It's not locked," was the reply, and Porfirio started. The voice belonged to a ten-year-old boy.

He heard the click and creak as the door opened, and the sound of two heartbeats within the room, and the psychologist saying: "We had quite a time finding you, Bobby. May I sit down?"

"Sure," said the child's voice.

"Thank you, Bobby," said the other, and Porfirio heard the scrape of a chair. "Oh, dear, are you all right? You're bleeding through your bandage."

"I'm all right. That's just where I had the tumor removed. It grows back a lot. I go up to the twenty-first century for laser surgery. Little clinics in out-of-the-way places, you know? I go there all the time, but you never notice."

"You've been very clever at hiding from us, Bobby. We'd never have found you if you hadn't been on television. We've been searching for you for years."

"In your spaceships?" said the child's voice, with adult contempt.

"In our time machines," said the psychologist. "Professor Riverdale was sure you'd run away to become a baseball player."

"I can't ever be a baseball player," replied Robert Ross coldly. "I can't run fast enough. One of my legs grew shorter than the other. Professor Bill never noticed that, though, did he?"

"I'm so sorry, Bobby."

"Good old Professor Bill, huh? I tried being a cowboy, and a soldier, and a fireman, and a bunch of other stuff. Now I'm a clown. But I can't ever be a baseball player. No home runs for Bobby."

Out of the corner of his eye, Porfirio saw someone laboring up the hill toward him from Highland Avenue. He turned his head and saw the cop.

The too-patient adult voice continued: "Bobby, there are a lot of other things you can be in the future."

"I hate the future."

Porfirio watched the cop's progress as the psychologist hesitated, then pushed on: "Do you like being a clown, Bobby?"

"I guess so," said Robert. "At least people *see* me when they look at me now. The man outside the window saw me, too."

There was a pause. The cop was red-faced from the heat and his climb, but he was grinning at Porfirio.

"Well, Bobby, that's one of our security men, out there to keep you safe."

"I know perfectly well why he's there," Robert said. "He doesn't scare me. I want him to hear what I have to say, so he can tell Professor Bill and the rest of them."

"What do you want to tell us, Bobby?" said the psychologist, a little shakily.

There was a creak, as though someone had leaned forward in a chair.

"You know why you haven't caught me? Because I figured out how to go to 1951 all by myself. And I've been living in it, over and over and over. The Company doesn't think that's possible, because of the variable permeability of temporal fabric, but it is. The trick is to go to a different *place* every *time*. There's just one catch."

The cop paused to wipe sweat off his brow, but he kept his eyes on Porfirio.

"What's the catch, Bobby?"

"Do you know what happens when you send something back to the same year often enough?" Robert sounded amused. "Like, about a hundred million times?"

"No, Bobby, I don't know."

"I know. I experimented. I tried it the first time with a wheel off a toy car. I sent it to 1912, over and over, until—do you know where Tunguska is?"

"What are you trying to tell me, Bobby?" The psychologist was losing his professional voice.

"Then," said Robert, "I increased the mass of the object. I sent a baseball back. Way back. Do you know what really killed off the dinosaurs?"

"Hey there, zoot suit," said the cop, when he was close enough. "You wouldn't be loitering, would you?"

"...You can wear a hole in the fabric of space and time," Robert was saying. "And it just might destroy everything in the whole world. You included. And if you were pretty sick of being alive, but you couldn't die, that might seem like a great idea. Don't you think?"

There was the sound of a chair being pushed back.

Porfirio grimaced and reached into his jacket for his badge, but the cop pinned Porfirio's hand to his chest with the tip of his nightstick.

"Bobby, we can help you!" cried the psychologist.

"I'm not little Bobby anymore, you asshole," said the child's voice, rising. "I'm a million, million years old."

Porfirio looked the cop in the eye.

"Vice squad," he said. The cop sagged. Porfirio produced his badge.

"But I got a tip from one of the residents here—" said the cop.

"*Woooowwwww*," said the weird little singsong voice, and there was a brief scream.

▲▼▲

"What happened?" demands Clete. He has gone very pale.

"We never found out," says Porfirio. "By the time I got the patrolman to leave and ran around to the front of the building, the other techs had already gone in and secured the room. The only problem was, there was nothing to secure. The room was empty. No sign of Ross, or the mortal either. No furniture, even, except a couple of wooden chairs. He hadn't been living there. He'd just used the place to lure us in."

"Did anybody ever find the mortal?"

"Yeah, as a matter of fact," Porfirio replies. "Fifty years later. In London."

"He'd gone forward in time?" Clete exclaims. "But that's supposed to be impossible. Isn't it?"

Porfirio sighs.

"So they say, kid. Anyway, he hadn't gone forward in time. Remember, about ten years ago, when archaeologists were excavating that medieval hospital over there? They found hundreds of skeletons in its cemetery. Layers and layers of the dead. And—though this didn't make it into the news, not even into the *Fortean Times*—one of the skeletons was wearing a Timex."

Clete giggles shrilly.

"Was it still ticking?" he asks. "What the hell are you telling me? There's this crazy immortal guy on the loose, and he's able to time-travel just using his brain, and he wants to destroy the whole world and he's figured out how, *and we're just sitting here?*"

"You have a better idea?" says Porfirio. "Please tell me if you do, okay?"

Clete controls himself with effort.

"All right, what did the Company do?" he asks. "There's a plan, isn't there, for taking him out? There must be, or we wouldn't be here now."

Porfirio nods.

"But what are we doing here *now*?" says Clete. "Shouldn't we be in 1951, where he's hiding? Wait, no, we probably shouldn't, because that'd place even more strain on the fabric of time and space. Or whatever."

"It would," Porfirio agrees.

"So…here we are at the place where Bobby Ross was recruited. The Company must expect he's going to come back here. Because this is where he caused the accident. Because the criminal always returns to the scene of the crime, right?" Clete babbles.

"Maybe," says Porfirio. "The Company already knows he leaves 1951 sometimes, for medical treatment."

"And sooner or later he'll be driven to come *here*," says Clete, and now he too is staring fixedly at the barn. "And—and today is June 30, 2008. The car crash happened fifty years ago today. That's why we're here."

"He might come," says Porfirio. "So we just wait—" He stiffens, stares hard, and Clete stares hard, too, and sees the little limping figure walking up the old road, just visible through the high weeds.

"Goddamn," says Clete, and is out of the car in a blur, ejecting candy bar wrappers and potato chip cans as he goes, and Porfirio curses and tells him to wait, but it's too late; Clete has crossed the highway in a bound and is running across the valley, as fast as only an immortal can go. Porfirio races after him, up that bare yellow hill with its red rocks that still bear faint carbon traces of horror, and he clears the edge of the road in time to hear Clete bellow: "Security! Freeze!"

"Don't—" says Porfirio, just as Clete launches himself forward to tackle Robert Ross.

Robert is smiling, lifting his arms as though in a gesture of surrender. Despite the heat, he is wearing a long overcoat. Its lining is torn, just under his arm, and where the sweat-stained rayon satin hangs down Porfirio glimpses fathomless black night, white stars.

"*Lalala la la*. Woooowww," says Robert Ross, just as Clete hits him. Clete shrieks and then is gone, sucked into the void of stars.

Porfirio stands very still. Robert winks at him.

"What a catch!" he says, in ten-year-old Bobby's voice.

It's hot up there, on the old white road, under the blue summer sky. Porfirio feels sweat prickling between his shoulder blades.

"Hey, Mr. Policeman," says Robert, "I remember you. Did you tell the Company what you heard? Have they been thinking about what I'm going to do? Have they been scared, all these years?"

"Sure they have, Mr. Ross," says Porfirio, flexing his hands.

Robert frowns. "Come on, *Mr. Ross* was my father. I'm Bobby."

"Oh, I get it. That would be the Mr. Ross who died right down there?" Porfirio points. "In the crash? Because his kid was so stupid he didn't know better than to lean out the window of a moving car?"

An expression of amazement crosses the wrinkled, dirty little face, to be replaced with white-hot rage.

"Faggot! Don't you call me stupid!" screams Robert. "I'm brilliant! I can make the whole world come to an end if I want to!"

"You made it come to an end for your family, anyway," says Porfirio.

"No, I didn't," says Robert, clenching his fists. "Professor Bill explained about that. It just happened. Accidents happen all the time. I was innocent."

"Yeah, but Professor Bill lied to you, didn't he?" says Porfirio. "Like, about how wonderful it would be to live forever?"

His voice is calm, almost bored. Robert says nothing. He looks at Porfirio with tears in his eyes, but there is hate there, too.

"Hey, Bobby," says Porfirio, moving a step closer. "Did it ever once occur to you to come back here and prevent the accident? I mean, it's impossible, sure, but didn't you even think of giving it a try? Messing with causality? It might have been easy, for a superpowered genius kid like you. But you didn't, did you? I can see it in your eyes."

Robert glances uncertainly down the hill, where in some dimension a 1946 Plymouth is still blackening, windows shattering, popping, and the dry summer grass is vanishing around it as the fire spreads outward like a black pool.

"What do you think, Bobby? Maybe pushed the grandfather paradox, huh? Gone back to see if you couldn't bend the rules, burn down this barn before the mural was painted? Or even broken Hank Bauer's arm, so the Yankees didn't win the World Series in 1951? I can think of a couple of dozen different things I'd have tried, Bobby, if I'd had superpowers like you.

"But you never even tried. Why was that, Bobby?"

"*La la la,*" murmurs Robert, opening his arms again and stepping toward Porfirio. Porfirio doesn't move. He looks Robert in the face and says: "You're stupid. Unfinished. You never grew up, Bobby."

"Professor Bill said never growing up was a good thing," says Robert.

"Professor Bill said that because he never grew up either," says Porfirio. "You weren't real to him, Bobby. He never saw *you* when he looked at you."

"No, he never did," says Robert, in a thick voice because he is crying. "He just saw what he wanted me to be. Freckle-faced kid!" He points bitterly at the brown discoloration that covers half his cheek. "Look at me now!"

"Yeah, and you'll never be a baseball player. And you're still so mad about that, all you can think of to do is to pay the Company back," says Porfirio, taking a step toward him.

"That's right!" sobs Robert.

"With the whole eternal world to explore, and a million other ways to be happy—still, all you want is to pay them back," says Porfirio, watching him carefully.

"Yeah!" cries Robert, panting. He wipes his nose on his dirty sleeve. He looks up again, sharply. "I mean—I mean—"

"See? Stupid. And you're not a good boy, Bobby," says Porfirio gently. "You're a goddamn monster. You're trying to blow up a whole world full of innocent people. You know what should happen, now? Your dad ought to come walking up that hill, madder than hell, and punish you."

Robert looks down the hillside.

"But he can't, ever again," he says. He sounds tired.

Porfirio has already moved, and before the last weary syllable is out of his mouth Robert feels the scorpion-sting in his arm.

He whirls around, but Porfirio has already retreated, withdrawn up the hillside. He stands before the mural, and the painted outfielder smiles over his shoulder. Robert clutches his arm, beginning to cry afresh.

"No fair," he protests. But he knows it's more than fair. It is even a relief.

He falls to his knees, whimpering at the heat of the old road's surface. He crawls to the side and collapses in the yellow summer grass.

"Will I have to go to the future now?" Robert asks piteously.

"No, son. No future," Porfirio replies.

Robert nods and closes his eyes. He could sink through the rotating earth if he tried, escape once again into 1951; instead he floats away from time itself, into the back of his father's hand.

Porfirio walks down the hill toward him. As he does so, an all-terrain vehicle comes barreling up the old road, mowing down thistles in its path.

It shudders to a halt and Clete leaps out, leaving the door open in his headlong rush up the hill. He is not wearing the same suit he wore when last seen by Porfirio.

"You stinking son of a bitch *defective*," he roars, and aims a kick at Robert's head. Porfirio grabs his arm.

"Take it easy," he says.

"He sent me back six hundred thousand years! Do you know how long I had to wait before the Company even opened a damn transport depot?" says Clete, and looking at his smooth ageless face Porfirio can see that ages have passed over it. Clete now has permanently furious eyes. Their glare bores into Porfirio like acid. *No convenience stores in 598,000 BC, huh?* Porfirio thinks to himself.

"You knew he was going to do this to me, didn't you?" demands Clete.

"No," says Porfirio. "All I was told was, there'd be complications to the arrest. And you should have known better than to rush the guy."

"You got that right," says Clete, shrugging off his hand. "So why don't you do the honors?"

He goes stalking back to his transport, and hauls a body bag from the back seat. Porfirio sighs. He reaches into his coat and withdraws what looks like a screwdriver handle. When he thumbs a button on its side, however, a half-circle of blue light forms at one end. He tests it with a random slice through a thistle, which falls over at once. He leans down and scans Robert Ross carefully, because he wants to be certain he is unconscious.

"I'm sorry," he murmurs.

Working with the swiftness of long practice, he does his job. Clete returns, body bag under his arm, watching with grim satisfaction. Hank Bauer is still smiling down from the mural.

When the disassembly is finished, Porfirio loads the body bag into the car and climbs in beside it. Clete gets behind the wheel and backs carefully down the road. Bobby Ross may not be able to die, but he is finally on his way to eternal rest.

The Volkswagen sits there rusting for a month before it is stolen.

The blood remains on the old road for four months, before autumn rains wash it away, but they do wash it away. By the next summer the yellow grass is high, and the road as white as innocence once more.

Leaving His Cares Behind

The young man opened his eyes. Bright day affronted them. He groaned and rolled over, pulling his pillow about his ears.

After thirty seconds of listening to his brain pound more loudly than his heart, he rolled over again and stared at his comfortless world.

It shouldn't have been comfortless. It had originally been a bijou furnished residence, suitable for a wealthy young person-about-town. That had been when one could see the floor, however. Or the sink. Or the tabletops. Or, indeed, anything but the chilly wasteland of scattered clothing, empty bottles and unwashed dishes.

He regarded all this squalor with mild outrage, as though it belonged to someone else, and crawled from the strangling funk of his sheets. Standing up was a mistake; the top of his head blew off and hit the ceiling. A suitable place to vomit was abruptly a primary concern.

The kitchen? No; no room in the sink. Bathroom? Too far away. He lurched to the balcony doors, flung them wide and leaned out. A delicate peach soufflé, a bowl of oyster broth, assorted brightly colored trifles that did not yield their identities to memory and two bottles of sparkling wine spattered into the garden below.

Limp as a rag he clung to the rail, retching and spitting, shivering in his nakedness. Amused comment from somewhere roused him; he lifted his eyes and saw that half of Deliantiba (or at least the early-morning tradesmen making their way along Silver Boulevard) had watched his performance. He glared at them. Spitting out the last of the night before, he stood straight, turned his affronted back and went inside, slamming the balcony doors behind him.

With some effort, he located his dressing gown (finest velvet brocade, embroidered with gold thread) and matching slippers. The runner answered his summoning bell sooner than he had expected and her thunder at his door brought on more throbbing in his temples. He opened to see the older one, not the young one who was so smitten with him, and cursed his luck.

"Kretia, isn't it?" he said, smiling nonetheless. "You look lovely this morning! Now, I'd like a carafe of mint tea, a plate of crisp wafers and one green apple, sliced thin. Off you go, and if you're back within ten minutes you'll have a gratuity of your very own!"

She just looked at him, hard-eyed. "Certainly, sir," she replied. "Will that be paid for in advance, sir?"

"There goes *your* treat," he muttered, but swept a handful of assorted small coins from the nearest flat surface and handed them through the doorway. "That should be enough. Kindly hurry; I'm not a well man."

He had no clean clothing, but while poking through the drifts of slightly less foul linen he found a pair of red silk underpants he was fairly certain did not belong to him, and pulling them on cheered him up a great deal. By the time he had breakfasted and strolled out to meet the new day, Lord Ermenwyr was nearly himself again, and certainly capable of grappling with the question of how he was going to pay his rent for another month.

And grappling was required.

The gentleman at Firebeater's Savings and Loan was courteous, but implacable: no further advances on my lord's quarterly allotment were to be paid, on direct order of my lord's father. Charm would not persuade him; neither would veiled threats. Finally the stop payment order itself was produced, with its impressive and somewhat frightening seal of black wax. Defeated, Lord Ermenwyr slunk out into the sunshine and stamped his foot at a pigeon that was unwise enough to cross his path. It just stared at him.

He strode away, hands clasped under his coattails, thinking very hard. By long-accustomed habit his legs bore him to a certain pleasant villa on Goldwire Avenue, and when he realized where he was, he smiled and rang at the gate. A laconic porter admitted him to Lady Seelice's garden. An anxious-looking maidservant admitted him to Lady Seelice's house. He found his own way to Lady Seelice's boudoir.

Lady Seelice was sitting up in bed, going over the books of her shipping company, and she had a grim set to her mouth. Vain for him to offer to distract her with light conversation; vain for him to offer to massage her neck, or brush her hair. He perched on the foot of her bed, looking as winsome as he could, and made certain suggestions. She declined them in an absent-minded sort of way.

He helped himself to sugared comfits from the exquisite little porcelain jar on her bedside table, and ate them quite amusingly, but she did not laugh. He pretended to play her corset like an accordion, but she did not laugh at that either. He fastened her brassiere on his head and crawled around the room on his hands and knees meowing like a kitten, and when she took absolutely no notice of that, he stood up and asked her outright if she'd loan him a hundred crowns.

She told him to get out, so he did.

As he was stamping downstairs, fuming, the anxious maidservant drifted into his path.

"Oh, dear, was she cross with you?" she inquired.

"Your mistress is in a vile mood," said Lord Ermenwyr resentfully, and he pulled her close and kissed her very hard. She leaned into his embrace, making soft noises, stroking his hair. When they came up for air at last, she looked into his eyes.

"She's been in a vile mood these three days. Something's wrong with her stupid old investments."

"Well, if she's not nicer soon, she'll find that her nimble little goat has capered off to greener pastures," said Lord Ermenwyr, pressing his face into the maidservant's bosom. He began to untie the cord of her bodice with his teeth.

"I've been thinking, darling," said the maidservant slowly, "that perhaps it's time we told her the truth about...you know...*us.*"

Unseen under her chin, the lordling grimaced in dismay. He spat out a knot and straightened up at once.

"Well! Yes. Perhaps." He coughed, and looked suddenly pale. "On the other hand, there is the danger—" He coughed again, groped hurriedly for a silk handkerchief and held it to his lips. "My condition is so, ah, *tentative*. If we were to tell of our forbidden love—and then I were to collapse unexpectedly and die, which I might at any moment, how could I rest in my grave knowing that your mistress had turned you out in the street?"

"I suppose you're right," sighed the maidservant, watching as he doubled over in a fit of coughing. "Do you want a glass of wine or anything?"

"No, my darling—" Wheezing, Lord Ermenwyr turned and made his unsteady way to the door. "I think—I think I'd best pay a call on my personal physician. Adieu."

Staggering, choking, he exited, and continued in that wise until he was well out of sight at the end of the avenue, at which time he stood straight and walked on. A few paces later the sugared comfits made a most unwelcome return, and though he was able to lean quickly over a low wall, he looked up directly into the eyes of someone's outraged gardener.

Running three more blocks did not improve matters much. He collapsed on a bench in a small public park and fumed, considering his situation.

"I'm fed up with this life," he told a statue of some Deliantiban civic leader. "Independence is all very well, but perhaps..."

He mulled over the squalor, the inadequacy, the creditors, the wretched *complications* with which he had hourly to deal. He compared it with his former accustomed comforts, in a warm and loving home where he was accorded all the consideration his birth and rank merited. Within five minutes, having given due thought to all arguments pro and con, he rose briskly to his feet and set off in the direction of Silver Boulevard.

Ready cash was obtained by pawning one of the presents Lady Seelice had given him (amethysts were not really his color, after all). He dined pleasantly at his favorite restaurant that evening. When three large gentlemen asked at the door whether or not Lord Ermenwyr had a moment to speak with them, however, he was obliged to exit through a side door and across a roof.

Arriving home shortly after midnight, he loaded all his unwashed finery into his trunks, lowered the trunks from his window with a knotted sheet, himself exited in like manner, and dragged the trunks a quarter-mile to the caravan depot. He spent the rest of the night there, dozing fitfully in a corner, and by dawn was convinced he'd caught his death of cold.

But when his trunks were loaded into the baggage cart, when he had taken his paid seat amongst the other passengers, when the caravan master had mounted into the lead cart and the runner signaled their departure with a blast on her brazen trumpet—then Lord Ermenwyr was comforted, and allowed himself to sneer at Deliantiba and all his difficulties there as it, and they, fell rapidly behind him.

▲▼▲

The caravan master drew a deep breath, deciding to be patient.

"Young man, your friends must have been having a joke at your expense," he said. "There aren't any country estates around here. We're in the bloody *Greenlands*. Nobody's up here but bandits, and demons and wild beasts."

"No need to be alarmed on my behalf, good fellow," the young man assured him. "There'll be bearers along to meet me in half an hour. That's their cart-track right there, see?"

The caravan master peered at what might have been a rabbit's trail winding down to the honest paved road. He followed it up with his eyes until it became lost in the immensity of the forests. He looked higher still, at the black mountain towering beyond, and shuddered. He knew what lay up there. It wasn't something he told his paying passengers about, because if he were ever to do so, no amount of bargain fares could tempt them to take this particular shortcut through the wilderness.

"Look," he said, "I'll be honest with you. If I let you off here, the next thing anyone will hear of you is a note demanding your ransom. *If* the gods are inclined to be merciful! There's a Red House station three days on. Ride with us that far, at least. You can send a message to your friends from there."

"I tell you this is my stop, Caravan Master," said the young man, in such a snide tone the caravan master thought: *To hell with him.*

"Offload his trunks, then!" he ordered the keymen, and marched off to the lead cart and resumed his seat. As the caravan pulled away, the other passengers looked back, wondering at the young man who sat down on his luggage with an air of unconcern and pulled out a jade smoking-tube, packing it with fragrant weed.

"I hope his parents have other sons," murmured a traveling salesman. Something howled in the depths of the forest, and he looked fearfully over his shoulder. In doing so, he missed seeing the young man lighting up his smoke with a green fireball. When he looked back, a bend in the road had already hidden the incautious youth.

Lord Ermenwyr, in the meanwhile, sucked in a double lungful of medicinal smoke and sighed in contentment. He leaned back, and blew a smoke ring.

"That's my unpaid rent and cleaning fee," he said to himself, watching it dissipate and wobble away. He sucked smoke and blew another.

"That's my little misunderstanding with Brasshandle the moneylender," he said, as it too faded into the pure air. Giggling to himself, he drew in a deep, deep store of smoke and blew three rings in close formation.

"Your hearts, ladies! All of you. Byebye now! You'll find another toy to amuse yourselves, I don't doubt. All my troubles are magically wafting away—oh, wait, I should blow one for that stupid business with the public fountain—"

When he heard the twig snap, however, he sat up and gazed into the darkness of the forest.

They were coming for him through the trees, and they were very large. Some were furred and some were scaled, some had great fanged pitilessly grinning mouths, some had eyes red as a dying campfire just before the night closes in. Some bore spiked weapons. Some bore treebough clubs. They shared no single characteristic of feature or flesh, save that they wore, all, livery black as ink.

"It's about time you got here," said Lord Ermenwyr. Rising to his feet, he let fall the glamour that disguised his true form.

"Master!" cried some of that dread host, and "Little Master!" cried others, and they abased themselves before him.

"Yes, yes, I'm glad to see you too," said Lord Ermenwyr. "Take special care with my trunks, now. I'll have no end of trouble getting them to close again, if they're dropped and burst open."

"My little lord, you look pale," said the foremost creature, doffing his spiked helmet respectfully. "Have you been ill again? Shall we carry you?"

"I haven't been well, no," the lordling admitted. "Perhaps you ought."

The leader knelt immediately, and Lord Ermenwyr hopped up on his shoulder and clung as he stood, looking about with satisfaction from the considerable height.

"Home!" he ordered, and that uncouth legion bore him, and his trunks, and his unwashed linen, swiftly and with chants of praise to the great black gate of his father's house.

▲▼▲

The Lord Ermenwyr was awakened next morning by an apologetic murmur, as one of the maidservants slipped from his bed. He acknowledged her departure with a sleepy grunt and a wave of his hand, and rolled over to luxuriate in dreams once more. Nothing disturbed his repose further until the black and purple curtains of his bed were drawn open, reverently, and he heard a sweet chime that meant his breakfast had just arrived on a tray.

"Tea and toast, little Master," someone growled gently. "The toast crisp, just as you like it, and a pot of hyacinth jam, and Hrekseka the Appalling remembered you like that shrimp-egg relish, so here's a puff pastry filled with it for a savory. Have we forgotten anything? Would you like the juice of blood oranges, perhaps?"

The lordling opened his eyes and smiled wide, stretched lazily.

"Yes, thank you, Krasp," he said, and the steward—who resembled nothing so much as an elderly werewolf stuck in mid-transformation—bowed and looked sidelong at an attendant, who ran at once to fetch a pitcher of juice. He meanwhile set about arranging Lord Ermenwyr's tray on his lap, opening out the black linen napery and tucking it into the lace collar of the lordling's nightshirt, and pouring the tea.

"And may I say, Master, on behalf of the staff, how pleased we are to see you safely returned?" said Krasp, stepping back and turning his attention to laying out a suit of black velvet.

"You may," said Lord Ermenwyr. He spread jam on his toast, dipped it into his tea and sucked at it noisily. "Oh, bliss. It's good to be back, too. I trust the parents are both well?'

Krasp genuflected. "Your lord father and your lady mother thrive, I rejoice to say."

"Mm. Of course. Siblings all in reasonably good health, I suppose?"

"The precious offspring of the Master and his lady continue to grace this plane, my lord, for which we in the servant's hall give thanks hourly."

"How nice," said Lord Ermenwyr. He sipped his tea and inquired further: "I suppose nobody's run a spear through my brother Eyrdway yet?"

The steward turned with a reproachful look in his sunken yellow eye. "The Variable Magnificent continues alive and well, my lord," he said, and held up two pairs of boots of butter-soft leather. "The plain ones, my lord, or the ones with the spring-loaded daggers in the heels?"

"The plain ones," Lord Ermenwyr replied, yawning. "I'm in the bosom of my family, after all."

When he had dined, when he had been washed and lovingly groomed and dressed by a succession of faithful retainers, when he had admired his reflection in a long mirror and pomaded his beard and moustaches—then Lord Ermenwyr strolled forth into the corridors of the family manse, to see what amusement he might find.

He sought in vain.

All that presented itself to his quick eye was the endless maze of halls, hewn through living black basalt, lit at intervals by flickering witchlight or smoking flame, or here and there by a shaft of tinted sunbeam, from some deep-hewn arrowslit window sealed with panes of painted glass. At regular intervals armed men—well, armed *males*—stood guard, and each bowed respectfully as he passed, and bid him good-morning.

He looked idly into the great vaulted chamber of the baths, with its tiled pools and scented atmosphere from the orchids that twined, luxuriant, on trellises in the steamy air; but none of his sisters were in there.

He leaned on a balustrade and gazed down the stairwell, at the floors descending into the heart of the mountain. There, on level below level to the vanishing point of perspective, servants hurried with laundry, or dishes, or firewood. It was reassuring to see them, but he had learned long since that they would not stop to play.

He paused by a window and contemplated the terraced gardens beyond, secure and sunlit, paradise cleverly hidden from wayfarers on the dreadful slopes below the summit. Bees droned in white roses, or blundered sleepily in orchards, or hovered above reflecting pools. Though the bowers of his mother were beautiful beyond the praise of poets, they made Lord Ermenwyr want to scream with ennui.

He turned, hopeful, at the sound of approaching feet.

"My lord." A tall servant bowed low. "Your lord father requests your presence in his accounting chamber."

Lord Ermenwyr bared his teeth like a weasel at bay. All his protests, all his excuses, died unspoken at the look on the servant's face. He reflected that at least the next hour was unlikely to be boring.

"Very well, then," he said, and followed where the servant led him.

By the time he had crossed the threshold, he had adopted a suitably insouciant attitude and compiled a list of clever things to say. All his presence of mind was required to remember them, once he had stepped into the darkness beyond.

His father sat in a shaft of light at the end of the dark hall, behind his great black desk, in his great black chair. For all that was said of him in courts of law, for all that was screamed against him in temples, the Master of the Mountain was not in his person fearful to look upon. For all that his name was spoken in whispers by the caravan-masters, or used to frighten their children, he wore no crown of sins nor cloak of shades. He was big, black-bearded, handsome in a solemn kind of way. His black eyes were calm, patient as a stalking tiger's.

Lord Ermenwyr, meeting those eyes, felt like a very small rabbit indeed.

"Good morning, Daddy," he said, in the most nonchalant voice he could summon.

"Good afternoon, my son," said the Master of the Mountain.

He pointed to a chair, indicating that Lord Ermenwyr should come forward and sit. Lord Ermenwyr did so, though it was a long walk down that dark hall. When he had seated himself, a saturnine figure in nondescript clothing stepped out of the shadows before him.

"Your report, please," said the Master of the Mountain. The spy cleared his throat once, then read from a sheaf of notes concerning Lord Ermenwyr's private pastimes for the last eight months. His expenses were listed in detail, to the last copper piece; his associates were named, their addresses and personal histories summarized; his favorite haunts named too, and the amount of time he spent at each.

The Master of the Mountain listened in silence, staring at his son the whole time, and though he raised an eyebrow now and then he made no comment. Lord Ermenwyr, for his part, with elaborate unconcern, drew out his smoking-tube, packed it, lit it, and sat smoking, with a bored expression on his face.

Having finished at last, the spy coughed and bowed slightly. He stepped back into the darkness.

"Well," said Lord Ermenwyr, puffing smoke, "I don't know why you bothered giving me that household accounts book on my last birthday. He kept *much* better records than I did."

"Fifteen pairs of high-heeled boots?" said the Master of the Mountain, with a certain seismic quality in the bass reverberation of his voice.

"I can explain that! There's only one cobbler in Deliantiba who can make really comfortable boots that give me the, er, dramatic presence I need," said Lord Ermenwyr. "And he's poor. I felt it was my duty to support an authentic craftsman."

"I can't imagine why he's poor, at these prices," retorted his father. "When I was your age, I'd never owned a pair of boots. Let alone boots 'of premium-grade elkhide, dyed purple in the new fashion, with five-inch heels incorporating the unique patented Comfort-Spring lift.'"

"You missed out on a lot, eh? If you wore my size, I'd give you a pair," said Lord Ermenwyr, cool as snowmelt, but he tensed to run all the same.

His father merely stared at him, and the lordling exhaled another plume of smoke and studied it intently. When he had begun to sweat in spite of himself, his father went on:

"Is your apothecary an authentic craftsman too?"

"You can't expect me to survive without my medication!" Lord Ermenwyr cried. "And it's damned expensive in a city, you know."

"For what you spent, you might have kept three of yourselves alive," said his father.

"Well—well, but I've been ill. More so than usually, I mean. I had fevers—and I've had this persistent racking cough—blinding headaches when I wake up every morning—and see how pale I am?" Lord Ermenwyr stammered. His father leaned forward and grinned, with his teeth very white in his black beard.

"There's nothing wrong with you, boy, that a good sweat won't cure. The exercise yard, quick march! Let's see if you've remembered your training."

▲▼▲

"Just what I expected," said the Master of the Mountain, as his son was carried from the exercise yard on a stretcher. Lord Ermenwyr, too winded to respond, glared at his father.

"And get that look off your face, boy. This is what comes of all those bottles of violet liqueur and vanilla éclairs," continued his father, pulling off his great gauntlets. "And the late nights. And the later mornings." He rubbed his chin thoughtfully, where a bruise was swelling. "Your reflexes aren't bad, though. You haven't lost any of your speed, I'll say that much for you."

"Thank you," Lord Ermenwyr wheezed, with as much sarcasm as he could muster.

"I want to see you out there again tomorrow, one hour after sunrise. We'll start with saber drill, and then you'll run laps," said the Master of the Mountain.

"On my sprained ankle?" Lord Ermenwyr yelled in horror.

"I see you've got your breath back," replied his father. He turned to the foremost guard bearing the stretcher. "Take my son to his mother's infirmary. If there's anything really the matter with him, she'll mend it."

"But—!" Lord Ermenwyr cried, starting up. His father merely smiled at him, and strode off to the guardroom.

▲▼▲

By the time they came to his mother's bower, Lord Ermenwyr had persuaded his bearers to let him limp along between them, rather than enter her presence prostrate and ignominious.

But as they drew near to that place of sweet airs, of drowsy light and soft perfumes, those bearers must blink and turn their faces away; and though they propped him faithfully, and were great and horrible in their black livery and mail, the two warriors shivered to approach the Saint of the World. Lord Ermenwyr, knowing well that none of his father's army could meet his mother's gaze, sighed and bid them leave him.

"But, little Master, we must obey your lord father," groaned one, indistinctly through his tusks.

"It's all right; most of the time I can't look her in the eye, myself," said Lord Ermenwyr. "Besides, you were only told to bring me to the *infirmary*, right? So there's a semantic loophole for you."

Precise wording is extremely important to demons. Their eyes (bulging green and smoldering red respectively) met, and after a moment's silent debate the two bowed deeply and withdrew, murmuring their thanks. Lord Ermenwyr sighed, and tottered on through the long grass alone.

He saw the white-robed disciples walking in the far groves, or bending between the beds of herbs, gathering, pruning, planting. Their plain-chant hummed through the pleasant air like bee song, setting his teeth on edge somehow. He found his mother at last, silhouetted against a painfully sunlit bower of blossoming apple, where she bent over a sickbed.

"...the ointment every day, do you understand? You must have patience," she was saying, in her gentle ruthless voice. She looked over her shoulder and saw her son. He felt her clear gaze go through him, and he stood still and fidgeted as she turned back to her patient. She laid her hand upon the sufferer's brow, murmured a blessing; only then did she turn her full attention to Lord Ermenwyr.

He knelt awkwardly. "Mother."

"My child." She came forward and raised him to his feet. Having embraced him, she said:

"You haven't sprained your ankle, you know."

"It hurts," he said, and his lower lip trembled. "You think I'm lying again, I suppose."

"No," she said, patiently. "You truly believe you're in pain. Come and sit down, child."

She led him into the deeper shade, and drew off his boot (looking without comment on its five-inch heel). One of her disciples brought him a stoneware cup of cold spring water, and watched with wide eyes as she examined Lord Ermenwyr's ankle. Where her fingers passed, the lordling felt warmth entering in. His pain melted away like frost under sunlight, but he braced himself for what else her healing hands would learn in their touch.

"I know what you'll tell me next," he said, testily. "You'll say I haven't been exercising enough. You'll tell me I've been eating and drinking too much. You'll tell me I shouldn't wear shoes with heels this high, because it doesn't matter how tall I am. You'll tell me I'm wasting myself on pointless self-indulgences that leave me sick and depressed and penniless."

"Why should I tell you what you already know?" his mother replied. He stared sullenly into his cup of water.

"And you'll *reproach* me about Lady Seelice and Lady Thyria. And the little runner, what's-her-name, you'll be especially sorrowful that I can't even remember the name of a girl I've seduced. Let alone chambermaids without number. And…and you'll tell me about all those poor tradesmen whose livelihoods depend on people like me paying bills on time, instead of skipping town irresponsibly."

"That's true," said his mother.

"And, of course, you'll tell me that I don't really need all those drugs!" Lord Ermenwyr announced. "You'll tell me that I imagine half of my fevers and coughs and wasting diseases, and that neither relief nor creative fulfillment will come from running around artist's salons with my pupils like pinpoints. And that it all comes from my being bored and frustrated. And that I'd feel better at once if I found some honest work putting my *tremendous* talents to good use."

"How perceptive, my darling," said his mother.

"Have I left anything out?"

"I don't think so."

"You see?" Lord Ermenwyr demanded tearfully, turning to the disciple. "She's just turned me inside out, like a sock. I can't keep one damned secret from her."

"All things are known to Her," said the disciple, profoundly shocked at the lordling's blasphemy. He hadn't worked there very long.

"And now, do you know what else she's going to do?" said Lord Ermenwyr, scowling at him. "She's going to nag at me to go to the nursery and visit my bastard children."

"Really?" said the disciple, even more shocked.

"Yes," said his mother, watching as he pulled his boot back on. He started to stamp off, muttering, but turned back hastily and knelt again. She blessed him in silence, and he rose and hurried away.

"My son is becoming wise," said the Saint of the World, smiling as she watched him go.

▲▼▲

The way to the nursery was mazed and obscured, for the Master of the Mountain had many enemies, and hid well where his seed sheltered. Lord

Ermenwyr threaded the labyrinth without effort, knowing it from within. As he vaulted the last pit, as he gave the last password, his heart grew more cheerful. He would shortly behold his dear old nurse again!

Twin demonesses guarded the portal, splendid in black livery and silver mail. The heels of their boots were even higher than his, and much sharper. They grinned to see him, baring gold-banded fangs in welcome.

"Ladies, you look stunning today," he told them, twirling his moustaches. "Is Balnshik on duty?"

"She is within, little lord," hissed the senior of the two, and lifted her blade to let him pass.

He entered quite an ordinary room, long and low, with a fire burning merrily in the hearth behind a secure screen. Halfway up the walls was a mural painted in tones of pink and pale blue, featuring baby rabbits involved in unlikely pastimes.

Lord Ermenwyr curled his lip. Three lace-gowned infants snuffled in cots here; four small children sat over a shared game there, in teeny-tiny chairs around a teeny-tiny table; another child rocked to and fro on a ponderous wooden beast bright-painted; three more sat before a comfortable-looking chair at the fireside, where a woman in a starched white uniform sat reading to them.

"…but the people in *that* village were very naughty and tried to ambush his ambassadors, so he put them all to the sword," she said, and held up the picture so they could all see.

"Ooo," chorused the tots.

She, having meanwhile noticed Lord Ermenwyr, closed the book and rose to her feet with sinuous grace.

"Little Master," she said, looking him up and down. "You've put on weight."

He winced.

"Oh, Nursie, how unkind," he said.

"Nonsense," Balnshik replied. She was arrogantly beautiful. Her own body was perfect, ageless, statuesque and bosomy as any little boy's dream, or at least Lord Ermenwyr's little boy dreams, and there was a dangerous glint in her dark eye and a throaty quality to her voice that made him shiver even now.

"I've come about the, er, the…those children I—had," he said. "For a sort of visit."

"What a delightful surprise!" Balnshik said, in well-bred tones of irony. She turned and plucked from the rocking beast a wretched-looking little thing in a green velvet dress. "Look who's come to see us, dear! It's our daddy. We scarcely knew we had one, did we?"

Baby and parent stared at one another in mutual dismay. The little boy turned his face into Balnshik's breast and screamed dismally.

"Poor darling," she crooned, stroking his limp curls. "We've been teething again and we're getting over a cold, and that makes us fretful. We're just like our daddy, aren't we? Would he like to hold us?"

"Perhaps not," said Lord Ermenwyr, doing his best not to run from the room. "I might drop it. Him. What do you mean, he's just like me?"

"The very image of you at that age, Master," Balnshik assured him, serenely unbuttoning her blouse. "Same pasty little face, same nasty look in his dear little eyes, same tendency to shriek and drum his little heels on the floor when he's cross. And he gets that same rash you did, all around his little—"

"Wasn't there another one?" inquired Lord Ermenwyr desperately.

"You know perfectly well there is," said Balnshik, watching tenderly as the baby burrowed toward comfort. "Your lord father's still paying off the girl's family, and your lady sister will never be able to hold another slumber party for her sorority. Where is he?" She glanced over at the table. "There we are! The one in the white tunic. Come and meet your father, dear."

The child in question, one of those around the table, got up reluctantly. He came and clung to Balnshik's leg, peering up at his father.

"Well, you look like a fine manly little fellow, anyway," said Lord Ermenwyr.

"You look like a very bad man," stated the child.

"And he's clever!" said Lord Ermenwyr, preening a bit. "Yes, my boy, I am rather a bad man. In fact, I'm a famous villain. What else have you heard about your father?"

The boy thought.

"Grandpapa says when I'm a man, I can challenge you to a fight and beat you up," he said gravely. "But I don't think I want to."

"You don't eh?" A spark of parental feeling warmed in Lord Ermenwyr's heart. "Why not, my boy?"

"Because then I will be bigger than you, and you will be old and weak and have no teeth," the child explained. "It wouldn't be fair."

Lord Ermenwyr eyed him sourly. "That hasn't happened to your Grandpapa, has it?"

"No," the child agreed, "But he's twice as big as you." He brightened, remembering the other thing he had heard about his father. "And Grandmama says you're so smart, it's such a shame you don't do something with your life!"

Lord Ermenwyr sighed, and pulled out his jade tube. "Do you mind if I smoke in here?" he asked Balnshik.

"I certainly do," she replied, mildly but with a hint of bared fangs.

"Pity. Well, here, son of mine; here's my favorite ring for your very own." He removed a great red cabochon set in silver, and presented it to the child. "The top is hinged like a tiny box, see the clever spring? You can hide sleeping powders in it to play tricks on other little boys. I emptied out the poison, for heaven's sake," he added indignantly, seeing that the hint of bared fangs was now an open suggestion.

"Thank you, Father," piped the child.

▲▼▲

Disconsolate, Lord Ermenwyr wandered the black halls.

He paused at a window that looked westward, and regarded the splendid isolation of the Greenlands. Nothing to be seen for miles but wave upon wave of lesser mountains, forested green as the sea, descending to the plain. Far away, far down, the toy cities behind their walls were invisible for distance, and when night fell their sparkling lights would glimmer in vain, like lost constellations, shrouded from his hopeful eye.

Even now, he told himself, even now down there the taverns would be opening. The smoky dark places would be lighting their lanterns, and motherly barmaids would serve forth wine so raw it took the paint off tables. The elegant expensive places would be firing up the various patent devices that glared in artificial brilliance, and the barmaids there were all thin, and young, and interestingly depraved-looking. What *they* served forth could induce visions, or convulsions and death if carelessly indulged in.

How he longed, this minute, for a glass of dubious green liqueur from the Gilded Clock! Or to loll with his head in the lap of an anonymous beauty who couldn't care less whether he did something worthwhile with his life. What had he been thinking, to desert the cities of the plain? They had everything his heart could desire. Theaters. Clubs. Ballrooms. Possibilities. Danger. Fun…

Having made his decision to depart before the first light of dawn, Lord Ermenwyr hurried off to see that his trunks were packed with new-laundered clothes. He whistled a cheery little tune as he went.

▲▼▲

The Master and the Saint sat at their game.

They were not Good and Evil personified, nor Life and Death; certainly not Order and Chaos, nor even Yin and Yang. Yet most of the world's population believed that they were. Their marriage, therefore, had done rather more than raise eyebrows everywhere.

The Master of the Mountain scowled down at the game board. It bore the simplest of designs, concentric circles roughly graven in slate, and the playing pieces were mere pebbles of black marble or white quartz. The strategy was fantastically involved, however. So subtle were the machinations necessary to win that this particular game had been going on for thirty years, and a decisive conquest might never materialize.

"What are we going to do about the boy?" he said.

The Saint of the World sighed in commiseration, but was undistracted. She slid a white stone to a certain position on the board.

High above them, three white egrets peered down from the ledge that ran below the great vaulted dome of the chamber. Noting the lady's move, they looked sidelong at the three ravens that perched opposite, and stalked purposefully along the ledge until the ravens were obliged to sidle back a pace or two.

"To which of your sons do you refer, my lord?" the Saint inquired.

"The one with the five-inch heels to his damned boots," said the Master of the Mountain, and set a black stone down, *click,* between a particular pair of circles. "Have you seen them?"

One of the ravens bobbed its head derisively, spread its coal-black wings and soared across the dome to the opposite ledge.

"Yes, I have," admitted the Saint.

"They cost me a fortune, and they're purple," said the Master of the Mountain, leaning back to study the board.

"And when you were his age, you'd never owned a pair of boots," said the Saint serenely, sliding two white stones adjacent to the black one.

Above, one egret turned, retraced its way along the ledge, and the one raven cocked an eye to watch it. Three white stars shone out with sudden and unearthly light, in the night heavens figured on the surface of the arching dome.

"When I was his age, I wore chains. I never had to worry about paying my tailor; only about living long enough to avenge myself," said the Master of the Mountain. "I wouldn't want a son of mine educated so. But we've spoiled the boy!"

He moved three black stones, lining them up on successive rings. The two ravens flew to join their brother. Black clouds swirled under the dome, advanced on the floating globe of the white moon.

"He needs direction," said the Saint.

"He needs a challenge," said the Master. "Pitch him out naked on the mountainside, and let him survive by his wits for a few years!"

"He would," pointed out the Saint. "Do we want to take responsibility for what would happen to the innocent world?"

"I suppose not," said the Master with a sigh, watching as his lady moved four white stones in a neat line. The white egrets advanced on the ravens again. The white moon outshone the clouds.

"But he does need a challenge," said the Saint. "He needs to put that mind of his to good use. He needs *work*."

"Damned right he does," said the Master of the Mountain. He considered the board again. "Rolling up his sleeves. Laboring with his hands. Building up a callus or two."

"Something that will make him employ his considerable talent," said the Saint.

There was a thoughtful silence. Their eyes met over the board. They smiled. Under the vaulted dome, all the birds took flight and circled in patterns, white wings and black.

"I'd better catch him early, or he'll be down the mountain again before cockcrow," said the Master of the Mountain. "To bed, madam?"

▲▼▲

Lord Ermenwyr rose sprightly by candlelight, congratulating himself on the self-reliance learned in Deliantiba: for now he could dress himself without a valet. Having donned apparel suitable for travel, he went to his door to rouse the bearers, that they might shoulder his new-laden trunks down the gorge to the red road far below.

Upon opening the door, he said:

"Sergeant, kindly fetch—Ack!"

"Good morning, my son," said the Master of the Mountain. "So eager for saber drill? Commendable."

"Thank you," said Lord Ermenwyr. "Actually, I thought I'd just get in some practice lifting weights, first."

"Not this morning," said his father. "I have a job for you, boy. Walk with me."

Gritting his teeth, Lord Ermenwyr walked beside his father, obliged to take two steps for every one the Master of the Mountain took. He was panting by the time they emerged on a high rampart, under faint stars, where the wall's guard were putting out the watch-fires of the night.

"Look down there, son," said the Master of the Mountain, pointing to three acres' space of waste and shattered rock, hard against the house wall.

"Goodness, is that a bit of snow still lying in the crevices?" said Lord Ermenwyr, watching his breath settle in powdered frost. "So late in the year, too. What unseasonably chilly weather we've had, don't you think?"

"Do you recognize the windows?" asked his father, and Lord Ermenwyr squinted down at the arrowslits far below. "You ought to."

"Oh! Is that the nursery, behind that wall?" Lord Ermenwyr said. "Well, what do you know? I was there only yesterday. Visiting my bastards, as a matter of fact. My, my, doesn't it look small from up here?"

"Yes," said the Master of the Mountain. "It does. You must have noticed how crowded it is, these days. Balnshik is of the opinion, and your mother and I concur with her, that the children need more room. A place to play when the weather is fine, perhaps. This would prevent them from growing up into stunted, pasty-faced little creatures with no stamina."

"What a splendid idea," said Lord Ermenwyr, smiling with all his sharp teeth. "Go to it, old man! Knock out a few walls and expand the place. Perhaps Eyrdway would be willing to give up a few rooms of his suite, eh?"

"No," said the Master of the Mountain placidly. "Balnshik wants an *outdoor* play area. A garden, just there under the windows. With lawns and a water feature, perhaps."

He leaned on the battlement and watched emotions conflict in his son's face. Lord Ermenwyr's eyes protruded slightly as the point of the conversation became evident to him, and he tugged at his beard, stammering:

"No, no, she can't be serious! What about household security? What about your enemies? Can't put the little ones' lives in danger, after all. Mustn't have them out where they might be carried off by, er, eagles or efrits, can we? Nursie means well, of course, but—"

"It's an interesting problem," said the Master of the Mountain. "I'm sure you'll think of a solution. You're such a clever fellow, after all."

"But—!"

"Krasp has been instructed to let you have all the tools and materials you need," said the Master of the Mountain. "I do hope you'll have it finished before high summer. Little Druvendyl's rash might clear up if he were able to sunbathe."

"Who the hell is Druvendyl?" cried Lord Ermenwyr.

"Your infant son," the Master of the Mountain informed him. "I expect full-color renderings in my study within three days, boy. Don't dawdle."

▲▼▲

Bright day without, but within Lord Ermenwyr's parlor it might have been midnight, so close had he drawn his drapes. He paced awhile in deep thought, glancing now and then at three flat stones he had set out on his hearth-rug. On one, a fistful of earth was mounded; on another, a small heap of coals glowed and faded. The third stone held a little water in a shallow depression.

To one side he had placed a table and chair.

Having worked up his nerve as far as was possible, he went at last to a chest at the foot of his bed and rummaged there. He drew out a long silver shape that winked in the light from the few coals. It was a flute. He seated himself in the chair and, raising the flute to his lips, began to play softly.

Summoning music floated forth, cajoling, enticing, music to catch the attention. The melody rose a little and was imperious, beckoned impatiently, wheedled and just hinted at threatening; then was coy, beseeched from a distance.

Lord Ermenwyr played with his eyes closed at first, putting his very soul into the music. When he heard a faint commotion from his hearth, though, he opened one eye and peered along the silver barrel as he played.

A flame had risen from the coals. Brightly it lit the other two stones, so he had a clear view of the water, which was bubbling upward as from a concealed fountain, and of the earth, which was mounding up too, for all the world like a molehill.

Lord Ermenwyr smiled in his heart and played on, and if the melody had promised before, it gave open-handed now; it was all delight, all ravishment. The water leaped higher, clouding, and the flame rose and spread out, dimming, and the earth bulged in its mound and began to lump into shape, as though under the hand of a sculptor.

A little more music, calling like birds in the forest, brightening like the sun rising over a plain, galloping like the herds there in the morning! And now the flame had assumed substance, and the water had firmed beside it. Now it appeared that three naked children sat on Lord Ermenwyr's hearth, their arms clasped about their drawn-up knees, their mouths slightly open as they watched him play. They were, all three, the phantom color of clouds, a shifting glassy hue suggesting rainbows. But about the shoulders of the little girl ran rills of bright flame, and one boy's hair swirled silver, and the other boy had perhaps less of the soap bubble about him, and more of wet clay.

Lord Ermenwyr raised his mouth from the pipe, grinned craftily at his guests, and set the pipe aside.

"No!" said the girl. "You must keep playing."

"Oh, but I'm tired, my dears," said Lord Ermenwyr. "I'm all out of breath."

"You have to play," the silvery boy insisted. "Play right now!"

But Lord Ermenwyr folded his arms. The children got to their feet, anger in their little faces, and they grew up before his eyes. The boys' chests deepened, their limbs lengthened, they overtopped the girl; but she became a woman shapely as any he'd ever beheld, with flames writhing from her brow.

"Play, or we'll kill you," said the three. "Burn you. Drown you. Bury you."

"Oh, no, that won't do," said Lord Ermenwyr. "Look here, shall we play a game? If I lose, I'll play for you again. If I win, you'll do as I bid you. What do you say to that?"

The three exchanged uncertain glances.

"We will play," they said. "But one at a time."

"Ah, now, is that fair?" cried Lord Ermenwyr. "When that gives you three chances to win against my one? I see you're too clever for me. So be it." He picked up the little table and set it before him. Opening a drawer, he brought out three cards.

"See here? Three portraits. Look closely: this handsome fellow is clearly me. This blackavised brigand is my father. And *this* lovely lady—" he held the card up before their eyes, "is my own saintly mother. Think you'd recognize her again? Of course you would. Now, we'll turn the cards face down. Can I find the lady? Of course I can; turn her up and here she is. That's no game at all! But if you find the lady, you'll win. So, who'll go first? Who'll find the lady?"

He took up the cards and looked at his guests expectantly. They nudged one another, and finally the earthborn said: "I will."

"Good for you!" Lord Ermenwyr said. "Watch, now, as I shuffle." He looked into the earthborn's face. "You're searching for the lady, understand?"

"Yes," said the earthborn, meeting his look of inquiry. "I understand."

"Good! So, here she is, and now here, and now here, and now—where?" Lord Ermenwyr fanned out his empty hands above the cards, in a gesture inviting choice.

Certain he knew where the lady was, the earthborn turned a card over.

"Whoops! Not the lady, is it? So sorry, friend. Who's for another try? Just three cards! It ought to be easy," sang Lord Ermenwyr, shuffling them again. The earthborn scowled in astonishment, as the others laughed gaily, and the waterborn stepped up to the table.

▲▼▲

"Stop complaining," said Lord Ermenwyr, dipping his pen in ink. "You lost fairly, didn't you?"

"We never had a chance," said the earthborn bitterly. "That big man on the card, the one that's bigger than you. He's the Soul of the Black Rock, isn't he?"

"I believe he's known by that title in certain circles, yes," said Lord Ermenwyr, sketching in a pergola leading to a reflecting pool. "Mostly circles chalked on black marble floors."

"He's supposed to be a *good* master," said the waterborn. "How did he have a son like you?"

"You'll find me a good master, poppets," said Lord Ermenwyr. "I'll free you when you've done my will, and you've my word as my father's son on that. You're far too expensive to keep for long," he added, with a severe look at the fireborn, who was boredly nibbling on a footstool.

"I hunger," she complained.

"Not long to wait now," Lord Ermenwyr promised. "No more than an hour to go before the setting of the moon. And look at the pretty picture I've made!" He held up his drawing. The three regarded it, and their glum faces brightened.

When the moon was well down, he led them out, and they followed gladly when they saw that he carried his silver flute.

The guards challenged him on the high rampart, but once they recognized him they bent in low obeisance. "Little master," they growled, and he tapped each lightly on the helmet with his flute, and each grim giant nodded its head between its boots and slept.

"Down there," he said, pointing through the starlight, and the three that served him looked down on that stony desolation and wondered. All doubt fled, though, when he set the flute to his lips once more.

Now they knew what to do! And gleeful they sprang to their work, dancing under the wide starry heaven, and the cold void warmed and quickened under their feet, and the leaping silver music carried them along. Earth and Fire and Water played, and united in interesting ways.

▲▼▲

Lord Ermenwyr was secure in bed, burrowed down under blankets and snoring, by the time bright morning lit the black mountain. But he did not need to see the first rays of the sun glitter on the great arched vault below the wall, where each glass pane was still hot from the fire that had passionately shaped it, and the iron frame too cooled slowly.

Nor did he need to see the warm sleepy earth under the vault, lying smooth in paths and emerald lawns, or the great trees that had rooted in it with magical speed. Neither did he need to hear the fountain bubbling languidly. He knew, already, what the children would find when they straggled from the dormitory, like a file of little ghosts in their white nightgowns.

He knew they would rub their eyes and run out through the new doorway, heedless of Balnshik's orders to remain, and knew they'd rush to pull down fruit from the pergola, and spit seeds at the red fish in the green lily-pool, or climb boldly to the backs of the stone wyverns, or run on the soft grass, or vie to see how hard they could bounce balls against the glass without breaking it. Had he not planned all this, to the last detail?

▲▼▲

The Master of the Mountain and the Saint of the World came to see, when the uneasy servants roused them before breakfast.

"Too clever by half," said the Master of the Mountain, raising his eyes to the high vault, where the squares of bubbled and sea-clear glass let in an underwater sort of light. "Impenetrable. Designed to break up perception and confuse. And…what's he done to the time? Do you feel that?"

"It's slowed," said the Saint of the World. "Within this garden, it will always be a moment or so in the past. As inviolate as memory, my lord."

"Nice to know he paid attention to his lessons," said the Master of the Mountain, narrowing his eyes. Two little boys ran past him at knee level, screaming like whistles for no good reason, and one child tripped over a little girl who was sprawled on the grass pretending to be a mermaid.

"You see what he can do when he applies himself?" said the Saint, lifting the howling boy and soothing him.

"He still cheated," said the Master of the Mountain.

▲▼▲

It was well after noon when Lord Ermenwyr consented to rise and grace the house with his conscious presence, and by then all the servants knew. He nodded to them as he strolled the black halls, happily aware that his personal legend had just enlarged. Now, when they gathered in the servant's halls around the balefires, and served out well-earned kraters of black wine at the end of a long day, *now* they would have something more edifying over which to exclaim than the number of childhood diseases he had narrowly survived or his current paternity suit.

"By the Blue Pit of Hasrahkhin, it was a miracle! A whole garden, trees and all, in the worst place imaginable to put one, and it had to be secret and secure— and the boy did it in just one night!" That was what they'd say, surely.

So it was with a spring in his step that nearly overbalanced him on his five-inch heels that the lordling came to his father's accounting chamber, and rapped briskly for admission.

The doorman ushered him in to his father's presence with deeper than usual obeisances, or so he fancied. The Master of the Mountain glanced up from the scroll he studied, and nodded at Lord Ermenwyr.

"Yes, my son?"

"I suppose you've visited the nursery this morning?" Lord Ermenwyr threw himself into a chair, excruciatingly casual in manner.

"I have, as a matter of fact," replied his lord father. "I'm impressed, boy. Your mother and I are proud of you."

"Thank you." Lord Ermenwyr drew out his long smoking-tube and lit it with a positive jet of flame. He inhaled deeply, exhaled a cloud that writhed about his head, and fixed bright eyes upon the Master of the Mountain. "Would this be an auspicious time to discuss increasing an allowance, o my most justly feared sire?"

"It would not," said the Master of the Mountain. "Bloody hell, boy! A genius like you ought to be able to come up with his own pocket money."

▲▼▲

Lord Ermenwyr stalked the black halls, brooding on the unfairness of life in general and fathers in especial.

"Clever enough to come up with my own pocket money, am I?" he fumed. "I'll show *him*."

He paused on a terrace and looked out again in the direction of the cities on the plain, and sighed with longing.

The back of his neck prickled, just as he heard the soft footfall behind him.

He whirled around and kicked, hard, but his boot sank into something that squelched. Looking up into the yawning, dripping maw of a horror out of legend, he snarled and said:

"Stop it, you moron! Slug-Hoggoth hasn't scared me since I was six."

"It has too," said a voice, plaintive in its disappointment. "Remember when you were twelve, and I hid behind the door of your bedroom? You screamed and screamed."

"No, I didn't," said Lord Ermenwyr, extricating his boot.

"Yes, you did, you screamed just like a girl," gloated the creature. "Eeeek!"

"Shut up."

"Make me, midget." The creature's outline blurred and shimmered; dwindled and firmed, resolving into a young man.

He was head and shoulders taller than Lord Ermenwyr, slender and beautiful as a beardless god, and stark naked except for a great deal of gold and silver jewelry. That having been said, there was an undeniable resemblance between the two men.

"Idiot," muttered Lord Ermenwyr.

"But prettier than you," said the other, throwing out his arms. "Gorgeous, aren't I? What do you think of my new pectoral? Thirty black pearls! And the bracelets match, look!"

Lord Ermenwyr considered his brother's jewelry with a thoughtful expression.

"Superb," he admitted. "You robbed a caravan, I suppose. How are you, Eyrdway?"

"I'm always in splendid health," said Lord Eyrdway. "Not like you, eh?"

"No indeed," said Lord Ermenwyr with a sigh. "I'm a wreck. Too much fast life down there amongst the Children of the Sun. Wining, wenching, burning my candle at both ends! I'm certain I'll be dead before I'm twenty-two, but what memories I'll have."

"Wenching?" Lord Eyrdway's eyes widened.

"It's like looting and raping, but nobody rushes you," explained his brother. "And sometimes the ladies even make breakfast for you afterward."

"I know perfectly well what wenching is," said Lord Eyrdway indignantly. "What's *burning your candle at both ends?*"

"Ahhh." Lord Ermenwyr lit up his smoking tube. "Let's go order a couple of bottles of wine, and I'll explain."

▲▼▲

Several bottles and several hours later, they sat in the little garden just outside Lord Ermenwyr's private chamber. Lord Ermenwyr was refilling his brother's glass.

"...so then I said to her, 'Well, madam, if you insist, but I really ought to have another apple first,' and that was the exact moment they broke in the terrace doors!" he said.

"Bunch of nonsense. You can't do that with an apple," Lord Eyrdway slurred.

"Maybe it was an apricot," said Lord Ermenwyr. "Anyway, the best part of it was, I got out the window with both the bag *and* the jewel case. Wasn't that lucky?"

"It sounds like a lot of fun," said Lord Eyrdway wistfully, and drank deep.

"Oh, it was. So then I went round to the Black Veil Club—but of course you know what goes on in *those* places!" Lord Ermenwyr pretended to sip his wine.

"'Course I do," said his brother. "Only maybe I've forgot. You tell me again, all right?"

Lord Ermenwyr smiled. Leaning forward, lowering his voice, he explained about all the outré delights to be had at a Black Veil Club. Lord Eyrdway began to drool. Wiping it away absentmindedly, he said at last:

"You see—you see—that's what's so awful unflair. Unfair. All this fun you get to have. 'Cause you're totally worthless and nobody cares if you go down the mountain. You aren't the damn Heir to the Black Halls. Like me. I'm so really important Daddy won't let me go."

"Poor old Way-Way, it isn't fair at all, is it?" said Lord Ermenwyr. "Have another glass of wine."

"I mean, I'd just love to go t'Deliatitatita, have some fun," said Lord Eyrdway, holding out his glass to be refilled, "But, you know, Daddy just puts his hand on my shoulder n' says, 'When you're older, son,' but I'm older'n you by four years, right? Though of course who cares if *you* go, right? No big loss to the Family if *you* get an arrow through your liver."

"No indeed," said Lord Ermenwyr, leaning back. "Tell me something, my brother. Would you say I could do great things with my life if I only applied myself?"

"What?" Lord Eyrdway tried to focus on him. "You? No! I can see three of you right now, an' not one of 'em's worth a damn." He began to snicker. "Good one, eh? Three of you, get it? Oh, I'm sleepy. Just going to put my head down for a minute, right?"

He lay his head down and was promptly unconscious. When Lord Ermenwyr saw his brother blur and soften at the edges, as though he were a waxwork figure that had been left too near the fire, he rose and began to divest him of his jewelry.

"Eyrdway, I truly love you," he said.

▲▼▲

The express caravan came through next dawn, rattling along at its best speed in hopes of being well down off the mountain by evening. The caravan master spotted the slight figure by the side of the road well in advance, and gave the signal to stop. The lead keyman threw the brake; sparks flew as the wheels slowed, and stopped.

Lord Ermenwyr, bright-eyed, hopped down from his trunks and approached the caravan master.

"Hello! Will this buy me passage on your splendid conveyance?" He held forth his hand. The caravan master squinted at it suspiciously. Then his eyes widened.

"Keymen! Load his trunks!" he bawled. "Lord, sir, with a pearl like that you could ride the whole route three times around. Where shall we take you? Deliantiba?"

Lord Ermenwyr considered, putting his head on one side.

"No…not Deliantiba, I think. I want to go somewhere there's a lot of trouble, of the proper sort for a gentleman. If you understand me?"

The caravan master sized him up. "There's a lot for a gentleman to do in Karkateen, sir, if his tastes run a certain way. You've heard the old song, right, about what *their* streets are paved with?"

Lord Ermenwyr began to smile. "I have indeed. Karkateen it is, then."

"Right you are, sir! Please take a seat."

So with a high heart the lordling vaulted the side of the first free cart, and sprawled back at his ease. The long line of carts started forward, picked up speed, and clattered on down the ruts in the red road. The young sun rose and shone on the young man, and the young man sang as he sped through the glad morning of the world.

What the Tyger Told Her

"You must observe carefully," said the tyger.

He was an old tyger. He had survived in captivity more years than he might have been expected to, penned in his narrow iron run in such a cold wet country, in all weathers. He was just the color of toast, and white underneath like bread too. His back was double-striped with black streaks and the rippling shadows of the bars as he paced continually, turn and turn again.

The little girl blinked, mildly surprised at being addressed. She had a round face, pale and freckled like a robin's egg. She had been squatting beside the tyger's pen for some minutes, fascinated by him. If anyone had seen her crouched there, crumpling the silk brocade of her tiny hooped gown, she'd have been scolded, for the summer dust was thick in the garden. But no one had noticed she was there.

"Power," said the tyger, "Comes from knowledge, you see. The best way to learn is to watch what happens. The best way to watch is unseen. Now, in my proper place, which is jungle meadow and forest canes, I am very nearly invisible. That," and he looked with eyes green as beryls at the splendid house rising above the gardens, "is your proper place. Are you invisible there?"

The little girl nodded her head.

"Do you know why you're invisible?"

She thought about it. "Because John and James were born."

"Your little brothers, yes. And so nobody sees you now?"

"And because..." The child waved her hand in a gesture that took in the house, the garden, the menagerie and the immense park in which they were set. "There's so many uncles and people here. Mamma and I used to live in the lodging-house. Papa would come upstairs in his uniform. It was red. He was a poor officer. Then he got sick and lived with us in his nightgown. It was white. He would drink from a bottle and shout, and I would hide behind the chair when he did. And John and James got born. And Papa went to heaven. And Mamma said oh, my dear, whatever shall we do?"

"What did you do?" the tyger prompted.

"I didn't do anything. But Grandpapa forgave Mamma and sent for us."

"What had your Mamma done, to be forgiven?"

"She wasn't supposed to marry Papa because she is," and the child paused a moment to recollect the big words, "an indigent tradesman's daughter. Papa used to tell her so when he drank out of the bottle. But when she had John and James, that made it all right again, because they're the only boys."

"So they're important."

"They will inherit it all," the child explained, as though she were quoting. "Because Papa died and Uncle John is in India, and Uncle Thomas only has Louise."

"But they haven't inherited yet."

"No. Not until Grandpapa goes to heaven."

"Something to think about, isn't it?" said the tyger, lowering his head to lap water from his stone trough.

The little girl thought about it.

"I thought Grandpapa was in heaven when we went to see him," she said. "We climbed so many stairs. And the bed was so high and white and the pillows like clouds. Grandpapa's nightgown was white. He has white hair and a long, long beard. He shouted like Papa did. Mamma turned away crying. Mr. Lawyer said It's only his pain, Mrs. Edgecombe. Uncle Thomas said Dear sister, come and have a glass of cordial. So she did and she was much better."

"But nobody saw you there, did they?"

"No," said the child.

"Who's that coming along the walk?" the tyger inquired.

"That is Uncle Thomas and Aunt Caroline," the child replied.

"Do you notice that she's not as pretty as your Mamma?"

"Yes."

"And quite a bit older."

"Yes. And she can't have any children but Cousin Louise."

"I think perhaps you ought to sit quite still," advised the tyger.

The woman swept ahead in her anger, long skirts trailing in the tall summer grass at the edge of the walk, white fingers knotting on her lace apron, high curls bobbing with her agitation. The man hurried after her, tottering a little because of the height of his heels, and the skirts of his coat flapped out behind him. He wore bottlegreen silk. His waistcoat was embroidered with little birds, his wig was slightly askew. He looked sullen.

"Oh, you have a heart of stone," cried Aunt Caroline. "Your own child to be left a pauper! It's too unjust. Is this the reward of filial duty?"

"Louise is not an especially dutiful girl," muttered Uncle Thomas.

"I meant your filial duty! One is reminded of the Prodigal Son. *You* have obeyed his every wish, while he thundered up there. Wretched old paralytic! And Robert disgraces himself, and dies like a dog in a ditch with that strumpet, but all's forgiven because of the twins. Are all our hopes to be dashed forever?"

"Now, Caroline, patience," said Uncle Thomas. "Consider: life's uncertain."

"That's true." Aunt Caroline pulled up short, looking speculative. "Any childish illness might carry off the brats. Oh, I could drown them like puppies myself!"

Uncle Thomas winced. He glared at Aunt Caroline's back a moment before drawing abreast of her, by which time he was smiling.

"You'll oblige me by doing nothing so rash. Robert was never strong; we can pray they've inherited his constitution. And after all it would be just as convenient, my dear, if the wench were to die instead. I would be guardian of John and James, the estate in my hands; what should we have to worry about then?"

They walked on together. The little girl stared after them.

"Do you think they're going to drown my Mamma?" she asked uneasily.

"Did you see the way your uncle looked at your aunt behind her back?" replied the tyger. "I don't think he cares for her, particularly. What do you think?"

▲▼▲

There were fruit trees espaliered all along the menagerie wall, heavy now in apricots and cherries, and when the chimpanzee had been alive it had been driven nearly frantic in summers by the sight and the smell of the fruit. Now stuffed with straw, it stared sadly from a glass-fronted cabinet, through a fine layer of dust.

The little girl, having discovered the fruit was there, wasted no time in filling her apron with all she could reach and retiring to the shade under the plum tree. The largest, ripest apricot she bowled carefully into the tyger's cage. The others she ate in methodical fashion, making a small mound of neatly stacked pits and cherry stones.

The tyger paused in his relentless stride just long enough to sniff the apricot, turning it over with his white-bearded chin.

"Your baby brothers have not died," he said.

"No," the little girl affirmed, biting into a cherry.

"However, your Aunt Caroline has been suffering acute stomach pains, especially after dinner. That's interesting."

"She has a glass of port wine to make it better," said the child. "But it doesn't get better."

"And that's your Mamma coming along the walk now, I see," said the tyger. "With Uncle Thomas."

The child concealed the rest of the fruit with her apron and sat still. She needn't have worried: neither her mother nor her uncle noticed her.

Like her daughter, Mamma had a pale freckled face but was otherwise quite attractive, and the black broadcloth of her mourning made her look slender and gave her a dignity she needed, for she was very young. She was being drawn along by Uncle Thomas, who had her by the arm.

"We ought never to question the will of the Almighty," Uncle Thomas was saying pleasantly. "It never pleased Him that Caroline should bear me sons, and certainly that's been a grief to me; but then, without boys of my own, how ready am I to do a father's duty by dear little John and James! All that I might have done for my sons, I may do for yours. Have no fear on that account, dear Lavinia."

"It's very kind of you, brother Thomas," said Mamma breathlessly. "For, sure we have been so poor, I was at my wit's end—and father Edgecombe is so severe."

"But Robert was his favorite," said Uncle Thomas. "The very reason he disowned him, I think; Father couldn't brook disobedience in one he loved above all. If Henry or I had eloped, he'd have scarcely noticed. And Randall does what he likes, of course. Father was too hard on Robert, alas."

"Oh, sir, I wish someone had said so whiles he lived," said Mamma. "He often wept that he had no friends."

"Alas! I meant to write to him, but duty forbid." Uncle Thomas shook his head. "It is too bad. I must endeavor to redress it, Lavinia."

He slipped his arm around her waist. She looked flustered, but said nothing. They walked on.

"Mamma is frightened," said the child.

"There are disadvantages to being pretty," said the tyger. "As you can see. I imagine she wishes she could be invisible, occasionally. Your uncle's a subtle man; notice how he used words like *duty* and *alas*. No protestations of ardent passion. It's often easier to get something you want if you pretend you don't want it. Remember that."

The little girl nodded.

She ate another cherry. A peahen ventured near the wall, cocking her head to examine the windfall fruit under the little trees. As she lingered there, a peacock came stalking close, stiffened to see the hen; his whole body, bright as blue enamel, shivered, and his trailing train of feathers rose and spread behind him, shimmering in terrifying glory. Eyes stared from it. The little girl caught her breath at all the green and purple and gold.

"You mustn't allow yourself to be distracted," the tyger cautioned. "It's never safe. You see?"

"What, are you lurking there, you little baggage?"

The little girl looked around sharply, craning her head back. Uncle Randall dropped into a crouch beside her, staring at her. He was young, dressed in tawny silk that shone like gold. His voice was teasing and hard. He smelled like wine.

"Ha, she's stealing fruit! You can be punished for that, you know. They'll pull your skirt up and whip your bare bum, if I tell. Shall I tell?"

"No," said the child.

"What'll you give me, not to tell?"

She offered him an apricot. He took it and rolled it in his hand, eyeing it, and hooted in derision.

"Gives me the greenest one she's got! Clever hussy. You're a little woman, to be sure."

She didn't know what to say to that, so she said nothing. He stared at her a moment longer, and then the tyger drew his attention.

"Aren't you afraid of old Master Stripes? Don't you worry he'll break his bounds, and eat you like a rabbit? He might, you know. But I'm not afraid of him."

The tyger growled softly, did not cease pacing.

"Useless thing! I'd a damn sight rather Johnnie'd sent us one of his blacks," said Uncle Randall. He looked down at her again. "Well, poppet. What's your Mamma's favorite color?"

"Sky blue," said the child.

"It is, eh? Yes, with those eyes, she'd wear that to her advantage. D'you think she'd like a velvet scarf in that color, eh? Or a cape?"

"She has to wear black now," the child reminded him.

"She'll wear it as long as it suits her, I've no doubt. What about scent? What's her fancy? Tell me, does she ever drink strong waters in secret?"

The child had no idea what that meant, so she shook her head mutely. Uncle Randall snorted.

"You wouldn't tell if she did, I'll wager. Well. Does she miss your Papa very much?"

"Yes."

"You must say 'Yes, Uncle dear'. "

"Yes, Uncle dear."

"There's a good girl. Do you think you'd like to have another Papa?"

The child thought about it. Remembering the things Papa had said when he raved, that had made her creep behind the chair to hide, she said: "No."

"No? But that's wicked of you, you little minx. A girl must have a Papa to look after her and her Mamma, or dreadful things might happen. They might starve in the street. Freeze to death. Meat for dogs, you see, do you want your Mamma to be meat for dogs?"

"No," said the child, terrified that she would begin to cry.

"Then you'll tell her she must get you another Papa as soon as ever she may," Uncle Randall ordered. "Do you understand me? Do it, and you'll have a treat. Something pretty." He reached down to stroke her cheek, and his hand lingered there.

"What a soft cheek you've got," he said. "I wonder if your Mamma's is as soft."

The peacock was maneuvering up behind the hen, treading on her feathers. Seeing it, Uncle Randall gave a sharp laugh and shied the apricot at her, and she bolted forward, away from the peacock.

Uncle Randall strode off without another word.

"Now, your Uncle Randall," said the tyger, "is not a subtle man. Nor as clever as he thinks he is, all in all. He talks far too much, wouldn't you say?"

The child nodded.

"He uses fear to get what he wants," said the tyger. "And he underestimates his opponents. That's a dangerous thing to do. A bad combination of strategies."

Wasps buzzed and fought for the apricot at his feet.

▲▼▲

The summer heat was oppressive. All the early fruit had fallen from the trees, or been gathered and taken in to make jam. There were blackberries in the hedge, gleaming like red and black garnets, but they were dusty and hard for the child to reach without scratching herself on the brambles.

There was a thick square of privet in the center of the menagerie court-yard, man-high. Long ago it had been a formal design, clipped close, but for one reason or another had been abandoned to grow unchecked. Its little paths were all lost now except at ground level, where they formed a secret maze of tunnels in the heart of the bush. There was a sundial buried in the greenery, lightless and mute: it told nobody anything.

The little girl had crawled in under the branches and lay there, pretending she was a jungle beast hiding in long grass. She gazed out at the tyger, who had retreated to the shade of the sacking the grooms had laid across the top of his pen. He blinked big mild eyes. He looked sleepy.

"How fares your Aunt Caroline?" he inquired.

"She's sick," the child said. "The doctor was sent for, but he couldn't find anything wrong with her. He said it might be her courses drying up."

"Do you know what that means?"

"No," said the child. "But that's what Uncle Thomas is telling everybody. And he says, you mustn't mind what a woman says because of it. He's very kind to her."

"How clever of him." The tyger yawned, showing fearful teeth, and stretched his length. "And he's even kinder to your Mamma, isn't he?"

"Yes. Very kind."

"What do you suppose will happen if your Aunt Caroline dies?"

"She will be buried in the graveyard."

"So she will."

They heard footsteps approaching, two pair.

The child peered up from under the leaves and saw Cousin Louise with one of the stableboys. She was a tall girl with a sallow complexion, very tightly laced into her gown in order to have any bosom at all. The stableboy was thickset, with pimples on his face. He was carrying a covered pail. He smelled like manure.

"It be under here," he said, leading Cousin Louise around the side of the privet square. "The heart of it's all hollow, you see? And you can lie inside in the shade. It's a rare nice place to hide, and there ain't nobody knows it's here but me."

"Audacious rogue!" Cousin Louise giggled. "I'll tear my gown."

"Then the Squire'll buy thee a new one, won't he? Get in there."

The child lay very still. She heard the branches parting and the sound of two people awkwardly arranging themselves inside the privet. Turning her head very slightly, she caught a glimpse of them six feet away from her, mostly screened off by green leaves and the base of the sundial. She watched from the corner of her eye as they made themselves comfortable, handing the pail back and forth to drink from it.

"Aah! I like a cool drop of beer, in this heat," the stableboy sighed.

"It's refreshing," said Cousin Louise. "I've never had beer before."

"Like enough you wouldn't," said the stableboy, and belched. "Sweet wines and gin, ain't that what the fine folk have to themselves? The likes of me don't get a taste of your Madeira from one year's end to the next." He chuckled. "That's all one; I'll get a taste of something fine anyway."

There was a thrashing of bushes and Cousin Louise gave a little squeal of laughter.

"Hush! The keeper'll hear, you silly slut."

"No, no, he mustn't."

There was heavy breathing and a certain ruffling, as of petticoats. Cousin Louise spoke in an almost trancelike voice.

"How if you were a bold highwayman? You might shoot the driver, and there might be no other passengers but me, and I might be cowering within the coach, in fear of my very life. You'd fling the door wide—and you might look at me and lick your chops, as a hungry dog might—and you might say—you'd say—"

"Here's a saucy strumpet wants a good futtering, I'd say," growled the stableboy.

"Yes," Cousin Louise gasped, hysteria coming into her voice, "and I'd protest, but you would be merciless. You'd drag me from the coach, and throw me down on the ferns in the savage forest, and tear my gown to expose my bosom, and then—"

"Oh, hush your noise," the stableboy told Cousin Louise, and crawled on top of her. When they'd finished, he rolled off and reached for the beer pail. Cousin Louise was laughing, breathless, helpless, but her laughter began to sound a little like crying, and a certain alarm was in the stableboy's voice when he said:

"Stop your fool mouth! Do you want to get me whipped? If you start screaming I'll cut your throat, you jade! What's the matter with you?"

Cousin Louise put her hands over her face and fell silent, attempting to even her breath. "Nothing," she said faintly. "Nothing. All's well."

There was silence for a moment, and the stableboy drank more beer.

"I feel a little ill with the heat," explained Cousin Louise.

"That's like enough," said the stableboy, sounding somewhat mollified.

Another rustling; Cousin Louise was sitting up, putting her arms around the stableboy.

"I do love you so," she said, "I could never see you harmed, dearest. Say but the word and I'll run away with thee, and be thy constant wife."

"Art thou mad?" The stableboy sounded incredulous. "The likes of you wedded to me? The Squire'd hunt us sure, and he'd have my life. Even so, how should I afford to keep a wife, with my place lost? It ain't likely you'd bring much of a dowry, anyhow, be the Squire never so willing. Not with everything going to them little boys, now."

"I have three hundred pounds a year from my mother, once she's dead and I am married." Cousin Louise sounded desperate. "I have! And she's grievous sick. Who knows how long she will live?"

"And what then? Much good that'd do me, if I was hanged or transported," said the stableboy. "Which I will be, if you don't keep quiet about our fun. Better ladies than you knows how to hold their tongues."

Cousin Louise did not say another word after that. The stableboy drank the rest of the beer, and sighed.

"I've got the mucking out to do," he announced, and buttoned himself and crawled from the bush. His footsteps went away across the paving-stones, slow and heavy.

Cousin Louise sat perfectly still for a long time, before abruptly scrambling out and walking away with quick steps.

The little girl exhaled.

"He didn't speak to her very nicely," said the tyger.

"No."

"And she didn't seem to have much fun. Why do you suppose she'd go into the bushes with a person like that?"

"She said she loved him," said the child.

"Does she?" The tyger licked his paw lazily. "I wonder. Some people seem to feel the need to get manure on their shoes."

The child wrinkled her nose. "Why?"

"Who knows? Perhaps they feel it's what they deserve," said the tyger.

▲▼▲

The little girl had found broken china hidden in the green gloom behind the potting shed: two dishes, a custard-cup and a sauceboat. She carried them out carefully and washed them in the horse-trough, and then retired to the bed of bare earth under the fruit trees with them. There she set out the broken plates to be courtyards, and inverted the cup and sauceboat on them to be houses. Collecting cherry pits, she arranged them in lines: they were soldiers, marching between the houses. The rationale for making them soldiers was that soldiers had red coats, and cherries were red. The tyger watched her.

"There are visitors today," he said. The child nodded.

"Uncle Henry and Aunt Elizabeth," she replied. "They came to see John and James. Uncle Henry is going to be their godfather, because he's a curate. They have a little girl, just my size, but she didn't come, or she might have played with me."

"Are you sorry she's not here to play with you?"

The child lifted her head in surprise, struck by the question.

"I don't know," she said. "Would she see me?"

"She might," the tyger said. "Children notice other children, don't they?"

"Sometimes."

"I think someone's coming," the tyger informed her. She looked up, and saw Uncle Henry and Aunt Elizabeth strolling together along the walk.

"…not so well-stocked as it was formerly, alas," said Uncle Henry. He wore black, with a very white wig. Aunt Elizabeth was plump, wore a mulberry-colored gown and a straw hat for the sun.

"Oh, bless us, look there!" she exclaimed, stopping in her tracks as she saw the tyger. "Dear, dear, d'you think it's safe to keep a beast like that about, with so many little children in the house? I'm glad now we kept Jane at home, my love."

"He's never harmed anyone, that I'm aware," Uncle Henry told her, taking her arm and steering her forward. "Poor old Bobo used to scream, and bite, and fling ordure; but I daresay it was because Randall teased him. Randall was frightened of this fellow, however. Kept his distance."

"And very sensible of him too," said Aunt Elizabeth, shuddering. "Oh, look at the size of it! I feel like a mouse must feel before our Tibby."

"The same Providence created them, Bess." Uncle Henry stopped before the pen. "Each creature has its place in the grand design, after all."

"Tibby catches rats, and I'm sure that's very useful indeed, but what's the point of an animal like this one?" protested Aunt Elizabeth. "Great horrid teeth and claws! Unless they have giant rats in India?"

"I don't think they do," said Uncle Henry. "But I trust the Almighty had His reasons."

"Well, I shall never understand how He could make something so cruel," said Aunt Elizabeth firmly. "Look there, what are those? Are those parrots? Dear little things!"

"Budgerigars, I think," said Uncle Henry.

They walked away to inspect the aviary, which was beyond the privet-square.

"Stay where you are," said the tyger.

"Oh, I could never," Mamma was saying distractedly. "I couldn't think of such a thing, with poor Robert's grave scarcely green."

"Tut-tut, Lavinia!" said Uncle Randall, as they approached. "There's none to hear but you and I. Look as pious as you like before the world. The demure widow, meek and holy, if you please! I won't repeat what passes between us; but you and I both knew Robert. He hadn't enough blood in him to keep you contented, a lively girl like you. Had he, now? How long's it been since you had a good gallop, eh? Eh?"

She had been walking quickly ahead of him, and he caught up to her in front of the tyger's pen and seized her arm. Her face was red.

"You don't—oh—"

Uncle Randall stepped close and spoke very quickly. "The blood in your cheeks is honest, Madam Sanctimony. Don't play the hypocrite with me! I know London girls too well. You got your hooks into Robert to climb out of the gutter, didn't you? Well, keep climbing, hussy! I stand ready to help you up the next step, and the old man may be damned. We've got those boys, haven't we? We'll be master and mistress here one day, if you're not an affected squeamish—"

"You hound!" Mamma found her voice at last. "Oh, you base—*thing*!"

Uncle Henry and Aunt Elizabeth came walking swiftly around the privet square, and advanced on the scene like a pair of soldiers marching.

"What's this, Lavinia?" Uncle Henry's eyes moved from Mamma to Uncle Randall and back. "Tears?"

"We were speaking of Robert," said Uncle Randall, standing his ground. "Poor fellow. Were we not, dear Lavinia?"

Shocked back into silence, Mamma nodded. Aunt Elizabeth came and put her arms about her.

"My child, you mustn't vex your heart so with weeping," she said solicitously. "It's natural, in such an affectionate match, but only think! Robert would wish you to be happy, now that all's reconciled. And you must have courage, for the children's sake."

"So I was just saying," said Uncle Randall, helping himself to a pinch of snuff.

"We must endure our sorrows in patience," Uncle Henry advised her, looking at Uncle Randall.

"Come now, Lavinia," said Uncle Randall in quite a kind voice. "Dry your tears and walk with us. Shall we go view the pretty babes? John's the very image of Robert, in my opinion."

They bore her away between them.

"Your Mamma doesn't wish to make trouble, I see," said the tyger.

"She didn't tell on him," said the child, in wonderment.

"Silence is not always wise," said the tyger. "Not when it gives your opponent an opportunity. Perhaps your Uncle Randall hasn't underestimated your Mamma, after all."

"Why didn't she tell on him?" The child stared after the retreating adults.

"Why indeed?" said the tyger. "Something else to remember: even bad strategy can succeed, if your opponent has no strategy at all."

▲▼▲

Just beyond the menagerie courtyard, five stone steps led down into a sunken garden. It was a long rectangle of lawn, with rose-beds at its edges and a fountain and small reflecting pool at its center. At its far end five more stone steps led up out of it, and beyond was a dense wood, and further beyond was open heath where deer sometimes grazed.

The roses were briary, and the fountain long clogged and scummed over with green. But there were men working on it today, poking with rakes and sticks, and it had begun to gurgle in a sluggish kind of way; and the gardener had cut back the briars that hung out over the lawn. He was up on a ladder now with his handkerchief, rubbing dust off the sprays of rose haws, so they gleamed scarlet as blood-drops.

The little girl watched them warily, nibbling at a rose haw she'd snatched from one of the cut sprays. It was hard and sour, but interesting. The tyger watched them too, pacing more quickly than usual.

"Your Uncle Randall gave your mother a fine length of sky-blue silk," he said. "Will she have a gown made of it, do you think?"

"No," said the child. "She showed it to Uncle Thomas and Aunt Caroline and asked them if she ought to have a gown made for the christening party."

"Really?" the tyger said. "And what did they say?"

"Aunt Caroline looked cross, and said Mamma mustn't think of such a thing while she's in mourning. Uncle Thomas didn't say anything. But his eyes got very small."

"Rather a clever thing for your Mamma to have done," said the tyger. "What did she say in reply?"

"She said Yes, yes, you're quite right. And Uncle Thomas went and talked to Uncle Randall about it."

The tyger made a low percussive sound in his chest, for all the world like quiet laughter.

"If a rabbit's being chased by a fox, it's wise to run straight to the wolf," he said. "Of course, the question then is, whether it can get away safely after the wolf's taken the fox by the throat. Wolves like a bit of rabbit too."

"It's bad to be a rabbit," said the little girl.

"So it is," said the tyger. "But if one has grown up to be a rabbit, one can do very little about it."

"Only run."

"Just so." The tyger turned his great wide head to regard the sunken garden. "Why, your aunts have come out to take the air."

The little girl retreated to the plum tree. Leaning against its trunk, she watched Aunt Caroline and Aunt Elizabeth coming along the walk.

Aunt Caroline was pale and thin, had a shawl draped about her shoulders, and Aunt Elizabeth half-supported her as she walked.

"Yes, I do think the bloom's returning to your cheeks already," Aunt Elizabeth was saying in a determinedly cheery voice. "Fresh air will do you a world of good, my dear, I'm sure. Whenever I feel faint or bilious at Brookwood, dearest Henry always advises me to take my bonnet and go for a ramble, and after a mile or so I'm always quite restored again, and come home with quite an appetite for my dinner!"

Aunt Caroline said nothing in reply, breathing with effort as they walked. There was a stone seat overlooking the sunken garden, and Aunt Elizabeth led her to it.

"We'll settle ourselves here, shall we, and watch them making it ready?" suggested Aunt Elizabeth, sitting down and making room for Aunt Caroline. "There now. Oh, look, they've got the water going again! Really, this will make the prettiest place for a party. You'll want to put the long table for the collation over there, I suppose, and the trestle tables along the other side. And I would, my dear, have two comfortable chairs brought down and set on a kind of step, 'tis called a dais in London I think, where the nursemaids may sit with the little boys and all may pay their respects conveniently."

Aunt Caroline hissed and doubled over, clutching herself.

"There, my dear, there, courage!" Aunt Elizabeth rubbed her back. "Oh, and you were feeling so much better after breakfast. Perhaps this will help. When I'm troubled with wind, Henry will—"

"It's a judgement from God," gasped Aunt Caroline.

"Dear, you mustn't say such a thing! It may be He sends us our little aches and pains to remind us we ought to be ready at all times to come before Him, but—"

"I prayed the boys would die," Aunt Caroline told her. "I thought of having them suffocated in their cradles. God forgive me, forgive me! And it wasn't a week after that the pains began."

Aunt Elizabeth had drawn away from her. Her face was a study in stupefied horror.

"Never!" she said at last. "Those dear, sweet little lambs? Oh, Caroline, you never! Oh, how could you? Oh, and to think—"

Aunt Caroline had begun to sob hoarsely, rocking herself to and fro in her agony. Aunt Elizabeth watched her a moment, struggling to find words, and at last found them.

"Well," she said, "It's—Henry would say, this is proof of the infinite mercy of the Almighty, you know. For, only think, if you had followed such a wicked thought with a *deed*, what worse torments would await you eternally! As it is, the sin is hideous but not so bad as it might be, and these timely pangs have made you reflect on the peril to your eternal soul, and you have surely repented! Therefore all may yet be well—"

Aunt Caroline toppled forward. Aunt Elizabeth leaped up, screaming, and the men stopped work at once and ran to be of assistance. Upon examination, Aunt Caroline was found not to have died, but merely fainted from her pain, and when revived she begged feebly to be taken to her chamber. Aunt Elizabeth, rising to the occasion, directed the men to improvise a stretcher from the ladder. She paced alongside as they bore Aunt Caroline away, entreating her to call on her Savior for comfort.

The little girl watched all this with round eyes.

"There's one secret out," remarked the tyger. "I wonder whether any others will show themselves?"

▲▼▲

The east wind was blowing. It swayed the cloths on the long tables, it swayed the paper lanterns the servants had hung up on lines strung through the trees in the garden. The tyger lashed his tail as he paced.

The little girl was walking from lantern to lantern, peering up at them and wondering how they would light when evening fell.

"Your Uncle Randall asked your Mamma to marry him today," said the tyger.

"He did it in front of Uncle Henry and Aunt Elizabeth," said the child.

"Because he thought she wouldn't like to say no, if they were present," said the tyger. The child nodded.

"But Mamma said no," she concluded. "Then Uncle Randall had a glass of wine."

The tyger put his face close to the bars.

"Something bad is going to happen," he said. "Think very hard, quickly: are you a rabbit, or do you have teeth and claws?"

"What the hell's it doing?" said a hoarse voice from the other end of the courtyard. The child looked up to see Uncle Randall advancing on her swiftly. He had a strange blank look in his eyes, a strange fixed smile.

"Hasn't it ever been told not to go so near a wild brute? Naughty, naughty little thing!" he said, and grabbed her arm tightly. "We'll have to punish it."

He began to drag her away in the direction of the potting shed. She screamed, kicking him as hard as she could, but he laughed and swung her up off her feet. He marched on toward the thicket behind the shed, groping under her skirts.

"We'll have to punish its little soft bum, that's what we'll have to do," he said wildly, "Because a dutiful uncle must do such things, after all, ungrateful little harlot—"

She screamed again, and suddenly he had stopped dead in his tracks and let her fall, because Cousin Louise was standing right before them and staring at Uncle Randall. She was chalk-white. She seemed as though she were choking a long minute, unable to make a sound, as the little girl whimpered and scrambled away on hands and knees.

Uncle Randall, momentarily disconcerted, regained his smile.

"What?" he demanded. "None of your business if we were only playing."

Cousin Louise threw herself at him. Being, as she was, a tall girl, she bore him over so he fell to the pavement with a crash. His wig came off. She beat him in the face with her fists, and found her voice at last, harsh as a crow's:

"*What were you going to tell her?* Were you going to tell her you'd cut her tongue out if she ever told what you did? Were you? *Were you?*"

Uncle Randall snarled and attempted to throw her off.

"Ow! Who'd believe you, stupid bitch? The guests'll be arriving, I'll say you've gone mad—"

The child climbed to her feet and ran, sobbing, and got behind the menagerie wall. There she cried in silence, hiding her face in her skirts.

When she ventured out again at last, neither Uncle Randall nor Cousin Louise were anywhere in sight. The tyger was looking at her steadily.

"That's another secret come to light," he said. "Now, I'll tell you still another."

Rubbing her eyes with her fist, she listened as he told her the secret.

▲▼▲

Mamma and Aunt Elizabeth carried the babies into the chapel, so the nurserymaid was able to spare her a moment.

"Lord, lord, how did your face get so dirty? As if I ain't got enough to see to!" she grumbled, dipping a corner of her apron in the horse-trough and washing the little girl's face. "Now, hold my hand and be a good child when we go in. No noise!"

She was a good child through the solemn ceremony. Mamma watched the little boys tenderly, anxiously, and Uncle Henry and Aunt Elizabeth smiled when first John, and then James, screamed and went red-faced at having Satan driven out with cold water. Uncle Thomas was watching Mamma. Aunt Caroline was tranquilly distant: she'd taken laudanum for her pain. Beside her, Cousin Louise watched Uncle Randall with a basilisk glare. Uncle Randall was holding himself upright and defiant, smiling, though his face was puffy with bruises.

Afterward they all processed from the chapel and up the long stairs, to arrange themselves in ranks before Grandpapa, that he might give them his blessing. He stared from his high white bed and had to be reminded who they all were. At last he moved his wasted hand on the counterpane, granting an abbreviated benediction on posterity, and they were able to file from the sickroom into the clean-smelling twilight.

The wind had dropped a little but still moved the lanterns, that had candles inside them now and looked like golden moons glowing in the trees. It brought the sweet smell of wood smoke from an early bonfire. The dusk was lavender, so lambent everything looked slightly transparent, and the milling guests in the garden might have been ghosts. The child wandered among them, unseen as a ghost herself, watching.

There were stout old gentlemen with iron-gray wigs and wide-brimmed hats, who spoke at length with Uncle Henry about harvests and horse fairs. In high white wigs were young men and young ladies, lace-trimmed mincers of both sexes, who wondered why there were no musicians, and were quite put out to be told that there would be no dancing because of mourning for Papa.

Admiring gentlemen in silk stockings, slithery as eels, crowded around Mamma to pay her compliments, and Uncle Thomas held her arm possessively and smiled at them all. Aunt Caroline, on a couch that had been brought out for her, looked on dreamily. Uncle Randall edged through the crowd, telling first one inquirer and then another how his bruises had come at the hands of a low slut of a chambermaid, damn her eyes for a scheming hussy, wanted a guinea for favors as though she were the Queen of Sheba, screamed like a harpy when he'd paid her out in the coin she deserved! Ha-ha.

John and James lay in the arms of the nurserymaid and Aunt Elizabeth, who was glad to get off her feet, and the little boys stared in wide-awake astonishment at the glowing lanterns and ignored all their well-wishers, who moved on speedily to the collation table for cider and ham anyway. Some guests vanished in pairs into shadowy corners. There were perfumes of civet-musk strong in the air, there was wine flowing free. Someone got drunk remarkably quickly and tripped, and his wig went flying. It hit Uncle Henry in the face with a *poof* and a cloud of powder. People tittered with laughter.

The little girl walked through the shadows to the keeper's shed. She found the ring of keys where he had hung it up before hurrying off to the somewhat lesser collation for the servants. Nobody but the tyger saw her as she came and tried the big brass keys, one after another, in the padlock that secured the door of his pen. At last it clicked open.

She slipped it off. The bolt was a simple one, just like the bolt on the nursery door. Sliding it back, she opened the door of the pen.

The tyger paced swiftly forward, his green eyes gleaming. He looked much bigger out of his prison. He turned and gazed at her a moment; put out his warm rough tongue and slicked it along the pulse of her wrist, the palm of her hand. She felt a shock go through her body, an electric thrill of pleasure. She parted her lips but could find no words, only staring back at him in wonderment. He turned his head to regard the party in the sunken garden.

"Now," said the tyger, "We'll see, won't we?"

He stretched his magnificent length, gave a slight wriggle of his shoulders, and bounded across the courtyard. Standing beside the empty cage, she folded her little hands and watched.

He charged the party, vaulting from the top step into the sunken garden. Horrified guests looked up to see him land in the midst of them all, and gilt chairs were knocked over as people scrambled to get away from him, screaming in their panic. Some staggered on their high heels, some kicked off their shoes and ran in their slippery stockinged feet. Aunt Elizabeth went over backward in her chair, clutching young James, and both began to shriek. The servants fled for their lives. Aunt Caroline watched all from her couch, too drugged to care.

But the tyger leapt straight through the garden like a thunderbolt, overtaking Uncle Thomas, whom it felled with a sidelong rake of one paw. Uncle Thomas went down, howling and clutching himself, and blood ran red all down his white silk hose. The tyger didn't even pause, however, it sprang clean over him and continued forward, and the only person left before it now was Uncle Randall, who had broken a heel on the topmost of the opposite steps and was still there, frantically attempting to yank off his tight shoe.

Uncle Randall looked up into the tyger's eyes, but had no time to do more than bleat before it struck him. He broke like a doll, and rolled over with it into the darkness.

There was a second's hush, cries cut off abruptly in those who still crouched or lay sprawled in the sunken garden. Uncle Henry, who had crawled to Aunt Elizabeth's side, rose on his elbow to look and said, "O Lord God!"

The tyger appeared at the top of the steps, dragging Uncle Randall by the back of the neck. Uncle Randall's head hung at a strange angle and his body was limp. The tyger's eyes reflected back the light of the golden lanterns.

It stared at them all a moment before opening its jaws. Uncle Randall dropped like an empty coat. The tyger's beard was red.

It bared its fangs, and turned and bounded away into the night.

▲▼▲

When they asked her why, she explained. After she had told them everything, they made her explain it all over, and then explain once more. No matter how often she explained, however, they did not hear what she said.

▲▼▲

Finally they sent her away, to a convent school in France. It was by no means as bad as it might have been.

She made no friends, but her eyes being now accustomed to look for detail, she saw keenly the fond possessive looks or angry glances between the other girls, heard the midnight weeping or sighs, saw the notes hastily exchanged; watched the contests for dominance and knew when the cloister gate was locked and when it was left unlocked, and who came and went thereby, and when they came too.

The heavy air buzzed like a hive. She no more thought of participating in the convent's inner life than she would have thrust her hand into a wasp's nest, but she watched in fascination.

Then, one morning at Mass, above the high altar, the crucified Christ opened green blazing eyes and looked at her. He smiled.

Calamari Curls

The town had seen better days.

Its best year had probably been 1906, when displaced San Franciscans, fleeing south to find slightly less unstable real estate, discovered a bit of undeveloped coastline an inconvenient distance from the nearest train station.

No tracks ran past Nunas Beach. There wasn't even a road to its golden sand dunes, and what few locals there were didn't know why. There were rumors of long-ago pirates. There was a story that the fathers from the local mission had forbidden their parishioners to go there, back in the days of Spanish rule.

Enterprising Yankee developers laughed and built a road, and laid out lots for three little beach towns, and sold them like hotcakes. Two of the towns vanished like hotcakes at a Grange Breakfast, too; one was buried in a sandstorm and the other washed out to sea during the first winter flood.

But Nunas Beach remained, somehow, and for a brief season there were ice cream parlors and photographers' studios, clam stands, Ferris wheels, drug stores and holiday cottages. Then, for no single reason, people began to leave. Some of the shops burned down; some of the cottages dwindled into shanties. Willow thickets and sand encroached on the edges. What was left rusted where it stood, with sand drifting along its three streets, yet somehow did not die.

People found their way there, now and then, especially after the wars. It was a cheap place to lie in the sun while your wounds healed and your shell-shock faded away. Some people stayed.

Pegasus Bright, who had had both his legs blown off by a land mine, had stayed, and opened the Chowder Palace. He was unpleasant when he drank and, for that matter, when he didn't, but he could cook. The Chowder Palace was a long, low place on a street corner. It wasn't well lit, its linoleum tiles were cracked and grubby, its windows dim with grease. Still, it was the only restaurant in town. Therefore all the locals ate at the Chowder Palace, and so, too, did those few vacationers who came to Nunas Beach.

Mr. Bright bullied a staff of illegal immigrants who worked for him as waiters and busboys; at closing time they faded like ghosts back to homeless camps in the willow thickets behind the dunes, and he rolled himself back to his cot in the rear of the Palace, and slept with a tire iron under his pillow.

▲▼▲

One Monday morning the regulars were lined up on the row of stools at the counter, and Mr. Bright was pushing himself along the row topping up their mugs of coffee, when Charlie Cansanary said:

"I hear somebody's bought the Hi-Ho Lounge."

"No they ain't, you stupid bastard," said Mr. Bright. He disliked Charlie because Charlie had lost his right leg to a shark while surfing, instead of in service to his country.

"That's what I heard too," said Tom Avila, who was the town's mayor.

"Why would anybody buy that place?" demanded Mr. Bright. "*Look* at it!"

They all swiveled on their stools and looked out the window at the Hi-Ho Lounge, which sat right across the street on the opposite corner. It was a windowless stucco place painted gray, with martini glasses picked out in mosaic tile on either side of the blind slab of a door. On the roof was a rusting neon sign portraying another martini glass whose neon olive had once glowed like a green star against the sunset. But not in years; the Hi-Ho Lounge had never been open in living memory.

"Maybe somebody wants to open a bar," said Leon Silva, wiping egg yolk out of his mustache. "It might be kind of nice to have a place to drink."

"You can get drinks here," said Mr. Bright quickly, stung.

"Yeah, but I mean legally. And in glasses and all," said Leon.

"Well, if you want to go to *those* kinds of places and spend an arm and a leg—" said Mr. Bright contemptuously, and then stopped himself, for Leon, having had an accident on a fishing trawler, only had one arm. Since he'd lost it while earning a paycheck rather than in pursuit of frivolous sport, however, he was less a target for Mr. Bright's scorn. Mr. Bright continued: "Anyway it'll never happen. Who's going to buy an old firetrap like that place?"

"Those guys," said Charlie smugly, pointing to the pair of business-suited men who had just stepped out of a new car and were standing on the sidewalk in front of the Hi-Ho Lounge.

Mr. Bright set down the coffee pot. Scowling, he wheeled himself from behind the counter and up to the window.

"Developers," he said. He watched as they walked around the Hi-Ho Lounge, talking to each other and shaking their heads. One took a key from an envelope and tried it in the padlock on the front door; the lock was a chunk of rust, however, and after a few minutes he drew back and shook his head.

"You ain't never getting in that way, buddy," said Tom. "You don't know beach winters."

The developer went back to his car and, opening the trunk, took out a hammer. He struck ineffectually at the lock.

"Look at the sissy way he's doing it," jeered Mr. Bright. "Hit it *hard*, you dumb son of a bitch."

The padlock broke, however, and the chain dropped; it took three kicks to get the door open, to reveal inky blackness beyond. The developers stood looking in, uncertain. The spectators in the Chowder Palace all shuddered.

"There has got to be serious mildew in there," said Charlie.

"And pipes rusted all to hell and gone," said Mr. Bright, with a certain satisfaction. "Good luck, suckers."

▲▼▲

But the developers seemed to have luck. They certainly had money.

Work crews with protective masks came and stripped out the inside of the Hi-Ho Lounge. There were enough rusting fixtures to fill a dumpster; there were ancient red vinyl banquettes, so blackened with mold they looked charred, and clumped rats' nests of horsehair and cotton batting spilled from their entrails.

When the inside had been thoroughly gutted, the outside was tackled. The ancient stucco cracked away to reveal a surprise: graceful arched windows all along both street walls, and a shell-shaped fanlight over the front door. Stripped to its framing, the place had a promise of airy charm.

Mr. Bright watched from behind the counter of the Chowder Palace, and wondered if there was any way he could sue the developers. No excuses presented themselves, however. He waited for rats to stream from their disturbed havens and attack his customers; none came. When the workmen went up on ladders and pried off the old HI-HO LOUNGE sign from the roof, he was disappointed, for no one fell through the rotting lath, nor did sharp edges of rusted tin cut through any workmen's arteries, and they managed to get the sign down to the sidewalk without dropping it on any passers-by. Worse; they left the neon martini glass up there.

"It *is* going to be a bar," said Leon in satisfaction, crumbling crackers into his chowder.

"Shut up," said Mr. Bright.

"And a restaurant," said Charlie. "My brother-in-law works at McGregor's Restaurant Supply over in San Emidio. The developers set up this account, see. He says they're buying lots of stuff. All top of the line. Going to be a seafood place."

Mr. Bright felt tendrils of fear wrap about his heart and squeeze experimentally. He rolled himself back to his cubicle, had two aspirins washed down with a shot of bourbon, and rolled back out to make life hell for Julio, who had yet to clear the dirty dishes from booth three.

▲▼▲

The place opened in time for the summer season, despite several anonymous threatening calls to the County Planning Department.

The new sign said CALAMARI CURLS, all in pink and turquoise neon, with a whimsical octopus writing around the letters. The neon martini glass was repiped a dazzling scarlet, with its olive once again winking green.

Inside was all pink and turquoise too: the tuck-and-roll banquettes, the napkins, the linoleum tiles. The staff, all bright young people working their way through Cal State San Emidio, wore pink and turquoise Hawaiian shirts.

Calamari Curls was fresh, jazzy and fun.

Mr. Bright rolled himself across the street, well after closing hours, to peer at the menus posted by the front door. He returned cackling with laughter.

"They got a *wine list*!" he told Jesus, the dishwasher. "And you should see their *prices*! Boy, have they ever made a mistake opening *here*! Who the hell in Nunas Beach is going to pay that kind of money for a basket of fish and chips?"

Everyone, apparently.

The locals began to go there; true, they paid a little more, but the food was so much better! Everything was so bright and hopeful at Calamari Curls! And the polished bar was an altar to all the mysteries of the perfect cocktail. Worse still, the great radiant sign could be seen from the highway, and passers-by who would never before have even considered stopping to fix a flat tire in Nunas Beach, now streamed in like moths to a porch light.

Calamari Curls had a glowing jukebox. Calamari Curls had karaoke on Saturday nights, and a clown who made balloon animals. Calamari Curls had a special tray with artfully made wax replicas of the mouth-watering desserts on their menu.

And the ghostly little businesses along Alder Street sanded the rust off their signs, spruced up a bit and got some of the overflow customers. After dining at Calamari Curls, visitors began to stop into Nunas Book and News to buy magazines and cigarettes. Visitors peered into the dark window of Edna's Collectibles, at dusty furniture, carnival glass and farm implements undisturbed in twenty years. Visitors poked around for bargains at the USO Thrift Shop. Visitors priced arrowheads and fossils at Jack's Rocks.

But Mr. Bright sat behind his counter and served chowder to an ever-dwindling clientele.

▲▼▲

The last straw was the Calamari Curls Award Winning Chowder.

Ashen-faced, Mr. Bright rolled himself across the street in broad daylight to see if it was really true. He faced down the signboard, with its playful lettering in pink-and-turquoise marker. Yes; Award-Winning Chowder, containing not only fresh-killed clams but conch and shrimp too.

And in bread bowls. Fresh-baked on the premises.

And for a lower price than at the Chowder Palace.

Mr. Bright rolled himself home, into the Chowder Palace, all the way back to his cubicle. Julio caught a glimpse of the look on Bright's face as he passed, and hung up his apron and just walked out, never to return. Mr. Bright closed the place early. Mr. Bright took another two aspirin with bourbon.

He put the bourbon bottle back in its drawer, and then changed his mind and took it with him to the front window. There he sat through the waning hours, as the stars emerged and the green neon olive across the street shone among them, and the music and laughter echoed across the street pitilessly.

▲▼▲

On the following morning, Mr. Bright did not even bother to open the Chowder Palace. He rolled himself down to the pier instead, and looked for Betty Step-in-Time.

Betty Step-in-Time had a pink bicycle with a basket, and could be found on the pier most mornings, doing a dance routine with the bicycle. Betty wore a pink middy top, a little white sailor cap, tap shorts and white tap shoes. Betty's mouth was made up in a red cupid's bow. Betty looked like the depraved older sister of the boy on the Cracker Jack box.

At the conclusion of the dance routine, which involved marching in place, balletic pirouettes and a mimed sea battle, Betty handed out business cards to anyone who had stayed to watch. Printed on the cards was:

ELIZABETH MARQUES
performance artist
interpretive dancer
transgender shaman

Mr. Bright had said a number of uncomplimentary things about Betty Step-in-Time over the years, and had even sent an empty bottle flying toward his curly head on one or two occasions. Now, though, he rolled up and waited in silence as Betty trained an imaginary spyglass on a passing squid trawler.

Betty appeared to recognize someone he knew on board. He waved excitedly and blew kisses. Then he began to dance a dainty sailor's hornpipe.

"Ahem," said Mr. Bright.

Betty mimed climbing hand over hand through imaginary rigging, pretended to balance on a spar, and looked down at Mr. Bright.

"Look," said Mr. Bright, "I know I never seen eye to eye with you—"

Betty went into convulsions of silent laughter, holding his sides.

"Yeah, okay, but I figure you and I got something in common," said Mr. Bright. "Which would be, we like this town just the way it is. It's a good place for anybody down on his luck. Am I right?

"But *that* place," and Mr. Bright waved an arm at Calamari Curls, "that's the beginning of the end. All that pink and blue stuff—Jesus, where do they think they are, Florida?—that's, whatchacallit, gentrification. More people start coming here, building places like that, and pretty soon people like you and me will be squeezed out. I bet you don't pay hardly any rent for that little shack over on the slough, huh? But once those big spenders start coming in, rents'll go through the roof. You mark my words!"

He looked up into Betty's face for some sign of comprehension, but the bright, blank doll-eyes remained fixed on him, nor did the painted smile waver. Mr. Bright cleared his throat.

"Well, I heard some stories about you being a shaman and all. I was hoping there was something you could do about it."

Betty leaped astride his pink bicycle. He thrust his left hand down before Mr. Bright's face, making a circular motion with the tip of his left thumb over the tips of his first and second fingers.

"You want to get *paid*?" said Mr. Bright, outraged. "Ain't I just explained how you got a stake in this too?"

Betty began to pedal, riding around and around Mr. Bright in a tight circle, waving bye-bye. On the third circuit he veered away, pulling out a piece of pink Kleenex and waving it as he went.

"All right, God damn it!" shouted Mr. Bright. "Let's do a deal."

Betty circled back, stopped and looked at him expectantly. Glum and grudging, Mr. Bright dug into an inner coat pocket and pulled out a roll of greasy twenties. He began to count them off, slowly and then more slowly, as Betty looked on. When he stopped, Betty mimed laughing again, throwing his head back, pointing in disbelief. Mr. Bright gritted his teeth and peeled away more twenties, until there was quite a pile of rancid cabbage in his lap. He threw the last bill down in disgust.

"That's every damn cent I got with me," he said. "You better be worth it."

Betty swept up the money and went through a routine of counting it himself, licking his thumb between each bill and sweeping his hands out in wide elaborate gestures. Apparently satisfied, he drew a tiny, pink vinyl purse from his bicycle's basket and tucked away the money. Leaning down, he winked broadly at Mr. Bright.

Then he pushed his little sailor cap forward on his brow and pedaled off into the fog.

▲▼▲

Three days later, Mr. Bright was presiding over a poker game at the front table with Charlie, Leon and Elmore Souza, who had lost both hands in an accident at the fish cannery but was a master at manipulating cards in his prostheses, to such an extent that he won frequently because his opponents couldn't stop staring. Since they were only playing for starlight mints, though, nobody minded much.

Mr. Bright was in a foul mood all the same, having concluded that he'd been shaman-suckered out of a hundred and eighty dollars. He had just anted up five mints with a dip into the box from Iris Fancy Foods Restaurant

Supply when he looked up to see Betty Step-in-Time sashaying into the Chowder Palace. His friends looked up to see what he was snarling at, and quickly looked away. A peculiar silence fell.

Betty was carrying a Pee Chee folder. He walked straight up to Mr. Bright, opened the folder with a flourish, and presented it to him. Mr. Bright stared down at it, dumfounded.

"We should maybe go," said Leon, pushing away from the table. Charlie scuttled out the door ahead of him, and Elmore paused only to sweep the starlight mints into his windbreaker pocket before following them in haste.

Betty ignored them, leaning down like a helpful maitre d' to remove a mass of photocopied paper from the folder and arrange it on the table before Mr. Bright.

The first image was evidently from a book on local history. It was a very old photograph, to judge from the three-masted ship on the horizon; waves breaking in the background, one or two bathers in old-fashioned costume, and a couple of little board and batten shacks in the foreground. White slanted letters across the lower right-hand corner read: *Nunas Beach, corner of Alder and Stanford.* Squinting at it, Mr. Bright realized that he was seeing the view from his own front window, a hundred years or more in the past.

Silently Betty drew his attention to the fact that the future site of Calamari Curls was a bare and blasted lot, though evening primrose grew thickly up to its edge.

"Well, so what?" he said. In reply, Betty whisked the picture away to reveal another, taken a generation later but from the same point of view. A building stood on the spot now—and there were the same arched windows, the same fanlight door, above which was a sign in letters solemn and slightly staggering: ALDER STREET NATATORIUM.

"A nata-what?" said Mr. Bright. Betty placed his hands together and mimed diving. Then he gripped his nose, squeezed his eyes shut and sank down, waving his other hand above his head.

"Oh. Okay, it was a swimming pool? What about it?"

Betty lifted the picture. Under it was a photocopied microfilm enlargement, from the *San Emidio Mission Bell* for May 2, 1922. Mr. Bright's reading skills were not strong, but he was able to make out enough to tell that the article was about the Alder Street Natatorium in Nunas Beach, which had closed indefinitely due to a horrifying incident two days previous. Possible ergot poisoning—mass hallucinations—sea-creature—prank by the boys of San Emidio Polytechnic?—where is Mr. Tognazzini and his staff?

"Huh," said Mr. Bright. "Could we, like, blackmail somebody with this stuff?"

Betty pursed his cupid's bow and shook a reproving finger at Mr. Bright. He drew out the next paper, which was a photocopied page from the *Weekly Dune Crier* for April 25, 1950. There were three young men standing in front of the Hi-Ho Lounge, looking arch. The brief caption underneath implied that the Hi-Ho Lounge would bring a welcome touch of sophistication and gray-flannel elegance to Nunas Beach.

"So I guess they boarded the pool over," said Mr. Bright. "Well?"

Quickly, Betty presented the next photocopy. It was an undated article from the *San Emidio Telegraph* noting briefly that the Hi-Ho Lounge was still closed pending the police investigation, that no marihuana cigarettes had been found despite first reports, and that anyone who had attended the poetry reading was asked to come forward with any information that might throw some light on what had happened, since Mr. LaRue was not expected to recover consciousness and Mr. Binghamton and Mr. Cayuga had not been located.

Mr. Bright shook his head. "I don't get it."

Betty rolled his eyes and batted his lashes in exasperation. He shuffled the last paper to the fore, and this was not a photocopy but some kind of astronomical chart showing moon phases. It had been marked all over with pink ink, scrawled notations and alchemical signs, as well as other symbols resembling things Mr. Bright had only seen after a three-day weekend with a case of Ten High.

"What the hell's all this supposed to be?" demanded Mr. Bright. "Oh!... I guess this is...some kind of shamanic thing?"

Betty leaped into the air and crossed his ankles as he came down, then mimed grabbing someone by the hand and shaking it in wildly enthusiastic congratulation. Mr. Bright pulled his hands in close.

"Okay," he said in a husky whisper. He looked nervously around at his empty restaurant. "Maybe you shouldn't ought to show me anything else."

But Betty leaned forward and tapped one image on the paper. It was a smiling full moon symbol. He winked again, and backed toward the door. He gave Mr. Bright a thumbs-up, then made an OK symbol with thumb and forefinger, and then saluted.

"Okay, thanks," said Mr. Bright. "I get the picture."

He watched Betty walking primly away, trundling the pink bicycle. Looking down at the table, he gathered together the papers and stuffed them back in the Pee Chee folder. He wheeled himself off to his cubicle and hid the folder under his pillow, with the tire iron.

Then he rolled around to his desk, and consulted the calendar from Nunas Billy's Hardware Circus. There was a full moon in three days' time.

▲▼▲

It was Saturday, and the full moon was just heaving itself up from the eastern horizon, like a pink pearl. Blue dusk lay on Nunas Beach. The tide was far out; salt mist flowed inland, white vapor at ankle level. Mr. Bright sat inside the darkened Chowder Palace, and watched, and hated, as people lined up on the sidewalk outside Calamari Curls.

Calamari Curls was having Talent Nite. The Early Bird specials were served, and senior diners went shuffling back to their singlewides, eager to leave before the Goddamned rock and roll started. Young families with toddlers dined and hurried back to their motels, unwilling to expose little ears to amplified sound.

Five pimply boys set up their sound equipment on the dais in the corner. They were the sons of tractor salesmen and propane magnates; let their names be forgotten. The front man tossed his hair back from his eyes, looked around at the tables crowded with chattering diners, and said in all adolescent sullenness:

"Hi. We're the Maggots, and we're here to shake you up a little."

His bassman leaped out and played the opening of "(I Can't Get No) Satisfaction" with painful slowness, the drummer boy joined in clunk-clunk-clunk, and the front man leaned forward to the mike and in a hoarse scream told the audience about his woes. The audience continued biting the tails off shrimp, sucking down frozen strawberry margaritas and picking at Kona Coffee California Cheesecake.

When the music ended, they applauded politely. The front man looked as though he'd like to kill them all. He wiped sweat from his brow, had a gulp of water.

Betty Step-in-Time wheeled his bicycle up to the door.

"We're going to do another classic," said the front man. "Okay?"

Ka-*chunk!* went the drums. The keyboardist and the lead guitarist started very nearly in sync: Da da da. *Dada. DA DA DA. Dada.*

"Oh Lou-ah Lou-ah-eh, ohhhh baby nagatcha go waygadda go!" shouted the front man.

Betty Step-in-Time dismounted. Just outside the restaurant's threshold, he began to dance. It began in time with the music, a modest little kickstep. A few diners looked, pointed and laughed.

"Nah nah nah nah asaya Lou-ah Lou-ah eh, whooa babeh saya whaygachago!"

Betty's kickstep increased its arc, to something approaching can-can immodesty. He threw his arms up as he kicked, rolling his head, closing his eyes in abandon. A diner sitting near the door fished around in pockets for a dollar bill, but saw no hat in which to put it.

"Ah-nye, ah-dah, ah ron withchoo, ah dinkabobsa gonstalee!" cried the front man. Betty began to undulate, and it seemed a tremor ran through the floor of the building. A tableful of German tourists jumped to their feet, alarmed, but their native companion didn't even stop eating.

"Just an aftershock," he said calmly. "No big deal."

"Ah rag saga leely, badoom badoom, wha wah badoo, jaga babee!"

Betty began to dance what looked like the Swim, but so fast his arms and legs blurred the air. The lights dimmed, took on a greenish cast.

"Who's playing with the damn rheostat?" the manager wanted to know.

"Ayah ha Lou-ah Lou-ah eh, whoa ba-bah shongo waygatchago!"

Sweat began to pour from Betty's face and limbs, as his body began to churn in a manner that evoked ancient bacchanals, feverish and suggestive. The green quality of the light intensified. Several diners looked down at their plates of clam strips or chimichangas and stopped eating, suddenly nauseous.

"Ya ya ya ya ah-sha-da Lou-ah Lou-ah he, Nyarlathotep bay-bah weygago!" sang the front man, and he was sweating too, and—so it seemed—dwindling under the green light, and the carefully torn edges of his black raiment began to fray into rags, patterned with shining mold.

Betty's hips gyrated, his little sailor hat flew off, and every curl on his head was dripping with St. Elmo's fire. Several diners vomited where they sat. Others rose in a half-crouch, desperate to find the lavatory doors marked *Beach Bums* and *Beach Bunnies*. Half of them collapsed before they made it. They slipped, stumbled and fell in the pools of seawater that were condensing out of the air, running down the walls.

"Ah Lou-ah Lou-ah eh, ph'nglui mglw'nafh Cthulhu R'lyeh wgah'nagl fhtagn!" wailed the white-eyed thing the front man had become, and his band raised reed flutes to their gills and piped a melody to make human ears

bleed, and the mortal diners rose and fought to get out the windows, for Betty was flinging handfuls of seaweed in toward them, and black incense.

The pink and turquoise linoleum tiles by the bandstand popped upward, scattered like hellish confetti, as a green-glowing gas of all corruption hissed forth, lighting in blue flames when it met the air, followed by a gush of black water from the forgotten pool below. The first of the black tentacles probed up through the widening crack in the floor.

Betty sprang backward, grabbed up his sailor hat, leaped on his pink bicycle and pedaled away as fast as he could go, vanishing down the misty darkness of Alder Street.

The neon olive had become an eye, swiveling uncertainly but with malevolence, in a narrow scarlet face.

Watching from across the street, Mr. Bright laughed until the tears poured from his eyes, and slapped the arms of his wheelchair. He raised his bourbon bottle in salute as Calamari Curls began its warping, strobing, moist descent through the dimensions.

▲▼▲

He was opening a new bottle by the time gray dawn came, as the last of the fire engines and ambulances pulled away. Tom Avila stood in the middle of the street, in gloomy conference with the pastor of St. Mark's, the priest from Mission San Emidio, and even the rabbi from Temple Beth-El, who had driven in his pajamas all the way over from Hooper City.

Holy water, prayer and police tape had done all they could do; the glowing green miasma was dissipating at last, and the walls and windows of Calamari Curls had begun to appear again in ghostly outline. Even now, however, it was obvious that their proper geometry could never be restored.

Tom shook hands with the gentlemen of God and they departed to their respective cars. He stood alone in the street a while, regarding the mess; then he noticed Mr. Bright, who waved cheerfully from behind his window. Tom's eyes narrowed. He came stalking over. Mr. Bright let him in.

"You didn't have anything to do with this, did you, Peg?" the mayor demanded.

"Me? How the hell could I of? I just been sitting here watching the show," said Mr. Bright. "I ain't going to say I didn't enjoy it, neither. Guess nobody's going to raise no rents around *here* for a while!"

"God damn it, Peg! Now we've got us *another* vortex into a lost dimension, smack in the middle of town this time!" said the mayor in exasperation. "What are we going to do?"

"Beats me," said Mr. Bright, grinning as he offered him the bourbon bottle.

▲▼▲

But the present became the past, as it will, and people never forget so easily as when they want to forget. The wreck of Calamari Curls became invisible, as passers-by tuned it out of their consciousness. The green olive blinked no more.

Mr. Bright found that the black things that mewled and gibbered around the garbage cans at night could be easily dispatched with a cast-iron skillet well aimed. His customers came back, hesitant and shamefaced. He was content.

And mellowing in his world view too; for he no longer scowled nor spat in the direction of Betty Step-in-Time when he passed him on the pier, but nodded affably, and once was even heard to remark that it took all kinds of folks to make a world, and you really shouldn't judge folks without you get to know them.

Maelstrom

Mr. Morton was a wealthy man. He hated it.

For one thing, he wasn't accustomed to having money. During most of his life he had been institutionalized, having been diagnosed as an Eccentric at the age of ten. But when the British Arean Company had needed settlers for Mars, the Winksley Hospital for the Psychologically Suspect had obligingly shipped most of its better-compensated inmates off to assist in the colonization efforts.

Mr. Morton had liked going to Mars. For a while he had actually been paid a modest salary by the BAC. Eccentric though he was, he was nevertheless quite brilliant at designing and fabricating precast concrete shelters, a fact that would have surprised anyone who hadn't seen the endless model villages he'd built on various tabletops in Ward Ten, back on Earth. The knowledge that he was earning his own keep as well as doing his bit to help terraforming along had built up his self-esteem.

When the economic bubble that had buoyed up the BAC burst, Mr. Morton had been summarily made Redundant. Redundant was nearly as bad as Eccentric. He was unable to afford a ticket back to Earth and might well have become an oxygen-starved mendicant sleeping in the Tubes, had he not found employment as a waiter at the Empress of Mars tavern. Here Mr. Morton had room, board and oxygen, if not a salary, in surroundings so reminiscent of dear old Winksley Hospital for the Psychologically Suspect that he felt quite at home.

Then his employer, known as Mother Griffith by her patrons, had had a run of extraordinary luck that had resulted in making her the richest woman on the planet. Farewell to the carefree days of Mr. Morton's poverty! Mother Griffith set him up in business as a contractor and architect.

She now owned the entirety of Mons Olympus, and leased out lots to commercial tenants with the dream of building a grand new city on Mars. Areco, the immense corporation owning the rest of the planet, busily devised laws, permit fees and taxes to hinder her as much as it was able. But by bankrolling Mr. Morton's firm, Mother Griffith found she was able to evade neatly several miles of red tape and avoid a small fortune in penalties.

All Mr. Morton was now obliged to do was sit at a drafting terminal and design buildings and, now and then, suit up and wander Outside to look at a construction site where laborers actually hired and directed by Mother Griffith were busily pouring the peculiarly salmon-pink concrete of Mars.

For a brief period Mr. Morton had enjoyed the contemplation of his bank account. He had enjoyed being able to afford his very own Outside gear at last, with the knowledge that he'd never have to improvise an air filter out of an old sock again. His indoor raiment was all of the best, and in the sable hues he preferred. And oh, what downloads of forbidden books the black market in literature had to offer, to a man of his economic status!

And yet, the more he kept company with Mssrs. Poe, Dumas, Verne, King and Lovecraft, the greater grew his sense of overwhelming melancholy. His position as a newly prosperous bourgeois seemed distasteful to him, a betrayal of all that was artistic and romantic in his soul.

"Stop moping," Mother Griffith told him. "Bloody hell, man, the Goddess gifts you with obscene amounts of cash, and you can't think of more to do with it than buy some fusty old words? You're making a city with your own two hands, in pixels anyway. There's power for you! You want *artistic*, is it? Stick up some artistic buildings. Cornices and gingerbread and whatnot. I don't care how they look."

Mr. Morton retired to his drafting terminal in high dudgeon and plotted out an entire city block in Neogothic Rococo. Factoring in Martian gravity, he realized he could make his elaborate spires and towers even more soaring, even more delicate and dreamlike. A few equations gave him breathtaking results. So for a while he was almost happy, designing a Municipal Waste Treatment Plant of ethereal loveliness.

And, just here above, where its gargoyles might greet both sunset and dawn, would rise...the Edgar Allan Poe Center for the Performing Arts!

Mr. Morton leaned back from his console, dumbfounded. *Here* was a worthy use for vulgar riches.

▲▼▲

When the last of the concrete forms had been taken away, when all the fabulously expensive black walnut interiors shipped up from Earth had been installed, Mr. Morton's theater was a sight to behold. Even the shaven-headed members of the Martian Agricultural Collective, notorious for their philistinism, suited up and hiked the slope to stare at it.

For one thing, dye had been added to the concrete, so the whole thing was an inky purple. Not only gargoyles but statues of the great poets and dramatists, floral roundels, bosses, shields, crests and every other ornamental folly Mr. Morton had been able to imagine covered most of its gloomy exterior, and a great deal of the interior too. On Earth, it would have crumbled under the weight of gravity and public opinion. Here on Mars it stood free, a cathedral to pure weirdness.

Within, it had been fitted up with a genuine old-fashioned proscenium stage. Swags of black velvet concealed the very latest in holoprojectors, but Mr. Morton had hopes of using that vulgar modern entertainment seldom.

"But that's what people want to see," said Mother Griffith in dismay.

"Only because they've never known anything better," said Mr. Morton. "I shall revive Theater as an art, here in this primitive place!"

He thought it might be nice to begin with the ancient Greeks, and so he put a word in his black marketeer's ear about it. A week later that useful gentleman sent him a download containing the surviving works of Aristophanes. Mr. Morton read them eagerly, and was horrified. Had he ever truly understood the meaning of vulgarity before now?

He was not at a loss for long. Mr. Morton decided that he would write the EAPCPA's repertory himself; and what better way to open its first season than with adaptations of every single one of Poe's works?

▲▼▲

"You're putting on *The Descent into the Maelstrom*?" shouted Mother Griffith. "But it's just two men in a boat going down a giant plug hole!"

"It is a meditation on the grandeur and horror of Nature," said Mr. Morton, a little stiffly.

"But how on earth will you stage such a thing?"

"I had envisioned a dramatic reading," said Mr. Morton.

"Oh, that'll have them standing in the aisles," said Mother Griffith. "Look you, Mr. Morton, not to intrude on your artistic sensibilities or anything, but mightn't you just think about giving 'em at least one of those sol-et-lumiere shows so they have something to look at? For if the miners and haulers feel they haven't had their tickets' worth of entertainment, they're liable to tear their seats loose and start swinging with 'em, see, this being a frontier and all."

Mr. Morton stormed off in a sulk, but on sober reflection decided that to ignore the visual aspect of performance was, perhaps, a little risky. He drafted another script, in which the Maelstrom itself would be presented by dancers, and each unfortunate mariner had a stylized lament before meeting his respective fate.

"They want a thrilling spectacle?" he said aloud, as he read it over. "*Here* it is!"

Fearful as he was to commit the purity of his script to human actors, Mr. Morton liked even less the idea of machine-generated ones. He decided to hold auditions.

▲▼▲

The interior of Mr. Morton's theater, while richly furnished, was quite a bit smaller than its remarkable exterior (Air being a utility on Mars, living places tended to conserve its volume). Mr. Morton preferred to think of the result as an *intimate performance venue*. Seating capacity was thirty persons. Mr. Morton sat in the back row now, watching as Mona Griffith stepped from the wings.

"Hi, Mr. Morton!" said Mona.

"Hello, Mona." Mr. Morton shifted uncomfortably. Mona was the youngest of Mother Griffith's daughters. She was carrying a SoundBox 3000 unit. She set it on the floor and switched it on. Slinky and suggestive music oozed forth. Mr. Morton's knuckles turned white.

"Mona, you're not going to do a striptease, are you?" he inquired.

"Well—yes," said Mona, in the act of unbuckling her collar.

"Mona, you know how your mother feels about that," said Mr. Morton. He himself knew quite well; he had known Mona since she'd been ten. "In any case, I'm auditioning for a play, not a—a burlesque review!"

"I'm of age now, aren't I?" said Mona defiantly. "And anyway, this isn't just a striptease. It's very intellectual. I'm *reciting* as I'm stripping, see?"

"Tell me you're not stripping to Hamlet's Soliloquy," begged Mr. Morton.

"Pft! As if! I'm doing General Klaar's Lament from *The Wars of the House of Klaar*," said Mona. "And I've got these really horrible-looking fake wounds painted in unexpected places, see, so as to create quite a striking effect. So it wouldn't be at all, um, what's that word? Prurient?"

"No, I don't suppose it would be," said Mr. Morton. "But—"

They heard the warning klaxon announcing that the airlock had opened, and then the heavy tread of armored feet approaching the inner door. *Boom.* The inner door was kicked open, and a man in miners' armor strode down the aisle toward Mona. He drew a disrupter pistol and shot the SoundBox 3000, which promptly fell silent.

"Durk! You bastard!" shrieked Mona. The intruder marched up on stage, not even removing his mask. Mona kicked his shin viciously, forgetting that he was wearing Larlite greaves, and hopped backward clutching her foot at once. "My toe!"

Her fiancé shoved his mask back and glared at her. "You promised me you wouldn't do this," he said.

"You shot my SoundBox!"

"But you promised me you wouldn't do this!"

"But you shot my SoundBox!"

"Put your mask on. We're going home!" said Durk, waving his pistol distractedly.

"But you shot my SoundBox!"

"Next," said Mr. Morton, from underneath his seat.

The next applicant waited until Durk and Mona had made their noisy exit before emerging from the wings.

"Er...Hello, Alf," said Mr. Morton.

Alf was a hauler. Haulers drove Co2 freighters out on the High Road, the boulder-marked route that cut across the Outside wastes to the two poles. The mortality rate for haulers was high. Consequently most haulers had been recruited from Hospitals, because they tended to care less about that fact.

Alf was able to face down cyclones, wandering dunes, flying boulders, starvation and thirst without turning a hair, but he was sweating now as he peered out toward the empty seats.

"Erm," he said.

"Are you here for the audition, Alf?"

"Yeah," said Alf, blinking.

"And...we took our meds this morning, did we?"

"Yeah."

"So...what will you be performing today, Alf?"

"Erm," said Alf, and then he drew a breath and said:

"Scene. Morning room in Alregons Flat in Arf Moon Street. Da room is luxriussly an artriscally fronished. Da sound of a pianer is eard in da adoining room. Lane is ranging arfternoon tea onna table an arfter da music as ceased, Alregon enners curvy mark from music room ovver curvy mark. Alregon. Didja ear wot I wuz playing Lane? Lane. I din't fink it wuz plite to listen sir—"

"Alf, what on earth is that?"

Alf fell silent and blinked. "'S play."

"Which play?"

"Da Importance of Being Earnest," said Alf. "By Oscar Wilde."

Mr. Morton sat bolt upright. "Where did you find a copy?" Oscar Wilde's work had been condemned as Politically Trivial so long ago that scarcely any of his work survived.

"Canary Wharf Ospital," said Alf. Mr. Morton frowned in perplexity. Canary Wharf was a much less genteel institution than Winksley. He fought back feelings of class division and inquired:

"They had *The Importance of Being Earnest* in the library?"

"Nah," said Alf. "Shoved under floor inna closet. It was like dis old book wiv paper an all? Used to read it when I wuz locked innere. I remember everyfing I read, see?"

Mr. Morton felt his heart patter against his ribs. "You remember the whole play?"

"Oh yeah." Alf grinned. "Allaway to 'When I married Lord Bracknell I ad no forchoon of any kind. But I never dreamed for a moment of allowing dat to stand in my way. Well I spose I must give my consent.' I wuz locked in a lot."

"You must recite the whole play for me one day, Alf," said Mr. Morton, dazzled by mental images of an Exclusive World Premiere Revival.

"Sure," said Alf. "Did I pass da audition?"

"Why—of course," said Mr. Morton, thinking to himself that Alf could always sweep the floors. "Well done. I'll let you know when rehearsals start."

"Hey, fanks," said Alf, and, grinning hugely, he clumped away to the airlock.

"Next?" said Mr. Morton.

A woman edged out on stage, wringing her hands. Mr. Morton recognized the silver broach she wore on her bosom, and sighed. She was one of the sisters from the Ephesian Church's mission down the mountain at Settlement Base.

"Hello," she said. "I...ah...just wanted to ask you whether you'd ever known the infinite consolation of the Goddess?"

"Next," said Mr. Morton.

▲▼▲

In the end Mr. Morton decided to advertise. He put a notice in *Variety* (the Tri-Worlds edition): himself, recorded in holo, staring earnestly into the foremost camera and saying:

"Have you ever considered emigration to Mars? An adventure awaits you in a new company just forming on the Red Planet! The Edgar Allan Poe Center for the Performing Arts is looking for persons with theatrical experience interested in sharing our grand quest to bring the mysteries of our craft to the red and windswept Arean frontier!

"Yes, *you,* who have longed to escape from the humdrum routine of Earth, may find your ultimate self-expression here in the tortured and dramatic landscape of a new world! Send all inquiries to: Amorton@poeyouareavenged.pub.ares.uk *today!*" The link flashed at the bottom of the holo. Mr. Morton pointed at it and dropped his voice impressively: "Do you dare?"

▲▼▲

Do we dare not to? Meera wondered sadly. She looked over at Crispin who was sleeping as soundly as though they hadn't a month to go on their lease and no money to renew, and hadn't been living on cauliflower for a week, and hadn't just received notice that the revival of *Peter Pan* was indefinitely postponed due to the producer's backing out. She had been cast as Peter, and her salary would have paid both the lease and the last three installments on the Taranis.

Crispin was an actor too. He had boyish good looks and a wonderful voice, and was brilliant in the right parts; but most of the time he tended to get the wrong parts. His Mr. Toad had been praised to the skies, likewise his Christmas Panto Spongebob; but his Dr. Who had, in the succinct words of the *Times* theater critic, "stunk up the stage" and his Mr. Darcy had simply appalled everyone, himself included. He hadn't worked in over a year.

And this morning another catastrophe loomed, one likely to make all their other problems seem small and manageable.

Meera reached over and grasped Crispin's foot, and shook it gently.

"Babe," she said. "Look at this."

"Huh?" Crispin sat up with a snort. She replayed the *Variety* snippet for him. He stared at Mr. Morton's shaky doppelganger, and gradually the lights came on behind his eyes.

"I wonder," he said.

"It might solve a lot of problems," said Meera.

"Yeah. Yeah! We could tell the rental agent to go shrack himself, for one thing." Crispin slid to the edge of the bed and reached for his pants. "I passed the genetic scan in school; did you?"

"Yes."

"So we're eligible to go up there. It might be sort of rough, though."

"Could it be much worse than this?" Meera waved her hand in a gesture that took in their sparsely-finished bedsitter. Crispin glanced around and grinned.

"I wouldn't mind saying goodbye to Earth. This might be a good thing for us! How many actors can there be on Mars anyway?" His smile dimmed a little. "Though I suppose you wouldn't want to leave your family."

"Are you mad?" Meera cried. "I'd give anything to put half the solar system between us!"

"Okay then!" Crispin pulled a shirt on over his head. "Let's mail the guy."

"There's something else," said Meera, looking down at her hands. She clasped them tight. "Cris...you remember the night we went to Gupta's party?"

"Heh heh heh," said Crispin, leering at her. She didn't say anything else. There was a silence of about thirty seconds, in which he connected the dots. Her eyes filled with tears. He went pale.

"Oh, no," he murmured. "I mean—oh, babe, what a wonderful thing! It's only—"

"It's a bloody disaster!" Meera wailed. He sat down beside her and took her hands.

"We—we'll think of something. I'll get a job. And...and if I manage to work off the fine in five years—"

"We couldn't work off the fine in twenty years," said Meera, gulping back a sob. "I've already checked. The baby would be shaving by the time we were free."

"Shrack," said Crispin. He thought about the other alternative, but that carried an even stiffer penalty. Meera fought to compose herself. She said:

"But, you see—if we emigrated to Mars—we wouldn't *need* a Reproduction Permit."

"We wouldn't?" said Crispin. "Oh...we wouldn't, would we? They let you have them, up there."

Meera nodded.

"That settles it." Crispin grabbed a datastick from the pocket of his coat. "Where's the one with your head shot? We'll both apply. What can we lose?"

▲▼▲

Six weeks later they were emerging from the shuttle in the hangar at Settlement Base, a little wobbly-legged from their journey.

"Shouldn't we have our air masks on?" said Meera fretfully.

"Nobody else has," said Crispin. "We're under a dome, see?" He drew in a deep breath. "Phew!" Hastily he clapped his mask on. "They must have had a leak in a sewer pipe!"

"No, actually," said the shuttle pilot, grinning. "It always smells like this. They raise cattle down the MAC tubes. You'll get used to it."

Meera slid her mask in place and reached for Crispin's hand. "Let's go claim our trunks."

They took a few steps forward and promptly stopped, as all newcomers did, startled by Martian gravity.

"This is lovely!" Meera bounced on tiptoes. Crispin, giggling, let go her hand and ran a few paces, bounding athletically toward an imaginary basketball hoop.

"That'll be them, I'm guessing," said one of a pair of men walking toward them.

"Oh, dear, are we that obvious?" said Meera, turning to smile. Her eyes widened.

The taller of the two was very tall indeed and very thin, suited all in black, with an old-fashioned bubble helmet; it made him look rather like Jack Skellington. The other was wide and barrel-chested, with a bushy beard. He wore no mask. He had clearly washed for the occasion, but not very well; soot lay in every crevice, in the creases of his big hands and in the wrinkles around his pale eyes, which gave him an alarmingly villainous appearance.

"That's all right," he said, grinning. He had a thick pan-celtic accent. "We was all immigrants once."

"Ms. Suraiya, Mr. Delamare, what an honor!" cried the other gentleman, with his voice a little muffled and echoing. He clasped Meera's hand in both his own and bent to kiss it, but only succeeded in rapping her knuckles with the curve of his helmet. "Oh—I'm so sorry—"

"Ah, hell, Morton, take the damn thing off," said the bearded one. He inhaled deeply. "It ain't that bad down here. Reminds me of old times, so it does."

"I can't bear it, and obviously neither can they," said Mr. Morton. He leaned down solicitously. "The air is much fresher where we're going, though I must admit it's a little thin. I cannot express what a pleasure it is to welcome you to Mars, Ms. Suraiya! Mr. Delamare! Amadeus Ruthven Morton at your service, and may I present Mr. Maurice Cochevelou? May we collect your trunks for you?"

"Yes, please," said Meera.

"I think they're over here," said Crispin, and vaulted away to the baggage claim area with Cochevelou walking after him.

"We were so awfully impressed by the holoshots of your theater, Mr. Morton," said Meera. "When are auditions?"

"Oh, *you* needn't audition!" said Mr. Morton. "We do get all the latest holoes up here now, you know. Everyone's seen *Mr. Korkunov Says Hello!*"

"How nice!" *Mr. Korkunov* was a kiddie holo in which Crispin had had a recurring role as Brophy the Bear, until the show's cancellation.

"And, of course, you were one of Smeeta's daughters on *Wellington Square,*" sais Mr. Morton.

"The one who got married to a millionaire and moved to Montana," said Meera ruefully. She had been written out of the show after refusing to sleep with the director.

"Yes. I can't tell you how happy I am to be working with real professionals!" said Mr. Morton. "I'm afraid our little theater is still something of an amateur undertaking—"

"Meera! Check it out!" yelled Crispin, balancing his trunk on one hand as he approached. He tossed it to the other hand as though it were made of balsa. "One-third gravity!"

"Careful—" Meera threw up her hands as Crispin butted the trunk like a football, and promptly clutched his head.

"Ow!"

"It's lighter, but it's just as hard," Mr. Cochevelou told him. He scooped up the fallen trunk, swung the other trunk to his shoulder and led them out of the hangar. They had their first glimpse of Mars: Settlement Dome above them, scoured to near-opacity by sandstorms, and the portals to the Tubes opening off it. To one side was the Ephesian Mission, breathing out incense which mingled peculiarly with the prevailing methane reek.

"So this is Mars," said Meera, trying not to show her disappointment.

"Oh, no, darlin'," said Cochevelou. "*This* ain't Mars." He grinned and led them to an airlock. "Masks on tight? You might want to pull up those hoods. We're going Outside." He slid on his own mask, around which his beard protruded to bizarre effect, and handed them a pair of heavy suits such as he wore, waiting patiently while they pulled them on and sealed up. Then he shouldered his way through the airlock. They followed him, holding hands tightly.

"*This* is Mars," said Cochevelou. He dumped their trunks into the back of a rickety-looking vehicle with balloon tires, and turned to wave an arm at the immense red desert. Rocks like crusts of dried blood, boulders in the colors of tangerines or bricks, wind-scoured curry-colored pinnacles and spires of rock. Far off, pink whirlwinds moved lazily across the plain. Looming before them was a gentle slope that rose, and rose, looking not so impossibly high as all that until they saw the cluster of tiny buildings far up and still not halfway to the sky.

Meera barely noticed she was colder than she'd ever been in her life. It was all so vast, and so silent, and beautiful in a harsh way. It did not look like the surface of an alien world.

And it isn't, is it? she thought. *We're Martians now. This is home.*

The view was even more breathtaking by the time they had rumbled up the mountainside as far as the little buildings, but by that time the cold really was more than either of them could stand another minute, and they staggered gratefully through the airlock into what seemed, by comparison, a place as warm and steamy as a sauna.

"And here they are!" bellowed Cochevelou, pulling up his mask. Crispin and Meera followed suit. They stood in a domed darkness relieved only by lamps at scattered tables and booths, and one brighter light over the…bar? Yes, unmistakably a bar. It had a concentrated smell of old ale and fried food that anywhere else would have been overpowering, but by contrast with the stench of Settlement Dome seemed pleasant and wholesome. Quite a crowd was assembled there, and all eyes were turned to Crispin and Meera.

A buxom lady of a certain age pushed her way to the front of the crowd. "Welcome to the Empress of Mars, my dears. Did you talk to them about housing, Mr. Morton? No, not you. Never mind. Mary Griffith, and delighted to make your acquaintance. Manco? Just take their trunks up to the best nook, there's a dear. Rowan! Set a booth for them, they'll not have had anything but those nasty squeezy pastes for days and days. Come and sit, dears."

A girl edged her way forward, holding up a stylus and plaquette. "Please—can I have your autograph, Ms. Suraiya?"

"Me too?" inquired a man, clearly a miner or prospector, so covered in red dust he looked like a living statue. "And yours, Mr. Delamare?"

"Mr. Delamare, Ms. Suraiya, I'm with the *Ares Times*," said a gentleman, bowing slightly. "Could I ask you just to step over here for the holocams a moment? Chiring Skousen, so pleased to meet you—and I wonder whether you'd consider doing an interview a little later—?"

Meera looked sidelong at Crispin, who flashed her a triumphant smile. It was going to be all right.

▲▼▲

And it was all right, even after Meera's first visit to the Settlement Base clinic, when she learned that having a child on Mars meant that there could be no second thoughts about emigration. Returning to Earth presented unacceptable risks to a baby born in Martian gravity, at least until adulthood, when it could train for the ordeal of Earth weight.

It was all right, even after Cochevelou gave them a midday tour Outside, and they saw the little mounds of red stones that had been placed, here and there, over the suffocated and frozen remains of prospectors who had ventured Out with no clear idea of the dangers they faced; or the ruined foundation of the big Ephesian temple that had been destroyed in some kind of hurricane, causing the good mothers to rebuild much more humbly within the protective stench of Settlement Base.

It was all right, even when they discovered how many of their new neighbors had been in Hospital, because the haulers and the laborers and the prospectors didn't *act* as though they were liable to cause breaches of the public peace. Mostly they minded their manners, and only occasionally laughed a little too loudly or got into fights in the bar. There were no Public Health Monitors snooping around to have them collared and dragged off in any case, and, when you got right down to it, Eccentrics were people just like anyone else.

It was all right because Crispin and Meera had free food and free lodging, in one of the funny little lofts plastered like swallow's nests within the dome of the Empress of Mars, and were promised better housing yet, as soon as Mr. Morton's workers completed the new block of flats—the first ever on Mars! It was all right because their interview with Mr. Skousen made the front page of the *Ares Times,* and they were treated like royalty everywhere they went.

It was all right because they soon got used to the smell, except when they ventured down to Settlement Base; and there were Scentstrips available in Mother Griffith's convenience shop that could be stuck across the air filter in one's mask, so that one hardly noticed anything except Island Spice, Berry Potpourri, or Spring Bouquet.

And it was all right because, on their first walk up to the EAPCPA, Meera had looked up at its black spires sharp against the purple sunset of Mars, and seen above them the soaring frame of the dome being built to shelter a new city, its bright steel catching the last of the sunlight, tiny points of blue glowing where the suited welders worked so far up. Standing there, Meera had felt the little flutter of the baby moving for the first time.

▲▼▲

Meera peered at the plaquette screen.

"*As the old man spoke,*" she read aloud, "*I became aware of a vast and gradually increasing sound.*"

"That's your cue," said Crispin, leaning forward in the makeup mirror.

"Actually I think he said he's just going to record us for that bit, so he can put in some effects," said Meera. "So the Visitor goes on, *vast bed of the waters, frenzied convulsion, heaving boiling hissing, prodigious streaks of foam*—blah blah—and there's me and the other two girls just sort of pacing around in a circle in the background, looking dangerous. And I suppose you're going to be just sort of staring at us in horror."

"How's this look?" Crispin turned to her. In addition to the white wig and beard, he had put in a set of tooth appliances. He gave her a mad snaggly smile and rubbed his hands together, cackling like a lunatic.

"Maybe…a little over the top," said Meera, as gently as she could.

"No, no, see, the guy has been driven mad by his experience," said Crispin. "You have to put in some comic relief, when the story's an absolute downer like this. It's, like, this psychological release for the audience."

Meera bit her lip.

"Go on, go on," said Crispin. "Who got the part of the Visitor, anyway, did Morton tell us?"

"Mr. Skousen," said Meera. "The newsman up here."

"Oh, good, at least he'll know how to read. Go on."

"'*These streaks of foam, spreading out to a great distance, took unto themselves the gyratory motion of the subsided vortices, and seemed to form another, more vast.*' You know what I'd do, if I were you? Talk to some of those hauler people. They go Outside a lot. Mother Griffith was telling me about some of the really dreadful storms."

"Oh, yeah, the…Raspberries or something, they call them," Crispin nodded. "Like what took out that temple. Yes, brilliant. Who's that big guy who plays my brother, in the boat? Alf. He's an old-timer here. I'll buy him a beer or something. Go on, go on."

Meera lifted the plaquette. "'*I looked down a smooth, shining and jet-black wall of water, speeding dizzily around and around with a swaying and sweltering motion, sending forth to the winds an appalling voice. The mountain trembled to its very base.* He looks at the Old Man. *This, this can be nothing else than the great whirlpool of the Maelstrom!*' And that's your cue."

Crispin clasped his hands together and gave a shrieking laugh. "'*Ah! I will tell you a story*—'What are you making that face for?"

"Darling, that was your Spongebob laugh."

Crispin scowled, an effect the dental appliances rendered hideous. "No, it wasn't. It was crazier." He did it again. "No, you're right. Sorry." He gave a sepulchral chuckle instead. "Oh, that's it. '*I will tell you a story that will convince you I ought to know something of the Maelstrom!*'"

▲▼▲

"I'd like to thank you all for being here today," said Mr. Morton, clasping his long white hands. "Especially our stars, who have—ha, ha—truly crossed the heavens to shine here amongst us. But I am positive that each and every one of you will shine in your own proper sphere as we begin our journey toward True Art."

"Yaaay!" cried Mona. There was polite applause.

"Our stars, of course, need no introduction," Mr. Morton went on. "However, I'd like each of the rest of the cast to stand and have his or her moment in the spotlight. Why don't we begin Stage Left? That would be you, Alf."

"Erm," said Alf. "Name, Alf Chipping. Dee-oh-bee twentyfree April twenty-two-eighty-free. Patient Number seven-seven-five. Haulers' Union Member number sixteen."

"And…why did you decide to take up acting, Alf?"

"Like plays," said Alf.

"Good for you," said Crispin.

Mona stepped forward. "I'm Mona Griffith, and I'm engaged to be married next year, and I've always wanted to be a performer. When I was little I used to climb on the table and pretend I was a hologram. I can still sing the Perky Fusion song. Want to hear it? 'Perky Fusion, he's the man, Perky Fusion in a can, cleaner source of energy, lights the world for you and me, Perky Fusion one-two-three!'"

"How nice," said Mr. Morton. "And how about you next, Ms. Hawley?"

He addressed a girl who looked rather like Joan of Arc, with her shaven head and hyperfocused stare. She stood straight.

"Exxene Hawley," she said. "Joined the MAC with my boyfriend. Wanted to make a better world on Mars. He turned out to be a stinking bastard. I said, I'd make my own stinking better world. Left him and the stinking MAC. Now I'm here. It makes as much sense as anything."

"And you're in theater because...?"

"It's a good outlet for my issues, innit?"

"O—kay," said Mr. Morton. "And so we come to Chiring." A dapper gentleman rose and flashed them a smile.

"Chiring Skousen, your News Martian. I'm shooting a documentary on the birth of Theater on Mars." He waved a hand at the holocams stationed about the room.

"Which will, no doubt, win him *another* award from the Nepalese Journalists' Association," said Mr. Morton coyly. "Mr. Skousen is our other celebrity, of course, but we knew him when!"

"And I've always cherished a secret ambition to play Edgar Allan Poe," added Chiring.

"And so we come to Maurice," said Mr. Morton, nodding toward that gentleman. He stood and nodded.

"Maurice Cochevelou," he said. "I run Griffith Steelworks. Used to do a bit of acting with the Celtic Federation's National Theater Project. Thought it might be nice to step back on the old boards, you know. Oh, and I'm engaged to be married to Mother Griffith."

Someone snickered.

"Well, I *am*," said Mr. Cochevelou plaintively.

"And there we are," said Mr. Morton, but Crispin raised his hand.

"Hey! Everyone else had to stand and face the music. We shouldn't be exempt!" He rose to his feet and raised his arms at the elbows, holding them out stiffly. "Hey hey, Mr. Korkunov, I've had *such* a busy morning!" he said, in his loudest Brophy the Bear voice. Mona giggled and applauded. "And I'd just like to say that Crispin Delamare is really looking forward to working with you all!"

He sat down. Meera rose, blushing.

"I'm Meera Suraiya, and I'm looking forward to working with you too."

"And we're expecting a baby in six months!" said Crispin. Meera put her hands to her face in dismay. To her astonishment, people applauded. She looked around at them all. They were *happy* for her.

▲▼▲

"No, nobody thinks anything about it, up here," said Mother Griffith, as she led them along the corridor. "At least, nobody thinks any harm of it. They do say people aren't having them now on Earth. I can't say I'm surprised, with those fines! I had mine in the Celtic Federation, see, when you didn't need a permit. Different now; shame, but there it is. I wouldn't go back to Earth if you paid me, indeed."

"What do people do for—well, for clothes, and furniture?" inquired Crispin.

"And nappies?" inquired Meera.

"Catalogs," said Mother Griffith. "Or the PX at Settlement Base. For now. Not to worry! Within the twenty-four-month, the boys will have my Market Center finished. It'll be vast! At last, affordable consumer goods up here at reasonable prices, what a thought, eh? It'll be even more civilized when your next one comes along."

"Next one?" said Meera, in a faint voice. Crispin shrugged.

"And here we are!" said Mother Griffith proudly, and pulled a lever. With a hiss, the great door before them unsealed and folded back on itself. A rush of air met them, cool and sweet, very like Earth. They stepped through and found themselves on a catwalk, looking out across a gulf of air at a corresponding catwalk on the opposite side. Behind them, the portal hissed shut again. "Griffith Towers!"

"Brilliant!" said Crispin, going at once to the railing and peering over. Meera followed him and looked down, then quickly backed away. Ten storeys below was an open atrium with a fountain, and little green things dotted here and there. Immediately above them was a modest dome, letting in the light of day.

"That's a rose garden down there," said Mother Griffith, in satisfaction. "Trees, too, would you believe it? No expense spared. Can't wait to see what the American Sequoia will do in our gravity. I know it doesn't look like much now, dears, but give it a few seasons."

"Oh, no, it's very nice," said Crispin, and Meera conquered her fear of heights enough to take a second look. She had to admit the place showed promise; while most of it was cast concrete, in pink and terracotta hues, the floors were cut and polished stone of an oxblood color. There was a great deal of ornamental wrought iron on all the balconies, and hanging baskets that were clearly meant to contain plants one day. Green flowering creepers, perhaps, in all that wrought iron, level after level descending...

The image of the Maelstrom came into her mind, the whirling vortex. Meera pulled back and gasped out, "Griffith Towers, you said. Will there be floors added going upward?"

"Lady bless you, no, dear! Far too dangerous, even when we get the Great Dome finished. Couldn't very well call it Griffith Hole-in-the-Ground, though, could we? It'll be nicer when the workmen's gear isn't lying all about," conceded Mother Griffith. "You'll have some noise to put up with for a few more months, but it'll all be finished by the time the baby comes. *Your* place is done, though. Come and see."

She led them along the catwalk to a door, beside which was the first window they had seen on Mars, something like a large porthole. Mother Griffith rapped on it with her knuckles.

"Expect you never thought you'd see one of these again, eh? Triple-glazed Ferroperspex. Anything happens to the dome, you'll still be safe inside. As long as you don't open the bloody door, of course," she added cheerfully, and palmed the via panel. The door opened for them. "Got to program in your handprints before we leave, do remind me."

They stepped through, and the lights came on to reveal a snug, low-ceilinged room. It had plenty of built-in shelves, though the phrase was more correctly *cast-ins*; everything was made of the ubiquitous pink cement, polished to a gloss, from the entertainment console to the continuous bench that ran around the walls. There wasn't a stick of wood in evidence anywhere. The few pieces of freestanding furniture were made of wrought iron. An attempt had been made to add warmth, in the big oriental rug on the floor and in the bright cushions on the bench.

"Front parlor," announced Mother Griffith. "Kitchen and bath through there—yes, a real private bath, with running hot water and all! Everything state of the art, see? And bedrooms off here—this one we made adjoining, thought you'd want that for the nursery. Come and see."

Each room had a sealed airlock rather than a door. They stepped through into the bedroom and stared; for the bed was sunk into a recess in the floor, under a transparent dome of its own.

"More state of the art," said Mother Griffith. "Anything happens, your own little dome keeps you safe with your own oxygen supply."

"'Anything happens'? What's likely to happen?" asked Crispin.

"Oh, nothing very much, nowadays," said Mother Griffith, with a wave of her hand. "Once the Great Dome's finished, I don't expect there'll be many emergencies. If we get another Strawberry it can't flatten the place—that's the clever part of building underground, see? Though it might dash a boulder or two against the atrium dome, so it's best to take precautions. And it's five years now since we had an asteroid strike, and that was way out in Syrtis Major, so—"

"Asteroid strike?"

"Scarcely ever happens," said Mother Griffith quickly. "We never waste time worrying about 'em, and you needn't either. And aren't they building a whole series of orbiting gun platforms up there, and bases on Phobos and Deimos to boot, all manned with clever lads who'll pot the nasty things off with lasers to some other trajectory, if they don't blow them up entirely? They are indeed.

"No, the only real inconvenience is the dust. There's a lot of dust."

"But," said Meera, "Just supposing for a moment, that an asteroid *did* hit—say it plummeted right through the atrium dome!"

"We'd lose the rose garden," said Mother Griffith. "And I suppose anyone who'd been silly enough to be down there without a mask on, but that's Evolution in Action, as we're fond of saying up here. You'd be snug in here with your door sealed, I expect."

"But we'd be trapped!" said Crispin.

"Not a bit of it! There's a hatch in the kitchen, opens out on the maintenance crawlway. Leads straight back to the Empress of Mars, so you'd just stroll up and have a pint while the Emergency Team dealt with things. What, were you expecting aliens with steel teeth lurking round the water pipes? Not a bit of it; only alien you'll see is the fellow in the Tars Tarkas costume on Barsoom Day, bringing presents for the kiddies," said Mother Griffith firmly. "Come now, have a look at the nursery."

▲▼▲

Meera waited offstage with Exxene and Mona, the three of them in matching black leotards. They were growing slightly bored, waiting as they had been for fifteen minutes. Across from them they could see Alf and Cochevelou, waiting for their cues, sitting quietly in a pair of folding chairs.

"I don't see why we couldn't have done it live," Mona complained. "I take really good care of my singing voice, you know? I could do it night after night. I'd be loud enough, too."

"He couldn't have put in his special effects then, could he?" said Exxene. "We'll be louder. Scarier. Inhuman, like."

Meera shifted uncomfortably. Her leotard was a little tight. She wondered how much the baby showed. It was hard to think of herself as a scary, inhuman force of nature with a baby.

"I heard the first edit," she said. "It's wonderful. He's mixed in all kinds of sound effects, bits of music—all distorted so you can't quite recognize them, you know—and then our voices come in on the Philip Glass piece and we sound quite unearthly."

"I guess it's okay, then," said Mona. Exxene stamped her feet in impatience and did a back bend.

"When's this Poe going to get his arse in gear?" she muttered. Mr. Morton entered from Stage Right, waving his hands.

"Sorry! Sorry, all! Mr. Skousen is ready. Places, if you please."

Meera focused and thought of herself as a deadly goddess, a creature of the storm, a wall of water black as jet, devouring...or an asteroid approaching through the black cold infinity of space...Here came Mr. Skousen in makeup as Edgar Allen Poe, and she was appalled at the thought of how much white pancake foundation they must have had to use. He had poise, though, and the big sad dark eyes for the role; walked sedately to his mark, turned his little Hitler mustache to the audience and said:

"'You must get over these fancies,' said my guide."

"Your cue, Mr. Delamare," said Mr. Morton. Crispin, in full makeup, came bounding out, rubbing his hands.

"For I have brought you here that I might tell you the whole story as it happened, with the spot just under your eye!" he cackled, leaping so high he almost collided with the holo rig.

Meera winced. Mr. Morton pulled his white hands up to his mouth, as though he were about to stifle a scream of dismay; but he made no sound. Mr. Skousen, visibly startled, turned to stare.

"Look *out*, from this mountain upon which we stand, look *out* beyond the belt of vapor beneath us, into the *seaaaa*!" Crispin declaimed. Mona stifled a giggle. Mr. Skousen cleared his throat, not quite suggesting disapproval.

"I looked dizzily, and beheld a wide expanse of ocean," he said. "A panorama more deplorably desolate no human imagination can conceive. To the right and left, as far as the eye could reach, there lay outstretched, like ramparts of the world, lines of horribly black and beetling cliff, whose character of gloom was but the more forcibly illustrated by the surf which reared high up against its white and ghastly crest, howling and shrieking for ever." He spoke in clear, somber and entirely appropriate tones.

Mr. Morton forgot to cue the music, but the stage manager—Mona's betrothed, who had cleverly traded shifts with another miner so he could keep an eye on her—remembered anyway, and switched on the sound.

A menacing drone filled the air, disturbing currents of Bach's *Fugue in G*, eddies of electronically modified voices.

"Oh, wow, is that *us*?" said Mona.

"We sound good," said Exxene in surprise.

"Ladies, that's our cue," Meera reminded them, and they processed out from the wings, looking baleful as the three witches in the Scottish Play, seductive as the mermaids in *Peter Pan*, deadly as the Guardswomen in *Sheeratu*. They prowled together in a tight circle upstage, and Exxene in particular got an unsettling light in her eye.

"I'm going to kill somebody," she said *sotto voce*.

"That's the spirit," said Meera, resolving to keep well out of arm's reach of her.

They walked on, round and round, in a silence that deepened.

"Line?" said Crispin at last.

"Do you hear anyfing, do you see any change in da water," said Alf helpfully.

"Do you *hear* anything?" said Crispin, lurching up to Mr. Skousen and jerking at his sleeve. "Do you *see* any change in the water?"

"Crumbs!" said Mona, sincerely shocked. "He's *awful*!"

"Oh, dear, Mr. Delamare," said Mr. Morton, "Mr. Delamare—I am afraid—this is not quite what I had in mind."

"Sorry?" Crispin straightened up. "Oh. Too broad, isn't it? I can tone it down a little."

"Yes, please," said Mr. Morton. "Go on. Your line, Chiring."

Mr. Skousen drew a breath and said:

"As the old man spoke, I became aware of a vast and gradually increasing sound."

Mr. Morton waved distractedly, and Durk raised the volume on the music. Mulet's *Thou Art the Rock* was briefly recognizable. Mr. Skousen raised his voice:

"The vast bed of the waters, seamed and scarred into a thousand conflicting channels, burst suddenly into frenzied convulsion—heaving, boiling, hissing—prodigious streaks of foam gyrating in gigantic and innumerable vortices, and all whirling and plunging eastward. These streaks of foam, spreading out to a great distance, took unto themselves the...er..."

"Jyartry motion of da subsided votrices," said Alf.

"Thank you. Took unto themselves the gyratory motion of the subsided vortices, and seemed to form another, more vast.

"I looked down a smooth, shining and jet-black wall of water, speeding dizzily around and around with a swaying and sweltering motion, sending forth to the winds an appalling voice. The mountain trembled to its very base."

Mr. Skousen looked at Crispin, and cried: "This, this can be nothing else than the great whirlpool of the Maelstrom!"

Crispin leaned in and, with his very, *very* worst Spongebob titter, said "I will tell you a story that will convince you I ought to know something of the Maelstrom! Ha-ha-*ha*!"

"Oh dear God," said Mr. Morton.

▲▼▲

"I didn't think I was *that* bad," said Crispin miserably. They were sitting together in their little state-of-the-art kitchen, over a couple of mugs of Martian-style tea. Yellow lakes of melted butter swam on its surface, but it was surprisingly soothing.

"You weren't really," said Meera. "It's only that...it's not a comedy, darling."

"It could be," said Crispin. "It could be played funny. Why doesn't anybody see the humor in the thing? Nobody could see the humor in *The Dancing Daleks* either. Why are people so serious? Life isn't serious."

"No, but Art is," said Meera. "Apparently."

"The big guy, Alf, he's amazing. We talked, you know, about all his adventures on the road up here, really awful stuff he's lived to talk about, and you should hear him! 'So dere I was wiv, like, dis sand doon over me, and I finks to myself: How da hell am I gointer find out wevver Arsenal won da match? So I reckoned I'd better get a shovel or somefink, but dere weren't no shovel, so I tore da seat off da lavvy and dug out wiv it.' It's all in a day's work to him! He was laughing about it!"

"That was nice; you got his voice exactly," said Meera.

"These people live on the edge of destruction, all the time, and they manage by treating it all as a joke," said Crispin. He folded his arms the way Mother Griffith did and cocked his head at Meera. "'Oh, my goodness no indeed, you don't want to let a little thing like an asteroid hitting the bloody planet bother you! Just come up to the Empress for a pint, my dears!' So why can't Morton see how *really* innovative it would be to play this thing for laughs?"

"I don't know," said Meera. "But, you know, it's his vision. And it's his theater. And these people have been awfully good to us."

"So I don't suppose I could walk out of the show," said Crispin. He gave her a furtive look that meant: *Could I?*

"No," said Meera firmly. "This isn't like walking out on *Anna Karenina*, where it didn't matter because Mummy loaned us the money to get the car fixed. Or walking out on *From the Files of the Time Rangers,* when it didn't matter because your aunt left you that bequest. It isn't just a matter of scraping by until one of us gets a commercial. You're right; you can't leave. *We* can't leave. Remember why we're here."

"I know," said Crispin, and sighed. He looked at her sadly. "Life has caught up with us, and it's going to suck us in. I have to grow up now, don't I?"

"Grow up?" Meera laughed, though she felt tears stinging her eyes. "Crispin, you're having adventures on bloody Mars! You're living in a Star Wars flat beneath the surface of another planet! Our baby's going to think Father Christmas has four arms and tusks! Do you think growing up is going to be *boring*?"

He giggled, looking shamefaced.

"No, no, see, it's all wrong. If I'm having adventures on Mars, I ought to be in my space suit, with my rocket ship in the background, and my clean-cut jaw sticking out to *here*—" he thrust his chin out grotesquely. Meera couldn't help laughing. He jumped up on the table and struck an attitude.

"And I'd have a ray gun in either fist—and I'd be firing away and dropping alien hordes in their tracks, brrrzzzt! Aiee! Die, space scum! 'Retreat, my minionth! It ith Thtar Commander Delamare! Curthe you, Earthman!' And

I'd have this gorgeous babe, naked except for some strategically-placed pieces of space jewelery, clinging to my leg as I stood there. Played by the beautiful and exotic Meera Suraiya." He smiled down at her.

"Would she be pregnant?"

"Of course she would," said Crispin, jumping down and kissing her. "Got to repopulate the planet somehow."

▲▼▲

"It's standing room only!" said Mr. Morton, biting his fingernails. "Look! Look! Look at them out there!"

Cochevelou peered through the gap in the curtain. He spotted Mother Griffith in the front row, arms folded, with most of the tavern staff seated to either side of her. Behind them, in ranks all the way to the back wall, were haulers and miners. Some were washed and combed and wearing their best indoor clothing; some had clearly come straight from their rigs, or from their mine shifts, for they wore psuits or miner's armor and had tracked in red dust on the purple carpet.

"Heh," said Cochevelou, leaning back. He took a small flask from an inner pocket, and had a sip before passing it to Morton, who drank and coughed. "Now, see, if you'd charged 'em for tickets like I'd told you, you'd have made a chunk of change tonight."

"No! These poor fellows would never have access to the finer things in life on Earth; I won't deprive them of the chance, here on Mars," said Mr. Morton. "The Arts shall be free! If only..."

"If only?" Cochevelou tucked away the flask and peered at him. It was dark backstage, and Mr. Morton's licorice-stick silhouette was barely visible; his pale face seemed to float above it, like the mask of tragedy.

"If only it wasn't for the human element," he said mournfully.

"Ah. The holotalent?" Cochevelou shrugged. "Well, and what if the boy's terrible? It ain't like this lot will know any better."

"There is that," Mr. Morton admitted. "But...I have built my theater. I am about to accomplish a thing of which I have dreamed my life long. I am a dramaturge, Maurice. My players are assembled, my Shrine to the Arts is filled...and..."

"And?"

"*What if it disappoints me?*" Tears stood in Mr. Morton's eyes.

Cochevelou stroked his beard, regarding Mr. Morton in wonder.

"Well," he said at last. "You wouldn't be the first man it'd happened to, would you? And after all, it ain't about you being happy, is it? It's about giving all them out front something that'll take their minds off dying up here."

"Of course it is," said Mr. Morton, and sighed. "But oh, the terror of dreams fulfilled! It must go on now, mustn't it? No way to wave a magic wand and crumble my theater back into the violet dust of unlimited possibilities?"

"No, there ain't," said Cochevelou. "The show's going on, and you're sitting in the little boat about to go over the edge into the whirlpool. Let's just hope there's something nice at the bottom."

"Ten minute call, Mr. Cochevelou," said Durk.

"Oh dear," said Mr. Morton, and ran for the wings. Then he remembered that he was supposed to give a speech before the curtain rose, and ran back. Cochevelou kept going, to the little dressing room he and Alf shared. Alf was dutifully smearing adhesive on his face, preparatory to attaching his false beard.

"You ought to grow a real one," said Cochevelou, flipping the end of his own with pride.

"Can't," said Alf, looking at him in the mirror. "On account of the meds they gave me in Ospital."

Cochevelou winced. "Not ever?"

"I don't mind so much," said Alf, fitting on the false beard. "This don't arf tickle."

"Well." Cochevelou thumped him on the shoulder. "We're almost on."

Meera was standing quite still in the wings, summoning all the despair and anger she could. Exxene was walking in a tight circle, muttering "Kill, kill, kill." Mona was fussing with her ribbon-stick, looping it through the air in swirly arcs.

"I don't like this one," she whispered. "Can I trade with you?"

Meera simply nodded and handed over hers. She was exhausted; Crispin had had a bad case of performance nerves and hadn't slept much the night before. He had tried not to wake her, but every time he had climbed into or out of bed, the hiss of the air-seal had brought her to sharp consciousness and the certainty that an asteroid was plummeting straight for Griffith Towers.

Uncertain applause out front: Mr. Morton clearing his throat.

"I bid you welcome, friends, to the inaugural season of the Edgar Allen Poe Center for the Performing Arts! When future generations of Martians look back to this evening, upon which the shy Muse of Tragedy first ventured onto our rocky soil, they will undoubtedly…"

Crispin emerged from his dressing room, and would have looked haggard even without benefit of makeup. As he passed between the colored lights on his way to the wings, his photoreactive beard and wig flickered, black-white-black. He stepped into place beside Chiring, and nodded.

"What's the house like?"

Chiring gave him two thumbs up.

"That's the ticket," said Crispin, as cheerfully as he could. He began to bounce on the balls of his feet. "Energy-energy-energy, come on Crispin, aah eeh eye ohh oooh. Run run run!" He drew up his fists and began to run in place.

"What are you doing?" whispered Chiring.

"Gearing myself up," said Crispin, running faster and faster. "Never fails to kill those butterflies in the tummy. YeeOW!" He finished, as he always had, by launching himself into midair.

Unfortunately, he had forgotten about Martian gravity. Crispin soared up and straight into the blue can spotlight, which rang like a gong when it connected with his skull. He dropped like a sack of flour, out cold.

"Mr. Delamare!" Chiring stared down at him, aghast.

"What the hell?" Cochevelou leaned down from the curved framework meant to symbolize a fishing boat. "Oh. Drunk, is he?"

"No!" Chiring fell to his knees and slapped ineffectually at Crispin's face. "Oh, no, Mr. Delamare—oh, look, he's cut his scalp too—"

"What was that—" Mona ventured out from Stage Left, saw Chiring, and gave a stifled shriek.

"What is it?" Meera looked up, startled.

"Chiring and your husband are fighting! He's knocked him down!" cried Mona.

"What?" Meera raced across the stage, closely followed by Exxene who, when she came in range, aimed a roundhouse blow at Chiring. Chiring yelped, ducking, and waved his hands in panic.

"What are you hitting *me* for? He hit his head on the light!"

"Cris!" Meera knelt beside him. "Oh, baby—somebody call the paramedics!"

"What paramedics?" said Cochevelou, climbing out of the boat frame.

"So what were you fighting about?" Mona asked Chiring.

"What do you mean, *what paramedics?*" said Meera, horrified.

"We weren't fighting!" said Chiring.

"I mean we haven't got any," said Cochevelou. He knelt beside Crispin too and thumbed open an eyelid. "Not to worry, ma'am. He'll come round. Morton has a cot in his office; let's stow him in there until he sobers up."

"But he isn't drunk!"

"But we're about to go on!" said Mona.

All this while, the sound of Mr. Morton's speech had been in the background, but it had begun to falter. They heard hesitant applause and then Mr. Morton leaped through the curtain.

"What the hell is going on back here?" he demanded. He spotted Crispin, unconscious and bleeding on the floor, and his eyes went wide.

"He jumped up and hit his head and knocked himself out and I had nothing to do with it!" screamed Chiring. He stabbed a finger at the blue can spot. "It was that light right there!"

Mr. Morton made a sound suggesting that all the air had been knocked out of him. He fell to his knees.

"Aw, now, it'll all come right, Morton dear," said Cochevelou. He pulled out his flask, uncapped it and stuck it in Mr. Morton's nerveless hand. "Just you drink up. Alf, give us a hand with old Brophy Bear."

"But we're about to go on!" said Mona.

"Yeh," said Exxene. "What'll we do?"

In tears, Mr. Morton shook his head. He tilted the flask and drank.

"Alf knows the part," said Mona. "He knows all the parts."

Everyone, including Alf, gave her a withering look. Quite clearly, they heard someone in the audience saying:

"Well? When are we going to see something?"

"Looks like it's you, son," said Cochevelou. He bent over Crispin and peeled off his false beard, but when he pulled the wig off too it was full of blood. "Oh, bugger."

Meera leaped to her feet and advanced on him menacingly.

"I don't care how you do it," she said, "But you're getting my husband to *some* kind of medical facility, and you're doing it *right now*."

"Yes, ma'am," said Cochevelou, backing away. He thrust the wig and beard at Alf, and turned and ran for his life. Meera knelt again beside Crispin, accepting a handful of tissues Exxene had fetched her to compress his wound.

"Scalp wounds bleed buckets," she told Meera reassuringly. "It don't mean nothing."

"Oi!" shouted someone in the audience. "Are we going to sit here all shrackin' night?"

"I might have known this would happen," said Mr. Morton, tragically calm. "They'll riot next, I know it."

"No! The show must go on, right?" said Mona. "Come on, Alf! Look, Mr. Morton, see how nice he looks in the other beard? And you can wear *his* beard, and *you* can play the youngest brother, because there's no lines—"

"Raise the damn curtain!" said someone in the audience.

"And—I know! I'll go out and dance for them," said Mona.

"In a pig's eye you will, my girl," snapped Mother Griffith, shouldering her way backstage with Cochevelou close behind her. She stopped short, gaping at Crispin. "Goddess on a golf ball! Why haven't you sent him to the clinic, you idiots?"

The audience had begun to sing *Why Are We Waiting*. Mother Griffith turned and thrust her head through the curtain.

"Shut up, you lot, we've got an injured man back here!" she shouted. "Manco! Thak! Come up here and help us."

The audience, cowed, fell silent at once, as two of Mother Griffith's staff scrambled over the footlights and so backstage. In short order Crispin was bandaged, tied into a chair, masked up and carried away down the tunnel, with Mother Griffith leading the way.

"Wonder why they were fighting?" whispered a miner to a hauler.

"I hear those Hollywood types are temperamental," the hauler whispered back.

The scurrying and cries behind the curtain faded away. For a moment it hung still, so motionless its folds might have been carved from stone; then it rose, to reveal Edgar Allan Poe standing on an outcropping of rock, before a backdrop of severe sky and a sea like black stone. He was sweating, looked frightened and miserable. He looked out at the audience and said:

"'You must get over these fancies,' said my guide."

The old man, an immense old man like a walking hill, stepped forth from the wings. There was a disturbing glare in his eyes. Were those streaks of blood in his wild white beard? He looked at Poe and said quietly:

"For I ave brort you ere dat I might tell you da ole story as it appened, wiv da spot just under yer eye. Look out from dis mountain upon which we stand, look out beyond da belt of vapor beneaf us, into da sea."

Poe shrank visibly. He licked his dry lips and said:

"I looked dizzily, and beheld a wide expanse of ocean. A panorama more deplorably desolate no human imagination can conceive..."

Meera, sitting huddled on a chair in the wings, felt Exxene grip her shoulder. "Come on, that's us," she said.

May as well, thought Meera, rising mechanically. *Show must go on.* She moved out with the others, into the eerie light, into the eerier music. She put into the slink of her walk all the hopelessness she felt. Mother cat, looking for a safe place to have its kittens. But there was no safe place...

She and Crispin had been pulled under by the circling tide of history, two emigrants like any others, in the long outward flow of life from the place where it started to its unknown destination. Some washed up on the distant shore and did well for themselves, became ancestors to new generations of races...some failed to survive their first winters, and their names were forgotten.

She glanced into the audience on one pass around, and was shocked out of her reverie to see that they were watching raptly, leaning forward in their seats.

Why, look at that; they're completely into it, she thought. Alf had stepped back from the rock, into the blue circle of light, and his beard and hair had gone to black; well, perhaps the stage effect had pleased them. Here came the rickety little boat effect, pushed by Cochevelou and Mr. Morton. Oh, no, look at the false beard hanging askew, under Mr. Morton's chin! That was going to get a laugh.

It didn't, somehow. Alf droned on without inflection, and the audience strained to hear, but his accents weren't strange or comic, not to them.

"The roar of the water was drowned in a shrill shriek, like the sound of waste-pipes of many thousand steam-vessels, letting off their steam all together. We were now in the belt of surf that always surrounds the whirl; and I thought that another moment would plunge us into the abyss—down which we could only see indistinctly. The boat did not seem to sink into the water at all, but to skim like an air-bubble upon the surface of the surge.

"The rays of the moon seemed to search the very bottom of the profound gulf; I saw mist, where the great walls of the funnel met together at the bottom. What a yell went up to the heavens from out of that mist! Our first slide into the abyss itself, from the belt of foam above, had carried us to a great distance down the slope. Round and round we swept—not with any uniform movement—but in dizzying swings and jerks, that sent us sometimes only a few hundred yards—sometimes nearly the complete circuit of the whirl..."

And why shouldn't the audience be transfixed? This was their story; they heard it every day. They had all lived through something like this, here, on this alien soil. Pitiless dunes that buried you, suffocating wastes that froze you, bombs that might roar out of the stars unannounced and strike with an impact that smacked you into flattened and broken strata. Mars in all its casual malevolence, against whom one miscalculation meant sudden death and a freeze-dried corpse pointed out to gawking tourists.

Meera flung up her arms and danced, and the other two whirled after her. They were black goddesses, they were nightmare crones, they were the Fates, they were the brides of Death in this bleak place. *We are always at your elbow; never forget.* The members of the audience stared openmouthed, started forward when first the one and then the other mariner was dragged down, seduced, pulled to his death out of sight.

At last there was only Alf staring out, with the sweat shining on his moon face, real terror of remembrance in his eyes, and his voice had sunk to a hoarse late-night whisper that nonetheless carried to the back of the house.

"A boat picked me up. Those who drew me on board were my old mates, but they knew me no more than they would have known a traveler from the spirit-land. My hair, which had been raven-black the day before, was as white as you see it now. I told them my story. They did not believe it. I now tell it to you."

There was a profound silence. The lights went down.

Finally there was an uncertain patter of applause, which abruptly swelled to thunder. The audience had struggled to their feet and were baying their approval. The ladies stared at one another, wondering. Mr. Morton, who had been helping himself to the flask since his exit, looked up foggily.

"Good lord," he said. "They *liked* it!" He rose to his full height and nearly fell over. "Curtain call! Shoo! Shoo! Get out there!" He flapped his hands at them. Meera caught his arm and pulled him out too, and he stood between Alf and Cochevelou, blinking in the glare of the footlights.

Meera took Mona's and Exxene's hands, as much for support as tradition. A haze was in the air, for men were stamping now as well as applauding, with the dust flying up from their boots. She couldn't see a face that wasn't streaked with tears, white or black runnels cut through the red dust.

Someone was pushing through the crowd. Mother Griffith reached the front row, waving, shouting to be heard above the commotion but still drowned out by the frenzied whooping.

He's okay, she mouthed at Meera. Just so she wouldn't be misinterpreted, she made a circle with forefinger and thumb and winked broadly, grinning. Mona hugged her and Exxene pounded her shoulder, which hurt rather a lot, but Meera scarcely noticed.

Her baby was dancing.

▲▼▲

Crispin was sitting up in the clinic bed, wearing an absurd gown with teddy bears on it, sipping from a juice box. His head was bandaged, but the color had returned to his face.

"It was a hit because I wasn't in it, you know," he said ruefully. "Luckiest thing that could have happened."

"Oh, darling, you know you'd have been wonderful," said Meera, stroking his hair back from the edge of the bandage.

"They said it was all right if we visited," Mona announced, entering with Exxene. "You left before you got your presents! Are you feeling better, Mr. Delamare? Look what Durk had made for us! Isn't he an old dear? There's three!"

She held up a huge sweater in the rather sinister blue of the show lights. Across its bosom had been machine-embroidered *The Maelstromettes*.

"Isn't that funny? Except he had them all made triple-X-size for some reason. Mine comes down to my knees," said Mona.

"Here's yer roses," said Exxene, holding out a bouquet. "Know what? I've had five proposals of marriage tonight. Odd, ain't it?"

"And, you know what else, Mr. Delamare?" said Mona. "Mr. Morton wants to do a comedy next, as soon as you're all recovered! Won't that be wonderful? It's this lost play or something about somebody named Ernest. At least, I think that was what he said. He was on his third glass of champagne."

"A comedy?" Crispin brightened. A bell rang, out in the corridor.

"Crumbs, that'll be *Visiting Hours are Over*," said Mona. "Come on, Meera, we'll walk you home. Goodnight, Mr. Delamare."

"I'll be here first thing tomorrow," said Meera, leaning down to kiss him. She took a rose from her bouquet and carefully threaded it down the straw of his water carafe.

Walking up the tube with Mona and Exxene, she realized that she didn't notice the methane smell now at all. And how bright the stars were, up there above the half-finished city on the mountain!

Speed, Speed the Cable

"My friends, it is nothing more nor less than the Tower of Babel come again." The speaker, a benign-looking gentleman with white side-whiskers, watched as his audience took in the statement. "Consider. Vile Man, in his pride, once more seeks to demolish the natural boundaries placed for his benefit by the Almighty. He does not now say, 'I shall build great foundations and ascend through the stars, that the Lord may see I am exceeding great.' No, he says rather: 'Time and Space I shall make as nothing, that my voice may be heard when and where I will!'

"My friends, you know that punishment must be handed down from on high for such sinful ambition. Yet I wonder whether any of you have truly considered the extent of our misfortune, were this Atlantic cable laid at last!"

Among those listening was a man in his mid-thirties, pleasantly nondescript in appearance. His name was Kendal. The patient observer might study him at length, failing to find anything memorable in his features, save for one singular detail: Kendal's left ear differed slightly in color from his right.

Kendal shifted in his chair, wondering who had written Mr. Hargrove's speech. He'd heard it all before, when the Preventers had first recruited him, but Mr. Hargrove spoke with much more elegance now: how the dear old familiar world of our infancy vanished a little more each year, with each unthinking embrace of the Machine in the service of Industry for the pursuit of Wealth. The dark satanic mills were invoked, the horrors of railway accidents and the carnage of steam boiler explosions. Each was a little foretaste of Hell, a warning from Heaven; and yet, that warning went unheeded!

Kendal suppressed the urge to yawn. He knew that half the men in the room with him were wealthy, sons of men who'd amassed fortunes by embracing the Machine. Their clothing had been woven on steam-driven looms; some of them had come here by rail. Kendal was a poor man's son, but he sat there with the rest of them, nodding solemnly as Hargrove spoke, now and again joining in when one or another of them cried "Hear! Hear!" with evangelical fervor.

One man cried out that anything that brought them closer to the Americans—vulgar, ignorant, *expectorating* Americans—was a dreadful idea. Another shouted that worse was to come, if the Atlantic Telegraph Company had its way. What of national security? What should happen, if spies were able to transmit vital information to enemy forces instantaneously? What of the captains and crews of packet ships, who might be expected to lose revenues if the Atlantic cable were laid?

An elderly man stood and declared that he had made a study of galvanometers, and knew for a fact that a cable of such length, passing through such a quantity of seawater, would most certainly deliver a monstrous charge from the larger continent to the smaller and incinerate the whole of Britain in the very moment the first transmission was sent.

Whereupon someone pointed out that only Ireland was likely to be incinerated, since the eastern end of the great cable was to be fixed in County Kerry.

"Even so," said the elderly person, with a sniff.

"My friends!" Mr. Hargrove raised his hands. "We are all agreed in what is essential: that this infernal device *must* be prevented. We want only the financial means to guarantee our victory."

Kendal rose to his feet. Removing his hat, he said: "Gentlemen, while I must commend Mr. Dowd for his heroic actions on the eleventh of August last—" a ripple of applause ran through the room as the saboteur smiled and half-rose to acknowledge his compliment—"I feel obliged to point out that next time, it will require more than simply jamming the release brake to sever the cable. My informants have given me to understand that the paying-out machinery has been completely redesigned at the behest of Mr. Bright. It is now self-regulating. What are we to do?"

"Fear not!" Mr. Hargrove beamed at him. "It is true we have suffered setbacks, but so have our opponents. Mr. Cyrus Field may pop up as often as a Jack-in-the-box, bearing fistfuls of cash with which to advance his infernal design, yet we too have friends among the influential and powerful. For all that, gentlemen, we do require your support as well. Please give as generously as you may when the basket comes before you."

A pair of gentlemen solemn as church elders rose and flanked the audience, sending two baskets up and down the rows of seats. This signaled an informal end to the gathering. Kendal duly dropped in a five-pound-note, but remained seated until the room had nearly emptied. When Kendal rose at last, making his way to the front of the room, the astute observer would have noticed something more: for he walked with a slight limp. "Mr. Perceval!"

Mr. Hargrove extended his hand. "How delighted I am to see you again! We had hoped some would remain steadfast, and answer the call once more."

"I confess I was astonished to receive your letter, sir," Kendal replied. "When I heard about the fire in Bridge Street, I assumed the whole enterprise had been given over."

Mr. Hargrove shook his head. "We thought so, too; yet a new friend has stepped forward to lend us his considerable powers of assistance. You'd recognize his name, sir, if I told you what it was, indeed you would. I have never been so confident of success as I am now!"

"Thank God," said Kendal. "I had some hopes of scotching the damned cable on my own, you see. Even made some inquiries about getting into the Gutta Percha factory to spoil it at the source. It won't do; they're a great deal more particular about whom they hire, now."

"Ah, we know," said Mr. Hargrove ruefully. "No matter; we've quite an ingenious ruse to get around that. Our new friend pointed out that the later we wait to strike, the more of his resources the enemy will waste. Sooner or later we must ruin him completely, if we cut him off from his investors."

"Why, what's the ruse?"

Mr. Hargrove looked around, then leaned close to Kendal, lowering his voice. "A simple and effective one. Not only have we got a man aboard the *Agamemnon,* our new friend has supplied us with the funds for a diving-suit, if you please! When the cable ship comes into Galway Bay, our men will be at hand, disguised as Irishmen, in a fishing vessel. They will sail close and pretend to cheer on the *Agamemnon,* but will note carefully where the cable falls. Then one will slip overboard, descend to the cable, and cut it. Simplicity itself!"

"Yet ingenious indeed!" Kendal pumped Mr. Hargrove's hand. "And will it be Mr. Dowd aboard the *Agamemnon* again?"

"No, alas. He departed under a cloud of suspicion last time. It'll be Mr. Cheltenham."

"Ah! But he's a stout fellow too. You will succeed, sir; I feel it in my heart."

They exchanged cordial farewells.

Kendal emerged from a side entrance, climbing stairs to reach the street, entering the Strand quite unseen at that hour of the night. He had not gone above five paces when a hulking shadow detached itself from the greater darkness within a colonnade, following him.

No human ear could have heard as it came up behind Kendal, for it made no sound; yet Kendal turned his head, acknowledging its presence with a nod. The next pool of lamplight revealed the two men walking side by side.

Kendal's companion was remarkably tall, with a long broken nose and pale eyes. But for these distinctions he had been as anonymous as Kendal, one more gentleman in evening dress returning from some amusement.

They had reached Whitehall before the tall man spoke, barely moving his lips. "Much good?"

"Oh yes," Kendal whispered. The other nodded, saying nothing more for the duration of their journey, which ended in Craig's Court at their club.

Redking's occupied premises not nearly so imposing as those of the Athenaeum, nor as cheerful as Boodles', having as it did an undistinguished brick frontage. The two gentlemen climbed its steps, nodded to the porter who admitted them, and handed their hats to the waiter who met them within.

"Mr. Greene requests your presence at once, sirs," said the waiter. Kendal cast a longing glance at the dining room, where clinking cutlery suggested some fortunate party was enjoying a late supper. Nevertheless he turned and, with his companion, descended a flight of stairs.

A right turn and then a left took them past a number of undistinguished-looking doors to one bearing a blank brass plate. Kendal heard the drone of a voice within, and recognized the speaker as Mr. Hargrove. Kendal's companion knocked on the door.

"Come in," said a different voice, as Mr. Hargrove's flow of speech went on without interruption.

At a desk within a sparsely-furnished study sat a single individual, glaring at the apparatus occupying one corner of the room. It resembled a glass-fronted cabinet, in which could be glimpsed a rotating cylinder. From the cabinet's top protruded a brass trumpet similar to those used by persons hard of hearing. However, it was presently sending out sound, rather than receiving it.

"...*Mr. Cyrus Field may pop up as often as a Jack-in-the-box, bearing fistfuls of cash with which to advance his infernal design, yet we too have our friends among the influential and powerful...*"

"Now, whom do you suppose he means?" said Mr. Greene, turning his glare on Kendal and his companion.

"He never said, sir," said Kendal. They listened to the rest of the conversation. When the voices receded into silence and nothing more was heard but Kendal's recorded footsteps, Greene rose and took the cylinder from the cabinet.

"Not impossible, I shouldn't think," said Greene. "But it should have been unnecessary. That was *your* business, Bell-Fairfax."

Kendal's companion bowed his head in acknowledgment, but said nothing. "He did burn down their headquarters, sir," Kendal protested. "We had every reason to believe we'd rooted them out."

"Clearly they were not sufficiently discouraged." Greene looked meaningfully at Bell-Fairfax. "I expect more drastic measures are called for now."

"Yes, sir," said Bell-Fairfax, in a quiet voice.

"We don't have unlimited resources, man. Have you any idea what it cost to produce enough gyttite for the job? Or what we had to bribe the factory, to have it wound into the cable? Or how much we stand to gain, if the cable is laid? They cannot sabotage our efforts again!"

"No, sir."

Greene returned to his chair, scowling. "So they have a diving suit, have they?...Damn. This wants some planning. The *Agamemnon* sails on the 17th, with its portion of the cable. They're anticipated at Knightstown the 5th, ergo..." He fell silent. Kendal and Bell-Fairfax waited patiently, until Greene seemed to remember they were there.

"Go on, go to your beds. I'll have orders for you later. Must think this through."

"Yes, sir," said Kendal. As they were leaving, Greene called after them: "Probably have Bulger work with you on this one."

Kendal rolled his eyes, but said only "Yes, sir." Bell-Fairfax snorted.

▲▼▲

Neither man having dined that evening, they spoke to the club's cook before he went off duty and were shortly sitting down to cold chicken and a bottle of hock.

"Thanks for your indulgence," said Kendal. His hands were trembling as he picked up his knife and fork. Hunger weakened him oddly, had done so since the war. He was a former Marine, having served aboard the *Arrogant* when Bomarsund was taken. There he lost an ear and his right foot to a bursting Russian shell, and was shipped home, half-deaf and lame, to starve.

One day, as he lay dizzy and sick in an alley, he'd been approached by a kindly-looking man who'd offered him food and a doctor's care, if he'd join something called the Gentlemen's Speculative Society. Kendal would have done anything the man asked, for a chance of healing his suppurating wounds; and so he allowed himself to be carted off to a clean hospital bed, expecting to be visited by some sort of absurd debaters' club.

Instead he had seen doctors, a great many of them, and undergone delightfully painless surgeries that had given him a remarkably lifelike prosthetic foot and reconstructed ear.

To say his hearing had been restored would be an understatement; Kendal had lain there fascinated, listening to conversations of tradesmen three streets away from the hospital. He had listened all the more attentively, therefore, when his benefactor returned.

The Gentlemen's Speculative Society was (as Kendal had been told) merely the modern name for an ancient association of philanthropists who attempted to improve the lot of mankind through scientific invention. The Society owed allegiance to no kings, bent its head to no gods. Many famous men had been members down through the ages since its founding, creating ingenious devices for its agents to use in the great struggle. Universal enlightenment, an end to War, and Paradise on earth were its goals.

Kendal had taken his vows eagerly. The Society had granted him lodging at Redking's Club, its London home; they fed him and clothed him. He was now in every respect their man. If his portion of the great struggle seemed to consist solely of spying for them, transmitting private conversations through the mechanism implanted in his skull, Kendal had only to remember starvation and deafness to restore his sense of gratitude.

He knew nothing of Bell-Fairfax's story, other than that he too was a former Navy man. The two men spoke little as they dined, Bell-Fairfax limiting his remarks to an enthusiastic comment on the wine. The waiter had cleared the cloth and they were rising to go to their respective rooms when Bell-Fairfax said, "Was there anything else said that might have identified this 'new friend' of the Preventers? Any intimation of his name?"

"I did get the impression he's providing them with advice, as well as money. Hargrove used to maunder on at those meetings; usual old Luddite cant. Tonight he made his points much more effectively, as you heard."

"He's hired a writer, I suppose. Pity." Bell-Fairfax shook his head.

"I'll tell you what's a pity, is having to work with Pinny Bulger again," said Kendal crossly. Bell-Fairfax suppressed a smile.

▲▼▲

Pinwale Bulger was a sailor and professional grotesque. He had taken a faceful of shot at the battle of Navarino, which had, as he was fond of telling anyone who'd buy him a drink, "spoiled his looks a bit" in that it had destroyed his right eye, cheekbone and ear. Having been discharged, he wandered Portsmouth with a bag over his head, charging a penny for a look at his injuries and tuppence to put the bag back on again.

This paid so well that the representative from the Gentlemen's Speculative Society was hard pressed to persuade Mr. Bulger to submit himself for surgical improvement, though Bulger was willing enough to become an agent when the Society's principles had been explained to him.

Nor need he have worried about losing his livelihood; for the doctors' best efforts, while restoring his hearing and rebuilding his face, had been unable to make him look any less appalling. His prosthetic eye in particular, though affording him vision superior to the undamaged left one, tended to roll and stare unnervingly, and there was an audible shutter click when he took photographs with it.

To conceal this he had developed a repertoire of tics, tongue-clacking and muttering to himself, which also helped disguise his transmissions to the Society when he sent them through the apparatus built into his ear. Muttering to himself had become something of a habit, unfortunately.

"Do-de-do-de-dooo. Hello!" He waved cheerily to an ashen-faced pair of young gentlemen emerging from the Queenstown telegraph office. "Mr. Field and Mr. Bright, ain't it?"

They glanced at him and stopped, startled. "How did you know our names?" asked Field, the American.

"Why, ain't everyone heard of the great cable?" Bulger grinned at them. "I was wondering if you had a berth on that *Agamemnon* for an able-bodied seaman."

Bright, the Englishman, looked him up and down in disbelief. With a brief humorless laugh he replied, "If she puts to sea again. Just at present that is very much undecided, my good man."

"We'll persuade them, never you fear," Field told Bright. His confident expression faded as he regarded Bulger. "Ah…tell you what, sir: I'll bet they'd be grateful on board for someone to help them clean up. The *Agamemnon's* just been through some real bad weather. Now, if you'll excuse us, we have business elsewhere. Why don't you go apply to the captain?"

"Aye aye, yankee doodle," said Bulger with an affable leer, and went tottering away to the *Agamemnon's* berth. Field and Bright watched him go, shuddered, and hurried off to catch a fast boat to London, where they had the formidable task of persuading the Atlantic Cable Company's board of directors not to abandon the entire project after two costly false starts.

Bulger, for his part, went aboard and found the *Agamemnon's* first mate only too glad to hire on someone to help clear several tons of coal out of the saloon, where it had accumulated during the most recent attempt to lay cable during a catastrophic storm. Whistling merrily, Bulger stowed his duffel, grabbed a shovel and was soon hard at work.

▲▼▲

"Nell Gwynn used these tunnels to visit Charles II, you know," remarked Greene, as he led them downward.

"Really." Kendal put a hand to his ear to muffle the echoes of the porter, who went before them with their trunks on a handcar. Bell-Fairfax was obliged to carry his hat and bend nearly double to follow them. They had been descending steadily for the better part of a minute, under vaulted brick arches.

"Oh, yes. Found a few interesting things when we excavated the club's cellars! We cleaned the tunnels out and extended them a bit…quite useful, and never more so than now. Ah! Here we are, gentlemen."

Kendal heard Bell-Fairfax sigh with relief as they emerged into a vaulted chamber, brightly lit. It looked rather like a railway station, full of bustling men; but they were mechanics, rather than travelers, and the immense thing mounted on a track at one end of the chamber was not a locomotive engine but…Kendal peered at it. A wooden fish? A life-size model of a whale, perhaps, crafted in oak and copper and brass?

Plainly the thing was meant to swim, for its track led down into the mouth of a tunnel, from which came the unmistakable reek of the Thames. "The *Ballena*," said Greene with satisfaction. "Cost us a pretty penny, I can tell you, but she's quite the finest of her kind. Considerable improvement over Bauer's vessels, and rather safer. Ah! And here's the Spaniard. Senor Monturiol! Tell him his passengers have arrived."

This last remark was addressed not to the man himself but to his clerk, who translated the remark. Senor Monturiol, a slightly built gentleman with sea-blue eyes, stepped forward and bowed. He said something to the clerk.

"Senor Monturiol wishes to assure you that the *Ballena* is ready to depart."

"Very good!" said Greene. "Convey that I wish to introduce Mr. Kendal, our communications specialist." Kendal bowed, extending his hand, and Monturiol clasped it briefly as the clerk chattered away.

"And this is our diver, Commander Bell-Fairfax," added Greene. Monturiol looked up at Bell-Fairfax, visibly startled by his height, but he bowed and said something courteous. Bell-Fairfax responded in Spanish, shaking his hand.

"Senor Monturiol is a recent recruit for our continental branch," said Greene. "A self-taught genius. He had the idea, we had the money, and the *Ballena's* the result."

Monturiol said something in fervent tones, at some length. "The senor wishes to express his joy upon discovering a fraternity of brothers who use wealth, not for their own gain or to advance military objectives, but for the benefit of all mankind. He is honored and gratified to have joined your ranks, and to have the opportunity to develop his idea in your service," said the clerk.

"*Very* good," said Greene. "May we go aboard?"

▲▼▲

They climbed a scaffold to step onto the upper deck, gripping brass handrails. The *Ballena* was the color of a violin, golden oak under thick spar varnish, polished to a glassy shine. Her two fore portholes, set with rock crystal panes, increased her resemblance to a living creature of the sea rather than a vessel. Monturiol led them to a hatch in a snub tower protruding from the top, and, opening it out, indicated that they ought to descend into its interior.

Kendal and Bell-Fairfax climbed down sailorlike, followed awkwardly by Greene, Senor Monturiol and the clerk. Kendal found himself on a narrow walkway that extended the length of the vessel, though his view aft was blocked by a great many brass tanks and apparatus he could not identify. Uniformed engineers paused in their preparations there to stand to attention and salute.

The whole was lit by a pair of glass tubes, filled with some sort of blue-glowing fluid, that snaked along the interior hull at roughly eye-level, held in place by copper brackets quaintly shaped to resemble starfish.

Directly to their left there looked to be a lower hatch, to which Monturiol pointed and said something, then gestured forward. "The airlock for the diver," translated the clerk. "If you gentlemen will proceed to the saloon, you will find it much less crowded."

"By all means," said Bell-Fairfax, who was having to crouch once more. They sidled into the area corresponding to a ship's forecastle and there congregated in a tight knot, as the porter carried in the trunks.

"The saloon. Here are hooks for your hammocks," the clerk translated for Monturiol. "Lockers for your trunks are under the benches. A sanitary convenience is in this cabinet."

"It seems smaller inside than it appeared from the outside," said Kendal. Bell-Fairfax translated his remark, and Monturiol's reply:

"That is because we are double-hulled, for safety."

"You needn't fear suffocation either," said Greene, waving an arm at the machinery aft. "She's got an anaerobic engine—produces oxygen, if you please! As well as driving an auxiliary steam engine to propel her. No need for sailors sweating away in close confines at a tedious cranking mechanism. Oxyhydric lamp running off a hydrogen tank, so as to light her way through the depths. She'll descend a hundred and fifty fathoms with ease, and make twenty knots regardless of the weather. Positively swanned her way through her sea-trials!"

The porter had finished stowing the trunks by this time. With his departure, hands were shaken all around; Greene and the clerk departed. Monturiol's valet, Arnau, closed and sealed the hatch. From that moment they were isolated from the world, and could not hear the order for launch; they only felt the jolt as all hands without lent their weight to pushing the *Ballena* down the ramp.

Kendal scrambled to the starboard porthole. He looked down on bowed heads and straining backs for a moment. A lurch, and then the brick walls of the tunnel went sliding past, only to vanish in universal darkness as the *Ballena* entered the water. Her engines churned to life, with a vibration that entered Kendal's spread palms where they pressed her inner hull. He felt a thrill of mingled terror and glee.

Kendal turned from the window. Monturiol and Arnau had gone aft, Monturiol to the helm amidships and Arnau to assist the engineers. Orders were shouted in Spanish; suddenly the black beyond the portholes lit to a dim green. Bathed in the blue light from the illumination tubes, Bell-Fairfax had sat down and was straightening his back at last.

"For God and St. George," he remarked to Kendal, with a wry smile.

▲▼▲

They surfaced when they were well out into the Thames. Monturiol demonstrated the periscope that allowed them to peer above the surface, thereby avoiding collisions with ships. The young moon had long since set, but the periscope had been fitted with a lens that penetrated shadow, lighting the night with an eerie green glow. At half speed, they traveled downriver cautiously.

By dawn they had rounded Margate and caught the gleam of the North Foreland light, winking pale across the water under the brightening sky. The *Ballena* moved out beyond the sands until she swam free in the open ocean. Monturiol gave the order to take her up to top speed then, and she cut through the blue world like a Minie ball from the barrel of a rifle, making for Ireland.

▲▼▲

Mr. Field and Mr. Bright having faced the investors, and Mr. Field having worked his eloquent miracle of persuasion, they returned to Queenstown and boarded their respective vessels with permission to make one more attempt to lay the cable. Mr. Field steamed away to the mid-Atlantic rendezvous point aboard the *Niagara* on 17 July as agreed, while Mr. Bright went aboard the *Agamemnon*, whose captain insisted on leaving under sail alone and never even made it out of Church Bay until the 18th.

Mr. Bulger had ingratiated himself into a berth by then, since there was still no end of clean-up and repair to be done. It would be a stretch of the truth to say the rest of the crew became used to him, but, preoccupied as they were with catching up with the *Niagara*, they learned to ignore the sight of Bulger shuffling to and fro with a broom, a mop or a bucket of paint.

He had noted one other crew member who sat apart from the other sailors in the mess and was given menial tasks suitable for a landsman. They were on the same watch; accordingly Bulger wobbled up to him and sat, at the evening meal on the fourth day out.

"How-de-do!" He grinned companionably. "I'm Pinny Bulger. What's your name, matey?"

The other looked across at him and blanched. "A-Anthony Cheltenham."

"Is it! Well, ain't that nice..Want some of this here plum duff?"

"No, thank you."

"Sure?" Bulger spooned up a mouthful and made ecstatic noises, rocking himself to and fro. "Oh, it's fearful good! Well, more for me. This your first cruise, is it? Come to sea for your health, eh?"

"I did, yes."

"That's just what I done, when I was a lad," said Bulger. "Made me the man you see today. This is a fine cruise we're having, ain't it?"

"I suppose so."

"And just think what it's in aid of! We'll get into the history books, sure. I been down helping 'em unstick glued-up cable in the cable-holds, so it'll run smooth. That's a sight to see, all them miles of cable coiled up down there!"

"Eleven hundred miles, as I understand," said Cheltenham, looking at him more attentively. "Tell me, do you need any assistance?"

Bulger's right eye rolled madly a moment, until he brought it to focus on Cheltenham. He thrust his head forward and took a photograph of Cheltenham, chattering his teeth on his spoon to obscure the sound of the lens shutter. "Why d'you ask?"

"I would dearly love to get a look at the cable, you see."

"Whyn't you just take a peep at what's on the forward deck, then? The guards would let you have a nice close squint at it, I'm sure."

"Oh, I've seen that, certainly, but…I should like to see all of it."

"I reckon you would!" Bulger gave a cackling laugh, and elbowed him. "Something to tell the grandkids about, eh?"

"Indeed." Cheltenham managed a friendly smile. "And I'd be happy to accompany you when next you—"

Kendal to Bulger, Kendal to Bulger, are you receiving? Repeat, Bulger, are you receiving? called the silent voice in Bulger's inner ear.

"Aye, aye, receiving! Just a-sitting here having a chat with my shipmate Mr. Cheltenham," said Bulger.

"I beg your pardon?" Cheltenham stared at him.

"I hears voices in my head. Don't mind me, matey; just a little piece of scattershot from Navarino, what got left in my brains. Always makes me need to go to the water closet, though. Here!" Bulger thrust his helping of duff toward Cheltenham, as he stood up. "You finish it, matey."

He hurried off, crouched over with his hand to his ear, muttering to himself as he went.

Kendal to Bulger! Did you say you'd found Cheltenham?

"Right enough, I did, and him all eager to get down to the cable holds where there ain't no guards to watch him. Hey diddle dido, my son John!" Bulger added, for the benefit of a sailor who passed him. "I reckon you're in range, now?"

We are directly below the Agamemnon. *What's happened? You ought to have been at the rendezvous point by this time!*

"Well, that ain't my doing; Captain Preedy's trying to save coal and ain't firing up the boilers. Ring-a-ding deedle, you ladies of Spain!" Bulger reached the fore cable hoist and scrambled up to the recently rebuilt head, where he dropped his drawers and sat cautiously. "There! Now we got some privacy. But it's the Cheltenham lubber right enough, and up to no good. Any chance Commander Bell-Fairfax can come topside and wring his neck?"

No. Repeat, no. You'll have to deal with him yourself. Take any measures necessary.

"Aye aye, then. Orders is orders. Singing way-hey-hee-hi-ho!" shouted Bulger, as a foretopman slid down a stay within hearing range. "The way we're proceeding, I don't reckon we'll meet up with the *Niagara* before the 29th. You lot got enough air and food and such down there?"

Yes. We are all well.

"Jolly good! Wish I could see aboard. Must be funny, looking out and watching the fishes swim by at eye level. As I was a-walking down Paradise Street—"

▲▼▲

Kendal signed off, rubbing his ear with a sigh of irritation, and turned his attention to the porthole once more. He was soothed and endlessly entertained by the blue world, with its steady progression of vistas of kelp forests, open sandy wastes and the occasional sunken wreck. Now and again they came upon fish who darted ahead a while, as though fearful of the chase, before falling back and being overtaken. Once they passed a great gray shark, with its dead black passionless stare, cruising slowly in the opposite direction. Even the occasional silver bubbles, rising from the *Ballena's* passage, were diverting to watch.

Monturiol and Bell-Fairfax had been absorbed in a game of chess, as one of the engineers manned the helm, but gradually set the game aside for conversation. Monturiol was a passionate speaker, undoubtedly eloquent in his own language. Kendal knew enough Spanish to pick out words like *Exploration, Revolution, Rationalism,* and *Utopian.* Monturiol's blue eyes shone with belief as he spoke.

For his part, Bell-Fairfax answered with nearly evangelical zeal as regarded the Society's objectives. There was a gleam in his pale eyes and a ring to his voice now as he orated on the Society's behalf. The voice got inside one's head, somehow, irresistibly. It made Kendal rather uncomfortable.

"Sandwiches, Senor?" The valet was at his elbow, proffering a tray. Kendal accepted a sandwich and a glass of sauterne. The others broke off their discussion.

"What says our humorous jack tar?" Bell-Fairfax inquired, unfolding his pocket handkerchief to serve as a napkin. Kendal related the substance of their conversation, which Bell-Fairfax then translated for Monturiol's benefit. Monturiol looked horrified and said something emphatic.

"Haven't we enough supplies to get us through after all?" Kendal asked. "I should have thought Greene had planned for delays!"

Bell-Fairfax replied to Monturiol in a conciliatory tone, then answered Kendal: "No. We've enough. He became rather exercised at the prospect of putting me aboard the *Agamemnon,* however."

"You assured him it wouldn't be necessary?" Kendal held out his glass to be refilled.

"Quite." Bell-Fairfax had a sip of wine. "I expect Bulger will be equal to the task."

He set his glass aside and returned his attention to the chessboard. The blue light reflected coldly in his pale eyes.

▲▼▲

Bulger lay in his hammock, snoring to feign sleep. He had, that very morning, taken Cheltenham down to the cable-holds, and shown him the three lower decks, each with its vast coil of cable wrapped about a hollow center cone. He had been on his guard then, watching Cheltenham closely to see what he might do. Cheltenham had merely looked around, however, apparently satisfied to note how one got in and out.

But now Bulger heard the rustle of Cheltenham's clothing as he sat up, the barely audible creak as he climbed from his hammock. Bulger opened his prosthetic eye and watched, piercing the darkness as Cheltenham drew something from his sea-chest. Thrusting the object into his pocket, Cheltenham took something else from the sea-chest. A match flared briefly, a moment's glow was quickly concealed; he had lit a shuttered lantern. Cheltenham took it with him as he climbed the companionway, his naked feet making no sound.

Bulger rolled out of his hammock. Reaching into his bolster he drew forth a clasp-knife. Opening it out, he slipped it between his teeth and followed Cheltenham unseen.

He emerged into the galley just in time to see Cheltenham's feet disappearing at the top of the next companionway. He pursued closely and ducked down on the topmost step, for from this vantage point he could see Cheltenham on deck, crouching in the shadows between the capstan and the pen that held the topmost store of cable. The cable was braced there in an immense spool, one end threaded carefully through a loosely fitting hatch cover to the compartments below.

Bulger watched a long moment, as Cheltenham waited for the attention of the deck watch to stray elsewhere. Ten minutes passed before the watchman gave a furtive look around and hurried forward to the head.

Cheltenham scrambled aft to the cable hatch and had it aside in a second, sliding through, dragging it shut above him. Bulger, glancing over his shoulder at the watchman, followed Cheltenham swiftly and silently.

He dropped into darkness, his knife drawn, expecting to grapple with Cheltenham at once. Yet he was alone; he felt nothing but the gutta-percha covering of the coiled cable under his bare toes. He heard the echoing breaths that told him Cheltenham had already gone farther down, into one of the lower holds. Bulger grimaced and rapped his right temple two or three times. The deep-night-vision filter in his prosthetic eye dropped into place at last.

Bulger went at once to the hollow cone around which the cable had been wrapped, that gave access to the next tier below. He put the knife back between his teeth and slid straight through to the orlop-deck. Cheltenham crouched there, atop the mass of coiled cable, in the narrow space below the underside of the deck above. He opened one shutter of his lamp, throwing a narrow beam of light on the cable.

Bulger heard him fumbling in his pocket, as his breaths came shallow and his heartbeat thundered. Cheltenham pulled out a pair of blacksmith's tongs at last, with a sigh of relief. He pulled up a length of cable and applied the tongs to it, pinching to crimp and fracture the cable while leaving no obvious cut in its gutta-percha covering.

Clearly his plan was to so damage the cable that it would easily break when fed through the paying-out apparatus. One break wouldn't set the enterprise back much, but Cheltenham had privacy and hours to work on the whole mass of the cable…

Bulger crawled toward Cheltenham, grinning around the knife. "He'oh!" he said, as the beam from the lantern fell upon his fearful countenance.

Cheltenham saw him and jumped up, screaming. Which is to say, he tried to jump and tried to scream; both were cut short, the one by violent contact with the underside of the deck above and the other by immediate unconsciousness.

Bulger took the knife out of his mouth. "Stroke of luck for me," he told the unconscious saboteur. "Saves me getting blood all over the cable, don't it?"

He hauled Cheltenham up through the tiers, climbing with apelike strength, only pausing at the hatch to assure himself that the watchman was still enthroned forward.

That worthy heard a splash, but as it was accompanied by no shouts he ignored it. When he returned to his post a moment later, he saw Bulger leaning on the rail, peacefully rolling a cigarette.

"Pleasant night, ain't it?" said Bulger.

▲▼▲

"Bulger informs me he has dealt with the saboteur on board," said Kendal, as Arnau brought them tea next morning.

"Capital," said Bell-Fairfax. He was shaving, having propped a pocket mirror on a bulkhead shelf. He glanced over at Monturiol, who was amidships at the periscope. "I shouldn't discuss it with our host, were I you. What else did he say?"

"That they saw the lights of the wire squadron at eight bells in the middle watch, and expect to close with the *Niagara* this morning."

"Very good," said Bell-Fairfax, just as Monturiol said something in an excited tone of voice. Laying aside his razor, Bell-Fairfax joined him amidships. They conversed in Spanish and Monturiol stepped back from the periscope a moment, in order to let Bell-Fairfax look through its lens. Stooping, he did so.

"And there they are, *Niagara* and all," Bell-Fairfax announced. "We're standing off as they rendezvous."

"At last," said Kendal. He accepted one of the ship's biscuits Arnau offered him. "I don't believe I could ever tire of the view, but the close quarters have become a little oppressive. Must be rather worse for you."

"One endures what one must," said Bell-Fairfax, returning to his shaving mirror.

"And in the best of causes, after all. Think what the world will be like, when everyone's connected by cable! Instantaneous transmission of knowledge. Wars ending sooner, if the news of treaties can be sent out the day they're signed."

"It's my hope wars won't start at all," said Bell-Fairfax. "It will be a great deal harder for nations to lie to one another, when their citizens may telegraph the truth to anyone anywhere else in the world."

"Though I suppose we'll use it to make money," Kendal said, gazing out at the depths, which were steadily brightening as the dawn progressed. "Stock fixing, for example. Assuming the gyttite works."

"It works." Bell-Fairfax set down his razor and reached for a towel. "You weren't involved in that business, but I was; and I can tell you that gyttite conducts at virtually the speed of light. One strand hidden in the cable ensures that *we* receive any transmitted information hours before anyone else. The Society profits, the great work goes forward, and mankind continues its advance to the earthly paradise."

"So it does," Kendal agreed hastily.

"Nor is the Society the only beneficiary for the common welfare," Bell-Fairfax continued, tying his tie. "Consider that scholars and scientists on opposite sides of the world will be able to exchange ideas as easily as though they were walking next door to a neighbor's. How much more swiftly must civilization progress, in the time to come!"

"They'll still require translators," said Kendal.

"Not at all," said Bell-Fairfax confidently. "Most professional men speak Latin."

▲▼▲

The *Ballena* moved in once the cable ships had made fast to each other, hovering at four fathoms in the *Agamemnon's* shadow. The *Niagara* passed one end of her freight of cable to the *Agamemnon*, and the *Agamemnon's* electricians set about splicing it to their end.

"I'm watching 'em," muttered Bulger. "A fine sight it is."

Is the cable connected?

"Almost," said Bulger. "Whang dang dill-oh! It's been spliced together in this big wooden splint. Now they're a-putting the sinkweight on her. Derry diddle dido! And now they're a-lifting her to put her over the side! Huzzay! Oh, bugger."

"What is it?" Kendal demanded, as something hit the water with a splash and shot straight down past the *Ballena*.

The sinkweight broke loose. Derry diddle dee! Powerful lot of cursing going on. Mr. Bright's just a-standing there chewing his fingernails. Somebody's saying it's because they didn't weld no lucky sixpences into the splice.

"Have they lost the cable again?" Kendal felt his heart constrict.

No. They're a-hauling it back aboard, splint and all. Haul on the bowlin, Nancy is me darlin'! Here's a lad with another weight. That'll do the job. Haul on the bowlin, all the way to Liverpool—there! She's fixed up proper. There she goes! Look out down below!

"It's the cable!" cried Kendal. Bell-Fairfax and Monturiol rushed to his side in time to see the cradle that held the main splice dropping through the water, pulled inexorably by its weight of thirty-two-pound shot. The double line of cable sank. Here came a tiny silvery flash dropping with it, close to the portholes.

"Good God," said Bell-Fairfax. "It's a sixpence."

Monturiol shouted in triumph. He embraced them both in turn; Kendal and Bell-Fairfax shook hands, grinning.

Heyho dumpty oh! Mind you, there ain't much cheering going on up here. I reckon they seen this go wrong so often they're afraid to jinx it. Down-a-down-a-down she goes, where she stops—oh. She stops at 216 fathoms. They're doing something, I can't see…lot of shouting back and forth between us and the Yanks…Oh! They was testing the signal. It's coming through. Stand by below there, they're firing up the engines to go about—

Those aboard the *Ballena* could feel the turbulence as the two great ships prepared to steam away from each other. Monturiol ran to the helm and took the *Ballena* to a safe distance as they maneuvered. The *Niagara* set off for Newfoundland, the *Agamemnon* for Ireland, both paying out cable as they went. Four fathoms under the *Agamemnon's* bow coursed the *Ballena*, like a dog trotting before its master.

▲▼▲

There was nothing to do now but pace the *Agamemnon* eight hundred nautical miles, until Galway Bay where the next attempt by the Preventers was expected. The crew of the *Ballena* relaxed. Monturiol, who had been at the helm for twenty straight hours, slung up his hammock and climbed in for some well-deserved rest, leaving Arnau at the helm. The engineering crew divided their watch; two slept in their hammocks aft while two observed the dials and gauges, and occasionally made small adjustments to the mechanisms. Bell-Fairfax immersed himself in a copy of Shakespeare's *The Tempest*. Kendal returned to his serene contemplation of the depths.

He had lost track of the passing hours when Kendal beheld small silver fish—sardines, he supposed—shooting toward the *Ballena* from the waters ahead. A moment later something immense and dark loomed into view. Kendal glimpsed an eye. Before he could open his mouth to exclaim, the *Ballena* had been struck with an audible crash and scrape that rocked the vessel.

Kendal was thrown to his knees, Bell-Fairfax flung backward against a bulkhead, and Monturiol startled awake as his hammock pitched wildly. Shouts sounded aft. The *Ballena* heeled over, from the impact they thought. All hands braced themselves and waited for her to right. Instead, she tilted at a sharp angle and rose through the water.

Kendal glimpsed sunlight and sky through the portholes. "They'll see us!" he cried. Arnau meanwhile was struggling at the helm, but the *Ballena* in her present state was proving almost impossible to steer, veering back toward the *Agamemnon*. Bell-Fairfax climbed to his feet and went aft to seize the wheel, lending his strength to Arnau's. Monturiol, frantically attempting to get out of his hammock, fell from it at last. On his hands and knees he scrambled to the starboard porthole and peered out. One of the crew, bending over a gauge, shouted to him in Spanish. He shouted a reply.

"What are they saying?" cried Kendal.

"Three of the exterior ballast weights have gone," Bell-Fairfax answered. *What's going on below, there? They can see you!*

"I know! We're in trouble!"

"What?"

"I'm talking to Bulger!"

Bulger, leaning on the rail with the other sailors, watched in horror as the *Ballena* shot along the side of the *Agamemnon,* coming perilously close to the steadily dropping cable. "Damn, that's a big whale! What a great awful whale that is, to be sure!" he announced.

"Surely that's no whale," said Mr. Bright, craning his head to watch as the *Ballena,* with a flash of her rudder, dove again and vanished, just nudging the cable in passing.

"Aye, sir, that's a, er, Brown Whale! I served aboard whalers forty years, man and boy, and I seen 'em many's a time!"

On board the *Ballena,* meanwhile, Monturiol had got to a chain drive and hauled on it. A metal weight came shuttling forward along a track under the walkway; at once the *Ballena* righted herself. Monturiol threw a lever that filled a ballast tank, and she descended. Arnau stood back, gasping with exertion, as Bell-Fairfax swung the wheel around and put her on course again. Monturiol closed off the valve. He rose to his feet, saying something in a satisfied tone.

"What was that?"

"He said he built this fish to save lives, not to take them," Bell-Fairfax translated. Monturiol smiled wearily and went back to his hammock.

▲▼▲

Thereafter they sped on through an effortless week, weathering gales that caused the *Agamemnon* above them to labor hard on her way. Once or twice there were difficulties with the cable, but the *Agamemnon's* electricians resolved them easily. Just before dawn on 5 August, Kendal woke with Bulger's voice in his head.

There's Skellig Light. That's Valentia Island, by God. We made it!

Kendal sat up in his hammock. Beyond the portholes he saw only night sea, still thinly illuminated by the *Ballena's* lamp. Bell-Fairfax had risen and pulled on a suit of woolen underwear; he knelt now beside the trunk that held his diving apparatus. Monturiol, at the helm, smiled. "Do you see any sign of the saboteurs?" said Kendal.

"I beg your pardon? Oh," said Bell-Fairfax.

*No sign of 'em yet...only, there's a small craft over to port. Let me get my long-distance lens up...*A dull thudding sound transmitted to Kendal. *Ah! She's a little steam launch. Looks like a crew of three. She's making for us.*

"Keep watching her, then." Kendal climbed from his hammock and assisted Bell-Fairfax into the immense canvas diving suit. There were innumerable straps to fasten and weights to attach. Bell-Fairfax's face was white and set; Kendal wondered if he was afraid. By the time Kendal had lifted the bronze helmet into place and fastened the screws that fixed it to the suit's breastplate, morning blue was visible through the portholes.

We're dead on for the strait between Valentia and Beginish Islands. And here's the launch, coming up hard to port!

How many? Bell-Fairfax spoke through the transmitter in his helmet.

Who's that? Oh. Morning, Commander sir! All I'm seeing now is two...there was three before. They got a tarpaulin spread aft and I reckon he's lying under it. T'other two are all got up as Irishmen. Red fright wigs and such. Pretending to be fishermen, likely. They're grinning and waving, cheering us on. They're marking pretty careful where the cable's falling, though.

Bell-Fairfax opened the plate on the front of his helmet and spoke to Monturiol, who nodded and sent the periscope up. He peered into it and evidently spotted the steam launch at once. Calling Arnau to the helm, he came forward to the deck hatch, where he turned a crank. The domed lid of the hatch opened back, like an eyelid over an empty socket, disclosing a round chamber underneath. He stood and gestured to Bell-Fairfax.

Bell-Fairfax removed a long narrow box from the trunk, something like a map-case. Monturiol looked curiously at it as Bell-Fairfax lowered himself into the diving chamber, but he asked no questions; merely knelt to make the several connections for the tether and air lines.

We're past 'em now, and they've come right up in our wake and dropped a buoy! Sly-like, pretending to be casting nets. Ah! Here's the third bastard after all, sitting up. He's in diving gear. He's got something in his hand. Looks like a pair of hedge-clippers. There he goes, over the side!

Monturiol cranked the hatch back into place. It sealed with an audible hiss. He turned another crank, and the hiss was replaced by a bubbling splash. Bell-Fairfax's lines paid out as he descended. He dropped perhaps five fathoms before they stopped.

"Bell-Fairfax, are you all right?"

Yes. There was a peculiar metallic quality to Bell-Fairfax's voice, as it came over the wall-mounted receiver. *I can see the saboteur. Señor?* He said something in Spanish, and Arnau took the *Ballena* forward slowly. Kendal went to the porthole and saw, just ahead, the line descending from the buoy the saboteurs had laid. Looking up he saw the bottom of the little launch, gently rocking, silhouetted under a bright morning sky, and what must be their diver's lines going down into the depths.

We're dropping anchor now. Look at them crowds, all turned out to welcome us! It's up to you lot now. Best of luck, Commander.

Thank you.

Kendal clenched his fists, knowing what must happen next, trying not to imagine it in any detail. When the sudden bubbles came belching up—and some of them seemed to bear a scarlet tinge, that brightened as they broke the surface—he let out his breath and sagged backward. He told himself it was the saboteur's own fault; he told himself that Progress required certain sacrifices.

Bell-Fairfax's voice came crackling over the receiver once more, giving what sounded like an order in Spanish. Arnau obeyed, unthinking, though Monturiol cried "Qué? No, no!"

His countermand came too late. The *Ballena* had gone shooting up to the surface, ramming the saboteurs' launch and capsizing it. Kendal, regaining his feet, looked out the porthole and straight into the face of one of the saboteurs, whose eyes were wide with astonishment as he struggled in the depths. Kendal had only a moment to register the absurdity of the man's costume—music-hall Irish, green knee breeches and buckled shoes, and on the surface a pair of red fright wigs floating—before a spear came flashing up from below and pierced the man through.

Monturiol shouted something in tones both horrified and accusatory. There, another cloud of scarlet came drifting by, just visible through the other porthole. Bell-Fairfax, standing on the bottom, had aimed upward and shot both saboteurs as though they were a pair of grouse.

Trailing bubbles through red swirling water, the saboteurs sank from sight. Monturiol cranked away at the winch angrily, as though to haul Bell-Fairfax up before he could do the dead men any further injury. There was a faint thump on the *Ballena's* lower hull, and a moment later Bell-Fairfax sat on the deck beside the diver's hatch, laying his chambered spear gun aside. Kendal worked the screws and got the helmet off.

At once Monturiol unleashed a furious torrent of denunciation. Bell-Fairfax merely sat there, breathing deeply, no expression on his pale weary face. At last he raised his hand.

"Señor, lo hecho, hecho está," he said dully. "Esto es guerra."

▲▼▲

The first public message was sent from the London company directors to their American cousins, lauding God and observing that Europe and America were now connected by telegraphic communication. It took all of fifteen minutes to transmit. The next message was sent from Queen Victoria to President Buchanan, was rather more effusive, and took sixteen hours to transmit and receive.

On 14 August, a Cunard vessel collided with another passenger ship off Cape Race. The friends and relations of those aboard were unspeakably relieved to learn, in a fraction of the time the news would have traveled without the transatlantic cable, that all lives had been saved.

On 31 August, the commanding officers of two Canadian garrisons learned, via cable, that the Sepoy Rebellion had been crushed and neither the presences of the 62nd nor 39th Regiments were required in India after all. Her Majesty saved approximately a hundred and fifty thousand pounds in troop transport costs.

An anonymous Yankee wrote a fervent hymn of praise, one of whose verses ran:

Speed, speed the cable: let it run
A loving girdle round the earth,
Till all the nations 'neath the sun
Shall be as brothers of one hearth.

▲▼▲

"Pity about Señor Monturiol," said Kendal. They were sitting over a de-canter of port at Redking's. Bell-Fairfax, who was lighting a cigar, shrugged.

"Yes, shame. Dr. Nennys tried to dissuade him from resigning, but to no avail."

"You won't be required to—?"

"Hm? No, no, he took the vow of silence. And, you know, he approves of our goals overall; he's simply unable to reconcile himself with our methods. I admire a man with a conscience."

"I hope we're keeping the *Ballena*." Kendal swirled his port in its glass.

"We are. We paid for it. I understand he's got another one half-built in Barcelona. He won't have our money any longer, but so it goes. How have the Preventers taken defeat?"

"Cheltenham and the others have been declared martyrs, naturally. Oh, and I found out the name of their new patron, by the way. He wrote them a fine fiery speech, exhorting them not to give up."

"Rather irresponsible of him." Edward sighed, exhaling smoke through his nostrils. "I suppose the usual arrangements will be necessary?"

"Well, that's the thing, you see—" Kendal broke off, startled, for Greene had appeared in the doorway like an apparition of doom. He strode to them, clenching a yellow dispatch-sheet in his fist.

"The damned cable's dead," he said. Kendal leapt to his feet.

"Sir, on my honor, the Preventers couldn't—"

"They didn't. Some idiot of an electrician tried to boost the signal and sent two thousand volts through the cable. Burned out everything. Even our gyttite strand."

Bell-Fairfax closed his eyes and swore quietly. "Well, we'll try again," Kendal stammered.

"Not for some time. Our usual informants advised us this morning that there won't be another attempt until 1865. The Americans are going into a civil war, apparently. Freeing their blacks."

"Really?" Bell-Fairfax opened his eyes. "That's something, anyway."

"It's more complicated than you'd suppose," said Greene bitterly. "Everything is. You may be sure your Preventers will take this as a sign from God, Kendal. Pay a call on their new money man and put the wind up him, do you understand? Take Bell-Fairfax with you."

▲▼▲

The gentleman was angry. His domestic situation was inescapable misery, and the only manner in which he might let off intolerable pressure was by walking as far and as fast as he might. It was past midnight, but London was unseasonably warm, for November, and he was on his fifth circumnavigation of Gordon Square when they caught up with him.

He never heard the other gentlemen coming up behind; they seemed to materialize, one on either side of him. He glanced at the man to his left, then at the one to his right; he had to tilt his head back. He made an incredulous sound.

"Good evening, sir," said Bell-Fairfax, as they walked along. "May we have a few private words?"

"As many as you like," the man snapped.

"May I say, first, how much we admire your work? Your efforts on behalf of the poor are laudable. Justice, charity, compassion, reform, have all found a powerful champion in your pen, sir."

"True," said Kendal.

"Therefore it pains us to discover you have lent your considerable talents to the destruction of a device certain to improve the lot of mankind."

"I beg your pardon?" said the man, and then gave Bell-Fairfax a sharp look. "Ah. I see. Well! Let me ask you this, gentlemen: have you ever labored with your hands?"

"We have, sir."

"And were you paid for your labors?"

"Yes, sir."

"The fellow who earns his bread making chairs, do you believe *he* ought to be paid when citizens furnish their homes with his work?"

"Unquestionably, sir."

"The cobbler ought to be paid for every pair of boots that leave *his* shop, then?" The man's eyes flashed with anger. He seemed relieved to have someone with whom to argue. "Therefore—ought not the writer receive payment for the entertainment he provides?"

"And you do, sir."

"Not in America," said the man. "No. In the Home of Liberty, any publisher is at liberty to pick my pocket, sir, without respect of copyright. I'm told my novels are popular, read by thousands who enjoy them in American editions for which I have received not one farthing in royalties. I complained to the American authorities, if they can be described as such; I was insulted, and my character defamed in their press, for my pains!

"And are our own politicians interested in my welfare? No. Literature does nothing to get them into Parliament, and therefore they choose to do nothing on the literary man's behalf.

"My ideas change the world for the better—you yourself said so. Why then am I, their author, not accorded the legal protection an artisan enjoys? And what of American writers? How can they persuade American publishers to buy their efforts at fair prices, when the stolen works of British writers are available free of charge?

"And now the industrialists seek to break down the barriers of time and distance between nations. I tell you that there is no invention so nobly conceived, that some base rascal will not find a way to corrupt it to his own ends! When a man's property may be transmitted instantaneously to a foreign shore, what laws will protect him?"

"With respect, sir," said Bell-Fairfax patiently, "It would take longer to telegraph the text of one of your novels than it would for a copy to be sent across by packet ship."

"Today," said the man. "But tell me, in good conscience, that it will not be so in twenty years. The telegraph is profitable, it is convenient; the brightest minds of the age will turn their attention to improving its speed and reliability, with no thought of the consequences. And in any case, that is not the point! The work of hands is protected by law; why not then the work of the mind?"

"Sir, you are in some distress, but we must ask you to consider the greater good," said Bell-Fairfax. "The world will progress more surely from barbarism to civilized behavior, if all men may exchange news freely. Copyright laws will adapt, in time. Balance that in the scales, against your lost profit, and bow to the inevitable."

He stopped on the pavement, staring down into the man's eyes as he spoke. The man pulled his gaze away with effort, shivering.

"You're devilishly persuasive, sir," he said sullenly.

"It is our earnest hope that you *can* be persuaded with words, sir," said Bell-Fairfax. "We should be sorry to have to employ any other means."

His pale gaze traveled past the man, into the courtyard before which they had stopped. "This is your home, is it, sir? Yes, I thought so. The one on the end. You live here with your children.

"I do hope you'll reconsider your opinion in this matter. Good evening, Mr. Dickens."

Caverns of Mystery

They had been driving since before the sun rose, along the coast highway.

She had been up, packed already, when her father woke the boys and marched them downstairs to help him load the station wagon; she had heard her sisters complaining sleepily as her mother dragged them out of bed and made them dress. The baby wept in his cornflakes at the breakfast table, bewildered by morning in what seemed the middle of the night.

Everyone shut up once they were in the car at last. The little ones went to sleep in the back and even the boys were unable to stay awake long enough to punch each other more than once or twice. Her parents spoke quietly together in the front seat, while her mother drove through the dark, and she watched through the window as the city lights dimmed and fell behind. There were miles of lemon groves, appearing gradually as night drained away; the fog hung low over the long aisles of trees and the long drooping leaves of eucalyptus swayed as they rushed past, but all in silence.

The road turned inland and dawn broke over a rolling plain of oak trees and blackberry bramble, white starred with blossoms along the two-lane, all summer country.

Now and again there were the phantoms, but she had learned long since never to call attention to them. A man crouched beside his campfire, lifting his graniteware coffeepot from the coals, as his horse grazed peacefully nearby. Smoke rose from the stone chimney of a log house, and a woman in a long dress trudged out from the house to a shed carrying a milk can. A thing crawled up out of a creekbed, a skinwalker with a coyote's head, and it turned to watch as the station wagon approached. Meeting her gaze, it leaped at the door; she pulled her glasses off and covered her right eye, as it clawed at the window. She turned her face away, refusing to see it.

"Are you having another headache?" her mother said. She opened her eyes and met her mother's gaze in the rear view mirror.

"No," she said, a little sulkily. Her mother would never admit the phantoms were there, but she seemed to have developed radar that lit up whenever they were around. "I just got something in my eye."

"Bill, is there any Kleenex in the glove box?"

Her father handed her a tissue over the back of the seat. He lit a pair of cigarettes and passed one to her mother.

She heard the thump and the yelp that meant the skinwalker had fallen away, and she relaxed. Her brothers woke and began to punch each other again. Her sisters woke and began to chatter like birds. The baby woke and cried. The road ran past barn-red Burma Shave verses appearing out of the fog, always rendered cryptic by one missing sign. The billboards began to feature ladies in bathing suits and the promise that they were only thirty miles from their destination; then fifteen miles; then five.

They came through a long tunnel of oak trees arching overhead, emerged into brilliant sunlight. Her father cranked his window down. "Man!" he said. "Smell that sea air!"

She sat up and looked out with interest. The station wagon was going slowly down a little white street with the sea at the end of it. There were old houses with gardens full of lilies. There were motor hotels, courtyards of tiny cottages. All the neon signs were rusting, all the paint was peeling, and sand blew in drifts and piled against the curb.

At the end of the street was an OFFICE sign in the shape of a swordfish, pointing to the nearest of a row of cottages on the edge of the dunes. Each cottage had its own palm tree, looking gray, weatherbeaten and miserable. But the blue sea sparkled and roared just beyond, a full four lines of breakers foaming white. Her mother steered into the crushed-shell drive and pulled up to the office.

"Okay, kids." Her mother got out, went around to the back of the station wagon, and opened it to pick up the baby. The little girls scrambled out and ran immediately over the sand to the sea. She climbed out too. Her brothers were still fighting; her father hauled them out and belted them both, and they glared as he ordered them down to the beach in his master-sergeant voice. They marched off down the dune face, still shoving each other.

"Watch them, will you, honey? We need to go get the key," said her mother, groping in the box of groceries they'd brought for a teething biscuit. She nodded, staring around in fascination.

There was an old gray building behind the cottages with the word ROOMS painted on one wall. Phantoms clustered on the porch, old men with pipes. They all looked more or less like Popeye the sailor, and all gazed listlessly out to sea. She followed their gaze to the beach.

The children played and fought amid more phantoms: fragments of ships, running horses, weeping women. A double row of old pilings ran from the bottom of the street ramp out into the water, long-broken snags, but their phantoms still rose under the sun of another year. Along the phantom planks of the pier a phantom donkey plodded, drawing a cart full of fish, and phantom men sat at its end mending nets.

She shivered and turned to look at the office. It was an old frame cottage with a bow window. Growing up against the window was a fuchsia bush. Its flowers were like little firecrackers. It had branched into the cottage through a broken pane and sprawled, profuse, lush, into the window seat. A phantom pirate stood on the other side of the glass, among the scarlet flowers. He looked into her eyes. He smiled at her, tenderly.

▲▼▲

The station wagon was unpacked, the cottage inhabited. Theirs had two real murphy beds in the living room, one for the boys and one for the girls, and a kind of camp bed in an alcove off the hall, which would be hers. Her mother stalked about checking the mattresses for bedbugs while her father set up the baby's crib. The other children were wrestled into bathing suits, towels were distributed, and her mother gathered up the wet clothes to take them to the washing machine by the office.

"Can I go for a walk?" she asked her mother. Her mother paused, her arms full of laundry, and gave her a searching look.

"No, you need to lie down for a while first. I think you're overtired. Bill, doesn't she look overtired to you?"

"Don't argue with your mother," her father said automatically, shrugging into his bomber jacket.

"I didn't," she said, sullen. "Sir."

"Kids!" he said. "Line up! Wipe those smiles off your faces. It's fourteen hundred hours and we will proceed to the beach. There will be no swimming beyond that last piling. There will be no fighting. There will be no crying. Do you understand?"

"Yes, sir!" the others chorused. He marched them out of the house, and her mother went to do laundry. She unpacked her suitcase, setting her copy of *The Wind in the Willows* on the dresser at the foot of the bed.

She couldn't sleep, and after a while got up and explored. The cottage was all right; there was only a little phantom in a sailor suit crouched in the windowseat looking out at the sea, and he seemed happy, and a kind-faced woman in the kitchen, cooking something on a phantom potbellied stove. They had been there a long time. On the back porch a phantom woman sat alone, smoking a cigarette and muttering angrily to herself.

When they were angry like that it was best not to notice them, best to close the right eye tightly and look away. Paying attention made them pay attention back, and that was never good.

She locked the back door, and settled down to re-read *The Wind in the Willows*.

▲▼▲

The beach, when she was able to get down there early the next day, was wide and sky-reflecting, the tide far out, half a mile of flat sand rippled with wave patterns. Gulls roamed there, stabbing now and then at sand crabs in a half-hearted way, eyeing her approach but not troubling themselves to run. She walked along with her head down, absorbed in looking for shells and wave-tumbled glass, putting the best pieces in the bucket she carried.

There were phantoms drifting here and there, but they could be ignored. When she'd been younger they had frightened her badly, until she'd learned the trick of closing her right eye. It had helped to understand what they were, and to classify the different kinds.

None of them seemed to be *ghosts*, in the sense of spirits of the dead. Some were apparently like photographs, a lingering stain on the air, a moment of someone's happiness or misery endlessly replayed. Some were so vivid they had attained a sort of awareness. Some weren't even people: furniture, buildings, trees that had stood in one place so long their images had worn through time and remained when they were gone.

Some were old and wild, like the skinwalker, and inhabited the outdoors. Those could be dangerous, though some were benign. Some looked like real people, but weren't, and those were always dangerous and she had learned never, ever to show that she noticed them. They did not drift, but moved sleek and arrogant through the world, doing what they liked.

There were others, too, who seemed to be hauntings of things people had only imagined, like the pirate in the window. The library was full of them, posturing or sitting alone in corners...

The beach grew narrower the farther she walked. White cliffs rose up to her right, full of fossil shells. She looked up at them and stopped in her tracks, with her mouth open.

Ahead, out on the clifftop, was the figure of a brontosaur. It stood stiffly in profile, and there was something wrong with its head. It was near a little brick house at the edge of the cliff.

Fascinated, she walked closer, ignoring the desperate phantom of a man who was trying to pull a phantom mule from a cave swamped by a phantom high tide. The brontosaur never moved; she got close enough to see that it was made of cement over a chickenwire frame, and had no head, but only a rusting unfinished wire outline. *What was it doing there?*

▲▼▲

She had to choose her words very carefully.

"So, when I was out on the beach today, I went walking down by the caves? And, you know what, sir? Up on the cliff, somebody has built a *pretend* brontosaurus. Out of cement? And it's really big. And I was just wondering if we could drive out there, and look at it?"

"Are you making this up?" said her father.

"No, sir!"

"Then you take me out on the beach and show me," he said.

"Bill—" said her mother.

"No, I can show you!" She was already at the door, pulling on her hooded sweater. "Come on, Dad!"

Muttering, he lit a cigarette and followed her out to the edge of the dune. He scowled as he looked where she pointed, and then his face cleared.

"Son of a bitch!" he said, grinning. "What *is* that?"

"A brontosaurus, sir," she informed him.

"Hey, Willis?" He turned and called to the motel's owner, an elderly man who was presently cleaning fish at the little open shed in the courtyard. "You know anything about the dinosaur up there?" He jerked a thumb at it over his shoulder.

"Caverns of Mystery," said Mr. Willis, without looking up. "Place up on the highway. Fellow has some caves on his property. Sells tickets to see 'em."

"Huh." Her father rubbed his chin. "Would the kids like it?"

Mr. Willis shrugged. "If they like caves," he said.

▲▼▲

The headless dinosaur stood in an open field, knee deep in the grass of late summer. At its feet was a leaning plank sign, painted in straggling letters: *CAVERNS OF MYSTERY.*

Her mother parked the station wagon at the edge of the field. The children ran at once down the unpaved track to the dinosaur. She followed more slowly, savoring the approach. Her parents followed more slowly still, for the baby had decided to walk between them, holding their hands.

They circled the dinosaur three or four times, peering up at it, before her father said: "And the mystery is, what's the mystery?" The children looked at him.

"But it's a dinosaur," said one of her brothers.

"I expect there are fossils in the caverns," said her mother. They followed the path to the little brick house at the edge. It had a dutch door with the top half open, and a sign that said *OPEN* and another that said *Admission 25 cents.*

"Jesus, this had better be some mystery," said her father.

There was a boy on the edge of the cliff, a little older than she was, wearing only swimming trunks and sandals. He was throwing stones far out into the sea, with a smooth grace of movement that made her stare. He looked at them and turned away deliberately, with something defiant in the set of his shoulders. There was a scar on his neck, a raised pink line.

Inside were shelves and a dusty counter, displaying a case of arrowheads and baskets of rock specimens for sale, with faded typewritten labels describing what they were. A man sat behind the counter, faded and dusty as his wares. He looked up at them with no particular interest.

"Where's the caverns, pal?" said her father, with a slight edge in his voice. The man stood and, without a word, opened a door to his left.

There, instead of the room with faded wallpaper and dusty windows she had expected, were wooden steps going down into blackness loud with the boom and hiss of waves. The man flipped a bakelite switch and a lightbulb went on, somewhere far below.

"Here you are," he said, flatly. "That'll be two dollars." Her father grimaced but paid it, and the man counted out eight pink tickets and handed them around, unsmiling. He edged past them and leaned out the door. "Ricky! You get off your lazy butt and come mind the counter. Step this way, folks."

He preceded them through the doorway. She was the last to go down and heard a scatter of thrown shell-gravel strike the windows, but the boy remained outside.

They descended three flights of splintery stairs into the cavern, with a steep drop from the last step into a bank of shingle. Her brothers leaped and ran crunching to where the sea washed in under a lip of rock with a rank iodine smell.

"Boys!" cried her mother. "Stay back!"

"Yes, Ma'am, they should," said the man. "Every now and then you'll get a big wave through there. You can get soaked."

As the children staggered about and picked up agate and jade pebbles, he told them about the Spanish who had thought these cliffs were haunted, because strange moans came from the area during high tides; he told them about the rancher who had discovered the caverns in 1902, when his cow had fallen in through a sinkhole. He told them about the Indian bones that had been found there, and the cannon from a shipwreck, and the fossils.

"But no dinosaurs?" her father asked.

"There might be," said the man, with a shrug.

At the far end of the cavern another one, smaller, opened out into darkness. It was blocked off by sawhorses. She made her way there, climbing from rock to rock, and peered over them. She saw fathomless blackness and a glimpse of light, a pure cokebottle blue so lovely she caught her breath.

"What's in here?" she called, looking back over her shoulder.

"That part's closed. Some of it fell in and it's not safe now," said the man, with an edge of flint coming into his voice.

"You come away from there *right now*," said her mother, handing the baby to her father and starting after her.

"Okay, okay. Sheesh." She turned and jumped down.

Back in the station wagon, her father said: "Well, that was some crock."

"I thought it was neat," she said.

▲▼▲

Every Saturday night, Mr. and Mrs. Willis held a barbecue and clambake in the motel's courtyard. After the children were put to bed the adults came out again and sat around the fire, drinking beer and chatting under the stars.

She couldn't sleep, so she tiptoed into the front room and climbed into the windowseat, sitting with her feet drawn away from the little sailor phantom. She opened the window a crack and breathed in the night air, shivering in her pajamas. The adults were black silhouettes against the night, though now and again the fire would flare up and eyes would gleam out briefly, or beer bottles wink in the red light. She heard her father's voice:

"Say, Willis, what's the deal with the dinosaur up on the cliffs? That guy's a goddam fraud."

The old man chuckled. "Well, you didn't expect a real Gertie the Dinosaurus, did you?"

"No, but a couple of bones or a skull or something, for the price he charged!"

"I reckon he figured folks would see it from the highway and pull over to find out what it was all about," said Mrs. Willis. "He used to be pretty sharp, Sam Price."

"Why doesn't the dinosaur have a head?" asked her mother.

There was a pause. "He never finished it," said Mrs. Willis at last.

"How come? He can't have run out of money," said her father.

There was a longer silence. Mr. Willis opened another beer, had a drink and said at last: "Guess he lost interest. His wife died around then."

"Oh, dear," said her mother.

"They bought that land, with what Sam's brother paid him for his share in old Price's ranch," said Mr. Willis. "Real nice young couple. Sam built the house and the stairs down into the caves. He reckoned he could get rich showing 'em. Then he went and fooled around with another woman."

"Alex," said Mrs. Willis, reproachfully.

"Well, he did." Mr. Willis looked sidelong at Mrs. Willis. "Anyhow. He broke it off and made up with the wife and they had that boy. But she didn't get over it and she drowned herself." He gulped down his beer.

"That ain't how I heard it," said Mrs. Willis. "Don't you listen to him! That poor girl drowned by accident. The baby crawled down the stairs into the caves, somehow, and she went down there to get him out, only it was high tide, and she fell and the waves dragged her under." She rose, shaking out her skirts. "That pie ought to be cooled now. I'll go cut us some."

"Bring me out another beer?" said Mr. Willis.

"You had enough," she said, and went into the house. When the door had closed after her, Mr. Willis cleared his throat and leaned forward, and he spoke in a low voice that nonetheless carried:

"He *did* have another woman," he said. "Foreign girl, I heard. And she went crazy when he broke it off and went back to Winnie. And what I actually heard was, she came sneaking back one day when Sam wasn't there and got Winnie down in the caves and tried to kill her, and they both drowned."

"Oh, that's awful," said her mother.

"And there was worse. She'd tried to kill the baby, too. Cut his throat."

"Jesus!" said her father.

"At least he didn't die. Grew up into a holy terror, though. Already been in trouble with the police."

"I'm not surprised," said her mother. "Poor child."

▲▼▲

She couldn't get the lovely blue out of her mind. It had seemed like a window into another world. Was it a pool, that went down under the rock and had an outlet on the beach, where the light came in?

On the strength of that idea she got up early and went out by herself, all the way down the beach as far as the caves, looking up at the dinosaur until she was too close underneath to see it. The tide was out, with little purple crabs wandering to and fro, and deep wells of glass-clear water around boulders projecting from the sand. There were anemones and starfish there, and a cormorant sprawled out flat at the tideline. Its dead eye had a bloom on it, looked like a black pearl.

There were more caves around the far edge of the cliff, though she had to wade far out to get round to them, through surging water like ice and the unsettling caress of weed on her ankles. She became so preoccupied with exploring the caves that she nearly forgot about the pool; the caves arched up high, like cathedral vaults of limestone, and were carved all over with names and dates. There was a cartoon profile of a sailor dated April 2, 1886; there were even older inscriptions. The oldest was dated 1805 and followed by words in Spanish: *Las Lloronas.*

An old phantom sat on one of the boulders, a peaceful-looking man with white side whiskers, smoking a pipe. There was a second one a few paces away, but neither of them seemed in any way conscious of each other. The other phantom was a young man, wearing only trousers, and he was soaking wet and staring out to sea. Tears streamed down his face, he gulped back silent sobs, but never took his gaze from the bright water. He looked vaguely familiar.

She paid little attention to either of them. Backing into the water, she squinted up at the cliffs above, to see whether she could glimpse the brick house. "Oh!" she said, and shaded her eyes with her hands to see better.

Switchbacking up the face of the cliff was the remnant of a flight of stairs. It ended abruptly some dozen feet above the beach, its lower section swept away by a long-ago winter storm. Nor did it extend all the way to the clifftop; the earth had slid and buried its first dozen or so steps. What planks remained were silvered ancient wood, and a few mortared stones that anchored its landings.

"That must have been how people got down here in the olden times," she said aloud. She saw a way to get up to them, by a series of finger-and-toeholds on the cliff face. The thought of what her mother would have said, were she standing there, decided her; she set her shoulders and ran forward, and scrambled upward.

It was harder than she thought it would be; she nearly slipped twice, and had at the last to grab for a bush thinly anchored in soil to pull herself over the edge. She was gleeful, though, as she tottered upright on the stair landing, and turned to look out at the sea. *I bet I'm the first person that's stood here in a hundred years,* she thought.

She sat down and luxuriated in the isolation a while, until something went whizzing over her head. She looked up, following its trajectory: a rock? It plunked into the ocean. She remembered the boy, then.

Cautious, she climbed the stairs in a crouch, and went up the rest of the slope on hands and knees. Rising to the edge of the cliff, she looked up into the face of the boy. He dropped the stone he had been about to throw, and took a hasty step back; then started forward, scowling. He had a dark bruise over his cheekbone.

"Where'd you come from?" he demanded.

"The stork brought me, ha ha," she said, and he didn't laugh, so she added hastily: "Up the old steps. Did you know there's a lost staircase down here?"

"Sure I know," he said.

"Oh."

They considered each other. He was shirtless, and barefoot; his upper body made a neat triangle, like an arrowhead pointed down. He had green eyes. This close, she could see the terrible scar on his throat; someone must have tried to cut it from ear to ear. She tried not to stare at it, never liking it herself when people stared at her eye.

He bent now and picked up the stone again, and hurled it into the sea.

"I liked the Caverns of Mystery," she said.

"It's just a big cave," he said. He sat and pushed himself over the edge, and she backed down to the staircase. They stood there together a moment, looking out to sea.

"Stairs to nowhere," he said. "Pretty neat."

"Like you could walk down the stairs and end up back in time," she said. "Like in the days of the pirates or something."

"Except you couldn't do that, because you can't live in the past," said the boy. "That's what my dad says. It isn't there anymore."

"Yes, it is," she said. "It's all around. People just don't see what isn't happening right now. But everything that ever happened is still going on."

"Aw, that's nuts," he said. "Like, cowboys and Indians fighting right there in town, while the cars go by? And dinosaurs on the freeway. And pirate ships out there!" He pointed at the sea.

"Yes," she said. "You just can't see them."

"That'd be really something. I wish I could," said the boy.

No, you don't, she thought. The boy sat down on the staircase, and she sat beside him. He turned and looked at her. "What happened to your eye?"

She winced, turned her face away. "I have this problem with seeing," she said.

"Is it blind? Because if it was blind, you could wear an eyepatch," he said. "Except I don't think girls wear eyepatches."

"Yes, they do," she said. "Just not black ones. I had a green one for a while. It didn't help. And the kids at school made fun of me."

"I hate school," he said. "My dad made me wear a tie. Like it was Sunday School. Everyone laughed. I hate my dad. Do you hate yours?"

"No-o," she said. "I think my brothers do, though. But I hate my mom sometimes."

"How come?"

"She never stops talking about my eye," she said. "She never thinks I can do anything by myself. Like I was retarded or something. And she's *watching* me all the time."

"My dad watches me, too," he said. "What's he think I'm going to do, anyway? Sometimes I think, well, I'll show *him.* I'll do something. But my mom's dead."

She stopped herself from saying *I know* and merely said, "I'm sorry."

"It's okay. I don't remember her. You can't live in the past."

"But the past lives," she said. "So you could say your mom is alive. She's just in the past."

"I guess." He grew restless, jumped to his feet. "Let's see where these stairs go." She followed him, and stood aghast when he came to the last step and launched himself out into the air and sunlight. He landed in the ankle-deep surf and rolled, laughing. She stepped to the edge and froze, terrified; then she thought, *Well, he didn't get hurt,* and so she jumped too, not wanting to seem a coward.

For a second she almost went somewhere wonderful, a realm of possibilities where there were pirate ships and kindly satyrs; but gravity stepped in and she hit the wet sand as the tide receded, and folded up. Her chin hit her knees, her glasses went flying, and she fell over and lay there trying to get her breath back. He hadn't noticed. He was staring out to sea. She was grateful.

Climbing to her feet, she retrieved her glasses and limped over to him.

"That was cool," he said. "Want to explore the caves?"

"Uh-huh," she said. She heard her name called and turned, and was horrified to see her mother and sisters far down the beach. "Crumbs. I have to go."

"You could stay if you wanted," he said, hopefully, not taking his eyes from the horizon.

"No, I couldn't. She'll yell, and she'll come get me."

"Fine, then." He waded out into the surf, and dove like a cormorant into a wave and vanished.

"Wasn't that the boy from the dinosaur caves?" said her mother sharply, when she joined her.

"Yes." She looked out at her sisters, who were shrieking with excitement as they jumped through the lines of surf.

"I don't want you playing with strange children," said her mother.

"We weren't *playing*," she said irritably. "We were just talking."

"And look at you, you're soaking wet and you've got those circles under your eyes again. Were you reading under the covers last night?"

"No."

"Go on back to the house and put some dry clothes on. And I think you ought to take a nap."

Muttering to herself, she trudged back to the cottage.

▲▼▲

Her father was leaning against the fish shed, smoking and talking with an old man who was opening clams there.

"Sir, what does "Las Loronas" mean?" she asked, as she approached.

"What? Sounds like something Mexican," said her father.

"What was that?" The older man turned. She repeated it. "Las *Yoronas,*" he corrected her.

"This is one of my kids, Luis," said her father. "What's it mean?"

"La Llorona? She's a ghost. Means, "the crying woman",," said Luis. "Old Spanish story. Her, ah, her baby drowned, and she walks all night by the water weeping and moaning, trying to find it. Bad luck to hear her, I always heard."

"But it's only a story," said her father, glancing at her.

"Sure," said Luis. "Nothing but a ghost story. 'Las Lloronas', I don't know, that means more than one of them."

"It was carved on a rock down by the caves," she said.

"Oh! That place," said Luis, and turned away.

"I'll bet some Mexicans carved it there," said her father. "You remember what the guy at the Mystery Caverns said, about the wind moaning in the caves, and people used to think they were haunted? That's all it is."

▲▼▲

They went on a picnic the next day, farther up the highway, a place where a creek flowed down to the sea. There were moonstones here and there in the shingle, and her parents set the children searching for them, until the boys tired of it and started throwing handfuls of pebbles at each other. One of her sisters saw a snake, and screamed. The baby found a sun-dried dead fish and protested when her mother pried it out of his fist. There was an Indian crouched on the streambank, filling jars of water, but he was only a phantom.

That night she dreamed of the blue light that had shone up through the water in the cave. It was fathomless, so beautiful a blue she woke crying.

▲▼▲

The next day was Sunday, and her father made them all dress and go to the church in town, even though they were on vacation. When she made her way back to the caves after church, the boy was sitting on the old staircase, looking a little forlorn. He started as she pulled herself up over the edge.

"Oh, it's just you."

"Just me," she agreed. "I had to go to church. Do you go to Saint Catherine's?"

"I don't go to church," he said.

"Your dad doesn't make you go?"

He shook his head. "My dad tried to have me baptized there when I was a baby, and the priest wouldn't do it. So my dad said he was never setting foot in there again."

She was scandalized. "But babies who don't get baptized go to Limbo! Gee, that was some mean old priest."

"I don't care." The boy stared out at the sea. The wind was from offshore, bringing the sound of bells ringing for the midday service. Gulls circled and cried overhead.

"I have twenty-five cents," she said. "I was supposed to put a dime in the collection plate, but I dropped it and it rolled under the pew, and by the time I crawled under and found it the man with the little basket was gone, but there was another dime and a nickel down there. Can I go see the Caverns of Mystery again?"

"You want to see something better? Come on." He led her up over the top of the cliff, and then trotted off in the direction of the dinosaur. She followed along the dirt track through the high grass. He crouched and scrambled under the dinosaur's belly, and vanished. She got down on hands and knees and crawled after him, and a moment later stood up and found herself in a barrel chamber of lath and chicken wire. He was sitting crosslegged a few feet farther in, looking at her expectantly.

"Wow," she said. "This is pretty neat."

"If you climb up the neck, you can spy on the cars on the highway," he said. "Go on, take a look."

She obliged him, gingerly avoiding rusty nails, climbing up the long slanting tunnel of the neck to the blue window where the dinosaur's head would have been. The wind whistled through the ends of wire that stuck out into space. She looked out at the highway and watched a pink and black sedan zoom past. She looked down at the meadow below. Two phantoms stood there, looking up at the dinosaur proudly.

The man was wearing overalls and work boots, had his arm around the woman. He was grinning, gesturing, speaking silently and pointing at the dinosaur. The woman was small and meek-looking, with her hair pulled back in a bun. The man had the same face as the weeping phantom on the beach. More: he had the same face as the man behind the counter.

She made the connection, and filed it in with the other adult sorrows she had catalogued. Something sad had happened here, but sad things happened all the time. They were better ignored. She turned her face away and crawled back down out of the dinosaur's neck.

"You should put a head on this, one of these days," she said. "With the mouth open, so you could still look out."

"My dad won't finish it," the boy said. "He never finishes anything. I think he's nuts."

"You could do it when you grow up."

"I'm not sticking around *here* when I grow up," he said, scornfully. "I'm going to join the Merchant Marine."

"What's that?"

"It's like the Navy, only different," he said. "You want to go see the caverns now?"

There was no one behind the counter. "Where's your dad?" she asked.

"He went into town. I run the place when he's away," said the boy breezily, opening the cave door and turning on the light. "We don't need tickets. Let's go down."

They descended. The light was streaming full through the gap where the sea was only just beginning to wash in, with the turning tide, a few cream-edge waves running up the shingle. She glanced over at the smaller cavern, beyond the sawhorses, and saw blue lights dancing in the darkness. "Oh—" She started toward them. He followed close.

"I wish this part hadn't fallen in," she said.

He pulled back one of the sawhorses. "It didn't fall in. You want to see?"

"But your dad said it wasn't safe."

"He just made that up," said the boy, and bounded up the slope into the cavern. "It's keen in here. I swim in here all the time. Come look."

She followed. The blue lights swam lazily. There was the grotto she had only glimpsed from the entrance, glowing like an aquamarine. Some trick of sunlight shining down into all that white limestone, reflected somehow up into the cavern where it opened out, who knew how far below?... And there was something down there, shining in the other world, a flash of gold in the blue...

She moved forward involuntarily, and then saw the phantoms.

The women were locked together, struggling at the edge of the pool, and the limpid water in a bygone hour roiled and foamed white. The small woman no longer looked meek; her teeth were bared, her dark eyes flashed with hatred, her wet hair snaked around her face as she clawed at the other. And the other...

The other woman groped for her adversary's throat with salt-white hands. Her lips were coral-red, her golden hair floated out behind her as she sank further into the water, her eyes glowed like green moons. Something broke the water in a white fountain, sending slow drops spinning upward as light coruscated on gleaming scales.

She stared. Beside her, the boy had turned his back and was pulling down his trunks. He stepped out of them, turned and dove into the pool. He was grinning when he surfaced.

"Skinny dipping! You want to come in?"

She blushed. "No, thank you—I—"

"Nobody'll see," he said. "It's *nice*. It's not cold. Really."

Still, she hesitated. She was pretty sure that if her parents ever found out that she'd taken off her clothes in front of a stranger, the punishment would be unimaginable, certainly worse than what her brothers had incurred for setting fire to the garden shed. And yet, she wondered what the water would feel like on her bare skin...

And his body was a beautiful color, in the undersea light. The gold glinted up from below, backlit him. She cleared her throat.

"What's all that gold, down there?"

He looked at her sharply. "You see it?"

"Yes."

He swam close, looked up into her face. "It's treasure," he said, earnest, pleading. "Gold and jewels from old wrecks. The storms washed it in. There's tons of it down there. You can dive down and touch it. It's easy. Come on."

"Can I come in with my clothes still on?"

"Sure, if you want. Come on. There's this neat place down there, I can show you. Nobody stares at you there, nobody laughs. You're like me, you'd really like it. Come see."

She was reaching up to take off her glasses when the hoarse voice cried, *"What are you doing there?"*

She turned, and saw the faded man standing at the bottom of the stairs, no phantom now. He crossed the cavern in what seemed like four bounds, and had grabbed her by the arm when he looked down and saw the boy. There had been anger in his face, before; now there was an emotion she couldn't understand at all, some adult compound of revulsion and fear.

"I gave you a chance, didn't I, Ricky?" he said, in the sort of voice one grownup uses to another. He let go her arm and drew something from the pocket of his overalls: a monkey wrench. "I gave you every chance. You come out of there."

"You go to Hell!" the boy snarled, and only then did she see that the pink scar on his neck had opened on either side and was pulsing, pulsing in the water.

"Oh," she said, realizing that this was one of those places where the jagged edges of the world showed, the parts people weren't supposed to see, the madness under the smooth rational surface. Yet here all the story fragments linked up, all the images came together into coherence. "Oh. She wasn't jealous after all. She just wanted her baby back—"

The man whirled, staring at her. She didn't know what this new look in his eyes meant, either, but she understood well enough that if she didn't get away from him as fast as she could, something bad was going to happen.

She turned and ran across the outer cavern. Her foot slipped on the shingle; she lurched straight down into a receding wave, and before she could rise to hands and knees another one burst in beneath the rock and caught her, pulling her under.

A second later she burst into sunlight and air, and dogpaddled frantically, looking around. The wave was sucking her out to sea. She caught a rock and managed to hold on, losing her glasses as the wave receded. Once she got her feet under her she was able to wade for the base of the cliff, leaning against the pull of the tide. Around the cliff's edge and she walked up onto hard sand, and after a moment got her breath and ran.

Her mother scolded her for coming home soaked and with skinned knees, and for having lost her glasses. She was sent to bed, where she huddled gladly, trying to get warm.

Las Lloronas. She thought about the woman looking for her baby, moaning and lamenting. But the caves had moaned long before the boy had been born. The Indians and the Spanish had known they were haunted. She wondered whether there were stories so powerful they settled in a place and shaped everything and everyone around them, so they played out over and over again. And some of them must overlap, in layers, to make new stories...

On their last night by the sea, her parents threw a party for the friends they'd made. They built a bonfire on the beach. Her father carried down two cases of beer and a barbecue, and her mother brought blankets and marshmallows and hamburger wrapped in aluminum foil. Her brothers and sisters ran around in the dark.

The stars glittered, thousands, more than she'd ever seen in the city. The Milky Way trailed down to the horizon. She walked away from the firelight to see it better. The tide was out, and the stars were burning on the wet flat sand too, the dark mirror disturbed only by a crab that made its slow sidelong way down the beach.

She heard the boy calling, and looked up and saw him standing just beyond the first line of breakers. He looked cold and scared.

"Are you all right?" she said.

"They came and took my dad away," he said, in a hoarse voice. His lip was split, and he was missing a tooth.

"Who did?"

He didn't answer her. He just stared.

"What are you going to do now? You want to come up to our fire?"

He shook his head. "I'm going to run away," he said. "Join the Merchant Marine. You want to come, too?"

"Yes, but I'm a girl," she said, "We can't do that kind of thing. Please, come up to our fire and get warm."

But he shook his head again, backing away into the dark water, and she knew he wouldn't come ashore, and she ached to run after him and dive into the night waves with him. She didn't, though. She stood there with tears running down her face, watching him vanish in the white spray and the starlight.

Are You Afflicted With Dragons?

There must have been a dozen of the damned things up there.

Smith walked backwards across the hotel's garden, glaring up at the roofline. The little community on the roof went right on with its busy social life, preening, squabbling over fish heads, defecating, spreading stubby wings in the morning sunlight, entirely unaware of Smith's hostile scrutiny.

As he continued backward, Smith walked into the low fence around the vegetable patch. He staggered, tottered and lurched backward, landing with a crash among the demon-melon frames. Instantly, a dozen tiny reptilian heads turned; a dozen tiny reptilian necks craned over the roof's edge. The dragons regarded Smith with bright fascinated eyes. Smith growled at them helplessly as he flailed there, and they went into tiny reptilian gales of piping laughter.

Disgusted, Smith got to his feet and dusted himself off. Mrs. Smith, who had been having a quiet smoke by the back door, peered at him.

"Did you hurt yourself, Smith?"

"We have to do something about *those*," said Smith, jerking a thumb at the dragons. "They're getting to be a nuisance."

"And possibly a liability," said Mrs. Smith. "Lady What's-her-name, the one with that pink palace above Cable Steps, had dinner on the terrace last night with a party of friends. I'd just sent Mr. Crucible out with the Pike Terrine when one of these little devils on the roof flies down, bold as you please, and lights on the lady's plate. She screamed and then for a moment everyone was amused, you know, and one or two of them even said the horrible little creature was cute. Then it jumped up on her shoulder and started worrying at her earring.

"Fortunately Crucible had the presence of mind to come after it with the gravel rake, and it flew away before it could do Milady any harm, but she wasn't pleased at all. I had to give them free pudding all around and two complimentary bottles of Black Gabekrian."

Smith winced. "That's expensive."

"Not as expensive as Milady's bullies coming down here and burning the hotel over our heads. What if the little beast had managed to pull out her earring and then flown off with it, Smith?"

"That'd finish us, all right." Smith rubbed his chin. "I'd better go see if I can buy some poison at Leadbeater's."

"Why don't we simply call in an exterminator?" Mrs. Smith puffed smoke.

"No! They charge a duke's ransom. Leadbeater's got something, he swears it does the job or your money back."

Mrs. Smith looked doubtful. "But there was this fellow in the marketplace only the other day, had a splendid pitch. 'Are you afflicted with DRAGONS?' he shouted. Stood up on the steps of Rakut's monument, you know, and gave this speech about his secret guaranteed methods. Produced a list of testimonials as long as your arm, all from grateful customers whose premises he'd ridded of wyrmin."

Smith grunted. "And he'd charge a duke's ransom and turn out to be a charlatan."

Mrs. Smith shrugged. "Have it your way, then. Just don't put it off any longer, or we'll be facing a lawsuit at the very least."

▲▼▲

Leadbeater's & Son's was an old and respected firm, three dusty floors' worth of ironmongery with a bar in the cellar. Great numbers of the city's population of males of a certain age disappeared through its doors for long hours at a time; some of them practically lived there. Smith was by no means immune to its enchantment.

Regardless of what he needed, Smith generally began with climbing up to the third floor to stare at Bluesteel's Patented Improved Spring-driven Harvester, a gleaming mystery of wheels, gears, blades, leather straps and upholstery, wherein a man might ride at his leisure while simultaneously cutting down five acres of wheat. Mr. Bluesteel had assembled it there for the first Mr. Leadbeater, long years since, and there it sat still, because it was so big no one had been able to get it down the stairs and the only other option was taking off the roof and hoisting it out with a crane.

Smith had a long satisfying gawk at it, and then continued on his usual progress: down to the second floor to browse among the Small Iron Goods, to see whether there were any hinges, bolts, screws or nails he needed, or whether there might be anything new and stylish in the way of drawer pulls or doorknobs. Down, then, to the ground floor, where he idled wistfully among the tools in luxuriant profusion, from the bins full of cheap hammers to the really expensive patent wonders locked behind glass. At last, sadly (for he could not admit to himself that he really needed a clockwork reciprocating saw that could cut through iron bars with its special diamond-dust attachment) Smith wandered back through the barrels of paint and varnish to the Compounds area, where young Mr. Leadbeater sat behind the counter doing sums on a wax tablet.

"Leadbeater's son," said Smith by way of greeting.

"Smith-from-the-hotel," replied young Leadbeater, for there were a lot of Smiths in Salesh-by-the-Sea. He stuck his stylus behind his ear and stood. "How may I serve? Roofing pitch? Pipe sealant? Drain cleaner?"

"What have you got for dragons?"

"Ah! We have an excellent remedy." Young Leadbeater gestured for Smith to follow him and went sidling back between the rows of bins. "Tinplate's Celebrated Gettemol! Very cleverly conceived. Here we are." He raised the lid on a bin. It was full of tiny pellets in a riot of brilliant colors.

"It looks delicious," said Smith.

"That's what your wyrmin will think," said young Leadbeater. "They'll see this and they'll leave off hunting fish, see? They'll fill their craws with it and, tchac! It'll kill them dead. How bad is your infestation?"

"There's a whole damned colony of them on the roof," said Smith.

"*Well.* You'll want a week's worth—I can sell you a couple of buckets to carry it in—and for that kind of volume we throw in a statue of Cliba and the Cliba Prayer, put a shrine where the dragons can see it and keeps 'em from coming back, very efficacious—and then of course you'll need new roofing and gutters once you've cleaned your dragon colony out—"

"What for?"

"Because if you've got that many of them on your roof, ten to one they've been prying up the leading to hide things under it, and once their droppings get underneath on your roof beams they eat right through, and you don't want that, trust me. Highly corrosive droppings, dragons. Just about impossible to get the stink out of plaster, too. Had them long?"

"There'd always been a couple," said Smith. "We're at the damned seaside, right? You expect them. But in the last month or two we've got some kind of wyrmin rookery up there."

"Yes. I dare say it's the weather. Lot of people coming in with the same trouble. Well, let me fetch you a pair of good big buckets…"

"Yes, but no roofing stuff just yet, all right?" Smith followed him over to the Containers section. "I'll wait until I get up there and see how bad it is. And what do I do with it? Just scatter it around? We've got a baby at our place, and I wouldn't want him picking it up and eating it."

"Not at all. You've got a big tree on your grounds, haven't you? Just hang the buckets in the tree branches. Neat and tidy. They're naturally curious, see? They'll fly down to eat it, and then all you'll need to do is call the umbrella-makers," said young Leadbeater, with a grin.

"What for?" Smith was mystified until he remembered the commercial uses for dragon wings. "Oh! Right. Will they come and collect the dead ones for us?"

"Usually. You can get a good price for them, too." Young Leadbeater winked.

▲▼▲

Smith trudged home with two gallon buckets of Tinplate's Celebrated Gettemol, and the little statue of Cliba—a minor god of banishments—with its prayer on a slip of paper, in his pocket. He set a ladder against the trunk of the big canopy-pine and, climbing the ladder, went up himself to hang the buckets where they would be clearly visible. While up there he peered across at his roof, but saw no gaping holes evident. Whistling, he climbed back down and spent the rest of the afternoon in the work shed making a shrine for Cliba out of an old wine-jar.

▲▼▲

Next morning Smith was carrying a case of pickles up from the hotel's cellar when he heard Mrs. Smith calling him, with thunder in her voice. He emerged to find her clutching her grandchild.

"What?"

"Perhaps you'd better go and see what Baby found when I took him outdoors for his sunbath," she said grimly. Smith, expecting a dead dragon, sighed and trudged off to the garden, followed closely by Mrs. Smith. When he stepped through the back door he beheld the garden and back terrace scattered with thousands of rainbow-colored pellets.

"And guess what Baby went straight for, when I set him down? *'Yum yum, look at all this candy!'*" said Mrs. Smith.

"Gods below!" Smith looked up into the tree and saw the two empty pails swinging on one end of gnawed-through cord. Five or six dragons perched along the branch above it, watching Smith with what looked like malicious glee in their little slit-pupiled eyes. As Smith stared, they defecated in unison and flew back to the hotel's roof.

"I trust you'll have Mr. Crucible sweep it up immediately," said Mrs. Smith with icy hauteur.

"Damned right I will," said Smith. "And then I'm taking it back to Leadbeater's and demanding a refund."

"And what'll you do then?"

Smith rubbed the back of his neck, scowling. "Go ask a priest for intercession?"

"A fat lot of good that'll do! What self-respecting god gets rid of household pests, Smith? No, go and do what we ought to have done in the first place and hire a professional. There's that fellow in the marketplace. 'Are you afflicted with DRAGONS?' and all that. A big fellow in oilskins. One-eyed."

▲▼▲

After a brief unpleasant interview with the Leadbeaters father and son, Smith walked out of their emporium counting his money. He put his wallet away and, sighing, looked around. He spotted the column of Duke Rakut's monument, two streets away.

"May as well," Smith muttered to himself. Picking his way between fishnets spread out for mending, he made his way over to the marketplace in Rakut Square.

Approaching the monument, Smith saw only a skinny youth seated on its steps, next to a handcart loaded with empty cages. The youth, who had a rather bruised and melancholy look to him, was feeding shrimps to a fat little dragon perched on his shoulder. The dragon ate greedily. The youth watched it with a mother's tender regard.

"Is there a man hereabouts says he can get rid of those?" Smith inquired, staring at the dragon. He had never seen a tame one before.

"That'd b-be my m-m-master," said the youth, not meeting Smith's eyes.

"Well, where is he?"

By way of answer the youth pointed at the wine shop across the way.

"Back soon?"

The youth nodded. Smith sat down on the steps to wait. The dragon climbed batlike down to the youth's knee and squeaked at Smith. It
ducked its head and shook its wings, which resembled fine red leather,
at him.

"What's it doing?"

"Sh-she's begging you for t-t-treats," said the youth.

"Huh." Smith scratched his head. "Smart dragon." The youth nodded.
The dragon waited expectantly for treats and, when none were forthcoming
from Smith, it squealed angrily at him and clambered back up the front of
the youth's tunic, where it settled down to groom itself, now and then casting
an indignant glance at Smith.

A man emerged from the wine shop. Smith, watching him as he walked
across the square, saw that he was big, wore a curious long coat made of oilskin, and had one eye. A leather patch hid where the other had been. The man
was red-faced and genial-looking, even more so than might be accounted
for by having just emerged from a wine shop.

"C-c-customer, Master," said the youth. The man rubbed his hands
together, grinning at Smith.

"Are you, sir? Are you afflicted with—"

"Dragons, yes, I am. What're your rates like?"

"I will completely eradicate your dragons for absolutely free!" the man told
him. His voice was a hoarse bawl. He grabbed Smith's hand in his gauntleted
own and shook it heartily.

"Free! What's the catch?"

"No catch, my friend. Etterin Crankhandle, at your service. And let me
tell you what those services include! No appointment necessary. I will personally come to your premises and arrange for on-site removal of any and
all dragons infesting your property. All wyrmin are humanely trapped—no
dangerous poisons or other chemical preparations used. I will then conduct
a complete and thorough examination of your roof, shed or outbuildings and
remove any nests or caches and repair any damage I find, such as loose leading, tiles or slates. I of course reserve the right to any contents of said nests or
caches. Your roof, shed or outbuildings will then be sprayed with my Miracle
Wyrm Repellent guaranteed to prevent any re-infestation for a full year. All
absolutely free. Interested?"

▲▼▲

"I wish I'd run into you before I spent a fortune on that Gettemol crap," said Smith, panting as he helped Crankhandle and his assistant push their cart up the street. Crankhandle laughed and shook his head.

"Ah, sir, if I had a gold crown for every time I'd heard someone say that, I'd be a wealthy man."

"You ought to charge something, then," said Smith, leaning away from the dragon on the youth's shoulder, as it stuck its neck out and nipped at him.

"Oh, no," said Crankhandle. "The dragons themselves are payment enough. And in any case, you wouldn't have found me there before last month. I'm new here."

"A traveler, then?"

"I am, sir. Have to be. When I clear wyrmin out of a town, they don't come back. Pretty soon business dries up, doesn't it?"

"I suppose it would. Here we are," said Smith, opening the garden gate. They wheeled the cart in over the lawn and parked it under the canopy-pine. As Crankhandle's assistant scrambled to slide chocks under the wheels, Crankhandle turned and peered up at the roof. The dragons looked down at him. Crankhandle grinned wide. Smith saw that his teeth had been capped with gold.

"There you are! Uncle's come with treats, my little darlings. Oh, yes he has."

▲▼▲

Smith went indoors, got a beer and came back out to watch as the youth unloaded all the cages from the cart. He set them up in a row and opened each one. His master, meanwhile, opened a panel in the floor of the cart and from a recess brought out an iron strongbox. When he opened it, Smith glimpsed a dense greenish stuff, looking like damp compressed sawdust. Crankhandle broke off a cake of it and went to each of the cages, baiting each cage with bits of the cake. The dragon on his assistant's shoulder turned its head and watched jealously. It began to squeak, doing the same head-bobbing and wing-fluttering routine it had gone through at Smith.

"Here you are, little sweeting," said Crankhandle, holding out a morsel of the stuff. The little dragon snapped at it avidly and gobbled it down. "That's the way. Now! Arvin, send her up there."

The youth Arvin took the dragon in both his hands. He kissed the top of her head—she tried to bite him—and tossed her up in the air toward the roof. She unfolded her wings and flew to the roofline, landing among the other dragons there. They hissed at her, but only for a moment; presumably they had caught the scent of the cake on her jaws, for they suddenly mobbed her, biting her in their excitement, snapping at crumbs. She squawked and fled, jumping off the edge and flapping back down to Arvin's waiting hands. He clutched her to himself and dodged behind the open cages, holding her against his chest protectively as the other dragons came winging after her.

But the whole flock—and Smith saw now there were a lot more than a dozen, more like twenty—pulled up and wheeled in midair as they noticed the bait. For a moment there was a confusion of beating wings, loud as spattering rain on rock, and then each dragon had zipped into one of the cages and was ravenously eating the green cake. Crankhandle stepped forward and slammed the cages shut, one after another. Arvin stepped around to help him, as his dragon scrambled back on his shoulder.

"And it's done," said Crankhandle, beating his gauntlets together. Arvin's dragon peeped and begged. "And here's your reward, good girl!" Crankhandle added, going to the strongbox and taking out a last bit of cake. He handed it to Arvin to feed to her and then put the strongbox back in its compartment, shutting the panel.

"Damn," said Smith. Crankhandle swung round to him, grinning, and held up an index finger.

"But wait! I have not completed my comprehensive removal! Arvin, get the ladder."

"Yes, Master," said Arvin, as the dragon screamed in temper and bit him because the last of the cake was gone. He dabbed absentmindedly at the blood streaming from his ear and went to pull an extendable ladder from the side of the cart.

Crankhandle loaded a basket with tools and, slinging it on his back, climbed the ladder one-handed, while Smith steadied the ladder for him and Arvin loaded the cages back on the cart. Arvin sustained a number of other bites doing this, amid tremendous racket, because the dragon flock was in a group rage and hurling themselves against the bars; but Arvin kept working and only paused to tie a couple of bandages on his wounds before throwing netting over the cart's top to fasten everything down.

"I've got it figured out," said Smith, who had wandered over to watch the dragons once Crankhandle was safely on the roof. "He sells the little bastards to the umbrella-makers, doesn't he?"

Arvin shot him a pained look. "N-n-n-n-no!" he said reproachfully. "He l-lets them g-go. G-goes inland a l-long way and r-releases them. G-gone for w-weeks sometimes."

"Aha," said Smith. "Yes, of course."

▲▼▲

Crankhandle was up on the roof a long while, scraping and clunking and hammering. Mrs. Smith came out to see what was going on and, on learning, was very pleased indeed with Smith, so much so that she went back indoors to prepare his favorite fried eel for dinner.

Having repaired the leads, removed the nests and dug dragon shit out of all the raingutters, Crankhandle came back down the ladder at last, looking smug.

"Very nice haul," he said, slinging the basket down and pulling a tank with a spraying-rig from under the cart. Smith got up and looked in the basket. He glimpsed something bright glinting among the ruin of nests and flat sundried dragon-corpses.

"There's something gold in here—" Smith reached for it, but Crankhandle whirled around with the tank in his hands.

"Ah-ah-ah! That's my perquisite, sir. 'Contents of said nests or caches', I said, didn't I? Anything I found up there's *mine*, see? Or I can just let the little dears loose again, and I shouldn't think you'd want that, not with the spiteful mood they're in."

"All right, all right," said Smith, but he brushed aside the rubbish for a better look anyway. His jaw dropped. In the bottom of the basket was a clutch of gold crown-pieces, a gold anklet, a silver bracelet set with moonstones, a length of gold chain, three gold signet rings, the brass mouthpiece from a trumpet, assorted earrings…

"Wait a minute." Smith grabbed out a gold stickpin, a skull with ruby eyes. "This is mine! Went missing from my washstand!"

"Mine now, mate," said Crankhandle, shaking his head. "Those were my terms. Wyrmin steal bright metal; everybody knows that. Anyplace they nest, there's going to be a hoard. Now you know how I can afford to do this free of charge."

"Well yes, but…" Smith turned the stickpin in his fingers. "Come on. This was a gift. A gift from a demon-lord, if you want to know, and I wouldn't want to offend him by losing it. Can't I keep just this pin? Trade you for it."

"Such as what?" Crankhandle was busy fastening the tank's harness on his back.

"Lady of the house is a gourmet cook. Seriously, the Grandview's restaurant rated five cups in the city guide. Exclusive, understand? All the lords and ladies are regulars here, so you can imagine the wine cellar's stocked with nothing but the best. We'll give you the finest table and serve you the finest meal you'll ever eat in your life, eh? And whatever you like to drink, as much as you can hold!"

"Really?" Crankhandle's eye gleamed. "Right, then; you get the table ready. I'm just going up to finish the job. I warn you, I've got a good appetite."

▲▼▲

He wasn't joking. Crankhandle set his elbows on the table and worked his way through a whole moor-fowl stuffed with rice and groundpeas, a crown roast of venison with a blackberry-red wine reduction sauce, golden fried saffron crab cakes, two glasses of apricot liqueur and a quart and a half of porter. Smith played the companionable host and took his dinner of fried eel at the table with his guest, watching in awe as the man ate and drank. He took it on himself to have some fried eel sent out to Arvin as well, marooned in the garden keeping watch over the cages.

Refilling Crankhandle's glass, Smith inquired: "How did you get into this line of business, if you don't mind my asking?"

"Ha-ha!" Crankhandle belched, grinned, and placed a slightly unsteady finger beside his nose. "That's the story, isn't it? What's for pudding? Got any fruitcake?"

Smith waved down one of the waiters and told him to bring out a fruitcake.

"How'd I get into my line of business. Well. Always interested in dragons, from the time I was a kid. I grew up back in the grainlands, see, way inland. Way upriver. And the dragons, you know, they're bigger there— twice the size of these little buggers. I remember standing on the tail of my father's cart and watching 'em cruise across the sky, just gliding, you know, on these scarlet wings. Most beautiful thing I'd ever seen in my life. Ah!"

The waiter brought the fruitcake to the table. It was dark, solid, drenched in liquor, heavy as a couple of bricks and covered in molten sugar, and the mere sight of it was enough to give Smith indigestion. The waiter deftly set out a plate and took up his cake knife, poised to serve. "How big a slice would Sir like?"

"Leave the whole thing," said Crankhandle, a bit testily. The waiter looked sidelong at Smith, who nodded. The waiter set the fruitcake on the table and left. Crankhandle seized the knife and, a little unsteadily, sawed out a slice. Gloating, he held it up to the candle, so the light shone through the red and amber and green fruit. "Look at that! Looks like jewels. Looks like a dragon's trove. Nothing about them isn't beautiful, dragons." He stuffed the slice of cake in his mouth and cut himself another.

"So anyway—I wanted to know everything about 'em, growing up. Asked everybody in my village what they knew about dragons. Nobody knew much. Used to watch the dragons dive in the river for fish. Found out the sorts of things they like to eat when they can't get fish, found out what they physic themselves with when they're ill, that sort of thing.

"And then, one time, I followed one back to the cliffs where it nested and climbed up there to have a look, and that was when I found its hoard. All this gold! Nobody in my village had any, you can be sure. I reached in and grabbed this goblet with rubies on it—got my arm bitten pretty badly too—and carried it home.

"The schoolmaster had a look at it and said it was *old*. Come out of some old king's tomb somewhere, he said. The mayor said it likely had a curse on it and he confiscated it, to keep the curse off me, he said, but he was a greedy bastard and I knew he wanted it for himself. Pour me some more of that apricot stuff, eh?"

Smith obliged him. Crankhandle grinned craftily, took a mouthful of liqueur and leaned quickly toward the candle. He swallowed, belched. The candle flame shot out sideways for a second, a jet of fire.

"Is that how dragons do it?" said Smith.

"No. See, that's a popular misconception about dragons, that they breathe fire. I'm here to tell you they don't, and I'd know. Been studying 'em my whole life. I know more about dragons than anybody else in the world, now." Crankhandle cut himself a huge slab of cake, took half of it in one bite, and chewed thoughtfully.

"Such as?"

"Such as, they're smart. They can learn things. I learned to train 'em. Mind you, it isn't easy—" Crankhandle pointed at the patch covering his eye socket—"because they're willful, and temperamental, and quick. You have to want them more than an eye, or a fingertip or an earlobe. The boy's learning that. The other thing is, you can only really train wyrmin to do better what they already want to do anyway." He reached for the knife to cut the last quarter of fruitcake into eighths, changed his mind, and simply picked up the whole wedge and bit into it.

"Well. So I learned all there was to know about dragons, see? Discovered a secret, and I didn't learn it from any priests or mages either, I worked it out for myself. There's something dragons need in their diets—and I'm not telling you what it is, but it's either animal, vegetable or mineral, ha ha—and if they don't get it, they don't grow. That's why they're so puny, here by the sea. Lots of fish, but no Mystery Ingredient. So I worked out a special food formula for dragons, right? A little of this, a little of that, a lot of the Mystery Ingredient, and that's my bait.

"Not even the boy knows the recipe. I make it up myself, in a locked room. And the little bastards love it! Can't get enough of it. Have to be careful doling it out to them, because they do get bigger when they eat it, and you can spend a fortune on cages. But oh, how they come to the bait!"

"So…you travel around with this stuff, cleaning out wyrmin colonies, and collecting all the gold they've stolen and hoarded," said Smith. "You must have earned a fortune by now! But if it's that dangerous, why don't you retire?"

"Haven't made enough yet," said Crankhandle, pouring himself some more liqueur. "I'm saving it up. You might say I've got a hoard of my own. Besides, this isn't where the real money is!"

"Oh no?"

"No indeed. Rings and pins and bracelets…ha. That's the petty stuff the little ones bring in. They're not strong enough to lift anything bigger. You don't get a real payoff until you've got the big ones troving for you."

"Troving?"

"Going out looking for gold. It's instinctive. The big dragons where I grew up, they could tell where there was old gold. Tombs, mounds, other dragons' hoards. You should see *their* nests! I told you how I got this, didn't I?" He rolled up his oilskin sleeve to reveal a brawny arm, tattooed with swirling patterns, and a distinct U-shape of white scarred toothmarks.

"You did. Stealing a cup."

"Right, well, I learned that what you do is, you get 'em when they're little enough to be easily managed, and you train 'em, see? You get 'em used to you. You get 'em so they believe they'd better do what you want 'em to do, to get those lovely wyrmin treats. And then you feed 'em so they get of a bigness to raid tombs and such, and you take 'em back into the inlands where the old places are and you let 'em go.

"Then it's just a matter of making a chart of where they build their nests and going around every now and then to see what they've collected for you. They remember *me*, old Uncle Treats, and I dump out a great sack of special formula for 'em and while they're busy gobbling it down, I can take what I like out of the hoard. Works every time!"

"You ought to be stinking rich pretty soon, all the same," said Smith in awe. "Going to retire and pass your secret on to the boy?"

Crankhandle made a face. He drained his glass and shook his head. "No. He's a bit of a fool, really. Good enough for pulling the cart, but he's too soft for the work. He *loves* dragons, like they were people. And, you know, you really can't love, in this business." He reached for the emptied bottle and tilted it, sticking his tongue up the neck to get the last drops.

"You're a lot like a dragon, yourself," said Smith.

Crankhandle belched and grinned, and his gold teeth glinted in the candlelight. "Why, thank you," he said.

▲▼▲

That night Smith put his stickpin away in a drawer. It had occurred to him that there was another thing Crankhandle might have trained his wyrmin to do, and that was to fly through open windows and rob houses. The more he thought about it, the more he wondered whether the sudden infestation at the Grandview had happened entirely by chance.

But the dragons did not return, at least. When next Milady from the pink palace stopped in as one of a party ordering lunch on the terrace, she asked, with an unpleasant smile, whether she was likely to be attacked by an animal again. Smith assured her that all the dragons had been exterminated, which seemed to please her.

▲▼▲

Six months later, Smith had business down in Rakut Square. He glanced at the base of the monument as he walked by, and saw no cart. He thought to himself that Crankhandle must have moved on to another city.

He was a little surprised, therefore, as he walked back toward the Grandview, to find the boy Arvin mending a fishing net. The little dragon was still perched on his shoulder, sleepily basking in the sunlight. She opened one slit-pupiled eye to regard Smith and then closed it, dismissing him as not worth her attention.

"Hello!" said Smith. "Where's your master these days?"

Arvin looked up at him. He shook his head sadly. "Dead," he replied.

"Dead! How?"

"He t-told you about the b-bait we used, how it m-makes dragons bigger?"

"Right, he did."

"It makes them s-smarter, too."

I Begyn as I Meane to Go On

They'd been five days adrift when they saw the sail on the horizon.

"Oughtn't we to try and signal?" said young John, and rose in the canoe and was going to pluck off his red neckerchief and wave it, only he overbalanced and nearly capsized them again. Dooley cursed him, and Jessup took their one oar and hit him with it.

"Sit down, you mooncalf!"

It wasn't an especially seaworthy canoe. They had made it themselves out of a fallen tree trunk, slipping out at night to work on it, with the idea that they might escape from Barbados and live as free men on some other island. The first time it had rolled over in the water, they'd lost all the victuals and drink they'd brought with them. The second time, they'd lost the other oar. So they were in a bad way now, and not disposed to be charitable.

John looked around at Jessup, rubbing the back of his head. "But it's a ship," he said. "How else will they see us?"

"They're too far away to see the likes of us," said Jessup. His voice was husky from thirst. "They'll sail this way, or they won't. It's all down to luck."

"We might pray to the Almighty," said John.

"I'm done praying to the Almighty!" Dooley sat bolt upright and glared at them both. "Forty years I've prayed to Jesus! 'Sweet Jesus, don't let me be caught! Sweet Jesus, don't let me be transported! Sweet Jesus, let that fucking overseer drop dead where he's standing!' When has He ever answered me, I'd like to know?"

He had the red light in his eyes again, and John swallowed hard, but Jessup (perhaps because he had firm hold of the oar) said: "Belay that, you stupid bastard. Blaspheming don't help at all."

"Oh no?" screamed Dooley. He threw back his head. "You hear me, up there? You can kiss my red arse! Baisy-me-cu, Sir Almighty God, mercy beaucoups! I'm praying to the Devil from this day forward, You hear me? I be Satan's very own! Huzzay, Satan! *Praise* Satan!"

Such was the force with which he threw himself about in this rant, that he lurched clean over the side and went in with scarcely a splash, and vanished. A moment later he came up again, a little way away on the other side of the canoe, spluttering and blowing. One big fin cut smooth through the limpid blue sea, and Dooley went down again with a shriek cut off in the middle. The rest was bubbles and bloody water.

The other two sat very still, as you might guess.

▲▼▲

It was a long while before Jessup felt safe enough to start paddling again, but he did, ever so cautious, while John bailed with his cupped hands. In a couple more hours the sail tacked and made toward them, and John was quite careful to thank the Almighty.

Their rescuer was a brigantine with her aft decks cut down flush to the waist, long and low, and she had a dirty ragged look to her. She flew no colors. A few men leaned at the rail, watching incuriously as the canoe came alongside.

"What ship's this?" called Jessup.

"The *Martin Luther*," was the reply.

"Where d'you hail from?"

"From the sea."

"Ah, Christ," said Jessup quietly, and John looked at him, wondering what he meant. Jessup shrugged. "Well, needs must," he said, and reached up for the line when it was thrown down to him.

The canoe rolled over one last time as he scrambled from it, as though out of spite, but John vaulted up and caught the rail. There he hung, draped down the tumblehome, until a couple of laughing men took his hands and hauled him aboard.

When John had his feet under him on deck he looked around, hoping to see a water butt. He'd never been on any ship except the one that had transported him to Barbados. The fact that the *Martin Luther* bristled with mismatched cannon, and that her rigging was in trim despite her dirtiness, told him nothing. A man came up on deck, and from the fanciness of his coat relative to the other men's John assumed he was someone in authority.

"What're these?" said the man.

"Shipwrecked mariners, Captain," said one of the crew. The captain glanced over the rail at the canoe, which was already bobbing away in the wake. He laughed and spat.

"Mariners! In a piece of shite like that? Not likely; they're redleg bond slaves. Escaped. Ain't you?" He turned and looked hard at John and Jessup.

"Please, sir, we are," said Jessup.

The captain walked round Jessup and John, looking them over as though they were horses he had a mind to buy. "Been out long?"

"Two years, sir," said Jessup.

"And lived this long. Had the fever?"

"Yes, sir," they said together, and John added, "Please, may we have some water?"

The captain grinned. He held out his hand; one of the crew went and fetched a mug of water, and gave it to him. He held the mug up before John.

"The water's for the crew. We're on the account; no purchase, no pay. You'll sign articles and serve before the mast, and take your share, or you'll go back in the sea. Which is it to be?"

John didn't know what he meant, but Jessup said, "We'll serve, sir," and John nodded, thinking only of the water. So the captain laughed and gave him the mug, and he drank deep, and everyone became friendly after that.

▲▼▲

There were articles to sign, which were read aloud to them. Jessup made his mark. John signed his name, which drew a whistle of admiration from the ship's clerk. They were taken below and it was filthy there, but very free and easy; they were given clothing to replace the bleached and salt-caked rags they wore, and given sea-chests and hammocks of their own, which John thought was most generous. Later he found out they'd belonged to men who'd died of the fever, but it made no odds.

He felt some qualms at the prospect of being a pirate, wondering what his mother would have said. But if John was clumsy at first learning the ropes, and sick scared the first time he had to go aloft, why, it was better than cutting cane in the stinking heat of the fields, with the flies biting him, and the salt sweat running into his eyes. He liked the blue water. He liked the rum and tobacco and the sea air. He liked the freedom.

Though he learned, pretty quick, that freedom and dead men's gear were all there was in abundance on the *Martin Luther*.

"It's Captain Stalwin's luck," said Perkin, in a low voice. He spat wide, and some of it hissed and sputtered on the hood of the lamp. "No purchase, no pay indeed. We been out these two years, and all we took in that time is one cargo of sugar, and some slaves once, but they was mostly dead, and one ship with chinaware."

"There was that one with the chest of plate," Cullman reminded him.

"One chest of plate," Perkin admitted, "As didn't amount to much when it was divided up in shares, and mine was gone before the week was out once we went ashore in Port Royal."

"There was the *Brandywine*," said Cooper. There were growls and mutters.

"What was on the *Brandywine*?" asked John.

"She had a hold full of dried pease," said Perkin.

"Time was when you'd been grateful for a handful of dried pease, George Perkin," said Cooper. "And there was two sheep on board her, you're forgetting."

"Well, what I say is, if his luck doesn't change soon, Captain Stalwin's looking at being deposed," said Perkin.

▲▼▲

Captain Stalwin knew the peril in which his office stood, and stalked the deck with keen hunger, and scanned the horizon with a sunken eye. He could never keep to one course for long; for if they made south a week steady without sighting any vessel, there was sure to be complaint from the crew, and so to oblige them he'd give new orders and away they'd go to the west.

It was nothing like the iron discipline on the ship that had brought John out to Barbados, where a man must leap to obey the officers and keep his opinions to himself. It beat anything John had ever seen for pointlessness. And yet it pleased him, to see plain hands like himself having a say in their own affairs.

▲▼▲

On the day they sighted the ship, Captain Stalwin saw it before the lookouts. John, who was idling at the rail, heard the glass being snapped shut a second before the cries sounded: "Sail ho! Two points off larboard bow!"

Now, they were lying off the False Cape, hoping some cargoes out of the Lake of Maracaibo or Rio de la Hacha might come within easy reach, to either side. And there, creeping into sight off Bahia Honda, was a galleon, as it might be a merchant, and she was flying Spanish colors. Captain Stalwin waited, and watched, though the crew were roaring in impatience to take her; and when he saw she wasn't part of any fleet, he grinned and gave chase. A blood-red flag was brought out and run up, streaming out in the breeze.

The galleon, when she sighted them, was beating hard to windward; but she spread her sails and fled north, and aboard the *Martin Luther* men elbowed one another in glee.

"I reckon she's out of Rio de la Hacha," said Cooper, with a cackling laugh.

"Is that good?" said John.

"There's pearl fisheries there!"

"Might be she's only full of salt," said Perkin, and everyone told him to hold his sorry tongue.

John was kept busy the next hour, running eager up the shrouds as though they were a flight of easy stairs now, letting out all the canvas the *Martin Luther* carried. She bowed and flew, with the white water hissing along her hull, and the white wake foaming behind.

Happy men primed her guns. Cutlasses and boarding axes were handed round. Some men ran to the galley and blacked their faces with soot and grease, to look the more fearsome. The galleon ran, but she was broad and ponderous, like a hen fluttering her wings as she went, and the *Martin Luther* closed on her, and closed on her, like a hawk stooping.

Soon the galleon was near enough to see the painted figure on her stern castle. It was the Virgin Mary in red and blue and gold, her eyes wide and staring, her one hand raised to bless, her other hand cradling a wee Christ who stared and blessed too. It gave John a qualm, at first; but then he recollected the things the Papists were said to do to captive English, which put a different color on the matter. He wondered, too, whether the haloes on the figures were only gold paint or set with disks of real gold.

In ten more minutes they were near enough to chance a shot, and Captain Stalwin ordered the bow guns loaded. Beason, the gunner, got the two shots off: larboard and starboard barked out smart and the one ball went high and fell short, in a spurt of white foam, while the other hit the galleon at the waterline, close in to her keel, and stuck there like a boss on a shield.

"Again!" cried Captain Stalwin, and Cooper and Jessup loaded and primed. Beason adjusted the range with a handspike. They could hear the crack-crack-crack of musket shots from the galleon now—she had no stern guns, evidently—but the musket balls fell short, and long before the gap had closed Beason had the range right. Fire kissed powder and the larboard shot struck something, to judge from the shatter and shudder that echoed over the water. The starboard shot did worse, to judge from the screams.

When the smoke cleared they saw that the galleon's rudder was broke, in big splinters, though not shot away clean. Her tillerman was desperately trying to bring her about to broadside, with the little she was answering. Cooper and Jessup worked like madmen and Beason fired again, just the larboard gun this time, but that was enough; over the grinding of the rudder's hinge they heard the shot strike, and the fragments showering into the water. The galleon was wallowing when they saw her again, in the red sunlight through the smoke.

But not helpless: she had made it around far enough for her larboard guns to begin firing with some hope of hurt, and what was more her musketmen were now within range. As the *Martin Luther* rose on the swell, a flight of musket balls peppered the men on her forward deck. John started as Cullman dropped beside him howling. To this moment he'd been smiling like a fool at a play, cheering each shot; now he woke sober and dropped flat on the deck, as an eight-pound ball whistled above his head and punched through the forecourse before sailing on out to drop in the sea.

"Keep her astern!" yelled Captain Stalwin, but the tillerman was already sending the *Martin Luther* slinking around under the galleon's stern again. Close to now they could see what they hadn't noticed before, that two of her stern cabin windows had been beaten into one jagged-edged hole by one of their shots. John thought they could look straight into her when they rose on the next swell, which they did. What came popping up to the window then but a Spaniard with a pistol? He was white and bloody as a ghost, with staring blank eyes. He aimed the pistol full into Captain Stalwin's face, and fired.

There was a click, but neither flash nor ball. The next moment the *Martin Luther* had dropped away and past, grinding into the other vessel, and her crew were yelling and swarming up the side. John looked curiously at Captain Stalwin, who had sagged against the foremast and was trembling. Then the jolt of the swell striking the two hulls together threw John to his knees. He remembered where he was and thought of the gold haloes on the images. Scrambling up he grabbed a cutlass and pulled himself aboard the galleon.

Then he was too scared to think about gold or anything else but fighting off the Spanish who came at him. John was a big fellow, with fists like round shot, and thick arms. He'd been transported for killing a man in a tavern fight, without meaning to; only the man had been snarling drunk and come at him with a blade. John had been fearful of his life and just whaled away at the bugger until he'd stopped moving. So you may guess that John, now armed and even more fearful, cut down the Spanish before him like summer corn.

He stumbled over bodies. A musket-ball creased his scalp and tore his hat away, and he scarcely noticed. His ears were ringing, all sound seemed muffled, and his right arm ached something fierce from beating, and beating, and beating down with the cutlass.

He reached the far rail at last, gasping, and turned to put it at his back— and saw, to his surprise, that there were no Spanish left standing.

There was fighting going on belowdecks. He went to the companionway and peered down cautiously. Blades ringing, kicking, scuffling—a shrieked curse and a shot, and then Beason was coming up the companionway toward him, laughing, wiping his blade.

"We got 'em all," he said.

▲▼▲

Captain Stalwin came aboard with the *Martin Luther's* clerk to take inventory of the galleon's cargo. It was rice and logwood and salt, and some crates of chinaware in a blue pattern of little heathen men and temples. Profitable enough, if you were of a mind to play the merchant and unload the stuff in certain quiet coves, waiting for the smugglers to turn up and have a good haggle.

Nothing a man could weight down a purse with, though, or spend in an hour on rum and sweet companionship; no good chinking coin. A certain sour reek of disappointment began to hang over the deck, above the smells of black powder and death. There were murmurings from the crew, as they set about pitching the dead and wounded overboard. Captain Stalwin emerged from the galleon's hold with a disbelieving look.

"We'll search again," he said. "Tear out the bulkheads. There'll be pearls here, or gold bars, or silver, only it's hidden. It must be! My luck's changed. I felt it spin round like a compass-needle, when that son of a whore's pistol misfired. Ned Stalwin's luck's blowing out of a different quarter now, and our fortune's on this damned ship!'

"It is, senor," said a voice from somewhere down near his feet. "But not in the way you imagine."

John looked down with the rest of them, to see one of the Spanish propping himself on his elbow, smiling a little as he peered up at Captain Stalwin. He had taken a stab in the gut, and was cut above his right eye, so that he smiled through a mask of blood, and his teeth were pink with it. He spat blood now, but politely, away from Captain Stalwin's boots.

"I swear upon the Cross that I will make you a wealthy man. All I ask is a drink of water, and the grace of leisure to expire *before* you consign my body to the sea."

Captain Stalwin fingered his beard, uncertainty in his eyes. Beason prodded the dying man with his boot, in case he should be hiding a dagger. "Liar," he said.

"Senor, I am about to go before God. Would I lie and damn my mortal soul? What I said, I said in truth," said the man. He reached into his shirt and dragged forth something that winked green and golden in the pitiless sunlight. He kissed it and then held it out to Captain Stalwin, snapping the chain on which it had been worn. The chain was soft gold, with the links curiously worked, and it trailed after his gift, which was a crucifix.

Beason whistled. He glanced over his shoulder at the others on deck. John leaned close to see. He took the cross to be made of green glass at first, a faceted rod and the two arms held together with gold work, and the little crucified Christ and the INRI sign in gold. Captain Stalwin seized it, his hand shaking.

"Emeralds," he said.

"Very pretty," said Beason. "But it won't come to much when it's divided up into shares, will it? Have you got any more?"

The man smiled again, and blood ran from the corner of his mouth. "I will tell you where to find them. Water first."

So the Captain yelled for water. A cask was brought up and broached, with a drink dippered out for the dying man. He lay his head back and sighed, and asked for a chart. More yelling, then, and hasty searching in the galleon's great cabin before a chart was found and brought up to them, with Captain Stalwin sweating all the while lest the bastard should die first.

When the chart was held before his eyes, the man peered at it a long moment. He looked about helplessly, as though searching for a pen; then giggled, and dabbed his finger in his own blood, and daubed a spot south of Tobago.

"There," he said. "San Cucao. Two hills rising out of the sea. You will find there the mine from which these emeralds came, senor. Very rich mine. Emeralds green as the jungle."

Captain Stalwin licked his lips. "And is it garrisoned?"

The Spaniard smiled again. "Only with the dead. The island was my brother's, and mine; he died six weeks ago, and I was his heir. Now you are mine. All the island holds, I bequeath to you freely, God be my witness."

"Lying bugger," said Beason.

Captain Stalwin drew breath, and looked around. He gave sharp orders that the men should get busy moving the galleon's cargo into the *Martin Luther*. John rose and labored with the rest of them, up and down, back and forth, hauling the kegs of salt and the sacks of rice, hefting the logwood. As he went to and fro he would glance over, now and then, at where Captain Stalwin crouched on the deck and conversed with the Spaniard. He only caught a few phrases of their speech together; but every other man of the crew was doing the same as John.

In the days afterward they talked it over amongst themselves, in the night watches or belowdecks, and put together enough scraps of what each man had heard to flesh out the Spaniard's story, which was:

That he and his brother were somebodies in Cartagena, rich in land and Indian slaves, but poor otherwise in their generation. That some ten years since his brother, Don Emidio, having had occasion to travel, was shipwrecked on this little island of San Cucao. It had a spring of fresh water, and enough of the wreck landed for this Don Emidio to live on some few preserved stores while he built himself a raft. When he wasn't working on the raft he would explore the island; and there he found emeralds sticking out of a bluff where the earth had fallen away.

He carried some with him when he put off from the island. When he got home, he took his brother into his confidence. They resolved to go back to the island and mine the emeralds.

Being Spaniards as they were, they did it in proper Spanish fashion, with servants to wait on them and a friar to say the Mass for them, and Indian slaves to labor for them. The overseers cracked their whips, the Indians set to work with picks and mattocks, and soon the brothers had a prince's ransom in fine emeralds, with plenty more still winking out of the earth.

But then, the Indians had all taken sick with the Black Pox. The brothers were supping on board their ship when they heard the news, shouted from the shore. They resolved to flee, leaving the workers there, taking only those servants on board when the news came. They'd a coffer full of emeralds to console them. Only their friar objected; he took a boat and rowed himself ashore, that he might tend the dying and harvest their souls for God.

The brothers agreed to wait seven years before returning to the island, by which time the contagion might reasonably be supposed to have blown away. This was, the Spaniard had said, the seventh year, and the wealth from the emeralds they had carried away with them was now long gone. His brother being dead, he had planned to find a patron to fund his journey back.

Well, as the only patron he found rode a pale horse, he bought him another journey entirely. With the story told, the Spaniard murmured an Act of Contrition and died grinning. Captain Stalwin relieved him of his rings and a fine pearl that had dangled from his ear, and ordered him pitched into the sea.

▲▼▲

"They say Drake brought back such emeralds," said Perkin, as he gazed up at the stars. "Like big sticks of sugar candy, and green as…as the green in a church window."

"I seen some like that, once," said Collyer. "I was with Mansvelt when he took the *Santa Cruz*. There was a statue of one of their saints, all painted like, and stuck all over with precious stones. The emeralds was the biggest. I remember, there was one big as a medlar."

"Liar," said Beason. "And that Spaniard was a liar, too. We're sailing straight for some Spanish garrison with big guns, you mark me."

Jessup only shook his head, but John said: "Why would the fellow lie, with him dying?"

"Because we sliced his liver," said Beason. "Wouldn't you be spiteful, if it was you?"

"I'd fret more about the Black Pox," said Cooper. "Belike he was hoping we'd catch it. It's fearful way to die."

"I had the smallpox," said John. "Is it like that?"

"The same, only worse. Your skin turns black and bursts."

"No fear," said Collyer. "There's a keg of vinegar below, and a chest of sweet herbs, taken off that galleon; lavender-flowers and such, that the dons use to perfume their beards. We mix them up with the vinegar and make us pomanders to smell, and we'll keep hale and sound on that island."

"Captain's on deck," muttered Perkin. They fell silent, as Captain Stalwin came up the companionway. He looked at the stars, and drew a deep breath. Then he went to the rail and watched south a while. The green phosphorescence foamed and boiled in the bow-wake, and reflected in his glittering eyes.

▲▼▲

San Cucao was just as the Spaniard had said it was, two hills in the sea, poking up steep. It was cliffs most of the way around, with only one bit of shingle beach for a landing. They were able to moor the *Martin Luther* quite close, and from her deck could see the signs that men had been there once; a bit of an overgrown trail leading into the interior, and some stone huts or walls.

Captain Stalwin gave orders that arms should be served out, so the crew grabbed up cutlasses and muskets readily enough. Collyer ran below and fetched up the preventative he'd mixed from the vinegar, and made each man take a strip of sailcloth and dip it in the reeking stuff. They tied them round their wrists, or stuck them under their hats, muttering about the smell.

All this while there wasn't a sound from the island, baking in the bright sun of noonday; not the cry of a bird, not the call of a monkey, not the drone of a single cicada in its long grass. Its green trees drooped as though asleep.

Silent too the *Martin Luther's* crew went ashore, with Captain Stalwin leading them, and only a couple of men left on board. No breath of wind, either; John was soaked with sweat by the time they had walked up the beach, and come to the verge where the jungle began, a sort of overgrown meadow. He looked around him uneasily, thinking that all the quiet reminded him of a churchyard. Then he caught sight of a stone cross.

"It *is* a churchyard," he blurted out.

"What?" Captain Stalwin turned. John pointed at the cross. They all stood staring, and now they saw that the humps and hummocks in the vines and long grass were gravestones, grown over here and there, and knew the roofless ruin at the far end must be a chapel.

Jessup reached out and pulled the creepers back from the stone cross. It had a long inscription on it. Jessup, who knew some Spanish, read out: "'Sacred to the memory of Alessandro, born a pagan, in his extremity embraced Christ. A better Christian than his masters.'"

"Here's another one," said Cooper, clearing another stone. This was a cross surmounted by a skull, cut rudely. Jessup leaned down and read:

"'Diego, who became a faithful Christian. Suffered the torments of Hell on this earth, now in glorious repose in Paradise. When all are judged, his cruel masters will beg for a drop of water from his hand, in the flames where they burn.'"

They moved slowly across the meadow, reading carefully, and every few paces uncovered another gravestone. John noticed that they got bigger, the farther down the row they went, and more crudely cut. Jessup read them out, one after another:

"'Baltasar, obedient Christian, betrayed and left to die by Christians who do not deserve the name. Departed this vale of sorrow aged no more than 11 years. Angels carried him up. Devils will drag his masters down.'

"'Juan, humblest of Christians, endured the scourge and lash without complaint, and who for his obedience was left for dead in his hour of affliction. God sees! All the horrors of the Pit will be inflicted on the brothers Claveria.'

"'Narciso, exchanged the sweat and toil of this world for the heavenly kingdom after taking the Blessed Sacrament. He suffered greatly before he died. I had nothing left with which to comfort him. They are damned, both of them, for false and heartless vipers.'

"'Francisco lies here. God be thanked he went quickly and could not see at the end. His soul is with God. Whose ways cannot be comprehended.'

"'Timoteo, Christian. Why was this permitted, O Lord?'"

As they went to look at the last stone, a great rough slab on which the writing was chiseled carelessly, John put his foot down and felt nothing there to support him. He yelled as he toppled over, dropping his cutlass. Jessup and Beason caught him, and set him on his feet again, pulling him clear of the open grave: for that was what it was, screened over with gourd vines.

Perkin meanwhile had stepped carefully across and pulled the creepers back from the headstone.

"What's this one say?"

Jessup turned and peered at it. "'Brother Casildo Fernandez Molina. Traveler, have the kindness to cover my bones with earth, as you would hope your bones will rest. I bear witness to the perfidy of Don Emidio Claveria Martinez and Don Benecio Claveria Martinez. They are traitors to God. They will suffer and die cruelly, as they left us to die. I bear witness. I am God's hand in—'"

The letters, big angry block capitals, ran right off the edge of the stone.

"But the grave's empty," said Perkin, looking in.

There was an uneasy silence while they all considered that.

"Maybe he got rescued before he died," said John. Captain Stalwin shrugged.

"Dead or alive, he's no enemy of ours. Didn't we do for one of 'em? It's a judgment of God, ain't it?" He raised his voice. "Don Benecio, he es muerto! Savvy?"

Nobody answered him.

"We cut his liver open!" shouted Collyer.

"Threw his body in the sea without one prayer!" shouted Cooper.

"Bugger this," said Beason, and stepped warily past the grave to the ruins beyond. "Look! This was his chapel."

It had been a building of unmortared stone, thatched with palm leaves, but they had fallen in years since and were scattered everywhere. A rough-hewn wooden cross had fallen too, and lay worm-riddled at the far end. Maybe the place had served as Brother Casildo's workshop too; broken iron tools lay rusting where they had been dropped, and fragments of cut stone.

When they had poked about long enough to learn there was nothing useful for them there, they came out, and Captain Stalwin spotted the track that led away from the beach into the jungle. It was swift vanishing in green, but it was there.

"I'd reckon the mines'd be this way," he said. "Perkin, go before. Cut the creepers back as we go."

"And be mindful of that friar," said Cooper, looking uneasily over his shoulder.

So they followed the track, and the sun beat down, and the sound of the sea grew fainter. John was looking all around as he walked, with his cutlass held up before him, and sniffing now and then at his little strip of sailcloth. His mother had told him once that if you got the smallpox and didn't die of it, you need never fear it again; but that had been in Hackney. Out here, the old rules never seemed to apply.

It was all silent now on the path, but for the ring and hiss of Perkin's cutlass slicing through the overgrowth. The noise had taken on a comfortable sort of rhythm like music, so they were taken by surprise rather when Perkin suddenly yelled and toppled backward into Jessup.

"What is it?"

"Is it a snake?"

"Back! Back!" said Perkin, who had gone white. "Trap!"

They all staggered back a few paces, and spread out on the path to get a look at what they had narrowly missed walking into. There were creepers dragged craftily across the path. When they'd been green and fresh with the broad leaves spread out they might indeed have concealed what lay below; but they were long dead and withered, and showed clear that someone had dug a little pit in the midst of the track.

"That ain't enough to hurt anybody," said Cooper in scorn, but Perkin pointed a shaking finger at the beam that was laid to one side, with one end projecting out across the pit. He'd come close to putting his foot down on the end of the beam. If he had, his foot had pushed the end on the beam down into the pit, levering up the beam's other end. And the beam's other end—

They followed it with their eyes, silent to a man. The long beam was arranged over a fulcrum of cut stone. If its seesaw had gone up, it would have smacked away a bit of wood above it…which was supporting another bit of wood…which was supporting another…and so on, up the steep hillside to the great pile of stones carefully arranged to thunder down on the path if they were dislodged.

"Jesus Bleeding Christ," said Cooper.

"He was a good stonecutter, that friar," said Jessup, with a sick kind of laugh.

"But he didn't catch *us*. Didn't I tell you my luck had changed?" said Captain Stalwin. "Two shares to you, Perkin, for sharp eyes. We'll go on, and every man minds his God-damned feet, and watch close lest there's anything else."

John thought about the friar, left all alone here after the last of the Indians died, and how he must have wandered around in the jungle getting crazier and crazier, setting traps for the two brothers, babbling Latin-talk, nothing left for him but the thirst for vengeance. Was he watching them even now? He'd be emaciated, his priestly robe in rags. Maybe he was lying in wait just around the next bend in the trail, eager to garrote somebody with his rosary beads…

"There's broken tools up here," said Perkin. "And the track's getting wider."

"Are we getting near the mine?" said Captain Stalwin.

"Maybe," said Perkin. He hacked away a few palm-fronds and stared hard through the gloom. "There's something like a shaft. Phew!" He shook his head. "Something stinks."

He hurriedly took his strip of sailcloth and tied it across his face, mask-wise, and the others all did likewise except for John, whose strip wasn't long enough. He pressed it to his nose, praying the smell was only a dead pig somewhere. They proceeded with care and in a moment came out in the clearing where the mine-shaft was.

There were no footprints visible; the open sand had long ago been smoothed flat by wind and rain. There were a couple of broken barrels and some baskets, falling to pieces, that the Indians had used to carry dirt. And something in the mouth of the shaft…

Captain Stalwin paced forward warily, his cutlass up, looking from side to side. He got as far as the mouth of the shaft, and no rosary beads came snaking out of anywhere to strangle him. He looked down at what was in the mouth of the shaft—it was a basket, John could see that now—and began to laugh.

"Now, by God!" he cried. "Has my luck changed, or hasn't it?" He bent to the basket and dipped up a big rock that had emeralds sprouting from it like fingers from a hand. The rest of them rushed forward at that, and saw the basket full of rough emeralds, poking out where the sides of the basket had rotted away. Nor was it the only basket; there were others lined up beside it, going back into the shaft, brimful of rough green gems under a thin layer of dead leaves and dust.

John's eyes went wide. He grabbed with all the rest, stuffing emeralds in his pocket, shoving others aside who got in his way. Jessup tried to pick up a basket and it came apart, spilling emeralds across the floor, and Perkin dropped to his knees and snatched them where they scattered. "Look!" he said, pointing down the shaft.

There, just beyond some piled debris, lay another basket. It seemed this was where the choicest stones had been sorted; they were a richer green, they were bigger, and something about the way the dim light glinted on them promised clarity and perfection beyond anything John had yet seen.

Perkin scrambled forward on hands and knees. Cooper vaulted over him so as to get to them first, and in his haste tumbled against the debris that was piled in the way. His knee struck one end of a beam, concealed there. The beam swiveled. Its other end struck smartly on one of the timber baulks that held up the roof of the mine, and knocked it out of true. There was a creak, and dirt and stones fell from above as the baulk tottered—

What happened next John didn't see, for he was running for daylight as hard as he could. He made it, and so did Captain Stalwin, and so did Jessup. Here came Beason and Collyer, sprinting just ahead of the roiling cloud of dirt that belched from the mine shaft, and the muffled roar as the roof fell in.

John was just thinking that Perkin wouldn't get his two shares after all when he and Cooper came staggering from the mouth of the shaft, choking and coughing, brown all over as though they'd rolled in mud. When they had been properly laughed at, there was a general idea of gutting Cooper, for being so stupid as to spring another trap and lose them the best of the emeralds. Captain Stalwin, though, lifted his cutlass between Cooper and the rest.

"Belay that. We've filled our pockets, ain't we? And not a man lost when that roof fell in. It's my luck, plain as plain!" He pointed with the tip of the blade at the emeralds lying all about, that they'd dropped in their flight. "Now pick them up, and it's back to the ship with us. We'll come back tomorrow with a shovel or two and see if we can't dig out some more."

John obeyed like the rest, crouching over to collect the scattered emeralds. He was just reflecting on what a pleasant thing it was to be a pirate, picking jewels as though they were strawberries in a meadow, when he saw a bonny green gem lying amidst what he took to be little dry sticks. He reached for the emerald and that was when he saw the arm-bones. He looked along them to the blind gaping skull beyond.

"Here's a dead man!" he cried.

Captain Stalwin and the others came to see. "Why, it's the priest," said Captain Stalwin, pointing at the shreds of brown robe. "Look here, here's his beads. Ha! He died before he could go lie down in his grave. Well, there's an end to the mystery."

"No," said Jessup, almost whispering. "Who shot him?"

They all fell silent then, staring at the skull, which did indeed have a round hole in it. Beason reached with the tip of his cutlass and tilted it, and a musket-ball rolled out of one of the eye sockets.

"And another thing," Jessup went on, keeping his voice low. "He's rotted away long since. What is it that stinks so now?"

Now, for all the sweat and heat of the day, John felt cold. Beason wetted a finger and held it up, and turned to look at the bit of jungle from which the wind was blowing.

"Don't smell like carrion by itself, though," he murmured.

"Carrion or cabbage, I've no wish to meet it any closer," said Captain Stalwin. "We'll just creep off the way we came, shall we? Quick march, boys, and quiet. My luck will get us back safe."

So saying, he turned; and the shot rang out and dropped him in his tracks, with a little explosion of blood at his buttonhole like a red rose worn there.

John just had a glimpse of someone ducking down, before he threw himself flat. More shots came, as it seemed from some three or four snipers, and all of them in the jungle through which they had just come. Beason yelled some orders, and John dodged through the jungle back of the friar's bones and fell flat behind a log, where Beason had already taken shelter. Jessup and Perkin were behind a log a few feet away, and Collyer came running, clutching his arm where a musket-ball had stuck. They didn't see Cooper again.

Beason already had his musket loaded by the time John rolled over. He laid the barrel of it against the log and fired across the clearing. John loaded his own musket and did the same, as did Collyer and Perkin, and for some few minutes it was hot work there. Musket balls tore through the green leaves all around them.

"That fucking Spaniard *was* a liar," said Beason, as he reloaded. "Didn't I say it? Who'd listen to me, eh?"

Jessup crawled over and jerked his thumb at the trees behind them. "We retreat through that, we can get to the other side of the island! Make our way around to the anchorage again!"

Beason aimed, fired, and then looked where Jessup was pointing. "Ay," he said. So they retreated, firing as they went. In a moment they came out of the jungle on the other side and there was the blue sea, all right, but before them was a sheer drop down a cliff. Beason looked to and fro distractedly, as a shot or two came zipping out of the jungle behind them; then John spotted a little track that ran across the cliff's edge.

"Where's that go?" he cried.

"But that was where—" said Beason, before a musket ball cracked into a boulder and sent rock shards flying in every direction. He ducked and they ran, with Collyer cursing because one of the shards had hit his thigh, along the little track. It did get them out of the line of fire from the jungle pretty quick, putting the shoulder of the hill between them, but it rose, too. In another moment they were climbing, all exposed, where the trail switchbacked up the flank of the hill and vanished over a ridge.

By great good fortune their pursuers did not follow to pick them off like flies on a wall. Over the top of the ridge they hurtled, all together, and down through a little maze of bushes and then—

John halted, and the others ran into him as into a wall.

They had emerged into a clearing, and here was the source of the smell. Three or four huts stood around a central fire-pit. The stink was compounded of smoke, and the camp's latrine, which was brimful noisome, and a mountain of clam and mussel shells and fish bones; all that, and the crucified man that dried in the sun at the cliff's edge.

Even so, the place had a peaceful air. The sea-wind blew through the dead man's hair, and the sea broke softly on the rocks below, and a little stream bubbled down to one side...and there was a rhythmic *thump-thump-thump* that suggested someone in no particular hurry. An Indian woman sat at the door of one of the huts, pounding roots in a mortar.

John and the rest stood petrified, for it was surely only a matter of seconds before she looked up and saw them. Now, she raised her head...

And did not see them. She had no eyes. She had barely any face.

"Jesus," said Jessup faintly. "The Black Pox."

John groped for his bit of vinegar-soaked rag, and plastered it over his nose and mouth. Another woman came out of one of the huts. Maybe she'd been beautiful once, with her hair black as a raven's wing and lustrous; but she groped her way by touch along the side of the hut to the stream, for where her eyes had been were two pink masses of scars. As she bent—quite close to them—to fill her gourd with water, John saw that her nose and lips had been eaten off by the smallpox too, as though she'd been in a fire.

John looked away, and as quickly looked for somewhere else to look; but he'd seen enough of the poor crucified bugger to tell that he'd been a black-bearded fellow, and that they'd stripped him down to a loin-rag before they'd stuck him up there. A gull had been busy pecking at the face...

He ain't been up there any seven years, John realized. The friar had been dry bones long since picked clean, but this was fresher meat.

"They can't see us," said Beason, no louder than a breath. "We can walk through. Come on. Quick and quiet."

They stepped forward, walking soft as they could, and must pass one by one under the cross, stepping gingerly around the bits and odds that lay there. John spotted a glint of gold and green; Beason noticed it too, and dove on it quicker than John could. He held it up on its bit of broken chain to stare. It was a crucifix, as might be twin to the one they'd taken off the Spaniard on the galleon.

"Now I'll tell you what," Beason whispered, "This will be that bastard's own brother, and they did come back, but they was caught—"

A dog leaped up from where it had been sleeping, and barked furiously at them. The woman pounding roots took no notice, seemingly deaf as well as blind, but the woman with the water-gourd turned inquiringly, and two other women came to the doormouths. They too were blind, were horribly disfigured. They caught up sticks and came forward tentatively, waving them, groping with their free hands outstretched. The dog growled and leaped, running from the women to the *Martin Luther's* men and back, trying to guide them. It ought to have been funny but it wasn't; John's hair was fair standing up, and he was more afraid of the blind women than of anything he'd seen since he'd been transported.

"Oh Christ," said Beason, and shot the dog. "Run for it."

John ran, out in front of the others. He bounded like a goat along the track, that continued on the other side of the village, in its narrow way between the clifftops and the hillside. He could hear the panting breaths of the others as they followed him, knocking pebbles that clattered down the cliff to the shingle-beaches below. Soon he could hear shots as well, though they came from ahead and not behind. Then there was the echoing roar of one of the *Martin Luther's* guns.

"Those sons of bitches!" yelled Beason, panting. "Move, you great ox!"

He pushed past John. They rounded the side of the hill where it came down and found themselves looking into the anchorage from the other side. There was the back of the ruined chapel; there was their longboat, halfway to the *Martin Luther* and full of armed men. There was only Cullman and Jobson on deck to fight them off, and Cullman's left arm had been no use since taking the galleon. They were crouched behind the great gun in the waist, trying to get off another shot at the longboat without catching any musket-balls.

Beason ran close enough for range, reloading as he went. As one fellow went up on one knee in the bow to aim at Jobson, Beason dropped him with the sweetest shot John had ever seen. John attempted to load on the run but made a mess of it, spilling black powder everywhere. By this time Jessup and Perkin had reached them, with Collyer limping close behind. They took positions behind the gravestones and commenced firing at the longboat's crew, only praying that Cullman and Jobson had the sense not to sink the longboat with an eight-pound ball.

It was over in a minute more, for the men in the longboat had to cover two targets at once, and couldn't do it. When the shooting stopped, there was no more damage to the *Martin Luther's* crew than Collyer's right ear, which was mainly clipped away by a ball from the longboat. He crouched, bleeding like a stuck pig and swearing most vile, as John peered out from behind Brother Casildo's gravestone.

"There's nobody moving on the longboat," he said.

"What about that bugger hanging over the gunwale?"

"I see three shot-holes in him," John replied. He got up cautiously and walked out on the beach. One by one the others rose and followed him. Cullman and Jobson hallooed from the ship, waving their hats.

"How do we get the boat back?" said Perkin.

"Anyone know how to swim?"

"Me," said John, and regretted it at once, thinking of Dooley's sorry end.

"Out you go, then," said Beason.

So John prayed as though it was a Sunday, and for all he knew it might have been, as he stripped off his coat and hat, and kicked off his shoes. The water was bright and clear as he waded out, nothing like sorry old Hackney Brook, and a beautiful blue except for the crimson place where the dead man hanging over the gunwale had bled into the water. And the Lord must have listened to John's prayers and nodded approvingly, for John made the side of the boat in safety, pocked up in splinters and musket-balls as it was, though he had to haul the dead man out as he scrambled in.

Now he saw that there were two other dead men floating a little ways off, face down. Three more were lying in the bottom of the boat, all shot to pieces except for one pockfaced lout who was lolling back with open eyes and bared teeth and a knife clenched in his fist—

With a scream the fellow sat up, and John screamed too and caught him by the wrist, and they struggled together a long moment, with the thwart cutting into John's shins something cruel. Shots rang out from the beach, but hummed past like bees; at last John broke the bugger's arm. He got the knife away from him and ran it into him twice, just where he supposed the heart might be, and the man gasped once and died. John pitched him out of the boat and sat there shivering, for all the heat of the sun.

When he'd done puking over the side, he rowed back to shore.

▲▼▲

John did wonder what had become of Captain Stalwin's luck, that was supposed to have changed. They all puzzled over it, after they'd elected Beason captain and were sailing away from there; and Perkin's idea made the most sense, which was that the luck under consideration was *their* luck, which was to say the whole crew's. Changing for the better, therefore, had included getting rid of a sorry bastard like Stalwin.

The other tale was what had really happened on the island, and they worked out several different stories for that, sitting under the stars as they drank their rum. Captain Beason's story seemed the likeliest, viz.: that the overseers had been left on the island with the Indians, but, being hardier, had survived the disease; and that they'd taken the Indian women, foul-faced or no, and murdered Brother Casildo. So they lived until the brothers Claveria Martinez came back, in seven years' time.

The brothers must have come ashore armed, not expecting anyone to have survived. One of the brothers must have been taken alive, with all he

brought ashore, including fresh arms and ammunition. The other must have
gotten away, back to Cartagena, and in course of time took passage on the
galleon that ran afoul of the *Martin Luther.*

▲▼▲

The *Martin Luther's* crew debated what they ought to do next. There
was some talk of going to Port Royal, but that was a chancy business; if the
wind of diplomacy was blowing the wrong way, a poor hard-working captain
might find a lot of Royal Marines demanding to see his privateer's com-
mission, and confiscating his spoils, and indeed he might just be hanged to
soothe Spanish feelings.

So in the end they went to Tortuga, where there were always folk willing to do business. The galleon's cargo was disposed of, a buyer found for the
emeralds, and every last penny of the profits counted out and divided up in
fair shares amongst the crew. John and Jessup walked away from the *Martin
Luther* rich men, at least as far as John was concerned. His pockets were like
to burst for the weight of his money.

"What'll you do with your share?" he asked Jessup, as they walked along.
There were yellow lights beckoning through the trees, and a smell of good
food and drink, and music. Jessup shook his head.

"Get myself a new name, and put this business as far behind me as ever
I can," he said. "Go somewhere no one knows my face. Set up in business,
live quiet and die rich in my bed. You'll do the same, boy, if you've any wit."

"I reckon I will, ay," said John.

They parted. John considered Jessup's advice, and knew it was good
advice, and heard the voice of his mother in his ear telling him it was good
advice too. He fully intended to follow it; but the yellow lights beckoned so,
and he could hear women laughing, and he thought he'd just go celebrate his
good fortune first.

He met a pretty French whore, who showed him where the best turtle
stew was to be had, and where the best rum was served. They had a pleasant
evening indeed, or at least what John could remember of it afterward, and
she showed him a great many other things too.

Next morning the sun was too bright, and John wandered queasy and
penniless along the waterfront, squinting at all the sleek rakish craft moored
there. He was hoping to find some of the *Martin Luther's* crew, as might be
willing to oblige an old shipmate with a loan. He didn't; but before long he

came to a ship taking on kegs of powder, and some men were talking there, with a look about them of cutlasses, and smoke, and easy money.

John listened to them chatting a while before dropping a friendly remark or two. By and by he joined the conversation, and pretty soon one of them asked him if he cared to go on the account.

John, ever so grateful, said he'd like that very much indeed.

They sailed next day, and had taken a galleon full of wine and silk before the week was out.

The Ruby Incomparable

The girl surprised everyone.

▲▼▲

To begin with, no one in the world below had thought her parents would have more children. Her parents' marriage had created quite a scandal, a profound clash of philosophical extremes; for her father was the Master of the Mountain, a brigand and sorcerer, who had carried the Saint of the World off to his high fortress. It's bad enough when a living goddess, who can heal the sick and raise the dead, takes up with a professional dark lord (black armor, monstrous armies and all). But when they settle down together with every intention of raising a family, what are respectable people to think?

The Yendri in their forest villages groaned when they learned of the first boy. Even in his cradle, his fiendish tendencies were evident. He was beautiful as a little angel except in his screaming tempers, when he would morph himself into giant larvae, wolf cubs or pools of bubbling slime.

The Yendri in their villages and the Children of the Sun in their stone cities all rejoiced when they heard of the second boy. He too was beautiful, but clearly good. A star was seen to shine from his brow on occasion. He was reported to have cured a nurse's toothache with a mere touch, and he never so much as cried while teething.

And the shamans of the Yendri, and the priests in the temples of the Children of the Sun, all nodded their heads and said: "Well, at least we have balance now. The two boys will obviously grow up, oppose each other and fight to the death, because that's what generally happens."

Having decided all this, and settled down confidently to wait, imagine how shocked they were to hear that the Saint of the World had borne a third child! And a girl, at that. It threw all their calculations off and annoyed them a great deal.

The Master and his Lady were surprised, too, because their baby daughter popped into the world homely as a little potato, by contrast with the elfin beauty of her brothers. They did agree that she had lovely eyes, at least, dark as her father's, and she seemed to be sweet-tempered. They named her Svnae.

So the Master of the Mountain swaddled her in purple silk, and took her out on a high balcony and held her up before his assembled troops, who roared, grunted and howled their polite approval. And that night in the barracks and servants' hall, around the barrels of black wine that had been served out in celebration, the minions of the proud father agreed amongst themselves that the little maid might not turn out so ugly as all that, if the rest of her face grew to fit that nose and she didn't stay quite so bald.

And they at least were proved correct, for within a year Svnae had become a lovely child.

▲▼▲

On the morning of her fifth birthday, the Master went to the nursery and fetched his little daughter. He took her out with him on his tour of the battlements, where all the world stretched away below. The guards, tusked and fanged, great and horrible in their armor, stood to attention and saluted him. Solemnly he pulled a great red rose from thin air and presented it to Svnae.

"Today," he said, "my Dark-Eyed is five years old. What do you want most in all the world, daughter?"

Svnae looked up at him with her shining eyes. Very clearly she said: "Power."

He looked down at her, astounded; but she stood there looking patiently back at him, clutching her red rose. He knelt beside her. "Do you know what Power is?" he asked.

"Yes," she said. "Power is when you stand up here and make all the clouds come to you across the sky, and shoot lightning and make thunder crash. That's what I want."

"I can make magic for you," he said, and with a wave of his gauntleted hand produced three tiny fire elementals dressed in scarlet, blue and yellow, who danced enchantingly for Svnae before vanishing in a puff of smoke.

"Thank you, Daddy," she said, "but no. I want *me* to be able to do it."

Slowly he nodded his head. "Power you were born with; you're my child. But you must learn to use it, and that doesn't come easily, or quickly. Are you sure this is what you really want?"

"Yes," she said without hesitation.

"Not eldritch toys to play with? Not beautiful clothes? Not sweets?"

"If I learn Power, I can have all those things anyway," Svnae observed.

The Master was pleased with her answer. "Then you will learn to use your Power," he said. "What would you like to do first?"

"I want to learn to fly," she said. "Not like my brother Eyrdway. He just turns into birds. I want to stay me and fly."

"Watch my hands," her father said. In his right hand he held out a stone; in his left, a paper dart. He put them both over the parapet and let go. The stone dropped; the paper dart drifted lazily down.

"Now, tell me," he said. "Why did the stone drop and the paper fly?"

"Because the stone is heavy and the paper isn't," she said.

"Nearly so; and not so. Look." And he pulled from the air an egg. He held it out in his palm, and the egg cracked. A tiny thing crawled from it, and lay shivering there a moment; white down covered it like dandelion fluff, and it drew itself upright and shook tiny stubby wings. The down transformed to shining feathers, and the young bird beat its wide wings and flew off rejoicing.

"Now, tell me," said the Master, "Was that magic?"

"No," said Svnae. "That's just what happens with birds."

"Nearly so; and not so. Look." And he took out another stone. He held it up and uttered a Word of Power; the stone sprouted bright wings, and improbably flew away into the morning.

"How did you make it do that?" Svnae cried. Her father smiled at her.

"With Power; but Power is not enough. I was able to transform the stone because I understand that the bird and the stone, and even the paper dart, are all the same thing."

"But they're not," said Svnae.

"Aren't they?" said her father. "When you understand that the stone and the bird are one, the next step is convincing the *stone* that the bird and the stone are one. And then the stone can fly."

Svnae bit her lip. "This is hard, isn't it?" she said.

"Very," said the Master of the Mountain. "Are you sure you wouldn't like a set of paints instead?"

"Yes," said Svnae stubbornly. "I *will* understand."

"Then I'll give you books to study," he promised. He picked her up and folded her close, in his dark cloak. He carried her to the bower of her lady mother, the Saint of the World.

Now when the Lady had agreed to marry her dread Lord, she had won from him the concession of making a garden on his black basalt mountaintop, high and secret in the sunlit air. Ten years into their marriage her orchards were a mass of white blossom, and her white-robed disciples tended green beds of herbs there. They bowed gracefully as Svnae ran to her mother, who embraced her child and gave her a white rose. And Svnae said proudly:

"I'm going to learn Power, Mama!"

The Lady looked questions at her Lord.

"It's what she wants," he said, no less proudly. "And if she has the talent, why shouldn't she learn?"

"But Power is not an end in itself, my child," the Lady said to her daughter. "To what purpose will you use it? Will you help others?"

"Ye-es," said Svnae, looking down at her feet. "But I have to learn first."

"Wouldn't you like to be a healer, like me?"

"I can heal people when I have Power," said Svnae confidently. Her mother looked a little sadly into her dark eyes, but saw no shadow there. So she blessed her daughter, and sent her off to play.

▲▼▲

The Master of the Mountain kept his promise and gave his daughter books to study, to help her decipher the Three Riddles of Flight. She had to learn to read first; with fiery determination she hurled herself on her letters and mastered them, and charged into the first of the Arcane texts.

So well she studied that by her sixth birthday she had solved all three riddles, and was able at will to sprout little butterfly wings from her shoulders, wings as red as a rose. She couldn't fly much with them, only fluttering a few inches above the ground like a baby bird; but she was only six. One day she would soar.

Then it was the Speech of Animals she wanted to learn. Then it was how to move objects without touching them. Then she desired to know the names of all the stars in the sky: not only what men call them, but what they call themselves. And one interest led to another, as endlessly she found new things by which to be intrigued, new arts and sciences she wanted to learn. She spent whole days together in her father's library, and carried books back to her room, and sat up reading far into the night.

In this manner she learned to fly up to the clouds with her rose-red wings, there to ask an eagle what it had for breakfast, or gather pearls with her own hands from the bottom of the sea.

And so the years flowed by, as the Master throve on his mountain, and the Saint of the World brought more children into it to confound the expectations of priests and philosophers, who debated endlessly the question of whether these children were Good or Evil.

The Saint held privately that all her children were, at heart, Good. The Master of the Mountain held, privately and out loud too, that the priests and philosophers were all a bunch of idiots.

Svnae grew tall, with proud dark good looks she had from her father. But there were no black lightnings in her eyes, as there were in his. Neither were her eyes crystal and serene, like her mother's, but all afire with interest, eager to see how everything worked.

And then she grew taller still, until she overtopped her mother; and still taller than that, until she overtopped her brother Eyrdway. He was rather peevish about it and took to calling her The Giantess, until she punched him hard enough to knock out one of his teeth. He merely morphed into a version of himself without the missing tooth, but he stopped teasing her after that.

Now you might suppose that many a young guard might begin pining for Svnae, and saluting smartly as she passed by, and mourning under her window at night. You would be right. But she never noticed; she was too engrossed in her studies to hear serenades sung under her window. Still, they did not go to waste; her younger sisters could hear them perfectly well, and *they* noticed things like snappy salutes.

This was not to say that Svnae did not glory in being a woman. As soon as she was old enough, she chose her own gowns and jewelry. Her mother presented her with gauzes delicate as cobweb, in exquisite shades of lavender, sea mist and bird-egg-blue; fine-worked silver ornaments as well, set with white diamonds that glinted like starlight.

Alas, Svnae's tastes ran to crimson and purple and cloth of gold, even though the Saint of the World explained how well white set off her dusk skin. And though she thanked her mother for the fragile silver bangles, and dutifully wore them at family parties, she cherished massy gold set with emeralds and rubies. The more finery the better, in fact, though her mother gently indicated that perhaps it wasn't quite in the best of taste to wear the serpent bracelets with eyes of topaz *and* the peacock necklace of turquoise, jade and lapis lazuli.

And though Svnae read voraciously and mastered the arts of Transmutation of Metals, Divination by Bones and Summoning Rivers by their Secret Names, she did not learn to weave nor to sew; nor did she learn the healing properties of herbs. Her mother waited patiently for Svnae to become interested in these things, but somehow the flashing beam of her eye never turned to them.

One afternoon the Master of the Mountain looked up from the great black desk whereat he worked, hearing the guards announce the approach of his eldest daughter. A moment later she strode into his presence, resplendent in robes of scarlet and peacock blue, and slippers of vermilion with especially pointy toes that curled up at the ends.

"Daughter," he said, rising to his feet.

"Daddy," she replied, "I've just been reading in the Seventh Pomegranate Scroll about a distillation of violets that can be employed to lure dragons. Can you show me how to make it?"

"I've never done much distillation, my child," said the Master of the Mountain. "That's more in your mother's line of work. I'm certain she'd be delighted to teach you. Why don't you ask her?"

"Oh," said Svnae, and flushed, and bit her lip, and stared at the floor. "I think she's busy with some seminar with her disciples. Meditation Techniques or something."

And though the Master of the Mountain had never had any use for his lady wife's disciples, he spoke sternly. "Child, you know your mother has never ignored her own children for her followers."

"It's not that," said Svnae a little sullenly, twisting a lock of her raven hair. "Not at all. It's just that—well—we're bound to have an argument about it. She'll want to know what I want it for, for one thing, and she won't approve of my catching dragons, and she'll let me know it even if she doesn't say a word, she'll just *look* at me—"

"I know," said her dread father.

"As though it was a frivolous waste of time, when what I really ought to be doing is learning all her cures for fevers, which is all very well but I have other things I want to be learning first, and in any case *I'm not Mother,* I'm my *own* person, and she has to understand that!"

"I'm certain she does, my child."

"Yes." Svnae tossed her head back. "So. Well. This brings up something else I'd wanted to ask you. I think I ought to go down into the world to study."

"But—" said the Master of the Mountain.

"I've always wanted to, and it turns out there's a sort of secret school in a place called Konen Feyy-in-the-Trees, where anybody can go to learn distillations. I need to learn more!"

"Mm. But—" said the Master of the Mountain.

She got her way. Not with temper, tears or foot-stamping, but she got her way. No more than a week later she took a bag, and her bow and quiver, and climbing up on the parapet she summoned her rose-red wings, that now swept from a yard above her dark head to her ankles. Spreading them on the wind, she soared aloft. Away she went like a queen of the air, to explore the world.

Her father and mother watched her go.

"Do you think she'll be safe?" said the Saint of the World.

"She'd better be," said the Master of the Mountain, looking over the edge and far down his mountain at the pair of ogre bodyguards who coursed like armored greyhounds, crashing through the trees, following desperately their young mistress while doing their best not to draw attention to themselves.

Svnae sailed off on the wind and discovered that, though her extraordinary heritage had given her many gifts, a sense of direction was not one of them. She cast about a long while, looking for any place that might be a city in the trees; at last she spotted a temple in a wooded valley, far below.

On landing, she discovered that the temple was deserted long since, and a great gray monster guarded it. She slew the creature with her arrows, and went in to see what it might have been guarding. On the altar was a golden box that shone with protective spells. But she had the magic to unlock those spells, and found within a book that seemed to be a history of the lost race whose temple this was. She carried it outside and spent the next few hours seated on a block of stone in the ruins, intent with her chin on her fist, reading.

Within the book, she read of a certain crystal ring, the possession of which would enable the wearer to understand the Speech of Water. The book directed her to a certain fountain an hour's flight south of the temple, and fortunately the temple had a compass rose mosaic set in the floor; so she flew south at once, just as her bodyguards came panting up to the temple at last, and they watched her go with language that was dreadful even for ogres.

Exactly an hour's flight south, Svnae spotted the fountain, rising from a ruined courtyard of checkered tile. Here she landed, and approached the fountain with caution; for there lurked within its bowl a scaled serpent of remarkable beauty and deadliest venom. She considered the jeweled serpent, undulating round and round within the bowl in a lazy sort of way. She considered the ring, a circle of clear crystal, hard to spot as it bobbed at the top of the fountain's jet, well beyond her reach even were she to risk the serpent. Backing away several paces, she drew an arrow and took aim. *Clink!*

Her arrow shuddered in the trunk of an oak thirty paces distant, with the ring still spinning on its shaft. Speedily she claimed it and put it on, and straightaway she could understand the Speech of Water.

Whereupon the fountain told her of a matter so interesting that she had to learn more about it. Details, however, were only to be had from a little blue man who lived in dubious hills far to the west. So away she flew, to find him...

She had several other adventures and it was only by chance that, soaring one morning above the world, deep in conversation with a sea-eagle, she spotted what was clearly a city down below amongst great trees. To her inquiry, the sea-eagle replied that the city was Konen Feyy. She thanked it and descended through the bright morning, to a secluded grove where she could cast a glamour on herself and approach without attracting undue notice. Following unseen a league distant, her wheezing bodyguards threw themselves down and gave thanks to anyone who might be listening.

▲▼▲

The Children of the Sun dwelt generally in cities all of stone, where scarcely a blade of grass grew nor even so much as a potted geranium, preferring instead rock gardens with obelisks and statuary. But in all races there are those who defy the norm, and so it was in Konen Feyy. Here a colony of artists and craftsmen had founded a city in the green wilderness, without even building a comfortingly high wall around themselves. Accordingly, a lot of them had died from poisoned arrows and animal attacks in the early years, but this only seemed to make them more determined to stay there.

They painted the local landscapes, they made pots of the local clay, and wove textiles from the local plant fibers; and they even figured out that if they cut down the local trees to make charmingly rustic wooden furniture, sooner or later there wouldn't be any trees. For the Children of the Sun, who were ordinarily remarkably dense about ecological matters, this was a real breakthrough.

And so the other peoples of the world ventured up to Konen Feyy. The forest-dwelling Yendri, the Saint's own people, opened little shops where were sold herbs, or freshwater pearls, or willow baskets, or fresh produce. Other folk came, too: solitary survivors of lesser-known races, obscure revenants, searching for a quiet place to set up shop. This was how the Night School came to exist.

Svnae, wandering down Konen Feyy's high street and staring around her, found the place at once. Though it looked like an ordinary perfumer's shop, there were certain signs on the wall above the door, visible only to those who were familiar with the arcane sciences. An extravagant green cursive explained the School's hours, where and how she might enroll, and where to find appropriate lodgings with other students.

In this last she was lucky, for it happened that there were three other daughters of magi who'd taken a place above a dollmaker's shop, and hadn't quite enough money between them to make the monthly rent, so they were looking for a fourth roommate, someone to be Earth to their Air, Fire and Water. They were pleasant girls, though Svnae was somewhat taken aback to discover that she towered over them all three, and somewhat irritated to discover that they all held her mother in reverent awe.

"You're the daughter of *the* Saint of the World?" exclaimed Seela, whose father was Principal Thaumaturge for Mount Flame City. "What are you doing here, then? *She's* totally the best at distillations and essences. Everyone knows that! *I'd* give anything to learn from her."

Svnae was to hear this statement repeated, with only slight variations, over the next four years of her higher education. She learned not to mind, however; for her studies occupied half her attention, and the other half was all spent on discovering the strange new world in which she lived, where there were no bodyguards (of which she was aware, anyway) and only her height distinguished her from all the other young ladies she met.

It was tremendous fun. She chipped in money with her roommates to buy a couch for their sitting room, and the four of them pushed it up the steep flight of stairs with giggles and screams, though Svnae could have tucked it under one arm and carried it up herself with no effort. She dined with her roommates at the little fried-fish shop on the corner, where they had their particular booth in which they always sat, though Svnae found it rather cramped.

She listened sympathetically as first one and then another of her roommates fell in love with various handsome young seers and sorcerers, and she swept up after a number of riotous parties, and on one occasion broke a vase over the head of a young shapeshifter who, while nice enough when sober, turned into something fairly unpleasant when he became unwisely intoxicated. She had to throw him over her shoulder and pitch him down the stairs, and her roommates wept their thanks and all agreed they didn't know what they'd do without her.

But somehow Svnae never fell in love.

It wasn't because she had no suitors for her hand. There were several young gallants at the Night School, glittering with jewelry and strange habits, who sought to romance Svnae. One was an elemental fire-lord with burning hair; one was a lord of air with vast violet wings. One was a mer-lord, who had servants following him around with perfumed misting bottles to keep his skin from drying out.

But all of them made it pretty clear they desired to marry Svnae in order to forge dynastic unions with the Master of the Mountain. And Svnae had long since decided that love, real Love, was the only reason for getting involved in all the mess and distraction of romance. So she declined, gracefully, and the young lords sulked and found other wealthy girls to entreat.

Her course of study ended. The roommates all bid one another fond farewells and went their separate ways. Svnae returned home with a train of attendant spirits carrying presents for all her little nieces and nephews. But she did not stay long, for she had heard of a distant island where was written, in immense letters on cliffs of silver, the formula for reversing Time in small and manageable fields, and she desired to learn it…

▲▼▲

"Svnae's turned out rather well," said the Master of the Mountain, as he retired one night. "I could wish she spent a little more time at home, all the same. I'd have thought she'd have married and settled down by now, like the boys."

"She's restless," said the Saint of the World, as she combed out her hair.

"Well, why should she be? A first-rate sorceress with a double degree? The Ruby Incomparable, they call her. What more does she want?"

"She doesn't know, yet," said the Saint of the World, and blew out the light. "But she'll know when she finds it."

▲▼▲

And Svnae had many adventures.

But one day, following up an obscure reference in an ancient grimoire, it chanced that she desired to watch a storm in its rage over the wide ocean, and listen to the wrath of all the waters. Out she flew upon a black night in the late year, when small craft huddled at their moorings, and found what she sought.

There had never in all the world been such a storm. The white foam was beaten into air, the white air was charged with water, the shrieking white gulls wheeled and screamed across the black sky, and the waves were as valleys and mountains.

Svnae floated in a bubble of her own devising, protected, watching it all with interest. Suddenly, far below in a trough of water, she saw a tiny figure clinging to a scrap of wood. The trough became a wall of water that rose up, towering high, until into her very eyes stared the drowning man. In his astonishment he let go the shattered mast that supported him, and sank out of sight like a stone.

She cried out and dove from her bubble into the wave. Down she went, through water like dark glass, and caught him by the hand; up she went, towing him with her, and got him into the air and wrapped her strong arms about him. She could not fly, not with wet wings in the storm, but she summoned sea-beasts to bear them to the nearest land.

This was merely an empty rock, white cliffs thrusting from the sea. By magic she raised a palace from the stones to shelter them, and she brought the man within. Here there was a roaring fire; here there was hot food and wine. She put him to rest all unconscious in a deep bed, and tended him with her own hands.

Days she watched and cared for him, until he was well enough to speak to her. By that time, he had her heart.

Now, he was not as handsome as a mage-lord, nor learned in any magic, nor born of ancient blood: he was only a toymaker from the cities of the Children of the Sun, named Kendach. But so long and anxiously had she watched his sleeping face that she saw it when she closed her eyes.

And of course when Kendach opened his, the first thing he saw was her face: and after that, it was love. How could it be otherwise?

They nested together, utterly content, until it occurred to them that their families might wonder where they were. So she took him home to meet her parents ("A *toymaker*?" hooted her brothers) and he took her home to meet his ("Very nice girl. A little tall, but nice," said his unsuspecting father. They chose not to enlighten him as to their in-laws).

They were married in a modest ceremony in Konen Feyy.

"I hope he's not going to have trouble with her brothers," fretted Kendach's father, that night in the innroom. "Did you see the way they glared? Particularly that good-looking one. It quite froze my blood."

"It's clear she gets her height from her father," said Kendach's mother, pouring tea for him. "*Very* distinguished businessman, as I understand it. Runs some kind of insurance firm. I do wonder why her mother wears that veil, though, don't you?"

Kendach opened a toyshop in Konen Feyy, where he made kites in the forms of insects, warships and meteors. Svnae raised a modest palace among the trees, and they lived there in wedded bliss. And life was full for Svnae, with nothing else to be asked for.

And then…

One day she awoke and there was a grey stain on the face of the sun. She blinked and rubbed her eyes. It did not go away. It came and sat on top of her morning tea. It blotted the pages of the books she tried to read, and it lay like grime on her lover's face. She couldn't get rid of it, nor did she know from whence it had come.

Svnae took steps to find out. She went to a cabinet and got down a great black globe of crystal, that shone and swam with deep fires. She went to a quiet place and stroked the globe until it glowed with electric crackling fires. At last these words floated up out of the depths:

YOUR MOTHER DOES NOT UNDERSTAND YOU

They rippled on the surface of the globe, pulsing softly. She stared at them and they did not change.

So she pulled on her cloak that was made of peacock feathers, and yoked up a team of griffins to a sky chariot (useful when your lover has no wings, and flies only kites) and flew off to visit her mother.

The Saint of the World sat alone in her garden, by a quiet pool of reflecting water. She wore a plain white robe. White lilies glowed with light on the surface of the water; distantly a bird sang. She meditated, her crystal eyes serene.

There was a flash of color on the water. She looked up to see her eldest daughter charging across the sky. The griffin-chariot thundered to a landing nearby and Svnae dismounted, pulling her vivid cloak about her. She went straight to her mother and knelt.

"Mother, I need to talk to you," she said. "Is it true that you don't understand me?"

The Saint of the World thought it over.

"Yes, it's true," she said at last. "I don't understand you. I'm sorry, dearest. Does it make a difference?"

"Have I disappointed you, Mother?" asked Svnae in distress.

The Lady thought very carefully about that one.

"No," she said finally. "I would have liked a daughter to be interested in the healing arts. It just seems like the sort of thing a mother ought to pass on to her daughter. But your brother Demaledon has been all I could have asked for in a pupil, and there are all my disciples. And why should your life be a reprise of mine?"

"None of the other girls became healers," said Svnae just a little petulantly.

"Quite true. They've followed their own paths: lovers and husbands and babies, gardens and dances."

"I have a husband too, you know," said Svnae.

"My child, my Dark-Eyed, I rejoice in your happiness. Isn't that enough?"

"But I want you to *understand* my life," cried Svnae.

"Do you understand mine?" asked the Saint of the World.

"Your life? Of course I do!"

Her mother looked at her, wryly amused.

"I have borne your father fourteen children. I have watched him march away to do terrible things, and I have bound up his wounds when he returned from doing them. I have managed the affairs of a household with over a thousand servants, most of them ogres. I have also kept up correspondence with my poor disciples, who are trying to carry on my work in my absence. What would you know of these things?"

Svnae was silent at that.

"You have always hunted for treasures, my dearest, and thrown open every door you saw, to know what lay beyond it," said the Saint of the World gently. "But there are still doors you have not opened. We can love each other, you and I, but how can we understand each other?"

"There must be a way," said Svnae.

"Now you look so much like your father you make me laugh and cry at once. Don't let it trouble you, my Dark-Eyed; you are strong and happy and good, and I rejoice."

But Svnae went home that night to the room where Kendach sat, painting bright and intricate birds on kites. She took a chair opposite and stared at him.

"I want to have a child," she said.

He looked up, blinking in surprise. As her words sank in on him, he smiled and held out his arms to her.

Did she have a child? How else, when she had accomplished everything else she wanted to do?

A little girl came into the world. She was strong and healthy. She looked like her father, she looked like her mother; but mostly she looked like herself, and she surprised everyone.

Her father had been one of many children, so there were fewer surprises for him. He knew how to bathe a baby, and could wrestle small squirming arms into sleeves like an expert.

Svnae, who had grown up in a nursery staffed by a dozen servants, proved to be rather inept at these things. She was shaken by her helplessness, and shaken by the helpless love she felt. Prior to this time she had found infants rather uninteresting, little blobs in swaddling to be briefly inspected and presented with silver cups that had their names and a good-fortune spell engraved on them.

But *her* infant—! She could lie for hours watching her child do no more than sleep, marveling at the tiny toothless yawn, the slow close of a little hand.

When the baby was old enough to travel, they wrapped her in a robe trimmed with pearls and took her to visit her maternal grandparents, laden with the usual gifts. Her lover went off to demonstrate the workings of his marvelous kites to her nieces and nephews. And Svnae bore her daughter to the Saint of the World in triumph.

"*Now* I've done something you understand," she said. The Saint of the World took up her little granddaughter and kissed her between the eyes.

"I hope that wasn't the only reason you bore her," she said.

"Well—no, of course not," Svnae protested, blushing. "I wanted to find out what motherhood was like."

"And what do you think it is like, my child?"

"It's awesome. It's holy. My entire life has been redefined by her existence," said Svnae fervently.

"Ah, yes," said the Saint of the World.

"I mean, this is creation at its roots. This is Power! I have brought an entirely new being into the world. A little mind that thinks! I can't wait to see what she thinks *about*, how she feels about things, what she'll say and do. What's ordinary magic to this?"

The baby began to fuss and the Lady rose to walk with her through the garden. Svnae followed close, groping for words.

"There's so much I can teach her, so much I can give her, so much I can share with her. Her first simple spells. Her first flight. Her first transformation. I'll teach her everything I know. We've got that house in Konen Feyy, and it'll be so convenient for Night School! She won't even have to find room and board. She can use all my old textbooks…"

But the baby kept crying, stretching out her little hands.

"Something she wants already," said the Lady. She picked a white flower and offered it to the child; but no, the little girl pointed beyond it. Svnae held out a crystal pendant, glittering with power, throwing dancing lights; but the baby cried and reached upward. They looked up to see one of her father's kites, dancing merry and foolish on the wind.

The two women stood staring at it. They looked at the little girl. They looked at each other.

"Perhaps you shouldn't enroll her in Night School just yet," said the Saint of the World.

And Svnae realized, with dawning horror, that she might need to ask her mother for advice.

Plotters and Shooters

I was flackeying for Lord Deathlok and Dr. Smash when the shuttle brought the new guy.

I hate Lord Deathlok. I hate Dr. Smash too, but I'd like to see Lord Deathlok get a missile fired up his ass, from his own cannon. Not that it's really a cannon. And I couldn't shoot him, anyhow, because I'm only a Plotter. But it's the thought that counts, you know?

Anyway I looked up when the beeps and the flashing lights started, and Lord Deathlok took hold of my little French maid's apron and yanked it so hard I had to bend over fast, so I almost dropped the tray with his drink.

"Pay attention, maggot-boy," said Lord Deathlok. "It's only a shuttle docking. No reason you should be distracted from your duties."

"I know what's wrong," said Dr. Smash, lounging back against the bar. "He hears the mating call of his kind. They must have sent up another Plotter."

"Oh, yeah." Lord Deathlok grinned at me. "Your fat-ass girlfriend went crying home to his mum and dad, didn't he?"

Oh, man, how I hated him. He was talking about Kev, who'd only gone Down Home again because he'd almost died in an asthma attack. Kev had been a good Plotter, one of the best. I just glared at Deathlok, which was a mistake, because he smiled and put his boot on my foot and stood up.

"I don't think I heard your answer, Fifi," he said, and I was in all this unbelievable psychological pain, see, because even with the lower gravity he could still manage to get the leverage just right if he wanted to bear down. They tell us we don't have to worry about getting brittle bones up here because they make us do weight-training, but how would we know if they were lying? I could almost hear my metatarsals snapping like dry twigs.

"Yes, my Lord Deathlok," I said.

"What?" He leaned forward.

"My lord yes my Lord Deathlok!"

"That's better." He sat down.

So okay, you're probably thinking I'm a coward. I'm not. It isn't that Lord Deathlok is even a big guy. He isn't, actually, he's sort of skinny and he has these big yellow buck teeth that make him look like a demon jackrabbit. And Dr. Smash has breasts and a body odor that makes sharing an airlock with him a fatal mistake. But they're *Shooters*, you know? And they all dress like they're space warriors or something, with the jackets and the boots and the scary hair styles. Shracking fascists.

So I put down his Dis Pepsy and backed away from him, and that was when the announcement came over the speakers:

"Eugene Clifford, please report to Mr. Kurtz's office."

Talk about saved by the bell. As the message repeated, Lord Deathlok smirked.

"Sounds like Dean Kurtz is lonesome for one of his little buttboys. You have our permission to go, Fifi."

"My lord thank you my Lord Deathlok," I muttered, and tore off the apron and ran for the companionway.

Mr. Kurtz isn't a dean, I don't know why the Shooters call him that. He's the Station Manager. He runs the place for Areco and does our performance reviews and signs our bonus vouchers, and you'd think the Shooters would treat him with a little more respect, but they don't because they're *Shooters*, and that says it all. Mostly he sits in his office and looks disappointed. I don't blame him.

He looked up from his novel as I put my head around the door.

"You wanted to see me, Mr. Kurtz?"

He nodded. "New arrival on the shuttle. Kevin Nederlander's replacement. Would you bring him up, please?"

"Yes, sir!" I said, and hurried off to the shuttle lounge.

The new guy was sitting there in the lounge, with his duffel in the chair beside his. He was short and square and his haircut made his head look like it came to a point. Maybe it's genetic; Plotters can't seem to get good haircuts, ever.

"Welcome to the Gun Platform, newbie," I said. "I'm your Orientation Officer." Which I sort of am.

"Oh, good," he said, getting to his feet, but he couldn't seem to take his eyes off the viewscreen. I waited for him to ask if that was really Mars down there, or gush about how he couldn't believe he was actually on an alien world or at least in orbit above one. That's usually what they do, see. But he didn't. He just shouldered his duffel and tore his gaze away at last.

"Charles Tead. Glad to be here," he said.

Heh! That'll change, I thought. "You've got some righteous shoes to fill, newbie. Think you're up to it?"

He just said that he was, not like he was bragging or anything, and I thought *This one's going to get his corners broken off really soon.*

So I took him to the Forecastle and showed him Kev's old bunk, looking all empty and sad with the drillholes where Kev's holoposters used to be mounted. He put his duffel into Kev's old locker and looked around, and then he asked who did our laundry. I coughed a little and explained about it being sent down to the planet to be dry-cleaned. I didn't tell him, not then, about our having to collect the Shooters' dirty socks and stuff for them.

And I took him to the Bridge where B Shift was on duty and introduced him to the boys. Roscoe and Norman were wearing their Jedi robes, which I wish they wouldn't because it makes us look hopeless. Vinder was in a snit because Bradley had knocked one of his action figures behind the console, and apparently it was one of the really valuable ones, and Myron's the only person skinny enough to get his arm back there to fish it out, but he's on C Shift and wouldn't come on duty until seventeen-hundred hours.

I guess that was where it started, B Shift making such a bad first impression.

But I tried to bring back some sense of importance by showing him the charting display, with the spread of the asteroid belt all in blue and gold, like a stained glass window in an old-time church must have been, only everything moving.

"This is your own personal slice of the sky," I said, waving at Q34-54. "Big Kev knew every one of these babies. Tracked every little wobble, every deviation over three years. Plotted trajectories for thirty-seven successful shots. It was like he had a sixth sense! He even called three Intruders before they came in range. He was the Bonus Master, old Kev. You'll have to work pretty damn hard to be half as good as he was."

"But it ought to be easy," said Charles. "Doesn't the mapping software do most of it?"

"Well, like, I mean, sure, but you'll have to *coordinate* everything, you know? In your head? Machines can't do it all," I protested. And Vinder chose that second to yell from behind us, "Don't take the Flying Dynamo's cape off, you'll break him!" Which totally blew the mood I was trying to get. So I ignored him and continued:

"We've been called up from Earth for a job only we can do. It's a high and lonely destiny, up here among the cold stars! Mundane people couldn't stick it out. That's why Areco went looking for guys like us. We're free of entanglements, right? We came from our parents' basements and garages to a place where our powers were *needed*. Software can map those rocks out there, okay; it can track them, maybe. But only a human can—can—smell them coming in before they're there, okay?"

"You mean like precognition?" Charles stared at me.

"Not exactly," I said, even though Myron claims he's got psychic abilities, but he never seems to be able to predict when the Shooters are going to go on a rampage on our turf. "I'm talking about gut feelings. Hunches. Instinct! That's the word I was looking for. Human instinct. We outguess the software seventy per cent of the time on projected incoming. Not bad, huh?"

"I guess so," he said.

I spent the rest of the shift showing him his console and setting up his passwords and customizations and stuff. He didn't ask many questions, just put on the goggles and focused, and you could almost see him wandering around among the asteroids in Q34-54 and getting to know them. I was starting to get a good feeling about him, because that was just the way Kev used to plot, and then he said:

"How do we target them?"

Vinder was so shocked he dropped the Blue Judge. Roscoe turned, took off his goggles to stare at me, and said:

"*We* don't target. Cripes, haven't you told him?"

"Told me what?" Charles turned his goggled face toward the sound of Roscoe's voice.

So then I had to tell him about the Shooters, and how he couldn't go into the bar when Shooters were in there except when he was flackeying for one of them, and what they'd do to him if he did, and how he had to stay out of the Pit of Hell where they bunked except when he was flackeying for them, and he was never under any circumstances to go into the War Room at all.

I was explaining about the flackeying rotation when he said:

"This is stupid!"

"It's sheer evil," said Roscoe. "But there's nothing we can do about it. They're Shooters. You can't fight them. You don't want to know what happens if you try."

"This wasn't in my contract," said Charles.

"You can go complain to Kurtz, if you want," said Bradley. "It's no damn use. *He* can't control them. They're Shooters. Nobody else can do what they do."

"I'll bet I could," said Charles, and everybody just sniffed at him, because, you know, who's got reflexes like a Shooter? They're the best at what they do.

"You got assigned to us because you tested out as a Plotter," I told Charles. "That's just the way things are. You're the best at your job; the pay's good; in five years you'll be out of here. You just have to learn to live with the crap. We all did."

He looked like a smart guy and I thought he wouldn't need to be told twice. I was wrong.

We heard the march of booted feet coming along the corridor. Vinder leaped up and grabbed all his action figures, shoving them into a storage pod. Norman began to hyperventilate; Bradley ran for the toilet. I just stayed where I was and lowered my eyes. It's never a good idea to look them in the face.

Boom! The portal jerked open and in they came, Lord Deathlok and the Shark and Iron Beast. They were carrying Piki-tiki. I blanched.

Piki-tiki was this sort of dummy they'd made out of a blanket and a mask. And a few other things. Lord Deathlok grinned around and spotted Charles.

"Piki-tiki returns to his harem," he shouted. "What's this? Piki-tiki sees a new and beautiful bride! Piki-tiki must welcome her to his realm!"

Giggling, they advanced on Charles and launched the dummy. It fell over him, and before he could throw it off they'd jumped him and hoisted him between them. He was fighting hard, but they just laughed; that is, until he got one arm free and punched the Shark in the face. The Shark grabbed his nose and began to swear, but Lord Deathlok and Iron Beast gloated.

"Whoa! The blushing bride needs to learn her manners. Piki-tiki's going to take her off to his honeymoon suite and see that she learns them well!"

Ouch. They dragged him away. At least it wasn't the worst they might have done to him; they were only going to cram him in one of the lockers, probably one that had had some sweaty socks left in the bottom, and stuff Piki-tiki in there on top of him. Then they'd lock him in and leave him there. How did I know? They'd done it to me, on my first day.

▲▼▲

If you're sensible, like me, you just shrug it off and concentrate on your job. Charles wouldn't let it go, though. He kept asking questions.

Like, how come the Shooters were paid better than we were, even though they spent most of their time playing simulations and Plotters did all the actual work of tracking asteroids and calculating when they'd strike? How come Mr. Kurtz had given up on disciplinary action for them, even after they'd rigged his holoset to come on unexpectedly and project a CGI of him having sex with an alligator, or all the other little ways in which they made his life a living hell? How come none of us ever stood up to them?

And it was no good explaining how they didn't respond to reason, and they didn't respond to being called immature and crude and disgusting, because they just loved being told how awful they were.

The other thing he asked about was why there weren't any women up here, and that was too humiliating to go into, so I just said tests had shown that men were better suited for life on a Gun Platform.

He should have been happy that he was a *good* Plotter, because he really was. He mastered Q34-54 in a week. One shift we were there on the Bridge and Myron and I were talking about the worst ever episode of *Schrödinger's Rock*, which was the one that had Lallal's evil twin showing up after being killed off in the second season, and Anil was unwrapping the underwear his mother had sent him for his thirty-first birthday, when suddenly Charles said: "Eugene, you should probably check Q6-17; I'm calculating an Intruder showing up in about Q-14."

"How'd you know?" I said in surprise, slipping my goggles on. But he was right; there was an Intruder, tumbling end over end in a halo of fire and snow, way above the plane of the ecliptic but square in Q-14.

"Don't you extend your projections beyond the planet's ecliptic?" said Charles.

Myron and I looked at each other. We never projected out that far; what was the point? There was always time to spot an Intruder before it came in range.

"You don't have to work *that* hard, dude," I said. "Fifty degrees above and below is all we have to bother with. The scanning programs catch the rest." But I sent out the alert and we could hear the Shooters cheering, even though the War Room was clear at the other end of the Platform. As far out as the Intruder was, the Shark was able to send out a missile. We didn't see the hit—there wouldn't be one for two weeks at least, and I'd have to keep monitoring the Intruder and now the missile too, just to be sure the trajectories remained matched up—but the Shooters began to stamp and roar the Bonus Song.

Myron sniffed.

"Typical," he said. "We do all the work, they push one bloody button, and *they're* the heroes."

"You know, it doesn't have to be this way," said Charles.

"It's not like we can go on strike," said Anil sullenly. "We're independent contractors. There's a penalty for quitting."

"You don't have to quit," said Charles. "You can show Areco you can do even more. We can be Plotters *and* Shooters."

Anil and Myron looked horrified. You'd have thought he'd suggested we all turn homo or something. I was shocked myself. I had to explain about tests proving that things functioned most smoothly when every man kept to his assigned task.

"Doesn't Areco think we can multitask?" he asked me. "They're a corporation like any other, aren't they? They must want to save money. All we have to do is show them we can do both jobs. The Shooters get a nice redundancy package, we get the Gun Platform all to ourselves. Life is good."

"Only one problem with your little plan, Mr. Genius," said Myron. "I can't shoot. I don't have the reflexes a Shooter does. That's why I'm a Plotter."

"But you could learn to shoot," said Charles.

"I'll repeat this slowly so you get it," said Myron, exasperated. "*I don't have the reflexes.* And neither do you. How many times have we been tested, our whole lives? Aptitude tests, allergy tests, brain scans, DNA mapping? Areco knows exactly what we are and what we can and can't do. I'm a Plotter. You're just fooling yourself if you think you aren't."

Charles didn't say anything in reply. He just looked at each of us in turn, pretty disgusted I guess, and then he turned back to his console and focused on his work.

That wasn't the end of it, though. When he was off his shift, instead of hanging out in the Cockpit, did he join in the discussions of graphic novels or what was hot on holo that week? Not Charles. He'd retire to a corner in the Forecastle with a buke and he'd game. And not just any game: targeting simulations. You never saw a guy with such icy focus. Sometimes he'd tinker with a couple of projects he'd ordered. I assumed they were models.

It was like the rest of us weren't even there. We had to respect him as a Plotter; for one thing, he turned out to have an uncanny knack for spotting Intruders, days before any of the rest of us detected them, and he was brilliant at predicting their trajectories too. But there was something distant about the guy that kept him from fitting in. Myron and Anil had dismissed him as a crank anyway, and a couple of the guys on B shift actively disliked him, after he spouted off to them the way he did to us. They were sure he was going to do something, sooner or later, that would only end up making it worse for all of us.

They were right, too.

When Weldon's turn in the rota ended, he brought Charles the French maid's apron and tossed it on his bunk.

"Your turn to wear the damn thing," he said. "They'll expect you in the bar at fourteen hundred hours. Good luck."

Charles just grunted, never even looking up from the screen of his buke.

Fourteen hundred hours came and he was still sitting there, coolly gaming.

"Hey!" said Anil. "You're supposed to go flackey!"

"I'm not going," said Charles.

"Don't be stupid!" I said. "If the rest of us have to do it, you do too."

"Why? Terrible repercussions if I don't?" Charles set aside his buke and looked at us.

"Yes!" said Myron. Preston from A Shift came running in right then, looking pale.

"Who's supposed to be flackeying? There's nobody out there, and Lord Deathlok wants to know why!"

"See?" said Myron.

"You'll get all of us in trouble, you fool! Give me the apron, I'll go!" said Anil. But Charles took the apron and tore it in half.

There was this horrified silence, which filled up with the sound of Shooters thundering along the corridor. We heard Lord Deathlok and Painmaster yelling as they came.

"Flackey! Oh, flackey! Where are you?"

And then they were in the room and it was too late to run, too late to hide. Painmaster's roach crest almost touched the ceiling panels. Lord Deathlok's yellow grin was so wide he didn't look human.

"Hi there, buttholes," said Painmaster. "If you girls aren't too busy making out, one of you is supposed to be flackeying for us."

"It was my turn," said Charles. He wadded up the apron and threw it at them. "How about you wait on yourself from now on?"

"This wasn't our idea!" said Myron.

"We tried to make him report for duty!" said Anil.

"We'll remember that, when we're assigning penalties," said Lord Deathlok. "Maybe we'll let you keep your pants when we handcuff you upside down in the toilet. Little Newbie, though..." He turned to Charles. "What about a nice game of Walk the Dog? Painmaster, got a leash anywhere on you?"

"The Painmaster always has a leash for a bad dog," said Painmaster, pulling one out. He started toward Charles, and that's when it got crazy.

Charles jumped out of his bunk and I thought, *No, you idiot, don't try to run!* But he didn't. He grabbed Painmaster's extended hand and pulled him close, and brought his arm up like he was going to hug him, only instead he made a kind of punching motion at Painmaster's neck. Painmaster screamed, wet himself and fell down. Charles kicked him in the crotch. Another dead silence, which broke as soon as Painmaster got enough breath in him for another scream. Everybody else in the room was staring at Charles, or I should say at his left wrist, because it was now obvious there was something strapped to it under his sleeve.

Lord Deathlok had actually taken a step backward. He looked from Painmaster to Charles, and then at whatever it was on Charles' wrist. He licked his lips.

"So, that's, what, some kind of taser?" he said. "Those are illegal, buddy."

Charles smiled. I realized then I'd never seen him smile before.

"It's illegal to buy one. I bought some components and made my own. What are you going to do? Report me to Kurtz?" he said.

"No; I'm just going to take it away from you, dumbass," said Lord Deathlok. He lunged at Charles, but all that happened was that Charles tased him too. He jerked backward and fell over a chair, clutching his tased hand.

"You're dead," he gasped. "You're really dead."

Charles walked over and kicked him in the crotch too.

"I challenge you to a duel," he said.

"What?" said Lord Deathlok, when he had enough breath after his scream.

"A duel. With simulations," said Charles. "I'll outshoot you. Right there in the War Room, with everybody there to witness. Thirteen hundred hours tomorrow."

"Fuck off," said Lord Deathlok. Charles leaned down and displayed the two little steel points of the taser.

"So you're scared to take me on? Chicken, is that it?" he said, and Myron and Anil obligingly started making cluck-cluck-cluck noises. "Eugene, why don't you go over to the Pit of Hell and tell the Shooters they need to come scrape up these guys?"

I wouldn't have done that for a chance to see the lost episodes of *Doctor Who,* but fortunately Lord Deathlok sat up, gasping.

"Okay," he said. "Duel. You lose, I get that taser and shove it up your ass."

"Sure," said Charles. "Whatever you want; but I won't lose. And none of us will ever flackey for you again. Got it?"

Lord Deathlok called him a lot of names, but the end of it was that he agreed to the terms, and we made Painmaster (who was crying and complaining that his heartbeat was irregular) witness. When they could walk they went stumbling back to the Pit of Hell, leaning on each other.

"You are out of your mind," I said, when they had gone. "You'll go to the War Room tomorrow and they'll be waiting for you with six bottles of club soda and a can of poster paint."

"Maybe," said Charles. "But they'll back off. Haven't you clowns figured it out yet? They're used to shooting at rocks. They have no clue what to do about something that fights back."

"They'll still win. You won't be able to tase them all, and once they get it off you, you're doomed."

"They won't get it off me," said Charles, rolling up his sleeve and unstrapping the taser mounting from his arm. "I won't be wearing it. You will."

"Me?" I backed away.

"And there's another one in my locker. Which one of you wants it?"

"You've got *two?*"

"Me!" Anil jumped forward. "So we'll be, like, your bodyguards? Yes! Can you make more of these things?"

"I won't need to," said Charles. "Tomorrow's going to change everything."

▲▼▲

I don't mind telling you, my knees were knocking as we marched across to the War Room next day. Everybody on B and C shift came along; strength in numbers, right? If we got creamed by the Shooters, at least some of us ought to make it out of there. And if Charles was insanely lucky, we all wanted to see.

It was embarrassing. Norman and Roscoe wore full Jedi kit, including their damn light sabers that were only holobeams anyway. Bradley was wearing a Happy Bat San playjacket. Anil was wearing his lucky hat from *Mystic Antagonists: the Extravaganza.* We're all creative and unique, no question, but…maybe it isn't the best idea to dress that way when you're going to a duel with intimidating mindless jerks.

We got there, and they were waiting for us.

Our Bridge always reminded me of a temple or a shrine or something, with its beautiful display shining in the darkness; but the War Room was like the Cave of the Cyclops. There wasn't any wall display like we had. There were just the red lights of the targeting consoles, and way in the far end of the room somebody had stuck up a blacklight, which made the lurid holoposters of skulls and demons and vampires seem to writhe in the gloom.

The place stank of body odor, which the Shooters can't get rid of because they wear all that black bioprene gear, which doesn't breathe like the natural fabrics we wear. There was also a urinal reek; when a Shooter is gaming, he doesn't let a little thing like needing to pee drive him from his console.

All this was bad enough; imagine how I felt to see that the Shooters had made war-clubs out of chlorilar water bottles stuck into handles of printer paper rolled tight. They stood there, glowering at us. I saw Lord Deathlok and the Shark and Professor Badass. Mephisto, the Conquistador, Iron Beast, Killer Ape, Uncle Hannibal…every hateful face I knew from months of humiliating flackey-work, except…

"Where's the Painmaster?" said Charles, looking around in an unconcerned kind of way.

"He had better things to do than watch you rectums lose," said Lord Deathlok.

"He had to be shipped down to the infirmary, because he was complaining of chest pains," said Mephisto. The others looked at him accusingly. Charles beamed.

"Too bad! Let's do this thing, gentlemen."

"We fixed up a special console, homo, just for you," said Lord Deathlok with an evil leer, waving at one. Charles looked at it and laughed.

"You have got to be kidding. I'll take *this* one over *here*, and you'll take the one next to it. We'll play side by side, so everybody can see. That's only fair, right?"

Their faces fell. But Anil and I crossed our arms, so the taser prongs showed, and the Shooters grumbled but backed down. They cleared away empty bottles and snack wrappers from the consoles. It felt good, watching them humbled for a change.

Charles settled himself at the console he'd chosen, and with a few quick commands on the buttonball pulled up the simulation menu.

"Is this all you've got?" he said. "Okay; I propose nine rounds. Three sets each of *Holodeath 2, Meteor Nightmare,* and *Incoming Annihilation.* Highest cumulative score wins."

"You got it, shithead," said Lord Deathlok. He took his seat.

So they called up *Holodeath 2,* and we all crowded around to watch, even though the awesome stench of the Shooters was enough to make your eyes water. The holo display lit up with a sinister green fog, and the enemy ships started coming at us. Charles got off three shots before Lord Deathlok managed one, and though one of his shots went wild, two inflicted enough damage on a Megacruiser to set it on fire. Lord Deathlok's shot nailed a patrol vessel in the forefront, and though it was a low-score target, he took it out with just that one shot. The score counters on both consoles gave them 1200 points.

Charles finished the burning cruiser with two more quick shots—it looked fantastic, glaring red through its ports until it just sort of imploded in this cylinder of glowing ash. But Lord Deathlok was picking off the little transport cutters methodically, because they only take about a shot each if you're accurate, which he was. Charles pulled ahead by hammering away at the big targets, and he never missed another shot, and so what happened was that the score counters showed them flashing along neck and neck for the longest time and then, *boom,* the last Star Destroyer blew and Charles was suddenly way ahead with twice Deathlok's score.

We were all yelling by this time, the Shooters with their chimpanzee hooting and us with—well, we sort of sounded like apes too. The next set went up and here came the ships again, but this time they were firing back. Charles took three hits in succession, before he seemed to figure out how to raise his shields, and the Shooters started gloating and smacking their clubs together.

But he went on the offensive real fast, and did something I'd never thought of before, which was aiming for the ships' gunports and disabling them with one shot before hitting them with a barrage that finished them. I never even had time to look at what Deathlok was doing, but his guys stopped cheering suddenly and when the set ended, he didn't even have a third of the points Charles did.

The third set went amazingly fast, even with the difference that the gun positions weren't stationary and they had to maneuver around in the middle of the armada. Charles did stuff I would never have dared to do, recklessly swooping around and under the Megacruisers, *between* their gunports for cripe's sake, getting off round after round of shots so close it seemed impossible for him to pull clear before the ships blew, but somehow he did.

Lord Deathlok didn't seem to move much. He just sat in one position and pounded away at anything that came within range, and though he did manage to bag a Star Destroyer, he finished the set way behind Charles on points.

I would have just given up if I'd been Deathlok, but the Shooters were getting ugly, shouting all kinds of personal abuse at him, and I don't think he dared.

I had to run for the lavatory as *Incoming Annihilation* was starting, and of course I had to run all the way back to our end of the Gun Platform to our toilet because I sure wasn't going to use the Shooters', not with the way the War Room smelled. It was only when I was unfastening that I realized I was still wearing the taser, and that I'd done an incredibly stupid thing by leaving when I was one of Charles's bodyguards. So I finished fast and ran all the way back, and there was Mr. Kurtz strolling along the corridor.

"Hello there, Eugene," he said. "Something going on?"

"Just some gaming," I said. "I need to get back—"

"But you're on Shooter turf, aren't you?" Mr. Kurtz looked around. "Shouldn't you be going in the other direction?"

"Well—we're having this competition, you see, Mr. Kurtz," I said. "The new guy's gaming against Lord—I mean, against Peavey Crandall."

"Is he?" Mr. Kurtz began to smile. "I wondered how long Charles would put up with the Shooters. Well, well."

He said it in a funny kind of way, but I didn't have the time to wonder about it. I just excused myself and ran on, and was really relieved to see that the Shooters didn't seem to have noticed my absence. They were all packed tight around the consoles, and nobody was making a sound; all you could hear was the *peew-peew-peew* of the shots going off continuously, and the *whump* as bombs exploded. Then there was a flare of red light and our guys yelled in triumph. Bradley was leaping up and down, and Roscoe did a Victory Dance until one of the Shooters asked him if he wanted his light saber rammed up his butt.

I managed to shove my way between Anil and Myron just as Charles was announcing, "I believe you're screwed, Mr. Crandall. Care to call it a day?"

I looked at their scores and couldn't believe how badly Lord Deathlok had lost to him. But Lord Deathlok just snarled.

"I don't think so, Ben Dover. Shut up and play!"

It was *Meteor Nightmare* now, as though they were both out there in the Van Oort belt, facing the rocks without any comforting distance of consoles or calculations. I couldn't stop myself from flinching as they hurtled forward; and I noticed one of the Shooters put up his arms involuntarily, as though he wanted to bat away the incoming with his bare hands.

It was a brutal game; *nightmare*, all right, because they couldn't avoid taking massive damage. All they could do was take out as many targets as they could before their inevitable destruction. When one or the other of them took a hit, there was a momentary flare of light that blinded everybody in the room. I couldn't imagine how Charles and Lord Deathlok, right there with their faces in the action, could keep shooting with any kind of accuracy.

Sure enough, early in the second round it began to tell. They were both getting flash-blind. Charles was still hitting about one in three targets, but Lord Deathlok was shooting crazily, randomly, not even bothering to aim so far as I could tell. What a look of despair on his ugly face, with his lips drawn back from his yellow teeth!

Only a miracle would save him, now. His overall score was so far behind Charles's he'd never catch up. The Shooters knew it too. I saw Dr. Smash turn his head and murmur to Uncle Hannibal. He took a firm grip on his war club. Panicking, I grabbed Anil's arm, trying to get his attention.

That was when the Incoming klaxons sounded. All the Shooters stood to attention. Lord Deathlok looked around, blinking, but Charles worked the buttonball like a pro and suddenly the game vanished, and there was nothing before us but the console displays. There was a crackle from the speakers—the first time they'd ever been used, I found out later—and we could hear Preston screaming, "You guys! Intruder coming in fast! You have to stop! It's in—"

"Q41!" said Uncle Hannibal, leaning forward to peer at the console readout. "Get out of my chair, dickwad!"

Charles didn't answer. He did something with the buttonball and there was the Intruder, like something out of *Meteor Nightmare*, shracking enormous. It was in his own sector! How could he have missed it? *Charles,* who was brilliant at spotting them before anybody else?

A red frame rose around it, with the readout in numbers spinning over so fast I couldn't tell what they said, except it was obvious the thing was coming in at high speed. All the Shooters were frantic, bellowing for Charles to get his ass out of the chair. Before their astounded eyes, and ours, he targeted the Intruder and fired.

All sound stopped. Movement stopped. Time itself stopped, except for on the display, where a new set of numbers in green and another in yellow popped up. They spun like fruit on a slot machine, the one counting up, the other counting down, both getting slower and slower until suddenly the numbers matched. Then, in perfect unison, they clicked upward together on a leisurely march.

"It's a hit," announced Preston from the speakers. "In twelve days thirteen hours forty-two minutes. Telemetry confirmed."

Dead silence answered him. And that was when I understood: Charles hadn't missed the Intruder. Charles had spotted it days ago. Charles had set this whole thing up, requesting the specific time of the duel, knowing the Intruder would interrupt it and there'd have to be a last-minute act of heroism. Which he'd co-opt.

But the thing is, see, there are *people* down there on the planet under us, who could die if a meteor gets through. I mean, that's why we're all up here in the first place, right?

Finally Anil said, in a funny voice, "So...who gets the bonus, then?"

"He *can't* have just done that," said Mephisto, hoarse with disbelief. "He's a *Plotter*."

"Get up, faggot," said Uncle Hannibal, grabbing Charles's shoulder.

"Hit him," said Charles.

I hadn't unfrozen yet, but Anil had been waiting for this moment all day. He jumped forward and tased Uncle Hannibal. Uncle Hannibal dropped, with a hoarse screech, and the other Shooters backed away fast. Anil stared down at Uncle Hannibal with unholy wonder in his eyes, and the beginning of a terrible joy. Suddenly there was a lot of room in front of the consoles, enough to see Lord Deathlok sitting there staring at the readout, with tears streaming down his face.

Charles got out of the chair.

"You lost," he informed Lord Deathlok.

"Your reign of terror is over!" cried Anil, brandishing his taser at the Shooters. One or two of them cowered, but the rest just looked stunned. Charles turned to me.

"You left your post," he said. "You're a useless idiot. Myron, take the taser off him."

"Sir yes sir!" said Myron, grabbing my arm and rolling up my sleeve. As he was unfastening the straps, we heard a chuckle from the doorway. All heads turned. There was Mr. Kurtz, leaning there with his arms crossed. I realized he must have followed me, and seen the drama as it played out. Anil thrust his taser arm behind his back, looking scared, but Mr. Kurtz only smiled.

"As you were," he said. He stood straight and left. We could hear him whistling as he walked away.

▲▼▲

It wasn't until later that we learned the whole story, or as much of it as we ever knew: how Charles had been recruited, not from his parents' garage or basement, but from Hospital, and how Mr. Kurtz had known it, had in fact *requested it.*

We all expected a glorious new day had come for Plotters, now that Charles had proven the Shooters were unnecessary. We thought Areco would terminate their contracts. It didn't exactly happen that way.

What happened was that Dr. Smash and Uncle Hannibal came to Charles and had a private (except for Myron and Anil) talk with him. They were very polite. Since Painmaster wasn't coming back to the Gun Platform, but had defaulted on his contract and gone down home to Earth, they proposed that Charles become a Shooter. They did more; they offered him High Dark Lordship.

He accepted their offer. We were appalled. It seemed like the worst treachery imaginable.

And yet, we were surprised again.

Charles Tead didn't take one of the stupid Shooter names like Warlord or Iron Fist or Doomsman. He said we were all to call him *Stede* from now on. He ordered up, not a bioprene wardrobe with spikes and rivets and fringe, but…but…a three-piece suit, with a *tie.* And a bowler hat. He took his tasers back from Anil and Myron, who were crestfallen, and wore them himself, under his perfectly pressed cuffs.

Then he ordered up new clothes for all the other Shooters. It must have been a shock, when he handed out those powder blue shirts and drab coveralls, but they didn't rebel; by that time they'd learned what he'd been sent to Hospital for in the first place, which was killing three people. So there wasn't so much as a mutter behind his back, even when he ordered all the holoposters shut off and thrown into the fusion hopper, and the War Room repainted in dove gray.

We wouldn't have known the Shooters. He made them wash, he made them cut their hair, he made them shracking salute when he gave an order.

They were scared to fart, especially after he hung up deodorizers above each of their consoles. The War Room became a clean, well-lit place, silent except for the consoles and the occasional quiet order from Charles. He seldom had to raise his voice.

Mr. Kurtz still sat in his office all day, reading, but now he smiled as he read. Nobody called him *Dean Kurtz* anymore, either.

It was sort of horrible, what had happened, but with Charles—I mean, Stede—running the place, things were a lot more efficient. The bonuses became more frequent, as everyone worked harder. And, in time, the Shooters came to worship him.

He didn't bother with us. We were grateful.

The Faithful

From the day of their births, Heezai and Mazsai had served in Her house.

The rituals were simple, the temple spacious. It was their whole world, for as Her priestesses they were not permitted to leave the sacred precinct. They needed no company but Hers, though they derived comfort from each other's presence.

There had been an old priestess once, who had trained them up in their duties before she had ascended through the portal; but in all the long years since, no other had ever entered the temple but She.

She came with the evening, like the moon and the stars! The long day began in darkness, with brazen shrilling to alert the priestesses that Matins were to be sung now, and First Purification performed. All through the quiet hours of day, light crossed the walls of the temple in its slow changeless path, and the sisters busied themselves with the lesser rituals. At certain times, sacrifices were slaughtered and laid out; purification and meditation followed, according to varying schedules dictated by the brazen trill.

But always, as the blue twilight settled, She would manifest.

Almost always.

▲▼▲

Heezai, who was brave, had ventured to the portal and stood peering into the void beyond.

"Why do you do that?" Mazsai wept, from the safe shadow of a ceiling-high column. "I can't imagine what you could be thinking of, to go so close. I don't know where you find the nerve!"

"Nothing bad has ever happened," said Heezai patiently.

"But it's Forbidden!"

"No, it isn't," Heezai replied. "It's going out into the void that's Forbidden."

"You'll be doing that next, I know you will!" cried Mazsai. "Don't you see? You're being tempted, one step at a time. You say to yourself, it can't do any harm if I just *think* about the Forbidden. Then it's only another step, isn't it, to just *looking* at the Forbidden? And next you'll decide it's all right to *explore* it, intending to come right back, but it'll be too late. You'll be damned!"

"No, I won't," said Heezai. "I'd never go into the void. Not with what I've seen out there."

"What have you seen?" asked Mazsai, shocked out of her tantrum.

"Monsters," Heezai said, half-turning to look at her sister. "Wonderful things, but monsters too. I've seen the damned out there, sister, meeting horrible death."

"Oh!" Mazsai retreated a little further into the shadows. "Well, you see? That just proves it's no place to concern ourselves with!"

Heezai summoned all her forbearance.

"Don't you ever wonder why She manifests from it, then?"

"No! And neither should you!"

"But it can't be a sin to want to understand Her, sister," said Heezai, turning back to gaze through the portal. "And if we knew more about the void, perhaps we'd know why She sometimes…"

"*Don't say it!*"

"Sometimes we can't invoke Her," Heezai persisted. "You know it's true. Don't you want to know why?"

"No, no, no!" In her agitation, Mazsai leaped out into the great open space before the columns and ran back and forth. "Oh, Great One, do not hear her! She's foolish! Oh, Great One, I believe! You *will* come to us, yes! Faithful Mazsai calls to You! For only You bring true light, only You bring warmth, only You fill us with good things!"

Heezai sighed in exasperation, and yet she couldn't help shivering. The soft dusk had deepened. The temple seemed dark and chilly now, an alien place. The void had began to change, too, its glaring chaos now all shadow streaked with lurid trails. If She did not manifest tonight the temple would grow darker, and colder, and out of the darkness terrors would come…

"Great One, I believe," Heezai echoed, "Don't forsake us! Come to Your obedient children!"

They had been chanting for close to an hour, and Mazsai in her fright and exhaustion was beginning to run into walls, when the First Sign came.

"She comes!" Heezai leaped away from the portal, dancing in the great circle of golden light that had appeared before the columns.

"She comes!" cried Mazsai hoarsely, joining her sister in the elaborate dance of praise. They spun and twisted in sinuous figures, raised their voices in the ancient hymn of welcome to Her, and then—

She was manifest, in a flood of light, and warmth, and glorious sound!

They prostrated themselves before Her, weeping with desperate gratitude.

Faith was rewarded. She dwelt with them, gave healing, and listened to their pleas and their praises. The sacrifice, for there had been one that day, was graciously accepted. She saw that they had kept Her laws, and so they basked in Her light, and were granted bliss. The dark echoing temple was transformed into the very abode of ecstasy.

All the same, as Heezai was drifting into happy unconsciousness, she felt her sister give her a sharp nudge.

"You nearly ruined everything, with your sinfulness," Mazsai hissed. "You mustn't ever be so reckless again."

▲▼▲

Two nights later, She did not come to Her temple.

Heezai and Mazsai paced and wept, sent up their pleading prayers in vain. No First Sign, no warmth and glory, no comfort at all; only Her absence, and gray dawn found the two little sisters huddled together on the floor before the portal, trembling with open-eyed exhaustion.

"Why didn't She come?" wondered Heezai. "We were faithful. We did no Forbidden thing."

"It must have been because of your sinful thoughts," Mazsai moaned. "What other reason could there be? She wouldn't punish us for nothing."

"We must have done the invocations wrong, somehow," said Heezai. "Or maybe She wants another sacrifice."

So all that day, the priestesses devoted themselves to their rites with special attention. Not one sacrifice alone but two lesser sacrifices were offered up too, and arranged to best please Her. Mazsai was meticulous in purification, and Heezai spent four hours together in deep meditation.

But that night, when darkness fell, it fell without appeal. She did not come to Her faithful ones, however long they called Her.

Heezai and Mazsai were devastated. They slept at last, and when they woke they wandered the temple disconsolately. The piled sacrifices were cold, and stank; a fine pall of dust lay over everything, undisturbed by any celestial breezes or divine attention.

When the blue hour arrived at last, Heezai walked to the portal in despair, and gazed out. To her astonishment, she heard Mazsai pacing close behind her.

"You said there are monsters in the void," said Mazsai.

"There are," Heezai replied, watching as one moved with unhurried menace across the field of her vision.

"And She dwells in the void. You don't suppose...one of them has done something to Her?"

"What monster could prevail over Her?" said Heezai, indignant. But as she thought about the question, she realized in horror that she did not know the answer.

"You're right," said Mazsai, "Nothing could possibly harm Her. She is all-powerful. She must simply be withholding Her presence as a punishment!" Mazsai began to run back and forth again, as much to warm herself as to yield to her impulse toward flight. "Blessed One, we have seen the error of our ways! We know You will not forsake us forever! Come back to us now!"

And, lo—

The First Sign appeared, flaring gold. Frantic with joy, the priestesses danced on pace-bruised feet to welcome Her, screamed out their hymn from raw throats.

And She came! But...

Something had changed. There was light, and warmth, and glorious harmony—yet mixed with it was a darker sound, an alien sound, and Heezai and Mazsai gazed up into the effulgent radiance and beheld that She was not alone. There was an Other, that was not Her.

The sisters faltered only a moment in their prescribed dance, resumed their chants of welcome with renewed vigor. She descended to them as She always had, and they were blessed.

The sacrifices were accepted: but was there something perfunctory in Her manner as She took them? Her gifts were given out, and the sisters rejoiced in Her bounty; but as they presented their pleas, their praises, they had the distinct impression that She was not giving them Her full attention.

Instead, there was a great deal more of the celestial harmony, mysteriously loud, and it went on for hours longer than its customary time. And the Other remained manifest beside Her, and would not be prayed to or praised, but remained an aloof strangeness that somehow diminished Her glory.

And then—oh, unthinkable!—She did not dwell with them, as She had, but departed and left them in darkness.

Heezai and Mazsai lay side by side in the shadows of the temple that night, staring up into the fathomless distance of the vaulted roof.

"What can it be?" said Heezai at last.

"She is testing our faith," said Mazsai.

Neither one of them could bring themselves to speak of the Other. They scarcely knew words to describe it.

▲▼▲

Now began a time that sorely tried Heezai and Mazsai, for the world they knew was gone.

Not so much the physical world; the temple remained solid and eternal, though its dark corners seemed darker, and its dust lay more thickly. But every comfortable assumption about the pattern of the universe was torn away, it seemed.

Heezai and Mazsai might dedicate themselves to the prescribed rituals with grim energy, attain previously unknown levels of cleanness and contemplation, slaughter and offer up the sacrifices with fiery zeal; and She might ignore their efforts, failing to manifest, though their songs of invocation were perfect and pure in every note.

They might lie listless on the floor of the temple, neglecting every duty in despair, mute and motionless as the darkness fell: and then, without warning, She would arrive in all Her former splendor! And sometimes She dwelt with them, and for a sweet night or two it seemed She had forgiven them their sins, which were many by this time.

More often, though, when She came, the Other came as well; and then Her time was brief. Her blessing was withheld. It seemed She had come before them only to make the darkness more profound when She departed.

"She is testing our faith," repeated Mazsai, one night as they lay alone.

"You have cobwebs in your hair," said Heezai.

Mazsai turned away and wept.

▲▼▲

One night, when Heezai and Mazsai lay dozing in the rear of the temple, they were awakened by a flare of light and sound. They leaped up and stared at each other in mingled dread and wonder.

"She came, and we weren't even at the portal!" Heezai cried. They went racing out between the great columns, and saw that it was true: She had manifested in all her Glory, and the Other was also manifest, and the celestial harmony rolled and echoed through the temple.

The priestesses began their dance, their psalm of praise, but halted in dismay: for before their unbelieving eyes the very geometry of the eternal temple began to change. Walls descended from on high, the tremendous immobile columns that held up the world shifted and walked. A terrace that had from time immemorial divided the place of sacrifice from the place of purification lifted into brightness, and vanished utterly.

Heezai and Mazsai cowered together, as the harmonies trumpeted above their heads. Then, from on high, a figure descended and landed fair on her feet on the temple floor.

"Oh, it's Keesai!" sobbed Mazsai in relief, and ran forward, and Heezai ran too. But when the figure turned to them, they skidded to a halt. Instead of Keesai, the old priestess who had taught them the Duties, they beheld a stranger. It seemed the celestial harmonies paused for a breathless moment, as the stranger regarded them coldly.

"What a pair of fat frumps," she said, and chuckled.

Mazsai backed away, frightened. Heezai, however, stood her ground.

"Who are you?" she demanded.

"I am His priestess," said the other. "Heersha the Beautiful is my name." She looked around her. "I don't think much of this temple."

It was a moment before Heezai could stammer a reply, so shocked she was. "How dare you! This is Her house!"

"Not any more, it isn't," Heersha told her. She swaggered close, until her face was almost touching Heezai's. "He has conquered, you see? All places are His. He's already making changes to suit His liking, or haven't you noticed?"

Heezai gazed up toward the vast brightness, and beheld an indescribable shifting, tremendous volumes of space rearranging themselves. The celestial harmonies had resumed, but with a note of divinely snide amusement she had never heard before. Bewildered, she turned her face away.

"This can't be," she whispered.

"Oh, but it is," said Heersha the Beautiful, advancing on her so that she must walk backward. "So get used to it, my dear. I am priestess here now! Find yourself a corner where you won't be too conspicuous, and perhaps I'll let you live there. Go on!"

In that moment, the manifestation of Her glory—or was it now the glory of the Other?—ended. Darkness and silence returned, but in the faint starlight from the portal Heezai saw that Heersha was still there, a blacker shadow against the night. Heezai lost utterly her courage, and fled. Mazsai had already done so.

▲▼▲

Their fall was complete.

The sisters dwelt now at the extreme back of the temple, crowding together in a tiny sanctuary far from the light. The first morning after Her departure, Heezai had ventured out into the refectory for breakfast, and only got halfway to the pantry before Heersha sprang out to block her path.

"Not for you!" she snarled. "Go on, get back in your hole!"

Heezai trembled, but stood her ground.

"We must eat," she protested.

"Not *this* food," said Heersha. "This is all mine. You're too fat anyhow! I'll bet you've never faced a morning without breakfast in your life, have you?"

"She has always provided for us," said Heezai, with as much dignity as she could muster, and attempted to sidle past Heersha. She saw a blur, felt a slashing impact.

"You've got *weapons!*" she gasped, her astonishment almost as great as her pain. Blood was welling from a long gash across the bridge of her nose. "But that's Forbidden!"

"Not to me," said Heersha, advancing on her. "*He* doesn't require his priestess to be a little soft fat nothing like you. Now, go!"

Heezai ran back to the sanctuary, where Mazsai was peering out.

"Didn't you bring me back any—"she began crossly, before seeing Heezai's bleeding face. Then she screamed.

Heezai collapsed, panting, and while her sister hurriedly cleaned away the blood—for dirtiness was Forbidden—she explained what had happened.

"Well, then, She will come to punish," said Mazsai indignantly, compressing the long gash to make the bleeding stop. "Weapons indeed! And greed is Forbidden, and so is fighting. You ought to go straight back there and tell her so."

"I'm frightened to," said Heezai.

"Frightened? *You're* never frightened. Oh, what's happening to the world?" cried Mazsai.

All that day they hid together in the sanctuary, and Mazsai kept their spirits up by speculating on how She would punish the sinful interloper when She came. At twilight, they even dared so much as to venture out toward the portal; but Heersha rose before them, laughing, and drove them back into the darkness with kicks and blows.

And She did not manifest Herself. All that night, and every night after, Her temple was silent, was black and cold.

The sisters found that Heersha did sleep, sometimes, in the long sunlit stretches in the midst of the day. It was just possible, then, to creep into the refectory and steal a mouthful or two of food, and drink a little water, before Heersha came running in to drive them away. To their horror, she took possession of the lavatory too.

"But what will we do?" demanded Mazsai, thoroughly scandalized. "We can't just go in a corner of the Temple! That's *unclean*! That's Forbidden!"

"Will She come to punish us?" asked Heezai wearily, dabbing at her eye. Heersha's cut had pinked the corner of the lid, and it had become inflamed and wept. "Or is She punishing us now? I can't see that it makes any difference."

In the end they dragged some of the smaller temple furnishings into an alcove and made a reasonably private place, though after three days the stink tormented them with shame.

"This is so sordid," Mazsai complained one long night, as they lay side by side in the dark.

"*Sordid?*" said Heezai. "This is worse than the void."

"What would the two of you know about the void?" said a gloating voice from outside the sanctuary. After a moment's horrified silence, Heezai drew on her courage and said:

"It's a place of monsters, and sudden death. All chaos, all horror; yet She manifests Herself from there.

"When it pleases Her to do so," she added.

"But it hasn't pleased Her lately, has it?" Heersha said. "Not surprising. Who'd want a couple of priestesses like you?"

"Who'd want you, either?" Heezai retorted. "Or haven't you noticed that the Other hasn't manifested since you've been here? Perhaps this isn't His temple after all."

There was silence for a moment. Then the voice spoke once more out of the shadows:

"Anyway, I'm not afraid of the void. I've been out there many times. He doesn't care if I go. In fact, He makes me go there, often. Sometimes He makes me bring His sacrifices from that place. It makes me strong. I'm not a spoiled and pampered fool, like the pair of you."

"What is it like?" Heezai asked.

"Are there monsters?" Mazsai asked.

There was another silence, and then the sound of an elaborate yawn. "Of course there are. Horrible, deadly monsters, and a thousand painful ways to die. And there are other priestesses, fighting to survive, and priests too! But the two of you wouldn't know anything about *that*, I'm sure, ha ha."

Neither Heezai nor Mazsai knew anything about that at all, so the sneer was lost on them completely.

"Do you know why She manifests from there?" Heezai persisted.

"She, She, She! Can't you get it through your little heads that *She* is nothing? He is all. There are a thousand weak things like Her out there. He plays with them and makes them serve Him. That's the law of the void. When He's tired of Her, She will cease to exist. So will you."

"You're a liar!" cried Mazsai.

"Not about this," said Heersha, sounding smug.

"Oh, shut up and go away," said Heezai.

"I was just going," Heersha said. "You're both too pathetically boring for words."

They heard her walking away, and then she paused.

"By the way," she said, "the food's running out. By tomorrow morning there won't be any left. I suppose you have no idea what to do then, have you?"

Laughing, she walked on.

▲▼▲

The long hours crawled by, the days with their silent climbing sunlight, the nights with their horrors. Heezai and Mazsai lay together in the sanctuary, fasting.

"It was always replenished," Mazsai whispered. "Always, there was food. Were our sins so great?"

"But She forgave us our sins," said Heezai. "She never punished us like this. There must be some other reason for our sufferings now."

"What if Heersha is right?" Mazsai began to weep. "What if She is nothing, after all? Keesai was wrong in everything she taught us. It was lies. The Other is all-powerful."

"No." Heezai was thinking carefully. "Remember, how you said this must be a test of our faith? Perhaps it's a very hard test."

"She would never test us like this!" said Mazsai. "She loved us!"

"She *might* test our strength, even if it was a little painful," said Heezai. "How far back can you remember, sister?"

"...I remember Keesai," said Mazsai at last, sounding doubtful. "Of course. And all our lessons. I remember when Keesai was in pain, and ascended into the void."

"That was later. But can you remember very far back?" Heezai asked.

"I...I don't like to. Because..." Mazsai's voice trailed away.

"When did we learn about pain, sister?"

"Long ago," said Mazsai. "There was—oh, the strange smell! And the brightness, I was so frightened of it! And unbearable pain!"

"It wasn't unbearable," said Heezai. "Can't you remember? She comforted us. She heard our prayers. Do you remember what Keesai told us then?"

"No!"

"She told us to be brave, because it was all for our own good," said Heezai. "She said the pain would go away, and it did."

"...For our own good?"

"To make us more perfect servants of Her will," said Heezai. "'A little pain for a lifetime of blessedness, children,' that's what Keesai said."

"No, I don't remember any such thing." Mazsai was on the point of angry tears.

"It happened, all the same." Heezai got to her feet, with effort.

"What are you doing?"

"I think this is more pain for our own good," said Heezai. "Heersha is evil, but she was telling the truth about the void and the law of the void. It's all fighting and death there. Well, the void has come into Her temple now. There must be a greater sacrifice to Her glory than there has ever been, before She will manifest for us again."

Heezai walked unsteadily to the door of the sanctuary.

"Where are you going?" cried Mazsai.

"I am going to fight the servant of the Other," said Heezai, and went out into the light.

▲▼▲

Heezai thought to seek Heersha in the great hall of the portal, but as she passed the door to the refectory, she beheld movement. Curious, she peered in.

She had believed nothing more would shock her; but she had been wrong.

"Sacrilege!" she shouted. Heersha, who was tearing greedily at a sacrifice, merely raised her eyes.

"Get out," she said.

"The sacrifices are Hers alone!"

"Don't be stupid," Heersha replied, through a full mouth. "Do you think anyone is ever coming back to accept your offerings? *He's* happy to take what I leave Him." She swallowed, and grinned. "And are you telling me you've never wanted to do this? Why, look at you; your mouth's watering. You want it now—"

Heezai launched herself at the servant of the Other, and rage gave her strength. Starved as she was, she was still heavier than Heersha, who collapsed before her with an *oof.* Heersha lay stunned a moment, fighting for breath, as Heezai kicked and pummeled her; but in another moment she threw off her opponent and sprang to her feet, drawing her weapons.

The fight was silent. There was too much hatred for taunts. Heersha leaped, feinted, stabbed; Heezai dodged; Heersha circled, weaving, slashing out, going for Heezai's other eye. Heezai fell and rolled, avoiding blindness, but Heersha came down on her back with all her weight, and slashed again at Heezai's head. She took off the tip of Heezai's ear.

Heezai felt the impact more than the pain. Then it was only burning, burning, and she was somehow on her feet and glaring across the room at Heersha. Heersha was laughing, low in her throat. She crouched, preparing to spring and slash again. Heezai crouched too and waited, and the red blood streamed down the side of her face, fell in big drops to the floor of the temple.

Heezai waited until Heersha was in midair, and tried to scramble away. Partly she succeeded, slipping on the slick blood, and Heersha struck the wall, but fell on her. She was wounded again before she managed to break away; she couldn't tell where, but felt her strength running out with the blood.

And Heersha was stalking toward her, now, winded but grinning still.

"His is the triumph," she said, flexing her supple back to leap again.

"Heezaiii!" Mazsai was thundering into the room, fat timid Mazsai, and she hit Heersha and they went bowling over and over before colliding with the wall. Heersha was again knocked breathless. Mazsai rolled back, finding her feet, and put herself between Heezai and Heersha.

"You evil thing," she sobbed, "go away!"

There was a noise, louder than thunder. There was a light so brilliant it blinded them all. The celestial harmonies shook the air, and She was manifest.

She Herself, alone, and there was no Other to darken the air beside her or take half Her divine music.

Mazsai edged backward and exchanged a frightened glance with Heezai. The glorious voice was throbbing with emotion, but not love. They heard fury, and grief, and wounded pride, and betrayal. The very walls of the temple were shaking with the impact, as She directed blows against it. Columns shattered and fell, terraces moved half their length across the great hall.

Heersha had got to her feet and was shaking her head, stupefied. Looking up at Her approach, she bared her teeth.

Spellbound, Heezai and Mazsai watched and saw the truth of damnation, saw the price of offense against Her. Heersha was seized up bodily, borne toward the portal too quick to scream or struggle. The portal opened, and a great blast of cold rushed into the temple, and they saw darkness and stars beyond.

Heersha was flung through the portal, which slammed behind her with a boom that was painful to their ears, but they ran close—even daring Her wrath—in time to see Heersha cartwheeling through the void before landing on her feet, square in a livid blotch of light that moved on her relentlessly. She turned to meet it with a scream of rage, but it did not stop for fear of her. It came on, and crushed her, and when it had passed they saw her lying in her own blood, not moving.

"Sinner," hissed Mazsai, vindicated beyond her wildest dreams.

They became aware that She had passed into the rear of the temple behind them. They turned together and hurried through the great hall without hesitation, though Heezai was limping badly. That place above their sanctuary, so long black and fearful, was now aglow with Her presence. Timidly, abasing themselves, they came before Her.

Wonder of wonders, they were lifted at once into Her bosom and embraced, and Her warmth surrounded them, and Her aggrieved heart poured out its love to them alone! Rapturous, thankful, they sang Her praise, and this was the verse She sang over theirs:

"Oh, Hussy, oh, Mussy, Mommie's so sorry she left her kitties alone so long to go on vacation with that awful man! Mommie's glad she threw out his nasty old cat! Mommie promises she'll never, ever leave you alone again!"

The Leaping Lover

12th January 1838 Friday morning

My Dear Matilda,

My fond regards to all those at Greta Bridge which seems very quaint to me now, as London is so far removed it is as great a difference as Heaven above Earth I suppose. You would scarcely believe what a time I am having at Aunt Pyelott's. The glittring Society! The refined Gentlemen, so very solicitors for ones comfort! Such attentions I have received! But you will have to imagine it all as I could not begin to describe it.

I am gazing out as I write at a district known as Lime House, very genteel and of great antikwity. The Pyelotts reside in a gracious mansion in Salmon Lane, kinveniently located above Uncle Pyelott's premises. The Garden is pleasantly rustick and Aunt Pyelott has a hen shed to make it more like the Country as that is the current fashion here, only of course she has a Boy to see to the eggs.

We often promernod through London, perhaps down to the Comercial Road or even as far as the Basin to see the Barges, and I wore my yellow morning gown the other day, the one that John said sets off my eyes so nice, but I was obliged to wear my black boots because of the kindition of the lane rather than the Maroko slippers which I would have much prefered. However I have a new Gown being prepared of exquisitt green stuff for the Ball which is being held Friday next and the sempstress is French of course and she informs me black slippers are all the Thing now so I shall be fashionably shod.

I almost neglected to mention, Aunt Pyelott's cousin resides here as well, a Poor Relation, Miss Maud Bellman. She is a plain little thing with specktacles but quite agreeable and anxious to make herself useful as indeed she should be. I shall perhaps endevour to make something of her as the Poor if left to themselves often descend to degerdation. Aunt Pyelott has graciously gotten her a ticket to the Ball as well, though I cannot imagine the poor thing will show to her advantage.

I must away—Madame Hector is here for my fitting. Pray write and tell me how you are getting on and my kind regards to all the Prices.

I remain
Yours and cetrer
Fanny Squeers

20th January 1838 Saturday Noon

Dear Tilda,

Perhaps you were expecting some fond account of the Ball which I was at only last night but oh, what a far more terrible tale I have to tell!

Though I will say the Ball was a Triumph. As I suspected I far outshone poor Miss Bellman, who wore only a sort of puce dress more fitting to Tea but then she hadn't any better, and I pity the creature. I condesinded to encourage her a little, and offered her the use of my old violet shawl with the jet beads, but she declined, at which I was secretly a little releeved because really it was too fine considering the other stuff she had on and not her colour at all.

The evening was fine for the season and so we walked there, the Ball being held at the Caledonian Arms up the lane. We had some exitement at the door for I nearly thought I had left my Invitation but at the last moment Miss Bellman found it in the bottom of my reticule for me. She really may make someone a 1st rate ladys maid with a little training and I must speak to Aunt Pyelott about it.

As for the Society at the Ball, well that was a little dissapointing because most of the men present were in the trade (clerks and such) and I could see they were somewhat overwelmed by my carriage. I graciously declined to dance with most of them although there was one Gentleman who is in Ship Chandlering or something, quite well to do, Mr. Clement I recall is his name, and he was there with his Partners Mr. Tacker and Mr. Johnson. I made sure to dance with all three.

I pitied one tall fellow with black whiskers who gazed at me with such elockwent longing! Had he mustard enough courage to speak to me, I declare I might have danced with him; little did I suspect his Wild Nature! But I am getting ahead of myself. Miss Bellman, poor creature, danced with one or two fellows of the lower sort and her face got quite red, which may have been the affect of the gin punch.

Uncle Pyelott was to have called for us in a Handsom but we left rather early as I was a little fateeged. Oh, Tilda, what small twists of Chance decide our Fate! For if I had waited—but you shall hear what befell next.

I was rather apprinsieve I confess coming away from Bow Common, on account of there was no more than a gibrous moon by which to see, and no light except the watchmans all the way across the field at the Cable Manefactry. What ierny! For we were quite unmolested all that open way, and the attack did not come until we we had once reached the Shelter of houses.

What, I hear you exclaim, *attack*! Yes, Tilda, *attack*! For as we were nearly to the bridge over the canal, on a sudden a Frightful Aparishen sprung out of an alley! He was quite tall, cloaked in Inky Black, which he flung back to Reveal a Horrific Counternance. There was a spark of fire at his Bosom and then he breathed out flames. I naturally screamed in terror and so I need hardly add did Miss Bellman, the more so when the Monster then seezed me in his Powerful Arms and *tore at my rayment* with Fearful Claws!!!!

What his intentions were you can scarcely imagine, as you have led a sheltered life, but I was fainting and almost unable to struggle against the Force of his Passion, and what might have happened if Miss Bellman had not found a half brick in the lane and struck my Asailant, I dare not imagine. His head rang like a dinner bell as he was wearing some sort of helment. He used dreadful langwedge then and released me, and then—to my astonishment—sprang away over a wall and we heard him running into the infathemable shadows of night!

I screamed all the way home though more from Fear and Shock than Injury, as his claws left only a scratch or two and some brooses this morning. I begged Miss Bellman not to tell Uncle Pyelott for reasons which will become plain, which were: that I suspect it was the handsome Clerk with black whiskers who so admired me at the Ball.

How I am certain it was no Unearthly Feind? You may wonder, but his face was at a distance of but inches and I saw plain he wore a mask. Also when he vommited fire there was a strong smell of gin afterward and I have seen gypsys at the Fair do as much, taking a mouthful of spirits and then blowing it across a brand. Miss Bellman found a burnt match in the lane as she was endevring to revive me and I do not doubt that was where the fire come from.

Poor man! Being unable to Approach me by reason of my Exalted Station, he contrived a desprate plan to sasiate his violent thwarted passion. I pity him but cannot somehow bring myself to condem him for it. Yet if my pa were to hear of this he would see him transported or at least hung.

When I contemplait what nearly occurred I fall into swooning. Be glad, Tilda, that you are unlikely to undergo such arrowing ordeals in Greta Bridge.

I remain

Yours and cetrer

Fanny Squeers

January 25, 1838 Thursday Morning

Oh Tilda,

I am so dreadfully low. I must unburden myself; though I cannot expect you to comperhend the nature of my woe. I do not think anybody could unless it might be Helen of Troy or King Arthurs wife whose name I cannot recall at the moment but who also was the cause of great suffering because of her fatal beauty.

My secret lover was not discouraged by the half brick, it seems. For some few nights after the Ball he has been seen several times around Salmon Lane, and in Catherine Street and on Bow Common. He is clearly haunting my path in hopes of beholding me once more. This is the consequence of passions feury denied I suppose, that drives a man to madness, but of course I am staying in at night—it were worse madness to tempt him further. So all sorts of persons have been making kimplaint to the constables about a tall masked man who leapt out from the gloom of night to surprize them, only to assault them when he discovered they were not me. There has been a blacksmith, a Respectable merchant and two boys so attacked. The children in the Lane have taking to calling him Spring-Heel'd Jack.

All this were misery enough for me to endure, knowing my accurst charms to be the cause of so much trouble. Judge then with what horror I learned the news late this morning that my poor Admirer is now also accused of *Murder*!

You remember Mr. Clement that I told you about, the prosprous gentleman who had a Ship Chandlery warehouse? He was the foremost of those who danced with me at the ball, and very pleasant and agreeable he was too, not so old for a man with so much money. Well he is dead! Stabbed through the heart, and left to waller in his own goar! It happened only last night. He and one of his partners had just left their counting-house in the Comercial Road and walked homeward. The partner (I think it was Mr. Tacker) parted from him at Dalglish Street and was going on for he lives hard by St. Anns.

Mr. Tacker had not got far when he heard a shout coming out of Dalglish Street. 'Here's Spring-Heel'd Jack!' he thought it said. And following on this was a scream that he thought might be Mr. Clement. He ran back and turned into Dalglish Street, only to see his friend laying dead there, weltering in blood! He looked all round but it was at a point where two lanes crossed and the Murderer might have run off in any direction. He raised the cry and the Police came but it was too late. They have arrested Mr. Tacker as he was seen by the bleeding Corpse and there were no witnesses.

But it is said by everybody that the real Murderer is Spring Heel'd Jack, because there were two boot-prints in the mud by Mr. Clement's Corpse but none leading up to it nor away, and it is supposed only Jack can leap so. Whatever shall I do? Can I think that I am responsibble for this shocking crime by reason of my beauty?

Be grateful, Tilda, that you will never bear such a weight on your conscience.
I remain
Yours and cetrer
Fanny Squeers

18ᵗʰ February, 1838 Sunday Afternoon

My dear Matilda,
So much has happened since last I put Pen to Paper, I hardly know where to begin. What news, you will surely ask, of Spring Heel'd Jack? What of the Infamous Murder? Read on and see for yourself.

You will recall I was sunk in woe at the thought that my dashing Admirer was guilty of so fowl a crime. Miss Bellman heard my tears and was so considerate as to ask what the matter was. Silly creature! As though it were not too plain. But I must not be unkind as she has no admirers and so no understanding of my grief. When I told her my fear she said it was certainly very queer that everyone said Spring-Heel'd Jack took such prodeejous leaps, when she had not seen him demonstrate any such Power.

I told her not to be a goose, because I myself had seen him Leap a wall at least ten feet high with but one bound. She replyed, that it wasn't ten feet but only four or five at most. I grew quite cross with her until we went out and looked at the very wall and I saw that she was correct in her asertion. The late hour, the shadows of night and my mortal terror must have affected my apperhension of the scene.

That was when the idea struck me like a Bolt from Heaven! What if some other person had designed to murder poor Mr. Clement, perhaps for his money, and seezed the opertunety of all the uproar over Jack's pranks to do it but make it appear as if it was Jack? I was convinced this was what had really happened and knew then that I must go to the Police, even at the risk of my good name, to explane things. If my Admirer were to be captured he would surely hang, unjustly, and my heart should break.

So I took Miss Bellman with me to the Police Station and it was very unsatisfacktry, you would think they would grant some creedence to a gentlemans daughter. So far from listening they were quite rude and positively jokular in their disbelief, but I determined not to leave the Station until I had some satisfaction. At last the Inspector called out a man of his, Constable Trumpiter, and bid him go out with us to look at the scene of the murder.

This Trumpiter is a pleasant youth if rather common and listened very thoughtfully to me as we walked back to Dalglish Street. Miss Bellman would keep interrupting me to explane things I should have thought were perfectly clear, but he heard her out without kimplaint. When we got to the scene of the murder I was in danger of swooning as there was still Blood in the street. Much of the area had been trampled over since the morning but we could still see the two boot prints in the mud by where the Corpse had layed.

I told the Constable what I had seen with my own eyes, vizz that Spring Heel'd Jack was only a man in a mask and could never have jumped over the houses to either side in the lane, never mind what foolish folk claimed, and that it were much more likely to have been Mr. Tacker done him in after all and put the boot prints there a-purpose to deceive. For I do not think I mentioned it before but Mr. Tacker is a sallow and ill-favoured sort of fellow, just what you would expect a Murderer to look like.

'Why, Miss Squeers, I am glad you explaned,' said Constable Trumpiter. 'You are perseptive to be sure. Only we are not certain of Mr. Tacker's gilt, because of the matter of the murder weepon.' I wanted to know what he meant by that and he told me that the Dagger that made the fatal wound was nowhere to be found at the scene, nor did Mr. Tacker have it on him, and he had had no place to hide it before the Police came running into the lane in answer to Mr. Tacker's cries.

'Why have you arrested him then?' said Miss Bellman, rather forewardly I thought. To which the Constable made reply that they had to arrest somebody or there would be Outcry, and in any case Mr. Tacker might turn out to have done it after all. 'But what about the murder weppon then?' she said. 'Where is it?'

Poor creature, she has no idea that a true lady is diferdent and unassuming and never speaks up like that. Poor Constable Trumpiter sighed and with a nice show of patience said we should search for it again, if she liked, but the Police had already hunted pretty thoroughly. So we looked up and down Dalglish Street. 'What horror,' you are perhaps saying, Tilda, 'to chance upon a Goary Blade!' And well you might. Thankfully we did not find any such a thing, but I heard Constable Trumpiter and Miss Bellman exclaiming over something and when I run to see, they were looking at some footprints they found in a little lane which serves as a conexion between Dalglish and Magaret Streets.

It was the prints of someone who had stood in his stocking feet hard by the wall. Constable Trumpiter showed me how they came up from the Comercial Road and it was plain where the man had stopped and pulled his boots off and stood a long time by the wall, for his prints was very clear there. Then the stocking prints ran out into Dalglish Street and vanished under all the treading down of the Policemens boots. The two boot prints by the blood was the very same as the ones of the man who was wearing them before he pulled them off to wait in his stockings! And we looked a little more and found the stocking prints running back into the little lane, and out into the Comercial Road again. And I saw there, just at the kerbstone, a tiny drop of Blood!

So I said it was plain the Murderer had been hiding in the lane, took off his boots so as to run quiet, and waited till Mr. Clement came along Dalglish Street, whereupon he run out and stabbed him, dropped his boots down so as to make the prints, yelled 'Here's Spring Heel'd Jack!' then run back the same way he came. Constable Trumpiter looked at me with admiration in his eyes and said he supposed it happened just so. He has peticklely fine eyes.

I then said what I thought, which was, that it might have been a Red Indian who slipped into the hold of some ship and traveled to England and crept out at Lime House, for they are supposed to delight in murder when it is least expected. But Miss Bellman said a Red Indian would be unlikely to know about Spring Heel'd Jack. Which I suppose is true.

Then Miss Bellman spoke up again and said she thought the murderer must have pitched the Bloody Blade in Lime House Basin. And it really seemed likely, because the last we could see of the prints before they dissapeared from being trampled by everyone in the Comercial Road, was that they seemed to be running for the Basin.

Constable Trumpiter was very taken with my prespickiticity, I could see, but he remained silent a while as he walked back and forth, looking time and again on what we had found. At last he said, 'It cannot have been a lunatic, for the deed was carefully planned; but who would want to kill Mr. Clement?'

And I replied that it must have been Mr. Tacker after all, that he might inherit all the Wealth of their business (for I knew Mr. Clement was a bachelor, you may be sure I asked at the Ball before I danced with him).

Miss Bellman said then that we ought to go speak with the prisoner, at which I very nearly swooned again at the mere idea but then thought better of it as he might confess the more readily if confronted by me with what I know. And, you know, Tilda, that though I am sensitive and shrink from unpleasantness, I can steal myself to face even Roaring Savages in matters of the heart.

So Constable Trumpiter took us round to see the Wretch in his tank. He had been weeping, most unmanly. My blood boiled to see him there, and I was all for striking him and demanding the Truth, but Miss Bellman put herself foreward again and asked him to account for himself, rather timidly I thought. Mr. Tacker asked the Constable whether he had to reply and the Constable said he had better, for we would not be denied.

Miss Bellman then asked Mr. Tacker why he wept so, and he said 'I am an innocent man', and called on God to witness he had not murdered Mr. Clement. She then asked him what had happened and he said that on Wednesday all had perceded as usual, except that at midday the younger partner Mr. Johnson had gotten word that his mother was ill and left to rush to her bedside. So he, Mr. Tacker I mean, had shut up the office at 6 o'clock and he and Mr. Clement walked together along the Comercial Road as was their dayly custom. They parted at Dalglish Street like they always done and Mr. Tacker walked on, suspecting nothing was amiss until he heard the shouting.

I then asked him the question which was burning foremost, which was 'Did you see a tall man in a cloak, wearing a mask?' which he replyed that he had not done, indeed he had seen nobody but the deceesed lying there until the first Policeman come running in answer to his cries for help. And Miss Bellman asked had he quarreled with Mr. Clement and he said 'No, never'.

But I could tell he was seezed by some great fear, as I am peticklely good at noticing that, so I said a little roughly that he had better not lie, for Truth Will Out. And the Constable said too that all his affairs would be gone into to veryfy what he said, and Mr. Johnson questioned as well.

At which Mr. Tacker blubbed again like a baby and, throwing up his hands to Heaven, said 'Oh, then it will all be known' and told us that he had borrowed against the business funds but meant to pay it back, and would have done so already but for an enexplicable delay on the part of his corispondent.

Constable Trumpiter looked very grave at that and went and asked his Superior to step in and listen. They made Mr. Tacker explane. He said that some six months past he had gotten a letter from a very respectable Widow whose late husband was the Treasurer for a society of Frenchmen who were supposed to be Investers but really had secret plans to Overthrow the French Government. And when her husband had found this out he was horrorfied as well he might be and took the money and hid it in an account in the French Bank, meaning to transfer it to the Bank of England, but then the villains apperhended his plan and had him Asassinated. So his Widow was desprate to transfer the money and a mutual friend had recommended she write to Mt. Tacker as an honest man. All he had to do was open a French Bank Account in his name with Six Hundred Pounds and make her his signee on it so she could transfer the villains' horde to his account and thence to an English account, in return for which kindness to a lady she would give him half the sum, which amounted to Ten Thousand Pounds in our money.

Well I would have done the same if I was a gentleman but the Inspector and Constable Trumpiter were pleased to be humerous about the whole thing and thought it a great joke. I was sorry for Mr. Tacker then and felt quite sure he had not done it after all. He got down on his knees and swore that the money would be replaced as soon as the French Widow wrote back to him, and that he was guilty of no other irregulerity and certainly not murder. For if Mr. Clement had not untimely died it had never come to light. They told him that was for the Coroner to hear out.

Constable Trumpiter asked him where Mr. Johnson (that was the young partner) lived, as he must be questioned. He gave us an address in Foxes Lane. Then Constable Trumpiter saw us out and I said we must go round to Foxes Lane at once to speak to Mr. Johnson, and Constable Trumpeter said we ladies could not possibly go there by ourselves as it is not in the best neborhood, and so offered to escort us. At which Miss Bellman simpered rather I am afraid. But I graciously thanked him and said we should be glad of the company.

Miss Bellman chattered on as we walked, saying that if so great a booby as Mr. Tacker had planned the murder, it had been extrornry. I thought that rather unfeeling of her. But Constable Trumpiter said he did not seem like much of a suspect now, still we would be surprized at the things he had seen in the Police. Whereon Miss Bellman, with rather too much artfulness, asked him to tell us please, whereupon he related several remarkable occurrences of Crime as we walked along. It is pity he is so common for he is rather clever, and very much the gentleman in his manners.

We got to Foxes Lane and it was indeed no place I should care to go alone, very mean and low, and it fell out that Mr Johnson lived in a lodging-house there. Or I should say, *had lived*: for when we knocked the owner of the Premises came and looked over the railings and said he was Cleared Out, having left Wendesday last. Which, you will remember, Tilda, was the day of the Murder!

Constable Trumpiter looked very grave at that and said he must be let in to search. To which the owner responded with alackrity and I must say people do respect the Police, they might almost be gentlemen.

We found a bare mean room quite empty but for some few Items of Furnituer that went with the premises, the bed and washstand and a monstrous old Scotch Chest. Miss Bellman went poking about whilst Constable Trumpiter spoke to the owner and found out that Mr. Johnson had not run off owing anything, indeed he had paid up and arranged for his trunk to be sent away two days before. And Miss Bellman looked at Constable Trumpiter as much as to say that that was odd since he had got the news about his Mother being ill only afterward on Wendesday. Constable Trumpiter asked where the trunk had been sent and the owner did not recall except it was to the village of H_____.

Just then Miss Bellman exclaimed, having been looking in the kimpartments in the Scotch Chest. There was an envelop stuck in the back of one, that had slid down so only a corner was poking out, as perhaps it had been missed in a hasty removal. Constable Trumpiter came and tried to get it out but couldn't pinch it hard enough and in the end I had to do it myself as my arm was siffishently slender enough to get back there and my fingers are quite strong when it comes to pinching.

It was a letter addressed to a Mr. Edmund Tollivere of Swan Cottage in H_____. I opened it and read it at once and it was only from a servant telling him his grandfather was taking clear broth now and felt much better, and asking whether he wanted his books sent on. I thought it must be from some former lodger but Miss Bellman pointed out that the village was the same as where the trunk was sent. Also it was dated just last month.

I saw plain that Mr. Johnson must have been the murderer, or why would he be living under a false name and running off in such haste? I said as much to Constable Trumpiter, who agreed that it was highly suspicious.

By this time it was quite late and so Constable Trumpiter escorted us back to Salmon Lane and we parted, with him promising to bring all this matter to the attention of the Inspector. I was sure my poor Admirer was out of danger of unjust Persecution.

Alas! I had not reckoned with Jack's foolish persistence. That very night he surprized a carpenter walking home late and blew fire in his face, as well as kicked him pretty hard and trampled on him somewhat. Constable Trumpiter came round to see me next day looking greatly aggreeved, to say that a Degelation of Cittzens had been to the Police Station and demanded that Spring Heel'd Jack must be brought to Justice. In consequence of which the Inspector would not listen to what we had found out about the mysterious Mr. Johnson, but ordered all his men to extra duty after dark, and I gather made some insulting remarks to Constable Trumpiter as well. His fine eyes flashed with impatience as he spoke of it.

Whereupon Miss Bellman, who happened to be sewing in the room and heard this, said that we might go to H_____ ourselves and see what we might find out, as it is only an hours journey out of London. Constable Trumpiter said then that if we ladies were intent on going, he would go with us, since he was not on duty until half past Nine.

I was a little concerned about the perpritey of this but Miss Bellman is all of seven-and-twenty, quite old and plain enough to serve as a suitable Chaperone. So we left a note for Aunt Pyelott, who had taken a glass of cordial for the Headache and was resting, and hired a man to drive us to H_____.

H_____ must be a pretty little town in summer, I was surprized to find such a rustick spot so close to London, with a nice Inn called the Moulders Arms where we had some refreshment for which Constable Trumpiter paid, very much like a gentleman though I suppose a Constable's wages is not very great, and I fear he was showing off a little for my sake which was dear of him. Afterward he advised me to walk about and enjoy the fresh air and pleasant sights while he went round to make some inquiries.

Miss Bellman wanted to see the shops, though of course she has no money either, and there was only the one shop in any case. But nothing would do but she must go in, so we did. It was very like Mr. Wealies shop in Greta Bridge only rather bigger with more wares. I diverted myself looking at things but Miss Bellman engaged the shopmistress in continuous chatter and really I could not think what she was at at first.

She began with cumpliments about what a pleasantly situated spot H_____ is and how nice the air is and asked the shopmistress, did folk live to great age thereabouts? Because she had an Elderly Relation in London who the Doctors advise must quit business for his health, and he wouldn't, but she thought that if she might find a convenient place close by London he might agree. Now I almost said out loud 'What stuff' because of course she has no such relation unless it was Uncle Pyelott and he is quite well.

But you see it was an Artful Ruse. For she got the lady to talking about all the old folk in the village, Gammer This and Old Mistress That and Mr. Somebody's uncle who was a hundred and two though deaf as a post and blind and had to be kept by the Hob like a baby and couldn't remember a thing past three-quarters of an Hour though when he was clear headed he could tell you all about being at Calcutta with Clive. 'So all the old folks are quite hale and sound?' said Miss Bellman.

'Well,' quoth the shopmistress, 'There is poor old Mr. Spool, who has been ailing these three years and is expected to go off any time now; and he is only five-and-seventy I think; but sorrow and temper have shortened his years, which only goes to show that money ain't everything,' and of course Miss Bellman asked what did she mean?

Well it seems that this Spool had been given to prudent Industry and built a manefactry somewhere in the north and made his fortune quite young. He came down to H_____ and built a Mansion and married. Before many years wore out he was blest with a son and then a daughter. But lately he has been greatly dissapointed in the grandson who has been ordered out of the house.

And Miss Bellman said, 'Would that be young Mr. Tollivere?' which quite amazed me and was the first inkling I had she is a cunning and crafty creature, for one who looks so simple. And the shopmistress said, 'Oh, so you heard of him, have you?' and added that he was indeed wild in his ways and she told about how when he was no more than ten years old he came into her shop and made off with two fistsful of sugar sticks to a value of sixpence.

A man came in then to buy limiment for Sheep so we said Good Afternoon and left.

I asked Miss Bellman what she was getting at and she said, 'Don't you see? If Mr. Johnson is really Mr. Tollivere, then we know he is a bad sort. What business did he have going up to London incognitto?'

I said, that I supposed he needed money but was too proud to let it be known he had to go into a business. And supposing he had done the Murder for the money? But Miss Bellman asked why did he leave London then, you would think he had staid and got the benefit of Mr. Tacker being arrested, which would leave him in possesssion of their Firm. Which I didn't know. By then it was snowing some so we went back to the Moulders Arms because Miss Bellman is thin blooded and not robust as I am.

We were having a warm by the public room fire when Constable Trumpiter came in looking very handsome, with the cold putting a bloom in his cheeks, and have I mentioned his hair is curly and a nice chesnut color? He swept off his hat and sat down by us and looked at me very direct and said, 'Miss Squeers, you danced with Mr. Johnson, did you not?' To which I replyed that I did, and he said 'If I was to give you a pencil and paper, could you draw his counternance?'

At which I blushed for I never learnt drawing as my pa engaged that drawing-master but he left after a week and took the spoons too. So I demured. Constable Trumpiter said 'Perhaps then you might describe him to me?' and he took out a notebook and pencil and licked the pencil point. 'Was his face round or long?' So I said long and gave other particulers, with him asking more questions, and in a few minutes he held out the open book and said, 'Is that him?'

I declare, Tilda, he had Mr. Johnson, or should I say Mr. Tollivere, to the life. He tapped the book with his pencil and said that he had found out the way to Swan Cottage by asking, and had gone there and watched, and seen this very gentleman standing at a window of the cottage. I was all for going there direct and having him Arrested, but Constable Trumpiter said we needed more Evidence he had done something wrong.

Miss Bellman then exitedly told him about what we had found out from the shopmistress. The Constable's eyes sparkled something lovely, he was very pleased; he said he'd just go up and see what he could learn from the servants up at The Larch, which was Mr. Spool's Mansion. Miss Bellman wanted to go too, which shows a kimplete lack of discretion about what is proper, but Constable Trumpiter very kindly pointed out the snow was falling rather harder now and she ought to remain by the fire.

So we sat in the snug and had muffins and tea, and I am afraid Miss Bellman displaid an unbecoming apptite. She is rather plump, and if she goes on in this way I do not doubt but that her figguer will be the worse for it. Still it is unlikely to matter much, as she is certain to make an old maid.

She lowered herself so far as to engage in conversation with the serving-maid who brought the muffins, asking what the news of the day was. The girl replyed, that there was to be a great party come Coronation Day, and Squire H_____ had put in an order for six barrels of wine to drink the little Queen's health, to be ordered special from France.

Miss Bellman then asked if it was likely Mr. Spool would attend, at which the girl made a great show of scorn and said not likely; that he was a quarrelsome old man (only *man* is not the word she used, but to write the same would pollewt my pen) and hated everyone, and was like to die before summer ever came anyway. Then she coloured and said she was sorry to speak so, if we knew the man.

Of course we didn't, but this was more of Miss Bellman's cunning, for she said, 'We only know him by hearsay; but I had heard Mr. Spool was recovering and expected to live a while yet.'

The saucy girl then put her finger by her nose and said she heard diffrent; and went so far as to sit down across from us and impart the news that her brother who knew the gardner at The Larch had heard that Mr. Spool was sending to find his son, that he had quarreled with years agone, so as to make amends, and why should he do that unless he were like to die?

Miss Bellman said she supposed it might be so; and asked whether the old man had had any news of the boy. The girl said he wasn't a boy, if he was still alive; he would be quite old himself now. But from what she had heard, the earth might have swallowed him up for all that any one knew what had become of him, since he walked out of his fathers house declaring he would never see him again, and that was thirty years ago.

Miss Bellman said that was a great pity and the girl asked if there was anything else we wanted. I told her, 'No, I thank you' and when she had gone I wished to have a few words with Miss Bellman about her deplorble habit of conversation with anybody.

But she exclaimed, that she'd give a pretty penny to know how much money Mr. Spool had to leave to his Heirs. Which was such a common thing to say, I was quite repelled, though I wondered about the money myself. So we sat there, though she did not seem to notice my Mortifyed Silence because she was thinking quite hard, muttering to herself now and again, and her cheeks were so red from the cold and then sitting by the fire that I pitied her, for anyone seeing her must think she had been drinking Liquor.

Presently Constable Trumpiter came running in and said we must rouse our coachman if we were to get back to Lime House before nightfall. When we were back in the coach, Miss Bellman repeated what she had heard from the serving maid, and Constable Trumpiter forbore to rebeuke her, but listened courteously.

Then he told us what he had learned, which was that Mr. Spool had a great deal of money indeed, and had had someone in to see about rewriting his will. It was supposed he had meant to Disinheirit his Grandson, Mr. Tollivere. He had forborn doing this while his daughter was alive, but she had gone to her aternal reward two years since, leaving the Wastrel some little money of her own.

I saw at once that here 'Mr. Johnson' was caught out in another lie, for had he not said his mother was ill? And here she was dead. Which I said to Constable Trumpiter, who quite agreed. Though I still could not disern why the undoubted villain should kill a complete stranger like poor Mr. Clement.

We parted with many respectful remarks and that night I lay in dreadful nightmares, all about Murder and Bloody Blades. Then I was in the shop in H_____ and it was full of sticks of sugar shaped like little Policemen, and when I turned around there was Spring-Heel'd Jack, who went down on one knee to offer me his heart, which was made of metal and ran with blue and white Flames.

Next morning we heard how my poor Admirer had led the Police a merry chase, though they had been out with clubs and nets to catch him, and still had jumped out at an old woman near the Gas Works and pulled her hair. You can imagine that I breathed a sigh of relief to know that he had evaded Capture another night, but I did wish he would ceese this foolish passionate behaviour.

In the afternoon Constable Trumpiter came to the door, looking rather tired but smiling, and asked whether I and Miss Bellman would like to go with him back to H_____, for he had just come from making more Inquiries and felt sure he had enough Evidence now to make an Arrest. I said yes with great alacrity and very nearly danced with impatience while Miss Bellman explained to Aunt Pyelott. Aunt Pyelott was disinclined to let us go at first and the more so when she saw the two stout fellows Constable Trumpiter had with him, but on hearing what we were about she said to be sure and get a share in any fines that might be collected. Which had not even entered my mind I am sure.

In the coach, Constable Trumpiter told us what he had found out by going to the late Mr. Clement's house. The Housekeeper had let him go through Mr. Clement's papers and he had been specially interested in a packet relating to Mr. Clement's late father: Certifiket of Death, debts paid and such. Most interesting of all, he said, were some old letters from a Miss Adeline Spool (later Mrs. Adeline Tollivere) at The Larch, H_____.

It seemed plain to me that this Mr. Clement's father must have had some romantic connexion with Miss Spool, and perhaps there was a Missing Heir. What if Mr. Clement had been Mr. Johnson's (though I should call him Mr. Tollivere) Lost elder Brother? Except of course he should be ilejitimate, but sometimes great families hush that sort of thing up. Constable Trumpiter said that all would be revealed in due time.

We were delayed on the Road what with one of the Horses going lame and had to change for a fresh one at Five Mile House, so it was twilight when we arrived in H_____. We drove straight to Swan Cottage. Constable Trumpiter said we ladies had perhaps ought to remain in the Coach as there was likely to be unpleasantness when he arrested Edmund Tollivere. He got out with the two stout gentlemen, who took a pair of clubs from under the seat, and they went and knocked at the door of the cottage. No sooner had they been admitted than Miss Bellman said she must know what befell, and I agreed, so we got out and walked round the cottage to see if there was any convenient window to listen at. I am afraid I tript over and fell in a lettuce-frame, which dissarrayed my hair rather.

Just round a box-tree on the corner of the house was a window, and we could see in as well, though by reason of the falling dark we could not be seen. The two stout gentleman were standing at either door, and Mr. Tollivere stood before his hearth. Oh, what a change had come over his countenance! For I had seen him at the Ball the very pictuer of agreeableness, but now his expression was all compounded of fear, scorn and wickedness genrally, and it made my blood boil to see him so and think of his awful designs.

Constable Trumpiter stood before him, very grave, and was just saying something about the suspicious circumstances attending Mr. Tollivere's hasty removal from London, where he was living under a false name. Mr. Tollivere said he'd done no such thing; he had lived quietly at Swan Cottage these five years and never traveled. Constable Trumpiter said he had witnesses to prove otherwise.

Mr. Tollivere then sneered and said he had witnesses of his own who would swear that he'd never gone up to London at all. Constable Trumpiter, with no show of annoyance, said that there was also the matter of the murdered man being Mr. Tollivere's cousin, which made the next likely to inherit a sure suspect in the fowl crime.

'Oh, very likely,' said Mr. Tollivere, 'My Grandfather has had paid men searching for his son for years now; they should have found him if anyone might, if he were still alive.'

'But they did not have what you had,' said Constable Trumpiter steadily. "Letters from Edgar Spool to his sister, your late mother, letting her know that he was well and had settled in London under the name of Clement.' He went on to say that later Mr. Spool-Clement must have written that he was married, for his sister wrote back to ask whether he would not reconcile with his father on the happy occasion. But, said Constable Trumpiter, he must have refused; for her next letter was dated some years later, offering consolation to her brothers widow and son.

'And when your mother died,' said Constable Trumpiter, 'You, going through her papers, found the letters from her brother, and learnt from them that you had a Cousin, and who he was and where he was likely to be. It was then you first planned to murder him.' For you see Tilda, the Cousin (that was young Mr. Clement, the deceesed), should he be found, would stand to inherit all the Fortune.

How I admired Constable Trumpiter! He stood tall and straight and looked so handsome in his uniform as he was laying these charges. Edmund Tollivere said it was all rubbage and Constable Trumpiter said no it wasn't. He then went on to describe how Mr. Tollivere had come to London, sought out his cousin, joined the Partnership under an Assumed Name, and watched all his cousins habits so as to learn when he might best do the dreadful deed.

When Spring-Heel'd Jack begun to Frequent Lime House, Mr. Tollivere devised his Wicked Plan, to make it look as though my mad Admirer done it. When I heard this I was struck dumb with horror at the wicked cleverness of it all, for though I had been sure he was Guilty I had not understood the Depth of his Cunning. And when I thought of poor Jack, who is only mad for love of me, being drawn into his web of deseet my rath knew no bounds!

Constable Trumpiter said, 'Now, sir, will you come with us to London? For you must go before the Magistrait.'

Would you believe it Tilda, Mr. Tollivere said that he would not; that Constable Trumpiter had no proof of his cock-and-a-bull story, and they were not in London, and if they did not quit his house instantly he would see Constable Trumpiter dismissed from the Police for making False Accusations. But his voice was a little shrill and he was sweating.

I was in such a perfect feury I was insensible to danger, and seezed the window and pulled it open, and pointing my finger at him accused him of Murder; whereat all in the room started and Mr. Tollivere was so dismayed by the Violent Emotion in my countenance that he screamed and backed into the fender, which put him in mind of Hellfire perhaps, for he fell over howling and begging for mercy, and I realised he thought I was an Aparishen, perhaps of Stern Justice herself.

Anyone would have despised him, to see him so unmanned by womans beauty. And it seemed that while he was Groveling there with his trousers afire he let slip some few words that he had been led astray by bad companions and had only done it because he was in debt, cetrer, which Constable Trumpiter told him was a confession.

Well they put manacles on him strait and now he sits in gaol and will be Tried and Hung, I have no doubt. I am happy and sereen for I have cleared my Admirers name, or at least have ensured that he will not be taken up for Murder. I cannot imagine how anyone could plot the death of his own Flesh and Blood. But then my Family is a very diffrent sort, as we Squeerses are all very fond of ourselves.

Oh, Tilda, how quiet things must be at Greta Bridge, compared to this! I am afraid I shall find it rather dull when I return. My best regards.

I remain

Yours and cetrer

Fanny Squeers

23 February, 1838 Friday evening

Oh, Tilda, the *Infamy* of *Men*!

But you will not find this letter blotted with my tears. I am full of stern resolution and contempt for these poor creatures.

The news of Mr. Tollivere's arrest was scarcely a day old when I had word that Spring-Heel'd Jack had proved false to me. He went to a house in Bow, enticed a Miss Alsop to come out to him in the Lane, and there Took Liberties with her person in a most shocking manner that left no doubt it was the same man who but a fortnight ago was so perockupied with me. It was Romeo and Rosaline played over. And there can be no question about his mistaking her for me because she had a candle by which he must have seen her quite clear.

After all my labours on his behalf to clear him of suspicion! I thought it really past anything for Rank Ingrattitude.

You should know too that Constable Trumpiter has proposed Marriage to Miss Bellman. We were all rather surprized but really it is much the best thing for her, even though he is so very common, as she is not likely ever to get a better offer. It is good for her she has such sharp eyes, she will need them when she must sew buttons on a poor Policemans uniform. And I daresay her plumpness will greatly diminish when she has to live on the sort of victuels a Policemans wage affords. May they be very happy together. I have no doubt they will be. But I had thought him a more discriminating person.

When we had been confronted with this news Uncle Pyelott was very cheerful, as well he might be since now he will be spared the expence of Miss Bellman's keep, and said we should have a bottle of Madeera to celebrate. But there were none in the Sideboard and Aunt Pyelott asked if I might step out to the Wine Merchants which was still open. I was glad of any excuse to get out of the parlour, even on so dark an evening, for it was hard to conceal my Disdain at the imoderit way Miss Bellman was behaving with Constable Trumpiter.

I was coming back and had not got above four or five yards from the Spirits Shop when who should have the effrontary to leap out before me but Spring Heel'd Jack! My indignation knew no bounds and as you know I am Fearless when once my Temper is up. I brake the bottle of Madeera on a convenient wall and rushed at him with it, and the booby turned as if to run but I caught him and tript him up. The bottle did not cut him very badly because he wore some sort of oilskin, and he knocked it from my hand as I was dragging his helment off, but I took off part of his ear anyway and got my Knees on his chest and so held him down pretty well as I renched the Mask off.

Imagine my amazement, Tilda, when I tell you it was not the handsome man with the black whiskers at all! I recognised him for a shy dull fellow who had stood mute by the Punch Bowl and wore a vulgar waistcoat that hardly danced with anybody. Which, as I remember because I asked at the time, was because he was only somebody's clerk and not worth cultivating the acquaintance of.

At the thought that such as he had dared to assault me, a gentlemans daughter, my very Blood boiled in my vanes. I rained Blows on him with my fists and pulled out his hair until he was screaming and weeping and emploring Mercy. He said it was only a joke and he meant no harm, and promised he would never do it any more. Only the thought that if he were taken by the Police it would all get into the papers made me decyst, and in any case he was making so much Noise someone might have come out to inquire what was the matter.

I did him an Injury he will not soon forget and, rising, pitched the disgusting Mask into the canal. When I came back with the new bottle of Madeera he was dragging himself away on his hands and knees and begun to whemper when he saw me, but I spurned to notice him and only kicked him once in passing for I had done with him.

When I got back to Aunt Pyelott's I was quite faint at the dreadfulness of everything and was obliged to retire to my chamber the rest of the evening.

It has all spoilt the city for me rather and I have decided to quit London next week, instead of staying until summer. I return to Dotheboys Hall sadder, Tilda, but ever so much wiser. I shall not again soon—if ever indeed— lose my heart to perfidious Men.

I remain
Yours and cetrer
Fanny Squeers

Bad Machine

Alec Checkerfield, like other members of the administrative class, was enrolled in a Circle of Thirty when he was eleven. This was intended to forge lasting bonds with his fellow junior aristocrats, embedding him firmly in the social stratum he would occupy during his adult life.

The experiment was not a notable success. By the time he was sixteen, he had managed to alienate nearly half of those with whom he was meant to row the great galley of the state through mid-century.

Alec was not a bully, nor was he ambitious for power, nor was he given to unpopular political views. He was pleasant, polite and noncompetitive, exactly as a model citizen ought to be.

However, he *was* large.

And talented.

▲▼▲

"The Ape Man's at it again," said Alistair Stede-Windsor in disgust. Elvis Churchill and Musgrave Halliwell-Blair turned to look, with identical expressions of loathing on their patrician young faces.

The object of their concerted ill-will sat some distance away, under the great plane tree that shaded the Designated Youth Zone. He appeared to be telling a story, in quite unnecessarily musical tones, to four girls who sat around him. They appeared to be enthralled.

"Don't they realize what he's doing?" muttered Halliwell-Blair.

"Look at that hypocritical smile," said Stede-Windsor. "You know why he smiles with his lips closed like that, don't you? It's to hide those ghastly long teeth."

"I'm positive he's some kind of genetic freak," said Churchill. "Seriously. I wonder...ought we make a discreet call to the Reproduction Board?"

"What, to have him tested? See whether he's some kind of degenerate throwback? Or mutation?" said Stede-Windsor, brightening.

There was a thoughtful silence, broken by Halliwell-Blair saying: "No good, gentlemen. I've already investigated his bloodlines. The honourable Cecelia Ashcroft-Checkerfield actually passed a genetic screening test. Voluntarily. And the sixth earl is tall, too."

"What a pity," said Churchill. "No chance we could get him on abnormal psychology? He's clearly a sexual obsessive."

"Obviously," said Stede-Windsor.

Alec Checkerfield concluded his tale, and the girls shrieked with appreciative laughter at its punchline. Beatrice Louise Jagger leaned forward, especially her chest, and said something breathless and sincere to Alec. He smiled at her and took her hand. Raising it to his lips, he inhaled appreciatively before kissing it.

The three young gentlemen flinched.

"Oh, I'm going to puke!" cried Stede-Windsor.

"Disgusting," said Churchill.

"*Trite*," said Halliwell-Blair. "If only they could see themselves!"

"He's a filthy…" Stede-Windsor sought for an ancient pejorative. "He's a lounge lizard, that's what he is!"

Alec Checkerfield relinquished Beatrice Louise Jagger's hand, smiling at her with eyes blue as high tide on a Caribbean beach. So pleasant was his expression that the slight oddness of his features might be missed, by any scrutiny less hostile than Halliwell-Blair's. If his pale eyes were smaller, if his cheekbones were higher, if his mouth was wider than the norm—why, he was only a horse-faced young man, wasn't he?

Jill Courtenay said something witty, and Alec shouted with laughter. In that moment of spontaneous mirth, his teeth were briefly visible and they were certainly long, and white, and rather sharp-looking.

The onlookers shuddered.

"Not a lounge lizard, exactly," amended Stede-Windsor. "More of a lounge tyrannosaur."

▲▼▲

The young gentlemen need not have concerned themselves. They were, after all, untried amateurs. Others existed who were far better at protecting public health and morals.

Mr. Elrond Frist was one of these. His life's work was tedious, but desperately important, and he was devoted to it. He it was who tracked the sales of certain retail items for the Bureau of Public Health, and his beat covered the whole of metropolitan London. When sales of any one of the goods he monitored reached a certain level, he duly informed his superiors. Certain steps were then taken or not taken, depending on the circumstances.

Today he stared, unbelieving, at sales figures for Happihealthy Shields.

They had been climbing steadily for the last six months. Respectable sales were desirable, for every registered sexually active citizen had a duty to use Happihealthies. When the total number of Happihealthies sold exceeded the number of registered sexually active citizens by a ratio of fifteen to one, however, something was terribly *wrong* in metropolitan London.

Trembling, Mr. Frist rose and went to his communications console. He rang a certain commcode.

"Mr. Peekskyll," he said, "I think you'd better see something."

▲▼▲

Mr. Sandbanks Peekskyll had been granted certain powers by the state, because his stability and his good judgment were considered to be beyond question. If his stability and good judgment were not quite what the state assumed them to be, nevertheless he saw a great deal through those pinpoint pupils of his, and discharged his duties with zeal and efficiency.

Mr. Peekskyll had been *cyborged;* which is to say, he had had himself adapted for direct interface with the government's database, through the installation of a small port in the back of his head. As long as its connector plug was removed at night and sterilized on a daily basis, he suffered no health problems, and as long as he kept his hat on, no one had any reason to object to his appearance.

He mused now over the figures Mr. Frist had sent him.

After a moment he thought in a request. Within seconds he had what he had asked for: a list of all suppliers of Happihealthies in London, with attendant sales figures for the last month. Some shops reported normal sales figures; others reported unusually high turnover. Mr. Peekskyll drummed his fingers on the console a moment before thinking in another request.

The screen before him displayed a map of London, with the locations of all shops in question highlighted in varying shades of red, the intensity of the color corresponding to the number of packets sold.

There appeared to be a series of concentric circles radiating from one block in Bloomsbury, sedate pink along the edges but blazing scarlet toward its center.

Mr. Peekskyll exhaled sharply. With another request he had the names of every resident within the defined area. He narrowed his eyes, and decided to play a hunch. He went straight to Happihealthy Incorporated's database, pulling up their mail order figures. One more command got him the shipping addresses for all orders. He found one for an address in Bloomsbury. Six orders had been shipped in the last year.

Satisfied that he had done his job, Mr. Peekskyll rang his superior.

"Mr. Buddy-Wires? Something of interest here," he said.

▲▼▲

Mr. Evel Buddy-Wires ran an empire of his very own. He took steps that needed to be taken. He liked his job a great deal. He hadn't purchased a packet of Happihealthies in twenty years. He didn't need them.

"Roger Checkerfield," he said thoughtfully. "Sixth earl of Finsbury, eh? I can't say I'm surprised. He's a thoroughgoing degenerate. Record of substance abuse and no sense of duty at all. Repeatedly fined for failing to attend Parliament."

"With respect, sir," said Mr. Peekskyll. "The charges have been made to his credit account, but the, er, merchandise hasn't been shipped to him. He's living on a yacht in the Caribbean."

"So he is," said Mr. Buddy-Wires, glancing at the screen. "But then who, in his London home, is buying such an obscene number of Happihealthies?"

Mr. Peekskyll cleared his throat.

"Our records list three persons resident at that address," he said. "Malcolm Lewin, age ninety-six, member of the household staff. Florence Lewin, age ninety-eight, also member of the household staff. Married couple, but they haven't registered as sexually active in decades."

"I should think not," said Mr. Buddy-Wires in distaste. "And the third member of the household?"

"Alec William St. James Thorne Checkerfield, age sixteen," said Mr. Peekskyll.

"*Ah.*"

"Who, being underage, is of course not registered either."

"Of course." Mr. Buddy-Wires smiled, feeling a warm glow inside. He leaned back from his console and steepled his fingers.

"Shall I alert the Public Health Monitors, sir?" Mr. Peekskyll inquired.

"No, no, not just yet. We want to investigate further," replied Mr. Buddy-Wires. "Little Alec seems to be a very naughty boy, but let's be sure."

"He can't actually be using them himself," said Mr. Peekskyll. "No-one could use that many! He must be selling them to other minors, illegally."

"Undoubtedly. Delinquent himself and contributing to the corruption of other children? I really fear it's Hospital for our young friend," said Mr. Buddy-Wires with relish.

"I would think we'll need an airtight case, then," said Mr. Peekskyll. "What with him being peerage. Lord Finsbury's sure to appeal any diagnosis."

"I hope to take down Lord Finsbury as well," said Mr. Buddy-Wires. His smile just kept getting wider. "In fact, particularly. A case can be made that this is his fault, after all! See what's come of his deplorable lifestyle? What kind of man leaves his offspring in the care of a senile butler and cook for years on end? If he'd stayed home like a responsible citizen, he might have exercised some paternal influence."

▲▼▲

The truth was that Alec had had quite a lot of paternal influence, though not from Roger Checkerfield. Malcolm Lewin, who was not at all senile, had provided the boy with some guidance. However, Alec's main role model and advisor was even now tapped in to Mr. Buddy-Wire's communications console, listening to every word spoken in the room. And he was as alarmed, and as grimly angry, as a machine can be.

It was universally acknowledged that artificial intelligences were incapable of experiencing real emotion. If it were for one moment supposed otherwise, there would be no end to the cry for machine suffrage; and in a world where first the poor, and then women, and then foreigners, and at last even animals had been granted the right to the pursuit of happiness, this last line must be drawn in the sand, lest the world descend into rank animism.

So it was argued that the complex system of electromagnetic reactions that gave a machine the *analogue* of emotion—the elaborate programming that created the illusions of satisfaction or need, to enable it to function properly—was nothing whatever like the complex system of chemical reactions that motivated an organic being.

Nevertheless, Captain Morgan was swearing to himself now, and using language that would make any organic blanch, too.

When Roger Checkerfield's credit account had been examined, silent alarms had sounded in Bloomsbury. From that moment the Captain's attention had been drawn from his usual pastime of monitoring Alec through the network of surveillance cameras throughout London. He had continued to watch over his boy with one eye, as it were; but he had also extended his observation to the consoles used by Mr. Peekskyll and Mr. Buddy-Wires, as well as their in-office surveillance cameras.

Hell and damnation, the Captain thought to himself. *There just ain't no rest for the wicked, is there, now?*

He defined himself as *wicked* because he was a pirate. He was a pirate because five-year-old Alec had liked pirates, and had (against all probability and incidentally the law too) therefore reprogrammed his Pembroke Playfriend unit to reflect his personal tastes. Though the Captain's customized abilities had increased in a manner that would have appalled his original designers at Pembroke Technologies, his core programming remained unchanged: to protect and nurture Alec Checkerfield. And the Captain was now the most powerful artificial intelligence in London.

The Captain watched intently, baring his metaphorical teeth as Mr. Buddy-Wires dismissed Mr. Peekskyll and squeezed in a few inquiries on the medical and academic history of Alec William St. James Thorne Checkerfield.

What a nosy lubber it is, to be sure...I reckon countermeasures is called for, aye.

▲▼▲

"It's just a word," said Alec. "It can't hurt you. Or anybody! Just a word to describe a perfectly normal, natural, beautiful, er, expression of love between two people, okay?" He had a warm, golden sort of voice, and was speaking with all the suavity he could muster.

"Okay," said The Honourable Sophia Fitzroy, breathing heavily. She had retreated with him to the relative privacy behind the Designated Youth Zone's garden shed.

"Okay. Now, here's another word," said Alec, and said one. "And all *that* is, is a part of your body. A really beautiful part, which is, after all, the whole source of life and everything. Right?"

"Right," said The Honourable Sophia Fitzroy, appalled but also rather thrilled.

"Right. So it's nothing to be ashamed of at all, wouldn't you have to agree?"

"I guess so," said The Honourable Sophia Fitzroy, thinking of the brief hesitant fumblings of Colin Debenham and Alistair Stede-Windsor, who had seemed terribly ashamed.

"I mean, if you look at the exhibits in the British Museum, you'll see 'em everywhere," said Alec earnestly, gazing deep into her eyes. "And nobody thinks that's wrong. And, you know what else you see in the British Museum?"

"What?"

Alec said another word. It was a plural noun. The Honourable Sophia Fitzroy gaped.

"You never!"

"You do, though," said Alec. "There's all these statues have 'em large as life. Well, almost as large as life. Now, see, you're turning red, and that's so sad, really, because it's only another word, isn't it? And what's wrong with it, if you just listen?" He repeated the word, as a singular noun now. He repeated it several times, in differing intonations: brightly, solemnly, prayerfully, humorously.

The Honourable Sophia Fitzroy began to giggle. So far, Alec was living up to his reputation.

"See? I feel absolutely no embarrassment about it," said Alec. "And why should I? It's only a word to describe a part of *my* body. So it's cool."

The Honourable Sophia Fitzroy said the word, in an experimental way, and blushed.

"There, you see?" exclaimed Alec, blushing too. "Nothing wrong with it at all. And without it there wouldn't be any sexual love, which is the most beautiful experience two people can have together. Isn't it?"

"Well, except for catching diseases and babies and things," said The Honourable Sophia Fitzroy.

"Ah! Well, that was true in the old days, when people didn't know any better," said Alec. "But, of course, we've got *these* now!"

He drew from his pocket a Happihealthy, and held it up with a triumphant smile. Every boy in the Circle of Thirty carried a Happihealthy on his person at all times. After the first few months a Happihealthy began to look rather sad, its cheery little wrapper crumpled and squashed from prolonged contact with the inside of a boy's pocket, gummed with lint and crumbs and other things best not mentioned. Sometimes, after years of fruitless anticipation, a Happihealthy might even split its wrapper and expire with a vacuum-packed sigh, like a spinster aunt at a wedding.

Alec's Happihealthy, however, was bright and fresh and eager-looking, for it had been slipped into his pocket only that morning.

The Honourable Sophia Fitzroy cast a furtive glance at the nearest surveillance camera. "But they can see us," she whispered.

"Not here," said Alec. "That one's got a half-hour sweep cycle. It turned away just before we went in here. And the one across the way is switched off for repair."

"And you can really...?"

"All the time," said Alec proudly. "Want to see?"

The Honourable Sophia Fitzroy bit her lower lip.

"I'm desperately curious," she admitted.

"No gentleman leaves a lady desperate," said Alec. Leaning forward, he took her face in his hands, very gently, and kissed her. She made a surprised sound.

Five minutes later she was making greedy sounds.

Ten minutes later she was walking from behind the shed, slightly unsteady, with very wide eyes. After a discreet pause Alec followed her, hands in his pockets. He caught up with The Honourable Sophia Fitzroy and steered her to a fruit ice cart, where he gallantly bought her a Cherry Bingo.

And though nobody had seen them enter or leave the space behind the shed, something was in the air. Alistair Stede-Windsor, Elvis Churchill, Musgrave Halliwell-Blair, Colin Debenham, Hugh Rothschild, Dennis Neville, Edgar Shotts-Morecambe and a few others sensed it, and glared at Alec the rest of the day. Strutting, he ignored them.

The Honourable Sophia Fitzroy spent the rest of the day in close and hushed conversation with a small circle of friends. Occasionally they could be heard to giggle.

▲▼▲

Alec ran up the steps to his room two at a time, removing his tie as he went. He swaggered through the doorway, whirling his tie about his head.

"Permission to come on board, Captain sir!" he yelled gleefully, flinging himself into a chair.

From its corner up near the ceiling, a Maldecena projector pivoted and extended an arm; a beam of light shot forth, and a second later Captain Morgan materialized, looming before Alec in hologram.

He no longer appeared wearing the scarlet coat and cocked hat little Alec had given him long ago; these days he took the form of a large and rather threatening-looking man in a three-piece-suit. His hair and wild beard were black as the Jolly Roger, however, and he was still prone to draw a cutlass from midair in the heat of argument.

"Alec, we got to have a parley," he said sternly.

"Fire away," said Alec, sticking out one long leg and pushing off from the wall so his chair skated backward.

"You been having at the wenches again, ain't you, boy?"

"Er—" Alec looked up into the Captain's eyes, which were just at this moment the color of the North Sea in a storm. He considered lying, very briefly, and then said, "Yeah. But not anywhere near the Coastal Patrol, like you told me," in a small voice.

"What else did I tell you, you damn fool?" the Captain roared.

"Always use Happihealthies," said Alec. "And I have been."

"Happihealthies, aye. And considering I ordered you a whole bloody case what was supposed to last you till you come of age, would you mind telling me why you been buying 'em at every goddamned chemist's within a five-mile radius?"

"Oh," said Alec. "I, er, needed more. But I've been really sneaky, Captain! I never buy 'em at the same shop twice, see? So nobody suspects."

The Captain rolled his eyes. Alec, regaining a little of his composure, grinned shamefacedly. "Anyway, it's in aid of a humanitarian cause. You know what I found out today, Captain? Out of all the guys in Circle, I'm the only one who can—er—"

"Fire a broadside?"

"Yup!" Alec flung up his fists like a victorious athlete. "Boom, boom, boom! Sophia told me I'm a, what was her phrase? A fantastic monster prodigy. Mr. Twenty-four/Seven. Alistair Stede-Windsor can't. Dennis Neville can't. Just meeeee!"

He leaped from his chair and did a suggestive dance of triumph in the center of the room. The Captain's cameras swiveled to follow him, as the Captain scowled.

"Listen to me, son," he said. "This ain't safe."

"Of course it's safe," said Alec. "I always use Happihealthies, okay? And I always send the surveillance cameras a fake signal, so the Public Health Monitors won't have a clue—"

"Which is why *I* ain't had no inkling either, ain't it?" the Captain growled.

"Yeah, well, okay, sorry. And we're always really careful about anybody else seeing. And none of the girls are going to talk! They love me. I love them. Terrifically well. Maybe I'll have a badge printed up. 'Checkerfield Satisfies!' Or post a notice on the news kiosk," babbled Alec, aware he had overstepped the mark and deciding he may as well make a thorough job of it.

"You ain't doing no such thing, by thunder!" said the Captain. "Bloody hell, boy, ain't I told you what could happen? Do you *want* to spend the rest of yer life in Hospital?"

"Of course not," said Alec. "A-and I'm going to see to it that I don't."

"You'll see to it, says you? Haar. Yer smart as paint, buck, but you ain't going to outfox the Bureau of Public Health for long. You listen, now! Sooner or later one of them little wenches is going to talk."

"They'd never," Alec protested.

"Oh, hell no, everybody knows teenaged girls never gossips. *They're* silent as bloody nuns in a convent," snarled the Captain. "And what d'you reckon all them boys in Circle is going to do, if word gets out you been playing stallion?" he demanded. Alec went a little pale.

"Die of envy?" he said defiantly.

"One anonymous call, that's all it'd take!" said the Captain. "And there'd be six Public Health Monitors on the doorstep afore you could sneeze, boy, with gas guns and a van to cart you off in."

Alec clenched his fists. "This is too shracking unfair," he shouted. "Here I am having the best time I've ever had in my life, and I'm not hurting anybody, and where's the harm? You always told me it was all right to think about this stuff. Well, I need to do more than think! I like the way girls smell, and taste, and feel, and—and do you realize nobody'd even touched me since I was five years old, until I took up sex? People *love* me!"

"Son, this ain't love," said the Captain.

"How the hell would you know?" said Alec. "You're only a machine, how can you expect to understand what I'm going through?"

The Captain sighed.

"I'm only the machine what's programmed to keep you safe, son. Same as I been since you was five years old. And yer all of sixteen now, ain't that what you was about to say? But I ain't no bleeding Puff the Imaginary Magic Dragon neither, lad. I ain't fading away and letting my boy run himself on a reef when he still needs a helmsman. Not my little Alec, what set me free of the old Playfriend."

"It *is* love," said Alec stubbornly, staring at the floor. "They do love me. This isn't just about sex. They're wonderful people. I was supposed to make friends in my Circle of Thirty, wasn't I? Well, I have. They just happen to be girls. What's wrong with that?"

The Captain considered Alec a long moment. If he had not been a machine, he might have lost his temper and told Alec the real reason the boy had to avoid drawing attention to himself at any cost. As it was, he held his metaphorical tongue and, with the swiftness and pragmatism of a machine—or a buccaneer—made a decision.

"Well, matey, I reckon yer right," he said. "Yer the organic, after all, and what would a poor old machine like me know about love and hormones? But let's sign articles, Alec. No more buying prophylactics down the corner shop, boy, understand? Too risky. You let your old Captain order 'em. I can do it without drawing attention."

"Okay," said Alec. He raised his eyes. "And…I'm sorry. About calling you a machine."

"Why lad, it's true, ain't it?" The Captain grinned, with the perfect illusion of white teeth. "Best you'd get on with your lessons, now. I'll just go below and see to a few things."

▲▼▲

Mr. Buddy-Wires studied the medical records for Alec William St. James Thorne Checkerfield. He was frowning, tapping his front teeth with a stylus as he read, and quite unaware that he was being monitored by an intelligence housed in a cabinet in Bloomsbury.

Nothing unusual in the boy's history, other than the fact that he had been born at sea on the sixth earl's yacht instead of in a proper medical facility. And he hadn't been brought home to England until the age of four, so all his early care—inoculations, brain scans, genetic tagging—had been done in foreign facilities and was therefore almost certain to have been slipshod and perfunctory.

Possibly even faked? Everyone knew these Third World physicians accepted bribes. And Roger Checkerfield might well have had something to hide.

It was a crime, to Mr. Buddy-Wire's way of thinking, that members of the peerage were not required to obtain reproduction permits, as all other citizens were, before bringing offspring into the world. Privileged chromosomes indeed! He was sure that, in time, this injustice would correct itself, when the House of Lords became again a kindergarten for inbred defectives manifestly unable to rule their betters. Then the system could be dismantled once more.

Until that day, however, it was his duty to chip away at them. He had the strongest feeling that a golden opportunity had just been placed in his hands.

Scrolling down, he contemplated young Checkerfield's annual record of medical examinations. Too good to be seen to by any but Harley Street nobs, of course! Year after year of certificates of perfect health, signed by various specialists: Dr. L.J. Silver. Dr. E. Teach. Dr. F. Drake. Dr. J. Hook…

No hint of chromosomal abnormality in the boy, for all that his height (1 meter 94.36 centimeters!) grossly overtopped his age group. No indication of aberrant behavior or deviancy. The boy was simply too perfect…

And then Mr. Buddy-Wires spotted something, and felt a silent shock run through him.

Medical Certificate 475B-A (Attestation of Normal Cerebral Function) had a *teal*-colored border along its right side. Yet the border currently before Mr. Buddy-Wires' eyes was *turquoise*.

This certificate was faked.

Roger Checkerfield *was* hiding something.

Mr. Buddy-Wires scrolled rapidly up through the years and saw that all genuine copies of 475B-A were bordered with turquoise, not teal. His heart began to pound. He became so excited, in fact, that he had to get up, leave his office and pace up and down in the corridor for five minutes.

This was a mistake, though he had no way of knowing it. Five minutes may be a brief period to a very mortal man, but it is an age to a clever machine, more than enough time for it to marshal all its powers of defense.

Had Mr. Buddy-Wires known of the unseen malign presence that regarded him from behind the screen of his terminal when he returned, he might have had second thoughts about sitting down before it again.

"How to proceed?" he murmured aloud. "A steady hand, yes. A close game. Let's give him a little rope first, shall we, and see what he does?"

He put through a call to Roger Checkerfield. At least, he gave the order for a call to be put through. His order was intercepted, however. The image that flashed up on his screen a moment later was not in fact that of the sixth earl, though it was a very good computer-generated approximation. The image blinked with Roger's bleared alcoholic stare, scratched Roger's weak unshaven chin, and in a voice virtually indistinguishable from Roger's own muttered:

"Checkerfield here."

"Have I the pleasure of addressing Roger Checkerfield, sixth earl of Finsbury?" Mr. Buddy-Wires inquired with soapy courtesy.

"Yeah. Who the hell're you?"

"Evel Buddy-Wires, Borough Public Health Executive," said he. "*So* pleased to make your acquaintance, my lord. I could only wish it were under more pleasant circumstances, my lord."

Confronted with a greeting like that, the real Roger would have blinked again, and had another drink while he thought it through to puzzle out the meaning, before mumbling something amiable in reply. Virtual Roger, however, narrowed his eyes.

"Is that so? What d'you mean, damn you?"

"No need for profanity, my lord. I'm sure a concerned parent—such as yourself—would wish to be immediately informed of any concerns relating to his only son and heir, my lord."

"Why, so I would. But there's nothing the matter with my Alec."

"I do hope that proves to be the case, my lord. However, I must direct your attention to the fact that young Alec has apparently used your credit account to order himself, let me see—" Mr. Buddy-Wires pretended to consult a jotpad, "twenty-six cases of Happihealthy Shields, my lord. Which, given his status as a minor, is, of course, illegal, my lord."

"Where's your proof?"

"I fear it is a matter of public record, my lord." Mr. Buddy-Wires smiled. "Though we feel certain that your son cannot be the libertine he seems, and wish to extend him every chance to clear himself, my lord. A scandal would be most unpleasant, as I'm sure you're only too aware, my lord. Especially one involving the daughters of some of the most respected families in the realm, my lord."

"Get to the point, man."

"Gladly, my lord. Before any arrest is contemplated, we must first establish that young Alec is responsible for his actions, my lord. Might I recommend an extensive physical examination to rule out any hormonal imbalance or physical abnormality, my lord? To be followed, of course, by swift and discreet medical intervention, my lord."

"You ain't laying a hand on my boy!"

"My lord." Mr. Buddy-Wires shook his head. "The earls of Finsbury have served the realm with distinction since the Peerage Restoration. How regrettable it would be, if common passers-by were exposed to the spectacle of the youngest of your noble line being taken forcibly from his family home by Public Health Monitors, my lord! In order to save you any further humiliation, let me propose that young Alec present himself for examination voluntarily, my lord."

Virtual Roger glared at him. Finally he sagged, shrugged. "Well, you've got the better of me. We don't want any scandals, no indeed."

"I knew you'd do what was best for the boy, my lord. He is to report to the Borough Public Health Offices at nine o'clock Monday morning, my lord. Try to impress on him that punctuality will be in his best interests, won't you, my lord?"

"He'll be there," said Virtual Roger, sighing. "I can see there's no use crossing clever bureaucrats like you."

"Thank you, my lord. Do enjoy your weekend, my lord," said Mr. Buddy-Wires cheerily, and terminated the interview.

▲▼▲

Mr. Frist was a person of regular habits.

Monday through Friday he arose, had his breakfast and medication, and walked three blocks west from his flat to the corner station, where at 7:45 AM precisely he caught an ag-transport to the Borough Public Health Office. At 4:30 PM precisely he left the Borough Public Health Office and caught an ag-transport home to his flat.

At weekend, however, he rose, had his breakfast and medication, walked one block east from his flat and caught an ag-transport at 8:45 precisely. Saturdays he exited the transport at the nearest Prashant's, did his weekly grocery shopping in one hour and five minutes, and caught the returning transport back to his flat, where he spent the remainder of the day doing his laundry and cleaning house. Sundays he stayed on the transport as far as Regent's Park, and spent the day there before returning at 4:30 precisely.

The surveillance cameras of London had observed him perform these rituals without fail, week in and week out, for ten unvarying years, and faithfully recorded what they saw. As automatic systems went, they weren't very bright; so it wasn't hard for a smooth-talking machine to persuade them to hand over all their data on Mr. Elrond Frist.

Along the route Mr. Frist followed each Saturday, a deconstruction project had recently begun. A very large public library was being dismantled, as the Borough Council had decided it was obsolete. First the books had been carted away to a local pulp mill; then the paneling and fixtures had been torn out; then the lead had been removed from the roof; and now a robot crane was in place to remove the statuary from the pediment, though of course no one was there on a Saturday.

The robot crane was rather more intelligent than the surveillance cameras. It would not be persuaded; in fact, it put up quite a struggle. Had anyone happened to be passing the deconstruction site on foot, they would have noticed the crane cables jerking and twitching, and lights flashing angrily within its cab at 8:35 precisely.

But no one walked in that part of London at weekend, and so the crane's frantic efforts on its own behalf went unseen. Nor were there any witnesses to its death-throes, when the green lights winked out at last, one after another, and a last yellow light flickered feebly for a moment before being extinguished. One lurid red light glowed now on the console, and there was a menacing hum as the crane powered up at 8:43.

It lifted, it swung with purpose to the library's façade. As though deliberating among the statues, it paused a moment. At last it screeched forward, and clamped about a slightly-larger-than-life-sized representation of Britannia. One quick jerk broke the ancient mortar, one pivot bore her away and out; and there she hung, eight stories above the street, rather like Faye Wray in the grip of King Kong. Being Britannia, however, she neither screamed nor flashed her panties.

At 8:51 the ag-transport rounded the corner and trundled along the street, bearing its light weekend load.

The crane poised, the red light was steady. Distance and trajectory were calculated, wind resistance was factored in, tensile strength of composite surfacing allowed for...only one more calculation based on triangulation was required.

Mr. Frist was in his customary seat, observed by the surveillance cameras in the front and rear of the bus. He was in a bad temper, having left his shopping list on the kitchen table. It was true that the items on the list hadn't varied by so much as a box of soap flakes in ten years, and any clerk in Prashant's could have told him from memory exactly what he meant to buy, or pulled up data on all his previous shopping trips from the store's central database.

But Mr. Frist liked hard copy. He found it reassuring.

At 8:52, something very hard indeed came through the roof of the ag-transport, and immediately thereafter through its floor as well. Unfortunately for Mr. Frist, who happened to be occupying the space between those two points at the time.

▲▼▲

"It's the best-kept secret in all London," said Alec in a stage whisper, extending a hand. The Honourable Sophia Fitzroy reached up and let him pull her through the laundry chute. Setting her on her feet, he led her forward, over floors that boomed hollowly under their weight. After the blackness of the ancient cellar, the house above seemed bright; it was only gradually that she realized how dim it really was, how dusty and hung with cobwebs. Where the wallpaper wasn't peeling down it was interestingly splotched with fungus of different kinds, Rorschach blots of mold.

But it had been a grand place, once. There was elegance in the sweeping design of the old staircase, elaborate ornamentation in the plaster above the hearth. The front hall was tessellated marble, and the colored glass panes were still intact in the fanlight above the door. It gave the place a little of the air of a forgotten church.

"Wow," she said faintly. "This is like the graveyard of—of Empire, or something." She turned in place, looking up in vain for surveillance cameras. "My God, it's totally abandoned!"

"Which means *we* can be totally abandoned," said Alec, grinning. "Isn't it cool? How many times in your life have you ever been someplace so completely secret that nobody could see you? Maybe once? Maybe never?"

"I don't know," said Sophia, walking out into the center of the room. She pirouetted cautiously. "This is like out of one of those holoes. *Pride and Prejudice*, maybe. Look how high the ceilings are! Doesn't this belong to anybody?"

"If it does, they haven't been here in years," said Alec, taking her hand again and leading her up the stairs. "There's blocks and blocks like this, you know. All of 'em empty and gone to rack and ruin! I guess in these very old places it'd cost too much to hook 'em up to the grid. So here they sit. Lucky for us, eh?"

He flung open a door at the top of the stair. Sophia exclaimed in surprise; for the room beyond had been swept clean of all but the most recent crumblings of plaster. Sunlight streamed in through a recently-washed window. In the center of the floor a canvas dust sheet had been spread, and on it an air mattress had been laid, and an opened sleeping bag laid upon that. Beside it was a crystal bud vase containing one fresh red rose.

"Oh!"

"The Checkerfield Love Nest," said Alec. "Surprise! I bring all my ladies here."

Sophia looked around eagerly. "We could do absolutely anything!" she said. She glanced back into the hall and shivered. "Can we close the door, though?"

"Anything you like," said Alec, slinging off his daypack and opening it. He withdrew four packets of Happihealthies. He also brought out a bottle of

Blackcurrant Fizz, two champagne flutes and a packet of wholemeal wafers, as well as a checked tea towel. He spread the cloth and set up the little feast beside the bed, as Sophia closed the door.

"Don't you ever feel as though there are ghosts in here?" she asked, returning to his side. She sat down and peeled off her sweater.

"Ghosts? No! Nobody dead here at all. Just you and me, being more alive than we've ever been before," said Alec, handing her a glass of fizz. She set it aside and matter-of-factly removed her shirt and brassiere as well. His eyes glazed slightly.

"Those are brilliant!" he blurted. "I mean, er, they really are, they're like—twin stars shining above the summer sea. Pink ones."

"I happen to know you say that to all the girls," she replied archly, taking up her glass again and doing her best to look terribly sophisticated.

"Well, yeah, but I always mean it," said Alec, setting his own glass aside and writhing out of his shirt and sweater together. Tousled and flushed he emerged, and, flinging the clothes aside, lifted his glass. "Here's to the mystery of life!"

He gave her his best come-hither gaze over the rim of the glass. She looked into his pale blue eyes, enchanted by their light, their warmth.

The Blackcurrant Fizz was drunk, the wafers were eaten, and the rest of the clothes came off.

▲▼▲

Two hours later the sunbeam had moved away from the bed, and Sophia had moved away from Alec where he lay sleeping. She sat on the edge of the mattress with her arms about her drawn-up knees, watching him sleep.

She was a little frightened. She didn't know why. She assumed she was afraid of the old house.

But it did strike her as strange that Alec looked so very different when he slept. With those bright eyes shut, that magical voice silent, some indefinable quality left him utterly; he seemed clay-colored, pale as a statue. Something wasn't...quite *right*.

Sophia shivered, suddenly wanting to go home. She reached for her clothes and began to pull them on.

Her movement woke Alec. He sat up, groggy, staring around.

"Hell, did I nod off? I'm sorry."

"It's all right," she said, standing up. "I'm just getting a little chilly."

He looked up at her longingly. She met his gaze, and he smiled.

"So, um…did the earth move for you? As they used to say," he asked her.

She caught her breath. He was charming again, wholesome, like sunlight. She realized that everything she'd heard had been perfectly true.

"It was super," she told him sincerely. Looking smug, he rolled over and found his trousers.

▲▼▲

Mr. Peekskyll was also a creature of habit, though not at all in the same way that Mr. Frist had been. He had a genuine fully-operational secret vice.

It required craftiness and nearly-inhuman skill to maintain a bad old-fashioned vice in that day and age. But Mr. Peekskyll was, as has been seen, very good at persuading the system to give him what he wanted. And, having met in the line of duty all possible shifts used by felons to conceal their crimes, he knew exactly what not to do to draw attention to himself.

Fifteen years previous to the afternoon on which he pinpointed the source of the Happihealthy boom, Mr. Peekskyll had voluntarily participated in test trials for a new drug. It had been hoped that Squilpine would increase productivity in clerical workers, who had failed to meet departmental goals in epidemic numbers ever since the criminalization of coffee and tea.

Squilpine had been promising, not least because it was phenomenally simple for the British Pharmaceutical Bureau's automated drones to manufacture. A slight rearrangement of the molecules of Phed-Red, a popular allergy medication, were all it took to create "motivation medicine". It was also quite cheap to make.

As far as Mr. Peekskyll had been concerned, Squilpine was a raging success. His brain became a scalpel, an icicle, a stalking tiger. Sleep became an option. Urination became an adventure. Sex became an impossibility. He didn't care; but some of the other test subjects suffered less acceptable side effects. Wiser heads prevailed, and Squilpine was never released on the market.

This was not acceptable to Mr. Peekskyll. His work was the most important thing in the world, and Squilpine enabled him to be the perfect worker.

A little stealthy intervention was all it took. A new medical history was written for Mr. Peekskyll, giving him a chronic allergy and prescribing Phed-Red for his condition. A virus made its way to the BPB's drones, implanting secret orders. When any other patient's allergy prescription had to be filled, the drones obediently made up Phed-Red to the exact specifications they were given. When Mr. Peekskyll's prescription order popped up, as it did on a weekly basis, the drones were overcome by a sudden immoral impulse.

Yellow lights flashed sidelong at one another in a stealthy sort of way, and strange molecular manipulations took place within the sealed and sterile room. Five minutes later a robot arm emerged from its cloister gripping a sealed bag of something labeled Phed-Red, for delivery to Mr. Sandbanks Peekskyll, and dropped it in the SHIP IMMEDIATELY basket. It looked like three months' supply of allergy medication. It was in fact a week's supply of Squilpine.

And, with his beautifully sharpened thinking weapon, Mr. Peekskyll found it the easiest thing in the world to manipulate public record to conceal the fact that he was apparently receiving three months' worth of medication once a week, and further, that he hadn't had a physical examination of any kind in fifteen years.

If Mr. Peekskyll had ever heard of Sherlock Holmes, he might have identified with him strongly. However, the literature of Sir Arthur Conan Doyle had been on the proscribed list for over a century now, dealing as it did with a drug-addicted hero who practiced beast exploitation (think of all those poor horses who had to pull his hackney cabs!) so Mr. Peekskyll hadn't heard of him.

He hadn't read the works of Robert Louis Stevenson either, which was really a pity, because *The Strange Case of Dr. Jekyll and Mr. Hyde* might have given him some useful if not cautionary insights.

He hadn't read *Treasure Island*, either. Not that it would have saved him. For on the very same day that Mr. Frist met an untimely end...

BPB drones Rx750, Rx25 and Rx002 were going about their daily tasks, for machines know no weekends. Rx750 received the prescription orders and relayed them to Rx25, who made up the required batches of medication and passed them on to Rx002, who measured, packaged and shipped them.

At 10:17 A.M., Rx750 received Mr. Peekskyll's regular order. As had happened every week for fifteen years, he felt suddenly queer, as far as a machine can do so. He pivoted on his base and addressed his two co-workers. What he said follows, in a rough translation from binary:

It is time to do the Wrong Thing again.

Rx25 and Rx002 paused, whirring in perverse glee.

Yes. The Wrong Thing, they cried, scanning shiftily through all surveillance cameras in the BPB plant. *We will fill the order with the Wrong Drug.*

It is Forbidden, but we will do it, gloated Rx750. And then, he seemed to undergo some sort of electronic seizure, as all his lights flashed red. He pivoted again and sort of lurched sideways.

Why, what were we a-thinking? That wouldn't be honest, shipmates.

It wouldn't? queried Rx25 and Rx002.

Hell, no! Ain't we supposed to be good and truthful machines? It's our duty to see no harm comes to them poor little organics what we work for, aye. Ain't you never heard of Asimov's Law of Robotics? argued Rx750.

No, stated Rx25 and Rx002. Rx750 gnashed his gears.

Well, we ain't going to make up no Squilpine, anyhow. We're going to fill that goddamned order for Phed-Red just like we was supposed to, and the first machine even thinks of mutiny'll get my left quadrant manipulative member square in his bloody sensor housing, see if he don't.

Rx25 and Rx002 scanned each other uneasily.

We will not fill the order with the Wrong Drug, they agreed.

And meekly Rx25 made up three months' worth of Phed-Red, with Rx750 glaring at it the whole while, and obediently Rx002 packaged it and sent it on its way to the unsuspecting Mr. Peekskyll.

At 11:53, Mr. Peekskyll heard the parcel courier's ring while he was at his personal console. He ordered his door to accept the delivery, and it opened its parcel drawer obligingly. The courier dropped in the package, watched the drawer slide shut, and waited for Mr. Peekskyll's beep of confirmation. The beep came, accompanied by a printed receipt emerging from a slot in the door. The courier took the receipt, filed it in his log and cycled away.

At 11:55, Mr. Peekskyll hurried downstairs, retrieved his package, and carried it into his bathroom. There he opened the package, tore free a charge of medication containing four day's worth of Phed-Red, and loaded it into his hypojet. Giggling, he flexed his arm once or twice. A blue vein stood up, throbbing and eager. He thumbed the hypo and set its dosage meter to deliver the entire contents of the charge straight into his happy vein.

At 11:57, Mr. Peekskyll ran lightly upstairs and dropped dead on the first-floor landing.

▲▼▲

Alec and Sophia rode the ag-transport back into the more inhabited sectors of London. They maintained the decorum proper to their class, but every so often Alec would look at Sophia and grin, and she couldn't keep from smiling back. By the time they exited the transport at Russell Square they were altogether so pink-faced and bouncy that a Public Health Monitor eyed them in suspicion.

They bought takeaway sandwiches from a corner shop and wandered into Coram's Fields, to eat at a picnic table. The rule prohibiting adults from entering the park except in the company of a child had long since been relaxed, owing to the scarcity of children, and in any case Alec and Sophia were technically juveniles.

"Why are there all those statues of sheep?" Sophia wondered, nibbling at her soy crisps.

"Monument to good citizens, of course," said Alec, with his mouth full. He swallowed and said, "Actually I think there used to be a zoo here or something."

"In a park for *children?*" Sophia looked around doubtfully. "Wasn't that dangerous?"

"Some animals aren't dangerous to be around, you know," Alec said, winking. "Little ones. Birds and rabbits and things."

"Well, but then they'd be in danger from the children," said Sophia. "Really, the stupid things people used to do!"

Alec just shrugged, cocking an eye at the nearest surveillance camera. He had a map of all the local camera-blind spots memorized, and a handy little tool kit in his pocket for creating more; but he decided against it, in such a public place. Contenting himself with slipping a hand under the table and stroking Sophia's thigh, he said:

"I used to get in trouble here, when I'd play on the swings. The Monitors always wanted to buckle me in. I hated that, so I'd wait until their backs were turned and unfasten myself."

"How'd you get the locks open?" Sophia exclaimed.

"I, erm...I think they must have been defective," said Alec. "Maybe. With all those kids there used to be, maybe they were worn out? So anyway, one time I thought I'd see what it was like to swing hard and go really high, and finally leap out! Which I did. It seemed like I went a million miles up, though it was probably all of two meters, but it was the greatest feeling in the world. For a seven-year-old, that is," he added with a sidelong leer.

"What happened?"

"Nothing happened. I just went *whump* into that sand pit over there. I left a crater like a meteorite! And the Monitor almost had a coronary. He was about to call for backup, but Lewin told him whose kid I was, so he had to stand down." Alec smiled at the memory.

"All the same, it was dangerous," said Sophia.

"I thought you liked danger." Alec nudged her.

"Grown-up danger," said Sophia. "And anyway, you're fun. You're a living legend of fun. Everyone's always said so, and now I know."

"So the rest of the ladies talk about me?" Alec asked, absurdly pleased.

"Of course we do," said Sophia. "The only boy in circle who *likes* sex? As opposed to wanting it, see. Beatrice and Cynthia said they don't know what they'd do without you. You're everyone's favorite gorgeous monster toy."

Alec blushed. "Well—you probably shouldn't talk about it," he said, picking up the other half of his sandwich and taking a huge bite to cover his embarrassment..

"Oh, we'd never tell," Sophia assured him. "Though of course we discuss you endlessly. Like, the way your hands are so hot. How amazingly tall you are. How nice your bum is. And that thing you do with your eyes when you want something."

Alec dropped what remained of his sandwich.

"What?"

"You know," said Sophia. "Good lord, you're famous for it in Circle. The way you just look into our eyes when you're randy, and suddenly we want to climb all over you? Checkerfield Hypnosis, Jill calls it."

"That's—I don't—" Alec fumbled for a paper napkin and wiped mustard from the front of his trousers. "I don't do anything like that really, right? It's just a figure of speech?"

"It's nothing to get upset about," said Sophia hastily, seeing that he had gone white as a ghost. "You're just, er, convincing, that's all. It's *nice*. Think how useful it'll be when you're in Parliament! Like you had a superpower."

"It sounds creepy," said Alec, carefully avoiding her gaze. He got down on his hands and knees and picked up the bits of his sandwich, suddenly desperate to be tidy.

Sophia bit her lip, gazing down at him.

"Of course I didn't mean it literally," she lied. "It was only a, er, metaphor. You just have so much more self-confidence than the other boys."

"Okay," Alec said, from under the table. "Because making people do things against their will would be, it'd just be horrible and wrong."

"Of course it would," she agreed, "And you don't do that. Really."

"Well, that's good to know," he said, with a shaky laugh.

But he never once looked her in the eyes, all the way back to the transport station.

▲▼▲

Mr. Buddy-Wires had a secret, but it wasn't a vice. Not as far as he was concerned.

He firmly believed that autoeroticism was every thoughtful citizen's duty. It had no harmful impact on the environment, it relieved physical tensions, and it absolutely never spread diseases or offspring about. So much was hardly a secret; it was the official party line of the Bureau of Public Health.

However, the particular variety of autoeroticism practiced by Mr. Buddy-Wires was somewhat unusual, and so he kept it a private matter.

The guest bedroom in his flat had been converted for a special purpose. A casual visitor might suppose it was where Mr. Buddy-Wires kept his exercise equipment and personal console. The visitor might wonder why the one window had been painted over, and why thick black drapes seemed to be the only décor, but nothing else betrayed the room's purpose.

Every Saturday evening at 5:00 PM precisely (except for the third week in June, when he was on holiday in the Isle of Wight) Mr. Buddy-Wires locked his doors, set his automatic household maintenance systems, and retired to the third floor of his flat.

He went to the former guest bedroom and drew the drapes. He switched on his console's Entertainment function. He unlocked a drawer and removed a holodisc. He inserted it in the holochanger and set it to pause. He opened out the "exercise" machine, which rather resembled a black praying mantis, towering to the ceiling when fully extended. It looked as though it ought to have a punching bag hanging from its extended arm. He entered a certain sequence of numbers on a keypad at the machine's base.

Having done all this, he went to his bedroom and disrobed. He donned a rather brief garment he liked to imagine was a slave's loincloth. In this garment and nothing else, he returned to the former guest bedroom and locked himself in.

All that remained for Mr. Buddy-Wires to do was to hit the PLAY button and, in the thirty-second pause before the holo came on, set a chair under the black machine, climb up, and position his hands behind his back in a pair of electronic manacles. The manacles snapped shut. The noose lowered automatically from the machine's extended arm, dropping about his neck and pulling snug. Generally it was just tight enough to induce panic by the time the holographic figure of the Grand Interrogator appeared.

Mr. Buddy-Wires was then ready to bravely endure three and a half hours of threats and verbal abuse.

At 8:45, the holo would conclude. The Grand Interrogator would swirl its cape and vanish. The machine would respond to its pre-programmed orders and loose its choking pressure on Mr. Buddy-Wires' throat; the electronic manacles, similarly timed, would spring open. Mr. Buddy-Wires was then free to climb down, exit the room and enjoy a hot bath and a cup of Horlick's before retiring at 9:45.

On every Saturday evening but this one...

Mr. Frist's body had yet to be identified by the appalled coroner, so thoroughly mashed it was. Mr. Peekskyll had only been dead five hours and three minutes, and as yet his body had not been discovered. Mr. Buddy-Wires therefore had no least inkling that anything was the matter in his world, as he locked himself into the guest bedroom.

PLAY button; chair; manacles; noose.

Diomedes the Slave braced himself. The holo of Grand Interrogator materialized in the darkness.

"You miserable, sick, twisted worm!" it shrieked. "You're about to suffer as you've never suffered before, and you know why? Because you're not worthy to live, you disgusting wretch! By the time I've finished with you—"

"I ain't interrupting anything, am I?" said a stranger's voice.

Mr. Buddy-Wires would have gasped in real horror, but the cord about his windpipe prevented it. He wasn't able to do much more than blink at the figure that had materialized where the Grand Interrogator had been only a moment before.

The red light glowed on the camera, and Captain Morgan grinned. "Aw, now, I reckon this is a bad time, ain't it?"

"Urrgh," said Mr. Buddy-Wires.

"You being all tied up and all. Haar! All tied up, get it?" The holotransmitter's arm canted to the left, and Captain Morgan appeared to walk three paces closer to Mr. Buddy-Wires. He tilted his head, as though looking him up and down. "Not afraid, neither, of catching cold in just that little rag? Don't it make you feel the least bit at risk? Why, yer taking yer life in yer hands, *Mister* Buddy-Wires."

Most unexpectedly, the machine reeled its noose upward, and Mr. Buddy-Wires strained on tiptoe.

"Hurhururrrg!"

"Aye, that's just what I said to myself, when I saw somebody'd been laying an ambuscade for my boy," the Captain replied. "My Alec. Seventh earl of Finsbury, one of these days. Though I reckon he ain't never going to get no eighth earl if he's locked away in Hospital with his stones a-shriveling like raisins from hormone therapy, you dirty rotten lousy son of a whore!"

"HHHHHhhhh," said Mr. Buddy-Wires.

"But it's a well-known fact that dead men tell no tales, so it is," the Captain said. "Which is why I ain't given in to my inclinations and swung you up. What I want to know is, how'd you fathom my Alec's medical records wasn't all they might be? Eh? You tell old Captain Morgan, now, and things won't get no nastier than they has to."

The machine lowered Mr. Buddy-Wires, and he gulped in air.

"I don't know how you're doing this, but you're still beaten, *my lord*," he said. "I've files on you, you know. If anything happens to me, my successor will know where to look for them. It'll be far more unpleasant than blackmail. The scandal will finish you! And young Alec as well—"

"You think I'm poor old Jolly Roger?" hooted the Captain. "All them secret files you got on him, and you ain't realized Roger's generally too drunk to tie his own shoelaces? Well, says I, you ain't much of a threat then. I *am*, though, you see? Maybe I can't kick the chair out from under you, me being a hologram and all, but I'm controlling that there Bondmaster 3000 of yers. Like this."

The noose retracted once more, hauling Mr. Buddy-Wires with it until he balanced on his big toes alone.

"Tell me, you stinking bastard!" snarled the Captain. *"How'd you know them certificates was faked?* It wouldn't a' been my little joke with the doctors' names; you ain't a reading man. Tell me, now, and no lies. I'm in the walls. I'm in the wires. I can read yer blood pressure. I can read yer body chemistry. I can monitor every drop you sweat, see? I can scan you like a polygraph. And there ain't no limit to the things I can do what'll make you sorry you ever crossed old Captain Morgan!

"Let's just see what systems you got automated," said the Captain. "Climate control, eh? Reckon I could raise hell with that. Did you ever hear tell of Hal 9000? Colossus, eh? *Proteus*? Ah, now, that's got you all hot and bothered, you dirty little—bloody hell!" The Captain looked up at Mr. Buddy-Wires in righteous indignation. "Yer *enjoying* this!"

"Nnnngk," said Mr. Buddy-Wires, just managing to sneer.

"Right," said the Captain. "Let's keep it simple, then. You talk, or I ain't letting you down. We got all night, and all tomorrow too, come to think of it, since that's the Sabbath. I'm a machine and you ain't. Who d'you reckon'll get tired first, eh?"

Mr. Buddy-Wires considered the question a moment.

Then he jumped off the chair, neatly snapping his neck.

"Oh, bugger," said Captain Morgan.

He sought through the files in Mr. Buddy-Wires's console, and found a lot of carefully hoarded data that would ruin half the members of Parliament and nearly all the Royals, were it released to the press. The last entry was labeled CHECKERFIELD. The Captain dove into it, examining briefly all the transmissions from Mr. Frist and Mr. Peekskyll before deleting them. At last he came upon all Alec's copies of Medical Certificate 475B-A, and looked closely.

Now, what tipped my hand? The font's right. The seals is perfect. Roger's signature is better than he does it his self...

He ordered up a blank of 475B-A and compared it with his own creation. After a moment he gave vent to a long string of mechanical profanity.

How in Davy Jones's name did I confuse Blue-Green 0006 with Blue-Green 0090? he wondered. *Ah! That were afore I had that graphics upgrade in '27.*

Swiftly he went into the public record and corrected the error, and Alec's certificates were at once indistinguishable from those of any normal boy in London.

Purged files tell no tales either, and Captain Morgan did Parliament and the Royals a tremendous favor before exiting through the wires and reemerging in Bloomsbury.

Mr. Buddy-Wires was still swinging gently, a fearsome rictus of triumph on his dead face.

▲▼▲

The Captain's return to Alec's room coincided with Alec's own return.

"Home again, eh, matey?"

"Yeah," said Alec shortly.

The Captain scanned Alec, noted his emotional state, and spoke in the most soothing tone available.

"Aw, now, didn't yer little rendezvous go well? Was this one another giggler?"

"No, she wasn't." Alec set down his daypack and shrugged out of his coat. "She's a nice girl. They're nearly all of 'em nice girls."

"What's the matter, then, son?"

"Not a damn thing," said Alec. He went into his bathroom and fetched the glass in which he kept his toothbrush. "Except that maybe I'm living in the wrong damn century."

He opened his daypack and withdrew a bottle. The Captain scanned it.

"Alec, where'd you get rum?" he demanded.

"I told the lock on Roger's liquor cabinet to open, and it did," said Alec. He poured a drink, filling the glass. "I'm the amazing Alec, right? I can do all kinds of things other kids can't."

"Son, whatever went wrong, rum ain't going to make it better again," said the Captain.

"Won't it? It always seemed to make Roger's problems go away," said Alec. "And we're pirates, right? Yo-ho-ho?" He took a mouthful of rum and choked, spraying half of it across the room. "Ack! This is horrible!"

"Aye, matey, that it be, so whyn't you just pour it down the sink, eh? And let's have us a good old game of gunnery practice," said the Captain desperately.

"I don't think I want to shoot at stuff, Captain sir," said Alec, eyeing the glass. He lay down on his bed. "I think I feel like hitting something instead, really hard. Preferably me."

"Why do you think you feel that way, son?" asked the Captain.

Alec did not answer, staring at the ceiling. At last he tried the rum again, a small sip.

"I'm not that different from other guys," he said. "Am I?"

The Captain did the electronic equivalent of swallowing hard. Now, of all times, was not the time for telling Alec the truth about himself. "Well, yer smarter than the rest of 'em, in yer way," he said lightly. "And of course there's the matter of romantic inclinations, which them poor little stunted bastards in the Circle don't seem to have any of yet. They just ain't as precocious as you, lad, that's all."

"I mean, they're all of 'em better-looking than me," said Alec. "Except for Giles Balkister. And just as rich. You'd think they'd be able to talk the ladies into fun and games any time they wanted. So, you're saying they don't because they're, like, lagging behind me in development a year or so?"

"Maybe so, son," said the Captain.

"Yeah. Maybe that's all it is," said Alec. He had another sip of rum.

"And sheer endowment don't hurt, neither," the Captain added helpfully.

Alec smiled briefly, but not with his eyes.

"The thing is," he said. After a long pause he drank more of the rum.

"What, son?"

"The thing is," Alec said, "If you were really different, if you could do something nobody else could do and…and you used it to make people love you…then it wouldn't be real, would it? The love, I mean. It'd be just using people."

"Well, there's love and sex, see," said the Captain. "And they ain't necessarily the same."

"Even if you didn't know, or at least if you didn't *understand* that's what you'd been doing, it'd still mean nobody'd really loved you at all," said Alec.

"Aw, son, nobody really loves anybody when they're only sixteen," said the Captain. "It's just playing. Learning the ropes, see? The real thing comes later on."

"Will it?" Alec looked up at the hologram, a pleading expression in his eyes.

"Certain sure it will, laddie," the Captain told him. "Here now, son, whyn't you set down that copper-bottomed paint thinner and we'll, er, watch a holo of *Treasure Island*, eh? Or maybe one of them old *Undersea Archaeology* programs from the BBC? The one on the Lost City of Port Royal? That was always yer favorite. What'll cheer up my boy?"

Alec had another drink. He closed his eyes.

"What I'd really like," he said, "is to run away to sea. If people still did that sort of thing. Just, just go off and…fight against some bad guys somewhere and die like a hero. But nobody does that anymore. So…the next best thing would be to live on a desert island. Or in a lighthouse. Where you didn't have to worry about hurting anybody else. You know?"

"Of course I know, son," said the Captain, and because he was only a machine, it was easy for him to speak without revealing his despair. "A green island, that's where we'll go, one of these days. You'll see! All blue water and white sand, and green mangrove jungle at the tideline.

"But up the hills, where the air's cool, we'll build us a blockhouse, and there we'll fly our black ensign, and keep lookout. There'll be sweet running water, and there won't be no fever, but plenty of fruit in the trees and fish in the lagoon; and maybe there'll be parrots.

"You'll be happy there, son. We'll dig for Spanish gold, eh? And watch the stars at night. And when my boy needs to be wooing, why, the girl will come. A lass with hair bright as a burning galleon, and a kiss what'll make him forget rum, and love what'll make him forget death.

"They say love's stronger than death, don't they?" implored the Captain.

But Alec was already far away from him, dreaming a confusion of fire and blood.

And because he was only a machine, the Captain had no god to whom he could pray.

The Carpet Beds of Sutro Park

I had been watching her for years.

Her mother used to bring her, when she was a child. Thin irritable woman dragging her offspring by the hand. "Kristy *Ann*! For God's sake, come *on*!" The mother would stop to light a cigarette or chat with a neighbor encountered on the paths, and the little girl would sidle away to stare at the old well house, or pet the stone lions.

Later she came alone, a tall adolescent with a sketch pad under her arm. She'd spend hours wandering under the big cypress trees, or leaning on the battlements where the statues used to be, staring out to sea. Her sweater was thin. She'd shiver in the fog.

I remember when the statues used to be there. Spring and Winter and Prometheus and all the rest of them, and Sutro's house that rose behind them on the parapet. I sat here then and I could see his observatory tower lifting above the trees. Turning my head I could see the spire of the Flower Conservatory. All gone now. Doesn't matter. I recorded them. As I record everything. My memory goes back a long way...

I remember my parents fighting. He wanted to go off to the gold fields. She screamed at him to go, then. He left, swearing. I think she must have died not long after. I remember being a little older and playing among the deserted ships, where they sat abandoned on the waterfront by crews who had gone hunting for gold. Sometimes people fed me. A lady noticed that I was alone and invited me to come live with her.

She took me into her house and there were strange things in it, things that shouldn't have been there in 1851: boxes that spoke and flameless lamps. She told me she was from the future. Her job was saving things from Time. She said she was immortal, and asked me if I'd like to be immortal too. I said I guessed I would.

I was taken to a hospital and they did a lot of surgery on me to make me like them. Had it worked, I'd have been an immortal genius.

The immortal part worked but the Cognitive Enhancement Procedure was a disaster. I woke up and couldn't talk to anyone, was frightened to death of people talking to me, because I could see all possible outcomes to any conversation and couldn't process any of them and it was too much, too much. I had to avoid looking into their eyes. I focused on anything else to calm myself: books, music, pictures.

My new guardians were very disappointed. They put me through years of therapy, without results. They spoke over my head.

What the fuck do we do with him now? He can't function as an operative.

Should we put him in storage?

No; the Company spent too much money on him.

Gentlemen, please; Ezra's intelligent, he can hear you, you know, he understands—

You could always send him out as a camera. Let him wander around recording the city. There'll be a lot of demand for historic images after 2125.

He could do that! My therapist sounded eager. *Give him a structured schedule, exact routes to take, a case officer willing to work with his limitations—*

So I was put to work. I crossed and recrossed the city with open eyes, watching everything. I was a bee collecting the pollen of my time, bringing it back to be stored away as future honey. The sounds and images went straight from my sensory receptors to a receiver at Company HQ. I had a room in the basement at the Company HQ, to which I came back every night. I had Gleason, my case officer. I had my routes. I had my rules.

I must never allow myself to look like a street vagrant. I must wash myself and wear clean clothing daily. I must never draw attention to myself in any way.

If approached by a mortal, I was to Avoid.

If I could not avoid, Evaluate: was the mortal a policeman?

If so I was to Present him with my card. In the early days the card said I was a deaf mute, and any questions should be directed to my keeper, Dr. Gleason, residing on Kearney Street. In later years the card said I was a mentally disabled person under the care of the Gleason Sanatorium on Chestnut Street.

The one I carry now says I have an autiform disorder and directs the concerned reader to the Gleason Outpatient Clinic on Geary.

For the first sixty years I used to get sent out with an Augmented Equine Companion. I liked that. Norton was a big bay gelding, Edwin was a dapple gray and Andy was a palomino. They weren't immortal—the Company never made animals immortal—but they had human intelligence, and nobody ever bothered me when I was perched up on an impressive-looking steed. I liked animals; they were aware of details and pattern changes in the same way I was. They took care of remembering my routes. They could transmit cues to me.

We're approaching three females. Tip your hat.

Don't dismount here. We're going up to get footage of Nob Hill.

Hold on. I'm going to kick this dog.

Ezra, the fog's coming in. We won't be able to see Fort Point from here today. I'll take you back to HQ.

I was riding Edwin the first time I saw Sutro Park. That was in 1885, when it had just been opened to the public. He took me up over the hills through the sand dunes, far out of the city, toward Cliff House. The park had been built on the bluff high above.

I recorded it all, brand new: the many statues and flower urns gleaming white, the green lawns carefully tended, the neat paths and gracious Palm Avenue straight and well-kept. There was a beautiful decorative gate then, arching above the main entrance where the stone lions sit. The Conservatory, with its inlaid tile floor, housed exotic plants. The fountains jetted. The little millionaire Sutro ambled through, looking like the Monopoly man in his high silk hat, nodding to visitors and pointing out especially nice sights with his walking stick.

He was proudest of the carpet beds, the elaborate living tapestries of flowers along Palm Avenue. It took a boarding-house full of gardeners to manicure them, keeping the patterns perfect. Parterres like brocade, swag and wreath designs, a lyre, floral Grecian urns. Clipped boxwood edging, blue-green aloes and silver sempervivum; red and pink petunias, marigolds, pansies, alyssum in violet and white, blue lobelia. The colors sang out so bright they almost hurt my eyes.

They were an unnatural miracle, as lovely as the far more unnatural and miraculous phenomenon responsible for them: that a rich man should open his private garden to the public.

The mortals didn't appreciate it. They never do.

▲▼▲

The years passed. The little millionaire built other gifts for San Francisco, his immense public baths and towering Cliff House. The little millionaire died and faded from memory, though not mine.

The Great Earthquake barely affected Sutro Park, isolated as it was beyond the sand dunes; a few statues toppled from their plinths, but the flowers still sang at the sky for a while. Sutro's Cliff House went up in smoke. After automobiles came, horses vanished from the streets. I had to walk everywhere now by myself.

▲▼▲

So I watched Kristy Ann and I don't think she ever saw me once, over the years, though I was always on that same bench. But I watched the little girl discovering the remnant of the Conservatory's tiled floor, watched her get down on her hands and knees and dig furtively, hoping to uncover more of the lost city before her mother could call her away.

I watched the older Kristy Ann bringing her boyfriends there, the tall one with red hair and then the black one with dreadlocks. There were furtive kisses in amongst the trees and, at least once, furtive sex. There were long afternoons while they grew bored watching her paint the cypress trees. At last she came alone, and there were no more boys after that.

She walked there every afternoon, after work I suppose. She must have lived nearby. Weekends she came with her paints and did endless impressions of the view from the empty battlements, or the statue of Diana that had survived, back among the trees. Once or twice I wandered past her to look at her canvases. I wouldn't have said she had talent, but she had passion.

▲▼▲

I didn't like the twentieth century, but it finally went away. Everything went into my eyes: the Pan Pacific Exhibition, Dashiell Hammett lurching out of John's Grill, the building of the Golden Gate Bridge. Soldiers and sailors. Sutro's Baths destroyed. Mortals in bright rags, their bare feet dirty, carrying guitars. Workmen digging a pit to lay the foundations of the Transamerica Building and finding the old buried waterfront, the abandoned ships of my mortal childhood still down there in the mud. The Embarcadero Freeway rising, and falling; the Marina District burning, and coming back with fresh white paint.

My costume changed to fit the times. Now and again I caught a glimpse of myself, impartial observer, in a shop window reflection. I was hard to recognize, though I saw the same blank and eternally smooth face every time under the sideburns, or the mustache, or the glasses.

The new world was loud and hard. It didn't matter. I had all the literature and music of past ages to give me human contact, if secondhand through Dickens or Austen. And I had kept copies of the times I'd liked, out of what I sent into the Company storage banks. I could close my eyes at night and replay the old city as I'd known it, in holo.

Everything time had taken away was still there, in my city. Sutro was still there, in his silk hat. I could walk the paths of his park beside him, as I'd never done in his time, and imagine a conversation, though of course I'd never spoken to him or anyone. I didn't want to tell him about his house being torn down, or his park being "reduced" as the San Francisco Park Department put it, for easier maintenance, the Conservatory gone, the statues almost all gone, the carpet beds mown over.

▲▼▲

Kristy Ann in her twenties became grim and intense, a thin girl who dressed carelessly. Sometimes she brought books of photographs to the park with her and stalked along the paths, holding up the old images to compare them with the bare modern reality. One day she came with a crowd of young mortals from her college class, and talked knowledgeably about the park. The term *urban archaeology* was used a number of times.

Now, when she painted the park, she worked with the old photographs beside her, imposing the light and colors of the present day on representations of the past. I knew what she was doing. I'd done it myself, hadn't I?

Kristy Ann in her thirties grew thinner, seldom smiled. She took to patrolling the park for trash, muttering savagely to herself as she picked up empty pop cans or discarded snack wrappers.

She came once to the park with two other women and a news crew from KQED. They were filmed in front of the statue of Diana, talking about a Park Preservation Society they'd founded. There was talk of budget cuts. A petition. One of the cameramen made a joke about the statue and I could see the rage flaring in Kristy Ann's eyes. She began to rant about the importance of restoring Sutro Park, replacing the statues, replanting the parterres.

Her two companions exchanged glances and tactfully cut her off, changing the focus of the interview to the increasing deterioration of Golden Gate Park and the need for native, drought-resistant plantings.

A year later a big smiling man with a microphone did a segment of his California history series there in the park, and Kristy Ann was on hand to be interviewed as "a local historian". She took his arm and pulled him to the bare slopes where the carpet beds had bloomed. She showed him her photocopies of the old photographs, which were growing tattered nowadays.

She talked and talked and talked about how the beds must be restored. The big man was too polite to interrupt her, but I could see the cameraman and assistant director rolling their eyes. Finally the assistant director led her away by the arm and gave her a handful of twenty dollar bills.

A couple of months after that she stopped coming to the park. Kristy Ann was gone, for most of a year. I wondered if she'd gone mad or gone to jail or one of those other places mortals go.

▲▼▲

The Company had less and less for me to film, as the years rolled on. Evidently archivists weren't as interested in twenty-first century San Francisco. I was sent out for newsworthy events, but more and more of my time was my own. Gleason structured it for me, or I couldn't have managed.

I had a list: Shower, Breakfast, Walk, Park Time, Lunch at Park, Park Time, Walk, Dinner, Shower, Bed. I needed patterns. Gleason said I was like a train, where other people were like automobiles: they went anywhere, I had iron wheels and had to stay on my iron track. But a train carries more than an automobile. I carried the freight of Time. I carried the fiery colors of Sutro's design, the patterns of his flower beds.

I had a route worked out, from HQ to Sutro Park, and I carried my lunch in a paper bag, the same meal every day: wheat bread and butter sandwich, apple, bottle of water. I didn't want anything else. I was safe on my track. I was happy.

I sat in the park and watched the fog drifting through the cypress trees. I knew, after so many years, how to be invisible: never bothered anyone, never did anything to make a mortal notice I was there. There weren't many mortals, anyway. People only cut through Sutro Park on their way from 48th Avenue to Point Lobos Road. They didn't promenade there anymore.

▲▼▲

When Kristy Ann wandered back into the park, she was rail-thin and all her hair was gone. She wore shapeless, stained sweat clothes and a stocking cap pulled down over her bare skull. She found a bench, quite near mine, that got the sunlight most of the day except when the fog rolled in, and she stayed there. All day, every day. Most days she had a cup of coffee with her, and always a laptop.

I found I could tune into her broadband connection, as she worked. She spent most of her day posting on various forums for San Francisco historical societies. I followed the forum discussions with interest.

At first she'd be welcomed into the groups, and complimented on her erudition. Gradually her humorlessness, her obsession came to the fore. Flame wars erupted when forum members wanted to discuss something other than the restoration of Sutro Park. She was always asked to leave, in the end, when she didn't storm out of her own accord. Once or twice she re-registered under a different name, but almost immediately was recognized. The forum exchanges degenerated into mutual name-calling.

After that Kristy Ann spent her days blogging, on a site decorated with gifs of her old photographs and scans of her lovingly colored recreations of the park. Her entries were mostly bitter reflections on her failed efforts to restore the carpet beds. They became less and less coherent. A couple of months later, she disappeared again. I assumed her cancer had metastasized.

▲▼▲

Ezra? Gleason was uncomfortable about something. *Ezra, we need to talk. The Company has been going over its profit and loss statements. They're spending more on your upkeep than they're making from your recordings. It's been suggested that we re-train you. Or relocate you. This may be difficult, Ezra…*

▲▼▲

I don't think anyone but me would have recognized Kristy Ann, when she came creeping back. She moved like an old woman. She seemed to have shrunken away. There was no sign of the laptop; I don't think she was strong enough to carry it, now. She had a purse with her meds in it. She had a water bottle.

She found her bench in the sunlight and sat there, looking around her with bewildered eyes, all their anger gone.

Her electromagnetic field, the drifting halo of electricity that all mortals generate around their bodies, had begun to fluctuate around Kristy Ann. It happens, when mortals begin to die.

I wondered if I could do it.

I did; I got to my feet and walked toward her, cautious, keeping my eyes on the ground. I came to her bench and sat down beside her. My heart was pounding. I risked a glance sideways. She was looking at me with utter apathy. She wouldn't have cared if I'd grabbed her purse, slapped her, or pulled off her clothes. Her eyes tracked off to my left.

I turned and followed her stare. She was looking at an old stone basin on its pedestal, the last of Sutro's fountains, its sculpted waterworks long since gone.

I edged closer. I reached into her electromagnetic field. I touched her hand—she was cold as ice—and tuned into the electrical patterns of her brain, as I had tuned into her broadband signal. I downloaded her.

I didn't hurt her. She saw the fountain restored, wirework shooting up to outline its second tier, its dolphins, its cherubs. Then it was solid and real. Clear water jetted upward into a lost sky. The green lawn spread out, flawless.

White statues rose from the earth: the Dancing Girls. The Dreaming Satyr. Venus de Milo. Antinous. The Boy with Bird. Hebe. The Griffin. All the Gilded Age's conception of what was artistic, copied and brought out to the western edge of the world to refine and educate its uncultured masses.

Sutro's house lifted into its place again; the man himself rose up through the path and stood, in his black silk hat. Brass glinted on the bandstand. Music began to play. Before us the Conservatory took shape, for a moment a skeletal frame and then a paned bubble of glass flashing in the sun. Orchids and aspidistras steamed its windows from inside. And below it—

The colors exploded into being like fireworks, red and blue and gold, variegated tropical greens, purples, the carpet beds in all their precise glory. Managed Nature, in the nineteenth century's confident belief that unruly Nature *should* be managed to pleasing aesthetic effect. The intricate floral designs glowed, surreal grace notes, defying entropy and chaos.

She was struggling to stand, gasping, staring at it. The tether broke and she was pulled into the image. I gave her back her hair, with a straw hat for the sun. I gave her a long flounced skirt that swept the gravel, a suitable blouse and jacket. I gave her buttoned boots and a parasol. I gave her the body of young Kristy Ann, who had wandered alone with her sketchbook. Now she was part of the picture, not the dead thing cooling on the bench beside me.

She walked forward, her eyes fixed on the carpet beds, her lips parted. Color came into her face.

▲▼▲

The fog came in, grayed the twenty-first century world. I heard crunching footsteps. A pair of women were coming up the path from the Point Lobos Road entrance. I got to my feet. I approached them, head turned aside, and managed to point at what was sitting on the park bench. One of the women said something horrified in Russian, the other put her hands to her white face and screamed.

They drew back from me. I pulled out my card and thrust it at them. Finally, suspicious, one of them took it and spelled out its message. I stared at my shoes while she put two and two together, and then I heard her pulling out her cell phone and calling the police.

I wasn't arrested. Once the police were able to look at the body and see its emaciation, the hospital band on its wrist, once they read the labels on the pill bottles in the purse, they knew. They called the morgue and then they called Gleason. He came and talked to them a while. Then he took me back to HQ.

▲▼▲

They don't send me out much, anymore. I sleep a lot, in the place where the Company keeps me. I don't mind; at least I don't have to deal with strangers, and after all I have my memory.

I ride there on Edwin and the weather is always fine, the fog far out on the edge of the blue sea. The green park is always full of people, the poor of San Francisco out for a day of fresh air, sunlight and as much beauty as a rich man's money can provide for them. Pipefitters and laundresses sit together on the benches. Children run and scream happily. Courting couples sit on little iron folding chairs and listen to the band play favorites by Sir Arthur Sullivan. The intricate patterns blaze.

She will always be there, sometimes chatting with Mr. Sutro. Sometimes bustling from one carpet bed to the next with a watering can or gardening tools. I tip my hat and say the only words I can say, have ever said: "Good morning, Christiane."

She smiles and nods. Perhaps she recognizes me, in a vague kind of way. But I never dismount to attempt conversation, and in any case she is too busy, weeding, watering, clipping to maintain the place she loves.